D0275281

Well Groomed

Also by Fiona Walker

French Relations
Kiss Chase

FIONA WALKER

Well Groomed

Hodder & Stoughton

Copyright © 1996 Fiona Walker

First published in 1996 by Hodder and Stoughton
A division of Hodder Headline PLC

The right of Fiona Walker to be identified as the Author of
the Work has been asserted by her in accordance with the
Copyright, Designs and Patents Act 1988.

10 9 8 7 6 5 4 3 2 1

All rights reserved. No part of this publication may be
reproduced, stored in a retrieval system, or transmitted
in any form or by any means without the prior written
permission of the publisher, nor be otherwise circulated
in any form of binding or cover other than that in which
it is published and without a similar condition being
imposed on the subsequent purchaser.

All characters in this publication are fictitious
and any resemblance to real persons, living or dead,
is purely coincidental.

British Library Cataloguing in Publication Data

Walker, Fiona, 1969–
   Well groomed
   1. English fiction – 20th century
   I. Title
   823.9'14 [F]

ISBN 0 340 61837 X

Typeset by Palimpsest Book Production Limited,
Polmont, Stirlingshire
Printed and bound in Great Britain by
Mackays of Chatham PLC, Chatham, Kent

Hodder and Stoughton
A division of Hodder Headline PLC
338 Euston Road
London NW1 3BH

For the Enfield diva, the Earl's Court dancer, the Compton stage manager, and for my sister, Hilary McDann.

One

AS TASH FRENCH FLUSHED the lavatory after her early-morning pee, a large icicle fell on to her head.

'Great. That's just . . . great.'

She was vaguely aware, as she staggered from the icy bathroom back to her fuggy, creased duvet and Niall's spread-eagled limbs, that there was a large white turkey peering at her through the lop-sided cat-flap at the base of the stairs, far too fat to fit the rest of its ample feathered bulk into the chilly comfort of the house. The rattling ground-floor windows were now too opaque with frosted condensation for it to look through those.

'Fattened for Christmas,' she murmured to herself as she carefully inserted her frozen extremities underneath Niall's warm, heavy legs and kissed his falcate, suntanned nose. In sleep, the long, curly eyelashes flickered as though stirred by a sigh and he burped mildly.

Christmas. The realisation finally hit Tash after an hour's fitful dreaming about Brussels sprouts, mistletoe and the latest festive Cliff Richard hit.

'Niall!' She sat bolt upright, her head reeling. The effort was too much and she sank back to the pillows with a groan, clutching her thumping brow.

'Mmmm?'

'What day is it?'

'Today, angel.' He stretched his stubbly face across to hers and, without opening his eyes, planted a sleepy, hungover kiss on her mouth. 'It's today, I think.'

'And would this "today" bear a passing resemblance to a certain important date in our religious calendar?'

'Give me a clue?' He was drifting back to sleep again, his sandpaper chin resting in the hollow of her neck.

'Like, yesterday was Christmas Eve.' Tash moved away to the edge of the bed.

'Ah.' Niall pulled a pillow over his head, one hairy armpit quivering as it was exposed to the frosty cold of the room.

'And my mother, step-father and Matty's unruly crew are due here for lunch.'

'Great,' came a muffled moan. 'What time is it?'

'Just after ten.' Tash squinted across to her watch, which was propped up between two dirty mugs on the bedside table.

'Good.' He resurfaced, stubble grazing her shoulder. 'That gives us time for a shag.'

'I'm freezing, Niall.'

'In that case,' he started to kiss his way down the rungs of her ribcage, 'let me show you what the Irish call central heating.'

After a lovely and slow, if rather fuzzy-headed, coupling, hangovers clearing, Niall pressed his lips into her moist stomach as Tash stretched across to gather up her watch.

'By the way, there's a very ugly white turkey outside.' She winced as she read the time.

'Yeah – we won him last night at the Olive Branch party – don't you remember?'

'I have a merciful blank after Marco Angelo started singing "The Girl From Ipanema", wearing nothing but a tea-towel and Jack Fortescue's deerstalker.'

'Yeah.' Grinning, Niall sagged back on the pillows. 'Great party, huh?'

'Glad you enjoyed it.' Tash winced again as she vaguely recalled regaining consciousness whilst being carried back the one hundred yards from the Olive Branch to the Old Forge by their kindly local publican, who was anxious to get to midnight mass. Come to think of it, she did seem to have a fleeting impression of Niall reeling around in a nearby ditch carrying a huge white turkey at the time. She had simply assumed she was hallucinating.

'What are we supposed to do with it?' she asked weakly.

'Well, as it's the day of our Saviour's birth and your greedy family are due for lunch in just over an hour, I'd recommend inviting it in to pull a cracker, wouldn't you?' Dark curls falling into his half-closed eyes, Niall staggered into the loo.

Tash was waiting anxiously outside when he emerged.

'I don't want you to kill it,' she pleaded.

'Fine.' Niall grinned lazily, kissing her on the forehead as he passed on his way down to the kitchen. 'I honestly don't think I'm up to it now, anyway. You go ahead – he's all yours. Hi there,' he added as he passed the cat-flap, from which an unspeakably ugly white face was peering, red eyes watering from the cold, caruncle hanging jauntily to one side like a slipping court jester's hat.

'I'm not going to kill it!' she protested, dashing after him.

'No, well then, there's no problem now, is there?' Having banged around in several cupboards for an Alka-Seltzer, Niall was searching the fridge for mineral water. The pipes were once again frozen, reducing the taps to a pitiful, burping dribble.

'Fine.' Tash sank down at the stone-topped table, her bottom making contact with a freezing cast-iron chair. 'Anyway, I bought a ready-stuffed, self-basting, idiot-proof frozen one – I guess I should bung it in the Rayburn as soon as I've translated the Paxo instructions.' She reached for her fags.

'Ah, now there's a thing.' Niall made do with dissolving two hangover tablets in Budweiser as the taps had now seized up completely, and there was nothing else to drink. 'Would this be a self-defrosting one too?'

'Shit!'

Tash watched in horror as Niall flipped open the freezer door with his knee to reveal several ancient pizzas, a bag of frozen peas, two empty ice-trays, a bottle of vodka and a vast idiot-proof turkey, as solid and frozen as a corpse in a glacier.

'Tash – she is a good cook, *non*?' Pascal asked as he cranked the hired Mercedes through a requiem of gears and crawled along in the Christmas Day traffic on the M6, his large Gallic nose wrinkling in anticipation of the gourmet treats ahead.

'I think so, darling,' his wife Alexandra answered distractedly as she frantically tried to wrap up presents in the passenger seat, sticking more Sellotape and gift tags to herself than to her gifts.

Their precocious eight-year-old daughter, Polly – squashed in the back seat with a very young, very nauseous puppy and a very old, very regal grandmother – was busy pulling revolting faces through the rear window at the shocked occupants of the car behind.

'Tell Polly to stop that, will you, Mother?' Alexandra reached for the Sellotape which was hooked on to the gear-stick just as Pascal tried to change into fifth.

'I'll do no such seeng, darleeng,' muttered Etty Buckingham, turning around and joining her grand-daughter in her tongue-poking fun, her grandiose fur hat falling on to her regal nose.

The skinny, biscuit-coloured puppy, anxious to join in, reeled around too and vomited liberally on to Pascal's cashmere jersey which Polly had been using as a knee cushion.

Matty French sulkily changed the wheel on his Audi as his wife crouched fearfully by the boot, pretending to read the *AA Road Map*.

'I think we're somewhere near Stroud,' she suggested hopefully as a wheel bolt flew past at nose level. 'Or it could be closer to Bristol. Hard to tell when everything's so white.'

'That's just fucking great,' hissed Matty, his fingers turning blue as he yanked at a stubborn nut. 'Tash and Niall live in Berkshire.'

'Oh, we came through there!' Sally realised excitedly, consulting the map again.

'I fucking know,' Matty hissed. His rather idiotic crocheted skullcap – a present from his long-suffering PA which he felt obliged to wear – rather lost him the edge when it came to patriarchal tyranny. He looked like a very trendy Hackney social worker searching for his inner child.

'Daddy said fucking!' chorused two excited small children from the warmth of the rear seat.

'Twice!' added the eldest, Tom, who could count.

The Frenches' third child, Linus, burst into noisy sobs as the car shook underneath his carry cot. He was wearing a large, colourful felt bonnet in the shape of a crocodile, his face protruding from its mouth as though recently swallowed.

Giving up on the map, Sally gazed delightedly at the paper-doily hedgerows and the frosted grass, spearing up in the cold, dry air like a rigid, peroxide-white punk hairdo.

'"I'm dreaming,"' she sang tunelessly, '"of a—"'

'"White Chrithmath!"' sang three-year-old Tor, who had recently added those two words to her repertoire of about twenty – most of them swear words.

'No, it is *not*,' muttered Matty, ever the pedant, particularly when, as now, his tether was nearing its end faster than a bolting goat's. 'White Christmases are so-called because it has snowed, covering everything totally in white. This is a sharp frost, which gives an appearance of snow but will fade as soon as it warms up.'

'Which, if the weather parallels your father's mood,' Sally said idly, 'will be sometime in March. I think we should get a place in the country, Matty. It's so beautiful.' Closing her eyes, she stabbed a dreamy finger into the map. 'We should buy a tumble-down brick and flint cottage in – er – Maccombe.'

'Don't move your finger!' Matty wailed, another wheel nut flying over his shoulder.

'Whyever not?' Sally looked up at him excitedly through her messy blonde fringe, wondering whether he was going suddenly, recklessly, to take her up on her idle dreams, a challenge he hadn't risen to since very early on in the heady idealism of their marriage. A cottage, an overgrown garden, local pub, fossil-like colonel, ancient jam-making spinsters, gymkhanas, coffee mornings . . . bucolic bliss! Yes, let's do it, Sals. Let's go ahead for the hell of it.

But Matty's big hazel eyes were narrowed, the retroussé nose still looked out of joint, and the wide, usually gentle mouth was set in a line as straight as a Roman road.

'That bastard Beauchamp lives in Maccombe.' Matty located the nut in a nearby patch of crisp, frozen hog grass. 'Tash's village is pretty near, I think. Fosbourne something. Look for Fosbourne.'

Sally sighed sadly and looked. 'There's a Fosbourne Holt here, and Fosbourne Dean.' Her finger homed into a corner of the map close to Maccombe. 'And a Fosbourne Dewkis.'

'Ducis!' Matty corrected. 'It's pronounced "dew-sis". You should know that. We've been there twice, after all.'

'Mmm, over a year ago,' Sally reminded him regretfully, wondering why he was so uptight.

'I wish to Christ we'd left it longer to go back,' Matty added tetchily under his breath. He hoped beyond hope that Zoe Goldsmith wouldn't make an appearance today.

'This isn't working.' Tash turned off her hairdryer and gazed forlornly at the idiot-proof turkey. 'It's still frozen solid.'

Niall, who had managed to gather enough icicles from the guttering to boil a pan and thus defrost the pipes, was blowing the froth from his hard-earned coffee and watching her with amusement.

'Sorry, Giblets, my son.' He looked across to the cat-flap from which a grubby beak still protruded. 'Your number's up. Twenty-five pounds, twenty-five days into December, twenty-five minutes now until Tash's mother's due to arrive.'

'Twenty-five minutes!' Tash gaped at her watch in horror. 'I must get dressed.'

'Stay as you are.' Niall wrapped her in a hug. 'I like to see you in the just-got-out-of-bed look. I find the idea of ripping off three jumpers, two t-shirts, two pairs of leggings, two pairs of socks and an old school scarf deeply exciting.'

'Do you think they'll mind that the heating's packed in?' Tash hugged him back for warmth.

'I'll light a fire.'

By the time she came back out of the bedroom dressed in a very warm trouser suit over her very warm thermals, with her hair sodden and her nose blue from an icy shower, Niall was immersed in some old newspapers that he had extracted from the coal cupboard as kindling for the fire, and had become so engrossed in reading that the fire was still unlit. The vast, black-stained forge hearth was still filled with soot, ashes, cigarette stubs and sweet wrappers.

Tash's eyes softened as she gazed at him. His curling black hair, in desperate need of a cut, was flopping all over his stubbled face, milk-chocolate eyes crinkling as he laughed at an A. A. Gill column dating back to September.

He'd had so little time to read the papers in the last few months, she realised; particularly the English ones that he adored, having spent so long filming in America, where his super-luxury trailer had been stuffed with scripts to be rejected. Here he was, dressed in nothing but a ratty striped dressing gown and bedsocks, hair on end, knees supporting a Sunday supplement as he stooped over an old television crit, guffawing as though he had watched the programme yesterday and agreed with every word. To Niall, everything was as fresh as he was, however jaded it – and he – appeared. He was the only man she knew who still laughed uproariously at old Marx Brothers jokes, and she loved him for it.

'Merry Christmas.' She held out a slightly damp package which she had just wrapped in the bathroom. She had forgotten to buy wrapping paper again this year, but doubted that he would recognise one of their drawer liners.

Niall looked up, his eyes uncrinkling for a moment.

'You look beautiful,' he sighed, taking in the red velvet suit, the long, long legs and wet, snaky brown hair curling over her huge, odd, blinking eyes and framing her lovely cleft chin.

She smiled shyly. 'Open it then.'

As he ripped at the package, Tash wandered across to the paint-stained portable radio that had been her only company when splashing white Dulux on the brick walls of the Old Forge six months ago, and surfed the dial until she found some carols.

'This is bloody wonderful!' Niall laughed as a flutter of poppy-strewn, damp paper finally landed on the floor and he held up a tiny miniature painting of them both together, framed in a fat, peeling antique gilt square.

Tash, puce with embarrassment, listened to a couple of bars of 'Good King Wenceslas'.

'You don't think it's a bit naff?' she asked nervously.

She had spent agonising hours the week before deciding whether or not to give it to him, and had only finally been persuaded when Gus and Penny, her dearest friends, had frog-marched her into the antique shop in neighbouring Fosbourne Dean and forced her to buy a frame – far more expensive than she could afford – insisting that if she didn't give it to him, they would sack her from her post as their working pupil.

'It's simply wonderful,' Niall sighed, echoing their words of a week earlier. 'And so small that I can take it with me wherever I work. Christ, I love you, Tash French.'

When she finally surfaced from a kiss far too long and raucous for one of Niall's standard celluloid love-scenes, she noticed a pair of red eyes peering at her critically through the cat-flap.

'Do you think we should let him in and give him something to eat?' she asked worriedly as Giblets let out an outraged gobble.

'Sure.' Niall shrugged, still staring at the painting in awe. 'God, this is great.'

'What the hell are we going to do for lunch?' Tash peered into the open-plan kitchen where three pounds of Brussels sprouts were still sagging from a hanging vegetable rack, confined in their plastic string supermarket bag with the lurid discount voucher on full show. 'Brussels sprout quiche?' She let in Giblets, who headed straight for the fireplace in disorientated excitement.

'We could.' Niall shrugged again. 'Or you could dash along to Penny and Gus's place and see if they can spare any extras, while I stay here and light a fire.' He propped the painting against a photograph of Tash and her event horse, Foxy Snob, taking a huge stone wall at last year's Highclere Horse Trials. Coaxing Giblets from the fireplace, he lit a cigarette in anticipation of the task ahead.

'I can't impose on them on Christmas morning,' Tash said worriedly. 'And they can hardly cut their turkey in half.'

'Afternoon.' Niall checked his watch. 'And why not? You can wish Snob and Hunk a Merry Christmas, and give the Moncrieffs their presents.' He nodded towards a large Selfridge's bag propped up by the door. 'We forgot to take them to midnight mass last night.'

'We went to midnight mass?' Tash looked confused.

'Mmm.' Niall nodded, heading back to the fireplace and throwing in his half-smoked cigarette. 'At least I think we did. Why in hell didn't you just take that cigarette off me, Tash? You know I've given up.'

'You're supposed to tell me to take them off you first, remember?' Tash, feeling slightly baited, headed for the door and stepped into her wellies as she reached for her ancient Puffa, which was oozing its lining through the tears like a clawed cushion. 'I'm not acting as fag cop without instruction since you locked yourself in Tom's bedroom with a packet of Rothmans at Sally's thirtieth.'

'You looked so sweet when you were soaked through – like a mermaid.'

'The terrapins weren't so chuffed to find themselves on dry land once their home had been deposited on me, though.' Tash pulled on her gloves sulkily.

Niall looked sheepish. 'Sorry.'

She grinned, able to forgive him anything when he looked at her like that. 'I'll see you in half an hour or so.'

An hour later, Alexandra and Pascal arrived to find Niall smoking a furtive Camel Light and reading an old copy of the *Marlbury Weekly Gazette* in the freezing cold. Tash was nowhere to be seen. A large white turkey was standing in the empty, black fireplace, its head cocked, listening to a droning Christmas sermon on the radio. A second turkey – smaller, plucked and frozen – was sitting on a polystyrene tray on the Rayburn, dripping on to the plate lids, from which a low hiss was burbling as the water ran down to meet the heat.

'*Allo, Niall, mon brave.*' Pascal picked his way into the tiny cottage, stepping over a tide of mess in his hand-made Italian shoes. '*Eet is cold, non?*'

But before Niall could look up and answer, Pascal was overtaken by his wife, wafting Arpège and flurried excitement.

'I've left Mother in the car with Polly – they're engaged in a frantic game of I Spy and won't come out until one is declared overall victor. Hi, Niall darling – Merry Christmas. Gosh, you're still in your dressing gown. I'm so sorry. Are we early? Is Tash still in bed?'

'No, you're late, Alexandra angel.' Niall rose from his knees and kissed her on both cheeks, admiring the butterscotch skin which was still as smooth as her daughter's. 'And I'm afraid you've caught me about my prayers, as it's the day of the birth of our Sacred Mary's only child, so it is.' He glanced guiltily down at the newspaper he had been reading and then beamed up at her.

'Gosh, how gloriously devout.' Alexandra looked at him in wonder and slight disbelief.

'And Tash is just at the Moncrieffs' farm saying hello to her horses now – giving them a Christmas carrot.'

'How lovely – she always did that for her ponies as a child.' Alexandra flicked back her short, glossy brown bob and caught sight of Giblets, who was pecking hungrily at the *West Berks Advertiser*.

'Good grief, is that lunch?'

'No, no.' Niall flipped a casual hand towards the turkey in the fireplace. 'He's a pet.' He headed towards the stairs, adding over his shoulder, 'That's lunch.' And he pointed out the dripping, goose-bumped pink lump on the Rayburn.

'The lunch, he ees frozen solid,' Pascal announced with a shudder as, still wearing his leather driving gloves, he prodded the wet, icy bird.

'Oh, dear!' Alexandra gazed around forlornly as she listened to Niall creaking about in the bathroom overhead. 'I mean, it's terribly romantic but it's a bit of a hovel, isn't it?'

'It's a bloody dump, *ma chérie*,' announced a warbling baritone from the door as Etty Buckingham tottered in, swamped by her squishy grey fox fur, bearskin hat worn at a rakish angle. She was an amazingly glamorous octogenarian, false eyelashes batting up a gale as she calmly took in the mess, hollow cheeks sucked in so that her cheekbones seemed higher and more angled than ever, like two wing mirrors. 'I weel take you all out to lunch in a local 'otel.'

'Rubbish, Mother,' Alexandra said kindly. 'You're far too poor, and everywhere will be booked up by now anyway. Pascal will cook.'

He puffed out his tanned cheeks, watery grey eyes widening under his chaotic mane of greying hair. Turning up the collar of his beautifully cut cashmere coat and shivering against the chill, he stalked into the tiny kitchen.

'I brought in ze wine, *Maman*,' chirruped Polly from the door as she came staggering in under the weight of two magnums of champagne. The raven-haired little girl, as delicate and ravishing as her mother, was wearing an elf's costume which was rather marred by the latest high-fashion trainers and the personal stereo attached to her leather elfin belt.

'Ah – what a lovely Christmas! I can tell it's going to be quite my favourite so far,' Alexandra sighed happily, reaching out for her daughter's load.

'You were the funniest thing at midnight mass!' Penny told Tash as they stuffed Snob with Polos, trying to keep hold of their wine glasses which he was keen to examine with his snapping pink muzzle. 'Lolling around in the back pew singing a solo rendition of "Santa Claus is Coming to Town" while the hip vic was giving yet another camp sermon about loving thy neighbour of either sex. Godfrey Pelham got such giggles he was eating his hassock.'

'Glad I was so entertaining,' Tash said weakly, ducking as Snob gnashed his teeth towards her hair, keen on the waft of apple shampoo. His startling zig-zag blaze bobbed like a stabbing sword.

The big chestnut stallion, as headstrong and temperamental as his stable companion, the Drunken Hunk, was mild and polite, rolled his purple-brown eyes and backed off sulkily, presenting Tash with a stained chestnut rump, flaxen tail twitching angrily, white hoof stamping almost silently into his thickly banked shavings.

Tash's two horses were the only ones not turned out for the day – Snob because he fought so much with all the others, and the yard comic, Hunk, because he was confined to stable rest with an injured tendon. Out in the Moncrieffs' hilly, frosted fields the rest of the yard's occupants were huddling together for warmth or nosing through piles of hay, swathed in heavy New Zealand rugs, some with protective hoods so that they resembled medieval chargers in low-budget armour. Tash noticed that the bottom field's trough, which Penny had smashed into with a hammer just minutes earlier, was already developing a thin crystal film of ice again.

'Come back in for another drink,' she urged, hooking her arm through Tash's. 'Zoe was still goose-stuffing half an hour ago, so lunch is yonks away. God, I wish you still lived here. Christmas was such fun last year.'

'I loved it,' Tash confessed, remembering a meal that had lasted from the Queen's Speech to Close Down, with no more domestic responsibilities than peeling the odd sprout and helping to wash up. Penny's sister, Zoe Goldsmith, was the farm's odd-ball cook and had produced a vast turkey stuffed with whole apples, garlic cloves, and, most controversially, green chillies. Last year, Zoe's kids had orchestrated a hysterically blue amateur Nativity play with Niall and Gus as the donkey, collapsing under the weight of a very tight Penny. Tash, as the Virgin Mary, had giggled so much that she'd burst out of the slinky underwear Niall had given her that morning – as ever two sizes too small; he had a flatteringly minimalist image of how slim she was every time he hit Rigby and Peller.

Penny and Gus Moncrieff ran their eventing and training yard on a thread of a shoestring. They were both immensely dedicated and professional, but long hours and talent only went so far in a profession that really required sponsors who did not mind pouring money into a sometimes bottomless pit as horses costing ten thousand pounds to buy and several thousand a year to keep, failed to make the grade, or got injured, or simply went stale. Very few horses became international, and Snob was one of the very few; Tash knew that she owed her job in part to her boisterous chestnut horse and his rapid rise to success, his stud fees and his popularity with spectators. She would be forever in his debt for enabling her to work for the tall fair-haired duo who kept laughing and joking throughout the season, whether they won or lost.

Tash adored Gus and Penny, who were always tired, always thin and too stressed, yet inevitably welcoming and willing to put themselves out for others. They were two of the best-liked people in the sport, and attracted friends and acquaintances like tourists to a sunny cove. Penny had once represented England in the World Equestrian Games, but she no longer rode at the top level, preferring to breed and train youngsters. Her sister Zoe lived with them, doubling as cook, groom and secretary and adding to the glamour of the yard with her London connections and minor celebrity as an erstwhile columnist and feature writer. They always attracted a huge crowd at Christmas, and this year was no exception. They had eighteen for lunch and Zoe was frantically cooking two geese and a twenty-pound turkey in the farm's unpredictable coke-fuelled range. Tash simply didn't have the heart to ask if she could borrow a couple of wings and the parson's nose.

'Matty's coming down today, isn't he?' Penny asked smoothly as they wandered towards the sagging farmhouse, their wellies crunching through frosted straw. 'Are you going to whistle him up a soya-bean drumstick?'

'God, I hadn't even thought,' Tash groaned. 'He'll just have to have a double helping of veg.'

She supposed that hosting a dinner for her mother's entourage plus her brother's brood was a tad ambitious as a first foray into independent yuletides. She wished now that she had stuck to Niall's idea of heading for Ireland and taking in the hospitality of his raucous family, or simply holing up in the Old Forge together and staying in bed all day. Either was preferable to the task ahead.

'I'd really better get back,' she sighed ruefully. 'My mother – given her unpunctuality – will just about be arriving now. My brother – given his – will storm into the village in less than an hour.'

'Just come in for one more drink, huh?' Penny's wet berry eyes gleamed cheerfully through her untidy dark-blonde hair, worn down for once. 'Gus will want another Christmas kiss, and you must collect your presents.'

'Oh God, I left yours at the Old Forge!' Tash remembered the Selfridge's bag with a wail.

Polly, who had by now opened all the presents destined for Penny, Gus and Zoe at Lime Tree Farm, was starting on the ones under the threadbare tree, which was still undecorated.

'Are these for my *maman*?' she asked, holding up the extremely flimsy lace underwear that Niall was intending to give to Tash far later that day, when once again alone with her.

'Don't be silly, *chérie*.' Alexandra was helping herself and Etty to two more huge gin and tonics as Niall clearly wasn't too good at refilling glasses. 'Those are far too young for me.'

'I don't know.' Pascal cocked a rather excited furry eyebrow as he placed garlic and salt-encrusted potatoes on to a roasting dish and doused them in olive oil and rosemary.

Perched on a very scruffy sofa beside her daughter, Etty shivered slightly from the cold and sniffed disapprovingly. The place smelled very stale, she noted, and there were five unwashed mugs gathering mould on the table beside her. She clutched her gin and tonic – smeary glass, too – to her fur chest, unwilling to place it amidst such contamination. Whilst fearfully dishy, her grand-daughter's Irish partner was rather odd. It was now after one and he still hadn't dressed.

Niall, who had built a large fire that was smoking slightly more than he was in Tash's absence, was tugging on his fifth Camel Light and wandering round in his striped dressing gown, getting under Pascal's feet as he tried to make them both a strong black coffee. They were now out of instant and the filter machine had broken weeks ago, so he was forced to improvise with grounds through a tea towel, generating a great deal of gritty brown mess.

'I wonder where Tash has got to now?' He looked up fretfully as there was a commotion of motorised clanks outside, followed by the sound of a car being reversed into a wheely bin.

This was soon replaced by the banging of car doors and the excited chattering of children. The next moment, Sally's pretty, rose-cheeked face was peering through the frosted windows and Matty, loaded down with baby equipment, elbowed his way through the front door.

'Hi, all.' He dropped a massive packet of nappies in at the door and scratched his head under his crocheted hat. 'Something smells good. Christ!' He caught sight of his grandmother and tried not to look too horrified.

Etty glowered back at him. They had never been the best of friends.

'Matty darling!' Alexandra sprang up from the sofa and rushed across the room to hug him which Matty, despite stiffening slightly, took in festive good humour.

'You look great, Mother.' He grinned, taking in the usual impracticality of her heavy silk jacket, bottle green wool trousers and high suede mules.

''Lo, everyone!' Sally appeared through the door carrying Linus in his carry cot, her messy honey-blonde mane already falling out of its scrunchy, grey eyes merry, denim dress covered in baby food. 'Merry Christmas! The kids are busy peering at the puppy in the Mercedes. Isn't it a bit cruel leaving it there in the cold?'

'Probably warmer than it would be in here,' Niall laughed, greeting his friend Matty with an affectionate arm around the shoulders and kissing Sally on both her pink cheeks.

'Christ, the puppy — I quite forgot!' gasped Alexandra, rushing outside to rescue her present and welcome her grandchildren.

'Get dressed, you lazy slob.' Matty grinned at Niall, pleased to see him looking so well. 'Tash still in bed?'

'Why does everyone think that we spend our entire time in bed?' Niall sighed, wandering back to his coffee-making.

'Because you more or less do,' Sally pointed out, kissing Pascal hello and making a tentative approach to Matty's grandmother. 'Hello, Etty. What a lovely surprise — we didn't expect to see you here. Are you well?'

'Closer to death than ever, *ma chérie*.' Etty, still wearing her bearskin hat, peered up from her gin. ''Xandra and James came to Scotland to rescue me from 'aving to spend anozer Christmas with Cass and 'er 'orrible 'usband.'

'Pascal, Grandmother.' Matty smiled weakly.

'I thought he was called Michael?' Etty gave him a cursory welcoming nod. 'You look too thin, Matthew.'

'Cass's husband is Michael,' Matty said patiently, watching as Niall, clutching his coffee, wandered up the narrow, twisting staircase to get dressed, followed by what appeared to be a large white turkey. 'My father is called James, Grandmother. Mother and he have been divorced for years. She's married to Pascal now.' He pointed to his step-father, who was grumpily teaching Polly how to peel sprouts. 'Xandra and *Pascal* came to rescue you from Scotland.'

'That's what I said, you stupeed child.' Etty stretched up a creased, rouged cheek. 'Now give me a kiss and bugger off and wash your hands – zey're filthy.'

'I had to change a tyre.'

Sally tried hard not to giggle as her husband's twitching face made contact with his grandmother's heavily made-up one. Matty loathed Etty, blaming her for bestowing the excesses of extravagance and bohemian wilfulness upon Alexandra. Etty, a ravaged French aristocrat who had been sent across the Channel by her impoverished family between the wars to marry a rich Englishman, was monstrously vain, bigoted and devious. She had made Matty's childhood hell by continually favouring his sisters above him and pretending that it was he and not herself who secretly laid into the gin supply during her stays with the Frenches. But Sally felt a great affection for the woman who had, if her stories were to be believed, spied for England during the Second World War, played poker with Lord Lucan, eaten oysters with the Mitford sisters, and been approached by a young Mitterrand as a potential mistress.

'Are you his latest, *chérie*?' Etty asked Sally rather grandly.

Sally gaped at her. 'I'm Sally – Matty's wife. You came to our wedding, Etty. And to Tom's christening.'

'Oh, did I?' Etty smiled blithely. 'I cannot remember. One attends so many society weddings that family ones seem rather piffling.' She gave Sally a huge wink and jerked her head towards Matty, who was testing Pascal's cranberry purée with a boot face, his rage barely controlled.

Sally grinned broadly.

Tash, who had cut through a rock-hard ploughed field to get back to the Old Forge in less time, clambered rather clumsily over a frost-dusted fence and suddenly caught sight of her mother's green wool bottom poking out of the rear door of a silver Mercedes, which was badly parked in the narrow lane. Attached to Alexandra's shapely ankle was the small, rotund shape of Tor, Tash's hyperactive blonde niece, her jaunty little pig-tails flopping over her chocolate-smeared face.

Tash drew in a guilty breath. That meant everyone had arrived, and she hadn't even begun to cook. She wished she hadn't spent quite so much time giggling with the Moncrieffs and their guests around the vast table in their warm, welcoming kitchen, putting off the moment she had to return to the icy forge. The slight body flush from two glasses of fizzy wine cooled to a shiver once more and, as she slithered off the railed fence, her gloved hands lost their grip on the bag Penny had given her. Her family's presence always sent her nerves through the roof. She could feel her fists clenching, and the cheap glass ring that she'd just won when pulling a cracker with Zoe's son, Rufus, scratched against the second and fourth fingers of her left hand. Faced with her turbulent family – especially Matty – Tash always felt like a shy, fat teenager again.

As she stooped to collect some of the presents that had tumbled out of her bag and on to the frozen verge, she spotted Tor's brother Tom galloping out from behind a green Audi – even more badly parked, Tash noted. Slithering to a leggy halt by the open boot, he saw her and let out an excited, war-like wail before stalking forwards and shooting her with one of his Christmas presents – a super-charged, repeat-action water rifle, of which his father strongly disapproved.

Drenched through, her Puffa as heavy as a bullet-proof vest, Tash mustered a brave smile.

'Hi, little rat.' She wiped her wet cheeks and bent down, kissing thin air as he ducked away with squirming shyness. 'I love your hair – it's really cool.'

'Think so?' Tom looked proud, beaming a toothy smile just like the one his father so rarely gave.

Tash actually thought the trendy cut made him look like a little thug, his shiny brown pudding basin having been shorn off to just a few stubbly millimetres. But she knew how to suck up to her younger relatives. At times, it seemed, they were her only allies in the pushy, selfish babble of her family.

'Tash!' Alexandra had backed out of the Merc and was trying to hide something that was squirming under her coat.

'Hi, Mummy – Happy Christmas!' Slithering across the frozen lane, Tash dropped all her presents and gave her mother a hug, experiencing, as ever, a sudden oil-geyser rush of affection.

But Alexandra backed out of her embrace with unexpected haste.

'You're soaking wet, darling.' She smiled rather awkwardly, and stooped to detach her grand-daughter from her ankle, into which Tor had been trying to sink her small, white teeth.

'I know,' Tash sighed, collecting the parcels that she'd brought back from Lime Tree Farm. They headed inside together, pursued by Tom and Tor. 'Did you have a lovely time in Scotland?'

'Lovely.' Alexandra smiled and dropped her voice. 'Mummy was a rogue – tried to nick the cutlery from every restaurant we took her to. Says she wants to move back to France with us, which is quite a ghastly idea.' She raised her voice again. 'Look who I found outside!'

Tash found herself the recipient of rather lack-lustre greetings as a result of her shoddy hostessing. Just as she started gibbering apologies to Pascal who, having got all the cooking on the go, was now sniffing one of Zoe's Christmas puddings with mistrust, there was a bellow from upstairs.

'Is that you, Tash?'

Quailing at the anger in Niall's tone, she crept towards the warped oak door that led to the steep, narrow wooden stairs.

'Yes. Look, I'm really sorry I was away so long, but Penny insisted that I—'

'Where the fock are my clothes?'

'Ah.' Tash stood on one foot and glanced awkwardly towards the kitchen. 'Well, all the stuff you brought back from LA is still in the machine, I think.'

'And the rest?'

She smiled nervously at her family, who were listening in with interest. 'Well, I gave a couple of your old suits to charity, and then I started sort of wearing the rest of your clothes to ride out in.'

'You what?'

'Back in a min,' Tash bleated over her shoulder and shot upstairs.

Matty looked across to Sally and rolled his amber eyes with despair.

Having clucked into Linus's carry cot for a few seconds, Alexandra sank down beside her mother again and readjusted the squirming bulge in her coat.

'Dreadful hole, isn't it, *chérie*?' Etty peered around the room critically, taking in the grubby, white-washed stone walls covered with Tash's colourful paintings, the threadbare furniture, curling rugs and amassed litter, which now included the stack of old papers that Niall had been reading.

'Must be terribly lonely for poor Tash while Niall's away.' Alexandra gazed around, noticing just how many paintings her daughter had been producing lately.

'She's away competing most weekends, I believe,' Matty pointed out, settling rather uncomfortably on a coffee table as there were no more available chairs.

'Not this time of year.' Sally pulled Tor on to her denim lap and wondered whether it would be terribly rude to help herself to a drink as no one had offered her one. 'Stop shooting Pascal and get the presents out of the car, will you, Tom?'

'If anyone gives me toiletries I weel make them eat them,' Etty threatened rather demonically. 'Ees the Queen's Speech on yet?'

But when Matty fiddled around with the several remote controls that worked the television, he managed to set the video recorder playing. In it was the blue movie that Tash and Niall had been giggling over the afternoon before. Etty almost ate her false teeth in shock.

When they had met two years earlier, Tash and Niall had fallen for one another as deeply and impractically as only they were capable of, believing that they had finally united two halves of the same huge, ludicrously romantic heart, but not realising quite how incompatible their lives were. Niall, a rising star in the acting world, spent a great deal of his working year on location or touring to publicise films. More recently, with a hefty American divorce settlement against him, he had been forced to take the roles that offered the fattest cheque, necessitating months on end living by West-Coast time. Tash, striving to build a career in eventing, lived a gypsy's life in summer, touring around the country in the Moncrieffs' vast horse-box from which she lived, ate and competed. Then in winter she was based in West Berkshire, training, schooling and teaching.

In the first year of their relationship, she and Niall had spent about two months together, and most of that in the company of others. Tash had visited him on location several times, but it was a closed, cliquey world in which he worked fifteen-hour days and lived so far beneath the skin of the character he was portraying that it was like visiting a stranger – and not a very nice one of late, as he was increasingly being cast as baddies in action movies. In turn, Niall battled to be there to support her when she competed, but he inevitably turned up too late to see her ride, or not at all as he was so often delayed on set. Once he had even travelled to entirely the wrong horse trials and had waited in vain for her to appear.

In despair they had arrived at the conclusion that the only way they were going to stand a chance of seeing one another was for Niall to move his permanent home from London to the tiny West Berkshire village in which Tash's team was based.

Huddling in the higgledy-piggledy hills that peaked and troughed alongside the far more graceful crest of the Wayfarer's Ridgeway, like muscles alongside a backbone, the Fosbournes were a clutch of villages within an ancient and remarkably unspoilt parish. It was a piece of anachronistic old Berkshire, almost untouched by the silicone valley industrial estates, business parks and out-of-town superstores that sprawled between identikit suburban housing estates further to the east. Too far away from a large town or flat land to be of much use, the Fosbournes housed a friendly if reactionary community which tolerated its few sacrifices to Thatcher's years well – the odd modern bungalow, DIY extension enthusiast or wailing weekday exterior alarm on a weekender's cottage. It was true that nowadays the narrow lanes were more often patrolled by Ford Escorts with thumping stereos and local entrepreneurs' flashy four-wheel drives than farmers' pick-ups or tractors, but Niall adored the place and had set about house-hunting like a zealot.

He had rented the old, converted forge six months earlier so that he and Tash had a base to be alone in together. Before then she had occasionally travelled up to his London flat when she had time, or more often he had stayed with her at the Moncrieffs' cramped farmhouse, where she was based for her work. Conducting their relationship surrounded by children, grooms, dogs, horses and the constant stream of visiting friends that the Moncrieffs attracted had been fun but frustrating.

He'd rented the cottage in mid-summer, when wistaria had curled seductively around its small, deep-set windows and pools of dappled sunlight had streamed into the vast, cool reception room. Once the village forge, it was bang in the centre of Fosbourne Ducis, equidistant between the pub and Lime Tree Farm, nestling in its rather ugly, squat way amongst barn conversions, brick and flint cottages, oak trees, high hawthorn hedges and narrow, patched-up Tarmac lanes. The long-neglected forge had been bought by weekending yuppies in the eighties and, with the addition of a loft conversion, bathroom and open-plan kitchen, they had transformed it into a stylish, if rather twee, love nest with a huge stone hearth which ate coal, a forest of knotted elm beams and more olde-worlde charm than Bilbo Baggins's cottage.

When Niall had first seen it drenched in sunlight, he'd fallen madly in love with it, rejecting the far grander old rectories and manor houses that his estate agent had deemed more fitting to his star status. He and Tash had moved there in late-July and experienced three heavenly weeks of love-nesting instincts, occasionally staggering out to the Olive Branch or the local post office store when they could be bothered to get dressed. Niall had then flown to the States to work on some terrible action adventure film, leaving Tash to divide her time between decorating and the autumn eventing season. It was then that she'd discovered the mould growing on their gingerbread cottage.

In autumn it was awash; in winter it was a freezing tomb. The roof leaked, the damp spread, the rot rose and the pipes froze. Set right on the main village lane just yards from the ford that allowed the little River Fos to trickle from the Lime Tree Farm fields down to Fosbourne Manor's lake and then on to Mill House, it flooded with alarming regularity. Tash had got used to keeping her wellingtons at the top of the stairs ready to don before she descended to breakfast each morning. She looked forward to travelling away to weekend events because the horse-box – even though on its last legs – was warmer and drier.

When Niall flew back for a rushed reunion, he found the forge's rustic drawbacks charming. He laughed as they squelched around on the sodden rugs and boiled kettles to fill the bath, finding the whole experience wonderfully refreshing after the anonymous, clinical luxury of five-star hotels and top-of-the-range location trailers, not realising how tough it was to live with such inconvenience seven days a week. Tash, in turn, was so pleased to see him and so preoccupied with enjoying every moment of having him around, that she couldn't bring herself to complain.

Alexandra was right. Tash had found it horrifically lonely without Niall and, in the last few weeks, had spent more nights than she cared to admit sleeping in her old room in Lime Tree Farm, which was tatty but warm, particularly when she was joined by the Moncrieffs' border collie, Wally, and Zoe's neurotic Dalmatian, Enid.

She spent so much time with the Moncrieffs – schooling and fittening the horses, taking her share of the day-to-day tasks in the yard, eating Zoe's eclectic food, filling in entry forms, travelling to competitions, working out diet and exercise plans for the horses, drinking and talking late into the night as they planned the year ahead – that there seldom seemed any point in staggering the half-mile home. And Niall knew that if she didn't answer the phone at the forge, she would almost inevitably be sitting on the splitting leather sofa at the farm with Wally's head in her lap and a glass of wine in her hand, laughing with Zoe or helping her kids with their homework.

'He's been doing the most Godawful work in order to pay off the divorce settlement – cast three times in the past eighteen months as a Middle-Eastern baddie in muscle-men war movies. It keeps them apart so much, and he loathes the scripts. I bet Lisette's grinning from Versace earring to earring. She wants him back, I'm certain.'

Sally, the most wildly indiscreet member of the family, was busily filling in Alexandra and Etty on all the latest gossip about Niall's and Tash's lives and those of anyone else that they mutually knew, when Niall re-emerged wearing what he had been dressed in the night before – a very grubby pair of white jeans and a vast navy blue Guernsey with cracked leather elbow patches and an unravelling hem. His dark locks were all over the place, he'd cut himself shaving and he was still squinting with hungover tiredness. Yet such was his presence and charm that when he smiled his big, lazy smile at Etty, she flushed delightedly under her bearskin and took a hasty swig of gin to calm her nerves.

Sally quickly shut up about Niall's ex-wife and asked Alexandra what she and Pascal were planning to do during the rest of their stay in England.

'Oh, darling, I wish we could cram everything in!' Alexandra was still clutching her coat around her oddly animated stomach, even though the fire was now heating the room to toasting point. 'There are so many old friends I want to catch up with, but we've got to fly back for New Year's Eve because Pascal's father is eighty and he's having a huge, boring old party in Paris. So we're whizzing to London the day after tomorrow for a quick stint at the Ritz and lots of drinks parties, then we'll take Mother back to Scotland and fly to Paris from there.'

Etty started grumbling rather heavily under her breath about Paris in January and perhaps never seeing it again, so Alexandra rushed on.

'Of course tomorrow is Sophia's usual Boxing Day do – so nice to be able to go for once. We usually can't get a flight over. You are going, aren't you?'

Sally swallowed awkwardly and shot a suspicious glance at Matty.

'We haven't actually been invited this year,' she admitted.

'Don't be ridiculous, darling!' Alexandra laughed. 'Of course you have. Sophia wouldn't not invite her brother, however snobbish she's been about the fact that you turned up in jeans the year before last. She always invites the entire family for Boxing Day. Always.'

Matty cleared his throat and looked away furtively.

'Well, we've agreed to go to some friends in London for lunch tomorrow anyway,' he muttered uncomfortably, toying with a button on his oversized cardigan. 'It would be a lot of effort to drive back to London tonight then Worcestershire tomorrow just to see more or less the same people again.'

'Nonsense!' Etty joined in the fight, loving an argument. 'You can stay 'ere tonight, *non*?'

'We couldn't possibly – it's far too small!' Matty snapped.

'Surely the Moncrieffs would put us up?' Sally suggested. She was rather excited by the prospect of getting another gawp at Matty's elder sister and her husband Ben's stately pile, which they so seldom visited. That would also get her out of lunch with Matty's interminably dreary, politically correct friends, Tony and Hetty.

'No!' Matty snarled rather too forcefully. 'It's Christmas night, for Chrissake. We can't just turn up uninvited at the farm and beg a bed.'

'Joseph and Mary did,' Alexandra pointed out smoothly.

'Sure, they wouldn't mind about that now,' Niall pointed out from the kitchen where he was at last pouring some drinks and once again getting under Pascal's feet. 'Would you like me to give them a call after lunch and ask? Better still, we could walk over there and say hi.'

'No, thanks.' Matty stalked towards the stairs. 'We haven't enough baby stuff to stay a night away. And besides, we're committed tomorrow. Mine's a huge scotch, Niall.' He stomped up, kicking the bare risers with his toes.

'Which means I'm the designated driver again,' Sally sighed. 'Boy, he's tetchy today – I'm sorry, everyone.'

'Always was a grumpy little milksop,' Etty grumbled, listening as, upstairs, Matty told off Tash in an embarrassed and huffy voice for not locking the bathroom door. 'Just like his 'orrible father.'

'Mother!' Alexandra shushed, shooting Sally an apologetic look.

'It hasn't got a lock,' Tash was explaining over her shoulder as she pounded downstairs, having changed from her damp trouser suit to a woolly red sweater dress.

'Ah, Tash – I've got your pressy—' Alexandra started to open her coat.

'I suppose that terrible man weel be there tomorrow?' Etty butted in, pursuing her own line of conversation.

'I expect so,' Alexandra sighed, closing her coat again.

'Who?' Tash kissed Niall on the cheek and helped him prise open the ice compartment of the freezer.

'Your father.' Alexandra wrinkled her nose as though talking about a strong smell.

'Oh, him.' Tash shrugged. 'Now who wants scotch and who wants gin and tonic? Only Niall seems to have poured about seven glasses of both.'

'How many are there then?' Niall looked up.

'Seven adults,' Tash counted. 'Three sprogs and Linus.'

'Ah, well, I know Linus likes a few chasers with his three o'clock bottle.' Niall held up his hands with a big grin and downed a scotch in one. 'You okay there, Pascal?'

'Hmmph.' Pascal – who had descended into understandable sulks sometime between peeling his eightieth and ninetieth sprout – looked up from his parsnip purée, grey eyes narrowed. 'Lunch, he is ready in *cinq minutes*.'

'That's great, so it is.' Niall was looking slightly worried. 'Tash . . .' He cleared his throat and jerked his head towards the stairs door.

Halfway up them, they went into a huddle.

'How many plates do we have exactly?' he whispered.

Tash covered her mouth, eyes widening as she gazed at him.

'Six settings,' she muttered through her fingers.

'Will that stretch to ten?'

Biting her lip, Tash shook her head. She knew her step-father's love of formal dining. Having so nobly set to work creating a lunch at which he was supposed to be a guest, and having cooked it with far more skill than she could ever have hoped for, Pascal would now want to sit at the head of a beautifully laid table, playing host with his usual bonhomie and aplomb, as though he was back in his Loire Valley *manoir* hosting a banquet for thirty.

They had the table – a grand, creaking, stone-topped one which Hugo Beauchamp had given Niall as a moving-in present and Tash generally used for spreading out her art equipment. And they had enough chairs – just, if they used the sofa, the bathroom laundry chair and the three garden chairs out of the shed, she worked out. But their crockery and cutlery would never stretch. Why hadn't she thought of that before?

'Okay.' She scratched her head, thinking fast. 'You dash along to the Olive Branch – they'll have finished serving lunch by now. Beg and borrow what you can – serving stuff too. Give Ange a present as a bribe – anything you can find. Or tell him I'll paint a picture of the pub as thanks. Steal if you have to. I'll set up what I can here.'

While Niall, still pulling on his shoes, dashed along the lane, Tash rushed around the cottage to the bemused speculation of her family, pulling a duvet cover out of the laundry cupboard and spreading it over the table in place of a cloth, and ramming bits of the already bedraggled Christmas tree into a chipped vase between the two stubby candles in the centre.

'Do you think she'll stop for a moment?' Alexandra hissed at Sally as Tash raced around in search of napkins. 'Only I want to give her this present.' She opened her coat a fraction.

'Oh, there it is,' Sally giggled. 'I was wondering what had happened to that. Don't show it to Matty, for God's sake. He'll start lecturing about one being for life, not just for Christmas.'

'Oh, that's so sentimentally English. This is a French pup, darling.'

'You *smuggled* it?' Sally balked.

'No, no – well, not exactly.' Alexandra glanced at Pascal who was whipping something in the kitchen now. 'This is one of Rooter's pups.'

'Rooter?'

'Great big hairy thing that one of Tash's admirers gave to her while she was staying with us in Champegny.'

'Yes, I remember.' Sally thought back. 'Looked like a large pampas grass arrangement on legs.'

'And Rooter was none too pretty either.' Alexandra cuddled her coat closer.

'Was?'

'Poor old darling breathed his last in Pascal's herb garden last month.' She looked rather tearful. 'He went out with a bang – literally. He was on the job with one of my spaniels at the time. Poor darling, I was rather attached to the old thing. He'd been with us almost two years.'

'Don't tell me that's the result?' Sally pointed to her stomach in shock.

'No, no – far too early for those to pop out, although God knows who we'll palm that litter off on this time. The whole valley is populated with Rooter's progeny now. There are shaggy yellow dogs of varying sizes on every street corner. No, this is an earlier vintage. My friends the Gallaghers – do you remember?'

'We had dinner with them when we stayed with you.'

'Yes, darling – and they had a little Manchester terrier called Bet with a very wet nose that was prone to point up unfortunate places?'

'I remember.' Sally crossed her legs.

'Well, the Gallaghers have moved back to Edinburgh now – Hamish's job, I think. And Rooter clearly rooted just a few days before they came back. Poor little Bet – Lord knows she must have winced, she's so small. Anyway, halfway through quarantine out popped five puppies. This is the runt. She's already four months old, but not as big as her ma. Hamish Gallagher saved her for me.'

'She's divine.' Sally lifted up the coat and looked at the strange little creature – a leggy mixture of black and tan fluff, pointy snout, vast opal eyes and big, petal ears the colour of golden biscuits. She was utterly endearing with her gamine Audrey Hepburn face and waifish, waggy tail, and was now quite settled in her fuggy hideaway.

Niall returned just as Pascal was threatening to throw the drying meal out of the window. He was weighed down with crockery, had knives and forks poking out of every pocket and smelled slightly of the two vast Bushmills that Marco Angelo, their local Italian landlord, had pressed upon him.

'He asked if you could do a portrait of Denise for her birthday next summer.' Niall hiccuped slightly, winking at Tash and setting his load down on the table with a clank. 'Says to make her look ten years younger and three stone lighter, or she'll never talk to you again.'

'Bless him.' Tash grinned, hastily setting places.

Marco and Denise Angelo ran the immensely successful Olive Branch with its Michelin-starred Italian restaurant. Known locally as Ange and Den, they were only slightly more famous for their food and hospitality than they were for their flamboyant bilingual arguments and smashing china. Today was obviously a harmonious day at *casa* Angelo, Tash surmised, from the stack of chip-free china that Niall had returned with.

'Now – at last – you can both have your present!' Alexandra gasped with relief and opened her coat, just as a small, fluffy bundle of long legs and big petal ears threw up on her expensive woollen trousers.

'*À table!*'

They were still madly opening presents when Pascal called them over to eat, leaving Polly, Tom and Tor sulky and frustrated as they were forced to relinquish new toys before trying to break them properly.

The meal was a glorious victory of skill over time. Pascal had taken the turkey off the bone to cook it quickly, poaching it in gallons of wine and double cream before grilling it in a cranberry glaze. The result was as moist and melting as watermelon, and surrounded by piles of glossy, crisp vegetables dripping with butter and black pepper.

Sally eyed the others' plates jealously as she ate the soggy pizza which Tash had hastily defrosted and microwaved when Matty announced that he and his family would not sacrifice their vegetarian ideals for Christmas. She was also sipping mineral water as she was the designated driver for the day.

'Can I have a piece of turkey?' Tom begged.

'No, you can't,' Matty snapped, pedantically picking pieces of pepperoni from his pizza slice before reaching across to do the same on Tor's. 'These pizzas aren't all veggie, Tash.'

'Aren't they?' she asked guiltily. She had realised that earlier, but had hoped that if she burned them enough they wouldn't notice.

Etty, who had called Pascal 'James' three times now, was eyeing Tash's left hand beadily.

Tash hoped she'd remembered to wash her hands since returning from the Moncrieffs'. She had a feeling that she hadn't. No wonder Matty was picking at his pizza like a medieval king's poison-tester.

The leggy puppy, whom Niall had named Beetroot, sat on Tash's lap throughout and was stuffed with turkey breast. She munched happily, her white teeth and pink tongue working furiously, and showed no more signs of nausea, for which Tash was relieved, having no desire to change yet again.

'Do you really like her?' Alexandra asked again over Christmas pud, anxious not to inflict an unwanted burden upon her youngest daughter.

'I love her – we love her.' Tash grinned at Niall and then her mother. 'I'm so sorry about Rooter, Mummy. He was a lovely character.'

''E smell like a *pissoir*,' Pascal pointed out, dousing the pudding in brandy for the third time and applying his lighter.

The two magnums of champagne were polished off with wildly indulgent speed and followed by several bottles of Chianti which Niall had bought for the occasion and which Pascal, who was a Gallic wine snob, pronounced 'undrinkable'.

Etty by far out-drank anyone and became quite raucous over Niall's sublime Irish coffee and Sainsbury's discount petits fours. Her bearskin and fur discarded, she turned out to be wearing a rather creased silk handkerchief dress and to have Carmen waves as even as corrugated iron in her gun-grey hair. Her face flushed from the booze and the heat of the fire, she watched Tash and Niall with her clever green eyes, liking the way they touched so often, passed glances as instinctively as two old carpenters working a double-handed lathe together. They weren't so silly and infatuated as to finish one another's sentences and call each other by sickly nick-names, she noticed with approval, but they had a simpatico rhythm, a way of reacting to one another, which denoted people so similar they could almost share identical genes.

As she settled in front of the fire with Alexandra and Pascal while the others started wrapping up for a cold, dark post-prandial walk with the kids, she caught her daughter's hand and squeezed it.

'I think we're going to have another family wedding soon,' she whispered in a very loud stage hiss, nudging her grey-pencilled eyebrows towards Tash who was trying to fit Tom into a pair of her wellies, and Niall who was tickling Tor until she dissolved into shrieking, delighted giggles.

'Really?' Alexandra looked terribly excited.

'Oh, yes.' Etty hiccuped slightly. 'I wouldn't be surprised if he's already asked her. I expect they'll announce it tomorrow – with the whole family gathered.'

'Gosh, do you think so?' Alexandra found she couldn't stop smiling. Whether it was from the champagne or her mother's certainty, she couldn't work out. Tash getting married to lovely Niall! The thought filled her with warm little shivers of hope.

'What makes you so sure, Etty?' Pascal puffed out his cheeks sceptically.

'Once one reaches my grand age, *chéri*, one knows it all,' she said haughtily. 'Besides,' she hissed under her breath, 'she ees wearing a ring on her engagement finger. One of those modern, trendy designers, I think. Probably Tiffany's.'

'What?' Alexandra and Pascal both craned around to gape, but Tash had pulled on her gloves and had Tom's hand in one furry mitt, the door latch in the other.

Sally, who hated walking and was afraid of the dark, plumped down beside her mother-in-law, certain that she had just caught the tail end of the most riveting piece of gossip.

'I think I'll stay here and chat, Matty.' She smiled blithely at her husband as he donned his crocheted hat once more. 'Keep an eye on Linus in the face of all this drunkenness.' She nodded towards Pascal, who was vaguely trying to offer his step-grandson a champagne cork instead of his dummy to stop him bawling.

'Sure,' Matty struggled into his cord jacket, unaware that Polly had tied the sleeves together.

'We'll only be half an hour or so,' Tash told her mother as she wandered out, letting in a rush of cold air in her wake. 'Just march this lot across the fields in the dark to see Zoe's kids' old ponies then back.'

''Bye, darling!' Alexandra waved her off and turned back to Pascal and Etty. 'This is so, so exciting. I can't wait to talk to James about it tomorrow.'

Etty and Pascal both exchanged horrified glances.

'About what?' Sally refreshed her glass of mineral water with a vast slug of brandy.

'Tash and Niall are engaged!' Alexandra confessed sotto voce as Matty followed the others out, having finally unknotted his sleeves.

'Ohmygod, how wonderful!' Sally whooped. 'Lisette will be so, so angry.'

Crunching over crisp, hard grass, Niall linked his fingers through Tash's and pressed a warm, steamy-breathed kiss into her cold ear.

'What's this?' He fingered a scratchy lump through her glove.

Tash looked down, trying to remember.

'Oh, that – I'd forgotten I still had it on,' she laughed. 'I pulled a cracker with Rufus this morning. It was my prize – he put it on me and proposed on Wally's behalf.'

'The little snake!' Niall pulled her closer. 'I hope you said no?'

'I said I'd think about it.'

'And have you?'

'Well, Wally's a great listener.'

'Bad breath.'

'Lovely brown eyes.'

'Farts in public, so he does.'

'Tremendously loyal.'

'To Gus.'

'Sleeps with me more often than you do.'

'Eats his own faeces.'

'I'll say no.'

'Good.'

When they got back, Etty was snoring on the sofa with a glass of brandy tipping into her silk cleavage, and Pascal was watching the blue video and furtively drinking the last of the Chianti. He hastily discarded it into a dead pot plant when the door opened.

Talking in hushed voices, Alexandra and Sally were side-by-side on the sofa having a cryptic conversation about sympathetic vicars which they instantly changed to Royal gossip when the walkers trooped in, blowing out steam and banging their palms together.

'You ready for the off soon?' Matty asked his wife, hangover already cramping his temples.

Sally hiccuped mildly and stretched an arm over the crocheted blanket on the sofa-back to clasp his.

''Fraid Alexandra and I got a bit bladdered, darling.' She went slightly cross-eyed as she smiled up at him, cheeks flushed from the fire which she'd recently banked up with logs. 'Looks like we'll have to shack up here for the night after all – go to Sophia's party tomorrow perhaps?'

Matty hissed through his teeth, but he couldn't really complain. He saw Niall, his oldest friend, so seldom. And they hadn't had a chance to catch up yet. He could argue out the Sophia thing tomorrow. But there was one thing that he was singularly determined upon: they were going to sleep on the floor here tonight, not in the Moncrieffs' vast, dog-smelling, draughty farmhouse.

'Where are you staying, Mother?' He looked down at Alexandra's glossy brown crown.

'Oh – some local hotel Pascal booked us into. The Royal Beech, isn't it, darling?'

'Oak, I think,' Pascal was sniffing around in the kitchen for more wine.

'But that's miles away!' Tash laughed. 'At least three-quarters of an hour's drive.'

'Oh dear, I suppose we'd better set off. Kick Granny, will you, Polly?'

'Niall,' Sally started cautiously as she returned from a trip to the loo, 'this might sound very odd, but there appears to be a large white turkey asleep on your bed.'

Two

'NIALL AND TASH ARE to be married, darling. Isn't it tremendously exciting?' were the first words that Alexandra had directed towards her ex-husband, James French, for almost two years.

He took them with remarkable calm, his rather dour and flabby but still patrician face scarcely affording a twitch of a muscle in response. His murky green eyes, tinged with the red cross-latticing from a boozy Christmas Day, flickered fractionally towards his tall younger daughter and her scruffy partner before returning to the excited, brimming gaze of his first wife.

'Really?' He could barely be bothered to utter the word.

Alexandra had cornered him in their elder daughter's more formal sitting room – an oppressive panelled tomb of crimson and oak, redecorated almost as often as Sophia herself. They were downing pre-lunch drinks as Sophia dashed around feigning panic, her black hair swept up to Ivana Trump heights, her long slim body swathed in Ralph Lauren wool, her face as exquisitely painted as the Old Masters adorning the panelled walls. Even though she had every finite detail of her lunch meticulously planned and listed on the schedule pinned to the fridge by a magnet, she could not relax.

Once a successful cover-girl who had been tipped for years to be a future supermodel and then grown too old to be super enough, she had achieved coffee-table tome fame instead by marrying into one of the oldest aristocratic families in the country – the hunting-mad, flat-chinned, acutely unacademic Merediths, who had square miles of estates attached to their several inherited titles, but barely enough realisable wealth to buy a square meal.

At first the family had staunchly disapproved of Sophia's middle-class connections and glitzy past, perceiving her as a 'showgirl'. Yet during the six years of her marriage to the amiable, oafish heir to the family's estates, Ben, she had proved herself to be far more commercially astute than the rest of the clan, who thought that opening one's house to the public was simply a matter of propping the front door ajar with a gumboot scraper and getting a local lout to direct cars into a flat field somewhere. Drawing on her celebrity-circuit and café-society connections, Sophia had transformed the Merediths' stately gothic pile, Holdham Hall, into a popular venue for charity functions, film location shoots and rich-at-play events, which in turn drew great swathes of the public for a nose around during the five summer months that the house was opened, hoping to spot a star – one of whom was Sophia herself, a *Tatler* and gossip-column regular.

The Merediths still saw Sophia as flighty and light-weight, but they could not deny the benefits of her tireless work. She was meticulously organised in everything she did – memorising names before parties, plotting exactly who to introduce to whom, researching the backgrounds of the most important or influential people in any one room. Even her own family Boxing Day drinks – held at Home Farm, where she and Ben lived, not the Hall which was still occupied by the incumbent earl – was organised with the same crib-sheet social skills.

The heating in Home Farm was turned to almost sub-zero because Sophia's dress was angora and made her glow as though straddling a radiator, the Christmas decorations glittered just as they had in the Harrods' seasonal display three weeks earlier and subtle strains of Elgar in her father's honour were battling to be heard over the guests' chatter (James loved Elgar for the simple and singular reason that he was British). In Sophia's vast Smallbone kitchen three local girls, the French nanny and a rather thick cousin of her husband's who had done a Prue Leith course recently were peeling, grating, basting, chopping – and bitching about her like mad. The house reeked of beeswax and Floris-scented candles. Even the dogs were sitting in a neat, bus-queue line by the closed kitchen door, looking as though they were fresh from a week with Dunbar. Yet still Sophia flapped and fussed and could not settle into conversations beyond a polite enquiry into someone's health at the same moment as she excused herself to check the pheasant soup.

Etty pursued her into the kitchen.

'Seet Niall next to your sister at lunch, *chérie*,' she demanded.

'Don't be silly, *Grandmère*,' snapped Sophia, dipping a little finger into the soup. 'That would ruin my seating plan.'

'Just do it,' Etty ordered, striding over to the range to help herself to more Glühwein, 'or I'll pretend to have dementia all afternoon.'

As Sophia raced off to swap around her place cards, Etty winked at the fat French nanny who was helping herself to a hunk of cooking chocolate. That, she reflected, would make their announcement far easier.

Tash and Niall, unaware that they were the subject of family scrutiny, were examining Sophia's Christmas cards, trying hard not to giggle at the more revolting photographs of chinless aristocratic children which various of Sophia's and Ben's friend had deemed picturesque enough for the front of their Season's Greetings. They certainly had a lot of cards – several hundred if counted – but not one from Tash and Niall who had missed the last Christmas post again this year.

'Of course it's all a complete secret – I'm not even supposed to know yet.' Alexandra took a huge slug of Glühwein and settled back into one of Sophia's sumptuous new brocade sofas while James perched uncomfortably on the arm. 'Mummy thinks they're going to announce it today. Doesn't she look well, by the way?'

'Needs a damned haircut.' James looked at Tash critically. She was excitedly waggling a card featuring Wills and Harry and whispering to Niall that Sophia must have forged it. 'So does her chap, come to that. Both look like a pair of gypsies.'

'I was talking about Mummy,' Alexandra said kindly, and then looked up to see James's wife hovering nervously in the doorway, the lipstick-stained glass of her third Glühwein already half-empty.

'Here, Henrietta darling!' she called out, patting the seat beside her. 'Come and sit down – you must be exhausted after all that cooking yesterday. How many did you have?'

'Oh, just James and the girls,' Henrietta swallowed nervously and perched as far away from Alexandra as possible, avoiding that warm, friendly gaze as she cast her blue eyes down to her knees, uneasily pleating her flowered Laura Ashley skirt with her fingers. 'Emily wanted to bring her boyfriend, but James felt we should just have family this year.'

'Chap's a dratted yob.' James cleared his throat, desperate to prod Henrietta into a more animated state. She was usually far more effervescent than this, but whenever she encountered Alexandra, his cool-headed, blonde second wife – to whom Alexandra could give almost twenty years – became ridiculously gauche, like a lower-third schoolgirl with a crush on a sixth-form lacrosse captain.

'Em adores Six Pack,' she said gently. 'And, after all, he's her third boyfriend since she went to university last October, so I don't think we need panic. You know what they're like at that age.'

'Gosh, yes – Sophia had loads of simply ghastly boyfriends before she met Ben,' Alexandra sympathised. 'Tell me, why is he called Six Pack? Is he a bit of a party animal or something?'

Henrietta shook her head. 'Something to do with his tummy, I gather. Em tried to explain, but I found it all rather baffling.'

'Is she here today?'

Alexandra looked around the gathered throng, a mixture of her own children and grandchildren, Sophia's in-laws and various honking Worcestershire locals that her elder daughter had deemed socially vital for Boxing Day lunch. The only noticeable absentees were various of the Merediths who were still out hunting, Ben's great chum Hugo who – usually a regular at Sophia's Boxing Day gathering – had Christmased in Australia this year, and, now Alexandra came to look, Henrietta's fractious but likeable elder daughter Emily was also not in evidence.

'She's spending the day with some friends.' Henrietta gave James a sideways look, but he showed no sign of guilt. There had been a huge row that morning as he'd tried to bully Emily into coming, culminating in his telling her that he wouldn't pay off her overdraft unless she came to lunch. She'd refused, and stormed away from the house in Henrietta's car.

'I see Beccy's here, though.' Alexandra grinned at Henrietta's younger, pudgier blonde daughter, who grinned back and then, blushing furiously, scuttled over to attack a tray of hors d'oeuvres. She reminded Alexandra of Tash at that age – shy, easily intimidated and desperate not to be noticed.

'Is she doing "A" levels this year?'

'Next.' Henrietta watched as her daughter crammed back three smoked salmon parcels on the trot.

'You and I must get our heads together soon.' Alexandra dropped her voice and touched Henrietta's arm. 'About the most exciting event of next year.'

'Oh yes?' Henrietta hoped it wasn't anything that might annoy James.

'Tash and Niall's wedding,' Alexandra whispered. 'I hope you'll chum up with me to organise it – I think we can give them quite a splash, don't you? Particularly if we keep the details a surprise. Pascal's agreed to pay for most of it, so I'm planning to spend a lot of time in England this spring. Gosh, we can be lavish!'

That, Henrietta realised, was truly going to annoy James.

'Lunch!' Sophia chimed at the same time as her synchronised antique clocks all pealed the first hour of the afternoon throughout Home Farm.

'Christ, it's like the Feast of Lanterns,' Sally muttered under her breath as they filed through to the long dining room to be faced with a table positively groaning under the weight of its piled goodies – most of them priceless crockery and silver rather than food.

Beside her, Matty, who was rebelliously donning his crocheted hat, was looking hugely sulky. They had spent a ludicrously uncomfortable night on the floor of the forge whilst the kids shared the sofa like Dickensian waifs. As a result they were both walking like rheumatic OAPs and Matty was convinced he had developed a chill. He was absolutely furious that his mother had called the forge from her plush hotel first thing that morning to pass on the news that Sophia was now expecting them for lunch and was delighted that they could make it after all. Knowing that Tash and Niall were likely to announce their Big News that day, Sally had insisted that they cancel their London lunch and go to Worcestershire.

'She told me there was nothing veggie here apart from bloody veggies,' Matty hissed under his breath.

'Great – can I have ham then?' Tom looked up at his father hopefully.

'No, you can't.' Matty grumpily sat down next to Niall, completely ignoring Sophia's placings.

Sighing, Sally winked at a downcast Tom and headed for the opposite end of the table where she realised happily that Sophia had placed her between her affable, easy-going husband Ben and a very dishy local who'd already filled her glass several times, told her some lovely gossip about the Parker-Bowleses and peered into her cleavage with surreptitious admiration, much to Matty's disgust – more because she had her cleavage on display than because he had looked, Sally suspected.

'Tom, you're eating in the kitchen with the other children.' Sophia smiled coolly at her nephew.

'But I'm nine!' he protested, looking deeply affronted.

'Quite,' Sophia waved him away impatiently. 'Beccy can eat with us this year, though.'

'Gee, thanks.' Beccy pushed back her alice band and noticed to her delight and terror that Sophia was booting Matty out of his chair and indicating for her to sit in it. This meant she would be sitting next to Niall. Next to her all-time hero, idol and crush. Next to the man she most wanted to take her breath away, take her virginity, and just basically take her away.

'I think I'd really rather eat with the children, actually,' she said in a terrified bleat.

'Nonsense!' Sophia looked aghast. 'You'll muck up my numbers.'

'Oh, do sit next to Niall,' encouraged a soft voice behind Beccy as Tash wandered back from washing her hands upstairs. 'He thinks your're great – and he's dying to give you all his opinionated clap-trap about horses and courses.'

Beccy blushed even more deeply. Try as she might to hate Tash for having Niall, she admired her riding too much to truly detest her. Beccy was on the lower rungs of eventing – just out of juniors and into young riders – and Tash was something of an idol.

'Besides, he's got Granny opposite him, and he's terrified of her.' Tash winked at Beccy and nodded towards Etty, still sporting her bearskin hat and fur coat to ward off the cold of Sophia's house. 'You can hold his hand and keep him distracted.'

Beccy gulped with gratitude and fear.

Tash was rather alarmed throughout the meal to find herself being peered at with avid interest by a number of her relatives. Her every move, from using the wrong spoon for her starter to dribbling red wine down the front of her cream jumper, was noted and contemplated by several sets of amber or green eyes.

She tried to catch Niall's eye for support, but he was wrapped up in flirting with Beccy on his far side, making Henrietta's daughter turn pink with delight as he flattered her like mad to cheer her up. Tash helped herself to more devilled turkey and dropped most of it in her wine glass.

By the time the dessert was circulating the table on a second lap, Sally had winked at her three times, her father had asked her if she had anything she wanted to tell him, and Etty loudly enquired why she wasn't wearing her lovely glass ring today.

'My what?'

'Your ring, *chérie*.' Etty waved her wine glass around in an expansive gesture which caused the men either side of her to duck. 'That lovely *bijou* that you were wearing *hier soir*.'

'Oh, that thing!' Tash laughed. 'I think I've lost it.'

There was a shocked silence at her end of the table.

Niall, who'd had rather too much wine, let out an enraged faux-theatrical wail as he turned to face her again. 'But that was your engagement ring, dammit!'

'And I told you yesterday that my answer was no.' Tash grinned at him.

'Ah, no, my darling.' Reaching out a hand, he lifted her chin and stared her out with relish. 'What you actually said was that you'd think about it.'

'I might change my mind then.' Tash pouted cheerfully, giving him a slight wink.

The rest of the table was hushed now. From the gloomy far end, Tash caught sight of her gossip-mad Aunt Cassandra frantically shushing various waffly locals.

'I might even say yes, just for the hell of it,' she half-heartedly pursued the role-play, increasingly aware that it was eliciting rather too much attention, particularly from her mother, who was almost in the flower arrangement in her attempt to listen in.

'Might you now?' Niall was growing aware of the attention too and relishing the prospect of playing to a crowd, although several glasses of Ben's best port was blurring the plot somewhat. He seemed to recall that Tash was entertaining a proposal from Wally the collie at Lime Tree Farm.

'Oh, yes, you must!' Alexandra joined in eagerly. 'You absolutely must!'

'Must what?' Tash and Niall both turned to her in confusion.

'Say yes.' Alexandra sounded slightly less sure of herself now. 'I actually thought you already had. I've told your father and he's terribly excited about it.'

'Is he?' Bewildered, Tash looked at her father.

James cleared his throat awkwardly. 'Very pleased. Yes,' he muttered grimly.

'What on earth are you all on about?' Sophia piped up from the end of the table, furious that this loud family dispute had just interrupted a wonderful, gossipy story she was being told about a local landowner's marijuana plants.

'Tash and Niall are going to get married!' Alexandra announced dreamily.

'We're *what*?' Tash gaped at her.

Niall started to laugh uproariously. Beside him, Beccy's face was fading with disappointment through the various shades of high blush like a dying sunset.

It was at this moment that Etty Buckingham realised that she might have started something of a faux-rumour. She dabbed her nervously puckered mouth daintily with her napkin as she let the gravity of her misapprehension sink in. Never one to take being proven wrong on the chin, she realised that hasty and drastic action was called for.

'Eeeeegh!' She let out a delighted, creaky wail which silenced the table from its increasingly excited, congratulatory babbling.

'You are going to make a dying woman so very, very 'appy, *ma jolie petite!*' She rose shakily from her seat, mustering a few tears as she stretched across the table to embrace Tash, hugging a lot of the flower arrangement at the same time. 'I sink zere is not a lovelier sing I could want to 'appen before I leave zis world.'

'But I – I mean we . . .' Tash fought to control the situation, but her grandmother was too forceful and too desperate.

'I weel pay for eet all,' Etty announced grandly, reaching for a handkerchief to dab her eyes. 'I weel spare no expense. I weel make thees the best—'

'We're paying, Mummy!' Alexandra chipped in. 'Pascal is quite delighted to help two such lovely young people start married life with every possible treat.'

Pascal cleared his throat unhappily.

'I say, congratulations, chaps—' Ben Meredith was trying to raise his glass at the head of the table, but his wife cut him off.

'By rights, Daddy should actually pay for Tash's wedding, Mummy,' she argued. 'He paid for ours.' She carefully didn't add what a fight he had put up to keep it cheap.

James's jowls were lifting like a bulldog cornered by honking geese. 'I'm not bloody paying.'

'But we're—' Tash stared hopelessly at Niall.

He was still speechless with giggles, lifting his palms upwards and shaking his head.

'You paid for my wedding!' Sophia pointed out.

'And damned nearly bankrupted myself in the process.'

'I weel pay!'

'You're absolutely penniless, Mother. Of course you can't pay.' Alexandra was beaming at Tash, tears edging her mascara into her crows' feet. 'I'm just so happy for you both, darling.'

'Mummy, I think there's been a terrible mis—'

'Shut up, everyone!' howled a loud bass from the head of the table, accompanied by the chiming of a coffee spoon against a port glass.

They all shut up and turned to look at Sophia's husband, Ben – a tall, rangy blond with soup stains on his shirt and his thinning mop of hay-like hair on end. He rose from his seat to his full six feet four inches, stooping to avoid the Christmas holly which was escaping from a picture frame behind his head, and grinned awkwardly.

'I think we should actually be congratulating Tash and Niall here,' he said, rather embarrassed now by his outburst, his weathered cheeks starting to pinken. 'Champagne all round, I say.'

'Have we got enough?' Sophia took a sharp breath. 'It won't be chilled.'

'It weel in this house, *chérie*.' Pascal shivered.

'Oh, Christ alive!' Tash whispered, kicking Niall, who was now bent double with delighted mirth. 'What are we going to do?'

Etty, who was pretending to be so carried away with emotion that she had her face buried in her handkerchief, held her breath and eyed them closely through the lacework.

'Well.' Niall straightened up with difficulty and buried his mouth in Tash's hair so that only she could hear, 'We could get married, I guess.' He was still fighting giggles.

'I guess,' Tash said hesitantly, worried that she was going to faint because her heart was beating so quickly that her blood was whooshing around her body like a white-water canoe run. 'Don't you think it's a bit drastic, though?'

'Not nearly so terrifying a prospect as telling your family that it's been a mistake.'

Niall kissed her ear through its curtain of hair and tried not to notice that Pascal had whipped out his camera and was snapping their embrace for the album. At least Polly, who was confined to the kitchen with the other children, couldn't video it.

He was still buoyed up by several glasses of scotch and a bottle of Burgundy, Tash realised. In this state he'd agree to sky-dive naked from the Holdham Hall ramparts if he thought it would make him popular with her family.

'This is ridiculous.' She bit her lip and then shook her head firmly. 'We must tell them, Niall.'

Pulling away, she turned to face the pairs of eager eyes trained on her. Even Sophia's helpers, staggering in with bottles of their employer's non-vintage champagne, were watching the couple with avid absorption. Niall's star status made this something of a coup – they'd undoubtedly be on to the tabloid press as soon as the corks had popped.

'Listen, everyone.' Tash took a deep breath. 'I have something to explain before this goes too far—'

The next moment a broad, warm hand had enveloped hers and she was swept out of the room, almost flooring herself as she fell over Sophia's pack of dogs, now lined up like the von Trapp children outside the dining-room doors.

Niall pulled her into the kitchen lobby and glanced around to check they wouldn't be overheard before clutching her shoulders and pressing her back against a hunting print. 'Don't tell them,' he urged.

'I must!' Tash stared into his chocolate eyes, wishing for a brief, honeyed moment that she didn't have to. 'This is all wrong. We can't get hitched just because my potty grandmother gets the wrong end of the stick. It's mad.'

'No more mad than me getting down on one knee and embarrassing myself by fluffing my lines, now.'

Tash pushed her hair out of her eyes and stared at him, her heart suddenly in her throat and using her epiglottis as a punch-bag.

'You weren't going to though, were you?' She swallowed her heart down so that she could croak out the words, but it continued beating madly in her windpipe like a ping-pong ball in a vacuum hose.

'Well, not today, no.' He shrugged, glancing away. 'Perhaps not at all. Not like that, no.'

Tash closed her eyes. She and Niall spent such long stretches of time apart, and were hopelessly impractical when together. Although lovely, their relationship had barely progressed in the two years they had been together. Each brief, snatched weekend still possessed the heady, heart-lifting feeling of a holiday romance. They weren't really capable of buying a toaster jointly, let alone starting married life.

'I went down on my knees to ask Lisette to marry me,' Niall was saying, his voice suddenly very quiet and serious.

'Was that before or after you tied the knot in the Las Vegas Elvis Chapel?' Tash bit her lip and fought a smile.

'Shhh!' Niall rolled his eyes. 'Don't remind me. We hardly saw that as a marriage – it was the family occasion in England that counted. I did everything the right way – father's permission, talking and planning through the night, not telling her where the honeymoon would be. Look where that got us.'

'I know.' Tash touched his cheek, trying to blot out the excited chatter coming from the nearby dining room.

'And you once agreed to marry someone you didn't love simply because you didn't want to hurt his feelings by saying no,' he reminded her with a crooked smile.

Tash guiltily bit her lip at the memory. She had agreed to get engaged to an ex-boyfriend once because she couldn't bring herself to tell him that the relationship was over. It had been one of the worst times of her life.

He pressed his forehead to hers. 'So I guess asking isn't always the best route.'

She gazed into his dark, honest eyes for a long time.

'What exactly are you saying here?'

Niall smiled. It was that big, loopy smile which creased his cheeks, crinkled his brown eyes and could stop her heart at fifty paces.

'That perhaps your mad bloody family have done us a favour. That perhaps this is fate. Neither of us is putting pressure on the other; the pressure is from outside. We could tackle this together. Think about this together. Enjoy this together. That's what marriages are about, Tash – committing to something together.'

'You're not saying that you're really willing to go through with it?' She gulped.

'Why not?' he laughed. 'We love each other, live together as much as we can. We now have dual custody of a dog and a turkey. And,' he rolled his eyes, 'I seriously think your grandmother would breathe her last if we tell them it's all been a misunderstanding now.'

'You really want to marry me?' Tash was aware that she was sounding rather thick, but she wanted to make sure she was reading this absolutely right.

'Depends if you want to marry me?' He raised a black eyebrow hopefully.

'It's certainly a thought.'

'Nothing need change.' He shrugged. 'Sure, you don't even need to change your name. And it'd make your family and mine extremely happy.'

'And us?'

Niall smiled. 'I don't know about you, but the only thing in the world that would make me happier would be a bit more time with you.'

'Same here.'

'So, shall we do it?'

Tash hugged him tightly, tucking the doubts and worries tightly away in her excited, leaping heart. 'Like you say, why not?'

Three

NIALL'S FAMILY WERE NOT as delighted as he'd anticipated. In their Catholic eyes, he was still, strictly speaking, married to Lisette, so could not be married again in their church. And, although they adored Tash, they felt she was too young and too daffy to make their son a decent wife.

'Sure, the girl's a mere slip of a ting, Niall,' his mother worried when he called them from the forge to break the news. 'And she's a hopeless cook, so she is. I'll never forget those sloppy pancake tings she served up on your birthday last year.'

'Fajitas.'

'Well, it certainly gave your father gas, now.' There was a deep sigh at the other end of the line followed by the sound of a hand-rolled cigarette being lit. 'Are you sure you're doing the right ting here, son?'

'Sure,' Niall said firmly, knowing just how to win her over. 'Tash can't wait to start a family.'

'Ah, sweet girl.' There was an ecstatic exhalation of breath followed by a hacking cough. 'I'm so pleased for you, my darling. Sure, it's about time you gave Nuala's nippers some young cousins to play with now.' She started coughing again.

'You should give up smoking, Mother,' Niall scolded. 'I feel so much better since I packed it in.'

As soon as he was off the phone, he lit up one of Tash's Camel Lights and wondered if feeding his mother the babies line had been a wise move. She was bound to be searching for her knitting needles already in anticipation of tiny socks and babygrows.

Through Lime Tree Farm's illuminated kitchen window, Tash caught sight of a neat, pudding-basin mop of blonde hair flopping over the table to scan a newspaper, and breathed a sigh of relief as she realised Zoe was there to offer coffee and advice. As she crunched up the drive, Zoe looked up and waved, smiling widely. She had a classically poised, northern European appearance that seemed icy-cool and imperturbable on the surface but cracked every time she smiled to reveal a bubbling geyser of warmth beneath. Tash thought her the epitome of sex appeal and longed to possess that effortless glamour.

Zoe Goldsmith was older than her sister, Penny, by a few years – she never specified how many – and had been something of a career and society glamourpuss in her time. For many years, she had been married to one of London's most successful designers. In the eighties, she'd had a showpiece house in Greenwich, a regular 'career mother' column in a Sunday broadsheet, feature pieces commissioned weekly, a designer wardrobe and two great kids who were so well behaved and good-looking that her friends had smarted with envy as they wiped snot and jam from the howling faces of their own plump brats.

Quite what had gone wrong was something Zoe kept a closely guarded secret. All Tash knew was that the dream marriage had ended very abruptly and acrimoniously, leaving her financially stymied as she lost both her house and the job practically in the same week. She and the kids had then decamped to stay with Penny and Gus temporarily until Zoe could find more work and get herself a small flat in London.

That had been seven years ago. So far as Tash could gather, Zoe had gone through some sort of breakdown shortly afterwards, and had stayed on to recuperate, paying her way by cooking and filing for her overstressed sister who in those days competed abroad for a great part of the year. Finding it impossible to get back into the closed shop of high-powered journalism, Zoe had tried instead to write fiction, failing to attract any interest in her work for several years before she accidentally bumped into an old friend who was setting up a new publishing venture.

That venture was now one of the most successful erotic fiction imprints in the industry, churning out hot, steamy tomes with short shelf-lives and high profits. Zoe – under the name Su Denim – was its flagship author, with over twenty books to her credit. She could now easily afford those things that had eluded her after her divorce:

a London house, smart social life and public-school education for her kids. But instead, she deliberately shunned such superficial trophies, preferring the settled, bucolic life with her sister and brother-in-law. The warmth of her friends within the eventing circuit and the good education that the local schools were providing for her kids could not easily be replaced by the slavishly fashionable and academically snobbish world she had left behind in the chattering dining rooms of her London circle. In truth, Tash also suspected that she stayed at Lime Tree Farm because she also knew how invaluable she had become to Penny and Gus. Without her calm, easy-going efficiency, unflappable common sense and occasional baling out when the bills turned red, the Moncrieffs would be bankrupt within weeks. Tash adored her, although she sensed a deep, enduring sadness that Zoe kept deeply hidden from her chaotic, dependent family.

'Can I borrow a fag? I left mine in the forge.'

Tash settled down at the Moncrieffs' cluttered table and reached for the nearest packet.

'Please do.' Zoe looked up from a pile of late Christmas cards and grinned. 'They're Rufus's. Since I confronted him about the cigarette butts in the guttering outside his window, the little brat now feels he can smoke openly in front of me. I have absolutely no authority.'

Rufus was the elder of her two children; at seventeen he was a big, blond charmer who loudly justified smoking, drinking and having four girlfriends as 'vital teenage experimentation'.

'Matty treated my mother the same way the moment he grew taller than her.' Tash was searching around for a lighter. 'It's just a height thing. Did you have a good Christmas?'

Zoe wrinkled her long, straight nose as she passed Tash a box of kitchen matches. 'Bit hectic. Gus had invited a load of people who he hadn't told me about, as ever.'

Even her voice was as warm and rich as butterscotch. Both sisters had cut-glass, almost antiquatedly clipped accents, harking back to hours of elocution lessons forced upon them by their snobbish parents. But whereas Penny had a high, slightly quacking voice that could split eardrums, Zoe's was so soft and velvety that she merely melted them.

'I was here when they arrived,' Tash reminded her. 'I saw Stefan Johanssen poling up along with Brian Sedgewick's mob. And two of Gus's brothers were arriving as I left.'

'So you were.' Zoe rubbed her forehead. 'Well, one chap got so paralytic he had to stay, and then Enid took a piece out of him when he came down for a glass of water during the night.'

'Poor thing.'

'It's okay, she calmed down once she realised he wasn't an intruder, didn't you, darling?' She blew a kiss to her nervy Dalmatian who was curled into a tight, uncomfortable knot in one of the tiny cats' beds by the Aga. Certifiably paranoid and singularly devoted to Zoe, Enid was wildly jealous of anyone her mistress touched or spoke to. Ears sinking back into her head, she blinked her pale amber eyes worriedly, anxious that she was being picked on.

'I was referring to him.'

'Oh, he'll live. Gus administered a tet jab with remarkable skill considering the number of bottles he'd sunk.'

'Christ, I'm glad I just had Matty and Sally snoring on our sofa.' Tash gazed around the kitchen, seeking comfort in the familiar, tatty paintings, over-stuffed shelves, piles of post and horse paraphernalia which littered every available surface. The room always smelled of hot coffee and wet boots.

'So Matty and Sally enjoyed Christmas with you, did they?' Zoe asked coolly.

'Sally did.' Tash gazed at the large, wipe-clean wall roster which had her marked as off work for the week. There was very little writing on it at all at this time of year as most of the horses were roughed off for winter and there were no events to attend apart from the odd hunt or indoor jumping competition. Come May it would be covered in bright felt pen marks like a toddler's mad doodling.

'And Matty?' Zoe was trying to coax Enid into eating a Bonio.

'Sulked throughout, as ever.' She sighed. 'I think they've got a lot of money problems at the moment. But Niall cheered him up in the end – he was wonderful, making everyone laugh so much.' She noticed that the list of next year's scheduled BHS trials was up on the wall at last, Blu-tacked beside the work roster with those competitions they were already entered for marked in red and those still pending in pencil. Eventing was so over-subscribed these days that sending off an entry fee was no longer a guarantee of competing – there was always a chance of being balloted out, and one had to choose which events to give top priority very carefully. Tash noticed to her delight that she was pencilled in for the biggest spring event, Badminton, on both of her top horses and a big grin spread across her face without her even noticing it.

Watching her, Zoe picked up a dead match and played with it thoughtfully. She knew Tash pretty well by now, realising that beneath the shy, rather clumsy exterior there existed a far tougher, more decisive heart. A heart that would tear itself out for something it loved and believed in, but with a good deal of self-preservation embedded in it too.

Tash was often embarrassed by the impact of her own physical presence. Despite an urge not to stand out, she was not a person who blended easily into the background. Extremely tall, curvy, and in possession of two huge, oddly coloured eyes, she inevitably drew attention as she dominated every crowd, her unkempt mop of hair several inches above everyone else's crown. These were not always admiring glances either: Tash had the natural hunched gaucheness of the self-conscious and seldom made an effort to dress up. She was renowned for looking dreadfully scruffy on almost all occasions. But this simply enhanced the effect whenever she did dress up. And, unusually, she had dressed up today.

Dark, smudgy kohl lines encircled her green and amber eyes, a beaded pin was holding her thick, curling hair up from her face to show off those high, pink cheek bones and long, long neck. She was even wearing a dress – the first time Zoe had seen her in one. Short, bias-cut and silky, it showed off her elongated curves and endless legs, although a tiny ladder was already threading its way up her tights.

'What's the occasion?' She smiled. 'I thought you'd just popped in for a coffee.'

'Niall's taking me out for dinner at the Olive Branch tonight.' Tash was staring at one of Zoe's daughter's GCSE drawings which was curling its way from its Blu-tacked position on the wall. 'That's a great picture – India just gets better and better.' She glanced at Zoe again. 'I was hoping the others would be here.'

'Well, Gus and Pen should be back any minute – they're raiding Tesco's wine department for New Year's Eve. You two are coming, aren't you?'

'To the party?' Tash grinned at her. 'Try and stop us.'

'Hugo will be back from Oz by then too – in fact, I think he's due back today, so he'll add to the glamour.'

'And to the drinks bill,' Tash sniffed.

'You two still not talking?' Zoe cocked her head critically. With her blonde, blunt-cut hair and thoroughbred features, she bore a rather startling resemblance to Joanna Lumley as Purdey. The cool, velvet voice and cat's eyes added to the illusion. There were moments Tash almost ducked for fear of getting a karate kick in the eye.

She pursed her mouth uneasily. 'Not sure. I've avoided him since the end of the season.'

'Mmm.' Zoe eyed her thoughtfully. 'I think Gus mentioned that you wouldn't even go hunting in case he was out with the field and tried to run you into a ditch.'

'Something like that,' Tash muttered. Although she had used the excuse of avoiding Hugo for not hunting this year, Tash had other reasons as well. A childhood accident and a general disapproval of the barbarity of the sport kept her away more than her tall, arrogant bête noire.

Hugo Beauchamp ran an eventing yard just a few miles away from Lime Tree Farm. He'd known Penny and Gus Moncrieff for years and they were mutually reliant upon one another, trading horses between the two yards, swapping advice, sharing the transport to many of the more distant events and helping one another out in a crisis. Hugo, who had a private income and a fat sponsorship deal, often benefited from the relationship more than the Moncrieffs, buying their best youngsters for the cash they desperately needed to keep the yard running. As a result, he was ranked amongst the top five riders in the country and had clocked up a large number of international honours to prove it. He even had an Olympic medal as the chain of his downstairs loo, which Tash thought horribly ostentatious.

Initially helpful when Tash had entered the sport, Hugo Beauchamp had been growing increasingly unpleasant of late. All had been well when she was a clumsy novice who seldom made it to the end of the cross-country phase, let alone into the money. Hugo, one of the sport's biggest stars, had coaxed her through her first year with rather condescending largesse, selling her his good novice, Drunken Hunk, giving her hours of coaching and ferrying her to events in his five-star lorry when Penny and Gus needed their dilapidated box elsewhere. But now that Tash was so regularly placed that she was climbing the overall leaderboard and getting ever-closer to making it into an international team, Hugo had gone right off her. He'd won last year's British Championship at the Gatcombe Open Trials just a weekend after Tash had moved into the forge with Niall, loudly rumour-mongering that she had done badly because she was thinking about kitchen cabinets and not the course. When she had beaten him into second place at Burghley three-day-event two months later, he had grown actively hostile, cutting her dead or putting her down at every opportunity. Hurt by his about-face, Tash now thought he was unspeakably spoilt and petty.

'Try to make friends again, huh?' Zoe uncurled her feet from beneath Wally the collie and stood up to put the kettle on.

'He's the one being unfriendly,' Tash pointed out tetchily.

'Well, I know.' Zoe was framing her words carefully, aware of how sensitive Tash could be about Hugo. 'But it does make things rather awkward for Gus when there's this ruck between you two. You know how much he relies upon Hugo's support.'

'Humph.' Tash stubbed out her cigarette. 'Hugo takes him for a ride almost as often as his own nags. Gus is better off without him.'

'Not really,' Zoe said kindly. 'I mean, I know that the majority of Hugo's actions are born out of self-interest, but he's not a bad ally for all his faults. He gets Gus liveries, gives him a lot of his time and cast-off equipment, sends Franny down here to help out when we're short-staffed.'

'I hardly think Hugo's forcing her!' she snorted.

Franny was Hugo's Rubensesque and rather terrifying head girl who dressed like an S & M mistress of pain and had a whip-like tongue to match. For the past six months she had been conducting a very public affair with Gus's much younger and less efficient groom, Ted. It paralleled and helpfully shielded the far more private liaison which Hugo was conducting with Gus's senior working pupil, Kirsty Judd, a Scottish event rider who used the yard as her southern base. Kirsty, who had worked in Australia for several years as a riding instructor, was engaged to a very rich, very macho Australian solicitor with whom she was spending Christmas. The fact that Hugo was also in Australia for the festive season had not gone unnoticed. Just as he took especial pleasure in riding dangerous horses, so, it seemed, he preferred his relationships with the heat on and the risk-factor high.

'Go easy on him on New Year's Eve, huh?' Zoe pleaded, handing Tash a chipped mug full of coffee. 'He's only mad at you because he's jealous.' She carefully didn't add what specifically he was jealous of. She privately doubted that it was just professional. Hugo was a far more complicated character than Tash gave him credit for.

'I'll try,' she sighed.

For years, as a teenager, Tash had lusted after Hugo from afar with a passion that only the hormonally confused youngster can harbour. A close friend of her brother-in-law Ben Meredith's, he had drifted around in the background of her family's social calendar like a beautiful spectre, and haunted Tash's dreams like a goading nightmare. His total disdain for her had been crucifying. While Tash had wept and daydreamed over pictures of him cut from *Horse and Hound*, Hugo had treated her with the curtest of uninterested scorn in return, hardly seeming to notice her existence.

It was only when they had been forced to endure one another's company during a long, lazy holiday with Alexandra, Pascal, and the rest of their assorted family and friends two years earlier that they had struck up an unexpected, if uneasy, friendship. Hugo, had helped her get to grips with the difficult, hot-headed Snob, given to his step-daughter by Pascal as a holiday challenge. Hugo had admired her courage and talent, and helped her get a job with the Moncrieffs as a result. For a brief and rather terrifying moment, he had even appeared to be attracted to her. The sense of amazed, disbelieving victory which Tash had experienced at that time had only been overtaken by the giddy joy of falling madly in love with Niall. Hugo had gone off her pretty quickly afterwards, and wasted no time in working his way through a string of staggeringly beautiful girlfriends, most of whom he treated appallingly.

Since then, Hugo had not shown the slightest interest in Tash as anything but a horsewoman and pupil, a fact which, in her very darkest, late-night moments, far away from Niall's comfortable, sleeping embrace, rather offended her. She knew that was fearfully disloyal to Niall, whom she loved with more depth and honesty than she had ever felt for Hugo during the agonising length of her fierce crush. But there was something competitive in her relationship with him that fed off a spark of sexual attraction. And, apart from that briefest of moments when he had wanted to take her to bed – in fact, Tash only guessed that he'd wanted to take her to bed, for he'd never actually stated the intention – all that attraction had been one-way. She had adored him for far, far longer than he'd ever fancied a quick night with her. Somehow, it left her feeling rather one down.

Zoe was still watching her closely as she stirred cream into her coffee from a plastic tub. 'You're not – no, no, forget it.'

'I'm not what?' Tash could hear Gus and Penny's grumbling old Land-Rover rattling over the frosted pot-holes in the drive outside.

Hearing it too, Zoe automatically reached for two more mugs.

'Not what?' Tash persisted.

'You'll bite my head off for this.' She smiled apologetically. 'But I have to ask to satisfy my insatiable curiosity. I was going to ask if you weren't just a little miffed about Hugo's affair with Kirsty? Because I rather get the impression that you still hold a bit of a torch—'

'No I do bloody not!' Tash could feel herself reddening.

'It's just that you've been far more anti-Hugo since it started.'

'The only reason his affair with Kirsty pisses me off is because she's stopped pulling her weight around here,' Tash pointed out piously.

'They can bonk morning, noon and night for all I care – until the suspension breaks on his ruddy horse-box, in fact. But if she asks me to exercise or muck out her bloody nags one more time, I'll shoot them both.'

'Right. Sorry. I was quite mistaken.' Zoe hid a smile. 'No torch, then.'

'Not even a match,' Tash insisted, disliking Zoe's smug smile. 'Anyway, how could I possibly feel a thing for that spoilt, stand-offish prig, when I'm going to marry Niall?'

'Quite.' Zoe was distracted by the banging of the back door as Gus and Penny staggered in, preceded by Wally who headed straight for Tash with a big, panting grin.

'Great to see you, Tash!' Gus greeted her with a whoop. 'I was hoping you might pole up and help out. We're bombed out with work. The horses need to come in to bed soon and most of them are crusted with frozen mud.'

'I – er – well, I just came for a chat really. I'm going out soon.'

'Oh, yeah, I see you're tarted up for once.'

Tash smiled weakly, wishing Gus Moncrieff would occasionally treat her with the same respect for feminine wiles as he did the other females in his circle. He always remembered to compliment his wife when she dressed up, was in constant awe of Zoe's understated sophistication, and positively drooled over his other working pupil, the red-headed, red-blooded and Monroe-chested Kirsty. But to Tash he gave the hair-ruffling, distracted attention of an owner patting his dog in passing. In fact, Tash reflected, he was more flattering to Wally than he was to her.

A tireless worker, Gus Moncrieff was in his early thirties but looked far older. He had a craggy, weathered face which was almost constantly dominated by a toothy smile, and a lanky frame which had far too little stuffing really to support it. A former point-to-point jockey, he still maintained his erstwhile anxiety to keep his weight down, aware that only the fittest, stockiest equines in his yard would be up to carrying his natural weight in the gruelling endurance phases of the sport. As a result, his skinny body had an apologetic stoop to it and his clothes, which had to be huge for his height and shoulders, hung off him like tent canvas after the guy ropes have been cut loose.

'I'll help you get some of your shopping in.' Tash leaped up quickly, aware that she had just been slagging off Kirsty for not pulling her weight around the yard.

'Thanks, hon.' Penny appeared in the doorway, buckling under a vast box of beer cans. 'Watch your step, it's really freezing over out there. You look nice.' She was momentarily distracted by a frantic hand-signal from Zoe, who was wide-eyed over her coffee pot, completely speechless.

Not noticing, Tash reached for her coat.

'Wish I'd agreed to give you that week off now.' Gus followed her out, scratching his very short, almost crew-cut, blond hair. 'Can you spare me a couple of hours to ride out Snob tomorrow? Ted's so frightened of him he keeps making up excuses not to.'

'I'll see,' Tash hedged. She'd had so little time off in the past year that she was unwilling to give it up.

By the time they'd slipped and struggled back into the house, Zoe had regained her senses and was gaping at Tash in astonishment. Penny, clearly in on her sister's sudden realisation, was hovering nearby and turning pink beneath her woolly hat, fleece jacket and thermal gloves as she whispered excitedly about it.

Zoe hushed her hastily and turned to Tash.

'Did you, um—' She cleared her throat, voice back down to its customary calm, fruity note. 'Did you say that you and Niall are going to be married?'

'Yes.' Tash set down a box of wine bottles on top of a pile of newspapers on the dresser.

'Really?' Penny was gaping at her as though she'd just said she was having a sex change.

'That's really what I said, yes,' she sighed, removing two party packs of crisps from the top of the box.

'You're joking, right?' Gus joined in the gaping.

'No!' she bristled, turning to face them. 'Why is everyone acting as though we've gone mad? Matty spent most of yesterday after-noon trying to talk Niall out of it, and he's my supposedly loving brother.'

'It's just,' Zoe hugged her apologetically, 'so sudden. Unexpected.'

'We've been together almost two years – and living together since last August.'

'Well, sort of, yes,' Penny agreed. 'In between living apart.'

Gus was trying hard not to laugh, which was even more insulting. Seeing Tash's hurt face, he battled with his amusement and looked at her earnestly. 'When exactly were you planning to get hitched?'

'Well, Mummy's keen on June.'

'Next June?' Zoe lifted a blonde eyebrow.

'In six months' time?' Penny lifted one of her own.

'In the middle of the bloody season?' Both of Gus's fluffy blond brows shot up in alarm too.

'Yes, yes and yes.' Tash wished she hadn't got herself quite so excited about telling them; their reaction was far from encouraging.

'Well, that's great.' Gus pulled himself together. 'Natasha O'Shaughnessy, huh?'

'I'm thinking of sticking with French.' Tash started nosing around in Tesco bags, eager for a comforting snack.

'And how does Niall feel about that?'

'He suggested it.' She located some crisps and ripped into the bag hungrily.

'Where is he, by the way?' Gus looked around. 'Writing guest lists?'

Tash poked out her tongue at him. 'He's walking the dog.'

They all stared at her. 'What dog?'

'Beetroot.' Tash grinned. 'You see, we have to get married. Give her a stable family home.'

'A shot-gundog wedding then?' Penny took off her woolly hat and ruffled her hair with a grin.

Once the news of their engagement had been announced at the Olive Branch that night, Tash and Niall were the grateful recipients of free champagne all evening.

'Ees so, so good.' Marco Angelo danced attendance around them, flapping serviettes and menus in between serving his ambrosial food. 'A wedding in the village! We haff not had a wedding for years!'

'Well, I'm not sure if we're getting married here,' Tash confessed, catching Niall's eye.

'Off course! You getta married in Catholic church – how could I forget?' The dapper little man smoothed back his pewter grey hair. 'You getta married in St Gabriel's in Marlbury, yes?'

'Er, no.' Niall cleared his throat. 'I've been married before, remember, Ange?'

'Oh, no worries. Father Quigley, he ees very sympathetic priest. He marry myself and Den, no?'

'I think my parents actually want me to marry from my old home.' Tash smiled apologetically. 'Near Windsor.'

'Oh.' Marco's mouth puckered slightly. 'Still, he is not far to drive. I arrange cover for that day, no?'

'Sure.' They both smiled up at him anxiously.

From the comments they had received that night, it seemed that all the congratulatory, excited locals were expecting an invitation to the reception at the very least. Once Tash and Niall added the eventers, film industry friends, mutual families and older friends, the reception was going to be simply colossal.

'Everyone wants to gawp at your film-star pals,' Tash giggled.

'Little do they know, I hardly have any.' Niall shrugged.

This wasn't strictly true – Niall made firm friends wherever he went and on whichever film he made. But he remained in close contact with just a few, knowing too well the trap of superficial, sycophantic relationships which had propelled so many other actors into an ever-decreasing spiral of cliquey self-destruction. Niall liked keeping a firm grasp on reality, on the world outside the privileged film industry, which by its very nature set up a false morality, an artificial ivory tower of wealth, sexual availability and immunity to guilt.

'Do you honestly think we're doing the right thing?' Tash asked as they walked very slowly and carefully back along the glacier-hard, slippery lane to the forge.

'No,' Niall confessed. 'But I'm quite happy about doing it.'

'Me too.' She grinned, listening to the delighted yelping from their small cottage as Beetroot sensed they were just yards away.

Giblets, now given permanent residency in the small, walled back courtyard, watched in confusion through the panelled glass of the kitchen door as Tash and Niall fell through the opposite door from the lane, stumbled as far as the sofa and, not bothering to undress beyond a cursory lifting and unbuttoning of layers, coupled with laughing, eager speed.

Beetroot, even more confused, bit Niall firmly on the ankle just as he was getting into his rhythm.

Moments later the telephone rang as Niall's agent, having tried to trace him all evening, finally tracked him down.

'We'll try this again later.' He kissed Tash on the mouth and, easing himself away, settled down to talk to Bob Hudson.

Giving his hair a final run through her fingers, Tash picked up Beetroot and wandered upstairs to warm up the bed in anticipation.

When Niall finally joined her almost an hour later, played out from arguing with Bob, she was asleep. Her long lashes swept towards her pale cheeks and her broad, slightly muscular upper arm was pressed to her mouth, guarding it from kisses. Curled into the small of her back, Beetroot let out an ominous growl.

'Why d'you hate me, huh?' Niall whispered, cocking his head and trying to stare the young dog out.

With her big, fluffy envelope-flap ears flattening to the small, black dome of her head, Beetroot's growl deepened.

Anxious not to wake Tash, Niall backed away and spent the night perched on the very edge of the bed, eyes wide open, heart heavy with guilt. Bob – as antisocial in his hours as ever – had passed on two pieces of information to him. The first was bad enough – a thankless task which he had to break to Tash in the morning. The second was a far trickier prospect, both to take in himself and to tell her. He was determined to keep it quiet for at least a few more weeks while he made up his mind.

Four

ON THE MORNING OF New Year's Eve, it snowed thickly in West Berkshire.

Zoe watched the feathery flakes drift almost aimlessly down to the frosted hoggin drive where they were settling with alarming speed. The trees had already turned into huge mushrooms, the hedges were just fat, piped trails of mashed potato and the fields stretched as uniformly white as fresh foolscap paper.

'We'll be lucky if even the locals can make it at this rate.' She turned to roll her eyes at her daughter India.

Fourteen years old and already as tall as her six-foot brother, India towered over her mother as she hovered nearby in the sitting room, trying to help tidy up for the party but anxious not to incur Gus's ire by moving a single back-of-an-envelope list or battered copy of *Eventing* magazine.

'I hope at least a few turn up.' She was twisting her long tangle of blonde hair under her chin like a beard. Even doing her goat impression, she looked unspeakably pretty and far more adult than her years. 'The more people we have in here,' she pointed out cheerfully, 'the warmer it'll be.'

'Nothing can compare to the chill factor at the forge.' Zoe shuddered. 'I popped in there this morning to give them some dog food – they've been feeding that poor little mite turkey leftovers all week – and I could barely talk for chattering teeth.'

'Are they really going to get married?' India curled her lengthy frame into the sagging velvet sofa and picked at a frayed cushion, downcast eyes veiled by lashes.

Zoe shrugged. 'Not sure, darling. Certainly not from the way they were both sulking earlier. Niall has to fly back to the States today to re-shoot some scene for that over-budget action thing that they're all in a panic about – Tough Justice, is it?'

'He won't be coming to the party then?' India was practically destroying the cushion.

'Shouldn't think so, darling. Tash was sulkily trying to phone round for flights when I left.'

'You know I don't want to go, angel,' Niall pleaded. 'I can't bear to leave you after so little time together – with ourselves not even announcing the wedding properly.'

Tash was throwing what few of Niall's clothes she could find into his battered leather hold-all. The zip wouldn't shut as it had become enmeshed in an airport luggage tag, chewing it into a sticky pulp. Fighting a losing battle with it, she was trying desperately not to cry, using her uncombed hair as a curtain to hide her unfocused, stinging eyes.

'I'll probably make it back for a few days next week,' Niall said with shattering lack of conviction. For a top-rated actor with two Baftas in the loo, he couldn't lie for toffee.

'You start shooting in Scotland on the sixth,' Tash reminded him, a catch in her throat.

'So I do.' He was scratching his stubble thoughtfully. 'But that's much closer to home, so it is. I'll be down here all the time. And you can come up to me.' He flashed a hopeful smile in the direction of her hair.

'Sure.' Tash's voice was wobbling so much that she shut up and wrestled some more with the stubborn zip.

'I love you.' Niall buried his face in the crown of her head, breathing in the comforting smell of her shampoo.

After the car had come to collect him, its driver grumbling that the lanes were almost impassable and the M4 a snowy death trap even at thirty miles an hour, Tash flopped on to the sofa with Beetroot. Shivering with misery as well as cold, she wept into the fragile dog's bristly black and biscuit coat.

When she noticed that Niall had left the little painting of them she had given him behind, she howled twice as loudly.

Penny phoned at lunchtime to ask if she could bring along any spare plates and glasses she had. Still buried in the sofa, Tash sniffed deeply and bravely and announced that she wasn't going to be at the party after all.

'Rubbish!' Penny was as brusque and unsympathetic as ever, like a jollying head girl telling a home-goal-scoring lacrosse player to 'buck up'.

'I can't, Penny,' Tash wailed. 'I know it's unspeakably wet, but I just want to go to bed and sniff his pillow. He's promised to call me the moment he's in LA.'

'And when will that be?'

Tash sniffed again. 'Not sure – he couldn't get a direct flight. 'Bout seven tomorrow morning our time, I think.'

'Which, by my calculations, gives him the chance to celebrate New Year there as well as in the air. Twice, in fact. The least you can do is celebrate it once.'

'He's doing it for both of us.' Tash hung up, feeling rotten.

She chewed the knuckles of her left hand and, looking down at her bare, calloused fingers with bleary eyes, remembered that Niall had promised to buy her an engagement ring on Monday. Somehow she didn't feel very engaged. Like a Mercury payphone, she felt totally unrung. She sometimes doubted that what they had together could be called a relationship at all.

When Alexandra called from London to say her farewells before flying back to France, Tash put on her brave 'nothing's wrong' voice.

'Tell Niall that I've been talking to Henrietta today,' Alexandra announced, cheerfully unaware that Niall was probably racing towards Heathrow at that very moment. 'And she's agreed to do a lot of the donkey work in England, bless her. She wants to meet you for a girly lunch soon to chat about what you want for the wedding reception, darling.'

'That's great,' Tash said weakly.

'And you mustn't worry about a thing. Promise me?'

'Not a thing, I promise.'

'Etty could talk about nothing but the wedding all week. She's so excited. Listen, I've had a little idea . . .'

Tash groaned. Her mother's ideas, however little, had a tendency to be on a grand scale.

'Pascal and I have decided that, if you and Niall are going to get married in June, you should have a lovely long holiday together with us in the Loire in May.'

'I can't.' Tash didn't even need to look at her diary. 'It's Badminton month – I'll be competing every weekend.'

'Three days' break midweek, then. You and Niall will need a pre-wedding rest. These things are frightfully stressful, darling.'

'We simply haven't got the time.' Tash was glancing up at her wall chart, cause of much misery. 'Niall will be on the publicity tour for Tough Justice then, and there's talk of him doing a British film around the same time.'

'Hmm.' Alexandra would clearly not be dissuaded by such trivialities. 'We'll just have to work out something closer to the time. Now, have you had a chance to turn your mind to bridesmaids yet? Do you think Tor can be trusted?'

Tash turned her eyes to heaven.

Zoe's son, Rufus – tall, sooty-blond and utterly without principle – did absolutely nothing to help arrange the party. Instead he nicked a couple of four-packs and stole across the snow-crusted courtyard to the flat above the stalls where Gus's lazy head groom, Ted, was back from Christmas with his parents and in dire need of blood-pollutants.

'Christ, I wish I'd stayed here again this year,' he moaned, ripping the ring off a lager can with desperate haste. 'One sweet sherry at six-thirty, then two stouts with my dad in front of the box, and a last-orders lager top with an illicit fag in the local pub if I was lucky.'

'Are your family a serious bummer, yeah?' Rufus pulled a face.

'Totally horrific, mate.' Ted put two fingers to his head and pulled an imaginary trigger, never for a moment considering the notion of admitting that his family were far more ashamed of his howling snobbery than he was of them – gnomes, stone cladding and all.

Ted liked to show off to Rufus, which largely involved boasting about how much alcohol he could ship, dope he could smoke and football trivia he could dredge up from memory. A self-styled 'bloke' in the *Loaded*, lager and Fantasy Football League mould, he cut an incongruous figure on the eventing circuit. But for all his laid-back, hard drinking attitude, horses had remained his only true love since the first time he'd clopped along Blackpool front on a donkey, aged six. His on-off girlfriend, the irascible Franny, often moaned that were he to treat her with the slavish love he bestowed upon Gus's horses, she'd chuck him for being too much of a wet New Man. Instead, Ted expected her to dress up for him, cook for him, perform extraordinarily athletic sex for him, and then visit the fridge for him immediately afterwards to fetch him a post-coital lager which he could sip in the bath that she would, of course, run for him. Franny was surprisingly meek in her compliance.

Rufus watched as, swigging lager, Ted crunched his way over his littered floors to examine his hair in the wardrobe mirror. He was totally paranoid about his hair – an obsession that sometimes seemed almost psychotic. He didn't so much have bad hair days as a bad hair lifetime; it was the one thing in which he lacked confidence. He had been known to spend an entire day in bed when he couldn't get his hirsute black curls to lie right.

But despite this, Ted was something of a hero-figure to Rufus who, at seventeen, was three years younger and, due to his cosseted background, far more naive. Ted had taught him how to smoke, drink, criticise videos, chat up women, drive off-road vehicles and roll a spliff. He liked Rufus's eager enthusiasm and devotion, but rather resented the way that the younger lad, even at seventeen, attracted women so effortlessly. Rufus, with his spidery height, big smile and sooty, long-lashed grey eyes, was something of a babe-magnet. Ted, who was well under six foot, stout, topped with a curly black thatch and in possession of a broken nose, fared less well. It was his humour, dogged determination and well-practised seduction skills which pulled, but – despite a phenomenal success rate – he still resented the youngster his natural looks and straight hair, so took every opportunity subtly to undermine them.

'You're not going to wear that tonight, are you, mate?' He turned around and studied Rufus's blue corduroy shirt critically.

'Hadn't really thought about it,' Rufus confessed. He seldom thought about his clothes beyond selecting them for warmth and practicality.

'Take a tip.' Ted tugged on his cigarette and rubbed his tired, red eyes. 'Blue's naff. Yellow. That's what you want, mate.'

'Yellow?' Rufus nodded, absorbing the information earnestly.

'Yup. Women can't resist yellow.' He turned back to the mirror again. 'D'you think I should get my hair cut?'

Later, dressed in one of Gus's yellow shirts which he had bartered tomorrow's mucking out for, Rufus looked pretty awful. The shirt was ridiculously big, and the colour clashed with his mouse-blond hair and lent his cream and pink complexion a sallow, jaundiced tinge. In contrast, Ted was sporting a navy Breton shirt which brought out the intense dark blue of his cheerful, roaming eyes. He'd tried to slick down his dark curls to his scalp with hair-gel, but they kept springing up like unravelling knitting wool.

Zoe had done her usual efficient, understated job of preparing both the house and herself for an influx of friends. Lime Tree Farm could never look tidy; it was a practical impossibility given the heaps of detritus which weighed down every available space and which had to remain in place for Gus to know where they were. But Zoe had an uncanny knack – acquired through years of living with the Moncrieffs – of making those piles of vital rubbish look artistic. She was helped on this occasion by the fact that so much could still be disguised with Christmas decorations. Cards perched on the top of piles of magazines and schedules, making them appear to be rather grand paper columns; holly was pinned neatly around feed charts on the walls, tatty lampshades on the ceilings and the numerous and rather frightening mounted antlers which Gus was absurdly fond of collecting. Even the most horrific Lime Tree eyesore – a wooden faux-flame candelabra which Penny was inordinately proud of stealing from their honeymoon hotel in Spain – could be disguised beneath a vast bunch of berryless mistletoe which Zoe had bought cheaply at Marlbury market. The gleaming white berries were in fact plastic pearls from a broken necklace of India's, but Zoe felt they were suitably convincing.

'You're not wearing that, are you, Mum?' Rufus bounded downstairs, blond hair on end. 'With your legs on show like that?'

'I certainly am.' Zoe smoothed down her red velvet dress as she headed towards the kitchen to put out glasses.

To add insult to injured pride, Tash could hear the Lime Tree party from almost half a mile away as she lurked unhappily in the chilly forge. In fact, she could hear stereophonic parties, as the racket from the Olive Branch's annual knees-up fought to compete with the Moncrieffs' raucous bash.

Tash, having wallowed self-pityingly in a luke-warm bath for nearly an hour, was swathed in Niall's stripy dressing gown and a head-towel, reading one of the scripts he had been sent before Christmas. She almost fell off the sofa when the door was pounded upon vigorously.

Shrinking back, she ignored it, glancing at the clock on the oven.

It was only ten-thirty. She groaned and tossed the script on to the rickety coffee table. God, she was bored.

The fist was still pounding a persistent tattoo, accompanied by a familiar voice calling her name with charmless superiority.

'Tash, I know you're bloody in there. Open up, you silly cow.'

Tash set her mouth angrily and continued to ignore him. She had no desire to greet Hugo with puffy eyes, red nose and a mascara-stained turban on her head.

'We've come to take you to the bloody party!'

Beetroot, who was barking herself hoarse on Tash's side of the door, let out a terrified yelp and scuttled away as the cat-flap flew open and a very tanned hand thrust a parcel through it.

'Your Christmas present.'

Tash's eyebrows shot up in astonishment. Hugo had never once bought her a present in her life. He seemed to derive particularly cruel pleasure from his failure to memorise her birthday, whilst his – 28 March – was a date which had once leaped out of her teenage diaries as though encircled in red.

She scuttled silently across the floor and looked at the package.

It was wrapped in luxuriously thick green and bronze paper, with a lot of loopy red ribbon and a large tag shaped like a figgy pudding. Silently, Tash reached out to flip over the tag.

At the same moment as she read the words '*For Penny and Gus, from Kirsty, with gratitude and love*', the tanned hand re-emerged from the cat-flap and gripped her firmly around the wrist.

'Ouch!' Tash tried to pull away but he was far stronger than she was.

'Now either we stay like this all night,' came the muffled drawl through the flap, 'or you let us in.'

Tash didn't like the 'us'. Peering through the open flap, she could see a lot of denim-covered upper thigh where Hugo was kneeling on the snowy front step, and could just make out the cruel, sharp line of his chin which was stretched downwards so that he could talk to her. There was also, however, a distinctly sickly waft of strong, feminine perfume and – yes – she could just make out the dim image of a strappy black shoe and a slim, ten-denier ankle in the background.

'Bugger off,' she muttered, looking around for something with which to hit his arm.

There was nothing within reach and Beetroot, who was proving to have a very warped sense of loyalty, had crept back to the door and was sniffing Hugo's sweater cuff with interest, snaky tail rising from between her back legs to wag excitedly.

'Listen, I'm only fucking here because Penny is upset that you haven't turned up. She sent me on an errand. Says I can't have a bloody drink unless I return with you in tow.'

'Don't be so wet, Tash,' came a purring Scottish lisp from behind Hugo. 'Just open the bloody door. We're freezing our balls off out here.'

'I always said you had balls, Kirsty,' Tash muttered under her breath.

'What's that?'

'Nothing.'

But Hugo had heard her childish retort and was gripping her wrist so tightly that her hand was in danger of turning blue. In fact it was going to turn blue anyway as a sharp blizzard came whistling in through the cat-flap. Tash, wearing only the dressing gown, was beginning to shiver. Beetroot, the disloyal minx, had started to lick Hugo's wrist now.

'Flattered as I am by your lust, Tash,' he drawled, 'I think I must warn you that it's rather misdirected.'

'That's my dog,' she grunted, trying again to pull away. 'Look, will you two just piss off? I'm not celebrating New Year this time.'

Sighing, Hugo let go of her wrist. 'Fair enough. Not sure I fancy sharing space with you in this bloody-minded mood anyway. Can I have my present back, please?'

Gritting her teeth, Tash ejected it at speed through the flap. She only just stopped Beetroot from following it out.

'Happy New Year!' Kirsty called huskily as their snow-muffled footsteps retreated.

Tash hoped Kirsty's heels sent her flying into a ditch. She crawled back to her sofa and wished that she didn't always feel so monumentally anti-social whenever Niall went away.

That had been her chance to be conciliatory to bloody Hugo, she realised. Her opportunity to fulfil her promise to Zoe and be nicer to him. If only he wasn't so effing arrogant. He'd made it perfectly clear that he'd only come to collect her under heavy duress. And he'd undoubtedly only agreed to do so because it gave him the opportunity to slope off with Kirsty for an illicit grope, far away from the eyes of so many gossipy friends. The sod!

She turned on the television to be confronted by Sir Harry Secombe warbling a hymn from on top of a Welsh mountain. She quickly turned it off again and flumped over to the fridge, which was almost bare because she'd already raided it twice that afternoon. Three cold roast potatoes and half a tub of brandy butter later and she felt no better. She just felt sick.

Penny phoned again twice to beg her to come over, but each time Tash just thanked her and told her gently and firmly that she was far happier at home waiting for Niall to call.

'But that won't be for hours – come over for just one drink at midnight, huh?'

Tash wouldn't be persuaded.

It was ten to twelve before she changed her mind. She'd just polished off her fifth fig roll and was washing it down with one of Niall's cans of Guinness – the only alcohol she could find. Burping with an indigestive spasm in her chest, she realised just how smug and snide Hugo would be over the next few weeks if she didn't pole up at all. He'd call her gutless and childish. It was just the sort of ammunition he devoured, storing it up for the perfect opportunity to put her down and mob her up.

She had no time to lose.

Dragging on the first outfit that came to hand, she ripped the towel from her tangled, half-dry hair, stepped into her Doc Marten boots – which were the only ones she could walk on ice in – and threw a chew to Beetroot before legging it towards the farm.

The Doc Martens might have given her a great grip, but the undone laces tripped her up three times. Tash landed twice on her bottom in deep snow and once nose down in a hedge. She sat in the middle of the lane, her wet backside soaking up yet more icy dampness, and hastily criss-crossed the laces around her ankles, her frozen fingers slowing her down to a hopeless fumble. Then, slipping her way upright again, she felt her buttocks clench against the cold air as she slithered and tripped towards the farm gates.

She arrived just as they were about to count down the hour.

'Thirty seconds to go!' came a scream from the sitting room to the left.

'Everyone into the sitting room – double quick,' called Gus.

For a moment, Tash was swept on a tide of familiar faces towards the huge, candle-lit room. Despite its size, however, it simply could not accommodate all of Gus's and Penny's guests and Tash was stranded with a dozen or so others in the hall, unable to squeeze inside. Amongst them was Kirsty Judd, balancing her long, curvy legs on the two strappy shoes Tash had spotted through the cat-flap earlier. She looked sensational – her freckled skin tanned in the Australian sun to a tawny gold, her fox-red hair freshly cut into a feathered urchin bob, her magnificent cleavage balancing like two rust-dusted golden globes on the wired corset of her tight little cocktail dress.

Looking down at her own inside-out and wrongly buttoned checked shirt – the same shirt that she had mucked out in a week earlier – Tash realised that she was in unflattering contrast on the looks front. Her thick, woolly tights, Doc Martens and frayed denim hotpants were too grunge student for words, her hair was a damp, chilly bird's nest of tangles, her nose a glowing beacon, her eyes as pink and puffy as two snapdragons. She looked unbelievably rough. The only kiss she was likely to get in the next minute was the kiss of life.

As the huge crowd in the sitting room started counting backwards from ten, Tash slunk towards the shadow of the stairs and tried to blend into the vast pile of coats slung over the banisters.

'Hi, Tash – so you made it after all,' purred that slinky little voice, as mellifluous as maple syrup sinking through a waffle. Kirsty would make Jean Brodie sound like a Glaswegian welder.

The counting had just reached seven.

Grabbing an abandoned half-full glass of red wine from a nearby bookshelf, Tash managed a very stiff half-smile aimed in the general direction of Kirsty's vast cleavage.

'Must find Hugo.' Kirsty melted away towards the sitting-room door just as he emerged from the kitchen, yawning widely and carrying a bottle of duty-free champagne.

Swinging her narrow-eyed gaze from Kirsty's enviously schoolboy bottom to Hugo's tall shadow, Tash drew in a sharp breath as she clocked his tan – as dark and smooth as chocolate praline. With his tortoiseshell flop of wavy hair, straight, straight nose and Barclaycard-blue eyes, he looked like a photofit of every schoolgirl's dream man. Tash's teeth gritted with hatred.

The count was now at five.

Hugo looked up from tugging at the champagne foil and, catching Tash watching him, smiled nastily before moving lazily towards her. 'So you made it after all?'

'She's gone that way.' Tash jerked her head towards Kirsty's retreating freckled back as the count reached two.

'Really?' he said flatly, standing opposite her now.

'One . . . Happy New Year!' came the shrieks from the sitting room as the sounds of greetings, kisses, popping champagne corks and whoops drowned out Big Ben on the radio.

Hugo hadn't moved a muscle. He barely seemed to notice that the year had turned at all.

Tash backed slightly away into the stairwell, alarmed by his uncharacteristic attention. He was smiling broadly and watching her with condescending interest, as a scientist watches a white mouse which he has just injected with a deadly virus.

The next moment she almost passed out as there was a loud bang inches in front of her. Suddenly, she was aware of icy, wet froth hitting her hot, breathless chest.

Laughing at her, Hugo lifted the bottle of champagne to his lips, lapping at the foaming rim before taking it in his mouth and swallowing a lengthy mouthful.

'Did I give you a fright?' he mocked, passing the bottle to her. 'Happy New Year.'

Holding up her chin, determined not to rise to his teasing, Tash took a hasty swig and thrust it back at him.

But Hugo was now gazing up at the ceiling.

'How extraordinarily inappropriate,' he murmured, cocking his head so that his tortoiseshell forelock flopped from left to right.

Following his gaze, Tash blushed crimson with mortification as she realised they were standing directly under Zoe's fat bunch of mistletoe which now bore only two pearl berries.

When she looked back at Hugo, he was smiling his most mocking smile, a curious look of concentration on his face.

Clutching tightly on to the bottle for support, Tash realised to her horror that he was moving even closer to her. For a terrifying moment his breath traced her cheek and she thought that he was going to kiss her. But he merely stretched up a hand and removed something from her hair.

'I shouldn't think this'll improve your chances, darling,' he said, dropping a pearl into the champagne bottle before turning away. 'Kirsty, darling! There you are! Now, I know you're practically a married woman, but humour an envious bastard with a New Year's kiss.'

In front of most of the eventing circle, none of whom could guess at their steamy affair, he drew Kirsty into his arms and planted a very respectable, if rather too long, closed-mouth kiss on her plump lips. Over his shoulder, Tash was appalled to see one of Kirsty's glittering blueberry eyes winking at her.

'Happy New Year, Tash!' Rufus lurched up, absolutely bombed out of his mind on vodka, his yellow shirt covered with pieces of quiche and party streamers.

Before Tash could respond, he had landed a huge, wet kiss on her gaping mouth and, even worse, inserted a warm, fat tongue into her mouth.

'You're a fucking great shnogger, Tash,' he hiccuped, backing away and reeling towards the downstairs lavatory from which, seconds later, came the unmistakable sound of retching.

Suddenly it was Auld Lang Syne time. Grabbed by Gus – with a far more warm and welcome New Year's peck on the mouth – Tash was propelled into the throng in the sitting room to link arms and sing. But luck was still not on her side as she found herself crossing her arms and clutching on to the small, manicured paw of Kirsty on one side and the damp, sweaty pudginess of

Ted's fingerlock on the other. His gelled hair was all over the place now.

'Been looking for you all night,' he hissed into her ear as she tried to sing along with the out-of-time, out-of-tune rabble. 'Hear Niall's gone away again – give me a call if you need a plug re-wiring.'

Tash rolled her eyes and tipped her head as far away from his stale breath as she could manage. Unfortunately this necessitated practically necking with Kirsty.

'No Niall tonight then?' she asked rather regretfully.

Still wrestling with 'sip a drink of kindness yet', Tash shook her head with another of her stiff little smiles. They were coming in remarkably handy tonight.

At last no one could remember any more words and Tash, released from her double half-nelson, escaped back to the hall, which was practically deserted. She found Hugo's bottle of champagne still sitting on the bookshelf where she had left it and, grabbing it by the neck, snuggled up by the familiar coats for a long, bolstering swig.

'You all right, darling?' Zoe asked as she swept from sitting room to kitchen, weighed down by trays. 'Happy New Year.'

'Blast!' Penny was following her with fingers full of glasses to be refilled. 'I forgot to post bloody Hugo outside to bring in the coal and the coins. I bet you the first stranger across the threshold will be that faggot Godfrey Pelham, and he's blue-rinsed, not dark. Plus he's so mean he never brings booze or grub with him.'

When the doorbell rang, everyone ignored it. No one who was welcome inside Lime Tree Farm would ever think to ring the doorbell. There was an unwritten rule at the farm that the doorbell was the domain of the VAT man and the bailiffs, giving Penny and Gus enough warning to hide. Everyone else just walked in.

'Happy New Year, sweetheart.' An eventing mate kissed Tash on the cheek. 'Perhaps this is the year you'll be capped, huh?' He drifted away towards the sitting room.

Tash was halfway down the bottle and perking up. She was just contemplating nipping upstairs to borrow an outfit from Penny and steal a bit of Zoe's make-up when Hugo the Cruel stalked malevolently up to reclaim his champagne.

Saying nothing to him, Tash thrust the bottle into his hand and moved away, but Hugo put up an arm to block her.

'Listen, I'm sorry I was a bit heavy earlier,' he said, not sounding particularly sorry at all. 'Penny's just told me about Niall's abrupt departure. Had no idea that was why you didn't want to come out. In fact, I'd not realised he'd been in England at all.'

'We *did* spend Christmas together.' Tash sighed. Sometimes Hugo could be ruthlessly self-centred; it was possible he'd even forgotten that she and Niall were still an item.

'Did you?' Hugo looked bored.

Realising that this was as much of an apology as she was likely to receive, and bearing in mind the ticking off Zoe had given her, Tash mustered yet another stiff smile. Any minute now and the wind would change, leaving her looking like Virginia Bottomley on Question Time for the rest of her life.

The doorbell was ringing again, and once again it was ignored.

'Have a good Christmas?' Tash humoured him, taking in the deepness of the tan again and deciding it looked a bit patchy and flaking. He was so vain, she was surprised he didn't use moisturiser.

'Pretty horrific.' Hugo's blue eyes narrowed tiredly at the memory. 'I stayed with Jim and Gail Reebok in their yard in New South Wales. Their little brats run around the stables like rats. No bloody discipline.'

'See much of Kirsty?' Tash asked casually, trying not to smile.

The blue eyes – even more searing when framed by golden-brown skin – crinkled at the corners for a moment before going dead-pan.

'A bit,' he answered, just as casually, then took a long swig of champagne.

The doorbell was ringing non-stop now.

'All right, all right! We surrender! I'm coming!' Penny yelled wandering into the hall still clutching a bottle of cheap plonk.

'Well, I'd better mingle.' Tash, feeling she had done her duty for Zoe's sake, looked around for a handy group to chat to.

'Haven't you forgotten something?' Hugo was still barring her way with a long arm, his green sweater pushed up to the elbow to show a lot of muscular, conker-brown arm.

'Forgotten wha—?' Before she could finish, his mouth closed on hers.

It was a brief, not entirely friendly kiss, but its effect still took both of them by surprise.

And Niall caught every second.

Framed in the doorway wearing a vast quilted coat, his nose puce from the cold, shoulders and hair dusted with snow, he looked both dishevelled and unspeakably handsome. His hands were full of Toblerone bars, claret bottles, loose change and lumps of coal stolen from one of the outhouses.

'Flights from Heathrow have all been cancelled because of the snow,' he announced with a big, unsteady grin. 'They kept us waiting hours at check-in then told us to go home. Happy New Year!'

'Niall!' Tash bounded across the hall, long legs flying as she leaped ecstatically into his arms.

Niall found he couldn't bring himself to look at Hugo.

It wasn't the kiss he minded. Everyone kissed everyone else on New Year's Eve. No, it was the guilty way Tash had snatched herself away when she'd caught sight of him, the gleaming blaze of something midway between fear and lust in her eyes.

Even as she surged forward, almost weeping with delighted excitement at his unexpected return, Niall's heart barely lifted. She was wearing unspeakable clothes, her hair was all over the place, her tights laddered and full of road grit. But her cheeks glowed, her eyes shone and she looked utterly beautiful. And, deep within his heart, he suspected that her radiance was not the result of his return.

Five

HENRIETTA, CONTRARY TO ALEXANDRA'S hype, was not wildly keen on the idea of orchestrating Tash's wedding from her side of the Channel. She had enough of a task keeping her own two daughters' lives within her grasp, without the added pressure of dabbling in the rather unconventional one of her step-daughter's. It wasn't as if Tash was a daughter that James had any particular time for. Tash was ludicrously close to her mother, and Henrietta sensed that James was somewhat intimidated by the link. In truth, she herself was too. Both she and James found it far easier to accommodate Sophia, who was glamorous, great to show off at parties and led a far more conventional life. Sophia, it had to be noted, also had far less time for her mother's bohemian antics than Tash.

Six years earlier, newly married to her former boss, Henrietta had willingly involved herself in the marriage of James's elder daughter to the rather raffish and supremely eligible Ben Meredith, now Viscount Guarlford. It had been one of those stressful but rewarding labours of love that the second wife feels obliged and gratified to take on. In those days Henrietta had a lot to prove to the back-biting gossips who hinted that James had only married his secretary in order to offset her against tax. The prospect of arranging Sophia's jet-set society wedding had terrified her, but thanks to weeks of sleepless nights and triple-checking, the whole thing had come off marvellously, ensuring her Sophia's devotion ever since. The fact that Alexandra – herself just remarried and wrapped up in her young toddler – had been involved to only the scantiest degree smoothed Henrietta's passage immeasurably. But Tash's marriage was a different matter.

Whereas Sophia had been James's favourite, Tash was something of an embarrassment to him. She in turn had always been perfectly warm and polite to Henrietta, but there was a rather unflattering lack of interest emanating from West Berkshire towards Tash's childhood home east of Bracknell. Unlike Sophia, Tash never telephoned for a chat or invited her father's new family over for a day in Fosbourne Ducis. Nor did she ever let them know where she would be eventing so that they could troop out to support her (not that James would really entertain the idea), or let slip any pieces of film gossip she had picked up through Niall. Henrietta, who was somewhat star-struck by Niall (at thirty-six he was closer to her forty years, after all, than Tash's twenty-seven), found this last negligence particularly galling.

When Henrietta's younger daughter, Beccy, had announced her intention to enter eventing professionally, Henrietta had braced herself nervously and telephoned Tash to ask her for lunch, adding that she'd really appreciate it if Tash could give some advice to Beccy. Tash had apologised profusely, but explained that it was the middle of the season and she simply hadn't the time.

Henrietta had felt absurdly snubbed.

The resentment had, to Henrietta's shame, been allowed to brood and bubble over the past six months, to the point where she now positively disliked Tash.

To add further to Henrietta's discomfort, the first two weeks of the new year brought a little flurry of postcards from Alexandra. It seemed to be one of James's first wife's favoured means of communication; a three-line scribble jotted on the back of a picture of the Loire Valley would arrive just a day after a single line jotted on a Mondrian print; the next day a reproduced watercolour of a wine bottle would be hiding in the Frenches' post box along with the usual credit card bills and circulars.

After a very bad financial slump in the mid nineties, James's finance company was at last out of the red and starting to fight its way back into competition with its larger rivals. But they were still extremely cautious with money. Many of the luxuries that Henrietta had delighted in when first married had now gone – the flashy cars, first-class flights, three-week holidays, designer clothes and weekends away. Henrietta's girls still went to fee-paying schools, but this was more to do with an investment fund which Henrietta's late father had set up than any contribution from James. He begrudgingly helped finance Beccy's eventing hopes, but had it been Emily who wanted to pursue the sport, Henrietta suspected it would have been different. However hard she tried to balance things out, it was clear to all that the relationship between James and his younger step-daughter was far healthier than that with Henrietta's troublesome elder.

Even today, Henrietta had spent most of the morning trying to locate Emily and her boyfriend, Six Pack, who had still not re-emerged from a raucous New Year party in Devon. That morning, three of their mutual friends had poled up the drive clutching ruck-sacks, claiming that they had been invited to stay for the weekend, a plan of which Henrietta had not even been warned let alone asked for permission. Lumping around the house in their slightly embarrassed, messy student way, they got under her feet and kept feeding crisps to the dogs. Henrietta found them very polite but extremely difficult to accommodate.

Consequently when the phone rang, she snatched it off the hook and reeled out the number with unaccustomed abruptness.

There was a short, confused pause at the other end before a soft, tentative voice spoke.

'Henrietta?'

'Yes,' she snapped, watching as one of the lolling students ambled over to the fridge and brazenly removed three cans of beer, nodding at her amiably.

'It's Niall here – Tash's Niall.'

Despite the miles of telephone cable separating them, Henrietta blushed as though given an unexpected peck on the cheek by Imran Khan.

'Niall!' She inched her way out of sight of the students. 'How lovely to hear from you. How are you?'

'Fine – a bit stressed,' he apologised. 'I'm just about to set out to the airport.'

'Are you heading to Scotland already?' Henrietta knew that he was due to start shooting some epic 'Celtic history' movie in the Highlands soon, a fact she had gleaned from Sophia, not Tash.

'America,' Niall explained. 'Just for two days. Listen, Tash asked me to call.'

'Oh, yes?' Henrietta would have felt it rather rude that Tash couldn't bring herself to call personally were it not for the fact that she was talking to a far preferable deputy.

'She's had to dash to meet the vet – one of her horses has a bad tendon that's gone puffy or something. Listen, are you free on the third Saturday in February? I forget the exact date.'

'Think so.' Henrietta was blushing more and more deeply. The sound of his voice was infuriatingly unsettling – deep, mellifluous and lilting; it should really only be allowed loose on the phone network after the nine o'clock watershed.

'Well, it's my one free weekend in England, so it is. Can you come over here for lunch? We've a great local restaurant I can book us into.'

Henrietta thought briefly and guiltily about a charity committee meeting she had arranged for that day, and then, mentally concocting a whopping lie about one of the girl's having 'flu as an excuse, said that of course she'd be delighted to go.

After she had arranged the time and directions, Henrietta rang off and danced around the flagstone lobby. Then, to the astonishment of the students, she offered them all enormous gin and tonics.

'Everyone's so madly in love with Niall,' Tash grumbled to Zoe the next day. 'It's not fair. Either they envy me like mad, or they simply don't think I'm good enough for him, or they smile that secret smile that says they're certain it won't last. Hardly anyone's congratulated me yet.'

'I have.'

'Only after questioning whether I was doing the right thing. Which, come to think of it, is pretty much how everyone has reacted.'

Zoe placed their requisite strong black coffees on the table and settled in front of her before speaking, kind blue eyes drinking her in. 'It's only because we love you both and care about you both and know how hopelessly hare-brained you both are. We just want to know that you're not both doing it because you're being pressurised into it.'

'Of course we're being pressurised into it,' Tash sighed. 'But the whole point is that neither of us mind – we're used to being bullied into things, it's the only way either of us knows how to live.'

She glanced at her watch. It was still before seven and hollow with icy darkness outside. She'd spent most of the night awake as she always did when Niall had just gone away, plus she had been worrying about Hunk who was still not trotting out levelly and looked likely to be out of action for the first few weeks of the year.

'Kirsty not up yet?' she yawned.

'Not back actually.' Zoe raised a blonde eyebrow. 'Sneaked off for a session at stud last night and clearly can't walk straight enough to get back here.'

Tash winced. 'Hugo's such a sod.' She shook her head. 'I thought Richie was coming out here in a couple of weeks?'

Richie was Kirsty's boyfriend from Australia. None of the occupants of Lime Tree Farm had met him yet, but photos of his butch, bull-necked person littered every surface and pin-board, more often than not featuring a girder-thick hairy arm draped around Kirsty's slender shoulders. When she had first arrived back in England, Kirsty's every sentence had been prefixed with 'Richie thinks' or 'Richie says'. Nowadays it was more often 'Hugo thinks'.

'My guess is there'll be fireworks when he does stagger off the red eye, poor chap.' Zoe scratched her chin unhappily at the prospect. Outside they could hear Penny telling Ted off for smoking a fag in the hay-barn. He complained loudly that it was the only way to keep warm.

'Do you think Hugo'll kick up a stink then?'

She shook her head. 'More likely Kirsty will. She's far more in love with Hugo than she wants to admit. Hugo being Hugo, he'll just get a kick out of the whole secrecy thing. It's Kirsty who'll crack under the strain.'

'Poor Richie.'

'Sounds like a prize idiot to me.' Zoe stood up to fetch her toast which had just popped out of the rusty toaster and on to the plate drainer. 'If he hasn't guessed what's going on then he must be pretty thick. Rumour has it Kirsty hardly saw him over Christmas. Too busy sloping off to meet up with Hugo in the bush or something.'

'Who told you that?'

'Penny heard it from Ted who heard it from Franny.'

'The bird in the bush telegraph then.'

Outside, Gus was leading out one of the horses to turn it out into the floodlit menage for a roll. They could hear its hooves sliding over the frozen cobbles, and Penny warning him that the sand in the menage was as hard as rock.

'How did Hugo take the news of your engagement?' Zoe asked lightly.

'Fine.' Tash shrugged. 'He just said: "I always thought you were a star-fucker, Tash, but I never had you down as the marrying type. How extraordinary." He's got a bet on with Stefan that it'll last less than six months. Stefan bet ten – but that's allowing for divorce proceedings.'

Stefan Johanssen was Hugo's unnaturally tall, hell-raising Swedish working pupil who was only marginally more morally principled than his boss.

Zoe started to laugh, but shut up as soon as she saw Tash's face.

'Do you think we'll last?' Tash asked worriedly.

Zoe stretched across to squeeze her hand, which was still icy cold from working outside. 'Of course you will, if you work at it and want it enough.'

Tash looked reassured, and pulled a face at Enid, who was lurking under the table and eyeing her nervously.

Zoe wished she could feel as sure as her words. As Tash heaved herself back up to resume work, pulling on that awful, ancient Puffa which looked as though a dog had slept on it for years, she could feel herself gradually filling up to the scalp with the icy chill of apprehension. She knew in her heart that she should have told Tash the truth; told her that no, she didn't think she and Niall had a cat in hell's chance – even given all of its nine lives.

But as she watched Tash gather up a sleeping Beetroot from Enid's bed and wander happily outside, she knew that as ever she had pandered to Tash's fragile self-confidence and told her a comforting lie. She just hoped that she'd be proved wrong about this one.

Most of the yard's horses were being clipped that day, a long, tedious job that required everyone to take a turn. It was the second major clip of the winter, which meant that the horses took to the unfamiliar buzzing of the electric blades more easily than they had in the autumn, and that the lines left from their previous clip still stood out on their coats as a guide. Tash, who was a notoriously asymmetric stylist, was grateful for them as she started on Gus's lazy old bay gelding, Fashion Victim, a gangly thoroughbred with a drooping lower lip and eyes that never fully opened, like a dope-smoking hippie. With one hind hoof propped up on its rim, he stood stock still throughout, looking like a bored hooker waiting on a pavement when trade was slow.

Clipping Snob, however, was a different matter. A thin-coated Selle Français with twitching skin and a brutal temper, he required the lightest of clips, but this took all of an hour and a half with both India and Ted clinging on to him for dear life as Tash tried to get anywhere near with the humming blades. His dark eyes rolling, red nostrils fluted and hooves stamping like a flamenco dancer in a sulk, he wasn't frightened so much as determined to have some fun and make them work hard.

'Can't we dope him?' Ted groaned as he was bitten for the third time.

Poor, injured Hunk was missing out on the fun as – confined to his stable all winter beneath a swathe of rugs – he didn't need another trim; his coat was still short enough to last through until spring. Pulling bored faces and whinnying for attention, he watched as his stable mate cavorted around causing bedlam.

Tash was puce in the face and utterly exhausted by the time she'd finished. Waiting for the clippers to cool, she heard a loud revving in the lane and, moments later, Kirsty was wandering up the pitted drive, an overnight bag slung over her shoulder and two tired bags slung under her baby blue eyes. Her red hair was looking uncharacteristically tousled and three of her shirt buttons were undone, displaying a lot of bouncy freckled cleavage and no bra. Her face was still flushed from the heating inside Hugo's car.

'You clipping?' she called out as she wandered past. 'Could you make a start on Betty for me, Tash? I'll take over when I've had a shower. Thanks, hen.' She tottered inside.

'Lazy cow,' Ted commiserated, heading towards Betty Blue's box. Kirsty's scatty, steel-grey mare was already looking goggle-eyed with trepidation as she backed away from the half-door over which she had recently been admiring Snob's antics.

Unable to face another battle, Tash told Ted to take a break and they headed through to the tack room to brew up a pot of tea.

'That woman has such a cheek.' Ted whistled as Tash filled the kettle at the chipped enamel sink. 'She's hardly ever here before eleven these days. I'm amazed Gus doesn't fire her.'

'She's the only one around here with any sponsorship,' Tash sighed. 'He can't afford to.'

'Can't you get Niall to sponsor you?' Ted gave her a cheeky look, his broken nose wrinkling thoughtfully. 'He must be worth a packet.'

But Tash shook her head. 'His divorce settlement was diabolical – his first wife was practically bankrupt when they settled, so she gets half of everything he earns.'

She winced at the memory. Although married formally in a Catholic church in England, Niall and Lisette O'Shaughnessy had in fact been married first at a drive-in chapel in America. Both had seen it as a private joke at the time. When Lisette chose to divorce him in the States instead of England, however, she was not just after the favourable exchange rate – she knew that she could claim for maintenance, which as a childless woman she would undoubtedly have been refused on the other side of the pond. With one of the best divorce lawyers on her side, she took Niall apart. Desperate to get things over with quickly, Niall had allowed Lisette to divorce him on the grounds of his adultery, even though she had left him for another man long before he met Tash. At the time he'd said he was happy for her to take every penny he earned so long as he was rid of her. She'd walked away with a Lottery winner's smile on her face.

'Did she marry him for his money?' Ted was examining his curly black hair in the cracked wall mirror now, scraping it back to see what he'd look like with a crew cut.

'Nope.' Tash plugged the kettle in. 'But she divorced him for the alimony. It's why he has to work in the States so much – they pay far better than anyone else.' She started examining the mugs to locate the two with the fewest tannin stains.

'Surely he could fork out for a few feed bills?' Ted pulled back his chin, not believing Niall could be that skint.

'He already owns Snob,' she confessed.

'He what?' He was so amazed he stopped examining his hair for a moment and gaped at her.

'I couldn't afford to import him,' Tash explained. 'Snob was given to me by my step-father in France, you see. There was tons of red tape and Niall sorted it all out for me, with Hugo's help. Snob had to be put in his name. It worked out simpler that way. We've never bothered to change it. Niall lent me so much money at the time that I thought it was fairer to keep Snob as his.'

'At least his ex-wife doesn't demand half his winnings,' Ted sniffed, returning his attention to the mirror.

'I'm sure she would if she knew.' Tash peered into a chipped mug. 'But she'd also have to pay half of his costs in return, and I can't see her being too keen. Anyway, I'm sure she has no claim on him.' Tash shuddered as she quickly dismissed the thought.

'What does she do?' Ted tried out a side parting.

'She's a producer.' Tash rinsed out the mug. 'Gets the backing for films – most of which she puts up herself, according to Niall.'

'So he pays for her to work and not you? That's a bit ripe, innit?' He pulled a curly tendril over one eye.

'Perhaps,' Tash hedged, watching him as he preened. 'D'you want me to cut your hair for you?'

Ted grinned. 'Yeah, why not? Fetch those clippers in here, would you?'

Kirsty almost fainted with shock when she re-emerged from the farm half an hour later to find Ted being clipped instead of her dizzy grey mare.

'What on earth are you doing?' she gasped.

'Tash is clipping my wings,' Ted laughed cheerfully, his black mop now shorn to a stubbly half-inch all over. 'To stop my hair being flyaway.'

Six

SALLY COULD EASILY ANTICIPATE one of Matty's black glooms. It would start with a general restlessness, a nit-picking inability to keep still as he wandered around the house finding fault with the smallest things – a pile of unpaired socks on the kitchen table, a packet of breakfast cereal put back into the larder empty, a final reminder that still hadn't been paid. He would quickly progress from these to more serious issues – Sally's over-zealous shopping, the children's reactionary teachers, the whingeing neighbour. Soon he would move on to the personal – their flaccid sex life, financial troubles, Sally's ghastly friends, his father's bullying during his childhood, Sally's spoiling of the children. Finally his black gloom would allow itself indulgently to encompass Big Issues – world poverty, the fall of socialism, the arming of volatile states, and Why Were We Put On This Earth In The First Place? More often than not, he blamed Sally specifically for all of these things.

Usually Matty could only contemplate such enormity for a few days before the black gloom played itself out and, after a brief spate of guilty penitence at his bloody-mindedness, he became his sweet, distracted self once more.

But this time the black gloom was taking a long, long time to lift, and Sally wished she was as good at anticipating its demise as its rise.

He had been sulky since Christmas, positively malcontent since Tash and Niall's announcement on Boxing Day, and utterly insufferable since New Year's Eve, which they had spent with Sally's rather weird parents

– a pair of ageing hippies who lived very comfortably in deepest Dorset, funding an affluent, if unconventional, lifestyle from their burgeoning shares. They represented everything Matty loathed. They were unpunctual slobs and he was a control freak; they adored junk television and the *Daily Mail*; Matty was an appalling intellectual snob and considered the *Guardian* grossly sensationalist these days. They loved the Momas and the Papas, while Matty considered blues to be the only respectable strain of modern popular music. He had done little during the stay to conceal his contempt for their taste.

To make things worse, he had now decided to work from home for a week and was driving Sally up the wall. Or, to be more accurate, into the cellar.

She would have never volunteered to clear the dreaded thing out had it not been for Matty's ever-prowling presence elsewhere in the house.

Since they had moved into the sprawling, tatty Richmond town-house four years earlier, Sally had ventured down to the cellar fewer than a dozen times. It was damp, dark, smelly and inhabited by an extraordinary army of spiders, wood lice, earwigs, silverfish and, occasionally, rodents. At this time of year it was also chillingly cold.

Most of the space – which stretched for the entire width and almost half the breadth of the house – was taken up with their old furniture, Matty's old files and film stock, and a great deal of rubbish left behind by the previous owners. When, in a moment of misplaced generosity, Alexandra had arranged to have their house completely redecorated while they were on holiday a couple of years earlier, the impeccably tasteful interior designer had taken one look at Matty's and Sally's amassed collectibles and ordered them struck from her sight. Now the cellar was host to several enormous bean-bags, Habitat shelf units, a vast number of raffia plant-pot holders and an old dentist's chair on which Matty had once brooded over the meaning of life.

Alone in the cellar, the sounds of John Lee Hooker and Matty's muffled footsteps seeping from the rafters overhead, Sally sank down into the dentist's chair and gazed up at the thin girder of light cutting its way through the dust on the high quarter-windows. Through them she could just make out the collection of weeds in the narrow wall beds outside and the shadow of the railings to the street.

'D'you want a coffee?' Matty yelled down from the top of the stairs to the kitchen lobby.

'No, thanks.' Sally knew for a fact that they had none in the house.

She had pilfered the last spoonful for a hasty half-mug while Matty was in the shower that morning.

'What on earth are you doing down there?'

'Oh, just having a bit of a tidy up.' She shivered, pulling her thick mohair cardigan around her.

'Tidying up? Are you mad? The house is a tip – why don't you tidy up here instead?'

'I'm looking for something.' Sally wished he'd go away and leave her in peace. Even here she couldn't escape from his nagging.

'Looking for what exactly?' He was halfway down the stairs now. Sally could make out his shadow curling menacingly around the far wall in a very Hitchcockian fashion.

'Oh – just things.'

'Christ!' He stomped back to the kitchen. 'I bloody give up.'

Sally huddled tighter in the chair and wondered whether to cry.

She'd been crying a lot lately, often for no real reason. The tiniest thing would trigger it off – getting her finger caught in the door of the dish washer, accidentally killing a spider when she was trying to throw it out humanely, a sad song coming on the radio, Linus crying – and cry he often did now that his teeth were coming through. At the root of her tears, she knew, were the first barbed scratches of the horns of a dilemma, but she wasn't sure that she was willing to face up to it right now.

What she needed was a real, close friend to discuss it with, but she was starting to realise just how shallow her friendships had become. During the years of her marriage her circle of friends had shifted and changed almost imperceptibly. The small, merry band of intimate confidantes she had once so relied upon – some old school and college cronies, a few close associates from her teaching days – had steadily drifted away as their lives no longer paralleled hers. They were either unmarried or, if they were in stable relationships, they had no children. And, while she was surrounded by nappies and lunch-boxes, washing and discarded toys, they had neat, minimalist houses with the latest high-tech stereo equipment to play all those CDs that their highly paid jobs allowed them to splash out on. They were free to meet up when she wasn't, they had great jobs, good clothes, more money, fewer sleepless nights – more fun, it seemed. Sally guessed she bored them with her out-of-date clothes, lack of street-wise nous, endless talk of children, nursery schools and baby-sitters. She was paranoid that they all talked about how dull she was behind her back.

Increasingly, she had peopled her world with other young mothers who, although scared of Matty and rather intimidated by Sally herself, were easier to feel comfortable with than her childless friends. They sometimes bored her with their bovine joy in motherhood, but she rather relished the fact that she often led in conversations, keeping them in stitches with her worldly gossip about Matty's hectic life producing documentaries and her other racy friends whom she still occasionally saw, especially Niall. Yet when it came to a crisis, she would lose far too much face by admitting it to them, and if she did, she suspected that their response would amount to nothing but embarrassed platitudes.

She needed someone who both respected and understood her. And she felt that she'd hidden so much of herself away of late that there were very few left who would recognise her voice of fear if it spoke out.

The person she missed most in the world right now was Niall's ex-wife, Lisette. When Sally had met Matty, he, Niall and Lisette had been the holy trinity of cosmopolitan style, wit and hell-raising charm as far as she was concerned. With Sally on board, they had made an invincible foursome: Niall, the dashing, romantic, daring leader; Matty, the clever, sensitive, idealistic foil; Lisette, the sexy, dangerous, funny siren; and Sally, the laughing, easy-going, caring diplomat. Together they had held endless raucous dinner parties, holidayed on the cheap all over the globe, attended every film, play and party they could get into without paying and talked out their wild dreams and ideals late into the night. Sally had adored Lisette for all her abrasive, aggressive ambition. She could cut steel on her acid humour, but she was astute, practical and incredibly incisive. And for someone often obsessed with blazing through life with blinkered disregard, she was a remarkably good listener. Sally and Lisette had become firm friends, talking for hours on the phone every day, meeting for gossipy lunches and sharing the most gruesome of secrets. It was from Lisette that Sally had developed her taste for shopping.

When Lisette had walked out on Niall to further her career with a dilettante Hollywood brat who had almost ruined it instead, the solid, four-square union had quickly become a three-legged horse. Niall had fallen apart, and as a consequence Matty and Sally's marriage had undergone tremendous strain. They had both tried valiantly to help him keep life and soul together, but the split between their greatest friends had merely served to highlight the widening fault-line in their own relationship. It had taken a lot of effort and talking to keep their marriage alive and kicking amidst the fall out. Niall was now back on an even keel and, to Sally's mind, utterly suited to Tash. But Matty had severe doubts about the union, and Niall and he no longer had the same close friendship they'd once shared.

Until recently, Sally had assumed that Lisette was still trying to get her off-on career as a producer re-started in the States.

Then, a few weeks ago, a promotional postcard had arrived on Sally's doorstep, hyping a low-budget British film starring some very classy young English actors along with a couple of fading American names. On the reverse side was a neat little logo featuring two director's chairs tipped together at angles with the words SLEEPING PARTNERS FILMS encircling them. A very brief, almost illegible note had been scribbled beneath: *Back in London. This is my work number. Let's do a two-bottle lunch very soon. Merry Christmas.'* There had been no signature. Flipping the card over, Sally had scanned the list of credits underneath the promotional still. Alongside the name of the director and the leading stars was '*Producer – Lisette Norton*'. It was her working name – her maiden one.

Sally had felt the strangest shiver of excitement and relief when reading it. In America, Lisette had worked under the surname Norton-O'Shaughnessy in the hope, no doubt, that she would be associated with Niall who was very much in vogue out there right now. Yet Niall was an even bigger name in England, and Lisette had dropped the name-drop. To Sally it was an unwritten sign that she might be getting her morals back on to an even keel.

Sally had been so tempted to call since the card had arrived, but a sense of loyalty to Niall had prevented her. It was ironic that were she to ask him, Niall would undoubtedly urge her to go ahead. He bore his grudges for only so long as the bruises took to fade. Yet Matty would react totally differently, taking umbrage on his easygoing friend's behalf. Sally daren't risk getting his back up even more at the moment; he would see the rekindling of the friendship as defection, not affection.

She rested her chin in the palm of her hand and closed her eyes. It was Matty about whom she most wanted to talk to Lisette. Lisette, who had known Matty for longer even than she had. Had, Sally suspected, been slightly in love with him once. Yet how could she contact Lisette when doing so would undoubtedly make the situation she wanted to talk about even worse?

Beneath a pile of old records, she located the postcard and pressed one of its angled edges to her nose as she dared herself to act.

She couldn't imagine what Lisette looked like now – stunning no doubt, sabre-slim definitely; she might have grown her sleek, dark hair.

Or had it hacked into a fashionable career-woman crop; she might even have had plastic surgery while she was in the States, nipping the odd laughter line, straightening her slightly beaky nose, plumping out the curling, narrow lips, enlarging her bust. Not that she needed anything doing to add to her beauty, but she was so easily bored that if change were on offer she might do it for the hell of it. Now she lived in London again, she probably shopped at Brown's, lunched at The Ivy, weekended in Champneys, and holidayed in Tuscany, taking a lap-top, fax and mobile phone with her. Sally could imagine her driving to work in an open-topped Audi – or would she go by cab?

'I bet she's got her eye on Michael Grade,' she said aloud with a giggle.

'Who?'

She craned around to see Matty halfway down the stairs again, steaming cup of tea in his hand.

'Who what?'

'Who's got their eye on Michael Grade?' Matty sounded strangely conciliatory, if a little condescending.

Realising that the black gloom was finally lifting, Sally carefully framed a smile.

'Oh, I was just, um, thinking up a bit of dialogue for a sort of Victoria Wood-type sketch.' She hummed slightly manically.

'Sally, we've got to talk.' He settled down beside her on the chair – one thigh placed awkwardly alongside hers, perilously close to Lisette's postcard.

'Oh, yes?' She stiffened, trying desperately hard not to glance down at it.

'Yes.' Matty hung his head. 'Listen, I know I've been a sod lately.'

'You certainly have.' Sally touched his cheek, shifting to cover up the card.

'I know. But you haven't helped, Sals.'

'No?' Sally looked at him sharply, biting back a comment about what a long-suffering, angelic and goddammit good egg she'd been in the past fortnight.

'You used to argue with me, Sals – tell me where to get off if I was being a git, throw things at me, yell at me. Lately, you just creep around avoiding me.'

'Oh, I see.' She snatched her hand away from his cheek, her hackles rising as though a key had been dropped down her collar. 'I seem to recall that you used to get pretty naffed off when I yelled at you.'

'Sure – at the time. But it always hit me afterwards that you were right to tell me off and I snapped out of it pretty damned quick. I don't know what's got into you these days – you don't seem to care any more. You know what a self-indulgent prick I can be, but you just let me.'

'Perhaps you're right,' Sally said slowly, not really knowing why she was telling such a lie. 'Perhaps I can't be bothered any more.'

There was a wail from upstairs as Linus woke up feeling hungry.

'I'd better go to him.' Sally made to stand up.

'No, Sals.' Matty pinned her down with his arm. 'We have to sort this thing out – we're falling apart here. Can't you see that?'

The wails were getting louder.

'Let me go, Matt.' Sally fought against him.

'Christ, we hardly talk any more, we never go out, never laugh together, never fuck.'

'Where's Tor?'

'In the garden with the sodding rabbit. Did you hear me, Sally?'

'Yes, you said we never fuck. Listen, I have to go to Linus.'

'He can wait!' Matty's voice was taut with anger and frustration. 'Don't you give a toss about this? I thought you'd want to talk it through – you've looked so bloody miserable lately.'

'I am miserable!' Sally pushed him away, grabbing the postcard as she stood up, her voice climbing scales. 'I want to laugh and talk and fuck. Of course I do! I'm just not sure I want to do it with you any more!'

Turning on her heel, she stumbled upstairs.

Clutching the wailing Linus to her chest, she wandered outside and watched as Tor fed strawberry laces to the rabbit through the mesh front of its hutch. It was freezing cold and her quick, short breaths streamed in front of her face like a dragon's in a deluge.

Sally clenched her eyes shut and started to shake. She hadn't meant what she said, but at the same time she was so itchy with frustration and boredom right now that she sometimes found Matty's presence physically repellent. She felt trapped. Utterly, utterly trapped.

Hearing the front door slam, she let her shoulders drop six inches as the tension eased out of her now that she knew he'd gone out. She jiggled Linus out of his tears and into a sort of catatonic half-snively state and walked purposefully back inside to feed him. It wasn't yet three o'clock – she had at least half an hour before she had to set out on the school run for Tom.

With Linus ensconced in his doorway-bouncer and looking vaguely drugged, as he always did when he'd grown bored of crying and wasn't certain what to do next, she drew out the postcard and settled by the phone.

The receptionist at Sleeping Partners Films assumed she was some crazed salesperson trying to sell space in *Variety*, so it took her a long time to get through to Lisette's office. Even then, she had to persuade a super-efficient PA to put her through, practically resorting to identifying Lisette's birthmarks in order to speak to her.

'Sally!' Lisette finally rasped. 'Listen – sorry to keep this short but I've got an office full of people. It's so, so lovely to hear from you. When can we meet?'

Hearing her familiar, rusty-hinge voice oozing warmth, Sally burst into tears.

'Okay, okay, darling. Calm down. What are you doing tonight?'

'Nothing,' Sally hiccuped. 'But Matty might—'

'Sod Matty. Tell him you've got a friend in a crisis and he's just got to babysit. I've got a drinks party at six, but I'll meet you afterwards. Can you make Coast for eight-thirty?'

'Which coast?'

Lisette laughed kindly. 'Christ, Sally, you are out of it! It's a restaurant. I'll send a cab for you to Richmond. Just stay calm till then – I'll be waiting with a big hug and buckets of wine.'

Without asking for confirmation, she hung up.

Once she'd found the door amid a sea of plate glass, Sally was rather miffed that they cross-questioned her at the reception desk of Coast – almost as though she was some sort of tart, she realised as she was finally and snottily allowed access to its hallowed interior and led to the allotted table. Of course, Lisette was late – Sally hadn't expected anything else. But at least she had called to leave a message that she was going to be there as soon as she could. And it gave Sally a chance to catch up on a few drinks. She ordered a vodka tonic and perused the menu. Then gaped at the menu. Then hid behind the menu as she wondered whether or not there was anyone else in the place who, like her, still possessed such a paltry item as a fifty-pound cheque guarantee card. She hoped to Christ that Lisette would cover the bill and let her post-date a cheque to her in the privacy of the loo or something.

'Sorry, sorry, sorry!' gushed a voice as husky as a rasp against iron, yet as soft as angora. 'Michael Grade cornered me and I simply couldn't get away. Shit! Don't cry, Sals. Please don't cry. Here – here's my hank. Darling, you look wonderful – so damned womanly and fulsome. I wish I had regular sex these days – I might have a glow like yours. Oh, God!

It's so fucking good to see you. Give me that hanky back, I'm going to pissing cry too.' Only Lisette could swear like that and still sound divinely feminine.

Sally looked up at the vision in front of her and wanted to stew in her own bile of envy.

Lisette was as thin as a sanded, filed-down rake, as glossy as a mirror and three times more carnal-looking than she'd ever been. The nose was new, the lips were new, the hair was different and, yes, the tits were almost twice as large, but the old Lisette sex appeal was as natural as water gushing and gurgling from a hot spring.

'Oh, God – you look so fantastic,' Sally wailed, handing back the handkerchief.

Lisette pushed it back at her and snatched up a napkin to dab her own tears.

'And you look unhappy as hell, even though you're popping out of that dress like Anna Nicole Smith with a brain. Shit, Sals – why d'you leave it so long to get back to me?'

Sally took a deep breath.

'I don't think I love Matty anymore.'

Lisette drew a very pink tongue across her dark red lips, pushed a long strand of straight, snaky black hair behind her small, pale ear, looked coolly up at the waiter and ordered a bottle of Pouilly Fuissé. Still saying nothing, she toyed with the mascara-smudged napkin and finally lit a very low-tar cigarette before answering.

'Can I have him then?' she joked lightly, then stretched across the table to clutch Sally's hand. 'I'm kidding, honey. Let's get pissed, eat like pigs and talk about it. Now start at the beginning and don't you dare say you're boring me once over the next hour.'

Almost an hour later, Sally finally played herself out and looked at Lisette with very bloodshot eyes, balking again at the sultry, understated power suit, the longer, slicker hair, the neat little nose.

'How long?' Lisette asked carefully, picking up on something Sally had thrown away as a final comment.

'Since I was three months pregnant with Linus.' Sally winced.

'And that is . . . ?'

'Over a year ago.'

'Christ! I thought you were blooming from too much of it.'

'I'm eating as a replacement activity.' Sally smiled sadly. 'You know weight always piles straight on my tits.'

'And I've got plastic in mine.' Lisette discarded a barely touched salad and reached for her oversized wine glass. 'Do you think he's having an affair?'

'Christ, no!' Sally laughed. 'He'd be so bloody guilty about it he'd jump on me at every opportunity to put me off the scent.'

'So you really think he's never strayed?' Lisette looked disbelieving, tapping her ash with a long thumb-nail.

Sally shrugged. 'Well, he's certainly had a few crushes. He was bloody infatuated with one director at the Beeb for months, but actual infidelity, no. At least I don't think so. Unless you . . . ?'

'God, no!' Lisette shook her head hastily. 'Not a sniff of a rumour. Although, we really don't have that many mutual contacts these days.'

Sally hung her head guiltily and wolfed down the last of her divine turbot.

'So tell me what you're up to? Are you in love?'

'No time.' Lisette grinned guardedly. 'I've been too shagged out getting Sleepers up and running to shag – we're working like mad on our second feature right now, with Channel Four backing which is terrific. In fact, our treatment has been so well received that we're getting the script written up in double-quick time and trying to get some big-name stars in place to secure the last of the backing. We're talking shooting schedule in place in weeks, baby.'

The pitch went right over Sally's head. She smiled encouragingly and tried to look knowledgeable. 'So what star names are you chasing?'

'Well, we think Kristin Scott Thomas is a possible – she'd be good as it's very Four Weddings in feel. The guy who wrote it is terrific – married to that Daytime TV presenter, by the way. It's called Four Poster Bed – a really zippy British Ealing Farce with a terrifically acerbic nineties treatment straight out of Shallow Grave. We're trying to get Liz Hurley optioned in, along with Saffron Burrows and Felix Sylvian, who has looks to die for although his acting is suspect. Alan Rickman and Jeremy Northam are keeping an open diary on the basis of the first dialogue script, and even Olly Reed might be lining up for a cameo role. But we really need some heavyweights on board to catch the American market.'

Sally was doing a nodding dog impersonation as she followed about half of what Lisette was saying.

'I was – er – thinking about Niall,' Lisette said cautiously.

'I adore Alan Rickman,' Sally said dreamily. 'Do you really think that he might – what?'

'Niall.' Lisette swallowed, looking terribly uncomfortable. 'I really need him on board, Sals, but I guess he still loathes me. It's so awkward.'

'He doesn't loathe you,' Sally said almost automatically, her confidence crumpling as she realised why Lisette had contacted her.

'He'd be so fucking perfect for the male lead – sort of Jeff Goldblum in The Tall Guy crossed with Mark Frankel in Solitaire for Two, with a dash of Jimmy Stewart in just about everything.' Lisette lit another ultra-low-tar cigarette. 'The director – I can't tell you who he is, because no contracts have been signed, but he's shit hot – is absolutely dying to approach Bob Hudson and woo Niall at this stage, but I just don't know how to tackle this one. I mean, he'll hear I'm involved and run a mile. There's no way he'll sign up once he realises I'm part of the package.'

'He might.' Sally shrugged listlessly. 'I mean – he hates working in the States. If this thing is shooting in the UK, it'd be an incredible selling point.'

'But what does he feel about me, Sals?' Lisette probed. 'How will he react when he sees my name on the script?'

Sally took a deep breath, and then another half-breath to muster courage until her lungs felt like a hot air balloon trying to clear Everest.

'He's getting married again, Lisette,' she said quietly. 'He's marrying Tash.'

Seven

TASH THREW HERSELF INTO her work for the first few weeks of January. With Hunk still out of action, she concentrated on starting the long, arduous process of getting Snob fit for the forthcoming season, plus helping to bring on a few of the youngsters Gus was hopeful would make future superstars.

One in particular, a gangly iron-grey gelding called Mickey Rourke, was looking likely to go far. He was still very babyish, with boggling eyes and too much leg, and possessed a tendency to trip himself up like a boy wearing long trousers for the first time. But he was gutsy and bold and adored his job. When Tash gently introduced him to jumping low grids on the all-weather menage (Gus couldn't afford an indoor school), he bounded around with such enthusiasm that she raced into the farmhouse afterwards to tell everyone how brilliant he'd been.

She was met with worried faces, as Gus, Penny and Zoe all looked up from the Sunday papers which they'd been poring over.

'I suppose you could call this your official engagement announcement.' Penny bit her lip as she held up the *People*.

'No going back now, kid.' Gus flapped out the *Sunday Express* for Tash to see.

She winced as she caught sight of a blurred photo of herself clutching nervously on to Niall's arm at a celebrity charity concert they'd attended the previous summer. Not only did she look tremendously uncomfortable amid such glamour, but she also looked appallingly fat. The headline read: *Niall O'Shaughnessy to Wed Girl Groom*.

'I'm not a bloody groom!' Tash wailed. 'And I look really ghastly.'

'No, you don't,' Penny reassured her as she examined the picture at close range. 'You look rather sweet – and you were in great shape last summer.'

'Oh God, I must be simply massive now,' Tash rolled her eyes down to her stomach which, now she came to look at it, did resemble one in the early stages of multiple-birth pregnancy. The zip on her cord breeches was straining gallantly against burgeoning flesh, and the seams were starting to give out toothy smiles as the stitches grimaced with effort.

'Well, you have put on a bit of weight over Christmas.' Penny eyed her critically, then catching Zoe's horrified look, added quickly, 'But everyone does. I've put on tons – it'll drop off while you get the horses fit.'

'And Niall looks great in these shots.' Gus was reading the lurid prose in one tabloid. 'Christ! They say you work for Mark Todd here – you have gone up in the world!'

'You look lovely, Tash.' Zoe gave her a reassuring hug. 'Fresh-faced, blossoming and sexy.'

'I want to be in bud, not blossom. I'm too young to blossom. I'm going on a diet.'

Later, Tash was sitting on the steps that led down to the forge's small kitchen, leafing through the Yellow Pages looking for slimming clubs and simultaneously diving her fingers in and out of a box of Frosties, when Beetroot started barking excitedly in the direction of the cat-flap.

Assuming that the little dog had just spotted Giblets, keen for a few scraps, Tash ignored her and tipped back her head to drop some more of the sugary cereal down her throat, wondering dreamily if they still had that tin of condensed milk in the cupboard. At that moment, Hugo let himself in through the front door and wandered inside.

Turning around at the sudden rush of cool air against her back, Tash almost choked.

'Tell me if you need the Heimlich manoeuvre within the next couple of minutes.' Hugo smiled frostily and stooped down to say hello to Beetroot who was greeting him with an ecstatic series of pirouettes.

Tash would have liked to smile frostily back, but she had far too many Frosties in her mouth. Coughing and spluttering fragments of orange cereal on to her chest, she stumbled upright and tried to look suitably outraged that he could walk in without knocking. Her wind pipe was far too blocked for her actually to voice the objection.

But, straightening up easily, his blue eyes watching her with amusement, Hugo pre-empted her.

'Sorry to barge in. I've got a fax from your fiancé – he seems to think that yours is up the spout.'

Tash looked briefly and guiltily at the fax, which she had broken an hour earlier while attempting to use it to photo-copy a full-length newspaper photograph of herself to stick on the fridge, food cupboard and freezer in an attempt to deter her from snacking. Embarrassingly, evidence of her earlier motivational attempts was still littered around the now dead contraption – curling reams of fax paper bearing very dark, grainy stats of her lumpy body.

'What have you been trying to do?' Hugo regarded them without great interest.

'Oh – this and that. Publicity, you know. Magazine questionnaires and such.'

He looked sceptical but said nothing, handing her the fax that he'd brought along.

Seeing Niall's messy, hastily scribbled handwriting, Tash felt the familiar hug of warmth and security fold itself tightly around her shoulders. She glanced irritably at Hugo. She didn't want him to hang around while she was reading it, but she supposed that she should thank him for taking the time to bring it over, perhaps even offer him a cup of coffee. It was uncharacteristically kind of him, she realised – far more in character would have been a curt call from his secretary asking her if she could come over and pick it up, adding that Hugo didn't want to encourage freeloaders using his fax to communicate with one another.

'Er – thanks for bringing it round,' she mumbled, suddenly feeling both grateful and awkward. 'Would you like a drink or something?'

'God, no.' Hugo was glancing around rather critically. 'I'm just racing to pick up Kirsty – we're going to the Cubitts' drinks party tonight. You not going then?'

Tash sucked in one cheek, aware that she was being put down and longing to have the wit for a quick-fire retort. She hadn't been invited, wasn't even aware that the Cubitts were having a drinks party. Had Niall been around, she realised glumly, they would have been top of the list. The locals were, as Gus continually pointed out, horrific star-fuckers.

'No,' she said lamely, noticing that his tortoiseshell hair was gleaming, his suit oozed understated class, and his neck was wafting out subtle, delicious tangs of aftershave. 'You look nice.'

One eyebrow shot up in astonishment. But, being Hugo, he found it impossible to return the compliment.

'Which is more than I can say for this place.' He nodded at the piles of mess. 'I don't know what's got into you lately, Tash. You've really let yourself go since you've been with Niall – I thought women were supposed to do that after they'd got married, not during their engagement. Has that turkey crapped in here?'

Wrinkling his nose, he wandered out again without a breath of a farewell.

'Bastard!' Tash hissed, her cheeks flaming, his words still ringing in her ears.

When she read Niall's fax, it only added to her misery and humiliation.

Tash darling,

Christ, I hate this sodding place. They've scheduled one more day in the dubbing studio, so no chance of flying back before Tuesday. Will have to head straight to Glasgow on Wednesday night red-eye. No weekends off until February – can you come up to see me in Scotland?

Will talk on phone as soon as I can get through to you. Have you switched it off or something? Call me.

Niall

Hugo must have read it, she reasoned. And he would have gloated over every word which spelled out her lack-lustre love-life as dictated by Niall's punishing schedule.

The following Tuesday evening, Tash had a rare chance for a night out. She was very careful about what she wore, she barely ate through worry beforehand and, an absolute first, she didn't knock back a swift bolstering drink to steady her nerves. She didn't even drink a cup of tea in case she developed water retention.

At seven o'clock she parked Gus's Land-Rover in Marlbury High Street and, doing a few star-jumps on the pavement, headed towards the United Reformed Church Hall. It was only as she was passing the brightly illuminated McDonald's windows that it occurred to Tash that perhaps she should have eaten before this particular date. In fact, not only should she have stuffed herself, but the more layers of very heavy clothing she was wearing the better. In weeks to come, she would thank herself for her forward planning.

She dashed back to the car and layered on Penny's holey jumper, which had been in the back of the Land-Rover for six months beneath her own tatty moleskin waistcoat, a filthy Husky she suspected had been a dog blanket for several years and Gus's ancient oilskin, which weighed a ton. Thus dressed like a rather unappetising explorer returning from a long, bath-free trek in Antarctica, she headed back to the church hall, stopping off first at the burger bar for a take-out.

The assistant wrinkled her nose as Tash took possession of her several thousand calories.

'You been lambing then?' She nodded at Tash's extraordinary garb, obviously assuming she was some rosy-cheeked local farmer's wife popping in for junk-food supplies to keep her menfolk going through the night.

'No – just off to Flab-busters actually.' Tash grinned amiably and took her burger and shake into a dark alley to wolf down before creeping into the church hall late.

She needn't have worried about her unpunctuality. The post-Christmas boom had brought an unprecedented number of newcomers to the weekly Flab-busters meeting, all eager to shed those extra pounds brought on by Christmas pud and double sherries.

The church hall was lined with drawings from local play-groups, tables of craft displays and stacks of plastic chairs. One end had been set up for the Flab-busters slimming club, consisting of a plump circle of plastic chairs (not reinforced, Tash noted), two three-sided screens covered with promotional material, and a table weighed down with measuring spoons and scales, low-cal tinned food and recipe books with glossy before-and-after pictures on their covers. Beside one screen a tall, very thin dyed blonde wearing a fake Chanel suit was weighing her influx of fatties on the type of scales Tash associated with pre-boxing-match weigh-ins. At her side a skinny assistant with mousy hair and a dribbly nose was filling in score cards of some sort. The dyed blonde – called Theresa according to her jaunty plastic name-badge – was doing a lot of cheerful tutting as her customers climbed guiltily on the scales and tried to stand on one foot as they assessed the festive seasonally adjusted damage.

Letting out a Big Mac burp, Tash joined the queue and eyed a suspect-looking cardboard snow-man, moulting cotton-wool and sporting a ragged beret. He looked like a victim of nuclear fall-out. She suspected he'd been made by one of the local play-groups and abandoned after Christmas. She knew how he felt.

Theresa was now getting quite overwhelmed with excitement as she ruled the scales, weighing her new charges and letting them know their target weights as she handed over an official welcoming pamphlet and home-made list of motivational Ryvita recipes while her runny-nosed assistant filled in their diet cards.

At the rear of the queue, Tash was lumbering worriedly towards the scales behind a vast woman who, despite the frosty weather, was wearing a summer tent dress. She had been eyeing Tash thoughtfully since her arrival, her nose twitching slightly under the assault of old farmyard clothing.

'You'll regret wearing all that in a few weeks' time,' she told her.

'Why?' Tash was already regretting the Husky jacket, which was smelling increasingly awful as she heated up. She was convinced a small, furry animal had been incontinent in it.

'Theresa's very strict at the weigh-in,' the woman warned, nodding at their leader who was arguing with a newcomer that she was definitely well over ten stones and needed to go on the 'quick-step' weight-loss programme, not the 'slow-shuffle' one. 'She makes you wear the same thing every week, otherwise your weight changes.'

'Oh.' Tash shrugged out of her oilskin which was also smelling pretty rancid. She was sweating rather hard now, so she might already be losing weight, she realised cheerfully. 'Have you been coming long then?'

'Since July.'

'Christ.' Tash tried not to stare at her still-bulging body. 'Have you lost much?'

'Twenty-eight pounds.' Tent Dress beamed. 'I want to be Gloria Hunniford-sized by my daughter's wedding in June.'

'Oh,' Tash swallowed miserably. She didn't want to think about weddings right now. Since she'd become engaged, she and Niall had spent less than a week in one another's company.

Tent Dress had reached the scales now and clambered on to them with some effort to be enthusiastically hailed by Theresa.

'How's my star slimmer then?' she gushed, adjusting her scales with long, scarlet fingernails. 'Not been tucking into too much Chrimbo cake in my absence, I hope?'

'No, Theresa, I haven't.' Tent Dress was suddenly as obsequious and coy as a first-year pupil talking to her favourite games mistress. 'Honestly not.'

'And did you follow that fromage frais and raisin pud alternative I gave you?' Theresa was staring sceptically at the scales, sliding the pounds reader grimly upwards.

'Um – yes, well, my husband wasn't too keen on that one.'

'Hmm.' Theresa's enthusiasm had evaporated as quickly as spit on an iron. 'You've put on two pounds this week. We'll have to pull our pop socks up, won't we?'

'Yes, Theresa.' Tent Dress hung her head as Theresa's skinny assistant blew her nose before filling in a card and handing it back.

When Tash ascended the scales, she was relieved to see that Theresa had to do a great deal of adjusting downwards to ascertain her weight.

'And who are we then?' Theresa beamed up at her, nodding for the minion to fill out an application form.

'Er, I'm alone actually.' Tash was slightly nonplussed.

Theresa let out a little tinkly laugh and peered at Tash's outfit, which was looking even more tramp-like without the oilskin. Her heavily mascara-ed eyes batted slightly, but she made no comment.

'Name?' croaked her assistant.

'Oh, my name?' Tash didn't like the way Theresa was creeping the slide back up again. 'Er, Natasha.'

'Second name?' the assistant said witheringly, blowing her nose again and adding a self-pitying cough for good measure.

'Elizabeth.'

'SURname?' The assistant was reduced to a bronchial wheeze.

'French.'

Theresa had achieved her balance now and glanced up at Tash with an air of surprise, as though trying to place her.

'Do I know your mother?' She crinkled her made-up eyes quizzically.

'I doubt it.' Tash looked dubious.

'Hmm.' Theresa clearly felt snubbed. 'Eleven stone three. We have got a lot of work to do, haven't we? How tall are you?'

Tash was gaping at her. She couldn't possibly be that heavy, could she? She'd been under ten last autumn. At this rate she wouldn't even need to use a weight-cloth across country; the shame would be torment.

'Perhaps I should take my boots off?' she wondered anxiously.

'How tall?' Theresa's eyes narrowed. 'Please spit it out, dear. I have a class to hold.'

'Five ten.' Tash could feel tears springing to her eyes. She suddenly felt like the side of a house, so vast in fact that she wanted to take the weight off her feet and lie down. Very quickly. In a dead faint.

'Okay, you should be aiming for ten stone two.' Theresa flicked her nails at her assistant before ramming some leaflets into Tash's hands. 'You're not a vegetarian or anything, are you?'

Feeling another Big Mac burp bubbling up, Tash shook her head, too tearful to speak. She was going to have her jaw wired, her stomach stapled and her fridge super-glued as soon as she found the time.

More chairs had been distributed to cater for the swollen ranks of dieters, making Theresa's neat circle into a rather chaotic open meeting. Tash found the only spare red plastic chair was right at the front of the 'class', next to the cardboard snow-man with scurf. She perched on the edge of it, now feeling so fat that she was certain it would collapse under her. As she brushed lightly against the snow-man, he keeled over, adding to her gloom.

'Welcome, welcome, welcome!' Theresa wafted nimbly to the centre of her circle, smoothing down the fake Chanel suit against her wafer-thin hips. 'So lovely to see so many new faces!'

The new faces were almost universally looking suicidal, having just been told how hugely overweight they were. Theresa swiftly cleared her throat and, reaching for a large photograph being held out by the fluey assistant, rushed on.

'This,' she paused for effect, clutching the photograph to her chest, 'was me before I joined Flab-busters six years ago!'

Turning the photograph around, she revealed a very grainy enlarged black and white shot of an extremely attractive, if curvy, brunette wearing a caftan and looking like a lost member of Manfred Mann.

There was a lot of gasping and giggling around the room – more, Tash suspected, as a reaction to the horrific dress-sense Theresa had once displayed than the extra pounds.

'I know, I know – I was SO overweight, but you see, if I can do it, anyone can.' Theresa beamed caringly as she propped the photograph up beside Tash. 'And I'm here to show you not only that I have got it off and kept it off, but that you can too. Together WE CAN!' With a theatrical flourish, Theresa nodded at her assistant who produced several tin cans from a plastic Tesco's bag and held them up. Each had 'I CAN', 'YOU CAN' or 'WE CAN' Tippexed on the side.

Tash settled back in her chair, no longer caring if it collapsed, and tried to catch someone's eye for a giggle. But everyone was looking quite rapt with enthusiasm now.

'What I am here to do is provide you not only with the know-how to shed those bulges, girls, but also the will power. And here he is.' Theresa made a lunge towards Tash. 'Mr WILL POWER!'

Giving Tash a dirty look, she extracted the collapsed snow-man, who was shedding cotton wool fast now, and held him up to her excited followers.

For the next hour, Tash stifled yawn after yawn, gave a few surreptitious Big Mac burps and correctly guessed the calorie content of a Kit-Kat (she ate three a day, and read that terrifyingly high three-figure digit each time she unwrapped one. It was a form of psychological torture).

'Well done, Natasha!' Theresa beamed at her insincerely, putting the Kit-Kat prop back into her assistant's Tesco's bag. 'For that you win a prize. Guess what it is?'

Tash raised an eyebrow. 'A Kit-Kat?' she suggested hopefully.

'No, no, NO!' Theresa laughed. 'What have I just said, Natasha? Chocolate is on what list in our Mental Munchy Map?'

'The once-a-week treat list,' Tash said with the flat by-rote boredom of a child reciting its times table.

'Quite.' Theresa crinkled her eyes fondly.

'Well, this is once a week,' Tash pointed out. She rather felt like a Kit-Kat now that the thought had been put in her head.

'And you've got a whole week to get through.' Theresa clearly felt she was exhibiting the patience of a saint. 'So you'll need your treat to look forward to, won't you? On Friday, you may be grateful that I told you not to have the choccy bar, because that means you can substitute it for the one alcoholic drink treat – say a gin and tonic. Hmm?'

Tash went pale. 'You mean I can only have one drink a week?'

Theresa shuddered with exasperation. 'Yes, I told you that. You can have ONE item from your once-a-week list, once a week. It's very simple, dear. Do try to concentrate.'

The rest of the class, also impatient with Tash's horrified lack of comprehension, was getting fidgety. Tash searched around for a sympathetic face, but after just one hour in her company they were all Theresa converts, possessing the same condescending expressions and slightly manic looks of enthusiasm.

'Here's your prize, Natasha.' Theresa clicked her fingers at her assistant, who reached into her Tesco's bag and extracted a Flab-busters fridge magnet which read 'TOGETHER WE CAN!'

After the hour was up, Tash couldn't be bothered to queue up in the long line of new devotees eager to buy scales and recipe books. Instead she took her oilskin and her fridge magnet back to the Land Rover, via the late-night newsagent's to buy a Kit-Kat.

'What's this?' India, who had called in on Tash to borrow some designer's gouache, fingered the Flab-busters fridge magnet with interest.

'Oh, nothing.' Tash pinkened slightly. 'Just some freebie I got with a Sunday supplement.'

'Isn't it a fridge magnet?' India stuck it back where she had found it.

'Yup.'

'So why have you got it on the fire guard? It's starting to melt.'

'I'm unconventional.' Tash went to the kitchen to make some hot chocolate, which she knew India adored. Then she remembered that, in her over-zealous post-Flab-busters blitz of all fattening foods the night before, she had thrown it out. All she had in the house was coffee, celery sticks and dog food. It was amazing how tempting Pal could be when one's stomach was performing back-flips of hunger.

'She's so gorgeous.' India had settled on the sofa now and was playing with Beetroot's huge envelope-flap ears. 'It's lovely to have an affectionate dog. Enid's so paranoid, she thinks a pat means a trip to the vet. Ted threw her a ball yesterday and she ducked for cover.'

'She totally adores your mother,' Tash pointed out. 'She's just a one dog woman. Wally's pretty friendly.'

'If you bribe him,' India sighed. 'You even have to offer him a choc drop to goose you these days, he's so spoilt for choice with all the eventers who troop through our kitchen. What's this?' She picked up a fat, dog-eared script from the sofa arm. 'One of Niall's?'

'Yup.' Tash squinted at it. She'd been so bored and lonely over the last few evenings that she'd been reduced to reading some of the scripts Niall had been sent. 'Actually that one's wonderful – so romantic.'

India scrutinised it with the critical eyes of an academic snob whose only recent reading had been the GCSE English syllabus – Jane Austen, Emily Brontë and Chaucer.

'Looks a bit schmaltzy – Four Poster Bed. Does he have to get his kit off?'

'Mmm – a bit, but it's far more of a witty English romance. Very sharp. I loved it.'

'Is he going to do it then?' India cast it to one side in favour of cuddling Beetroot some more.

'I'm not sure,' Tash confessed. 'I've not spoken to him about it.' She didn't add that she'd not in fact spoken to Niall at all for several days. He was never available, never in his hotel and never seemed to get her messages. When he did call her, she was invariably out working or fast asleep. They were currently communicating by answer machine alone, which was hugely frustrating, although it did give one the time to think up those witty little one-liners normally only mulled over long after the conversation has ended.

'You're so lucky having Niall,' sighed India. 'He's absolutely wicked to show off about.'

'And he's a lovely man,' Tash pointed out wryly.

'Yes, that too. He's an ace bloke. God, my friends at school are so jealous that I actually know him. They were sick as spun-dried cats when I told them you guys were getting hitched.'

Tash sucked her thumb uncomfortably. India, as long and leggy as an evening shadow, was looking doe-eyed with enthusiasm.

'I can't wait for the wedding,' she sighed happily. 'Mum's gone all dreamy about it too, you know.'

'I thought she didn't altogether approve.' Tash gave a ghost of a grin as she headed back into the kitchen to see what she could find in the absence of hot chocolate.

'I think she needs a man of her own.'

Tash, who had been in the midst of offering India a Diet Coke, swallowed the rest of her sentence and looked up from the fridge in shock.

'What makes you say that?'

'We-eell,' India looked shifty, 'it's just that she hasn't had a boyfriend for simply ages. And I was thinking . . .'

'She went out with Gus's friend Frank last year.'

'. . . of setting her up.'

'Who with?' Tash kneaded her spare tyre thoughtfully, wondering if it had gone down yet.

'Someone local actually.'

'Oh, yes?' Tash grinned. 'Like who? There's not exactly a plethora of available men in the village. Godfrey Pelham, I suppose, but he's a bit old and fusty—'

'He's gay, Tash!'

'Oh, yes; I suppose now you mention it he is a bit camp.'

'I was thinking of Hugo.'

'Hugo!' Tash's chin slammed back into her neck. 'Are you serious?'

India looked mildly insulted. 'Of course. I mean he's quite a bit younger than Mummy, but he's just her type and incredibly sexy, you have to admit.'

'Christ!' Tash was having trouble getting to grips with this. She badly needed some chocolate. 'Would you really fancy him as a step-father? I mean, it's not so long ago that you fancied him, full stop.'

'A silly teenage crush.' India dismissed it, sounding more forty than fourteen. 'Even you fancied him once. And anyway, he likes older women.'

'Sure – like Kirsty?'

'She's only three years younger than Mummy.'

'What?' Tash's chin hit her neck again.

'Didn't you know?'

'No – I mean I never asked.'

'She's thirty-seven.' India nodded. 'Gus says the only reason she wants to marry thick Richie is because she's desperate to have kids before she's forty.'

'Good grief,' Tash giggled delightedly. She'd always imagined that Kirsty was the same age as herself, she certainly looked no older. Although, she reasoned rather gloomily, it could just be that she herself looked no younger than thirty-seven.

'And Hugo's last long-term girlfriend was older, wasn't she?'

'Amanda?' Tash shuddered at the memory. She had been terrified of the diminutive, sharp-tongued Amanda who had a sub-zero manner with other women – particularly tall ones. 'She was a bit older, I think – not much.'

'There you go!' India seemed to think that this proved he and Zoe were positively star-destined in the lover stakes.

Tash busied herself looking for the desired gouache.

'I hardly think,' she ventured gently as she dug through her paint tin, 'that the fact Hugo has dated a couple of attractive older women makes him and your mother compatible. I don't even think she likes him very much – he can be pretty insufferable. And he'd make a lousy step-father.'

'I disagree.' India was marking Tash with her eyes. 'He'd pretty much let us get on with it, I should imagine. Anyway, I'm off to Art School as soon as I get my "A" levels, and Rufus and he get on brilliantly – they can talk about cricket and horses for simply hours.'

'And what if he wants kids?' Tash was trying to make sense of what appeared to be a ludicrous suggestion. She was amazed that India appeared to be taking it so seriously.

'Oh, Mummy'd probably go along with that too. She's always said she'd like a couple more once Rufe and I are old enough to help her out. She and Hugo would have beautiful babies.'

Tash wrinkled her nose. If their babies turned out anything like Hugo, they'd need to be thrust into the arms of a karate-trained nanny pretty smartly. She couldn't imagine anything more potentially brattish than a seven-pound replica of Hugo.

'So will you help me?' India was looking at her eagerly.

Tash gaped at her. It was at times like this that she wondered whether India came from another planet. She appeared so calm and serene for her age, so eminently capable of doing anything she put her mind to, so unrealistically mature and sane. Not only that but she was blessed with looks that Tash would have considered a miracle in her own youth. She was the most stunning-looking girl Tash had ever encountered, more flawless than one hundred faces staring out of the glossy magazines which mocked the overweight in dentists' waiting rooms and on newsagents' shelves. Yet for all these apparent gifts from God, she was as daft as a hairdresser'sworth of brushes.

'You want me to help you set your mother up with Hugo?' She clarified the situation in a croaking voice.

'Yup.' India smiled expectantly.

'Christ.' Tash looked down to see that she had dropped a large quantity of gouache on the floor and now appeared to be treading most of it in as she wandered around in a state of disbelief.

'Please, Tash. I really need your help – I mean, you know him far better than me, and I know he's best friends with your brother-in-law, so that could be useful.'

'No way!' She started shaking her head and walking towards the kitchen for some much-needed calories.

'Please?' India looked imploring.

'Why don't you put it to Penny and Gus and see how they react?'

'No, Mummy won't let me do that.'

'You mean your mother knows about this?'

'Of course.' India stood up, tipping Beetroot on to a cushion. 'I mean, she didn't suggest it or anything, but I think we can say she's given her tacit approval. If we do it this way we can palm it off as a silly schoolgirl thing if he shows no interest.'

Tash was completely speechless now. She knew that Zoe had seen a couple of men over the years she had lived with Gus and Penny, but she had always maintained that after her first marriage she had no intention of getting seriously involved again. She'd obviously been very badly hurt, although it was a topic she never offered much information about and Tash respected her too much to probe. She wasn't immune to men's charms, and she certainly had plenty of admirers – there were many of Gus's friends who had tried to become more to her than a coffee-in-the-kitchen chum and occasional dinner date. But they were all gently sent away by Zoe's polite, friendly indifference. The thought that she might be harbouring a private desire to hook Hugo – Mr Eligible Local Hell-raiser – was beyond belief.

'What exactly did you have in mind for me to do on her behalf?' Tash asked humouringly. 'Deliver a *mot d'amour* by horseback to his box at a competition? Slip a love-drug into his coffee next time he's at the farm trying to buy a cheap horse?'

'You'll do it then?' India looked ecstatic. 'Brilliant!'

'Well, I'm not . . .'

'I thought a Valentine's card to start off with. That's next week, isn't it? You can make one.'

'Me?' Tash laughed. 'That's ridiculous – I've painted some of his horses for him; he knows my style. He'll just think it's from me.'

'Well, if I do it it'll look like it came from a GCSE art student – which I am. I mean, I know I'm good, but I'm not as good as you.'

'Can't you just buy one?' Tash was beginning to think this wasn't just a daft schoolgirl idea. It was a very dangerous bad one.

'No, we can't.' India started to gather up squashed tubes of paint. 'You're going to do it because then you can say an anonymous local glamourpuss commissioned it from you if Hugo asks. I mean he'll *know* you didn't send it personally, won't he? You loathe him. And you're marrying Niall.'

'But I haven't time. I have to make Niall a card.'

India handed her a tube of leaking crimson. 'Better get started then.'

'You've been a long time.' Zoe greeted her daughter at the door and waited patiently for her to remove her shapeless man's overcoat, two cardigans, lambswool scarf and the thickest of her three jumpers before kicking off her wellies and wandering through to the sitting room to seek a place by the fire.

'I've been talking to Tash.' She looked victorious, gathering up a half-eaten Galaxy bar from Gus's littered desk. 'I think I might have done something rather brilliant.'

'What? Tidied up the forge?' Spurred by the thought, Zoe started gathering up mugs – of which there appeared to be several on every surface; Gus and Penny never took them back through to the kitchen. Two had been used as ashtrays.

'Nope.' India grinned over her shoulder as she plumped down by Wally, who thumped his tail and wriggled across the hearthrug on his belly to sniff interesting Beetroot smells lingering on her jeans. 'I've persuaded her to send Hugo Beauchamp a Valentine's card.'

'You what?' Zoe froze in horror. 'Whatever for?'

'Well, you were talking to Penny last night about thinking that Tash still fancies him rotten . . .'

'You were never supposed to hear that conversation!' Zoe's face flushed. 'It was just idle gossip over a bottle of wine.'

'I was next door, I couldn't help hearing it,' she pointed out. 'And I also heard you saying that you thought that Hugo was secretly wild about her too.'

'India, that gossip was so, so idle it was almost asleep. We were a bit tight and being very silly. It's all absolute rubbish.'

'I think you were right.' India played with Wally's ears, turning them inside out to expose their guava-pink centres. 'I think she really does have a thing about Hugo.'

'Oh, poor Tash,' Zoe sighed, shaking her head as she wandered out.

'Poor Niall.' India stared into the flickering fire, watching it spit tongues of sparks up into the sooty flue.

She didn't care what her mother said, she was certain that she'd done the right thing. And what's more, she was going to make sure Tash carried on believing that she was playing Cupid. Having just read *Cyrano de Bergerac*, India thought the whole idea of Cupid being shot by his own arrow impossibly romantic and sexy. At school, Valentine's Day was wildly influential, making or breaking relationships; she was certain the same was true throughout life, however sceptical her cynic of a mother was.

Eight

AS EVER THE QUEUE of traffic turning into Marylebone High Street from Regent's Park was banked up and beeping, as angry as a swarm of wasps trying to get at a maggot hole in a plum.

Lisette Norton wasn't unduly bothered. For once she didn't cut up a fellow driver or lean on her horn. She had just driven through a beautifully frosted park and had a wonderful conversation on the car phone with her production manager, Flavia Watson. It was the best possible news. Flavia had rung from Ireland where she was on location with the hottest director of the moment, David Wheaton. Lisette had been chasing Wheaton for weeks in the hope that he would come on board to direct Four Poster Bed but he had continually eluded her. He loved the script, adored Lisette's ideas and the suggestions for art director and DoP; he was also in total agreement as to who should be offered first refusal on the lead roles. But he wouldn't agree to go ahead with contracts until they had at least one of those lead players confirmed. And that elusive lead player refused to confirm until David had. That player was Niall O'Shaughnessy, and Lisette knew him well enough not to push him; he was extremely wary of making a film with her in the first place, despite the over-inflated fee she was offering him – three times that of the other actors and far more than she could really afford. She had only been able to offer so much by arranging a last-minute tie-in deal with a leading gossip glossy – an idea that she'd thought up during her recent dinner with Sally. If she put him under any pressure to commit, she suspected he would blow up in her face and defect back to the States, where he was being offered ten times as much for a third of the commitment. As such David Wheaton was her trump card and she had fought capped-tooth and acrylic nail to secure him.

Just as she had begun to despair of moving the stalemate situation on to fresh ground, Flavia had confessed an absolute dream of a secret. Three vast glasses of wine in Soho House and Lisette's rather uppity, super-efficient West Indian manager had carelessly let out a Freudian slip of the tongue of glorious dimensions. Safe, reliable 'I'm-not-a-fornicating-luvvie' Wheaton, who lived in a baby-infested house in Highgate and had a well-publicised marriage to a children's television supremo, had once been her lover and they remained on very friendly terms. Lisette had seized on the news with delight – dispatching Flavia to Ireland where Wheaton was shooting the last few location shots of a big-budget American nostalgia movie. Flavia had been very reluctant to pull strings, but as Lisette had pointed out, she either pulled them or pulled the plug on her job. Flavia had clearly pulled herself together into the bargain and, with Wheaton confirmed as on board, Lisette knew the project was now on full throttle.

She dialled through to Bob Hudson's office as she finally turned into Marylebone High Street, catching the eyes of a few good-looking men outside the street's bohemian cafes and wishing she had the time to fall in love these days.

'Bob – it's me. The *Cheers!* magazine deal has now been accepted as we discussed and – wait for it – Wheaton's a definite, so I'd like to confirm Niall for Daniel as soon as possible. Will you get the okay from him and ring me back today so that I can get the contracts out to you? Thanks.'

Ringing off, she turned her red Alfa into the small mews where her office was based and smoked a stealthy cigarette before scaling the external stairs to the glossy, first-floor rooms which housed Sleeping Partners Productions.

The team's production secretary, Lucy, was waiting eagerly for her at the door

'Bob Hudson's just called. We've definitely got Niall so long as he gets the publicity tie-in confirmed in the contract.'

'Niall wants that?' Lisette was momentarily surprised.

'Bob wants that.' Lucy checked her note-pad. 'He says he wants a copy of the *Cheers!* magazine offer before he gets Niall to sign.'

'Sure.'

Lisette smiled smoothly and headed into her office where she closed the door behind her and shuddered with happiness. Drawing a bottle of Bushmills out of her filing cabinet, she poured herself three fingers and downed it in one with another shudder of pleasure. The taste brought back such vivid sensory memories that it was like drinking a distilled essence of Niall.

She had often wondered how she would react to the news that he was to remarry. She had anticipated a mule-kick of jealousy in her belly, a stab of rejection in her temples. Not once had she imagined feeling quite so delighted at the prospect.

The timing of Niall's marriage, she reflected, was of supreme convenience to her marketing campaign.

When Tash finally heard Niall's voice, she almost broke down with happiness. He was calling from Glasgow where they were rehearsing for the swash-buckling swords-and-sporrans epic Celt, which was due to start shooting the following week.

'I've missed you so much!' she wailed.

'Shh, angel – I know, and I'm bloody sorry I've made such a cock-up of getting hold of you. Christ, but it's been hectic up here.'

'I can imagine – I got your fax. It was lovely. I've been writing back but you know how lousy I am at finishing anything.'

'Oh, so the fax is back together again then, is it?' Niall cackled. 'I wasn't sure if it had got to you.'

'I've borrowed Gus's – he says he doesn't know how to work it anyway. Oh, it's so lovely to hear your voice.'

'Yours too, angel, yours too. Listen, I can't talk long as I've a line rehearsal with Minty in a minute.'

'Minty?' Tash tried hard to sound cool and cheerful, but the age-old jealous demons were already clawing at her back. It happened every time he was working on a new film – the appearance of an unfamiliar woman's name, one she had never heard Niall mention before the shoot, yet undoubtedly one that she had seen on credits and fly-bills long before that. That name would crop up in their conversations over and over again, to vanish like a popped bath bubble the moment the film was wrapped.

'Yes, you know – Minty Blyth. Christ, that girl's a talent! She puts me to shame.'

So long as that was the only place she was putting Niall then Tash supposed it was all right. Minty Blyth was a fantastically pretty actress with a mane of black corkscrew hair, a body which curved as perfectly as an egg timer and eyes that acted out a bedroom scene even when

she was off set. Fresh, precocious and unbothered about stripping off
in every film she did, she also had a reputation for sleeping with her
leading men. Tash was extremely wary of her.

'Tell me what you've been doing?' Niall said softly. 'I want to hear
you speak a little longer.'

Considering he'd just hailed her with tales of missing luggage, a
suicidal set dresser, a coke-addict director and a film that was going
over-budget before shooting had started, Tash felt her news was slightly
paltry in contrast. She didn't really want to admit that her life was
currently consumed by weighing food and comparing it against a 'Once
A Week Treat' chart, doing sit-ups, reading endless low-fat recipes and
watching Elle MacPherson videos to depress herself. Nor did she think
Niall would be fascinated by a run-down as to the precise amount of
interval training she was putting the horses through to get them fit for
the forthcoming season.

'I went to the pub with Penny and Gus last night,' she said lamely.
'They're very on form. Ange had a black eye – he says he slipped in the
kitchen, but Denise was strangely quiet all night so Penny's convinced
she clocked him one. She kept sending Gus up to get her to pull pints
and look at her hands to see if she had bruised knuckles. Gus ended
up plastered.'

Niall burst into riotous laughter which Tash thought was something
of an over-reaction to a rather blandly told tale. She'd never possessed
his ability to make the mundane sound wonderfully ridiculous.

'God, I miss life down there. How are Zoe and the kids?'

'Very well. Rufus had a ravishing new girlfriend for about a week;
he brought her to the farm for dinner and she fell in love with Ted,
which rather depressed Rufus.'

'Poor lad – I bet Ted flirted with her all night. He's such a
young sod.'

'I don't think Rufus is too bothered. He's got two more girlfriends
now, apparently. He sees one for a snog in twenty-minute morning
break and the other at lunchtime in the common room. Neither seems
to mind, but he's forking out a lot on Valentine's cards.'

Niall sighed happily. 'Zoe okay?'

'Mmm – not bad.' Tash was unwilling to mention India's ludicrous
bit of match-making. She was supposed to be finishing off the first
instalment of their stupid Cupid plot that night, a prospect she'd been
putting off all week. She quickly changed the subject. 'Listen, you can
tell me where to get off here, but I've just read one of the scripts you
left lying around at Christmas and I think it's fantastic.'

'Oh, yes – hi, Minty. Be with you in a moment.' Niall was clearly distracted by the arrival of the long-haired curvy one. 'Which is that?'

Tash stretched across to pick it up. 'Four Poster Bed. It's seriously funny.'

'I know. I loved it too – we'll talk about that another time, yeah?'

'You mean, you're going to do it?' Tash asked excitedly. It hadn't escaped her notice that it was all due to be shot in England, which would keep Niall on her side of the Atlantic at least until autumn.

'I may – we'll talk about it soon, I promise.' He sounded terribly distracted now, and very eager to get her off the phone. 'Don't forget that lunch with your step-mother on Saturday – will you book a table somewhere? I'm flying down on Friday night. Patrick Guest's hired a chopper to get to his wife in Somerset and I'm cadging a lift as far as Thruxton in it.'

Tash finished the call and rang off feeling absurdly dejected. She could just imagine Niall in his hotel suite, rolling his eyes at Minty – Tash somehow saw the actress arriving in a black negligée, clutching chilled champagne and the script – eager to shake off the clingy girlfriend who had just bored him rigid about the romantic excesses of a lanky seventeen year old. Minty was probably being all soothing now and saying coy little things like, 'Well, people who don't know our profession can seem terribly staid at times, Niall darling. Shall we run through those lines or have a drink first? You look like you need a shoulder massage.'

Tash shuddered and wished she could eat something. But it was Flab-busters the next night and she'd been lapsing all week so she had to try and make up for it with a last-minute fast.

She hugged Beetroot and then suddenly laughed. Niall was coming down to the forge on Friday night. Valentine's Day! She was going to see him in less than three days! And she was going to be slightly thinner than last time. She was such an idiot for feeling jealous.

Now almost ecstatic, she twirled Beetroot around the forge, put the sheets in the machine to be washed and settled down to work like smoke on the Valentine's cards. If she got hers to Niall in the post tomorrow, he'd be guaranteed to get it on Friday morning, which would cheer him up during the flight from Scotland to Berkshire.

Miraculously, Tash had lost five pounds by the next Flab-busters meeting, most of which she suspected was body fluids through not drinking a single cup of tea all day. She was also wearing one less jumper and no socks. Theresa was nonetheless delighted.

'Well done, Natasha!' she beamed, her metallic eye make-up twinkling on her lids like two slug trails. 'We'll shift that tubby tummy in next to no time.'

Having arrived more promptly than the week before, Tash sat in the back row of plastic chairs and sulked. Earlier that week, she had prided herself that, even though overweight, she still had a fit, wash-board stomach. Now she realised that in fact it poked out further than her tits.

Despite this, she maintained a certain flush of pride throughout Theresa's class – blissfully ignoring the skinny woman's attempts to motivate her slimmers with a series of badly painted cardboard road signs which bore such heavy warnings as 'Slow Down At Refrigerator Chicane', 'Watch Out for the Ryvita Roundabout', and 'Never Exceed the 30 Cal Per Hour Limit'.

Back in Gus's Land-Rover, Tash listened dreamily to the latest groin-pumping Oasis track on the radio and distractedly put the two Valentine's cards in their written envelopes before gumming on first-class stamps and posting them in the town's main Post Office to fox their recipients. If she had posted them in the village, India had pointed out, it would have narrowed down the field of Hugo's admirers by far too much for their first move. The fact that letters posted in the village bore the same postmark as those mailed in the main market town bypassed Tash entirely.

She still harboured the gravest doubts about her involvement in the project. Consequently, she had heavily disguised both her handwriting and her artistic style as she had created a card for Hugo of quite revoltingly sentimental cuteness, covered with big-eyed ponies and Labrador puppies with a Byron quote she had hurriedly and carelessly dredged up from Niall's *Dictionary of Quotations*:

Merely innocent flirtation. Not quite adultery, but adulteration.

She couldn't pen anything more romantic, although she had promised India that she would dig up something truly passionate by Donne or Yeats or, at worst, Patience Strong. Nothing had seemed right however. She simply could not bring herself to write such things to the ignorant, unfeeling and philistine Hugo. So she had settled for the obtuse angle with far more pleasure, signing the centre of the card with a simple question mark and a hefty squirt of a hugely overpowering perfume that Sophia had given her for Christmas, called Fire of Desire.

Niall's card, by contrast, had taken hours to make, consisting as it did of a great collage of photographs of herself, Beetroot and Giblets – most of them very wonky Polaroid ones which she had taken the night before. These had been cut out Blue Peter-style and glued on to twee gold paper to be surrounded by pressed flowers, glittery stars which Sally's kids had left behind after their Christmas visit, and witty little cartoons of herself performing a dance of the seven veils. It was a wildly indulgent and really pretty naff card, but Tash knew Niall would appreciate the effort she had put into it and laugh uproariously at the result. There would be plenty of time to be more romantic and sultry together on Friday night. Just to be extra-careful she had marked the card 'Private' and 'Urgent' and 'Confidential' in several places and put the Lime Tree Farm address on the reverse to make sure he spotted it amongst the heaps of adoring red envelopes he would undoubtedly receive from fans. The year before Tash had learned her lesson when Niall, shooting an action adventure in Venezuela over Valentine's Day, had taken almost a week to locate her anonymous card amongst all the others that Bob had forwarded.

On the morning of Valentine's Day, Tash was up well before the post and, having settled Beetroot in the Lime Tree Farm kitchen with Enid, was out in the yard mucking out before six, accompanied by Wally, who had a rather kinky taste for fresh horse droppings. It was still dark, and the damp cobbles gleamed in the harsh neon working lights, contrasting with the warmth of the yellow lighting inside the stables which gave the shavings and feedbuckets a strangely Nativity look. Tash, dressed in several jumpers, three pairs of leggings beneath a pair of Niall's old jeans and a daft woolly balaclava shaped like a duck's head, felt far from Christ-like. Her occasional true-blue swearing through chattering teeth was quite unchristian too, particularly when Snob, a sulky riser, bit her on her well-padded behind several times. She knew him well enough to realise that this wasn't a savage attack – simply his grumpy, macho version of a hearty 'good morning' – but the pain was eye-watering and she longed for him to be like Hunk, who blew her raspberry kisses and handed her his water bucket with his teeth, a trick Ted had taught him, not realising that it would sometimes be half-full, which had a tendency to drench the ungrateful recipient.

For once Kirsty was up for the early shift and helping out, albeit grudgingly and between long fag breaks. She'd allotted herself the easy task of giving the horses a small net of soaked hay each to chew through before their hard feeds.

'Morning, Tash,' she sniffed, tightening a woolly scarf around her slender neck as she emerged from Mickey Rourke's box. 'Hunk any better this morning?'

Tash, who had just trotted him out across the yard, nodded with relief. 'His paces are so level now a spirit measure wouldn't move.'

The big, beak-nosed bay horse was on his last week's enforced stable rest, and had been suffering depression in his quiet, polite way as a result, no longer pulling so many silly faces to make Tash laugh or playing dead to get attention first thing in the morning. He was also off his food and had to be coaxed into eating with little treats like Polos and sugar cubes mixed in, of which Gus thoroughly disapproved. Having watched all the other horses getting tacked up and ridden out each day, he also craved attention, and Tash found more and more of her coffee time was being soaked up paying quick guilt visits to him as if he were an elderly relative. It would be great fun for them both to start working together again and she couldn't wait for the all-clear from Jack Fortescue, the vet.

'Hugo's thirtieth birthday party should be good fun, huh?' Kirsty continued breezily as they crossed paths heading for the manure bonfire.

'Er – sure,' Tash hadn't heard anything about it. 'When is it again?' she asked ultra-coolly. The effect was rather spoilt by the fact her wheelbarrow chose this moment to tip its uneven load on to poor Wally.

'The twenty-eighth of March, you clot. Don't you remember?'

'Not off hand – I might be in Scotland with Niall,' Tash said rather quellingly, disliking Kirsty's supercilious attitude. 'Is it going to be a big do?'

'Huge.' Kirsty, having dumped her load, leaned back against the corrugated patchwork on the side of the barn and lit a fag as she watched Tash still struggling to right her barrow. 'He's invited half the eventing world, plus loads of London cronies and most of his family. Should be terrific.'

Tash was doing some mental calculations. 'Won't Richie be over in England then?'

Kirsty looked shifty. 'Should be.'

'That'll be nice,' Tash enthused, shovelling the last of her dropped load back into the barrow. 'You'll be able to show him off. I must say, I'm dying to meet him.'

'I thought you were dieting to meet him.' Kirsty grinned and, giving her the ghost of a bitchy wink, headed off to the store-room to mix up the hard feeds.

When they stopped for breakfast, the post had arrived and India and Rufus, in their school uniforms and wolfing back toast, were examining their small piles.

'I've got three.' Rufus beamed up at Tash as she staggered in, her hands numb with cold. 'I must say, that duck's head is seriously unflattering.'

'Thanks.' Tash, collapsing into a sturdy chair by the cluttered table, was gaping at India's pile. 'Christ – did you advertise or something?'

India, looking pink with embarrassment and excitement, shook her head. 'I honestly can't think who sent them.'

'She sodding well got twelve!' Rufus whistled enviously.

'Wow!' Kirsty was examining her own three fat red envelopes.

Tash peered at the rest of the pile of post in mild hope, but she was fairly certain that Niall, if he remembered to send one at all, would have sent it to the forge. There was a great heap of bills for Penny and Gus, she noticed worriedly.

'Mum's got one too.' Rufus waggled a rather crumpled pink envelope at Tash. 'But she just pooh-poohed it, and refused to open it until she'd walked Enid. Bloody spoil sport! I bet she doesn't get back before the bus comes so we'll have to wait until this evening to see it.'

Tash looked across at India, who gave a flicker of a wink with one huge cobalt eye before re-examining her post in genuine amazement.

Sighing, Tash poured herself some coffee and decided that if she had looked anything like India at fourteen, she would have expected the postman to give himself a severe case of lumbago every 14 February. As it was, she had received precisely five Valentine's cards in her entire life, and three of those had been from her mother.

'Oh, look – Hugo's invites have arrived!' Kirsty whooped, having quickly cast aside a huge, flower-strewn card from Australia in favour of poring over an embossed mantelpiece weight. 'He's so wonderfully formal, don't you think. Like Mr Darcy?'

'There are similarities.' Tash drew the froth from her coffee through her still-chattering teeth and listened as Gus and Penny stirred upstairs. Gus was clearly having a shower as the downstairs sink was making hiccuping noises – a sure sign that someone was trapped inside the ancient, misted-up cubicle in the main bathroom. Penny was swearing loudly from the direction of the laundry cupboard, cursing the 'sodding bastard' who had yet again nicked all her extra-thick socks.

'That'll be Mum.' India stood up and started to search for her shoes. 'She wears three pairs at a time in this weather and borrows Rufus's Timberland boots. Where the hell are my Doc Martens?'

'In front of the fireplace where you left them last night,' Zoe announced smoothly as she walked in through the kitchen door, pulling back her thick red cowl, cheeks pink from a brisk walk. She was followed by a cowering Enid, who shot the massed crowd in the kitchen a distrustful look before slinking over to the Aga to curl into a tight foetal ball. A moment later, Beetroot dashed in through the door, trailing a long piece of binder twine which she presented to Tash as she wriggled in an ecstatic body-wag of welcome.

'She came along for the ride,' Zoe explained, sitting down beside Tash and nodding as she offered coffee. 'You kids had better step on it, hadn't you?'

'Open your card first.' Rufus grinned.

'Okay, okay.' Sighing, Zoe reached for it and ripped it open.

On the front was a glittery picture of an unrealistically fluffy kitten with eyes as big and blue as Pamela Anderson's attached to electrodes. Inside there was a riddle:

> My first is in **h**orse, but not in carriage,
> My second in **hum**p, but not in marriage,
> My third is in **nag**, but not in ride.
> My fourth in **bouquet**, but not in bride.
> I'm saying I just can't get enough,
> Be my Valentine, Hot Stuff.

'Wow!' Rufus was seriously impressed. 'That's so sexy, Mum.'

Zoe was trying hard not to laugh. India, deep inside the hood of her coat, had almost uncontrollable giggles.

'Christ – that's a bit direct, isn't it?' Kirsty was looking perplexed. 'Shall we try to work it out?'

She made a lunge for the card, but Zoe whipped it away and tucked it beneath *The Times*. 'Better not,' she said airily. 'It's just a joke from Gus, I think. Far too childish to bother with.' She hurriedly started to work her way through the rest of the mail.

Kirsty looked miffed, but soon cheered up as she caught sight of yet another one of Hugo's embossed invites.

'Oh, he's invited everyone here – even Ted. Isn't that great?'

Glancing at it, Tash noticed that her own and Niall's names were missing, but she dismissed it before her ego had a chance to be bruised. An invite would undoubtedly be waiting for her on the forge doormat when she got back, as would her Valentine's card from Niall.

'I'd better get on.' She struggled up, pulling her knitted duck warmer back over her nose. 'Snob was practically beating his door in when I left him. You coming for a hack, Kirsty? Ted's going to bring Fruit Chew.'

Kirsty was still absorbed in her invitation. She looked up, her eyes positively misted. 'Oh, yes, I suppose so.'

'Tash!' Rufus called as they made their way out.

'Yup?' She spun around.

'Duck!' He threw a screwed-up Hugo invitation at her. It ricocheted plum off her beak.

On the ride, Ted tried hard – if sleepily – to fish about the number of Valentines India had received. He was extremely fed up that he had missed breakfast by oversleeping, having yet again been involved in a three in the morning lock-in at the Olive Branch the night before. Tash couldn't be sure, but she guessed from his hints that he himself had sent India about half of the dozen cards, industriously changing his hand-writing in each before posting them from a different region of West Berkshire.

'She's so seriously unspoilt.' He was swiping idly at overhead branches with his crop as they made slow progress through one of the pitted bridleways that interlaced the undulating Fosbourne lanes.

'I think she's bloody wise for her years.' Tash was trying to stop Snob going into orbit as twigs assailed him in Ted's wake. 'She makes me feel about ten sometimes – and I can give her over a decade.'

'Yeah, wise – true.' Ted looked round at her. 'But wickedly innocent. I mean, you're kind of smutty, Tash – no offence. She's seriously sexy, but totally unaware of it. You're more deliberate.'

'Thanks.' Tash was deeply shocked at this statement. Admittedly, she had taken the odd kinky shot of herself with a Polaroid for Niall recently – which she now rather regretted – but she was far from a wanton. 'I thought you went for Franny's rubber fetish look?' she called after him, trotting forwards to catch up.

'I'm a man of extremes.'

'Extremely bad taste, I'd say.' Kirsty, following behind on Gus's top-grade horse, Sex Symbol, was only too happy to put Tash's mind at rest. 'And you're quite wrong about Tash's sex appeal, Ted,' she added, shouting loudly along the lane to be heard above the din of the horses' clattering hooves. 'She's not at all deliberate. I mean, she never dresses up to look sexy – not even for Niall. And she's no' even a wee bit smutty, are you, Tash? You're quite prudish really, aren't you?'

'Er – well. Maybe a bit. Sometimes.' Tash felt even more offended at this. She knew she was no sex siren, but she liked to think she was one up from Sister Wendy in the letting-it-hang-loose stakes.

'No, I don't mean Tash is provocative,' Ted argued cheerfully. 'She just tries harder than India, who doesn't need to try at all, she's so damned sexy. You need to make more effort, Tash – in a sweet way.'

'I see.' Tash was starting to redden with anger, but Snob chose this moment to try to rear up and exit the scene through a hazel bush, which prevented further discussion.

She sloped back to the forge at lunchtime, primarily under the pretence of tidying up for Niall's impending arrival, but in truth dying to get her mits on her post.

The Reader's Digest congratulated her on the fact that she had made it through the first round of their Prize Draw, and offered her a no-obligation opportunity to peruse their *Encyclopaedia of Offshore Marine Wildlife.* The local oil company reminded her that her tank would be almost empty now, and would she like to take advantage of their ten percent Freebie Feb offer to have a refill? Her mother had posted her a list of dress-designers in London she *must* get in contact with a.s.a.p., and Henrietta had sent her a postcard of Windsor Castle with a polite confirmation of their lunch on Saturday, written in her bold, round hand.

There was no Valentine's card, and no invitation to Hugo's party.

Tash was loth to admit it even to herself, but she was far more hurt by the latter. Niall always forgot Valentine's Day. He had forgotten last year, and had made up for it with profuse apologies and two tickets to see the latest Maggie Smith play, followed by dinner at the Arts Cafe and a sleazy night in a London hotel afterwards because they couldn't be bothered to make the taxi journey to his Chalk Farm flat to be alone and near a bed. Niall perennially forgot everything – her birthday, his birthday, his phone number, his pin number, Bob's secretary's name, his mother's maiden name when he lost his bank cards. It was part of his nature to forget things and somehow Tash loved him all the more for it. Hugo had a better memory than Nelly the Elephant and had deliberately left her off his guest list to hurt her. She wanted to throttle him. Better still, she wanted to have one of his poxy invites so that she could send him a curt little RSVP rejection letter thanking him for his kind offer but saying, although he desperately needed friends to join him in celebrating entering his ancient thirties – still single and unloved – she would be otherwise engaged, coupled up and very much beloved, in the arms of her gorgeous lover. The fact that the lover was six years older than Hugo could be glossed over for the purposes of Tash's malevolent intention.

She didn't feel like going back to the yard to work after such a shattering postal let-down, but she knew that Gus would not condone her self-pitying behaviour much longer. She had been taking a lot of afternoons – or more specifically, mornings – off recently to moon over photograph albums and miss Niall. That had been tolerated and forgiven in mid-winter when the season was a long way off and the horses were enjoying a well-earned rest. The working pupils were in theory supposed to be working just as hard at this time, helping to host clinics with other riders, doing some indoor show-jumping competitions with the novices, hunting the youngsters and sometimes helping Gus out with fact-checking or proof-reading on one of the occasional eventing manuals he wrote. Playing hooky on these things was chastisable, but forgivable. Damaging the horses' chances in the events to come by slacking on the all-important fittening process was nothing less than idiotic and self-destructive. And Gus was so strapped for cash at the moment that Tash was extremely expendable.

She spent a murderous afternoon trying to get Mickey Rourke to show some vestige of flat-work obedience in front of a critical Gus on the all-weather menage.

'I told you the horse was a clumsy tearaway!' he yelled in exasperation after just half an hour of Tash's fighting to make Mickey's star-gazing, feet-tripping paces look graceful. 'He may jump like a mutant flea, but he shakes his head as though he's got the buggers in his ears and he lollops about like a smashed young farmer at a disco. He'll never upgrade – he's going in *Horse and Hound* next week.'

'He's just young and over-eager,' Tash protested, but Gus had already stomped off.

Later, she tried to do some jumping work on a couple of Penny's intermediates, both of whom were overexcited after their winter break and had her off so many times that she was as bruised as a windfall by the time she limped inside for tea.

Having wolfed a pizza with India and Rufus (both in possession of a clutch more red cards from their school pigeon holes), she carried Beetroot the few hundred yards home along the pitch-black lane, almost having a heart attack when she walked into an overhead branch and mistook it for a rapist's baseball bat. Then, remembering that Niall would be with her in just a few hours' time, her heart started to lift like a hot air balloon given a jet of burning gas.

The forge was cold, damp and unwelcoming when she let herself in.

The only light came from the flashing red dot on the phone telling her that she had some messages.

Tash took off three or four layers and leaned against the range for a few moments to warm up before elbowing on a few lights. She found her bag, extracted the two bottles of claret that Zoe had pressed on her for Niall's homecoming, then guiltily remembered that she had promised to book a lunch table for Henrietta the next day.

Wandering over to the phone to make a quick call to Den at the Olive Branch, she remembered the messages and pressed the Replay button before she tried to call out.

'Hi, Tash, sweetheart – it's just me.' It was Alexandra. 'Did you get my letter, darling? Will you promise to set up an initial meeting soon with someone about the dress? It doesn't have to be anyone I suggest. Please call me this weekend – we're in Paris, by the way. It's *ages* since we've spoken and we've lots to discuss. I gather Hen's seeing you tomorrow, so I'll gossip to both of you afterwards. Oh – and I'm coming over for Henry's christening – I promised Sophia and Ben – although Pascal can't make it. We'll both get our heads together there. Your father is apparently keen for you to get married in that awful little flea-pit, St Ja—'

The machine, programmed to give callers thirty seconds in which to say their piece, cut her off mid-stream and bleeped perfunctorily before giving way to a stern, deep drawl that made Tash jump.

'Tash – Hugo,' he announced in his abbreviated, unfriendly way. 'I think we need to talk about this – er – extraordinary card thing. Call me, will you?'

He sounded both amused and faintly pissed off. Tash cursed as she realised that he'd seemingly rumbled her style despite all her careful attempts to cover it up. Damn! Well, she was going to tell all. There was no way she was going to let him think for a moment that she had voluntarily posted him a Valentine's card.

Her reasoning was brought to an abrupt halt as she realised that Niall was talking on the machine.

'—can't be helped,' he was saying in his sad, melodious voice. 'I'm so disappointed about this, angel, I simply can't tell you. Listen, I've got to go and do this bloody thing now – we're shooting all night so far as I know – and tomorrow's pencilled in even though it's a Saturday. Christ, is this thing over-budget! Still – it's not my problem, I suppose. I mean, not seeing you is my problem. Big problem. I'll call later – or try me at my hotel at around two or three if you're still up. I'll stay awake for you. I love—'

The machine cut him off too.

Tash kicked off her boots, fed the eager Beetroot, threw some celery out to Giblets, switched on the television and poured herself a vast glass of wine.

'Niall's not coming!' she wailed into the empty room. A tidy, empty room – with its vase of snowdrops in his honour, its fresh candles in anticipation of seduction, and small stack of carefully selected CDs ready to be thrown casually into the machine the moment he entered. She had bought two vast, juicy steaks and a vat of cream the night before at Sainsbury's (terrified that she would bump into a fellow Flab-buster at the express check-out, straining under their half-basket of bean shoots and cottage cheese). She had even washed the sheets, and dry-cleaned her sexy red dress which she could now just about zip up once more.

Tash took another slug of wine and let self-pity give way to furious indignation.

'Bastard!' She stood up slightly shakily and, zapping Family Fortunes with the remote, rammed a CD into the stereo. Moments later Enigma filled the room with a throbbing, sensual beat laid seductively over a hypnotic Gregorian chant. 'Bastard, neglectful Irish sod! After all my bloody efforts.'

Dancing funkily in time to Enigma, she headed upstairs and drained the rest of her glass of wine before wandering slightly woozily into the small, chilly bathroom and taking a long, chilly shower. At least the cool water chased the puffiness from around her eyes and faded the pink tinge of her nose somewhat. Afterwards, she drenched herself in Fire of Desire and struggled into the red dress, which was really far too tight. Still, it didn't matter as he wasn't coming. She was doing this purely for herself.

Rather too slewed to aim straight, she slapped on some off-centre eye make-up, which simply served to give her a strange squinty expression, although her eyes looked slightly smokier as well. She then trotted back downstairs and started to fry both steaks in almost half a pound of butter, continually tripping over Beetroot, who stood drooling beneath her. She tripped over to the stereo to change the music before grooving her way back to her heavenly-smelling comfort food.

'Neglectful Celtic dilettante!' she wailed along to the music. 'Stayaway crap boyfriend.'

She had just added almost an entire badly crushed head of garlic, half a glass of claret and several peppercorns to her sizzling mix when Beetroot shot over to the cat-flap and started her ecstatic wriggling routine.

Tash, when sober, would have been alerted to danger at this point. Half a bottle of claret the better and singing tunelessly along to the Pretenders, she was completely oblivious of the quick-fire rap on the door that preceded entry.

A moment later, there was a rush of cool air and Hugo strode inside, already stooping down to welcome his delighted reception committee.

Completely oblivious, Tash was waggling her frying pan, her bottom and her vocal chords as she got to grips with the sexier part of 'Sassy'. She flipped over the fat steaks and threw in a little more wine for good measure before lowering the heat in anticipation of hacking a few vegetables to boil-friendly proportions.

'Tash?'

'Mmm?' Nose deep in the fridge, she didn't bother to look around.

'Tash, are you feeling quite all right?'

Three new potatoes went flying into the cheese box as she slowly registered the presence, and the chill, in the room. Whether it was from outside, or from the occupant – or indeed from the fridge, in which she had been buried for some moments – was hard to tell. But the chill was nonetheless very chilling and entirely sobering.

Slowly, Tash straightened up. Then she carefully straightened her skirt, which had risen up alarmingly. Finally, she straightened her hair which, pinned up when wet, had now fallen over her nose like a condemned man's hood.

'Hugo – how unexpected!' She reeled around slightly too fast, so that her head seemed to spin on her neck for several more circuits before she pulled herself together. 'What brings you here?' She was aware that she was looking more than slightly slewed, but there was nothing for it but to brazen this one out.

Hugo was regarding her with something close to disgust. Dressed in his working garb – hay-flecked fleece jacket, black suede chaps and heavy dealer boots – he looked gloriously dishevelled, his eyes ringed with tiredness.

'Are you expecting someone?' He looked over her shoulder at the two sizzling steaks.

'Oh – no, just a quiet night in, you know.' Tash shrugged uncomfortably. Then she suddenly remembered the brief message he had left before the devastating one from Niall which had eradicated all those that had gone before.

'Listen, about that card. It was just a daft idea of India's really—'

'Well, yes,' Hugo butted in almost boredly, giving the room his usual look of disapproval. 'That was partly why I called round.'

'Like I say – it was a commission really.' Tash could feel herself start to babble as she always did when wildly embarrassed. 'I mean, it's not from me personally – Lord, no! I don't fancy you myself or anything. Uck! Quite the reverse, in fact. That is – not that you're not very attractive to certain people. I'm sure lots of people are falling over themselves to go to bed with you and suchlike. Well, the odd one. Just not me. Definitely not me. No. Um. Oh.'

At that moment the phone rang. Tash leaped on it as her saviour, leaving Hugo standing in the centre of the room looking incredibly confused.

There was a lot of crackling, which told Tash she was connected to a mobile in a remote region.

'Okay – I've got two minutes to lay my heart at your feet.'

It was Niall.

'Oh, darling. Am I glad to hear you!' Tash glanced triumphantly around at Hugo, who appeared to be helping himself to wine now, oblivious of her caller.

'Listen – I am so chronically sorry about not making it down tonight. If it's any consolation, you can't be nearly as upset as I am now.'

'Oh, I can,' Tash whimpered, 'but I do understand. I so wish you were here – they're so shitty for keeping you there.'

'You really don't mind?'

'No, of course not – I just feel for you, and wish so much I was with you.'

Why did she wimp out so easily? she thought in consternation. It was always the same when Niall was trying to see her from a location – disappointment after disappointment. And, as ever, she was just so pleased to hear his voice that she could forgive him anything.

'I 'clare, I'm not going to stand for it in future.' He seemed to echo her thoughts. 'But Nigel – that's the director – is so stressed out it's untrue. The set dresser threw himself off the peak of a Munro today.'

'What's a Munro?'

'A small mountain.'

'Christ! Is he dead?'

'Fractured ribs and bruised coccyx.' Niall, despite himself, was trying not to laugh. 'Poor little sod landed on a hill-walker. Still, he's on enforced bed-rest, so he's happy. God, I miss you.'

'Me too. When d'you think you can get down?'

'Well, I can't guarantee anything until we wrap the location shoot

– which looks like being the middle of March. I promise to try and make it for Henry's christening, though, and I hope to make it to old Hugo's birthday do, too.'

Tash stiffened slightly. 'You what?'

'Yeah, I got his invite today – thank him and say yes, will you? It was really thoughtful of him to send one up here as well as to you. He must know how out of touch I feel stranded here. Talking of which, I am SO SORRY, angel . . .'

'Sorry about what?' Tash, whose narrowed, Hugo-hating eyes had been watching over her shoulder as he removed her burning steaks from the heat and tried the sauce with a long, tanned finger, tried to focus on what Niall was saying.

'That I forgot Valentine's Day,' he laughed. 'You know me – I can never get with these things. You forgive me, don't you?'

'Course I do.' Tash shot Hugo another dirty look, still dwelling on the deliberately errant invitation. He was lapping up the sauce now, the sod. She hoped he bit on a peppercorn soon.

'I've sent some flowers by Data-post today, but I guess they'll take a couple of days to reach you.'

'You needn't have bothered,' Tash sighed, wishing that he didn't feel the need to guilt-trip quite so much. 'Did you get my card?'

Niall cleared his throat uncomfortably. 'Well, I think I did.'

'What d'you mean, you *think* you did?' Tash laughed, remembering all the personal snap-shots – including a couple of her in the sex-on-legs basque he had given her for Christmas. 'Wasn't it obvious? If you haven't opened it yet, I put my address on the back of the envelope.'

'Oh, I opened it.' Niall cleared his throat yet again, and then went quiet for a moment as someone spoke in the background, probably leaning in through the door of his trailer to issue an instruction. He sounded more hurried as he spoke again. 'I mean, it's a very charming wee picture, Tash – and I'm sure you went to a great deal of effort on my behalf, but I don't quite understand—'

'You ungrateful sod!' she yelled, suddenly finding her face was colouring as though dipped in red ink. She couldn't believe how insulting he was being. 'You bastard! I bet you've been having a good laugh at my expense all day, haven't you?'

'What?' He sounded pole-axed.

'Very charming wee picture, my ass! In fact most of the pictures were of my bloody ass!' she spluttered on. 'I know what you don't quite understand.' She could feel tears welling up now. She couldn't care less that Hugo was swigging wine and ear-wigging happily from less than three yards away – she was furious. 'You just don't understand what you're doing with a big-arsed old bag like me when you could be with Minty, or Sandra, or Julia, or Purdy, or whatever the latest starlet's called. That's what you don't bloody understand!'

Realising she had said all those resentful and jealous things that she had sworn to herself she would never say, she burst into tears.

There was a long pause at the other end, during which Tash could hear Hugo starting to knife and fork his way into the steaks in the background. She hoped he got BSE and croaked. Her back was prickling with embarrassment that he was overhearing all this.

There was more mumbling at the end of the phone and Tash suddenly realised to her increased shame and horror that, far from being stunned into silence by the searing insight and painful truth of her words, Niall was conducting a conversation with someone else whilst muffling the phone.

Finally he uncovered the receiver and started speaking with hushed urgency.

'I really have to go,' he whispered. 'But I truthfully think you've got the wrong end of the stick here, Tash – all I was saying now was that I didn't understand the quote about adultery. Were you trying to say something about me and Lisette, angel? Because you really don't have to worry yourself about that on any account.'

'But—' Tash was nonplussed for a moment.

'I mean, I know I've taken this part in Four Poster Bed with her producing, but I barely need to meet her during the film shoot. We'll hardly speak – in fact, my taking it is a sign of just how over her I am. For Christ's sake, I'll be marrying you a few days after the first location shoot's over! Some glossy magazine is photographing the wedding – that's how I'm getting paid. Lisette arranged it. That line about flirtation being adulteration really freaked me, angel.'

Tash barely took most of this in. Feeling as though her downward-bound free-fall had just been broken by a mid-air mattress, she suddenly realised what she had done.

'You got the Byron card!' she gasped.

'I got your card, Tash.' Niall sounded pressurised. 'A few stick-horses and a quote about flirting and adultery. I realise the Lisette news must have come as a shock but I didn't expect this.'

'Niall, I didn't mean you at all!' She was torn between confusion and amazement. She'd had no idea that Lisette was producing the comic film. Tash was horrified that she was, appalled that she was, but even more flabbergasted by how much Niall seemed to think he had told her without having uttered a word until tonight.

'I have to go, angel.' His voice was fading, as though he was already stretching away from the phone. 'Please, please don't worry – and, if I think about it, the card is really moving. Even more so because it shows how vulnerable you are and, believe me, I would never take advantage of that. I'll call you later if I can. I love you.'

And he was gone, leaving a curt dialling tone.

Tash replaced the receiver and, straightening her ridden-up skirt yet again, turned warily back to Hugo who had eaten almost an entire steak now.

'Help yourself,' she offered in a strangled voice, starting to realise the full, appalling implications of her rushed posting technique.

'Oh – so sorry.' Lazily, Hugo looked down at the ravaged pan, sounding not at all apologetic. 'You really weren't expecting anyone, were you?' He glanced at the unlaid table, and the piles of Tash's clothes strewn around.

She shook her head, tempted to say, 'Only you,' to scare him. But she stopped herself in time.

'Listen – about that card . . .' She coughed uncomfortably. 'There's been a bit of a mistake.'

'Oh, yes?' Sounding relieved, he offered her a refilled wine glass.

Looking straight at him, Tash saw that his blue eyes were unfriendly, his mouth curled into a taut bow of insolence.

'Yes – you see, it wasn't intended for you.'

'I see.' He plainly didn't believe her.

'Yes.' Tash made a grab for her wine and took a huge slug, most of which trickled down her wind-pipe. 'It was meant for Niall,' she spluttered.

Hugo's scornful gaze didn't flicker. 'I can imagine.'

'And I posted him the wrong one.'

He nodded slowly. 'I see.'

'Yes.' Tash's lips were starting to quiver as the awfulness of the telephone conversation started to sink in.

'You posted Niall a card you intended to send me?' he asked carefully.

Tash nodded blankly.

'So I take it the kinky self-portraits I received through the post this morning were intended for his eyes only?'

Carrying on nodding, Tash started to cry.

Hugo continued to watch her, not making a movement of sympathy or retreat. His handkerchief remained firmly in his pocket, his feet planted on the ground. He simply watched as Beetroot shuffled across to Tash's ankles and gazed up at her caringly.

'I suppose you laughed at me?' she hiccuped through her tears.

Hugo bit his curling lower lip and looked faintly mocking, but said nothing.

'He's taken a film part,' Tash found herself blurting, 'because Lisette is producing it.'

'Lisette the ex?' Hugo's eyebrows shot up with interest.

Tash nodded. It was something of a forte now.

'Well, well.' He took a slow draw of wine and glanced at his watch. 'Listen, I'm meeting someone at eight. I really popped round to give you this.' He started fishing in his pockets.

'Do you have that card on you?' Tash bleated desperately.

'Not on me, no.' Hugo extracted something from an inner pocket and, waggling it for a second in front of Tash's swimming eyes, placed it on a work surface.

'Can I have it back?'

'I'll see if I can find it tomorrow, but I can't promise anything,' he said dismissively. 'Listen, thanks for the drink. And the steak. I really must go.' He headed for the door.

Tash, aware that she was standing in her howlingly draughty sitting room wearing a ludicrously tight red dress, Medusa hair and wonky eye make-up, having just sent her bête noire near-nude photographs of herself, started to shiver uncontrollably with mortification.

'Oh – by the way.' Hugo turned at the door, stooping to give Beetroot a pat. 'I'll see what I can find out about Lisette for you, shall I?'

'Thanks,' Tash managed to splutter with a mouth-cracking smile, blindly aimed in the general direction of the door.

As soon as he was gone, she threw herself on to the sofa for another howl which was instantly curtailed as the sofa took on her momentum and crashed into the television which toppled over and then imploded dramatically.

Tash lay for several seconds, too numb for tears, wondering why on earth she was planning to marry a man she hadn't seen since the New Year. Then she cringed and wriggled and winced with shame as she realised that Hugo had that morning been gaping with snooty astonishment at photographs of her seductively draped over the same sofa she was now cowering in.

On her way to bed, she picked up the card Hugo had left and regarded it listlessly. It was an invitation to his birthday party. On the front, he had simply written 'Tash'. She tore it to shreds, fed the rest of the steak to Beetroot and went to bed, setting her alarm for half-midnight.

Between half-midnight and three in the morning, she lay awake waiting for Niall to call back, but he failed to oblige.

At two, she tried his mobile. It was switched off. She then called the third assistant director's mobile who – complete with loud partying background noise – told her that Niall had headed back to the hotel to call his girlfriend.

Tash stayed awake a little longer, nodding asleep and then jerking awake as though hanged by the neck from a rope until dead tired.

At three, she called his hotel. The phone rang for ages before a very tired-sounding Scottish man picked up the call and, grumbling under his breath, tried Niall's room for her.

'I'm afraid there's no answer there,' he came back to her. 'Would you like me to leave a message?'

'Can you just check if his key's been taken?' she asked.

'No – it's still here, my dear.' The man came back a few seconds later, giving a pert sniff which said a lot about his attitude to 'these film types'.

'Thanks – just say Tash called.' She rang off and, hugging her loneliness and tonight's shame to her, conked out to dream that she was riding directly after Hugo in the cross-country section of a one-day-event, stark naked and catching up with him fast as Snob bolted over the fences, totally out of control.

'Leave me alone, you desperate little freak!' Hugo yelled over his shoulder. 'You've always had a crush on me!'

Tash sat bolt upright, suddenly awake, sober and reeling with shock. As far as Hugo now knew, she realised with dismay, she had sent him a Valentine's card this year. It wasn't the card he had actually received, but it was a card nonetheless. From her. Sad, desperate Tash, who had always had a crush on him – even though she was now getting married to someone else. And, not only that, he still had the evidence – the card that she had intended only for Niall's lovely big brown eyes.

She sank back into the pillows and listened to her heart thud the milliseconds until it was time to head to the farm for work.

The next morning Kirsty was even more superior. In fact, she positively queened it over Tash. Being Kirsty, she was so nice about it that it could have been a big cuddle of a compliment, but Tash knew different.

'Tash – I bet you're feeling great today. Did Niall and yous talk until the wee hours, huh?' she asked as they cleaned tack – one of the dullest jobs in the world that everyone in the yard avoided.

'He couldn't make it back,' Tash muttered through gritted teeth as she soaped the same piece of rein over and over again.

'Och, that's a shame.' Kirsty's voice was as soothing as honey on a sore throat. 'Still, I bet you sent him a wonderful Valentine's card, eh?'

Ted, who was measuring out the feeds in a far corner, scoffed happily. 'Write him a kinky fantasy, did you, Tash?' he asked hopefully. 'Lots of sexy stuff about what you're going to do with him when you get your mitts on that famous arse?'

'Oh, no,' Kirsty giggled. 'I bet she sent him some revealing shots of herself. Reminded him of what he's missing.'

Tash bristled but said nothing, determinedly concentrating on the reins.

'Christ!' Ted sounded excited. 'Next time you're taking some of those, can I have the negs, yeah?'

'Sally, Sally – it's me, darling. Is he around?'

'Yup.'

'Damn. Listen – such exciting news! Niall has agreed to play Daniel in Four Poster, so we're going ahead.'

'Oh, that's wonderful!'

'And even better – I've arranged for *Cheers!* magazine to have exclusive coverage of Niall and Tash's wedding. They're paying literally tens of thousands, honey, which will cover Niall's fee. His agent, Bob, helped me set it up. That man is so shit-hot.'

'*Cheers!* magazine?' Sally gasped. 'I thought every married couple who appeared in that was jinxed? Didn't they do a huge spread on Liz and Larry Fortenski at home just a fortnight before the split?'

'Don't talk shit, darling – it's fucking fantastic publicity for the film. They're going to tie it all into the first location shoot if I'm lucky. Now I've just got to find the pissing location. We're currently dis-located.'

Sally giggled. 'When do you start?'

'May. Listen, d'you fancy helping me out? I could really use a good assistant on this one.'

'You don't mean that.'

'I damn' well do.'

'But I have no experience.'

'But you know me, know Niall, and could be a wonderful help if I need a mediator, which I'm sure I will. Please, Sally?'

'I'll think about it.'

'Okay – I'll ask no more for now. But I will demand one thing – come to Hugo Beauchamp's thirtieth as my guest?'

'You've been invited?'

'*Very* surprising, I know, but yes, he's just called, practically begging me to attend. Most odd, but also most damned well welcome. Lord, is that man divine! Will you come with me?'

'Christ, Lisette.' Her voice went hushed as she realised she'd uttered the forbidden L word within Matty's hearing, but he didn't appear to notice as she went on, 'You-know-who *loathes* that man.'

'Well, I took it as read that he wouldn't be invited, but I dearly want you to come with me.'

'Can't you take a dishy man?'

'Oh God, Sally! All the dishy men I know are either gay, or married, or both. I'd far rather take a good friend to giggle with.'

'Well, I'll try.' Her voice dropped even lower. 'But I'll have to lie.'

'You know what the Bible says, honey,' Lisette laughed before ringing off: '"And though shalt definitely lie with thine husband."'

Nine

LUNCH WITH HENRIETTA WAS not a success.

Tash was still at Lime Tree Farm when Henrietta poled up to the forge at twelve-thirty sharp. Having totally forgotten about the assignation, Tash was coaxing one of the novices – a very nervous but talented mare called Groupie – around a few low jumping grids when Henrietta telephoned the farm. The noise of the outside klaxon hailing the call sent Groupie over the menage perimeter fence in a huge, tight, catjump that unbalanced Tash, spinning her through the air to land bang on a pole, almost knocking her teeth out with her knee.

It set the tone for the afternoon. Because Tash had forgotten to book, Marco Angelo at the Olive Branch could not squeeze them into the restaurant however hard he tried to pressurise three businessmen into paying their bill and leaving. Instead, they were forced to perch at a draughty table by the door and eat in the main bar. Several local farm hands were drinking pints, swearing like troopers and smoking rollies nearby; all of them greeted Tash as an old chum, which terrified Henrietta. She tried hard to be polite and hide her disappointment, but it was obvious that she was quite put out by Niall's non-appearance.

'He truly couldn't make it,' Tash apologised on his behalf. 'He was really miserable to let you down – but they were shooting through the night yesterday and he was totally trapped up there. He sends you his love and promises to make up for it next time.'

Henrietta, having dressed up in his honour in a rather risqué Laura Ashley trouser suit in plum cord that plunged at the front, fought valiantly not to hang her head during their cheek-bulging lunch of warm goat's cheese salad and mackerel poached in cider cream, but she was not on top form. Tash, bug-eyed with a hangover and bruised from two days' falling off, was far from her best too.

They barely mentioned the wedding, except to agree on a few points that it was obvious neither of them cared about.

'Your father agrees that you should marry somewhere close to here – a local hotel with a licence or something?'

'Fine – I'll ask around.'

'Your mother called to suggest GTC or Peter Jones for the wedding list. I thought the latter, as I always shop there and know a few of the assistants by name.'

'Fine – whatever.'

'I have a chum who's a terrific florist. She did the Earl of—'

'Fine – tell her to go ahead.'

'Have you been for any dress fittings yet?'

'Mummy sent me a list – I'll call around next week.'

'Well, you'd better get a move on. Let me know as soon as you've decided – we have to tone in bridesmaids and pages. Have you decided those yet?'

Tash was staring blankly at her uneaten mackerel, empathising with its glazed eyes and gaping mouth. It was precisely how she had looked for hours on end the night before.

'Tash?'

She looked up and, realising the topic of bridesmaids had been raised, spoke off the top of her head.

'Whichever of Sally's and Sophia's can walk – I suppose that's Tom, Tor, Lotty and possibly Josh. Plus Niall's sister's brood – that's three girls under ten, I think. And his brother's two boys – they're three and seven. And Polly, of course. That should do it.'

Henrietta looked slightly pale. 'Adult bridesmaids?'

Tash shook her head. 'No way. I went through that at Sophia's wedding. Too awful. I'll inflict it on no one. But I want Zoe to be my matron of honour – although she must wear what she wants. Absolutely no cerise taffeta or anything. And she can sit down during the ceremony if she gets bored.'

Henrietta looked appalled, but stifled her objections. 'Best man?'

She shrugged. 'Up to Niall. Matty, I should imagine.'

'Ushers?'

'Well, Rufus is paying me a tenner to make him one but I should put Gus down really – Rufe can assist. And Niall will come up with another – his friend Donal probably.'

'Will they all need to hire morning suits?'

'God knows.' Tash gazed at a hunting print and wished more than anything that Niall was with her. She felt no excitement as it was – just a nervous, almost deadened, sense of pressure.

Henrietta, although the soul of politeness, felt exactly the same. As Tash drifted further and further into a state of near-catatonia, she tried to plug a couple of her real reasons for hurtling along the M4 that day. Beccy badly needed a few tips about making eventing a career. Could Tash help? Perhaps Beccy could come to Lime Tree Farm during her Easter vacs and help out for a meagre wage and a bit of experience?

'Um – not sure, really.' Tash thought about the bills she had seen on the kitchen table the morning before, and knew that Gus and Penny, far from wanting to fork out a meagre wage for a teenage hopeful, would be realistically thinking about dumping one of their working pupils instead. That meant either her or Kirsty.

'I'm sorry.' She grimaced. 'I'll ask, but I wouldn't hold your breath. Perhaps Hugo might help?'

'Oh, would you ask him?' Henrietta looked eager at the prospect, secretly thinking him far more professional and successful than Gus and Penny Moncrieff.

'Well, I honestly think it would be far better coming from Ben and Sophia,' Tash confessed, unwilling to let too much of Hugo's and her distaste for one another slip. 'They're much closer to him.'

'I see.' Henrietta looked slightly boot-faced at Tash's reluctance.

Feeling mean, she insisted both that she pay for the meal, and that Henrietta have a dessert.

They tackled the puddings in silence – Tash slipping from her '30 Cals Per Hour' speed limit by diving into a gutsy old-fashioned bread-and-butter mountain; Henrietta was far more abstemious with a light lemon soufflé.

Finally, she broached the other favour.

'Do you think that Niall would be able to get Emily a couple of days' work experience on a film set?' she asked, slightly shame-faced at her cheek. 'I know it's a bit much, but she's terribly keen and wouldn't get in the way. She's set her heart on working in films or telly after graduating, you see.'

Again, Tash was worried about asking. With the current tension between herself and Niall, she wasn't brave enough to petition a favour that encroached upon his career. He was always very distant when she tried to talk about the film world, as though she was Guinevere asking Merlin to show her a simple magic trick.

'I'll ask him,' she promised lamely.

'What's he got lined up? Anything exciting? Is he going back to America soon?' Henrietta was eager for gossip. She found the film industry wildly exciting and elusively sexy.

'He'll finish this over-budget Scottish epic thing, Celt, then fly off to promote Tough Justice in the States,' Tash recited flatly, having told umpteen people of Niall's future movements of late. 'Then he's back working for the Beeb in Yorkshire with The Tenant of Wildfell Hall, doing Mill On the Floss for Radio Four, promoting Tough Justice in the UK, then off to the States again promoting Celt – and poling up to the Oscars, I should imagine. And then he's shooting an English film called Four Poster Bed.'

'Oh, that sounds great fun!' Henrietta was almost beside herself with the glitz of it all.

'His ex-wife is producing the bed romp,' Tash said, feeling a bit mean at her bluntness. But sometimes she got so wound up relating Niall's work schedule to eager ears who listened as avidly as though it was The Archers. She often felt she spoke *about* Niall – how he was, what he was doing, what gossip he had told her and what he had lined up – far more than she ever spoke directly *to* him. Sometimes she felt just like his press secretary.

Henrietta had completely missed the bitterness in Tash's last comment.

'So will you be going to the Oscars with him, or will she?' she asked eagerly.

'Who?' Tash wrinkled her brow.

'His ex-wife?'

Tash tried hard to smile, but found that it wavered on her lips and faltered into a worried wobble as though she'd had an injection at the dentist's which hadn't quite worn off.

'That,' she said slowly, 'is like asking whether you will be sitting next to Daddy at the wedding or whether you think Mummy should.'

Henrietta barely said a word over coffee and, forgetting even to broach the subject of catering for the reception, made up a lame excuse about a hair appointment to race home immediately afterwards. Hastily promising that they'd talk again at Henry's christening in a fortnight, she left Tash with the bill and a half-eaten dessert.

During the fortnight that separated her lunch with her step-mother from the far grander impending christening in Worcestershire, Tash cast off another four pounds – most of which was still the result of her craftily removing another layer before each Flab-busters session. She also continued to work laboriously on the horses, fighting a continual power struggle with Snob who had lost all respect for her since the autumn, and trying again and again to prove that the belligerent but supremely talented Mickey Rourke was worthy of keeping and bringing on. Gus was currently selling several horses to ease his debts, which worried her. Mickey was undoubtedly top of his list of four-legged burdens that he wanted to turn into five-figure sums. Ted had already descended into a serious and understandable fit of resentful surliness that week because Gus had sold Fruit Chew to America – a horse Ted had spent the previous year upgrading and bringing on in the hope that he would have a chance to event himself in the spring season. But Gus hadn't wanted to sell him either; he simply had no choice when offered tens of thousands.

'Right now I'd sell Wally for a few weeks' diesel money,' he sighed.

As Wally, the faithful heel-hugger, had developed raging mange which the vet put down to stress, Tash was convinced that he had understood every word.

It was screamingly obvious that cash was very tight at the farm. India and Rufus were both bursting out of their school uniforms, and whingeing non-stop that they were missing out on skiing trips and art excursions because Zoe refused to fork out as she sank all her money into covering her sister's outstanding debts for feed and vet's bills. Tash noticed that Zoe herself was still wearing the much-patched jumpers that she had worn all the time she had known her – most of which had belonged to Gus in their prime. Gus and Penny now shopped at jumble sales and relied on hand-me-down competition clothes offered by other eventers – frequently Hugo.

Even though it was still below freezing at night, the farm's central heating had been switched off for the 'summer' and the only heat came from the unpredictable, coke-guzzling range and the fire in the sitting room. The bedrooms were like refrigerated trailers. With no money for a supermarket stock-up, Zoe had served sausage and bean casserole three nights on the trot, simply varying the flavour by adding chilli one night, curry the next and – a legendary meal even by her standards – aniseed essence on the third.

Two days before Henry's christening, Gus came raging into the kitchen clutching a letter that he'd finally got around to reading, several days after it had arrived.

'Those bastards at Drover Clothing have pulled out of the sponsorship deal!' he howled. 'I can't believe it – it was worth thirty grand a year. They say the corporate image wasn't right. They're planning to sponsor some Welsh golfer this year.'

'Christ, I'm sorry.' Zoe, who had been gossiping with Tash about Ted stealing Rufus's girlfriends, turned to him in horror. 'Do they own any of the horses?'

'Thankfully, no.' Gus threw the letter on the table and stalked over to the damp larder to forage for biscuits which, knowing Gus, would constitute his lunch. 'But they subsidised a hell of a lot of food and their bloody coats kept Pen and me dry last year. Shit!' He took his anger out on a packet of Maryland cookies which split open and landed at a delighted Wally's feet.

'What are you going to do?' Tash looked up from *Horse and Hound*, which she had been slyly checking through to see if Mickey was advertised, which he wasn't. Four other of the yard's hopefuls were, however, including Groupie.

'Lord knows,' he sighed. 'I'm still waiting to hear from a couple of firms, but it's getting pretty late to expect anyone to come forward with a big wad of cash to get us through this season. I just don't know how in hell we're going to cope.'

'We'll have to win a lot – that's all.' She smiled with far more confidence than she felt.

'Don't be fucking facetious!' Gus snapped. 'How can we win anything when we can't afford the diesel money to get us to the competitions in the first place?' He stalked out of the room, crunching biscuits underfoot.

Tash winced. Although she and Gus got on well at a superficial level, she was always the first in the line of fire when he was uptight, confirming a niggling little fear she kept to herself that he was not really very keen on her. It also came out when he was pissed; he would pick on her and mob her up ceaselessly, delighting in her discomfort and fear of confrontation. She sometimes felt he resented her, although she had no idea why.

'Don't worry – he'll calm down soon.' Zoe rubbed her shoulder encouragingly. 'You know what he's like: so combative and grouchy about money.'

'Yes, I know.' Tash guiltily sloped back to work.

What she also knew only too well was that she was the most expendable member of the team. So far she had won relatively little compared to Gus, Penny and Kirsty and had no international experience at all, having bypassed the junior and young rider ranks by coming to the sport so late. She brought them in valuable stud fees through Snob, and was getting a fairly high-profile following in the sport – largely thanks to Hugo's early support and, latterly, her romance with Niall as reported in the national press – but these were superficial plus points compared to the day-in, day-out earning potential of a professional event rider. Gus was a seasoned international who coached as well as evented, added to which he designed courses, wrote books and rode horses for private owners. Penny, once a star in her own right, was the true horse-trainer who was invaluable in spotting talented youngsters, breaking them and bringing them on; she also ran the livery side of the business practically single-handed. And Kirsty was not only a high-ranking team member and long-standing professional, she was now the only rider in the yard with sponsorship – all three of her advanced horses were owned and supported by a City investment bank.

It was only a matter of time, Tash reasoned, before she was asked to leave and she, Snob and Hunk, were out on ten limbs. For now, she remained on tenterhooks.

Working very late into the night in the floodlit menage to gain Brownie points, she fell into bed without a second thought for the impending family gathering.

She had little time to plan what to wear to Henry's christening, although she knew she owed it to Sophia to smarten up for once. Sophia had bestowed the ultimate compliment upon them by asking Niall to be a godfather, along with one of her old modelling cronies.

Niall, who was filming late into the night on the Friday again, had agreed to fly to Birmingham airport on Saturday morning and meet Tash at the tiny church in Holdham village, which fell within the estate's grounds.

Leaving it as late as possible, Tash raced around the shops before her Flab-busters session, hawking her buys with her to the United Reform Church Hall.

'Two pounds – congratulations!' Theresa was beside herself to find someone among her regulars who had actually lost weight. This week, one of her motivational ploys was to pin a large star-shaped paper badge to each of her slimmers, emblazoned with the amount that they had lost over the past seven days.

Later that night, Tash pinned her glittery '2' to the fireguard beside the melted fridge magnet and wondered whether her life would really be as hunky-dory as Theresa promised if she were slim.

She scrunched her eyes closed and tried to imagine herself as a slinky size eight in the Lisette Norton mould, but superimposing her head on that consumptive-whippet figure just made her think of a character on a Cluedo playing card – all big, menacing face and tiny, matchstick body. The happiest, most level-headed and certainly the most sexy woman Tash knew was Zoe, and she was an elegant, voluptuous size fourteen with curves that a car designer could only dream of for a new prototype.

'The problem with me isn't weight,' she told a fascinated Beetroot, 'it's waiting. I spend my entire life at the moment waiting for Niall. If he was here more often it would be a wait off my bloody shoulders.'

Beetroot nudged her delightedly with her wiry muzzle, brown eyes glued devotedly to Tash's face.

'Niall used to look at me like that,' she sighed. 'You know, Root, I've started to think I'm weight-watching in vain.'

Ten

SHE BORROWED TED'S RICKETY Renault 5 to drive to Worcestershire, as Gus needed the Land-Rover to tow the trailer, delivering one of the youngsters he had just sold to a new owner for a much-needed four-figure sum. The Land-Rover was cheaper to run than the box, which was uneconomical for transporting just one horse.

'The clutch is a bit iffy,' Ted warned Tash as she fought her way inside past a lot of danging football paraphernalia and found herself sitting on several tape boxes and an old, gucky packet of fruit Polos. 'And she tends to cut out over seventy. Plus the accelerator cable has been known to snap, so be gentle. There's a coathanger in the boot in case you need to mend it.'

She nodded worriedly.

Ted rubbed his growing-out crew cut as he watched her. With his bullish neck and broken nose, the stubbly hairdo made him look like a squaddie. He claimed it had improved his pulling no end, but Tash thought he looked terrifying, and far more likely to pull a trigger than a woman.

'Are you seriously wearing that?' He regarded her outfit doubtfully.

'What's wrong with it?'

'Oh, nothing – it's pretty wild, that's all.' He gave her one of his seedy winks. 'You're looking well choice. See you later – take care of my baby.'

Trying hard not to go above sixty all the way to Worcestershire, and treating the accelerator pedal like a sewing-machine control during some delicate embroidery, Tash arrived at the sleepy Holdham village chapel ten minutes late.

It was immediately apparent that her outfit was not one of her best. The first person she encountered in the car park was Sally. Backing out of the Audi's passenger door, she burst out laughing.

'Christ – Sophia will go ape!' She looked Tash up and down. 'Not that she isn't already. One of the godfathers is already stoned, and the other one – your dear intended – hasn't turned up yet. She's spitting. Ben is trying to pacify her in the vestry, but Henry has just puked everywhere and the vicar says he's got a wedding at midday and can't hold things up any longer than twenty-past.'

Tash, still shaking from her nerve-racking journey, tried to take this in.

Sally was looking very merry and pink-faced in a lilac angora top and deep heather-coloured silk skirt. Her wispy blonde hair had recently been cut into a smart layered bob and was today topped by a squashy fake fur hat.

'You're looking fantastic,' Tash said admiringly.

'New friends and lots of influence at the hair salon.' Sally hooked her arm through Tash's and led her under the lych-gate. 'I just came out to fetch some teething gel for Linus – actually he doesn't really need it anymore, but he's addicted to the stuff, the little junky, and he's wailing so much in sympathy with horrible Henry that I thought it would shut him up. Perhaps I should squirt some at your sister.'

'Oh God, I hope Niall gets here.' Tash looked fretfully over her shoulder towards the car park, but amongst the flashy Mercs, BMWs and Discoverys, nothing stirred. She suddenly recognised Hugo's racy little green sportscar and winced. Why her stomach flip-flopped quite so much every time she spotted it she had no idea – she supposed it must be because she had once had a lift in it and almost thrown up at the speed he had driven.

'Is Hugo here?' she asked, even though she knew.

'Chatting up your mother,' Sally said dreamily. 'God, he's so good-looking it's unfair – when he walked in I almost died with desire until I realised who it was, the bastard! Matty has 'flu, by the way, so don't kiss him. Have you lost weight?'

'Some.' Tash felt slightly bucked, but Sally didn't pursue the topic enough to bolster her confidence further.

'Isn't this place heavenly? I'd quite forgotten,' she was babbling on as she admired the fat yew trees and crumbling graves that fronted the little flint chapel. 'Look at all those daffs coming out – Wordsworth would erect crowd barriers. They match your outfit.'

Yellow had never been one of Tash's best colours – it tended to make her look bleached out and pink-eyed; the only colour it brought out in her was that of her teeth. But she had been in a hurry in Marlbury, which only had one decent clothes shop. Having found nothing in there above a size eight, she had resorted to one of the cheap but cheerful bargain stores that littered Marlbury's unsuccessful shopping mall – shops that lasted just a few months before they sold off their stock cheap and were replaced by a bargain book store. The assistant in Frock Off and Die had been incredibly flattering, and Tash had been so amazed that she could once again get into a size twelve that she'd bought the little sixties-style suit without question, racing next door to buy some trashy but trendy footwear.

The latest fashion was for knee-length patent leather boots. Even more hardened fashion victims were wearing snakeskin ones. The shop in questionable taste had possessed a pair of snakeskin bunion-squeezers in Tash's size and another eager assistant had raved on about the fact that most people's legs were too short and fat to get away with them. Tash – who had long, gangly legs – had been absurdly pleased. What the assistant hadn't pointed out was the fact that knees as bruised as a prep school bully's were not a becoming addition to the look, or that they were desperate to get rid of the boots because they were a size eight. Coupled with her too-short, too-shiny and far too yellow suit, Tash was dressed more for a tarts and vicars party than a christening among the landed gentry. She was wearing two pairs of opaque tights to hide the bruises, and had added her black dressage top hat wrapped in a checked silk scarf to detract from the ghastly suit, but was nevertheless acutely aware of looking on the unflattering side of disgusting.

One glance at Ben Meredith's stuffy relations confirmed that it would be impossible to melt into the background today. Her glaring outfit stood out amongst the muted beiges and navy blues of the congregation like a Post-it note stuck to Monet's winter study of Rouen Cathedral. As she wobbled on the unfamiliar high heels into the dusty chill of religious worship, she received a lot of dumbfounded stares and one or two titters.

In the second pew from the front, Alexandra looked up from discreetly reading about the Princess of Wales's skiing holiday in *Cheers!* magazine and hailed her daughter enthusiastically. Beside her a familiar, Laughing Cavalier's face sneered from beneath a mop of tortoiseshell hair, a beautifully straight nose wrinkling with distaste, two swimming-pool blue eyes as chilly as the chapel thermostat.

'Tash darling – you look radiant, and so slim!' Alexandra gushed far too loudly. 'Oh, it's lovely to see you. Come over here, sweetheart, and squeeze in between me and Hugo.'

Tash cringed at the prospect, catching Hugo's horrified expression. But the looks from the rest of the congregation were so grim, she couldn't face the prospect of trying to cram herself in anywhere else. She grabbed an order sheet from a harassed-looking younger Meredith and shuffled towards her mother.

'Where is that rotten man of yours?' Alexandra was in the aisle now, waiting for Tash to squeeze past her. As slim and elegant as a Borzoi, she was the picture of sophisticated grandmotherly chic in a soft brown wool wraparound dress with her slim legs tapering to understated court shoes. Tash was aware that her snakeskin knee-high boots were attracting unflattering guffaws and comments from all sides and her top pair of tights had already snagged on the jagged interior of Ted's car.

'Talk about snakes and ladders.' Hugo too was enjoying a good look.

Tash gave him a withering glare, failing dismally to think up a witty crack about asp-holes.

'I do hope you'll wear those in competitions, Tash,' he muttered as she slid in beside him, trying hard not to let any part of her body make contact with his. 'They'd be far more effective than spurs – one glimpse of those from the corner of his eyes, and that chestnut of yours would accelerate like a Ferrari in a ram raid.'

'Have you spoken to him today?' Alexandra hadn't heard this and was settling in beside Tash, a squashy black coat across her slender knees.

'Who?' Tash wondered if her mother seriously thought she'd confess to talking to Snob as though he was human – even to a mother.

'That unpunctual, sexy man of yours!' Alexandra pressed her hand lovingly on top of Tash's, which was gripping the pew in front. 'Honestly, Tash – you are so vague sometimes.'

'Oh – Niall.' Tash watched the vicar flapping worriedly at the font, where Ben was looking stooping and stupid beside a tall, devastatingly broody blond hunk. 'No – but he sent a fax yesterday afternoon to say he'd definitely be here.'

'What an extraordinary relationship you two have.' Hugo, who was reading the order sheet with interest, didn't look up. 'Communicating through rolls of heat-sensitive paper. I suppose you could call it the fax of life.'

'I was riding out on the all-weather gallops when he called,' Tash said huffily.

'Riding out a storm then, I should imagine.' Hugo moved slightly away from her, clearly unwilling to make contact with the static that was emanating from her suit.

'Your father has already cornered me to demand to know whether or not he's expected to give you away,' Alexandra hissed to Tash, and shot the back of James's red, neatly clipped neck a nasty look. 'I mean to say, who else is going to? The silly man!'

Tash suddenly and guiltily realised that she had been so paranoid about the effect her outfit was having that she hadn't even noticed that her father and Henrietta were sitting in the pew in front. Not that they had exactly leaped up to greet her. Right now she felt that her father would be only too willing to give her away.

She tapped him lightly on the shoulder.

'Hi, Daddy.'

Stiffening, he craned around.

'Oh, it's you,' he muttered. 'You well?'

'Fine.' Tash wished he didn't always appear to be so ashamed of her. 'And you?'

'Reasonable,' he said brusquely, making to turn away again, relieved that he had done his duty.

'Mummy says you're worrying about giving me away,' Tash persisted, her anger piqued.

'Not worried,' he hissed, clearly unwilling to enter the conversation. 'Just making sure.'

'Well, it's okay. I don't want you to give me away.' Tash lifted her chin. 'I want Mummy to.'

She could hear Hugo spluttering with derision beside her, the pompous reactionary! She had a brief urge to add loudly that she wanted to marry in yellow PVC just to see if he'd fall off the pew completely, but bit her tongue.

'You what!' James swung around. At his side, Henrietta didn't turn, but the beige padded shoulders of her English Eccentrics jacket rose to her ears as though suddenly attached to her pearl earrings.

'I want Mummy to give me away,' Tash muttered. 'After all, she kept me after you two divorced, which rather gives her possession – nine-tenths of the mother-in-law and all that.'

'Oh, darling!' Alexandra enveloped her in a scented arm and hugged her close. 'That is so lovely!'

At that moment Sophia emerged from the vestry with a still-wailing Henry, both looking almost deranged with stress. Henry looked suspiciously likely to throw up again at any second, a sickly dribble emanating from his cherubic mouth.

'Tash!' Sophia spotted her sister in the crowd and closed in on her.

Even when demented, she looked gorgeous. Her huge green eyes were traced with the most subtle of tawny liner, but it still brought out the amber flecks so that they resembled unripe russet apples; her black hair had been lightly pinned into tumbling wisteria traces over her cheekbones, and her cream Amanda Wakeley suit was so understated yet well cut it allowed the slender perfection of her figure to rule the day in one of the most demure displays of sexual exhibitionism Tash had ever encountered. She felt like a great yellow neon 'Bargain of the Week' sign blazing from a car lot in contrast.

The only thing that marred this flawless beauty was Sophia's hysteria.

'Where is he?' she wailed, leaning over the pew towards Tash so that their mother's dress was threatened by Henry's impending puke. 'I mean, I know he's a star, but this is so dreadfully rude. It may look good to roll up late to a première or celebrity opening or charity ding-dong, but one has to keep a sense of proportion. This is a religious ceremony – I thought Catholics were supposed to take these things seriously?' She shot a wary look at the vicar, whom she hadn't pre-warned of Niall's denomination.

'He promised he'd be here,' Tash soothed. 'I'm sure he'll arrive any second now – he's probably stuck in traffic.'

'Well, tough.' Sophia gazed around the church frantically. 'We'll just have to get someone else to stand in for him – drat! Who is there? Hugo?'

He looked up, unworried. 'I'm already taken, darling – you used me for Josh, remember? Twice looks like heirlessness.'

'Dratty drat!' Sophia raked the room, her beautiful eyes suddenly settling on a very unwilling recipient of her attention. 'Matty!'

Jiggling Henry at her cream chest, she raced to the back of the chapel and pounced on her brother who was sulkily reading *Private Eye* in a rear pew, oblivious of the fact that Tom and Tor were loudly fighting to one side of him. He was again wearing his ubiquitous crocheted hat, which had now developed a strangely lumpy look and had a large coffee stain over one ear.

'No way.' Matty looked up in shock, instantly realising what she was asking. 'I'm an atheist – I'm only here under duress, and because Sally said there's going to be loads of food.'

'Oh, do dry up – this is an emergency. Get to that font!' Sophia practically had him out of the pew by his collarless grand-dad shirt.

In her panic, she didn't hear the throaty sound of a black cab arriving at speed in the car park outside. Marching Matty up the aisle, she whipped off his cap as they arrived at the vicar to effect hasty introductions.

With Matty standing sullenly by the font – slightly apart from his fellow god parents in an attempt to look detached and agnostic – the vicar hastily whipped out his Bible and, clearing his throat with a creepy series of hiccups, settled the congregation, which was largely made up of Ben's family all talking loudly about shooting. There was a resounding sound of crunching footsteps on gravel coming from outside now.

'Ladies and gentlemen,' the vicar droned in a dull, booming voice that appeared to resonate from the depths of his cassock, as though relayed via an implanted loudspeaker, 'I am delighted to welcome you all to our ancient parish for the delightful . . .'

'Christ and Lord above – am I glad I made it!' came a deep, sexy croak from the door.

Tash almost melted with pride.

Framed in the high arch of the doorway was a tall, broad figure, stooping slightly as he fought to catch his breath before entering. He was wearing a vast trenchcoat and jeans and, to Tash, had never looked more desirable and untamed, like a craggy, windswept horizon that only the bravest dared set out to reach. She felt herself rise up on her haunches with buttock-clenched delight.

Beside her, Hugo rubbed a finger over his chin, lounging back in the pew.

Niall's voice was like warm, soothing oil in an aching ear. 'I'm so sorry, everyone – my plane was delayed, and then the traffic out of Brum was hell on earth, so it was. God! There was a point back there when I thought the little sod'd be in his teens by the time I made it here. Hi, Sophia angel. Christ, you look glorious!'

Niall may have just blasphemed like a Satanist and stilled the room with his loud, happy raucousness, but such was his charm that he was instantly forgiven. Sophia went pink with delight, Ben greeted him with a great, slapping bear hug, and even the vicar looked quite skittish with excitement to have such a good-looking famous face in his church.

Shooting his friend a grateful wink, Matty passed him his pre-printed lines and sloped gratefully back to his pew, where Sally had now silenced Tom and Tor with two giant activity books, carefully hidden from view by some propped-up hassocks.

As Niall took up position, his eyes raked the room for Tash. Spotting her glowing in her undersized RTA police officer's yellow uniform, his eyes softened and he blew her a loud kiss. Sophia chose this point to have a slight coughing fit and a lot of Ben's relatives turned to stare at Tash with renewed amazement, suddenly registering that she was the unworthy recipient of this great man's affections.

Tash, however, had caught a hint of something that worried her far more than her general disfavour with the gathered Meredith clan. She gazed at Niall worriedly as he beamed out warmth and bonhomie to the room.

Hugo had spotted it too, and stretched across to trace Tash's ear with the warm, careless breath of his caustic observation.

'He's bloody pissed,' he hissed in an undertone.

She closed her eyes, appalled. Why, oh why, was Niall drunk at eleven in the morning?

Somehow Niall coasted through the ceremony, not fluffing a single line. Only Hugo and Tash noticed the unnaturally faraway look in his deep brown eyes, the slight lethargy in his delivery, and the husky catch in his voice that only ever appeared after his fifth Bushmills. The rest of the congregation watched in awe as he stole the show without intending to. His reading was so beautifully timed, heavenly on the ear and emotional to the soul, that even Ben's cold-hearted, pragmatic mother scrabbled in her Mulberry handbag for a handkerchief, finally extracting a very creased piece of loo-roll. When they finally filed out of the chapel, he was pressed upon from all sides by delighted family members eager to introduce themselves.

Trying to fight her way through, Tash couldn't get close to him. All she could hear as she found herself shunted past and out into the cold was the yakking praise of the local gentry.

'We met on Boxing Day – Clarissa and George, do you remember?' And: 'I hear you're practically going to be marrying into the family – I'm so delighted!' Or: 'Sophia has told me so much about you – I'm sure you'll be a simply splendid role-model to Henry.' Before long, he was being asked to do an after-dinner speech for the local hunt ball, and donate a personal item to the Guidedogs for the Blind auction.

Tash found herself out in the car park, standing between Hugo and

Ben, who both ignored her while they had a very boring chat about straw-burning generators.

Giving up on feigning interest, she caught sight of her father and Henrietta exchanging overly polite platitudes with the vicar, and suddenly realised that both Emily and Beccy were with them – the latter looking ludicrously studenty in a torn, crumpled mackintosh and Doc Martens. She was shooting James looks of frosty hostility from beneath a dyed black fringe. Tash cringed behind Ben as she remembered her silly, shrewish comments in the church. She quickly looked away and found herself almost nose-to-nose with her brother-in-law who had finally noticed her and was having a sly peek at her legs.

'Tash, old thing.' Ben, galvanised into courteous action by a sense of duty, gave her a stiff-backed hug – the closest he ever came to affection. 'You looked quite splendid – very choice.'

'Thanks.' Tash smiled bravely. It was a family joke that you knew you were looking truly awful when Ben paid you a compliment; he had simply diabolical taste in women's clothing, still believing that Pan's People were the be all and end all of feminine chic.

'I must say, I'm jolly pleased that you and old Niall are finally getting hitched – you make a premium couple.'

He made it sound like bovine artificial insemination.

'Don't you agree, Hugs? Tash and Niall are superbly matched?' He turned to his old friend, eager for confirmation.

Pushing a stray lock of walnut-coloured hair from his forehead, Hugo caught Tash's eye and, after a beat, flashed her a glacial smile.

'They seem to be custom-made for one another,' he said dryly, looking across the gravel sweep of car park as Niall, having finally extricated himself from the Meredith heavies, made his way towards Tash, tripping over Linus's baby buggy and pitching left into a small patch of crocuses.

Tash looked at him and, despite the dullness a few drinks had wrought to his dark, shining eyes, felt only relief and happiness that those milk chocolate holes on his soul told her he was as ridiculously pleased to see her as she was him.

'Hi, angel.' He drew her into a kiss that was so satisfyingly long and luscious it made up for the fact that his mouth tasted of whisky, and his chin badly needed a shave. Tash resurfaced short of breath and, although fizzing with excitement, she was mildly aware that the vicar was watching them with beady, jealous eyes as Niall went for a second take, tongue tasting her mouth as though re-visiting a favourite wine.

'Great reading, Niall old chap.' Ben cleared his throat awkwardly, clearly embarrassed by the kiss. Seemingly oblivious, Hugo had already wandered away to talk to Sally.

Niall barely seemed to notice Ben hovering uncomfortably nearby.

'Forgive me?' he breathed, nuzzling into Tash's neck.

'What's to forgive?' She pressed her face into his soft, cool hair. It badly needed a wash and was so long that it touched his shoulders, but it smelled so familiar that she shuddered with happiness.

'Lots, so there is.' He pulled away, his darting gaze suddenly shifty with guilt. 'Not making it back that weekend, not calling enough, not standing up for myself or demanding time off to spend with you, taking on the part in Lisette's film – ah!' He grinned uncomfortably as she stiffened involuntarily at the mention of the L word. 'I knew you were upset about that now.'

Tash shook her head, suddenly truthful. 'I'm secretly grateful to her.' She smiled. 'Because it'll keep you in England – and close to me.'

'Ah – there's a thing.' He enveloped her in a tight hug of happiness. 'Let's go home. I can't be facing this reception now. I want to go to bed with you.'

Tash wanted that very much too, but she knew that they would both have to face her sister for many years to come – and not going to her reception to pay a bit of lip service, even if it meant that they had to keep their lips off one another for a few hours, would be unforgivable.

'Just for five minutes,' she promised Niall as she led him towards the car.

Grumbling, he hung back and, so delighted to see Tash again that he was given to over-the-top gestures, blew Ben's mother a kiss. Lady Malvern, as she liked to be known at all times (even, it was reputed, in Woolworth's where she bought her horses' mints), almost fainted with shock. Her tightly crinkled, baby bloodhound eyelids opened fully for the first time in years to reveal two very bloodshot blue eyes.

Niall paddled Tash's hand and followed her past Hugo's boy-racer – 'Now there's a wonderful fucking car, Tash darling, I could do with one of those' – as far as her borrowed heap of rust, which was thankfully concealed from most of the gathered throng by a large four-wheel drive.

'What to Christ is this?' He gaped at the sagging metal death-trap.

'It's Ted's.' Tash turned the key and simultaneously kneed the driver's door in the place that Ted had demonstrated that morning. It obediently swung open.

'Lord, but we have to buy you a car.' Niall watched her fold herself with some difficulty into the driver's seat, her yellow bottom resting on a dog lead, a back copy of *Eventing* magazine, and an old packet of Marlboro Lights. 'Do you fancy one like Hugo's – or would you prefer something racier?'

'You're not buying me a car, Niall.' Tash let him in through the passenger's door by jabbing the handle with a de-icer scraper as Ted had taught her.

The reception was predictably grand and slickly managed. It was, Tash supposed, inevitable that someone who used to be as kill-for-it fashionable as Sophia (it was rumoured that she had once hired a fleet of taxi drivers in New York just to track down a scarce bottle of Chanel Rouge Noir nail varnish) would now hire chefs for a christening to produce the same almost inedible raw lamb, chilli-rich nibbles that were stinging the tongues of the clientèle of every fashionable media haunt in London. Ben's family wore the long-suffering, green-gilled expressions of boarding-school children in a refectory as they looked down on tray after tray of uncooked fish, marinated lime-leaves and lemongrass and kumquat marmalade tartlets.

Yet even though the food was more fashionable than Bjork, Tash had judged it totally wrong by wearing high-trash clothes to the christening; she would have made a better impression arriving in her usual work gear of Barbour and jods as much of Ben's family, it appeared, had chosen to do.

The reception was held in the oppressively ornate Holdham Hall long gallery. It was one of the few rooms in the Merediths' ancient family seat that was open to the public ('The Gawpers' as the Countess kindly referred to them) and was seldom used by the family at all. Although the security ropes and plastic walkways had been removed for winter, the tour-guide placards and plastic 'Exit' signs had been left in place, lending the reception the strange atmosphere of one held in a hired venue. Racing up and down the long, polished floors like speed skaters, all the under-tens – including Tor and Tom – were letting out great echoing shrieks. Tash was reminded of a bowling alley and was amazed that Sophia hadn't gone to greater lengths to tart the room up.

'*Huge* row with Mother about holding the party here,' Ben explained in an undertone when he brought her over a glass of champagne that was so cold it stuck to her hand. 'We were going to have it in the orangery, but Ma announced this morning that she'd hired it out to the local dog-training class for the afternoon and we'd have to come in here. Sophia is livid – there are dozens of Alsatian pups learning to sit and stay by bloody expensive flower arrangements as I speak.'

Tash stifled a giggle as Ben waggled a second glass around until it lost most of its contents. 'Brought this for Niall.' He seemed at a loss to know what to do with it.

'I'll take it for him,' she offered, privately wondering whether she could steer Niall towards orange juice when he returned from the loo.

At the far end of the room, Sophia was doing her usual sublime hostess act, introducing the right people to the far-right people and ignoring Sally and Matty who were looking very left out and very left-wing. Lying in state beneath a great awning of ivory silk by the door, Henry was wailing his lungs inside out and being largely ignored. Only the red-faced French au pair took any notice of him as she struggled to hold a five-foot teddy bear over the cot and wave it around. It was almost as portly as she was and Tash watched in amazement as she nearly flattened Henry, cot and all, with it before pitching off towards the drinks table, thoroughly off balance. Henry just screamed twice as loudly.

'The baby's crying, Bernadette!' Sophia shouted over her shoulder from within a social cluster. 'For God's sake, show him his new teddy like I told you!'

Tash took a brief respite from her killing heels by perching on a tatty old leather chair.

'Don't sit on that, dear,' Lady Meredith said curtly as she charged past to refill her glass. 'It's tenth-century – absolutely priceless.' Without another word, she headed for the red wine.

Tash sprang upright again and wandered towards Matty and Sally, then noticed at the last moment that they were chatting to Hugo. Backing away, she was forced to resort to Henrietta and the girls, who were looking worried and bored respectively.

Feeling she had to make up some ground after the sticky lunch and the daft vitriol in the church, Tash gave them all kisses on the cheek, noticing to her embarrassment that they all seemed as reluctant to accept her endearment as Jesus feeling Judas plant a wet one on his beard.

'Are you all well?' she asked cheerfully.

'Fine,' Henrietta said bleakly, not looking at all friendly.

Tash had never known her to be pointedly uncivil, and realised that she had hurt her far more than she'd intended by being so unhelpful the previous week. Henrietta was normally so timid and in desperate need of approval that she was overly polite to anyone and everyone. For a while when she had first married their father, Sophia, Matty and Tash had referred to her as the Nodding Dog. It was a childish slur that Tash now regretted, realising how tough it had been for Henrietta, always regarded just as Daddy's Secretary, to adjust to the role of Daddy's New Wife. James French's three headstrong, unruly children must have made it very hard indeed for her and her young daughters to fit in.

Desperate to make up ground, she made the mistake of tapping Henrietta right where the wound was rawest.

'I hear you want to work in films?' she asked Emily, unaware that Henrietta was flinching beside her.

'That's right.' Emily looked at her with lazy, narrowed blue eyes which seemed to be weighed down with half a bottle of black liner. The look didn't suit her. Beneath all the muck and hair dye, Tash knew she had the most glorious English rose looks which would propel her into a low-paid dogsbody assistant's job on a film in next to no time – production managers, especially male ones, couldn't resist having a fleet of Mollys, Pollys and general Sloaney jollies around the sets clutching clip-boards, gushing pointlessly and hanging on their every word – even if it was just a request for skimmed milk and two Hermasetas in their tea. But dressed as she was – in a shapeless, oversized and faded tea dress, Doc Martens, laddered tights and the old covert coat James wore to walk the dogs – she stood a better chance of getting a small extra role in the crowd scene of a Ken Loach film.

'Have you asked Niall then?' she asked Tash belligerently, her eyes squinting.

Tash bristled at the expectancy of her tone. Sometimes she was treated – especially by the more loosely connected members of her family – as though Niall was a Lottery jackpot she should dole out equal shares of whenever asked.

'He's around here somewhere.' She smiled encouragingly. 'Why don't you ask him yourself?'

She knew she sounded tight-lipped and schoolmarmy, but didn't like the way that Emily was up-and-downing her outfit as though she was wearing a body bag.

'And you're still eventing, of course.' She turned to Beccy, knowing she was on safer ground. 'I saw you at the Ruttleford trials last October. You did very well – I loved that youngster you were riding, the bay. Are you going to compete her this year?'

'No.' Beccy's face started to crumple.

'Your father sold her,' Henrietta said nastily. 'To one of your friends,

I believe. A Swedish chap.' She patted Beccy on the back, looking around in embarrassment in case anyone was witnessing her daughter's emotional display.

'Stefan?' Tash looked at Beccy sympathetically.

She nodded, clearly not trusting herself to speak as she fought bravely not to cry.

'Oh, you poor thing.' Tash touched her arm. 'That's so awful – losing a horse you really think is starting to go right for you. It's happened to me with Gus's horses so many times and it never gets any easier. It's such a mercenary business.'

Beccy sniffed miserably and shrugged, clearly not believing Tash had experienced anything close to her level of loss.

'If it's any comfort, Stefan is a bloody good rider – and very kind to his horses. And he's working at Hugo's yard this year, so she'll want for nothing.'

'Is he?' Beccy suddenly looked interested. 'Stefan Johanssen is staying at Haydown?'

Tash nodded. She had seen the lanky Swede only two days ago, when he had driven down to Lime Tree Farm from Maccombe to say hi, almost flattening Wally when he parked his motorbike in the yard and left most of its tyre rubber on the cobbles. Not yet twenty, he was competing for only his second year in England, but already was extremely popular with the other riders who fell for his lofty, blond looks, his enviable ability to ride competitively when hungover to the back of his immaculately straight teeth, and his strange, loopy vowel sounds. He had the huge-eyed, gauche look of a cartoon character which made everyone think he was a gullible pushover, yet he was as shrewd as a horse-dealing gypsy. Coupled with Hugo, who was one of the bravest and most accurate riders in the business, it was generally believed that he would really shape up this year, if he didn't die of alcohol poisoning first.

'Mummy's going to ask Hugo if he'll take me on as a working pupil,' Beccy said cheerfully, her near-tears forgotten.

Henrietta, who – despite admiring Hugo immensely – was secretly terrified of him, cleared her throat nervously.

'That would mean I'd be living near you, wouldn't it?' Beccy seemed to have forgiven Tash.

'Just four or five miles away. And there's lots of other eventing yards nearby.'

'Are Gus and Penny Moncrieff really going bust?' Beccy asked blithely.

Tash gaped at her. 'Where did you hear that?'

Again, Henrietta cleared her throat. She was beginning to sound as though she had a large batch of hatching frog's spawn in there.

Beccy quickly changed the subject. 'Have you really had horses sold on that you wanted to ride?'

'God – tens of them,' Tash sighed. 'It's always so heartbreaking, but you have to accept that it's a business as well as a sport and the only way the yard can run is by selling on some of the best horses.'

Beccy nodded, but her eyes kept darting to Hugo, who was standing just a few yards behind Tash, having an animated conversation with one of Ben's crusty, horse-loving relatives. He has the most beautiful profile I've ever seen, she realised dreamily. She tried hard to listen to Tash, but her concentration was desperately torn.

'My method now,' Tash was saying, 'is to concentrate on the tough nut horses who have just as much potential as the easy-going ones, but don't show it as fully at first – there's one at the moment I'm eager to keep on. He'll be simply fantastic soon.'

'Is he like Snob?' Beccy was almost as madly in love with Tash's big, potty chestnut as she was with Michael Hutchence, Johnny Depp, Niall, and – very secretly – Hugo Beauchamp. She noticed out of the corner of her eye that he was standing closer now, knocking back orange juice and looking divinely aloof.

'Mickey?' Tash thought about it. 'I guess he has the same stubbornness, and he gets bored easily too. But he's not as bright and wily as Snob. He's more eager to please, but he doesn't know how to do it yet and gets too excited to learn. He's got phenomenal raw ability, though. I know Gus sees pound signs every time I improve him – it's hell really.'

'Why?' Beccy had started to notice that Hugo's eyes darted towards Tash every so often, almost as though it was a habit – the same way she would look at her best friend at a party to check she was still enjoying herself. It struck her as odd.

'Because,' Tash explained, slightly thrown that Beccy kept looking past her ear, 'the better horses get, the more likely they are to be sold. It's catch twenty-two times table – you work your guts out on them because you want them to show you their true colours, and the moment they do, you lose them.'

'Christ!' Emily yawned loudly. 'I can't believe that grown women can be so excited about horseflesh.' She eyed Hugo thoughtfully as he made his way past them to refill his glass. 'Although I suppose it has its compensations.'

Beccy followed her sister's gaze and took a deep breath. 'Now's your chance, Mummy!' she hissed, watching as Hugo paused right in front of Tash to peer down the very flat cleavage of one of Sophia's modelling friends.

Tash clenched her teeth with tense foreboding as she remembered that she was under strict instructions from India to do some more matchmaking that day, mentioning Zoe's wonderful nature every time Hugo came within breathing distance, and telling him how lovely it would be if he popped into the farm more often. India had even suggested that she tell Hugo he was a fool to be dabbling with Kirsty when what he really needed was a good wife, but she could just imagine his reaction to that and it involved a large quantity of orange juice dripping from her own face.

Watching him listen intently to Henrietta's quiet, embarrassed approach, she was amazed to see that, instead of brushing her off like an unwanted fly on his jacket sleeve, he apologised profusely for not being able to help this year and then took out a pen from his breast pocket to scribble down the names of some friends who might be able to accommodate Beccy in their yards during her school holidays.

'Tell them I recommended her.' He smiled at Henrietta and then Beccy as he tore the scribbled sheet from his diary and handed it over. 'I saw you at Ruttleford trials last year – you were on that bay mare Stefan's riding now, weren't you?'

Beccy nodded, so pink in the face that she looked as though a huge bubblegum sphere had just popped in it.

'You've got a lot of guts.' Hugo winked. 'I admire that more than anything. Keep at it and you'll be terrifying the hell out of me in a couple of years. Just don't get too good, too soon.' He grinned and then started to walk towards the drinks table.

'Thank you!' Henrietta called after him, flushed with success and turning to shoot Tash a victorious look.

She was speechless with shock and burning with shame for not having done more for Beccy herself. It wasn't because she was mean, it was because she was gutless – she still felt like a complete tyro herself, battling to keep up in a game of draughts, while Hugo was a total chess-master.

'Tenner for your thoughts.' Niall had pushed through to her side and was eager to shake off the last few attention seekers who were still waggling arms and glasses at him.

Tash bit her lip and watched as Henrietta, having plucked up the courage with a swift swig of wine and flushed from her recent success, approached Niall now to elicit some help on Emily's behalf. Slouching beside her, Emily looked decidedly embarrassed at her mother's red-faced twitchiness. Tash felt her anger flare, thinking that Emily was really old enough to stand up and ask for herself.

Sally, who had dumped Matty by a display of medieval armoury, wandered up to stand beside Tash.

'I just overheard Sophia telling Ben's aunt that she needed to invest in a decent foundation,' she giggled in an undertone, swigging champagne. 'To which the aunt boomed, "Garment or fund? Because, I can assure you, I have both!" Sophia suggested Lancôme and legged it. What's Niall looking so constipated about?'

'Henrietta's just having a word with him about Emily's work experience,' whispered Tash, still feeling an acid-burn of shame drenching her cheeks for being so ungenerous to her step-sisters. No doubt Niall was now offering Emily a highly paid job as his script adviser, she realised unhappily.

But when she glanced at him, Niall was looking evasive.

'Sure, I'll ask,' he was saying vaguely. 'But you really need someone from the production side in your favour – that's the way in now.' He looked at Emily's silent, expressionless face dubiously. 'I'm just an employee really,' he apologised.

Embarrassed for him, Tash hung back and found herself standing next to Matty, who had pursued his wife and was glowering with disapproval as he always did at Sophia's parties, which was why he was invited to so few.

'But I thought you were the star on this Four Wheel Drive thing?' Henrietta was asking Niall anxiously, glancing towards Tash for support. 'Surely you could ask if Emily can just observe for a day?'

'It's not as simple as that,' he started, eyeing Emily's snarling mouth dubiously.

'Are you after a job then, Em?' Sally butted in, looking cheerfully at Henrietta's morose daughter.

'Yeah.' She shifted her bovver boots nonchalantly.

'On this film Niall's in?' Sally persisted.

'Yeah,' Emily continued, scuffing her shoes and looking at no one, seemingly transfixed by the cat's cradle of her laces.

'I can get you something to do on it, I should think,' Sally promised easily. 'I'm working on it myself.'

'You what?' Tash, Matty and Henrietta all gaped at her in disbelief.

Only Niall found this highly amusing. 'Christ – it's like the Redgrave family around here,' he whistled. 'Any second now, Tash my darling, and you'll tell me you're the stunt co-ordinator. I need another drink.'

Escaping to the long, cluttered drinks table to refill their glasses, Tash found herself queuing behind Hugo's straight, unfriendly back in broad-shouldered made-to-measure jacket. He was having a laughter-saturated conversation with a very rakish and razzled-looking older blonde who was flirting like mad with him, huge predatory eyes drinking him in like an ecstasy raver spotting a long, chilled Evian bottle. Neither turned to acknowledge her.

Hastily averting her gaze, Tash caught sight of her mother who, having cornered Henrietta to chat about weddings, was now eager to pull her back into the proceedings.

Shrugging apologetically, Tash held up her drinks glasses by way of an excuse and waggled them to emphasise her point. But she hadn't noticed that hers was still half-full and its contents spilled neatly down the centre pinstripe of Hugo's beautifully tailored jacket.

'What the Christ?' He spun around, his cool eyes taking in the yellow peril behind him and narrowing.

'I might have guessed,' he sighed. 'Really, Tash, if you want to attract my attention, you can just say my name.'

The rapacious blonde found this extremely funny. Tash failed to muster a glint of a smile.

'I'm very sorry,' she said as sincerely as she could, even though she was secretly rather pleased with her gaffe. 'Send me the dry cleaning bill.'

'Sure.' He made to turn away, but Tash – spurred by Henrietta's gallant nerve – decided that now was her chance to perform at least one of her duties, however reluctantly.

'I hear you and Zoe have been seeing quite a lot of one another?' she asked without subtlety, wanting to get her promise over and done with.

'Have we?' Hugo turned back unwillingly. 'No more than usual.' He shrugged carelessly.

'Oh.' Tash was rather taken aback. Perhaps he was being cagey. She decided to test the ground.

'She's lovely, isn't she?' she asked, just as Hugo stretched his empty glass towards a very hairy member of Bea Meredith's staff who was dispensing freshly squeezed orange juice from a jug.

Studying the fluffy-chinned woman, Hugo raised an eyebrow as his glass was filled. 'If you say so, Tash,' he said condescendingly.

Tash ploughed on. 'Yes – I mean, she has two teenage kids and a hell of a workload, and yet she still looks so glamorous all the time, and is tirelessly patient and friendly.' She held out her two glasses to the withered, hirsute hag in the white pinny who looked as though she should have been pensioned off at around the time of decimalisation.

Hugo, glasses refilled, lingered on, fascinated by the conversation. Behind him, the blonde had melted away, shooting Tash dirty looks. 'Do you really think so?'

'Of course.' Tash regarded him in mild astonishment, wondering if he saw another, less amiable side to Zoe – perhaps she was a secret sex siren. 'She's also wildly attractive, and she has that cool, blonde charm I'd just kill for,' Tash said ardently. 'I mean, I'm sure a lot of men would just die to be with her.'

His forehead creased, Hugo regarded the hairy waitress again, his face a study of attempted concentration. 'Well, she looks as though she's out-lived a fair few, yes.'

'That's a terrible thing to say!' Tash gasped. 'She looks incredibly young for her age. She's only two years older than Kirsty,' she pointed out indiscreetly.

'Now that *is* bitchy,' he murmured, his eyes dancing with sudden malice. 'I'd almost say you were trying to set me up here, Tash.'

She flushed, realising that she had been as utterly indiscreet as ever – blunderingly steering him to exactly where she had her feet glued into the deepest, stickiest of holes.

She shrugged as coolly as she could and scratched her nose. 'You could do a lot worse.'

Hugo laughed, still staring at her as though she was mad. 'Like what? A positively ancient Scottish event rider?'

Tash squirmed inside her yellow PVC, realising she was nosing far too far into his personal life. But, remembering her promise, she decided to go for broke. For some crazy reason her heart was going ten-fold to the baker's dozen in her chest and her cheeks were starting to flame with colour now. She realised to her amazement that she actually wanted to carry out India's ludicrous instructions.

'I know it's none of my business—'

'Quite,' he snapped.

'—but Kirsty is engaged,' Tash gabbled.

'I know that.' He took a slurp of his drink too quickly, showing a very pink tongue as he licked a drop of juice from his lip. His blue eyes were lapping hers up, one moment icily angry, the next conceitedly amused. Suddenly, he looked at her very worriedly, his head tipping forward so that his voice could drop to a breath and still be heard. 'Do you think I should give her up?'

Tash was slightly disturbed by the gravity of his question, but felt that it was a distinct moment of breakthrough on India's behalf.

'Well, I think it would be best for her sake,' she replied carefully. 'I mean, she stands to get really hurt if this goes on much longer. Richie is coming over to stay next month, after all.'

'Right – yes, so true.' He nodded earnestly, seeming to absorb this. 'I can see that. You really do have her best interests at heart, don't you, Tash?'

Tash didn't like the way he said that. And a flicker in his eyes startled her – they were like the flint sparks of a gas hob waiting for ignition. She had seen just that look before and knew for certain that it preceded an explosion of such velocity that she'd lose her eyebrows.

'I just thought—' she bleated, desperate to back-track and explain.

'And may I say how flattered I am that you take such a keen interest in my love life,' Hugo continued, his voice as icy as Sophia's champagne. 'To the point of trying to involve yourself in it directly by sending me a Valentine's card plastered with semi-nude pictures of yourself.'

'But that was a mistake—' Tash felt herself burning under an instant blush of mortification as she realised what he was saying and how loudly he was saying it. Niall was just yards away.

'Which I have to thank you for, incidentally,' he stormed on, 'as it's caused great amusement amongst my staff who've pinned it to the tack-room wall.'

'Oh, God!' Tash covered her eyes in shame. 'It wasn't—'

'But as I haven't the slightest interest in you sexually, darling,' he hissed, his voice again dropping to a snarl that only she could hear, 'I suggest you butt out and leave me alone before I ask Niall to prise you off.' He grinned maliciously. 'And I shouldn't imagine he'd be too pleased to hear how your affections wander so rampantly while he's away filming his little pics, would he?'

With that, he turned on his heel and left her mouthing at thin air like a trumpeter who's suddenly found his instrument whipped away.

'Tash darling!' Alexandra raced in from the left, bangles jangling. 'Henrietta and I have just been planning everything down to the last T. I think the reception flowers should be all white and buckets of rustic corn-structure things to represent your vocation, don't you? Have you been having a nice chat with Hugo? I heard Niall asked him to be an usher earlier today.'

'He did?' Tash asked weakly.

'Yes – Hugo seemed delighted. Said he'd always wanted to tell your family exactly where to go.'

Eleven

IN VERY HIGH DUDGEON, Matty was not talking to Sally at all. He was horrified that she had even met up with Lisette again, let alone taken a job with her behind his back. Within minutes of the revelation, he had packed all the children into the car and was waiting sulkily in it, listening to Any Questions on the radio at full blast.

Sally had two more drinks and did another circuit of the room to irritate him.

James had been hitting the red wine more often than he should have done because Emily was driving them all back to Berkshire later (she liked driving the Jag to these occasions because her step-father always got so pissed that he fell asleep and failed to notice the fact she was doing over a ton in the fast lane for most of the return journey).

He was also drinking too much because he found the family that his older daughter had married into intimidating. A Calvinist corporate achiever who had worked eighty-hour weeks throughout his thirties and forties to enjoy the benefits of an affluent life, he was continually aware of his own inadequacies – particularly his failure to be knighted, which always irked him. He was immensely proud of Sophia's progress, of her position and standing, yet found himself increasingly in her shadow nowadays. She was a gossip-column regular, whilst he very occasionally made it into the business pages. As the sternest of father figures, this unsettled him. He was aware of her continuing respect, her uncompromising love of him, but her aristocratic marriage and title tainted this. And her stuffy, stand-offish in-laws – particularly

Ben's terrifying mother, Bea, and deaf, barking father, Henry – made him feel about twelve. They were amazed and 'charmed' that he still had to work for a living. James, who ran one of the most successful venture capital institutions in the City, didn't want to charm people, he wanted to frighten them. This haughty, haw-haw world, although alluring and in many ways enviable, was not his own. He could sneer all he liked when he was away from it, but when he was confronted with it, as now, it made him feel left out.

He was therefore rather staggered that they all appeared to take to Niall so easily – his big-hearted charm and loud, riotous humour delighting them, his star-status exciting them. James was continually astonished that everything was so easy for this Irish braggart, just because he was good-looking, way out and gilded with that elixir of popularity – fame. They even seemed more willing to accept Tash by association. James had once been ashamed of his younger daughter; now he was appalled and angered to find himself jealous of her too. Her recent snub about not being given away by him – a topic he himself was aware of bringing up in a fit of petty spite – served to compound his niggling irritation with her. He was itching to air his animosity. And he was now very drunk.

They were gathered by the door as Tash and Niall made to leave – Sophia and Henrietta talking weddings, Alexandra and Ben talking holidays, and Tash and Niall talking cars. All spoke at once in a cacophony of noise – deep, light, husky and sharp voices all fighting for air space like multifarious plane engines at an airshow. Only Emily and Beccy, now bored to oblivion by the whole proceedings, kept silent. Lurching up with a full glass of red wine, James cut across them all.

'So – you're getting hitched at last, Tash,' he said forcefully, fighting not to slur his words. 'Wondered when we'd finally palm you off on some poor sod.'

Tash, hardened to his scorn, took a while to realise quite how sarcastic he was being; Niall was far too drunk to notice.

'Still, runt of the litter's always the last to go,' he muttered, patting her quite heavily on the back. 'Shame you've landed yourself with a chap who flirts with all the pretty women in the room, but I suppose that's part of the deal with this celebrity caper. I just hope he plays around a long way from home – these actor types all seem rather indiscreet.'

'James!' Alexandra was horrified. 'What are you saying?'

'Just saying she won't keep him faithful, that's all.' James shrugged, instantly realising that his hurt and anger had propelled him too far, but equally unwilling to repent and apologise. 'I mean, the chap's already been married once. And with all these actress totties around, he's hardly likely to want to come home to fat little Tash every night.' His eyes were focused in the middle-distance, still seeing the chubby toddler, superimposed with her adult face.

'For Christ's sake, James!' Alexandra snapped, looking to Henrietta for support. But she was gazing at the floor in shame, unwilling to move for fear of making things worse.

Sophia was still gassing on about the need for a matron of honour, unaware that no one was listening to her. Giggling with repressed delight at their step-father's drunken ire, Emily and Beccy shot furtive glances at one another. Beside Tash, Niall was looking mildly confused but uncomprehending, his main focus of attention still concentrated on a dud lighter with which he was trying to light the cigarette that dangled from his mouth. Ben, who had been wandering around with a bottle of champagne to refill glasses, cleared his throat noisily and examined a nearby oil painting as though seeing it for the first time.

Tash was mortified. Backing away, she felt a lump the size of a house brick gag her breath as the inevitable tears started to clog her vision. It was as though someone had kneed her hard in the chest; she could barely breathe, her lungs aflame.

'Don't take offence, Tash,' her father said almost amiably, his eyes fighting to focus on her as he swayed to one side. 'Just stating a few facts.'

'Is that really what you think of me?' she croaked, barely able to see him for the scalding well of tears. 'And of Niall?' She glanced towards him for support, but he had wandered off to cadge a light now, drunkenly approaching various of Ben's relatives.

'Don't be ridiculous,' her father snapped gruffly, trying to muster a laugh to gloss over his explosion. 'I just think you might have bitten off more than you can chew, poppet.'

'I see.' Her voice warbled ludicrously, as though limbering up for a yodel. 'In that case, I think I should spit something out fast. You *are* going to give me away after all, Daddy.' She wiped away her tears furiously as she glared at him. 'Forget what I said earlier. When Niall and I get hitched you can fulfil a lifetime's ambition – my lifetime to be precise. Because for every bloody second of it you've wanted to give me away and now you've got your chance. Sorry that it's twenty-seven years too late, but it's the best give-away offer you'll get all summer!'

Blindly, she tore away from the group and ran slap into Bea Meredith whose glass spun to the floor and shattered into smithereens.

'For Christ's sake, you great clumsy girl – that was Waterford!' she boomed.

Sobbing, Tash sprinted with streaming eyes along a side hall to the huge landing and then threw herself down the vast, ornate marble stairs two at a time.

Coming the other way, Hugo flattened himself against a mahogany banister and watched in alarm. As Tash passed him, she tripped blindly and almost fell down the last ten steps. Hugo grabbed her arm just in time, ripping the cheap yellow fabric to the shoulder where it gaped like a peeled banana.

'You okay?' he asked gruffly, then, taking in her tear-stained face, he looked genuinely worried. 'What's happened?'

'I'm fine,' Tash croaked in a strangled wail. 'Just throwing myself at you as ever, Hugo – and trying to get you to rip my clothes off me. Looks like it worked, huh?'

With that, she bolted off, sobbing even more loudly, her humiliation never more complete.

Racing outside for refuge, she found herself in the dusty Renault in embarrassingly close vicinity to her brother, who was still sulking in the Audi parked alongside, waiting for the errant Sally to join him, Any Answers blaring loudly. Thankfully he was buried in Umberto Eco and didn't look up, only moving when Jonathan Dimbleby started asking for comments on divorce statistics, when he cranked up the volume even more.

Smoking two cigarettes on the trot and feeling sick as a result, Tash waited ten minutes by which time she could see again, although her eyes were as puffy and raw as two fresh scalds from an iron.

She craned around to look for signs of Niall, but he was nowhere. Far from leaping to her defence, he appeared to be still partying with the enemy. She scrutinised the grand stone steps up to Holdham's gaping entrance for movement.

For a moment, her heart leaped with relief as she saw a tall, dark man swooping out in true romantic hero style, and then it plummeted towards the rubber floor mats as she realised who it was.

She shrank down in her seat as Hugo stomped outside, protected from the cold by a vast coat he appeared to have borrowed, banging his hands together for warmth and breathing out in great gusts. It lent him the wildly romantic look of a bygone Russian prince, hair flopping over his straighter than straight nose, collar turned up to his ears against the chill. Tash longed for a revolutionary Bolshevik to pop out from behind a bay tub and cosh him. Instead he strode towards his car unchecked, his breath clouding in front of him like a ghost indulging in a secret kiss.

For a moment she thought that he was going to drive home, but he merely unlocked his car with an electronic tweet, took out some fags and wandered back into the house again. Tash let out her trapped breath, relieved that he hadn't spotted her.

Niall had now failed to come in search of her for over quarter of an hour. Tash started to snivel again. Perhaps her father was right – he was probably glad to be rid of her and flirting like mad with some of Sophia's glamorous modelling cronies. Starting the engine with an elongated, throaty rattle, she reversed sharply out of her parking space, nearly ploughing down Ben's great-aunt who furiously tried to scrape the side of the Renault with her Zimmer frame. Tash accelerated down the long, shadowy drive in a flurry of gravel, forgetting to put on her headlights and consequently flattening two pheasants and a rat.

The air between Matty and Sally had no time to clear.

When he discovered that Tash had left without him, Niall begged a lift as far as London, planning to take the train on to Marlbury from there. Sally was booted into the back with the kids who sprawled loose-limbed and exhausted across her, unaware of the adults being childish overhead. Matty wanted to listen to Radio 4, Niall demanded Radio 1 and Sally put in a bid for Radio 2 just to be churlish. Matty wanted the windows closed, Niall open; he wanted to chain-smoke, Matty protested as a recent non-smoker; Matty thought the motorways would be the fastest way home, Niall preferred the scenic route. Sally suggested that they all get out and walk to save time. At least the children slept throughout, which eased her tension. And by the time they had passed Banbury on the M40, Niall was asleep too, his head flopping back between the seat and the passenger window so that Sally had a lapful of his hair and a bird's-eye view of his nose quivering under each breath.

'Poor sod's knackered.' Matty broke his silence momentarily as he looked across at Niall. 'Should we really drop him off at Paddington, d'you think, or bring him back with us for a sleep and a clean up?'

'Paddington,' Sally muttered, staring out at the strobe-like flashes of passing street-lights. 'He and Tash have so little time together as it is.'

'Would have had a damn sight more if she'd driven him home,'

Matty hissed, before resuming his stony silence for the remainder of the journey.

Sally pressed her face to her daughter's sleeping head and wished that she had told Matty about going to Hugo's party earlier. She'd have to lie now. There was no way he'd forgive her for a wild night out with Lisette.

Niall didn't make it to Marlbury until past nine that night. His mobile phone was out of charge and no taxis were waiting in the small rank to one side of the station. Shivering in a phone box that smelled of stale urine, he called the forge. No one answered and after about twenty rings the machine came on with Tash's cheerful breathy voice announcing that she was out. His name was no longer included, he noticed, which he supposed was fair as he was so seldom there.

Niall pressed Call Continue and dialled through to the farm, guessing that she would have poled up there for white wine, warmth and sympathy.

India answered, sounding startlingly like her mother, and shouted loudly for the radio to be silenced, deafening Niall far more than if it had been left pounding in the background.

'Sorry about that – it's Rufus's shitty music. Are you at the forge with Tash?'

'No, I'm at the station. Isn't she with you?'

'Nope.' India giggled, clearly mouthing his side of the conversation on to an interested party. 'Ted's hopping mad because he needed his car for a hot date with Franny's fangs tonight, and you haven't brought it back.'

'But I'm at the station.' Niall sighed, realising that Tash wasn't there. He was so tired that it was taking minutes for even the simplest facts to sink in.

'D'you mean the car broke down?' India giggled even more, always nervous when talking to Niall. 'Do you two need a lift or something?'

'No – there's just me . . .' He went quiet for a moment as he heard his predicament being discussed in the background before there was a series of loud clunks and muffled expletives as the phone changed hands.

'Niall, it's Zoe – what's going on?'

He repeated his rather foggy explanation, adding, 'Listen, if she's not there, I'll get a cab over from here. She's probably at home not answering the phone. She was a wee bit upset earlier, so she was.'

'She's not at home, Niall,' Zoe sighed. 'Ted walked over to your place about half an hour ago to search for his car and it was in darkness. He left a note for her to come straight round here when she gets back, so I'm sure she will.'

'Christ!' Niall watched the units ticking down in front of him and slotted in another twenty pence. 'Where on earth can she be?' He was seriously worried now.

'Well, let's not discuss it over the phone,' Zoe said practically, never one to waffle. 'I'll come and pick you up.'

The Lime Tree Farm kitchen was as welcoming as Niall had ever known it: messy, warm, full of people, dogs and cats, and smelling pungently of one of Zoe's odd-ball curries.

Rufus and Ted were at the table giggling over India's glossy magazines, Penny was filling in entry forms at the opposite end of the table, and Gus was slumped on the dogs' sofa with Wally and Beetroot asleep on his lap watching Alien on the ancient black and white portable by the dishwasher.

'Hi, mate.' He stood up, tipping the dogs on to the floor where they sleepily shook themselves and peered at the newcomer, their tails wagging tentatively as they eyed up who it was. 'Sorry to be all piled in here – we're cutting down on fuel so the sitting room is freezing.'

Wally had slunk over to Niall now, head dropped in obsequious greeting. Behind him Beetroot – who, to Niall, seemed to have doubled in size and become exquisitely pretty – bared her teeth and backed off hurriedly.

'Hi, Niall.' Penny squinted up over her glasses and blew him a kiss. 'Have a beer and sit down. Will you shift one of those cats, kids?'

India obligingly booted a fat marmalade farm cat from a wicker chair and kissed Niall hello before heading to the fridge to fetch him a beer.

'Actually I'd far rather have a coffee, if that's okay?' Niall was squinting with tiredness. 'So none of you've heard from Tash then?'

They shrugged apologetically, but no one seemed unduly worried, apart from Ted.

'She's stolen my motor!' he wailed in anguish. 'The old bitch. Now I won't get a shag tonight, because Franny's decided to go and see the latest Keanu Reeves flick in Marlbury instead of coming with me to Xcess in Newbury.' He gazed threateningly at Niall as though it was entirely his fault. With his squaddie haircut, he looked surprisingly menacing and Niall quailed slightly.

Zoe settled on the sofa beside Gus and smiled apologetically. She was wearing a perfectly ancient cardigan of Penny's which had no buttons left and cuffs as frayed as raffia, and her jeans were a mosaic of patches. Yet such was her sanguine sophistication that she still looked like Princess Diana heading to a late-night hostel undercover.

'So how was Scotland, Niall?' she asked tentatively. She'd asked the question several times in the car on the way back from the station, but he had merely gazed through the windscreen into the mid-distance, lost in thought.

'Cold and wet.' He smiled vaguely, about to tell her more, when Rufus butted in excitedly.

'Do you really get to snog Juliet Richards *and* Minty Blyth in this film you're making?' he asked, almost beside himself with envy.

'Yup.'

'And do they both get their kits off?' Rufus was agog with jealous admiration. 'Tash says Juliet's got silicone boobs – do they feel different from real ones?'

For the next hour, Niall tried hard to respond to the endless questions and enthusiasm of the Lime Tree contingent, but he was far too whacked, hungover and concerned about Tash's non-appearance to make much sense, or follow conversations to their logical conclusions. He found himself asking Penny twice whether they'd been competing that day, to be told twice that the first affiliated trials were the following weekend, and he repeated the same story about Minty Blyth's stalker three times.

'Can I call the forge again?' he asked.

'Sure.' Penny shrugged, having finally tucked all her entry forms into envelopes and settled back with Gus and the snoring dogs to watch Sigourney Weaver running around with a flame gun.

Niall wandered out to use the phone in the chilly, darkened study, but simply got Tash's voice on the machine again. He waited through to the beep and asked her to pick up the phone several times, but it was obvious she wasn't there. Dropping the phone back into the cradle, he stooped to the floor to pat Wally, who had followed him through – ever the one to suck up to a new arrival. In the silent gloom, he could just hear them talking about him in hushed voices in the kitchen.

Niall slumped against the desk, numbly letting Wally's warm tongue lap against his cold, stubbled cheeks. Sober now, he recalled only too vividly how Tash's despotic father had baited her in front of her entire family and he had just lolled around silently and stupidly in the background, neither defending her nor really caring to take in what was happening, so swamped was he in his own self-pity and self-doubt. He suddenly, rather manically, wondered if she was seeking comfort from someone else right now. His stomach seethed at the thought.

He buried his face in his hands and listened to the sound of the news drumming its way on to the screen in the kitchen as Alien took a break for light relief with Trevor McDonald and the latest on Eastern Europe.

'You okay?' Zoe's soft voice pervaded the room at far closer range.

She hovered by the door, about to turn on the light, but changed her mind and looked at him worriedly through the gloom. Wally, his loyalty divided, crawled on his belly halfway to her and then lay there like a stretched-out frog, chin resting on his forepaws, the whites of his brown eyes gleaming up at her in the dark.

'Well, it wouldn't take a genius to answer that now, would it?' Niall's voice was muffled by his hands before he pulled himself together, ran his fingers back through his dirty hair and looked up at her sadly.

'Want another coffee?'

He shook his head. 'Where the hell d'you think she's got to, Zoe?'

She shrugged. 'My guess is that clapped-out old banger of Ted's has croaked somewhere between here and Worcestershire and the poor darling is hanging around garages and exhaust centres sorting it out – or fighting her way back here via BR which, as you know, could take till next week.'

Niall nodded, only half seeming to believe it.

'You two had a row?' Zoe asked cautiously.

Niall rubbed his nose with the back of his hand and cocked his head thoughtfully. 'Not a row exactly, no.' He bit his lip. 'But I think I let her down badly today.'

Zoe was silent for a few moments, waiting for him to offer more information, which he didn't. She wanted to ask him to talk to her about it, certain that he had a lot he wanted to get off his chest right now, but she didn't feel it was her place. She didn't know him that well, or feel particularly impartial and objective where he was concerned – especially when it came to Tash. As one of Tash's confidantes, she would feel simply awful if he told her something which compromised their friendship, something which she felt she had to keep secret.

Niall was still silent, staring into the corner of the room. In the dim light from the hall, Zoe could see how pale and hollow his cheeks were, and the tight, knotted tension in the muscles of his jaw.

She started to back away.

'Do you think Tash would ever be unfaithful, Zoe?' he suddenly asked.

'Tash?' Zoe almost laughed, just stopping herself in time. 'Are you serious?'

'Of course I'm fucking serious!' He looked up at her sharply, his voice very low and utterly chilly. 'I wouldn't be asking you if I wasn't serious.'

Zoe flinched. It was the first time she had ever known the congenial, almost comically easy-going Niall to be angry and the transition from domestic pet to untamed predator was so total, it unnerved her.

'No, she never would,' she said, her voice shaking slightly. 'Never – I promise you, Niall.'

'You covering for her?' he snapped, his eyes narrowed as they squinted up at her through the shadows.

'No!'

'Sure.' He looked away dismissively. 'Cover her face; mine lies dazzle.'

When Tash finally let herself into the forge, it was in complete darkness apart from the red half-light of dying embers in the fire. She knew that Niall was inside because the post that she had been in too much of a hurry to pick up that morning was no longer underfoot, and the place smelled wonderfully of burning logs and coffee, but he made no move to greet her. As she closed the door quietly behind her, she was also aware that there was a strange stillness because Beetroot was still at the farm, not wriggling around her feet to welcome her.

'Niall?' She groped for the light switch but, her eyes adjusting to the gloom, spotted his shape slumped in the tattiest armchair just before she hit it.

'Niall?' She tip-toed through the dim room, now hearing his low, steady breathing.

He was fast asleep, a three-quarters empty bottle of John Power beside him. He must have bought it from the Olive Branch, she realised – Niall was forever complaining that it was the only Irish whiskey they stocked, although Ange did try to buy in a bottle of Bushmills whenever he knew that Niall was visiting.

When a few gentle nudges failed to rouse him, Tash threw the spare duvet over him, put up the fire-guard and crept upstairs alone.

Niall finally rose at midday – six hours after Tash had woken. He was still craggy with sleepiness and complaining loudly of a monumental hangover, but he didn't chew her out immediately for rushing away from the christening as she had anticipated. Instead he made coffee, moaned about the mess and, putting on two of Tash's jumpers which were hanging on the rail above the Rayburn, set about lighting a fire.

Tash hovered awkwardly in the tiny kitchen recess, wondering whether she should set to doing something loving and wifely like heating up croissants and squeezing oranges. But she had neither the enthusiasm nor the ingredients. In a fit of Flab-busters zest, she had packed the fridge with nothing but cottage cheese and salad. Somehow she had a feeling that Niall's hangover was compatible with neither.

When the fire was at last smoking into the tiny room like Bet Gilroy at the breakfast table of the Rovers Return, Niall retreated to the desk in the corner by the garden window and squared up to a pile of post as high as the table lamp. He had barely spoken a word to her and now he bore a look of such studied, angry concentration that the silence ached on.

Unable to bear the tension any longer, and guiltily aware that it was she who should really break it with an apology, Tash grabbed her purse and fled out of the door to the village shop.

It wasn't a wise move. Denise Angelo, the svelte, giggling landlady of the Olive Branch, was in there chatting to Godfrey Pelham, the gay ex soapstar who ran the little post office stores in his retirement as though it was Harrods Food Hall, with row upon row of exotic muesli, sun-dried tomatoes, olive purée and parma ham, but no Spam or Heinz in sight.

'Tash darling!' He fell upon her excitedly. 'I hear your gorgeous chap is in the village again. *Quelle* excitement – will you be having lunch in the pub?'

'I doubt it.' Tash scrunched up her face apologetically and picked up a basket.

'I quite understand,' Godfrey soothed happily. 'Still in bed, is he? Bet you've just popped in for some biscuits to keep your energy levels up.'

'Something like that.' Tash threw some Hobnobs into her basket to keep him happy.

'Niall popped into the pub last night,' Denise told her conspiratorially, as though she was a private detective imparting vital information. 'He looked awfully tired. Said you were too whacked to come out for a drink.'

'He's been working very hard on location.' Tash smiled weakly and headed for the breakfast cereals section which was tucked away from sight behind the upright fridge display.

'Ah, yes, location work is always the most draining!' Godfrey sympathised knowingly. 'All that hanging around in the cold, no decent canteen, desperately early starts – ghastly! I loathed it.'

'Good job you hardly did any then.' Denise giggled. 'Most of your scenes took place at that hospital canteen that wobbled when the door opened, didn't they?'

Godfrey sniffed sulkily. 'Well, of course, Niall does more work on seventy-five mil than I ever did.'

'Is that his fee these days!' Denise gasped in awe.

'It's a technical term,' Godfrey said witheringly. 'Isn't it, Tash sweetie?'

She was too busy reading the sugar content on a box of muesli to take this in.

When she re-emerged from behind the fridge, Godfrey and Denise were exchanging 'rude little madam' looks which they instantly changed to expressions of delighted rapture as Tash headed towards the fruit display.

'You two named the day yet, have you?' Denise simpered.

She looked up vaguely. 'It's Sunday, I think.'

Denise gave her an odd look before realising the mistake. She sensibly didn't pursue the matter further.

'Well, I must be getting back to the pub – we're booked out.' She cleared her throat. 'And Ange will be going spare without his pepper.' She rattled a bag of pepper corns at Tash to emphasise her point. 'Six ounces here for the price of a pound at the wholesaler's,' she tutted, stalking out.

'Blame the local Tesco's superstore!' Godfrey yelled after her huffily before turning his full attention on Tash for some second-hand industry gossip.

Tash couldn't be bothered with his bitchy, slightly derisive interest right now. She paid for the few things in her basket and wandered up to the farm to collect Beetroot, who was ecstatic to see her.

'Have you and Niall patched things up?' Zoe asked hopefully when she arrived.

Tash shrugged.

'Go back there and talk to him, huh?' Zoe squeezed her arm. 'He was in a terrible state last night – seemed to have convinced himself you were having an affair or something.'

'You're joking?'

She shook her head seriously. 'Get back there, Tash, and *talk* to him. He's so desperately insecure right now.'

Tash bolted back to the forge as though starting from blocks and burst in through the door.

'The car conked out – it took ages to get it towed and all the pay phones were . . .' she started to gabble before she realised that Niall was on the phone speaking in a hushed voice.

He hung up the moment he saw her, almost seeming to jump out of his skin with fright.

'Sorry,' Tash panted, grinning happily. 'You didn't need to do that – I'd have shut up.'

He grinned awkwardly. 'It was only Bob, so it was, you did me a favour. What were you saying?'

'Sorry, basically.' She bit her lip. 'For dashing off without an explanation yesterday and then not trying hard enough to get through – I honestly thought I'd be back here hours before I made it.'

'I'm sorry too.' He stood up and walked towards her, arms outstretched. 'For getting drunk and not standing up for you. Truth is, your family frighten me a little.'

'Me too.' Tash went into his arms, trying to ignore Beetroot growling jealously below. 'D'you still want to get hitched into the French mob?'

'Sure do.' He kissed her neck very gently, aware that his stubble was scratching her. 'Now, how can I persuade you to come up to Scotland next weekend?'

Tash sighed. 'I'm competing in Gloucestershire.'

'Afterwards?'

She wasn't keen, but she knew he would be hurt if she told him so. She found film sets terrifying, most of all because he did so little to help her out when she visited him there, simply assuming she'd love everyone in the cast as much as he did even though she'd never met them before. 'I'll see what Penny and Gus say.'

'Well, I'll ask them now, shall I?' Niall bounced back to the phone, suddenly as excited as Tigger told he was going on a picnic.

Tash paced around as he phoned the farm, inwardly groaning when Gus answered, not Zoe.

Moments later, Niall was doing enthusiastic thumbs up signs at Tash while at the same time apologising to Gus for being a bit off form the night before.

'Well, that's settled.' He grinned as he hung up. 'You can drive straight up to Scotland after the trials. Gus says he'll be glad to give us a break together.'

'What exactly will I drive up in?' Tash asked worriedly, her heart sinking at the thought of all those intimidating film types. She doubted Ted would lend her his Renault again.

'Ah, well, I'm going to buy you a car tomorrow morning.' Niall gripped her hand and started to lead her upstairs. 'Which only gives us about twelve hours in bed.'

Following him up, Tash started to laugh. He was just impossible to resist sometimes.

'I said I didn't want you to buy me a car, Niall,' she protested rather half-heartedly as he pulled her into the bedroom.

'Ah, but I insist.' He gave her a mock-serious look. 'I'm going to get you a little run-around so that you no longer give me the run-around.'

Twelve

TASH WAS OVER TWENTY minutes late for her next Flab-busters session. The drive there was a nightmare.

Niall had an impossibly impractical and romantic taste in cars. This did not involve souped-up boy-racers, classic Bentleys or little sports numbers straight out of The Avengers; his taste was far too subtle and eccentric for that. He had a vision of Tash behind the wheel of one car, and one car only – a sixties Citroën DS *décapotable*. Huge, angular and waspish, Tash's new motor was considered by those in the know to be a classic design icon. Most people, however – including Tash – thought it an ugly, noisy eyesore.

She had seen the car before in movies – Jean-Paul Belmondo had smouldered behind the wheel of one during an off-beat French road movie which Niall was particularly keen on (he had made her stay up until the early hours a year before to catch it on Channel 4).

'I know it's an ugly-looking bugger,' he enthused, 'but you have to admit, it has character in spades.'

'Ace of spades, perhaps.' Tash was certain it was a potential death-trap.

Niall seemed to have bought the rarest and tattiest one in West Berkshire – possibly the country, Tash suspected, from the odd looks she received whilst driving it. His purchase was not as lovingly and immaculately restored as the advert had promised. With its dull red paintwork and splitting, dusty leather upholstery, it looked more like an ancient mini-cab than a design classic; when first getting into the driver's seat, Tash expected to catch a whiff of chicken biryani or doner kebab, and to look in the rear-view mirror at a nauseous drunk asking to be taken to Camden Palace via a cashpoint. Niall enthused about the ground-breaking hydraulic system, the exaggerated lines, the gloriously Thunderbirds dash, the throaty cough of the engine. Gazing at the car, he was terrifyingly like Jeremy Clarkson on Ecstasy. Tash only wished that he occasionally looked at her like that.

Some of Niall's enthusiasm had initially rubbed off on her, however. She was immensely grateful for the gift, if slightly embarrassed by his generosity.

'Call it an engagement ring,' he'd said, and kissed her on the nose.

Tash supposed she was the only girl with an engagement ring that was bigger than she was, and which could do ninety downhill with the wind behind it. Or which fell apart quite so regularly.

In the three days since she had taken delivery of the DS, it had broken down twice, refused to start numerous times and failed to brake on one alarming occasion. And, as it was such a complicated 'design classic', there was only one mechanic within a fifty-mile radius who would touch it. The local garage threw up their arms in horror when Gus towed it to them. They had then gathered around the low-slung car like builders around a brazier, afraid to get too close yet magnetically drawn towards the red monster.

'You don't see many of those,' they'd clucked admiringly, as though gawping at a page three model. Then, after a good nose under the bonnet and a few circuits around the chassis, they'd refused to touch it.

Instead, Tash had waded through the Yellow Pages to discover that the only expert in classic Citroëns lived the other side of Reading and cost over one hundred pounds to call out. She had called him out several times already. Niall's present was proving extremely expensive to run and Tash was now quashing the ungrateful wish that he'd just bought her an old Fiesta run-around. Or a ring.

Two days later, Tash and Snob competed in their first trials of the season. They were held at the very grand country seat of an impoverished Gloucestershire landowner who was an old family friend of Hugo's. As such, Hugo occasionally boxed up his novices and drove them down the M4 to pound around the trials course during his spring training schedule. This was done on the understanding that Hugo would not be competing on the same horses at the trials, and that a case of claret would arrive on the landowner's doorstep as a thank you. In fact, Hugo always competed the same horses at the trials, and had won at least one section each year.

This year he surpassed himself by winning three of the four sections that day. His two top horses – Bodybuilder and Surfer – were already as fit as Grand National contenders, their muscles packed as tightly as fish in a Spanish trawler's net beneath the muted gloss of their clipped coats. The vast, athletic Bodybuilder was looking so unbeatable that he was instantly an odds-on favourite for Badminton. Seventeen hands of barely controlled black power, he had been with Hugo since he was a two year old and they possessed an almost telepathic understanding. Watching them was a hypnotic experience – the fluid, balletic grace and control of their dressage belied the titanic explosion of energy which took place later across country as they smoked over the muddy, pitted fields of the estate like medieval heralds trying to stop a battle.

Equally, Surfer – a nervy, ribby liver-chestnut with the worried eyes of a battered wife and a wiry, twisting ability to jump anything, however bad the stride – wiped all the competition aside in his own class. He was almost as impressive as Bodybuilder, but it was the big, unruly black thug whom Hugo really adored. Some of his more churlish, resentful rivals claimed that the bad-tempered black horse was the only thing in the world Hugo loved more than himself.

'Probably because they have so much in common,' sighed Lucy Field, a top female rider who knew Hugo of old. 'They're both mad, bad, and dangerous to say no to.'

'Hugo was offered three million for that horse before the last Olympics,' Kirsty told her proudly. 'But he turned it down flat.'

There were mass grumblings amongst the eventing community that Hugo dominated so much of the day's action, but it was generally agreed that, despite the advantage he held, he was on cracking form.

'Better than bloody ever,' Gus sighed as he watched Hugo collecting a vast blue and red rosette from a terrified local mayoress whose court shoes had firmly plugged her into the soft ground beside the twitching, hot-headed Bodybuilder.

Tash sat grumpily in the cab of the Lime Tree horse-box, swigging lukewarm tea from a plastic beaker and nursing her pride. Overexcited, overfresh and stronger than ever this year, Snob had towed her around the course at full throttle, finally dispensing with her services at the lake which he had decided to steer around instead of pound through. Tash had not actually fallen in the water but into the thick quagmire of mud and hoof marks on the take-off side, coating herself with mud so that she now looked like Will Carling after a particularly hefty tackle from Jonah Lomu.

'You were right to retire him.' Penny clambered into the box beside her. 'He went totally through the bit – I've never seen you struggling so much to hold him.'

Tash slouched into the ragged seat and gnawed uneasily at a cuticle.

'D'you think I'll be able to bring him back?'

'Well,' Penny looked sceptical, 'we could try him in a different bit again.' She didn't sound very hopeful.

'But . . .'

'We'll see.' Penny patted her muddy leg. 'It's early days. Lots of schooling ahead, I think.'

Tash knew that Penny wasn't optimistic. It had happened many times before to her and other female eventers – a bold, boisterous horse who was simply too strong for his rider. As they matured and grew in confidence, so they tested their strength in an enthusiastic battle to go faster and get ahead, thinking that now they were so good at it, they could dictate the pace. Changing bits and schooling endlessly could help to a certain extent, but often the only way to cure the problem was to sell the horse to a bigger, stronger male rider. And Tash knew exactly who was waiting in the Angel Gabriel wings as far as Snob was concerned.

She listlessly helped Ted rug and boot up Snob and the other horses ready to be boxed up to travel back to the farm.

'You not coming with us then?' He watched as she untangled a pile of thick woollen bandages. 'I wanted you to cut my hair again tonight.'

She shook her head. 'I'm driving up to Scotland to see Niall.' She wrinkled her nose at the prospect. 'He can't get away from filming, so he wants me to go there instead – meet everyone.'

'Lucky you,' he sighed enviously. 'I'd love to meet Juliet Richards.'

'Funny, I don't feel quite the same enthusiasm.' Tash scratched Snob's nose. She'd far rather go back home with the Lime Tree team, have a bath and get some sleep so that she could start some flat-work with Snob at first light the next day.

Thinking this, she scratched a muddy leg dispiritedly and wished she could freshen up.

If she had asked, Tash was certain that Hugo's landowner friend would have been only too willing to let her use one of his huge, chilly bathrooms. But she was too proud, and very eager to avoid Hugo's gloating presence right now. Instead, she made valiant attempts at a flannel wash in the living quarters of the horse-box but, as it was a one-day event, Ted hadn't filled the box's water supply up fully, and what was there was icy cold. Her progress was further hampered by Gus, Penny and Ted thundering in and out of the box to collect pieces of tack, schedules, jumpers and, when it started raining, their waxed jackets.

Finally, as the last horse was clattering into the box behind her, Tash gave up trying to get herself any cleaner. Her face was now pretty much mud-free, although her hair was looking suspiciously ratty and her finger-nails were lined with grit.

Listening to the horses shifting and blowing on the other side of the wooden partition, Tash threw on the velvet trouser suit that Niall liked and jumped out just as the ramp was heaved up with a clank.

'Are you sure you'll be all right in that car?' Gus looked anxiously at the now very muddy red Citroën which had caused much hilarity amongst other eventers that day.

'Fine – it was pretty good on the way here. And I'm now a member of the AA.'

'Stands for Anxiously Awaiting, in your case.' Penny kissed her on the cheek. 'Have a great time – give our love to the old bugger.'

'Thanks.' Tash could feel homesickness and trepidation already curling her toes and twisting her stomach into a knot of anxiety.

She and the car both bumped their way out of the parking field, unwilling to tackle the journey ahead.

Niall's hotel was an isolated old hunting lodge beside a small loch. Tash and the design classic had considerable difficulty winding their way around the perilously narrow, precipice-sided lanes towards it in the dark. At one point, they nearly flattened a sheep that wandered across the road in front of them, vacuous eyes a luminous blue in the headlamps.

'Like Hugo's,' Tash muttered malevolently as she swerved to avoid it.

The car had drunk three tanksfull of petrol on the journey and it was almost three in the morning by the time Tash turned into the broad drive in front of the lodge. She was drained, haggard, freezing cold and shaking from drinking so much service station coffee to keep herself awake. But even so she drew a breath and widened her eyes as she took in the beauty of the place. Set against an oil-spill sky and pitted steel loch, backed up by an anthracite-black forest, it was staggering in its splendour – a higgledy-piggledy medley of pillars, turrets and mullions which should have looked ridiculously twee and faux-Burns. It didn't. Floodlit so that it shone like an old steel blade in the night, it was gloriously real, powerful and slightly frightening.

It was also locked.

Despite the bright floodlights outside, there was only the gloomiest of glows from within, one low-watt bulb in a deep lobby. Tash tapped tentatively on the door and then gave up from nerves. The place seemed absolutely secure and sound asleep.

Huddling her shoulders against the cold, she searched in the dark for a bell. There was none. She wandered around the side of the building, walking straight into a tangled flowerbed from which she had considerable trouble extricating herself. Beyond that she could just make out the expanse of a tufted lawn leading to a stone wall, beyond which stretched the menacing black gleam of the loch.

On the other side of the crumbling lodge, a cloistered stone walkway ran alongside tall mullioned windows through which Tash could just make out a deserted, darkened dining room. Gnarled wooden railings to her right separated her from the loch, from which an icy wind bit into her skin.

She came to an abrupt halt as a chunky, low stone wall appeared from nowhere in front of her, jabbing her in the stomach and blocking her path like the steel of a turnstile. Beyond it appeared to be a cluster of balconies belonging to luxurious bedrooms in the hotel, cluttered with wrought-iron furniture and squat pots of alpine plants. From one, a cigarette end glowed.

Tash froze with sudden, shivering excitement. Someone was smoking a cigarette outside in the freezing cold at three in the morning. There was only one insomniac she knew who would do that.

'Niall?'

Cigarette jettisoned into the loch, he bounded across the walls that separated them, wearing only a pair of cotton underpants and an enormous greatcoat, its collar turned up against the wind.

'I thought you weren't coming.' He closed his damp woollen arms around her and clutched her desperately, a glacially cold cheek pressed to hers.

Tash hugged him back and, despite the vast, scratchy coat, could feel just how skinny he had become recently.

It was only when she coaxed him back into his room that she registered how plastered he was too.

Abstractedly she was taking in the ancient, baronial grandeur of the room, the vast, dark four poster bed, the hunting prints, the velvet curtains as heavy as Medusa's hair. But she barely noticed them as she watched Niall reel around the room, knocking into furniture and tripping over his own unbalanced feet as he fought to welcome her in the manner he drunkenly deemed fit – with a large measure of malt.

'I really don't want any.' Tash tried to dissuade him from his lurching search, desperate to make him sit down and look at her for the first time in weeks.

'Oh – fine.' He reeled on the spot for a few seconds before wandering over to the bed and sitting on it. 'Good journey?'

'Long.' Tash perched beside him as he flopped back on to the bed, one idle hand reaching out to stroke her leg as he gazed, unfocused, at the velvet canopy before closing his eyes.

'That's good,' he mumbled. 'I've got a six o'clock start tomorrow.'

The next moment he was asleep.

Having taken off his shoes and covered him with the quilt, Tash went back outside through the double windows and climbed across several private balconies to fetch her bag from the car.

When she came back into the room, he was curled into a tight knot, the quilt creased and wound around him like a tubigrip. When she tried to slip inside it too, he stiffened his back and arched away.

Feeling utterly rejected, Tash passed a sleepless night on a baronial settee, covered with a blanket she found in the vast wardrobe. It was almost five in the morning when, stiff and riddled with shivers from the cold, she crawled into bed alongside Niall, curling up against him for warmth. He was so still and leaden, it was like trying to cuddle a corpse. Absolutely exhausted, Tash free-fell into deep sleep.

Thirteen

THE NEXT MORNING, NIALL had been collected by his driver to travel to the Celt location shoot long before Tash woke, leaving her a note to explain exactly where they were filming and what time it was best to get there.

Propped up in bed, she squinted across the room at the evidence of his quick exit: a damp towel left on the floor after a hasty shower, a lidless can of deodorant beside her feet on the end of the bed, a rejected pair of socks lying inside-out on a chair, gaping like fledglings' mouths.

The unfamiliar room glared in the steely early-morning light. Heavily panelled with pock-marked oak, filled with dark austere furniture and clustered with macabre hunting prints, it was very grand and very unwelcoming. Cold and lonely, Tash cuddled deeper into the counterpane and squinted across to a broad, squat desk at the far end of the room. Even without her contact lenses in, she could see that it was coated in pages of the film script, call sheets and the copious character notes that Niall made before every job.

In Celt, he was playing a character called MacGinnen – a hell-raising, womanising rebel laird with a heart of gold, who led an eighteenth-century posse of outlawed Catholic Highlanders; a sort of Robin Hood set in Scotland. The whole film was Hollywood-backed and, as Niall openly admitted, historically inaccurate schmaltz. Loosely based around the 1715 rebellion, it was a good excuse for lots of long-shots of beautiful Scottish glens, passionate love-affairs between hairy Scotsmen and fragile French babes, and dramatic sword-clashing battles. According to Niall, the American market – its taste whetted by Braveheart and Rob Roy – couldn't get enough of romantic Scottish epics. He thought the Celt script stank, but he was being paid a lot of money to act in it, and cast and crew were undoubtedly excellent.

This was a world from which Tash felt totally alienated, however hard Niall had tried to persuade her of its prosaic banality. As ever, he had described this project in his pithy, sardonic one-liners, or rambled on about it for hours when he was frustrated and needed to use Tash as a vent. He always talked her through everything he did so that she didn't feel excluded, tried to put faces to the countless unfamiliar names that popped up with every new project – people who became temporary friends and drinking partners, or enemies, or butts of jokes, and then faded away after the wrap party. Tash felt she had a pretty good thumb-nail sketch of those involved and the scale of the project. But close to and faced with the reality of a film in progress, she always felt hopelessly shy and estranged from his working life.

His wake-up note suggested that she roll up around midday, when the shooting of a long fight sequence was due to end and they would break to re-set the cameras for a closer shot. He told her to seek out the third assistant director, Mel, who would point her to the catering truck, Niall's trailer, and some friendly faces. Tash quelled a childish desire to be pointed back to Berkshire.

The day's shooting was taking place on a windswept stretch of Highland moor a few miles away. It was undoubtedly a breathtaking backdrop – a head-spinning mix of heather shag-pile, folding glens, barbed pine forests and distant, snow-tipped peaks jagging up into bleak, grey mist. All were being lashed by a hard, spitting rain that felt like schoolboys throwing pebbles. Half a mile to the left, a sheet-metal loch was being pitted and corrugated by the skin-stripping wind, and overhead the clouds were pressing down as though God was sitting on his suitcase, desperate to pack the contents down further. Savage and romantic, it was a spot guaranteed to get the Americans into their day-glo shorts and over the Atlantic in droves to buy novelty sporrans. Tash wondered if the film had been sponsored by the Scottish Tourist Board. It was the ultimate in product placement

She, however, approached it from a less salubrious angle – behind the camera. Beside a tiny open lane, a muddy area had been cordoned off as the location's base and was teeming with action as well as rain. At the base of a wooded hill, it was relatively sheltered from the wind, and groups of stressed-looking film types were clustered around sipping tea from steaming beakers, huddling beneath the hoods of their brightly coloured kagoules. Dozens of cars had squelched up the ground and were parked beside rows of pantechnicons, caravans and smaller transit vans. To one side was a logo-covered catering lorry with a make-shift tarpaulin cafeteria hitched up to the side of it.

Wheels spinning in the mud, Tash parked the design classic beside a remarkably clean Jaguar and headed towards the tented eatery, wishing she had ignored vanity and put on her wellies as her ankle boots sank so deeply into the wet mud that it seeped inside over the rims.

To her immense relief, Niall was already in there, sitting at a table around which were crammed a large number of assorted eighteenth-century Highlanders, some of whom were incongruously wearing Puffa jackets and waterproofs over their long, muddy plaids and sodden shirts.

He was laughing his head off as he munched his way through an enormous baguette. Bright-eyed and wild-haired, he looked utterly removed from the tortured, drunken soul of the night before.

Tash paused in the gloom of the tented entrance, breathing in the combined smell of cooking, cigarette smoke and damp canvas, a curiously reassuring mix which reminded her of the competitors' tent at large horse trials where she would huddle with the Lime Tree team between phases, listening to the commentary, sipping milky tea and discussing all things equine as Gus nicked her fags.

Niall had polished off his baguette now and was helping himself to the large tag-end of one discarded by his neighbour. Tash caught her breath as she realised it was Minty Blyth, his corkscrew-haired co-star, huddled in a vast waterproof cape and sulkily smoking a Marlboro. Even dressed in scruffy Scottish garb, her glorious hair teased out like a furze bush, her face smudged with mud, she was exquisite – all curves and creamy skin.

As Tash watched her, she looked up, aware of the attention. Tash braved a smile, but Minty had already looked away, assuming she was some minor member of the crew or an extra fascinated by stardom. Turning back to Niall, she listened as he regaled the table with one of his raucous, exaggerated stories which rendered them all tearful with laughter as he hammed it up and acted out all the roles with grand gestures and big theatrical faces.

Tash moved forward, wishing that he would look up and welcome her to save her the embarrassment of general scrutiny as she crept up to tap him on the shoulder.

But he was far too absorbed in his storytelling to notice her. Minty did, however, watching Tash suspiciously from the corner of one big, dark eye, wary of the likelihood of a battered autograph book being thrust into their cosy clique.

As Tash approached the table, one of the assorted kilt-wearers said something that made the rest of them collapse in a delighted howl of riotous laughter. Tash tried not to feel a pang of worry as Niall's head lolled on to Minty's shoulder with familiar ease and he wiped away a tear of joy before stretching across her to extract a cigarette from her packet. Smiling a big, feline smile, Minty seemed totally at home with the gesture. There was something about the easy, tactile way that their bodies made contact which unzipped Tash's chest with jealousy and she had mentally to slap herself down for being so suspicious.

Squelching up to Niall, she cleared her throat awkwardly.

'Are we being called, darling?' One of the kilts looked up at her, assuming her to be an assistant to a third assistant or similar.

'Tash!' Niall looked round and leaped up with delight, tipping Minty so acutely to the right that she nearly fell off the bench. 'I thought you were never coming – great timing. We're all waiting for the rain to clear. Come here.'

He enveloped her in a great bear hug and indulged her in a rather perfunctory kiss before spinning her round to face the table. He'd transferred mud on to her cheek with the kiss, and pushed her hair into her eyes so that she was winking like a pervert in order to see, but she managed a hearty smile.

'Here – meet a great bunch of people. This is Tash.' He clutched her proudly, and she derived a certain amount of bolstering satisfaction from the fact that Minty was looking exceedingly huffy.

Various muddy faces peered up at her in fascination. Tash tried not to squirm around uncomfortably as she felt like a small child being eyed up by a new batch of classmates. Her eyes were still full of hair and watering madly, and she had the disconcerting feeling that she was something of a disappointment to them.

'Tash!' One of the kilts got to his feet and stretched across the table to shake her hand. 'You're *the* Tash, are you? Delighted to meet you. I'm Brian.'

There followed a lot of names and pointers for Tash to remember people by – 'He was in The Minister, remember?' – 'This is the one I told you about who fell off his horse twenty times on the first day's shoot' – 'Played alongside Gere in that political thriller last year' – 'She turned down the latest Sharon Stone role'. Tash tried to follow them all, but after a couple of minutes she was completely lost. Some of the faces were extremely familiar, but the one she was drawn to again and again was Minty Blyth's. Eyeing her through a cloud of hair and smoke, she seemed to take an instant dislike to Tash, and, with a sinking heart, Tash could guess why.

It often happened. In the secure, gang-like intimacy of a location shoot, actors who had to kiss and make eyes at one another daily on a film set were also eating together in the hotel at night, going through lines together afterwards in the bar, sharing a car ride together in the early hours of the morning, sitting in make-up together gossiping. Living in one another's air pockets, it was inevitable that the love-affair on-set often carried on in extra-curricular time. Or, if not, the feeling between the actors was often so strong and visceral that it seemed to eclipse other long-standing relationships away from the shoot. Tash knew that Niall had an appalling habit of unintentionally encouraging his leading ladies to fall for him, with his friendly charm, patience, tactile warmth and occasional glimpses of a deeper, more brooding side that they ached to understand. His was a lethal, aphrodisiac mix of ingredients guaranteed to induce dizziness in all who fell under its spell. Tash should know, as she herself had fallen for it. And she had a shrewd idea that Minty had too.

'So you're the jockey?' she asked, eyeing Tash's thighs sceptically.

'Eventer.' Tash smiled back. 'It's a sort of equestrian triathlon.'

'Oh.' Minty clearly wasn't interested enough to question her further.

'I'll get you some coffee, angel.' Niall loped off, indicating for her to sit down in the tightly gathered group.

Squeezing into the space that he had vacated, Tash found herself pressed next to the smoky-eyed actress in an involuntarily close pairing. Minty leaned pointedly away and lit another of the endless stream of cigarettes that kept her voice so low and husky.

'Is this your first visit on set?' she asked rather condescendingly.

'On this film, yes,' Tash nodded, deciding that she had to try and make herself like Minty for Niall's sake.

'I'm afraid you'll find it terribly dull.' Minty fiddled irritably with her plastic cup. 'Lots of hanging around and such.'

'Oh, I don't really mind that.' Tash smiled as Niall made his way back to her, a great big grin tugging at his craggy face. 'I'm here to see Niall, so the more hanging around the better. We can hang around together.' She felt bubbles of warmth popping inside her as she looked at him.

'You two not been together long, then?' Minty watched Niall too as he paused at another table to have a chat with a harassed-looking costume lady who had noticed pickle stains on his shirt.

'A couple of years.'

'Re-a-lly?' Minty's arched brows shot up, and then she flashed a bewitching little smile. 'Still keeping an eye on him then, huh? Very sensible – he's a dreadful tart, isn't he? I must check whether they're going to keep us hanging on any longer. C.U.L.'

With a swirl of damp petticoat and plastic mac, she wandered out of the tent.

'What's C.U.L.?' Tash asked one of the kilts.

'Some crap she's picked up in the States – stands for Catch Up Later or something.'

'Oh,' Tash said vaguely, still dwelling on the tart line. What had she meant?

'Ignore her, she's a complete bitch.' The kilt winked kindly. 'Cigarette?'

Tash took it gratefully, and relaxed as Niall settled in beside her and slung an easy arm around her shoulders as he pressed his face into her neck.

'It's great to see you, angel,' he sighed.

'You too.' She breathed him in happily, but as he played with the zip on her jacket and smiled roguishly into her eyes, she was uneasily aware that he was in character; he was MacGinnen, the rampaging, womanising Celt with the heart of fire. The real Niall had been the one she had encountered the night before in his hotel room, and that had been an altogether darker character.

It was, as Niall pointed out delightedly, a typical wet day on location. For every two minutes of frantic action, there were twenty of toe-twiddling inertia.

'And I'm being paid a fortune to drink tea and grope Tash!' He howled with laughter. 'Christ, but I love this job! It's God's own paradise this side of heaven, so it is.'

For the most part it rained, and Tash whiled away the time sitting in the tent with the others, swapping gossip, playing cards, reading the papers and drinking endless cups of tea. Niall was smoking in public again, she realised, as he worked his way through an entire packet of Marlboro in just three hours.

Despite this, he was on rip-roaring form, and gloriously attentive. When there appeared to be no immediate prospect of the next scene on the schedule being shot in the downpour, he whisked her off to his trailer for a bit of privacy.

It was a far drier and more luxurious waiting-room than the tent, but Tash knew why he preferred to hang around in the latter, which was raucous and friendly and full of stimuli.

The trailer would be uncomfortably cramped with more than four people in it. There was a small eating area with rather repulsive Dralon seats fitted around a plastic table. There was also a minute loo and shower, a small kitchenette with a microwave, and a portable television which was showing racing from an equally windswept Ayr.

Tash again found it familiar – it was just like the living accommodation of the horse-box she and the Lime Tree team travelled and lived in when eventing in two- and three-day events. It even had the same tendency to steam up on the inside during rain, and the same slightly chemical smell which came from exhaust fumes and plastic fittings.

Niall immediately headed for the kitchen area and located a bottle of Bushmills.

'Can I just have a coffee?' Tash watched him worriedly.

'Sure.' He flicked on the kettle and poured himself several inches from the bottle.

Tash longed to ignore the move, but she was worried about him. Close to, he was pale and drawn, his face pinched with tension, eyes darkly smudged from lack of sleep. He had also dropped an alarming amount of weight. The director had asked him to grow his hair for the part – a long, straggly mop of black ringlets, it hung round his head like Rembrandt's beret emphasising the haggard look. The camera simply piled on weight, so Tash knew that with his broad shoulders and sculpted features in high relief, he would look impossibly noble and romantic on screen, but in the harsh neon lights of the little caravan kitchenette, he cut a pathetically gaunt figure.

Shooting her a cheery wink, he knocked back almost half a glass of whiskey in one gulp.

'Shouldn't you lay off that until you know the scene definitely won't be shot?' she asked, trying to keep her tone light and breezy.

'I guess I should.' He drained the rest.

Tash sat on one of the repulsive Dralon seats and fingered a pile of script pages awkwardly as she watched him making coffee. His movements were clumsy and impatient, and he cursed under his breath, revealing the rawness of his nerves. But still MacGinnen's smile remained plastered to his mouth like a Band Aid holding back emotion.

'They seem like a nice bunch,' Tash started falteringly. 'The rest of the cast.'

'Sure – this lot are a great bunch,' he agreed happily, pushing his hair out of his eyes. 'Better than the Edinburgh lot, who were all a bit precious. D'you like Minty?' He looked up from his task expectantly. 'I saw you chatting away to her earlier.'

'She's very beautiful,' Tash said carefully.

'Bloody talented actress.' Niall brought her coffee over. 'This is only her third film since graduating from drama school, and she's incredibly professional. She's worked so hard on her character since being up here.'

Tash nodded, remembering. 'Yes, you were going through lines with her once when you called.'

'Was I?' He looked blank.

Tash blew on her coffee and said nothing, realising that he had forgotten the call altogether. She could remember it almost word for word. She had told him she'd loved the Four Poster Bed script, not knowing that Lisette was producing it; he had promised to fly down to Berkshire the following weekend, which he hadn't.

Smiling apologetically, he turned back for a nip of whiskey and then peeled off his oilskin. Beneath it, he was swathed in a vast speckled green plaid. It was wrapped around his waist beneath a thick leather belt before being hitched up over his shoulder where it was secured by a chunky brass buckle. Beneath it was a tatty, oversized cloth shirt, gaping at the front where the string had come unlaced. His lower legs were wrapped in what appeared to be long woollen bandages with cross-laced leather shin-pads on top. He wore the same ensemble on his forearms.

'You're soaking wet!' Tash reached out to touch the damp cloth.

Niall shrugged. 'This is my third costume of the day – the first got coated in mud in the battle scene, the second was soaked afterwards, and I had to put this on for the close-ups. Costume wanted to dry it off for me, but Nigel – the director – insisted I kept it on for the kiss.'

'The kiss?'

'That's what we were supposed to be shooting before the rain really set in.' Niall pulled on a huge Aran over the entire damp ensemble. It bagged in an extraordinary fashion over his costume, making him appear hunch-backed. 'MacGinnen – fresh from battle – returns with his posse to the nearby woods, where his love is waiting – that's Minty – and leaps off his horse to kiss her. Everything's set up – we just have to shoot the bugger.'

'I see.' Tash gnawed at a nail uncomfortably. She wished he hadn't invited her on set on the day he kissed one of the love-interests. She wondered vaguely if he'd done it deliberately.

'Don't tell me you shoot the sex scene tomorrow?' she joked.

'No, that was last week. Although there's one with Juliet Richards when we go back to Edinburgh in ten days' time.'

'I see.' Tash turned over a couple of pages of script, noticing the copious notes Niall had made in the margins. One of them read: *'Imagine she's T dressed in her old jeans.'*

She hid a grin as a warm wave of reassurance lapped her face. Then her smile dropped slightly as she noticed that the line read, 'D'ye think I'd want you now, huh?'

'Dialogue's a bit hard to read, isn't it?' She scanned the page.

'Hellish.' Niall had poured himself another drink and sat beside her. 'It was written by a Yank who thought he had a strong grasp of the vernacular based on three weeks' touring the Highland distilleries on some package holiday. But the voice coach is shit hot, so all might not be lost. Come here.'

Prising the script out of her hands, he pulled her into a rather rushed and clumsy kiss. He tasted of whiskey and cigarettes and Tash fought an urge to ask him to clean his teeth. She hoped he wasn't using her as a warm up for Minty. She just couldn't shake off this feeling of paranoia, however ridiculous she told herself she was being.

The kiss was becoming more aggressive by the second and Niall was pressing down on her with some force now, pushing her back against the seating and hitching her leg roughly up his side with a strong hand as he tried to force her to lie back. Tash wasn't enjoying it at all.

But before she could wriggle away from his grip and tell him off, the door burst open and Niall pulled abruptly away as Minty swept in, her beautiful face pink from the warmth of her own trailer.

'The rain's stopped, darling!' she announced in a breathless voice. 'Nigel says there's enough light to go for a couple of takes, so get into make-up *tout de suite* for a touch up. See you!' Without even a perfunctory glance at Tash, she whisked out again.

Tash felt a light stain of colour leaping to her cheeks, aware that she and Niall had been caught necking like teenagers. She briefly let herself indulge in a fantasy that Minty had a honking crush on Niall and was devastated to catch him indulging in carnal pleasure with his intended, minutes before she herself was going to steal a much-coveted and totally celluloid kiss with him.

'I'll just clean my teeth.' Niall headed into the bathroom, pulling off his jumper in his wake.

Tash took a great slug of coffee that ran down her chin, her fantasy image disappearing as quickly as a popped balloon.

'Niall around?' A bedraggled blonde poked her head around the door, clutching a clip-board in a plastic bag.

'He's just coming.' Tash nodded towards the bathroom.

'Great.' The girl grinned, her nose red from the cold. She was a young, soft-voiced American with incredibly white teeth that had probably cost thousands of dollars. 'You must be Tash – I'm Mel. Come and watch, you can stand with me.'

If Niall really wanted to impress Minty, Tash reflected sourly, he should invest in a set of teeth like Mel's.

The celluloid kiss was a long time coming. Tash had been on location with Niall before, and it never ceased to amaze her how much faffing, forethought and energy was expended for just a few seconds of film.

The shot had been set up on the edge of a tightly clustered pine wood. Beside it ran the tracks for the craned trolley cam which would swoop to earth as it captured Niall galloping in from battle followed by his gang, and then swing around to track him as he slithered to a halt on a marked spot where he would leap from his steed and straight onto Minty.

As ever, there seemed to be an enormous number of extraneous people hanging about swigging from beakers of tea, banging their hands together for warmth, or dragging on cigarettes. The techies were easily recognisable from their practical anoraks, baseball caps and occasional fleeting attentions to a wire or a piece of tracking. They huddled together talking through the technicalities of the scene, slightly apart from the artistes – themselves conspicuous by their costumes, inertia, and the preferential treatment they received from everyone else. Also hanging around the hub of the action were other more arty production types who were notable for their impractical outfits, loud voices and occasional temperamental fits.

Of them all, Nigel the director was the loudest and most tempestuous. Wearing a tatty Goretex coat and a baseball cap promoting one of his previous films, he seemed to derive a sadistic satisfaction from making everyone do three times as much as they really needed in order to satisfy his near-obsessive perfectionism. Gnawing at his lower lip, eyes darting madly, he stalked around barking orders like a despotic military leader conducting the last stages of a bloody coup. Terrier-like, he snapped and snarled at everyone in sight – Tash included – as he demanded that everything was triple-checked and set to go before they started the final camera rehearsal. Even rehearsing the actors through the scene – which, according to Niall he had already done before the rain broke earlier – was something of a five-act play.

'Don't suck her face off, Niall!' he screamed. 'Open wider, Minty darling – no, no, not like that. That looks revolting. For God's sake, use your tongues.'

Tash cringed under her shared umbrella as she watched Niall kiss Minty over and over again, and seem to enjoy it far too much. It was a strange experience, and something of a first. She had seen him kissing a multitude of actresses before – but that had always been in two dimensions, after the scene was cut and edited and projected on to a white screen. Watching the live performance was agony.

'Kinda odd for you, huh?' Mel watched her cheerfully.

Tash nodded. 'I guess I'll have to harden myself to it.' She shrugged. 'It's a bit like being married to the mob, isn't it?'

Mel, who had been looking across at Nigel's frantic hand signals to the horse trainer, turned back to her in amazement.

'Did you just say married?'

'Yes – well, not yet, I mean.' She blushed, realising she was spilling more beans than an overturned Heinz lorry. 'Later this year.'

'Christ!' Mel grinned, rubbing her red nose with a mittened hand. 'That was quick work, wasn't it? I thought you and Niall only met kinda recently?'

Remembering that Minty had said the same thing, Tash started to detect a lie. She swallowed uncomfortably. 'A couple of years ago, actually.'

'Oh.' Mel's eyebrows shot up. 'I see.' She was plainly astonished.

'But perhaps it would be better to keep quiet about it.' Tash smiled apologetically. 'I mean, if Niall's not eager for people to know.'

'Sure.' Mel was looking across at Nigel again. 'Here we go, they're in first positions.'

Tash looked up and saw that Minty was now in place under a pine tree, a costume assistant holding an umbrella over her until the last moment to stop drips from the trees landing on her nose. A make-up assistant was fiddling with the long black tresses, using a Polaroid picture as a guide.

In the distance, Niall and three more of the kilts were waiting on horseback for the hand-signal from a nearby walkie-talkie-wielding techie which would cue them to gallop into shot. Steam was rising

from the horses, who had already been pounded around a distant field
for twenty minutes to give them the sweated-up, battle-weary look.
Plumes of hot air puffed from their impatient nostrils as the assorted
actors – some with clearly limited equestrian skills – fought to keep
them in check.

Tash felt a sudden, aching pang of homesickness for Snob and the
Lime Tree Farm mob. She longed to be sitting in the warm, cluttered
kitchen at the farm right now, tucking into one of Zoe's off-the-wall
meals and talking about the progress of the horses and the gossip on
the circuit.

Nigel was barking into a walkie-talkie as he crouched beside the
swarthy director of photography, both looking into a monitor at the
base of the camera crane which displayed what the camera operator
had in frame. Up on the crane, the camera-man and his focus-puller
were sitting in a tight space, shoulders high as their ears against the
cold. Tash decided they looked like two grumpy sailors perching in
the crows nest at the top of a ship's mast.

Someone was yelling for silence on set behind her head.

'Okay – let's go for it on the first take, shall we?' Nigel yelled. 'Where's
the fucking clapper?'

Tash jumped, wondering whether she was supposed to applaud,
but the next moment a nervous-looking youth had darted in front
of the camera crane and was holding an electronic clapper-board over
his head.

'Not yet!' Nigel snapped witheringly. 'And get out of shot, Cynthia!'
The brolly-woman dashed away from Minty, who licked her lips in
anticipation.

'Turn over,' Nigel barked. 'Standby for take – everybody quiet,
please.' He pulled down the peak of his baseball cap so that it tipped
towards his nose in very Third Reich fashion. 'Okay. Camera?'

Up on his crane the focus-puller nodded and yelled back, 'To
speed!'

'Sound?'

A sound engineer crouching beside a lap-top computer which
was attached to various space-age master boards fiddled with his
headphones and glanced across at a man holding a furry mike on
a boom. 'Rolling,' he muttered.

'Mark it!'

With a breathless spiel of the slate and scene number from the
nervous-looking youth, the clapper came down and he loped gratefully
out of shot.

'And – action! Go in three, Jim!' Nigel squawked into his walkie-talkie, gazing fixedly at his monitor.

Moments later, Niall and his posse were thundering down the hill, sending up great divots of earth in their wake. The camera swept around on its crane, following their progress in a smooth downward sweep.

Tash stifled a laugh as she saw that one of the kilts, his face pinched with fear, looked dangerously close to falling off, or not stopping at all. Thankfully his mount was far more experienced than he was and, without any apparent guidance from its rider, slithered to an obedient halt behind Niall's huge, sweating chestnut as the camera dropped to head-height and filmed Niall jumping off.

Then it slid easily along its well-oiled tracks as it followed his short run to the delighted Minty who fell into his arms, her exquisite tulip-bud lips rising towards his.

Tash winced as the kiss seemed to go on forever. Craning her head to try and see whether they were using tongues, she fought a desperate urge to shout 'Cut!'

When Nigel finally yelled the blissful word, Tash had come to the conclusion that not only were they using tongues, but they were indulging in mutual mouth-washing and teeth flossing with them.

After a quick consultation with his camera-man and the sound engineer, Nigel squinted at the sky and shrugged. 'Print it?' He turned back to his DoP.

'Print it.' The swarthy DoP nodded and backed off to talk to the camera crew once more while Nigel addressed the group at large.

'That was fucking fantastic, guys – more fantastic than the fucking, in fact,' he yelled at the actors. 'The light's going. We're out of here, folks. Thank you, everyone. Grab your call sheets from Angie if you haven't already. See most of you tomorrow.'

Tash heaved a sigh of relief and watched as Niall slowly disentangled himself from Minty and tried to make his way over to her, big grin still firmly in place. But he was waylaid en route by Nigel who had suddenly shed his dictator role for oily, conciliatory father-figure.

'Terrific work, Niall – great passion. I think we should work on . . .'

Hoping he was going to say 'the scene where Minty loses all her teeth', Tash tried to listen in but Nigel turned his back to her so that his words were muffled.

As Mel sloped off to help with the wrap, dropping piles of paper in her wake, Tash huddled in the worsening drizzle feeling left out. Minty had joined Nigel's tight little congregation now and was preening delightedly under his increasingly unctuous praise. Tash loathed the way she touched Niall when she spoke, as familiar as a lover. She knew that this was typical of actresses, but it didn't stop a squat little green harpy of jealousy from crouching on her shoulder and whispering 'They're bonking' into her ear.

'Tash!' Niall waved her over. 'Come and meet Nigel. Nigel, this is Tash.'

Nigel, who close up was a weasely-nosed little man with darting eyes and an over-wet mouth, didn't look at her at all.

'Hi,' he muttered, walking off to chat to his location manager.

Niall laughed cheerfully. 'Bastard. Let's rip this plaid off, get my stuff together and go back to the hotel – you must be bored stiff. I said we'd give Minty a lift, okay? Her driver hasn't turned up yet.'

Tash gave Minty as big a smile as she could muster. 'Fine.'

At least the back seat of the design classic was tiny and covered with dog hair and sweet wrappers, she realised with some satisfaction.

Tash had hoped for a quiet meal together that evening. She badly needed to talk to Niall, to try to draw him out about his erratic behaviour, his drunken, near-comatose unhappiness of the night before, his relationship with Minty. It occurred to her in a moment of panic on the way back to the hotel that he had only kissed her in his trailer because he had spotted Minty approaching through one of the steamy windows and wanted to make her react. Worst of all, Tash was beginning to worry that his odd behaviour stemmed from the most disturbing of all reasons – his feet were getting colder than a Himalayan hill-walker's about the wedding.

But she had no chance to talk to him. The moment they were in their room alone, he peeled off his clothes and headed into the shower. As soon as he was out, he was dressing, eager to get to the bar, MacGinnen's smile still dancing on his lips.

'Can we go for a walk or something first?' Tash asked hopefully.

'In this weather?' Niall laughed, looking towards the vast window where the loch was almost in darkness and being lashed by another downpour. 'Tash, you're so gloriously hare-brained sometimes. Are you going to change, or shall we go now? I'm parched, so I am.'

'Can't we stay here and talk for a bit?' She snuggled against him imploringly.

He pulled a face, still boundlessly cheerful. 'We can talk in bed later, so we can. I want you to get to know everyone better, angel. They're a terrific bunch, you said so yourself.' He pulled gently away from her and walked over to the desk to glance at his character notes.

'Niall,' she bit her lip, following him, 'have you told them we're getting married this summer?'

''Course I have,' he gathered her into a hug and dropped his mouth to hers. The move seemed alarmingly perfunctory, as though it, too, was scripted.

Tash badly wanted the reassurance of the kiss, but the image of him using precisely the same moves on Minty over and over again in front of a crowd earlier made her feel jumpy and distanced. And when his mouth did close over hers it was greedy and boisterous, not at all gentle. She kissed him back, but nothing kicked inside her except for a great churning swell of panic.

'You,' he announced as he pulled away and headed for the mirror to check his hair, 'are going to cheer up tonight, if it kills me. You're so morose, angel, it's depressing me. I know you find film sets intimidating, but it'll get easier, I promise. The guys think you're a knock-out, and Minty adores you already.'

'Minty?' Tash croaked, gaping at him.

'Sure.' He grinned at her over the shoulder of his mirrored reflection. 'She told me earlier that she thinks you're priceless. I've invited her to the wedding.'

When he urged her to hurry up, Tash trailed into the shower and indulged in a long, thoughtful, lonely blast of hot water, listening to Niall chattering away in the other room or singing Rolling Stones hits very loudly. She wasn't sure if he was talking to her or on the phone, the shower made it impossible to hear a word. After five minutes he went quiet.

Wondering if he was okay, Tash wandered back into the main room, a toothbrush poking from her mouth as she tried to neutralise her breath from so much coffee on set.

He had gone already, leaving a selection of clothes on the bed which he was clearly eager for her to wear.

Tash sighed unhappily. Dear Niall had such romantic ideas, but his taste in women's clothing was appalling. He had laid out her nylon under-slip, thinking it some sexy little black number, plus her black riding jacket which she had been wearing at the trials the day before and had brought along by mistake. It reeked of horse and, on close inspection, had a line of scurf along the front from leaning into Snob's neck as they jumped. Added to this, he had put out her hold-up stockings which always fell down in minutes and her long boots from the christening.

She longed to pull on some jeans and one of his jumpers, but was too uncertain of him at the moment to risk it, guessing that it would be best to pander to him while she rode out his current mood.

When she looked in the mirror, she perked up slightly. The outfit was ridiculously tarty, but she had to admit it was absurdly sexy as well. The stockings made her legs look gloriously long, and the strappy slip clung to exactly the right curves of her body. Matched with her bruised, tired eyes and damp, dishevelled air, she felt both sleazy and sophisticated – a been-there, bored-by-that rock chick in the Marianne Faithful mould.

Having made up her face and dusted off the worst of the jacket's scurf, she headed to the bar with a rebellious swing of her hips, her nerves firmly held at bay.

The first person she caught sight of was Minty, lounging on a tartan sofa wearing threadbare jeans and a shrunken Fair Isle sweater which clung to every curve of her capacious bosom and minute waist. Her beautiful face free of make-up and her hair as wild as it had been on set, she made Tash feel like an over-primped tart trawling the hotel lounge for trade. Her fragile confidence started to ebb away.

'Tash darling!' Minty gave her a friendly wave. 'You look gorgeous. Doesn't she look gorgeous, everyone?'

She was draped partly over the sofa arm and partly over Niall who, scruffier than ever in his ancient jeans and Aran, was knocking back scotch and chatting to several other sprawling men. Tash assumed they were the kilts, now unrecognisable without their muddied faces and draped blankets. As Niall made no effort to move sideways and accommodate her, she dragged over a spare chair and plonked it beside one of the lounging men.

'Were you in the battle scene earlier today?' she asked, trying to imagine his face covered with mud.

'Hardly.' He looked put out. 'I'm the lighting camera-man.' Turning his back on her, he joined in an animated conversation about whether or not Nigel was shagging the young clapper loader.

Niall was still completely ignoring her as he laughed uproariously with Minty, MacGinnen's big grin tugging at his cheeks, gaze merrily soaking up that clean, scrubbed pink face with its ripe plum cheeks, kitten eyes and cocoa dusting of freckles.

Tash felt a tide of bile and panic surge at her throat. More than anything, she felt jealousy eating at her stomach. Their confidence and companionship left her hopelessly alienated. The entire group was chattering about the film and future scenes, a topic of which she knew precious little. Most of them, it seemed, were heading on to Edinburgh the next week to continue shooting there.

Gratefully recognising the man who had given her a cigarette in the tent earlier and told her that Minty was a bitch, she caught his eye and grinned.

'Edinburgh's beautiful, isn't it?' she said, unable to think up anything less banal in the brief second that she had his attention.

'So are you,' he growled wolfishly, and slithered his eyes along the entire length of her legs. Tash gulped uncomfortably and glanced at Niall, who was now playing with Minty's hair while he talked to her. When she looked back at her cigarette friend, he was once again embroiled in a loud conversation about Nigel's apparently rampant sex life.

She spent the ensuing two hours perched on the edge of a chair, draining her drinks far faster than everyone else. Her small talk needed a microscope to be spotted and went largely undetected.

When they all finally piled into the baronial dining hall to eat, she found herself sitting between two of the former kilts who had both forgotten her name and proceeded to talk across her as though she was a mildly irritating stone column. She had wanted to sit beside Niall, but he'd cheerfully insisted that she should get to know his friends better.

'You'll love these two guys,' he'd laughed as he posted her between them and kissed her on the top of the head, 'they'll keep you in stitches all night. You can charm them, angel, and make me wildly jealous.'

She tried gallantly not to let him down, cracking the odd joke and interjecting comments and questions when the conversation went anywhere near something she felt was common ground, but it was like talking to the television – they just chattered on regardless. The only thing they seemed to want to keep stitched was her mouth.

Tash tried to feign an interest in her soup, gazing at it as though it was doused in the cyanide of her own jealousy.

The only comment levelled at her by one of the name-forgetting kilts was, 'At least we know you won't do a Minty and chuck that all up later – you haven't eaten enough of it to get a purchase on any vomit.' Laughing with his friend, he proceeded to chatter about the crew on the last film he had done, none of whom Tash knew.

She looked at She Who Vomits – placed neatly between Niall and the best-looking of the kilts. Minty looked ravishing and regularly ravished. She kept leaning across to whisper into Niall's ear, that pretty, coquettish smile playing on her lips. Every time she spoke, he burst into gales of laughter.

I can't believe he's doing this, Tash thought murderously. He must know how much he's hurting me.

The flirtatious cigarette-donor, who was sitting directly opposite, was back on her case again.

'Devastating, isn't she?' he murmured, locking eyes with Tash.

She managed a wobbly smile. 'She's very beautiful.'

'And knows it.' He let out an indulgent, almost carnal sigh. 'I can't tell you how good that feels.'

Tash wondered what he meant. Perhaps someone was playing footsie with him under the table and he thought it was her? She scraped back her chair slightly and sat prudishly upright.

'What feels?' she asked.

'That,' he sighed, eyes sliding sideways and watching Minty pop one of Niall's breaded mushrooms into her lush little mouth. 'I was on the receiving end of that last week. You don't have anything to worry about.' He turned to Tash again with a sad smile. 'They're not shagging.'

'What d'you mean?' She looked at him in horror.

'I mean,' he dropped his voice and leaned forward intently, 'that she only flirts like that when she hasn't got someone into bed. The moment you do the business, she doesn't want to know. She's famous for it. She only had a go at me last week because Niall made it so patently obvious there was nothing doing.'

Tash glanced at Niall again. The only thing he was making patently obvious tonight was how hysterical he thought Minty's sense of humour was.

'Exactly.' Her confidant knew precisely what she was thinking and grinned across at her broadly. 'I was wondering why too. It only started yesterday – just after he said you were coming up to visit. If this is some sort of game you two guys play, then I'm only too happy to join in. I must say, you are a simply gorgeous creature.'

Suddenly a warm hand started to creep on to her knee. As Tash's stay-up stockings had again fallen down, it encountered nothing but wrinkled nylon and rubber. She whipped her chair back further, but the hand slid onward, fingering its way inside the stocking tops.

Her mouth full of mushroom soup, Tash started to splutter and cough in alarm.

Feeling childish tears prickling at her eyes now, she mumbled something about going to the loo, pushed away from the table and fled back to her room.

There, she paced around for twenty tearful minutes, wishing that Niall would follow her to check that she was okay. When he plainly wasn't going to appear, she lit a cigarette with shaking hands and stalked out on to the cloistered balcony to gaze at the loch and think up a way of winkling Niall away from Minty to bawl him out. It was perishingly cold and her flimsy nylon slip whipped back against her skin like a slap of water from a bucket. Tash closed her eyes and shivered, wondering what the hell he was playing at.

Inside the room, the phone rang.

Racing inside, Tash snatched it up within seconds, fighting resentment that Niall was calling her from the bar after his meal and not bothering to walk the fifty or so yards of lobby that separated them.

'Miss French – call for you,' announced a soft Scottish voice.

'Tash?' came a breathless pant.

'Penny, what is it?' She fought disappointment.

'Okay, don't get in a panic, but I knew you'd kill me if I didn't tell you. Snob's got a bloody awful bout of colic.'

She froze. 'How bad?'

She could hear Penny drawing in breath through her teeth.

'Well, Jack Fortescue thinks we've made it in time, but we're still battling, to be honest. Gus found him cast at eight – just couldn't get up. Poor devil's in agony.'

Tash clutched the bed for support, dragging acres of counterpane over her in her distress. Penny never minced words, and for that she was grateful, but she felt utterly panicked and helpless. Colic was at the least a painful bout of equine tummy ache, at worst life-threatening. Because a horse is physically incapable of being sick, any poison it eats causes distressing pain as its stomach distends with gas and its body tries frantically to expel it. If more serious, the stomach starts to spasm and the pain is excruciating. The risk is that the horse's bowel will twist during spasm, cutting off the blood supply and causing an internal rupture. It was this that could kill. Tash knew that for Penny to call, the colic had to be about as bad as it got.

'How long has he been like it?'

'Hard to tell – the trouble is he always paws in his stable so much and makes such a hullaballoo that no one realised the poor devil was in pain. And he's bloody difficult to treat. It took four of us to get him up.'

'But what – I mean, why?'

Penny drew in another sharp breath. 'Kirsty let him out for a leg-stretch in the menage this afternoon and then raced inside to take a call from Hugo. God knows what he found to eat in there – someone must have thrown down an apple core or something – but the stupid idiot seems to have eaten great fist-loads of sand along with it. Now it's all bunged up inside him.'

Tash closed her eyes, 'And Kirsty never thought to . . .'

'. . . never thought to mention that it might be sand until the horse was writhing in agony. No.' Penny sounded extremely angry.

'But Jack definitely thinks he'll pull through?'

Penny didn't answer for a few seconds. 'He's pretty certain, but the sand is blocking his gut so he's still in agony, poor lamb. Jack's working like mad – Gus is with him.'

Knowing what that meant, Tash almost broke down. 'I'm coming back.'

'Christ, no!' Penny sounded appalled. 'It'll take you simply hours. You're better off there with Niall. I'll call you the moment we know.'

'I'm coming home,' Tash sobbed, and slammed down the phone.

Not bothering to change, she piled all her stuff into her bag. As she raced towards the dining hall to tell Niall what had happened, she heard loud whoops of laughter and stopped in her tracks. She couldn't see the group's table through the door, but Minty's voice was ringing throatily above the cackles as she regaled the others with a series of acid comments.

Cowering behind a huge, baronial pillar, Tash didn't have to listen for long to hear who she was describing.

'Did you see her stockings? They were dangling around her knees like old hockey socks! I kept expecting her to bully off.'

'Instead she just ran off dribbling!'

'Poor thing,' Minty giggled. 'She probably had soup in her mous-Tash.'

Biting her lip, she backed away, feeling as though she'd been branded on both cheeks by a red hot iron that read 'LOSER'. She knew she'd behaved like a wimp all day, but couldn't believe Niall wasn't leaping to her defence. Fighting not to cry, she rushed back to the room again to leave a scribbled note of explanation.

Her only small pleasure was that she wrote it in thick black eye-liner all over a page of his dialogue script for the first scene scheduled the next day.

Reversing the design classic with a squeal of tyres on Tarmac, she didn't notice the glow of a cigarette end from the darkened garden as Niall, standing alone in the shadows, watched the car he had bought her speeding away from the hotel.

Fourteen

WEIGHED DOWN WITH THE most exclusive carrier bags Sally had ever had the pleasure of hooking over her arms, she and Lisette snatched a quick drink in the Fifth Floor at Harvey Nichols, sitting in a bright corner to watch Knightsbridge bustling below.

'So the wedding's all set for the first Saturday in June, is it?' Lisette took the top inch off a long gin and tonic with a delighted roll of her eyes. 'Only I have to liaise with the *Cheers!* magazine people soon to arrange their photo-shoot. They want loads of pictures of frothy bridesmaids and celebrity guests.'

Sally nodded. 'From Fosbourne, according to Henrietta, not James's place after all. They still haven't sent out invites – apparently Tash and Niall haven't bothered writing a list yet. Tash is even planning to compete at Badminton the weekend before the wedding.'

'And Niall will be in my bed.' Lisette gave her a wink.

'What?' Sally almost spat out a mouthful of vodka and orange.

'Four Poster Bed.' She lit one of her low-tar cigarettes. 'The film, darling. Try at least to learn the name if you're going to work on the fucking pic – that sort of thing impresses backers.'

'Sorry.' Sally grinned. 'So you're definitely going to try and change Hugo's mind?'

'What d'you think this is for?' Lisette nodded towards the plushest of her carrier bags in which nestled an acre of tissue paper delicately wrapped around one of the slinkiest dresses Sally had ever seen. Lisette had bought it especially for Hugo's birthday party, at which she was

planning finally to persuade him to relinquish his house for a fortnight
to let her team film there on location. She'd already asked him twice
and been turned down flat both times, but she was determined to win
through.

'It is a beautiful house,' Sally sighed, having driven past it with
Tash once.

'Beautiful owner.' Lisette's eyes twinkled.

Sally looked at her in shock, her mouth forming into an O.

'Not Hugo?'

'It might be fun.' Lisette smiled thoughtfully, indulging herself with
a mental image for a second or two. 'I've always wanted a crack at him,
but he's so fucking aloof, I can't read him.'

'Shouldn't think he's particularly well read either,' Sally said disparagingly.

'Maybe not, but that doesn't stop him being unfairly bright. I've never
met anyone with such a sharp tongue.' Lisette's luminous eyes twinkled
greedily.

'Sounds painful.'

'I reckon that beneath that six-inch steel veneer, he's incredibly
passionate.' She winked. 'And you have to admit, he's divinely
constructed.'

'My mother-in-law thinks he's the sexiest man on God's earth,' Sally
giggled. 'She spent ages trying to set him up with Tash one summer.'

'Hugo?' Lisette spluttered. 'Matty's mother tried to set Hugo up
with Tash?'

'More or less – she was certainly hinting hard. Anyway, Tash
went off with Niall in the end so . . .' She covered her mouth in
embarrassment.

But Lisette shrugged. 'Ancient history, darling. I always said I wasn't
set up to be a me-Niall house-wife. He needs someone much more
placid – Tash is great for him. Now tell me more about this wedding.
Is Tor going to be a bridesmaid? She'll look so fucking cute.'

A few minutes of wedding gossip later, Sally took a deep breath.

She flushed. 'Listen, now I'm working for you, I've been looking
through all those notes you gave me and I've come up with a bit of
a publicity idea for Four Poster Bed.'

'Oh, yes?' Lisette looked at her watch dismissively. 'The thing is, hon,
we've really worked out the publicity strategy alrea—'

'It might help you get in with Hugo too.'

'Oh, yes?' Lisette suddenly looked far more interested. 'Will it
cost much?'

'I'm not sure. It's a sort of a wedding present for Niall and Tash really. I was going to ask you whether you thought it might work . . .'

Tash had driven into the dawn and through the morning, slowing up as the traffic began to choke the roads and fatigue started to twitch at her tired eyes. After a snatched lunch, she had fought her way through the Birmingham motorway system and was now heading for home. She was absolutely shattered and driving so badly that she was amazed she made it to Berkshire at all. The design classic was in an even worse state, clanking and groaning as though trying to throw up its entire engine after bingeing out on so much high-octane petrol, its windscreen now bearing two gleaming, wash-wiped arcs amidst a thick coating of mud and grime. The batteries had gone flat on Tash's cassette player hours ago, and she was trying to keep herself awake and focused by singing Abba songs at the top of her voice – they were the only ones she could ever remember.

It was almost dark again by the time she reached the farm, her lungs hoarse as she belted out 'Fernando', somehow unable to stop even though she was home. She was so tired that she felt an over-riding urge to burst into tears of relief for having made it back, feeling like an Arctic explorer who's battled for hours and hours through a blizzard to make it to base camp. As she parked the car beside Zoe's never-used old Merc, Wally and Beetroot raced into the yard barking their heads off in greeting while Enid hid behind the Land-Rover, her spotty tail glued between her legs, amber eyes peering at Tash from beneath the chassis.

Noticing that the horse-box was missing, Tash almost fell out of the design classic and stumbled on cramped legs straight for Snob's box, pursued by an ecstatic Beetroot. Both of the doors were shut and her heart stuck in her throat like a bulimic's fingers as she slid back the top bolt with shaking fingers and peeked in.

With a juggernaut whicker, Snob's pink nose was thrust through the gap and rammed into her face, accompanied by an enormous amount of slobber coated with green slime. Tash almost fell backwards as he head-butted her grumpily, eager for a snack to appease his aching, empty stomach. His huge, purply eyes rolled with greed and bad temper.

'Hardly a model patient,' laughed a voice behind her. 'The bugger's almost had my arm off twice this evening. Gus says he's being disarming. Or was it armless?'

Tash spun round and spotted Ted, lounging against the box next door and scratching Mickey Rourke's grey lop ears.

'So he's all right?' she said anxiously, glancing at Snob who was trying to snap at her coat collar. She was still wearing her nylon slip and riding jacket; her hold-up stockings had slipped deep beneath her long snakeskin boots now.

'Not one hundred percent yet,' Ted said. 'Jack reckons he'll be feeling pretty rough for a couple of days. But he's not going to be Kit-e-kat, if that's what you're worried about. You look fantastically horny, by the way.'

To Ted's surprise, he was the sudden recipient of an enormous hug before Tash bounced back to hug Snob, who inserted his pink nose into her coat and bit off the strap of her slip.

'Now you're back, will you cut my hair?' Ted patted Mickey who, wildly jealous that Tash hadn't yet said hello, was whickering like a revving lorry engine, his big, pale face stretching towards Snob's stable to see what all the fuss was about, wall eyes bulging.

'I'd better show my face in the house first.'

'Gus and Penny are taking a clinic in Hampshire.' Ted started to wander back to the tack room, his denim behind coated in dust from sitting down on one of the feed bins to clean tack. 'But Zoe's around somewhere, cooking one of her killer curries. If you hurry, she'll count you in too – Kirsty's invited Hugo over for it, poor sod. I hope his guts are lined with more lead than a church roof.'

'Oh, I'm sure he's too keen to curry favour with Kirsty to care.' Tash gave Snob a final kiss before closing his top door.

In the kitchen, Zoe and India were chopping veg and watching *Neighbours* simultaneously.

'We've been expecting you.' Zoe looked up, her smooth, Slavic face not entirely friendly.

'Oh, yes?' Tash nicked a carrot and gathered up Beetroot, who was still weaving around underfoot. She had grown so big of late that Tash groaned as she lifted. Her back was aching from driving for so long.

'Niall called – said you'd done a bunk,' Zoe clattered through the cutlery drawer disapprovingly, selecting a huge chopping knife. 'He was beside himself with worry.'

Wincing, Tash sat at the table and started to gnaw at her carrot, letting Beetroot scrabble around to keep balance on her lap. She had tried to keep Niall from her head for the past few hours, determinedly concentrating on Snob. Now even the mention of his name made her stomach lurch with anguish and guilt.

'Ted says Snob's going to be okay.' She spoke between mouthfuls. 'I was so worried, I thought—'

'We spoke for quite some time, actually.' Zoe put down her knife on the table and glanced pointedly at India.

'I – er – said I'd look at Rufus's new CD Rom,' India explained before dashing upstairs, stealing a last, regretful look at *Neighbours*.

Sitting down opposite Tash, Zoe pushed her pudding-basin bob from her eyes and brushed a few imaginary crumbs from the table in front of her as she clearly braced herself to give Tash a ticking off.

'He says it was pretty tricky in Scotland.' She let out a long-suffering sigh.

'Yes, well, he was behaving a bit oddly. He—'

'Niall said you were very cold and distant. That you hardly made an effort with anyone.'

Tash stared at her, eyes widening.

Zoe covered her mouth and blew through her fingers as she regarded Tash thoughtfully before continuing.

'I get the impression that he's really very worried about you, Tash – he seems to think you've changed recently.' Her blue eyes were awash with concern and kindness, but there was a critical edge to her voice. 'He was incredibly hurt that you left without telling him. Penny would never have called you if she'd thought you were going to race back like this. I think Niall's really cut up that you seem to value your horse above him.'

'He wasn't himself,' Tash bleated rather pathetically, desperate not to mention her fears about Minty. 'He was all wrapped up in the film and his cast.'

'It's his job, Tash,' Zoe sighed, abandoning impartiality in her exasperation.

'He was drunk when I got there.'

'Did you ask him why?'

'I tried, but we were hardly alone at all. I tried to talk to him, but he kept shutting me out.'

'Christ, Tash.' Zoe rubbed her forehead in despair. 'You behave like a teenager on a first date with him sometimes. I can just imagine what you were like. He's probably as miserable as hell up there, missing you like crazy and dying for your support, some of your daft energy. Instead he got a timid schoolgirl who cowered as though he was about to say boo!'

Tash had never heard Zoe speak so harshly. She was so over-emotional and exhausted that she simply didn't know how to react.

'I see.' She stood up, still gripping Beetroot awkwardly to her chest, her voice hoarse with shame. 'You and Niall had quite a chat then?' She started to back out of the room.

'Is that all you have to say?' Zoe looked astonished.

'More or less.' Tash's face was aflame with humiliation. She couldn't believe that Niall had told all this to Zoe, her closest friend and ally. She was horrified that he had aired their problems – and such a one-sided version of them, too – to someone she considered to be her own confidante. He may well have wanted to use Zoe as a go-between, an emotional arbiter, but Tash was far too proud and angry with them both to comply. Instead she wanted to stamp her feet like a kid and run home to Mummy. She was shredded from the drive, hollow with hunger and aching to talk to Niall without a busy-body, curry-cooking interpreter present.

'We're all worried about you, Tash.' Zoe stood up, anxious for her interrogation to continue, clearly apologetic for her harshness. 'You *have* changed lately – snapping at people, disappearing off on your own, working more than usual, losing so much weight, mooning over Hugo.'

'I have not been mooning over Hugo!' she wailed, feeling a childish tantrum tugging at her temples.

'Well, Kirsty seems to think you have, darling.' Zoe moved over to her.

'Kirsty thinks every female over ten is after Hugo.'

A car door banged outside and Wally scrambled out of the kitchen, bark booming.

'Most of them are.' Zoe was trying make a joke out of it. She moved forward, her voice softening along with her eyes. 'Darling, you're engaged to Niall. I know it's only human to want one last fling, but Hugo of all people!'

Tash was almost purple with misunderstood, shattered pride. She clutched Beetroot, who was slipping fast.

'I am not after Hugo! I hate bloody Hugo,' she screamed. 'And I hate Kirsty, and I hate you too!' She dashed blindly out of the kitchen, almost flooring Kirsty and Hugo who were coming in from the main door, stripping off coats and boots.

'Ouch!' wailed Kirsty as Tash trod on her foot.

'Steady on!' Hugo laughed, spinning back as she slammed her way past. 'I think that dog wants a sick bag.'

With Beetroot pressed tightly to her chest, legs lolling, Tash raced into the yard and found to her horror that Hugo had blocked in the design classic with his muddy high-tech Range Rover.

'Bastard!' She kicked the offending car and its alarm went off, shooting Beetroot deep into her coat in fear.

'Tash!' Zoe came running out of the house in her wake, tripping over as she hastily pulled on her shoes. 'Please stay for supper – I'm sorry I had a go at you the moment you walked in. I want to help. I'm so worried about you!'

Ignoring her, Tash wrenched open the design classic's boot and dragged out her case before stumbling from the light of the yard and along the wet, muddy grooves of the track to the gates. Once her feet made contact with the more secure Tarmac of the shadowy lane, she ran all the way home.

Waiting for her on the mat at the forge was a large wad of post. In it was a long letter from Alexandra setting out her plans for the reception and announcing that she was planning to get Tash's dress made in Paris as she had plainly made no progress on it herself. There was also a long message from Henrietta on the answer-machine explaining that she had found out that there was a very grand commercially owned house in Fosbourne Dean which could host weddings, and that she would try and book it the next day unless Tash raised an objection.

'We simply have to have a venue,' she explained in her curt, cut-glass voice, sounding slightly hysterical. 'The invitations need to be printed and posted desperately soon, and without a venue it's hopeless. And if I haven't got your guest list by next week, I'm making it up myself!' With that she had given a manic sob and rung off.

The fax was spewing out a large number of wedding dress designs from France, beneath which was a very lewd fax from Rufus, who had a habit of sneaking into his school staff room when it was deserted to send them as a joke.

There wasn't a single message from Niall.

Despite eyelids that seemed to be weighed down with lead false eye-lashes of fatigue, Tash kick-started herself with a coffee that was more granules than water and called the loch-side hotel. She was told Niall was still out filming. But it was the usual round of switched-off mobiles, answering services, mechanical voice-mail-boxes and third assistant directors telling her he'd wandered off to get a cup of tea and they couldn't see him. In the end, drooping with tiredness, Tash called the hotel again and left a message apologising for her swift exit and asking him to call her the next day.

Despite several more messages, he didn't call her back for almost a week, and then it was MacGinnen who got in touch.

'Sure we were both in funny moods last weekend.' He glossed over the whole affair with a melodious laugh. 'I miss you so much, angel. I can't wait to see you again. Tell me everything that's been happening this week. How are Zoe and the kids? How's that chestnut of yours doing now? I just want to hear your voice kissing my ear.'

'I miss you too, Niall.' Tash fought tears, desperate for comfort. 'I love you so much.'

'I know you do, angel. And I'm blown away by it – I truly don't deserve you. Now tell me what you've been up to?'

For the first time ever, Tash found herself feeding him a pack of lies about how great things were. She simply couldn't bear to tell him the truth.

Relations between Tash and the Lime Tree Farm mob were in reality growing increasingly strained. She found it almost impossible to talk to Zoe, who made gallant efforts to be conciliatory. Tash was aware that she was sulking like a child, but felt hurt and very much alone. Gus and Penny were clearly worried about her too, but tactfully kept conversations practical and friendly. Neither of them wished to get involved in her personal problems, and both were too busy and distracted about money really to spare the time.

They had now been forced to sell three of their most promising youngsters to free up some cash, plus one of Gus's best internationals, Party Animal. This meant he was left with only two advanced horses to ride that season. One was the yard's vintage star, Sex Symbol, whom Gus worshipped because he had won Penny her last gold medal before she'd retired from top-flight competitions, but he was fifteen years old and only really had one more season in him before he retired to loll around in the Lime Tree fields and hunt for fun. The other was another gallant old-timer, the mule-faced, grouchy Fashion Victim, who was incurably lazy and unpredictable, so had remained unsold despite being on the market for almost a year. Neither was attractive to sponsors, team selectors, or likely to give Gus any long-term purchase on the sport, and he knew it. He became increasingly crabby and snappy, especially towards Tash.

She threw herself into working her own charges, battling with Snob who, as he got fitter, was growing stronger and more unruly by the minute, and bringing on kind-hearted, clumsy Mickey Rourke, who was still on the market but remained unsold, although Hugo had made a stupidly low offer.

Dear, long-suffering Hunk was at last being hacked out and lunged to strengthen his leg. Tash relished her time with the easy-going gentleman of the yard with his clever, stand-up comic's face and his incurable greed for Polos. Taking him out on slow, solitary hacks on the windswept downs, she could talk her heart out, certain that he was the most discreet of confidants and that, unlike Snob, wouldn't savage her with his teeth if she rambled on too long. With several other youngsters to exercise and weekly competitions to attend in an attempt to qualify for the bigger events later in the spring, Tash found she could keep her mind totally focused on the job, falling into bed at night too exhausted to dwell on Niall, the wedding or her own childish behaviour towards Zoe. She even gave up going to Flab-busters as she found it harder and harder to spare the time. Yet the weight still dropped off. At any other time, Tash would have been ecstatic. Now she barely noticed.

Which was pretty much the state in which Niall found her when he came back from the shoot a fortnight after her disastrous visit. The forge was a tip, Beetroot greeted him with a frenzied attack on his legs with her teeth, and his vast pile of post was being used as a draught-excluder behind the front door.

Tash was asleep on the sofa when he arrived, her feet, wearing much-darned, unmatched socks, poking up in the air where her ankles were propped on the arm, her head lolling close to the floor, nose-to-handle with a half-full cup of cold tea into which some of her hair was falling.

Niall sat on the old dog-eared chair opposite and, disengaging Beetroot from his ankle where she was starting to draw blood, took in the muddy cord breeches, the old jumper which he recognised as one of his own, the narrowness of her wrists which protruded from the rolled-over cuffs.

He stared up at the ceiling in despair. 'We're both a couple of fucking kids pretending to be adults,' he muttered, reaching for the script of the BBC adaptation of The Tenant of Wildfell Hall, in which he was due play the evil, tyrannical Huntingdon. He had three days off between the wrap of Celt and the start of the location shoot for Wildfell, which was taking place in Yorkshire. Then it was down to London for studio work and a week off before flying to America to promote Tough Justice. The prospect exhausted him.

When Tash awoke the next morning, she found that she was on the sofa, her hair sopping with wet tea, an excruciating crick in her neck and Beetroot asleep on her stomach. Opposite her a loud snoring sent her heartrate into triple figures. She peeped across the gloomy room and saw that Niall, still wearing his coat, was asleep in the armchair, its throw pulled over his legs for warmth, a script scattered around him where it had dropped from his lap and the plastic spine had broken off.

She longed to wake him, but it was past six already and she had a competition to get to in Wiltshire. She didn't even have time to shower as she pulled a clean shirt and jods from the washing machine – where they had lain damp and creased for days. She then grabbed her boots and, clicking her tongue for Beetroot – who had started to growl at the sleeping Niall – galloped along the lane. She competed three of Gus's young horses at the novice trials that day and returned exhausted, aching, and fully aware that she could have ridden far better had half her mind not been on Niall.

Their reunion that evening was fraught with awkwardness, but not as hellish as Tash had anticipated. They were both on their best, apologetic behaviour, trying desperately to please one another. Niall hardly drank at all as Tash cooked a luxury Marks and Sparks dinner which he ate his way through with a cheerful smile, even though she had forgotten to remove the cellophane cover before putting it in the oven.

Niall wanted to make slow, gentle love to her, but by the time he got out of the bathroom from hastily cleaning his teeth, she was already conked out in bed, her alarm set for first thing the next morning, her back a long arch of deep-sleep, as clear as a 'do not disturb' sign on a hotel door.

He settled in beside her and rested his cheek against the soft hair that lay across his pillow. It smelled of shampoo and straw. Closing his eyes, Niall longed for her to shift around and envelop him in a sleeping hug as she so often did. Instead, Tash muttered something in her sleep about spare bandages and then started to snore.

For the next few days, he barely saw her. He spent increasing amounts of time sitting in the kitchen with Zoe, bemoaning her absence and drinking Gus's scotch, which he replaced regularly before drinking it again.

'It's always like this at the start of the season. She has to qualify Mickey Rourke for some Intermediate events,' Zoe explained. 'And although Snob is technically qualified for Badminton because he won so much last year, she needs to give him some tough tests to prepare him this year. She's having one hell of a struggle with him at the moment – he almost broke her neck at Harewood last week.'

'I'll break her neck if she doesn't sit down and talk to me soon,' moaned Niall. 'I have to go back up to Scotland tomorrow, then straight to Shepperton for the dubs and on to Yorkshire for rehearsals. I won't be back until the end of March.'

'For Hugo's birthday party?' Zoe brightened.

'So it is.' Niall seemed to have forgotten. 'That should be fun.' He didn't sound at all enthusiastic.

'Ish,' she shrugged, not noticing his ironic tone. 'His bash is the day before Lowerton – the biggest advanced trials before Badminton. Apart from Saumur in April, it's absolutely the most vital comp for anyone hoping to give their horses a real test. Most of the eventers will be drinking like AA converts to keep their heads clear the next morning.'

'That should be fun,' Niall repeated, hardly listening.

Watching his pinched face, Zoe put down the entry forms she had been sifting through and sat down opposite him at the table. She was wary of probing too deeply. Yet he looked so tired and forlorn, she couldn't ignore him.

'It's not going too well at the moment, is it?' she asked gently.

A black eyebrow shot up and he smiled sadly. 'Not brilliantly, no.'

Zoe took a deep breath. 'You're not having second thoughts, are you? About the wedding?'

He looked at her for a long time, saying nothing, until Zoe squirmed with embarrassment at her nosy do-gooder inquisition. She had not forgotten his rude abruptness the night he had returned from the christening without Tash.

'Sorry – I'll butt out.' She made to stand up but he grabbed her arm to stop her.

'Has she said anything to you?'

Settling in her seat again, Zoe was as gentle and soft-spoken as Selina Scott drawing out a repressed royal in a one-off interview.

'I think she was very hurt by whatever happened in Scotland,' she murmured, her pale, focused eyes soaking up his face. 'She needs you to give her a lot of reassurance. I can tell she's desperate to talk things out, but she's clamming up because she's so afraid you don't love her as much as you did.'

'I adore her!'

'Then tell her,' Zoe said simply. 'She obviously feels horribly alone right now.'

'Then I wish she was as up front about it as you are.' Niall smiled sadly, letting go of her arm and sagging back in his chair.

'I'm not marrying you, Niall, so I can say what I like.' Zoe gave him a sage smile. 'A wedding's an enormously stressful thing to organise. Her mother and step-mother are putting her under a lot of pressure to come up with a guest list; there's less than three months to go now.'

'Shit!' Niall's face darkened.

Zoe bit her lip, on the verge of digging deeper, but he was staring broodily at the wall chart now, eager for a distraction.

'Fucking Gus is working her to death, so he is,' he sighed. 'She puts in more hours than a junior hospital doctor. That's why she's stressed out.'

'We're all working hard. The yard's in crisis.'

Niall rubbed his eyes. 'I know how it feels. I'm shattered. I owe the tax man thirty grand – Christ knows where I'll find it. And until I can get our settlement reassessed in the States my ex-wife takes practically every penny I earn – ironic as she'll be paying me in May. Or rather *Cheers!* will. I haven't had a holiday in months. It's one of the reasons I was so bloody wired in Scotland.'

'Tash said you weren't yourself.' Zoe picked at a pock-mark in the table.

'Nor was she!' He looked offended. 'She was extremely bloody-minded, so she was, stomping off like that.'

'I think she feels pretty guilty about that.'

'Did she say so?'

Zoe shook her head, not quite looking him in the eye. 'We had words, but she didn't say much. I bungled it, to be honest. I took your side rather.'

'My side?' He tilted back his chair despondently, eyes raking the ceiling. 'Jesus! I wasn't aware that we were that divided now.'

'Not side, exactly.' Zoe blushed. 'Sorry – bad choice of word. I was angry with her for doing a bunk from Scotland.'

Niall stared at the ceiling in silence for a few moments. He looked as though he was praying.

'I don't blame her to be quite honest,' he sighed, tipping the chair forward again and staring at Zoe's cat brooch. 'That's a sweet wee thing, now.'

'Why don't you blame her?'

He flipped a teaspoon over on the table and pressed his finger into its bowl.

'I think I've made a big mistake, Zoe.' He let the spoon go and rested his creased forehead in his palms.

She froze, guessing he was about to confess to not wanting to marry Tash. She wasn't at all certain that he should be telling her so.

'What makes you say that?' She cleared her throat anxiously.

'I always fuck up.' He looked at her with a lop-sided grin. 'I find Tash so hard to read – I mean, Christ, I love her but you know even when I first met her, I couldn't tell if she was attracted to me or not. She gives out very funny signals.'

'I know that.' Zoe smiled. 'She's the most bashful extrovert in the world.'

'So I thought she was all for this thing, but now I reckon she's not keen.' His palms hit his forehead again. 'In fact, I keep expecting her to beg me not to go through with it.'

'Things aren't that drastic, surely?'

Niall shrugged. 'She seemed really happy about it to start with, but I suppose she just wanted what I wanted. Now she's so frosty and uncommunicative, I think I should just call it all off – buy myself out of the contract.'

Zoe looked at him wonderingly. He was rather losing her here. She kept finding that her eyes were drawn to his hands – they were so bony and long-fingered that they seemed to have a life of their own, dancing around the table in search of distraction. She longed to stretch out an arm and still them for a moment.

'What exactly do you mean?' she asked, watching as his fingers played with the teaspoon.

Niall sighed deeply, reaching down to scratch Enid who had crept anxiously up to him, topaz eyes bulging as she contemplated dashing away again.

'I wasn't altogether honest with her,' he started. 'I just couldn't bring myself to tell her until it was too late and too difficult.' He stopped, biting his lip so that Zoe could see his lovely, uneven white teeth reddening the flesh to the colour of parma ham.

'What didn't you tell her?'

'That Lisette's behind it all,' he sighed, closing his eyes. 'And will be there throughout.'

'Who's Lisette?' Zoe asked. The name was only vaguely familiar.

'She's my ex-wife and still pretty predatory.' He grimaced. 'I can handle her but Tash goes to pieces when she's around. It could be a bit of a walking on eggshells situation.'

Zoe's mouth was hanging open. She was finding this hard to take in. His ex-wife persuading him to marry Tash? It seemed insane.

'Go on,' she murmured numbly.

'Well, I flunked telling Tash until I was in Scotland and then just blurted it down the phone during a row.' He groaned at the memory. 'She's been like a hurt dog ever since, cowering away from me. And I guess I've been pretty belligerent too, ashamed of myself for being so cowardly – drinking too much, flirting my bollocks off, acting the hell-raiser as of old. It's a defence mechanism. I know I do it, and I know it's madness, but it just feels so easy to slip into.'

'Like a bottle?'

He looked at her sharply and then shrugged. 'I guess. A little. Lisette used to give me a really hard time about it, but Tash tries to ignore it, which means I just do it all the more and that hurts her so badly.' He looked up guiltily. 'I was a bit of a sod in Scotland.'

Zoe nodded carefully, not knowing how to frame her next question but desperate to know.

'Niall . . .' She coughed. 'Tell me – why on earth is your ex-wife behind your decision to marry Tash?'

His dancing fingers momentarily stilled, Niall pulled back his chin in confusion, trying to figure out what she meant. Then, supposing she was asking him why his first marriage broke up, he shrugged.

'I adored Lisette – idolised her even.' He scratched Enid's nose, careful not to frighten her. 'I think I was a bit obsessive, a bit cloying for her, but I just loved her so damned much – she's alive and ambitious and in control whereas I've always been a bit of a dithering bugger. She supported me, believed in me; I think her faith in me helped me focus in those early years when I went after the jobs rather than them coming after me. Christ, I did everything from washing pots to driving cabs as I waited for adverts in *The Stage* and prayed for big breaks.'

Zoe watched in silence as he sat up again and poured himself another scotch, sending Enid scuttling back to her basket.

'She worked for the Beeb then,' he explained. 'Producing documentaries with Matty. That's how I met her – Matty and I go way back. But while Matty has the intellectual mind and didactic fervour, Lisette is far, far better at getting people motivated, at wining and dining and shining out as a talent. She went to work for an independent in the early-eighties and her career really took off – long before mine; she supported me for years and I loved her to distraction for it. Then when I started to get the breaks, to work away so much and receive acclaim of my own, the marriage started to lose its way.'

'Was she jealous maybe?' Zoe coaxed, but he shook his head.

'She was proud of me, and proud of her contribution to my success,' he explained. 'It was more about my abstraction, the fact I made friends with a new set of people on each job, took them under my wing and all but brought them to live with us. Our marriage became very crowded, Princess Diana-style. An actor is hell to live with, you know.'

'Sounds like living here.' Zoe smiled reassuringly.

'Well, I think she'd started to go off me a bit by then anyway.' He sighed. 'She was never very faithful – I knew that early on and went through every type of hell, alternately trying to make her stop and then trying to reconcile myself to it as a factor in our marriage. She never had serious affairs – they were more like quick fixes to make herself feel good, appease the jealousy she felt when seeing me in a clinch with some actress on stage.'

'But that was just acting.' Zoe gazed at him. 'Hers were the real thing.'

'Don't be so sure.' He smiled sadly. 'She liked the big, bad seductress role, but within our marriage she was far softer, in far greater need of reassurance. She could be a bloody bitch, don't get me wrong, but it's impossible not to forgive her – she's so damned funny and charming and sexy. She's got tremendous guts too. She would never flinch from owning up, coming clean and sitting down to talk out how we were going to work through something. And I wasn't altogether blameless.'

'In what way?'

He took a slug of scotch. 'I have a tendency to fall in love a lot,' he confessed. 'Don't get me wrong, I don't shag my way from film set to theatre to television studio. Lisette used to call them my "Rushes Crushes" because they generally petered out by the time the rushes of the love scene were shown the next morning, but my moping around like a love-sick teenager must have irritated the hell out of her.'

'How did it end?' She watched his animated fingers drawing intricate patterns on the table top.

He winced. 'She ran off with an American trustafarian who had convinced her he was the next Quentin Tarantino. Then he fucked off and left her to pick up a decimated career in the States. Even I wondered if she could do it. But she has – and now she's back to hire me.'

'She's hired you?' Zoe was completely confused, wondering for an awful, ludicrous moment whether Lisette was somehow paying Niall to marry Tash.

'I'm one of the leads in the next film she's producing,' he explained. 'Didn't I tell you? It's why Tash is so upset.'

'Because Lisette's given you a job?' Zoe suddenly realised what he'd been driving at and felt a complete fool for going so far up the wrong tree – like a by-pass protester realising she's been camped in an oak three miles from the chain-saws. She started frantically to back-track. 'You think that's why Tash was unhappy in Scotland?'

'Of course it is.' Niall didn't quite meet her gaze. 'My bloody awful timing has driven darling Tash into a silence that I can't shake her out of. I trust her a thousand times more than I ever trusted Lisette, I'd die for her, but she just can't see that. She's convinced I'd run back to Lisette if she were just to click her fingers.'

Zoe was watching his face and could see the taut tic of worry working in his cheek.

'Are you so sure you wouldn't?' she breathed, flinching as he looked up at her sharply.

But his answer was cut off as India's exquisite face appeared around the door.

'Mummy – er – hi, Niall. Actually you'd be better. Can I ask your advice?' She was hanging half-in the doorway, most of her body still on the third rung of the stairs.

Niall, staring angrily at Zoe, pulled himself together and smiled across at her.

'Sure, angel.'

'I've got a date,' India confessed, absolutely scarlet with embarrassment, 'and I rather hoped you'd let me know if you think this is a bit too tarty or not?'

As she shuffled into the room, tugging down a rather short skirt which revealed her endless legs, Niall let out a wolf whistle and shook his head. 'It's simply lovely – if I were ten years younger I'd fall for you myself.'

'Don't you mean twenty years?' India asked, with the polite tactlessness of youth.

'Yes, yes, I suppose so,' Niall laughed, not really minding. He had continually to remind himself that he was closer to forty than twenty.

India's long, blonde hair, worn in a fringe, framed her pale, smooth face with its clever blue eyes so that she looked almost too perfect – like a pretty heroine in a Japanese comic strip. Niall could suddenly see cool, poised Zoe as a younger woman – that same impassive, flawless face and wise eyes; she must have been stunning. He stared from daughter to mother in awe.

Zoe saw the way he was looking at her and felt absurdly flustered.

'Excuse me, I think Wally's trying to say something.' She extracted his drooling face from her lap and headed hastily through to the scullery to pick up the dog bowls, her shoulders high with tension as she fought to calm down from her tactless cross-questioning a moment earlier. She was convinced Niall had been about to lay into her. And she was equally convinced that he had not been entirely honest with her either.

Niall watched her snatched, nervy movements and realised that he had come close to confessing something he hadn't even admitted to himself. Raking his hand through his hair, he turned back to India and smiled.

'You look delectable, angel,' he assured her. 'Whoever it is, he's a lucky sod, so he is.'

Niall hoped he was also a very well-behaved sod; she was total jail bait in that simple, classic tunic dress which made her look at least eighteen. Tall, willowy and with features hewn like a smooth marble bust, India could never look tarty – she had too much poise and class, the sort of cut-glass looks that could earn her a fortune if she were spotted by a modelling agency. She could have a long and starved career as a coke-sniffing, chain-smoking model if she so desired. And tonight, looking as she did, she needed to be with a man who possessed tremendous self-control. Niall privately hoped he was a spotty fourteen year old who was terrified of her.

'Actually, I feel really mean because it's Ma's birthday and we usually all eat together,' India whispered, glancing across to the scullery. 'But I've fancied this man for ages and I never dreamed he'd ask me out.'

'Sure, your mother won't mind.' He smiled reassuringly. 'She was on a first date once too, and she's the others to keep her company now.'

India looked slightly doubtful as she dashed upstairs to check her reflection one last time and then clean her teeth once again.

With a blast of cool air, Ted sauntered in from the front door wearing his favourite navy blue shirt – always saved for hot dates – his knowing ladsy face grinning broadly. Tash had recently re-clipped his hair, but in her distraction she had cut rather too much off so that he looked like Brian Glover, his scalp gleaming through the lightest dusting of stubble like a white chocolate truffle sprinkled with cocoa. He reeked of aftershave and was carrying a card for Zoe.

'Where is she?' he asked cheerfully.

'In there.' Niall nodded towards the open door where Zoe was feeding the dogs.

'India?'

Niall gaped at him. 'You're India's date?'

'Sure.' He looked mildly offended. 'Why not?'

'Well, you're too old for one,' snapped Niall. 'And you're going out with Franny . . .'

'It's off. She doesn't like my new haircut.'

'And it's her mother's bloody birthday,' Niall blazed on, keeping his voice hushed but deadly. 'You could have been a little more thoughtful.'

Ted shrugged, unbothered. 'Zoe was all for it – says she doesn't want to celebrate turning forty other than by drinking herself silly and watching the box. Rufus is out too – some video sesh, I think, which basically means blagging his way into a pub in Marlbury with his schoolmates. And Pen and Gus are eating out with some potential sponsors.'

'You mean Zoe's all alone on her fortieth?' Niall was horrified.

'Way she wants it.' Ted tossed the card on the table and headed towards the stairs, yelling for India.

The moment they had set off in his rusty Renault 5, Niall stomped through to Zoe.

'That girl is far too young to be going out with the likes of Ted,' he declared. 'He's totally immoral.'

Leaving a spoon in a dog bowl, Zoe turned back to him, surprised by his anger, but trying to keep the atmosphere light.

'You sound like her father.' She smiled awkwardly. 'She's been badgering me all week about it and I rather caved in, to be honest.'

'He'll try and deflower her the moment they're away from here.' Niall was aware that he was using the prudish, pompous language of an old biddy fresh from a Moral Meeting with the WI but he felt wildly sanctimonious right now, possibly exacerbated by the recent admissions of his own infidelity.

'She knows that,' Zoe laughed, turning back to the dog bowls. 'When I tried to give her a gentle bit of advice about saying no when one was uncomfortable, she started reeling off the most extraordinary knowledge about how to say no, demand a condom, give a blow job and lift one's legs for deeper penetration. It's all those magazines she reads, I suppose.'

'Jesus!' He was appalled. 'And you still let her go?'

'She's not planning to have sex with him, Niall,' Zoe laughed, putting the dogs' dinners on the stone tiles. 'She was flabbergasted when I even broached the subject. She's so bloody sane it frightens me – she won't drink, loathes smoking, thinks Ecstasy is a death warrant and knows more about sexually transmitted diseases than I do.' She headed back through to the kitchen. 'The only thing she's dead set on finding out about tonight is French kissing – despite the threat of mouth-ulcers and cold sores, on which she is no doubt extremely well read. She's decided that Ted is a safe bet as he cleans his teeth regularly and never has bad breath.'

Following her, Niall was speechless.

'She never ceases to amaze me.' Zoe turned and watched his reaction with sparkling eyes. 'I'd trust her with my life, unlike my son whom

I suspect is right now drinking his way towards having his stomach pumped.'

Pressing his finger to his mouth, Niall tried to look shocked for a little longer but found himself laughing too. 'Christ, I'll never understand kids.'

'One never does – but it's quite good fun learning that at times.'

'I wonder if I ever will.' Niall shrugged, looking at the pictures of Zoe's kids through the years which littered the shelves and dresser.

'You and Tash will have great kids. She'll be a wonderful mum – scatty, but great fun.' Zoe started clearing away the debris on the table, eager to make up for her cross-questioning earlier. 'And you'll be a wonderful father.'

He didn't answer.

Aware that he was uncomfortable even with this line of conversation, she rattled quickly and rather indiscreetly on, not seeing Ted's unopened card as she stacked it into a pile of event schedules.

'Penny is desperate for children, poor darling, but they simply can't afford it, and there are some ghastly doubts about her fertility which have dragged on for years. If they ever want to go for it, it's pretty likely they'd have to go through IVF treatment which would be such a trauma for them, and so costly. I think she's beginning to panic a bit – she's already thirty-six.'

'Same age as me,' Niall mused absently, and then suddenly snapped to attention. 'And you are celebrating a birthday, sweetheart, which I knew nothing about. Happy returns!' He leaned across to peck her on the cheek just as she was wiping it with a dog-foody hand, so that he got a mouthful of Chappie-flavoured fingers.

'Thanks.' Zoe moved away in polite embarrassment, her hand suddenly burning hot. 'I'm not really celebrating this one.'

'Of course you are.' He followed her, taking the pile of papers from her hands. 'Go upstairs and smarten up – I'm taking you out to dinner at the Olive Branch.'

'Thank you, but I can't possibly,' she replied, flustered. 'What about Tash? She's coming back from this event soon.'

'We'll leave her a note to join us.' He was already binning the papers and searching for his coat. 'Now go and wash your hands while I call Ange and get him to squeeze in another table.' He dodged past Beetroot who was snarling at him whilst trying to eat at the same time, almost choking with the combined effort.

Laughing in resignation, Zoe headed upstairs, suddenly rather glad that she was celebrating her birthday after all. Life might not begin at forty, she mused, but that was no excuse not to get one.

Fifteen

ZOE FOUND THAT SHE couldn't possibly keep pace with Niall in drinks, although she made the mistake of starting out by trying to do so. Consequently she was pretty tight by the time they even looked at the menus.

A vast fire was crackling nearby, into which Niall tossed cigarette butts at regular intervals. Faces flushed from the heat and the booze, they chatted rather mindlessly about news and views as Ange dashed back and forth past them, occasionally stopping for a chat or to make a recommendation. He was on top form tonight having been highly recommended by Craig Brown the previous week. His peppery pelt of hair gleamed like the pewter tankards above his bar and his coffee-bean eyes were sparkling so brightly that he seemed to have undergone a sea change and replaced them with black pearls.

Zoe wasn't sure whether it was the alcohol loosening her tongue, or just his manner, but she found Niall remarkably easy to talk to. By the time she was chomping through a large plate of gnocchi, she had already described her childhood and was hinting at the unhappiness of her marriage, a subject upon which she seldom allowed herself to be drawn. There was something about Niall's big brown 'talk-to-me' eyes and astonishing, self-deprecating honesty about his own marriage which left her feeling she could keep nothing from him. She could see why Tash described him as a better listener than the Midland griffin.

'My ex-husband, Si, is a very driven, very clever man,' she explained. 'That was one of my greatest problems, really – he was a total workaholic throughout our marriage, and a perfectionist to boot. When he got home he simply couldn't accept the fact that his household didn't run as smoothly as his office.'

'What does he do?' Niall asked, refilling his glass.

'Well, he was a design architect – one of the best; very well respected. But he doesn't work anymore.'

'Retired?'

'In a sense.' Zoe was unwilling to let too much slip. 'He had a sort of breakdown in the eighties.'

'And took early retirement?'

She took a deep breath. 'Not voluntarily, no, but it was obvious he couldn't work anymore.' She glanced away uncomfortably. 'He developed schizophrenia. Paranoid schizophrenia, to be precise.'

'Christ!' Niall breathed out in horror.

'It was awful,' Zoe confessed. 'Total Jekyll and Hyde stuff. I said he was a perfectionist, didn't I? Well, it was rather more than that, really. He was so *good* at what he did, everyone knew him. I fancied him rotten for years before he asked me out – I'd been to interview him for a magazine profile. I was quite well known then.'

'I remember.' Niall grinned. 'I used to slobber over your by-line photo.'

'Really?' Zoe blushed slightly.

He nodded and, when she fell silent, prompted her to go on.

'Well, after we married, Si didn't want me to work – not in the nine to five sense that I once did, that is. I wrote a column for a while – it was amazing what schlock one could get away with in those days. A quickly dashed-off witty five hundred words about the washing machine breaking down earned me a fortune. I even wrote a novel – a decent one, not the tat I scribble now. But then I got pregnant with Rufus and was pretty ill throughout. Cue for marriage to go downhill.'

'He wasn't very supportive?'

She gave a rueful smile. 'We lived in this extraordinary house in Greenwich that Si had designed – totally minimalist; it won a couple of awards. It was supposed to be low-maintenance, nothing to dust etcetera, but it was actually impossible to exist normally in. There were no bookshelves, pictures, ornaments, nothing. If one left a newspaper lying around, Si would explode. I think Lime Tree Farm would be his idea of hell.'

Niall was watching her closely now, saying nothing, just letting her talk on.

'With kids comes litter – it's inevitable.' She sighed. 'And I was adamant that I didn't want a nanny, but I have to confess I wasn't a natural mother.'

'You're a great mother!' he protested.

'I'm fine now, but I was appalling to start with; I had killing post-natal depression for months after Rufus, I felt utterly trapped, cried all the time, and panicked if he so much as sneezed. I must have been hell to live with and Si was never the most sympathetic of listeners. Looking back at that time from his point of view, I suppose he equated children with dirt, noise, litter, and a tearful, abstracted wife.'

'Kids must take a lot of adjusting to.' Niall poured more wine into both of their glasses, although hers was still almost full.

'The trouble is, I don't think he was prepared to adjust at all,' Zoe went on. 'He was wildly jealous of my time and started to get a bit fanatical about tidiness and such like. I just thought he was being more of an old fusspot than usual, but by the time India came along, he was really manic about it – he would wash his hands twenty or thirty times after a meal, clean his teeth until they bled, throw away the kids' toys if they were left out and scream the house down if he found a speck of dirt anywhere. I think we went through about ten cleaners in as many months.'

Niall could see the pain in her face and guessed that, although she didn't admit it, she levelled a great deal of blame at herself.

'I talked it over with a psychologist friend and we came to the conclusion that it was obsessional neurosis.' She rubbed her mouth. 'She suggested Si should go for Behavioural Therapy. But it was ridiculous – he wouldn't even own up to having a problem. He'd become more and more withdrawn and unemotional; it was so hard to have a decent conversation with him because he spoke so quickly that his sentences sometimes didn't make sense – he'd get the words in the wrong order or use words that didn't even exist. But he was still as quick as lightning if I tried to fool him – I told him that I was going for stress counselling and wanted him to come too; the moment we arrived he realised it was a ruse and you couldn't see him for smoke.'

'Go on.'

'Then the voices started. He was behaving more erratically than ever – doing strange things, such as pulling the kitchen apart to look for some non-existent smell he thought was lingering, or following me to Sainsbury's because he'd convinced himself that I was having an affair. He even locked me in the bathroom for an entire day once because I was due to meet a friend for lunch and he didn't want me to go. I was frantic with worry because India was just a tot – Rufus had started school then. But when he let me out, India said she'd had great fun playing washerwoman with Daddy. He'd had her scrubbing and scrubbing her toys in a plastic bucket all day. A two year old! Whenever I tried to talk to him about it, he explained it away by claiming that he'd been told to do it. I honestly started to wonder whether he'd joined a cult or something.'

'But the voices were in his head?'

She nodded. 'Obviously other people had started to notice his instability as well – friends stopped asking us out, he began to lose contracts at work, his family backed right off too. His jealousy escalated to insane proportions – he went to one of those spy shops and bought all sorts of surveillance equipment to rig up around the house so that he could listen to what I was doing wherever I was. He bugged all the phones in case I was talking about him and his "madness". Instead of sleeping at night, he'd stay up listening to the tapes of calls I'd made while he wasn't around to listen in live. Then one day he found that I'd left a load of washing piled by the machine and went so bananas that he burned the lot – right there in the kitchen, using petrol of all things; the room was gutted and he scorched most of his hair and forehead off in the process.'

'Jesus! Didn't you get help?'

She nodded. 'Thankfully our doctor was an old friend and he coaxed Si into a psychiatric consultant's office in Harley Street by telling him that he thought he might need minor surgery on his burns – it was the only way to get him there, to pretend the man was a plastic surgeon. Si was in total denial, refusing to admit to a problem; he thought his behaviour was completely rational. The consultant couldn't believe that he'd been able to live such a relatively normal life – he also said he was unlikely ever to fully recover. The only reason he had hidden it for so long was because he was so bloody clever. Within a week, Si was taking so many drugs he was in a walking coma. His voice was slurred, he was clumsy and forgetful. I'd lost him.

'I can't tell you how guilty I felt afterwards – it was just indescribable. I tried to look after him for almost a year, but it almost drove me to madness too – it was like having three children and, despite the drugs, he was still dangerous and unpredictable. He would lock me in the house quite regularly, sticking postage stamps over the locks so that he could tell if I'd gone out. I walked around with spare keys and second-class stamps in every pocket. It was ridiculous, a lunatic life, living with a lunatic.'

'You still loved him?' Niall watched her wet eyes glittering as they reflected the fire.

'In memories, yes, but I confess they faded fast.' She shrugged. 'In that state he was bloody hard to love and very easy to hate. He was still clever and had snatches of such lucidity that I almost believed he was better again, but the next moment he'd be thrashing around like a wild thing, telling me I was contaminated or a whore or rank with some infectious disease. Then he'd be catatonic for hours afterwards. I was always afraid that he might hurt the children – particularly as he was so terrified of illness and they were going through the mumps, tonsillitis and chicken pox phase – so I lived on my nerves, never letting them out of my sight. I had no work – no one wanted me to write for them and I can see why now. Everything I submitted was dashed off in such a distracted hurry. At the time I thought there was some sort of conspiracy going on. I even convinced myself that Si had been ringing around all the newspaper and magazine editors warning them off. Of course he hadn't – it was a time of great change, papers under new ownership and editorship, moving out of Fleet Street, revolutionising their printing techniques and streamlining their teams. There was no call for the sort of happy, chatty house-wife column in an era when the career woman was starting to march into the boardroom and demand her rights. And that silly column I once did was all I was remembered for; I'd been labelled, all my earlier work seemingly forgotten.

'When Si finally agreed to move into a residential clinic we were practically broke.' She took a huge slug of wine. 'The only place he agreed to go was, of course, the most expensive in the country. So we sold the house and invested the money to pay his fees. I took the kids out of school and we moved in with Penny and Gus. I said it was for a few months and I'm still here – outstaying my welcome.'

'They'd be devastated if you left!' Niall protested. 'You hold the ship together.'

'Well, it's not my cooking they want me to stay for.' She managed a faint smile. 'Although I suppose I make a decent answering service, and the kids are useful spare grooms.'

'Plus you contribute a huge whack to the mortgage.'

Zoe shrugged. 'I think that's one of Tash's exaggerations. I get a few thousand pounds for each book and most of that goes into Si's account to keep it topped up.'

'He's still at the clinic?'

She nodded. 'He went through a spell of trying to live a normal life again – rented a flat in London and wrote some academic articles about architecture – but within weeks he was suffering all the old symptoms plus some. The fool had taken himself off all the drugs. It was so sad. He was taken to the police station at one point and sectioned under the Mental Health Act. One of his neighbours had caught him going nuts in the hallway, trying to tear up the floorboards because he thought there was a smell beneath. When she told him to stop, he attacked her.'

'And now?'

'He's still in deepest Staffordshire, designing modern houses that he will never get to build. I visit him every month – I can't bear to go more, to see the man I loved restricted so dreadfully by his own diseased brain. They really do take part in group basket-weaving sessions, you know?' She smiled up at him, acutely embarrassed to have spilled so much.

Niall took her hand, giving it a warm, reassuring squeeze.

'And how are you now?'

'Fine.' She gently pulled her fingers away. 'The kids are so wonderful – but I'm sure there are scars underneath. They were never loved by their father, India comes to see him sometimes and he doesn't even know who she is – he's just blanked her out. Rufus loathes him – begged me to get a divorce. He got sort of fixated on it, frighteningly like his father. It took me five years to convince Si to let me have one.'

'D'you think you'll ever remarry?'

Zoe laughed. 'Well, that's not why I got it – to make myself available. Gosh, no! It was a way of getting some control over my life again, of feeling less guilty about Si's awful, hellish life. Somehow it allowed me a little distance to evaluate the situation and work out where to go.'

'So where are you going?'

'Nowhere for now.' She pushed her dessert plate to one side, the perfect square of *tiramisù* untouched. 'The kids are happy at their schools. I could just about afford to send them to private ones again now, but when I asked them whether they wanted that they both refused point blank. Living with Penny and Gus gives them a lot of stability, a feeling of family unity. And I think Penny finds their presence a Godsend. Young kids might make her resentful and sad, but those gallumphing teens seem to give her the right sense of motherliness without the yearning for a tot. She adores them.'

Niall put down his glass and tilted his head. 'I asked about you, Zoe.'

'I'm happy enough.' She shrugged. 'Penny and India are forever trying to set me up with men before I get too wizened, but they've got hopeless taste.'

Niall laughed. 'Still you can't keep yourself hidden away in that farm forever. You're a beautiful woman, Zoe, you need someone around to appreciate that.'

She smiled gratefully, mildly embarrassed by the compliment but aware enough of her looks not to argue with false modesty. 'Well, I've got two big, noisy kids and very little time, which doesn't help. I've been out with a couple of men in the last few years – I saw one for several months actually – but I find it very hard to trust people after Si, and to be honest I'm more of a London intellectual than a country wife type. Most of the men I meet are locals, or eventing friends of Pen and Gus. I know this sounds monstrously snobbish, but I find them rather shallow and arrogant as a rule. I love living around here, but I think looking for a man is like shopping for coats – one needs to go to London.'

'That sounds pretty bloody damning to me,' Niall laughed, leaning back as Ange whisked up personally to remove their plates, mouth pursed with irritation as he saw that Zoe hadn't touched her dessert.

'Ees no good?' he looked at her, eyes lugubrious with mock-hurt.

'I'm certain it was lovely,' Zoe apologised. 'I just have an upset tummy right now, Ange.'

'Hmmph – why you come and eat here then?' He flounced off.

But Zoe was gazing into her wine glass thoughtfully, watching the dim, orange light from the fire play in the depths of the Chianti.

'There was one man,' she murmured as Niall opened his mouth to speak. He promptly shut it again.

'Yes?'

'No – I shouldn't have mentioned it.' She took a huge gulp of wine and coughed as it streamed into her wind pipe. 'Too close to home. It was a silly mistake, really.'

'Please tell me if you want to.' He leaned forward anxiously. 'I won't mention it to a soul.'

Zoe glanced around, keen not to be overheard

'I met him at a party,' she whispered, eyes still glued to her glass. 'At the farm. It was just after Tash had moved in. You were in Puerto Rico or something glamorous – we hadn't met then.'

'I remember. I had half a scene in a Stallone blockbuster. I came to stay a couple of weeks later.'

'That's right. Well, it was Gus's birthday, so we had a huge barbecue all day. Tash was a bit new and nervous so Penny got her to invite a load of friends and family.'

'I think I recall Gus warning her never to let her cousin Marcus over his threshold again.' Niall grinned. 'Didn't he give Wally a hash cake?'

'That's right.' Zoe nodded, too absorbed in her painful memory to muster a smile. 'Well, one of her lot arrived late in a very black mood and hardly socialised at all. He came into the kitchen while I was washing up some glasses – we'd run out as usual. I think he just wanted to get out of the throng. Anyway he sat and chatted and drank his way through an entire bottle of red wine. We got on tremendously well – he was so bright and witty, very dry. I suppose we were both terribly tight but you know how it is when you have a good old flirt for fun – there were no fireworks or turtle doves, just laughter and too much looking at one another. I felt like a teenager.'

'I know the feeling exactly.' Niall nodded and played with his wine glass.

'Well, I'm deeply ashamed to admit this, but I behaved like a silly teenager too.' She hung her head even more. 'I went into the back pantry for something or other and we were having such an animated conversation that he followed me while we talked. The next moment we were necking like fifteen year olds. It was all rather undignified but tremendous fun. That's when the fireworks went off – it was so stupid and dangerous, but we were all over each other.'

'So?' Niall grinned. 'Where's the harm in that?'

'He was too drunk to drive back, so he decided to stay the night,' she went on, her face aflame. 'He kept looking at me in a way that said sex after lights out – it was still very teenage but incredibly erotic. Everyone was pissed and tired – you know what it's like after parties – so they pitched off to bed. He conked out on the sofa for a nap. I stayed up to clear away stuff and dear Tash helped me, practically keeling over with tiredness. She said she'd had a lovely time and was so pleased that I'd looked after her brother, Matty. Then she explained that he was in a terrible funk when he arrived because the babysitter had let them down at the last minute and his wife had insisted on staying in London instead of dumping the kids at a friend's which he'd wanted. Apparently they'd had a flaming row and he'd only come down at all to spite her.'

Niall's eyes were huge. 'Matty? You necked Matty in a larder?'

Zoe covered her face with her hands and nodded. 'He and Sally brought the kids down one Sunday when you were staying, remember? It was just a couple of weeks after the party. We couldn't even look at one another.'

'Christ!' He was still trying to take this in. 'Matty? Christ!'

'I feel so ashamed. I'd had no idea he was married. I hadn't known Tash that long, so she hadn't told me much about her family. I knew he had kids because he'd mentioned them when we were talking, but I'd just assumed they were from a previous relationship. When Sally turned up two weeks later with a child on each arm and a bump in the middle, I could have killed Matty. She was eight months pregnant and far too lovely to cheat on.'

'She is lovely. The bloody idiot!' Niall banged his wine glass. 'What the hell did he think he was playing at?'

Zoe rubbed her eyes tiredly and shrugged. 'He was drunk – we both were – and he was mad at her for digging her heels in. Plus I was flirting for England that day. I found him wildly attractive after the ham-fisted approaches of all those thick farmers. Men do very strange things when their wives are heavily pregnant. He used me as a bit of momentary escapism, I suppose. You can't really blame him for that.'

'I bloody can.'

'Are you saying you never do it?' Zoe sighed, looking up. 'Flirt for escapism? What about your Rushes Crushes?'

Niall tried to stare her out but found his eyes dropping guiltily away.

'I don't entirely believe your line about Tash behaving bloody-mindedly in Scotland,' she said gently. 'It's not like her – she might be hellishly stubborn at times but I know how timid and willing to please she is, and she'd cut out her heart for you, she loves you so much. She needed a jolly good reason to behave as she did.'

'Well, she didn't have one.' Niall picked up his glass and drained it. 'I'll get another bottle.' He looked around impatiently for Ange, then his face suddenly darkened with worry.

Zoe was about to badger him a little more when she followed his gaze and caught sight of Tash wavering in the doorway, still wearing muddy breeches and a tatty baseball cap. Spotting them, she grinned broadly and bounded towards their table, knocking a chair over in her wake. Zoe drank in her scatty enthusiasm – she was as chaotic and lovable as a spaniel puppy desperate to say hello to everyone at once.

Niall watched her progress with a far more guarded expression.

'Happy birthday!' she panted, handing over a battered parcel. 'Sorry it's squashed. Kirsty sat on it in the Land-Rover on the way back.'

'How did you get on?' Zoe asked, noticing that when Tash kissed Niall, he didn't respond. Her stomach twisted with concern.

'Fine.' Tash pulled a spare chair over and flopped down on it. 'Mickey won his class so is now a fully fledged Intermediate which puts a few more grand on his asking price, so keep it quiet from Gus, will you? Snob towed me around at twice the speed of light and came eighth in his class – his dressage was hopeless. Hugo and Bodybuilder won again. That horse is simply phenomenal! Plus Hugo won the other open class with Surfer and scooped up most of the novice classes as well. He's bloody unstoppable. Kirsty had a fall . . .' She was breathless with excitement, still high from the exhilaration of competing. It always took her hours to come down.

'Is she okay?'

'Fine, thank God – bruised bum and pride mostly.' Tash grinned up at Ange as he sashayed over and gave her a very gallant kiss on the hand.

'Ees my favourite bride to be.' He puckered his mouth slightly as his lips made contact with the taste of horse sweat and hoof oil. 'You are joining your handsome fiancé and the matron of honour, no? Not long to wait now, huh?' He gave her a wrinkly wink.

Tash swallowed awkwardly. 'Three months.'

'Ah!' Ange pressed his hands together with delight. 'And all the village weel be watching. Ees so lovely – our two local stars. I take many photos. Maybe I sell them, no? More wine.' He dashed off excitedly, leaving Tash in flabbergasted silence.

Later, Tash was rather browned off that Niall insisted on walking Zoe back to the farm to guard her against local rapists, even though she herself undertook the same walk nightly alone. She considered tagging along for the company, but felt rather alienated by the strangely conspiratorial air that had suddenly sprung up between them.

Instead she called after Niall to bring back Beetroot, who was shacked up with Wally and Enid by the Aga, and then let herself into the forge.

The Rayburn had gone out, so she trudged into the back yard and collected enough coke to get it going, huddled beside it and wondered if she would ever beat Hugo again. He seemed to be able to win blindfold at the moment. Today when she had been hacking back to the horse-box after a disastrous cross-country round on Snob in which he had almost pulled her arms from her sockets and overshot two fences by going too fast, Hugo had walked past them on his unbeatable new horse, Surfer, his muddy face wreathed in victorious smiles.

'That stallion of yours still pulling like a bridal train, I see?' he'd called. 'I blame it on too much sex.'

'You what?' Tash bristled.

'The horse is covering too many mares,' he laughed. 'You didn't think I was talking about his rider, did you?'

Chance would be a fine thing, Tash had thought sadly.

Niall took ages to come back and then guiltily confessed that he'd had a coffee at the farm as India was back from her date and keeping them all in stitches with descriptions of Ted's attempts to seduce her.

'Did Penny and Gus get the sponsorship?' Tash asked hopefully.

Niall shook his head. 'Poor Gus is in a pretty evil mood. He said he was going to have to sell some horse called Mickey Rooney or something.'

Tash froze. 'Rourke?'

'That's it.' He pressed his palms to the warming Rayburn.

She fell into an uneasy silence. Gus had said that before – many times – but it still frightened her afresh when he repeated it.

'Zoe's a funny creature, isn't she?' Naill squatted beside her.

Tash looked up. She had decided to forgive Zoe today – it was part of a new think positive regime she had determined for herself, although the news about Mickey had already started to erode that. 'In what way? I think she's lovely.'

'Sure she is,' he nodded. 'But she's a lot more complicated than I gave her credit for. She's had a bloody hard life – I think she carries a lot of unhappiness around with her.'

Tash nodded in agreement. 'I've been a bit sulky with her lately,' she confessed. 'I should make it up – we had a childish fight.'

Niall grinned. 'You've been a bit sulky with me too.' He cocked his head.

'True.' She wondered whether to challenge him about Minty, but didn't have the heart. He was looking so soft-eyed and loving that she felt like doing back-flips and laughing instead of spoiling for a fight. He hadn't looked at her like that since he'd been down from Scotland.

'I suppose I should make it up to you too,' she said gutlessly, knowing she should really be suggesting a serious where-are-we-going-here talk. But when his eyes were drinking her in like this all she wanted to do was dive into them and drown. She felt giddy with relief, her long-buried libido leaping out of its lair and bouncing around delightedly.

'I suppose you should.' His nose was almost against hers now, breath caressing her upper lip.

'Niall,' she took a deep breath, 'I really think we need to . . .'

He planted a long, languid kiss on her lips, silken tongue tasting sweet and cool in her mouth.

'. . . kiss like that more often,' she panted, hormones drenching her body and pulses leaping like fleas on a dog.

They made love for the first time in weeks, but it was not altogether successful. Despite stubbing his toe on the bed-frame as he climbed in, Niall soon got into the mood again, but was somehow distanced and more technically demanding than usual, insisting that she contort herself into a hunched, squatting position which was more like natural childbirth than sex and not at all enjoyable. She gently eased him around so that she was on top and was starting to enjoy herself thoroughly when she noticed that the curtains were still open and she could be seen bouncing around on top of him from the lane.

'Oh, don't stop,' he groaned as she started to crouch forwards on her elbows.

'I'm not.' She pressed her forehead to his hot, fluctuating chest, hoping that no one was having a late-night dog walk outside.

At a moment of mutual near-ecstasy, Tash got cramp, which didn't help, and then Niall started to perform a strange, if erotic, finger massage around her inner thighs and pelvis which he had never done before and she wondered exactly where he'd learned it. Just as Niall twisted her beneath him once more and was getting into his smooth, fluid rhythm, Tash remembered something and wriggled into a half-sit.

'Where's Beetroot?'

He paused for a moment and looked down at her, his hair all over the place. She suddenly noticed how red and sweaty his face looked. And rather old, too.

'She wouldn't come with me,' he muttered, starting to get into his stride again as he plunged on, pushing her back against the pillows once more.

Tash tried to get into the swing, but found herself disturbingly haunted by the image of Niall looking sweaty, red and old – like Jimmy Savile after a marathon run, wearing a black curly wig. It rather put her off and she felt guiltily relieved when he finally came and rolled off her, for once not carrying on for lazy, fun-filled minutes afterwards until she herself came. Instead he kissed her on the shoulder and pulled her into a hug.

That night as they lay in a moist, post-coital tangle, Niall told her some of what Zoe had confessed to him, although he didn't mention that the person she had kissed at Gus's party was Matty.

Tash lay awake long after he had started snoring wondering who it could have been. Racking her brains, she only recalled talking to the eventer Brian Sedgewick for most of the afternoon – a big, flirty Welshman with a face like a caved-in prop forward's. She had hardly seen Zoe at the party. The only person she had seen even less of was Hugo. She was surprised how disturbed she was by the connection.

Sixteen

THE BUILD-UP TO HUGO'S thirtieth birthday party on the eventing circuit was tremendous. It seemed that everyone, from the riders to the grooms to the organisers, course-builders, trainers and owners, was going. Tash had to admire his democratic guest list. It was going to be such a huge bash that it was rumoured he had even hired bouncers to check invitations at the door. Remembering that she had torn hers up, Tash wondered whether she would get in.

As March brightened the flowerbeds and fattened the treetops, she started to feel a fanatical hatred for him. For one thing, he beat her at every competition; he was winning so much with the invincible Bodybuilder and the diminutive Surfer that he was considered a definite for next year's Olympics. For another, he had finally bought Mickey Rourke from Gus.

'You can't let Hugo have him!' Tash screamed when she found out, so demented with fury that she didn't care if Gus sacked her on the spot. 'He'll try to break his spirit – Mickey is totally the wrong sort of horse for Hugo. He needs lots of loving patience and encouragement.'

'I'm sure Mickey will be very loving and patient with Hugo,' Gus had said witheringly.

'I'll buy him!' Tash bleated desperately, close to tears. 'I'll match whatever Hugo has offered. I'll get a bank loan.'

But when Gus told her how much Hugo was paying, she fled the farm in tears. She couldn't lay her hands on that sort of money even if she held up one of the Marlbury High Street banks, let alone asked for a loan. It was probably twenty thousand more than the horse was worth.

She missed the big clumsy grey with his gangly legs and desperate willingness to please; the Lime Tree yard was less fun than ever without him. She was certain that Hugo had only bought Mickey because he knew she adored him so much. She kept having to stop herself slashing the tyres of his lorry.

At most competitions he pointedly ignored her. Only occasionally did he make a remark as he passed – mostly asking after Niall which was a sore point, as he was now in the States on a gruelling publicity tour for Tough Justice and called less and less often. But then, in a sudden volte face at a recent competition, Hugo had wandered up, all smiles, and cornered her by a fence as they walked the course.

'I've been doing a bit of detective work for you on Lisette O'Shaughnessy – or Norton, as she now likes to be known.'

'Oh, yes?' Tash had almost fallen into the fence with surprise. She had quite forgotten his promise on Valentine's Day; it had been such an embarrassing encounter that she had blocked it from her mind.

'Well, she's actually been after me.' He gave her a sideways look. 'Or rather, my house. She's already been around for a recce and is planning to bring several of her cronies to the party. She wants to use the place for her film.'

'Oh, no!' Tash covered her mouth and gaped at him.

'I thought you'd be pleased!' Hugo laughed at her, not altogether unkindly. 'I've already refused, but I thought I'd see what you said. I mean, it gives us all a great opportunity to keep an eye on them – and I'm certain she's up to something. I'm just worried that a load of actors romping around the place will frighten the horses.'

But Tash couldn't think beyond the immediate ramifications of his statement.

'You've invited Lisette to your party?' she gasped.

''Course I have.' He sighed irritably. 'I've always got on well with her – she's very funny. You'll just have to be brave, darling, and if you can't, don't come. You can always lock Niall up at home.'

Tash had stomped off in a huff at that point.

Worse still, Gus had now arranged for her to get a lift with Hugo to the Lowerton trials the day after the party. His own Badminton hopefuls, Fashion Victim and Sex Symbol, were already well qualified and being saved for the big event, so he and Penny were competing at a smaller set of trials nearby with a clutch of novices. In truth they could barely afford the diesel to Lowerton, which was over two hundred miles away.

'Can't I take the Land-Rover and trailer?' Tash begged.

'And sleep in it?' Gus laughed. 'It's a two-day trials, Tash. You might be willing to bunk down in a trailer covered in a horse blanket for the night – God knows I've done it myself enough times – but Ted would resign if I made him do it. Go with Hugo.'

'Can't Kirsty go with him and I'll go with the Stantons?'

'Too risky – thick Richie's coming over next week, remember? We're keeping Kirsty and Hugo well apart during his stay – I can't risk the horses being hurt if big, dumb boyfriend spots the connection and throws a wobbly. You go with Hugo. He's not sleeping in the horse-box – you know what he's like. He's shacking up with some friends as per usual. You'll be quite safe from his wicked ways.'

Tash pulled a face and walked out.

The wedding plans were raging on, despite precious little input from either Tash or Niall. Alexandra faxed several reports as to the state of The Dress, which Tash was due to be fitted into when she and Niall spent a few days in France with her mother and Pascal just before the wedding.

Tash allowed her to run riot – entirely acquiescing to her judgement and that of the super-efficient Henrietta who, in truth, was doing far more of the practical organisation. She had now booked the venue, the caterers, marquee hire firm, waiting staff and registrar, but was getting increasingly hysterical that there was no guest list and consequently no invitations and nobody buying presents from the list – which she herself had composed – that had been lodged with Peter Jones for almost a month.

'But it's only March,' Tash said vaguely.

'We should have sent the invitations out by now,' Henrietta told her. 'People are starting to buy their own presents – I know for a fact that your Aunt Cassandra has bought you a Dualit combi-toaster.'

'Whatever for?' Tash was amazed. 'I already have a toaster.'

Henrietta chose to ignore that. 'At this rate everything will be doubled up. I only just stopped James's brother from getting a bread maker.'

'Lucky escape then. I'm far too young to meet my bread maker.'

She had started to screen her calls to avoid wedding conversations, listening each night to a tape filling up with messages detailing rehearsal schedules and seating ideas. She became increasingly slack about returning calls, feeling horribly guilty but unable to face up to an hour-long debate about whether or not to sit Great-uncle Cornelius next to Great-aunt Germaine in case their hair rinses clashed. And she had more pressing things to worry about than her uncle's impending purchase of a bread maker.

Right now she felt that the most useful present that anyone could give the bride and groom would be a course of sessions at Relate. Niall had flown straight from Los Angeles to London without bothering to call in on the forge – by phone or in person.

Yet when he returned the night before the party, he was in roaring spirits despite an all-day rehearsal for The Tenant of Wildfell Hall. Racing into the forge, he gathered Tash into a fireman's lift and heaved her straight upstairs.

'Christ, but I've missed you!' he growled, dropping her down on the bed and starting to undress.

Rather blown away by his enthusiasm, Tash laughed with delight, pulling off the several jumpers she was wearing in excitement.

'And you can butt out.' Niall booted the door shut on Beetroot, who had pursued him upstairs, hackles drawn.

Later he told Tash off for continually leaving the answer machine on.

'But you never call!' she grumbled. 'I'd pick up if you did.'

'I do call – I just hang up when I get that irritating bloody message. I want to talk to you, angel, not a tape. I'm fed up of conducting my relationships by phone and fax.'

'Relationships?' she repeated, emphasising the plural teasingly.

But instead of laughing he looked cornered for a moment. 'And you really have to change that message, Tash,' he told her critically. 'You sound like you're being stabbed to death. You don't include me on it at all.'

'That,' she said truthfully, 'is because you're hardly ever here.'

Tash and Niall travelled to the party with Zoe, who had volunteered to drive.

'Sure, you'll be wanting to drink, won't you?' Niall protested. 'Let's all get a cab.'

'No, I'd better stay sober,' Zoe sighed. 'I have to keep an eye on the kids. Rufus is bound to mix everything and throw up on some of Hugo's exquisite furniture – not that he hasn't thrown up on most of it himself over the years. Really, I don't know how the laws of justice can let a philistine bounder like that live in such an exquisite house.'

They could hear the pounding of music even before they drove into Maccombe village, a gloriously remote cluster of brick and flint houses which nestled in a wooded perch on the edge of the Berkshire downs.

Of them all, Haydown was the grandest, if the most decrepit. Set behind a high brick and flint wall and imposing wrought-iron gates, it was bang in the middle of the tiny village, its land spreading out behind it in a wide, downward-sweeping fan. Tash simply adored it, but kept that quiet for fear of adding to the Hugo-idolatry myth. When first clapping eyes on it, she had felt a little like Lizzie Bennet clocking Pemberley.

Tonight it was looking spectacular – like a grande old dame tarted up for a rare jaunt on the town. Every window glowed a winking welcome as figures moved in and out of the light behind them. There were cars parked everywhere. As Zoe pulled into the drive behind a heaving Merc which had pounding music to rival that coming from the house, Niall whistled.

'One forgets quite how spectacular it is,' he breathed. 'Jesus, he's a lucky sod – no wonder every woman's after him.'

'Very draughty.' Zoe crinkled her nose. 'And the plumbing's buggered.'

Hugo's father had died several years earlier, leaving the house to his eldest son, with whom he had conducted an extremely stormy relationship. The rest of his considerable estate – including all his investments and the family company – had been left in the more capable hands of his younger son and his widow, Alicia, who now lived in a cottage on the edge of Haydown land. Without any cash resources apart from a small private income, and trapped in the coils of death duties, Hugo had initially struggled to keep the place on and continue eventing. Even now that he was so phenomenally successful, his sponsorship money and winnings were all poured into the horses and the house had been left more or less to rot. Hugo lived by the philosophy that all was well so long as the door closed behind him, the bed was hard, the dogs fed and the cleaner came twice a week.

Tash had always thought there was something grand about the house's tatty state of repair, its ancient furniture and nineteenth-century wiring. Tonight it added a rather bohemian splendour to the party.

The house was already heaving with people as they entered. The first couple Tash recognised was Kirsty and Richie – the Australian boyfriend, to whom she had been engaged longer than a teenager's phone-line. Kirsty was always far friendlier to Tash when Niall was around and even more so now that she had her future husband in tow. Wearing a sparkling bottle green dress which set off her slender frame and glorious hair like a shiny crocus stem, she glided up, dragging Richie by the hand.

'Tash, you know Richie. Darling, this is Tash's gorgeous fiancé, Niall

O'Shaughnessy. They're getting married this summer, so they can give us lots of tips for next year.'

'Great to meet you, Niall mate.' Richie stretched out his arm. He was an enormous man – well over six foot four and as broad as a rugby international. He had gargantuan square shoulders, a square red face, square broken nose, and even square-cut blond bottle brush hair.

'Likewise.' Niall looked up at him, for once dwarfed.

'We must get our heads together for a wee bit of wedding gossip, huh?' Kirsty drew Tash to one side.

'Er – sure,' she gulped. It was the first time Kirsty had shown any interest in the subject.

'Hugo's really fucking me off,' Kirsty hissed as soon as they were out of Richie's earshot. 'If you see him, tell him to back off, will you?'

'Why? What's he been doing?'

'Stirring things up.' Her blue eyes flashed like panda lights. 'He keeps flirting with some predatory wee anorexic brunette with a nose-job.'

About to say she didn't blame him, Tash caught Richie shooting her an odd look and went pink. 'That's right – cream silk. Listen, I must say hi to some people and introduce Niall.'

'I think he's already introducing himself to the drinks waiter,' Richie laughed, joining them again, his square face redder than ever. Tash thought he looked like a big, walking-talking pillar box.

As soon as she could extricate herself from Kirsty's sudden need to talk about weddings, Tash went in search of Niall. But it was impossible to find him in the heaving throng as she was assailed over and over again by eventing cronies. In the end she gave up and, collecting a glass of white wine from a local girl who had been roped in to help, she milled around chatting to old friends.

It was a splendid, rip-roaring occasion. Hugo had got the right idea for hosting a party – there was no silly theme or carefully mixed crowd. He hadn't decked the house in decorations – or even had it cleaned from what Tash could see. He had simply opened it up, invited all his friends and laid on enough booze and food to keep everyone uproariously happy for the night.

She was amazed by how many people she knew, but supposed that living in the same area and competing in the same sport gave them a lot of mutual acquaintances. She was delighted to be pounced upon by Stefan, Hugo's lofty Swedish working pupil who was the heartthrob of the circuit. Many eventers pretended to disapprove of his flirtatious, philandering ways, but he was too young, overexcited and adorable to dislike.

'Tash!' He bounded up, kissing her on both cheeks and then the mouth. His short, spiky blond hair was teased upwards so that he looked taller and thinner than ever. He was one of the only men Tash knew who made her feel petite. 'You look lovely!' His cartoon-character eyes were so playful they almost tickled when they looked at you.

Tash flushed with embarrassment, but felt hugely bucked by the compliment. She had made a supreme effort that night in an attempt to look as glamorous as the Minty Blyths of this world, aware that Lisette would be in evidence to appraise her ex-husband's future bride with her usual scorn. She also knew that Lisette was guaranteed to look phenomenal and, however much she hated herself for being competitive, didn't want to let Niall down by making her usual slapdash effort. Dressed in a new slinky red satin party dress which she could hardly believe was actually a size twelve and not too tight, she had spent hours coaxing her unruly hair into a sleek Audrey Hepburn chignon and had then painted her eyes as carefully as a porcelain artist gilds a Wedgwood miniature so that they looked huge and cat-like. Matched with red Cupid's bow lips and a wildly flattering smoke-grey jacket that Sophia had given her years ago, Tash knew she was having one of her rare on-nights.

'Jesus!' Niall had whistled when he'd walked into the forge bedroom to change. 'You look sensational. I don't think I should take you out at all tonight; there might be men with weak hearts there.'

'There's only one man I'm interested in, and his heart's as big as Africa.' She'd looked at him nervously, not certain how he would react.

'And he's not going to let you out of his sight all night.' He'd watched her, eyes glittering with lust.

Tash was ebullient. The result of her unusually lengthy preening was about as good as she got, although she wished she'd had time to go out and buy some strappy little sandals instead of resorting to the jinxed snakeskin boots again, but time had been on her back rather than her side. Yet, despite the rush, she was bubbling over with confidence. Her only disappointment was that, far from keeping his eyes glued to her, Niall had sloped off at the earliest opportunity to eye up the drinks tray.

'Great party, huh?' Stefan was gazing around at the talent, of which there seemed to be a brimming surplus.

Tash had always thought that female eventers looked far sexier in their tight jods and jackets than party mufti – herself included. Many of them were too muscular to get away with slinky dresses, their faces ruddy from working outside for most of the year, their hair limp, thin and flat from so much time trapped beneath a sweaty helmet. There was also a rather high bad-taste factor which predominated at eventing parties – Tash, slightly distanced from the inner enclaves thanks to her association with Niall and his fashionable world, had noted it from a distance with some discomfort. It seemed to be a social group trapped in a time warp – and sadly that was the glittery, shoulder-padded eighties. Tash supposed that if one lived in such a tight-knit clique, one followed its rules with little regard for the wider world. Eventers had little time to shop, read fashion magazines or watch television. As such they were insulated from new trends and still assumed the knickerbocker with sequinned tank-top look to be the height of chic.

Nevertheless they were a good-looking bunch and many had clearly made a great deal of effort on Hugo's behalf. Mixed in with locals, Hugo's multifarious friends and several of his ex-lovers, they were a giggling, chattering gaggle of fresh-faced, blue-eyed British fun.

But of all the guests, two women far out-classed the others in looks and sex-appeal.

One was Tash's elder sister Sophia, resplendent in the latest Versace satin shirt and Gucci hipsters, with her glossy black hair piled at the crown of her head like a generous ice-cream cone. The other was Lisette O'Shaughnessy.

Tash caught her breath when she spotted her. The last time they had met, Lisette had been on the wafer-thin side of skinny and rattling with nervous tension, her career in tatters around her. As with many women in a crisis, she'd had her hair shorn to a butch, defeminising crew cut and had taken to wearing boxy, powerful clothes that were far more intimidating than they were attractive. But even then she had packed such a carnal punch that men had drooled wherever she went.

Now Tash barely recognised her. She'd grown her hair to shoulder length where it rested on her creamy skin in a glossy, walnut brown flick – lightened either by the sun or by Nicky Clarke, Tash couldn't tell. Her body was still a long, lean whip of bone and sinew, but it seemed that hours in the gym had rendered it more sleekly proportioned and carnal than ever, and her skin glowed as though fresh from a balsam sauna.

Catching Tash watching, she turned and smiled in cool recognition before moving away.

Biting her lip, Tash scoured the room for Niall, but he was still nowhere to be seen.

'Now *she* is a seriously sexy woman,' Stefan whistled, also watching

Lisette as she shimmied towards a drinks tray. 'I wouldn't mind having a crack at her later.'

Tash hid a smile. Stefan had a fairly thick Swedish accent, but had picked up on Hugo's curt, public school manner of speaking; it could sound quite ridiculous at times.

'I think you'd be the first to crack, Stefan.' Tash saw Lisette shooting him a thoughtful, appraising look before drifting into an eager group which included Tash's brother-in-law, Ben, who was positively foaming at the mouth in admiration.

On cue, Sophia breezed up to Tash, regarding her outfit with some distaste.

'Hi – you look very slim.' She gave her a perfunctory kiss on each cheek. Tash always found Sophia's greetings confusing as she was a slavish follower of fashion and the number of kisses dictated by those in the know changed with the season's hot colours. At a family wedding, Sophia would kiss Tash three times, the last one catching Tash's earring as she moved away; on the next occasion she would plant a single kiss, leaving Tash holding her cheek up as though showing off a spot as she anticipated further smears of MAC lipstick which never came.

Tonight's double whammy left Tash dithering for a moment as she wondered whether a third delayed pucker was due, but Sophia was already reintroducing herself to Stefan and bitching about the drive there.

'Bloody Hugo asked us to give some eventer called Lucy Field a lift and she didn't stop yakking and swigging vodka the entire way.'

'Lucy's sweet.' Tash giggled as she watched Sophia's big, green eyes narrowing. She could just imagine her sister taking against the effervescent little blonde eventer who was far better bred, but had far worse manners and no dress sense whatsoever.

'Oh, I hardly know her.' Sophia shrugged, eyes scanning the room for someone interesting. 'Bit of a drab mix, isn't it? Although I've already had a fascinating chat with Lisette Norton. She is *so* predatory, that woman.' She dropped her voice and huddled close so that Stefan couldn't hear. 'I'm certain she's after a very dashing male we both know jolly well.'

Tash could feel the blood draining from her face as though someone had pulled the bath plug on her jugular.

'Oh, yes?' she warbled, certain that Sophia was loving every minute of this.

'She's definitely got her sights set on Hugo,' hissed her sister.

Swigging her glass of wine, Tash wondered why she still felt icy cold even though Sophia hadn't said the name she'd expected.

Seventeen

TASH TRACKED DOWN PENNY and Gus in the vast, echoing kitchen where they were listening politely to Hugo's mother, Alicia Beauchamp, ranting about what a ghastly party it was. Resplendent in eau de nil chiffon layers with the family pearls choking the loose skin of her neck, she had cornered her own supply of gin and friends and was holding court in what had once been her own kitchen, although she had not made so much as one cup of tea there in her entire married life.

'Tash darling!' Alicia hailed her with a bony, liver-spotted hand. 'So good to see you. You look too thin. Haven't seen my son, have you?'

Tash shook her head, kissing her on the soft, loose-skinned cheek. She smelled of cologne and Rothmans. 'Have you seen Niall?'

'Your dashing Irish chap?' Alicia peeked over her shoulder. 'He not with you, no?'

'No.' Tash smiled at Penny and Gus, who were both terrified of Alicia and quaking with deferential fascination at her every word.

Tash rather liked her – she was a saner, younger version of her own grandmother and tremendously high-octane, even though she was also blisteringly blunt. She was besides the only person Hugo deferred to, which gave her a lot of Brownie points in Tash's book.

'I saw him with Zoe somewhere.' Gus touched Tash's shoulder. 'Chatting to Hugo.'

'Ah.' It suddenly occurred to her that she hadn't seen Hugo at all and she'd been at the party over an hour. She also remembered with a wince that she and Niall had left his birthday card and present – a bottle of rare Macallan malt – back at the forge.

'Now, Tash, you must have a lovely single friend who would make Hugo a decent wife,' Alicia boomed at her. 'We've been chatting about how ghastly it is having two sons who refuse to get married off – I want some grandchildren before I'm too frail to pick the buggers up.'

Tash caught Penny's eye and tried not to giggle. Alicia was wildly indiscreet. She was glad Hugo wasn't within earshot.

'Well . . .' She cleared her throat, wondering if she dared mention Zoe, but deciding against it. 'Not really, no – most of my friends are married or living with someone or whatever.'

'Damn.' Alicia inserted a gnarled finger beneath her pearls to stop them pinching for a moment. 'Shame. You know, I don't understand what's wrong with the boy. He gets through more girlfriends than horses, but never seems to treat them as well. Thought he was pretty keen on one a couple of years back, but she pushed off. He's been even worse since.'

'Amanda?' Tash recalled Hugo's clever, tempestuous girlfriend who had ultimately chosen her career instead of him.

'No, no, not that outspoken harpy – Lord, no. I think he was glad to be shot of her.' Alicia headed for a refill of gin. 'Someone quite different, but he refused to squeak her name to a nosy old bat like me. Met her on holiday, I think. He was extremely cut up about it.'

Tash looked at Penny and Gus in bafflement, but they just shrugged and looked quickly away, catching one another's eye. They were clearly desperate for an escape route.

Tash spotted it in the form of her sister-in-law wandering past the kitchen door.

'Sally!' She bounded over, dragging the Moncrieffs with her. 'You look fantastic. Gosh, I didn't know you'd be here.'

'Well, I pop up all over the place.' Sally kissed her, laughing. She was looking far slinkier than Tash had ever seen her, her usually messy blonde hair slicked back into a chignon at the nape of her neck, her face painted with minimal but exquisite make-up that emphasised the wicked grey eyes and curling mouth. Her dress – a long, narrow tube of cream silk – emphasised her terrific curves whilst minimising the rounded belly which had never flattened after Linus was born.

She kissed Gus and Penny hello, then turned back to Tash.

'I said hi to Niall – he looks knackered, poor sod.' She nodded towards one of Hugo's panelled sitting rooms in which Niall was clearly ensconced. 'He says you guys are getting married in the village now. That's terrific. When are the invitations going out?'

'Soon,' Tash coasted vaguely. 'Is Matty with you?'

Sally shook her head. 'Babysitting very grudgingly. I've told him I'm on an assertiveness weekend. He says that if I assert myself any more, I'll be assertifiable.'

'Why didn't you tell him the truth?' Tash stared at her blankly.

Sally lifted her chin bravely. 'I'm here with Lisette – Matty disapproves of our friendship,' she explained, not quite looking Tash in the eye. 'You don't mind, do you?'

Tash was about to confess that, childish as it may seem, she did rather mind when there was a sharp blast of cold air behind her.

'What the –?' Sally gaped over Tash's shoulder and then started to laugh.

Turning around, she saw that the fat oak door which led from the kitchen to the long rear lobby was wedged wide open. A loud, roaring engine noise boomed from the narrow passageway and the next moment a glistening wet tyre capped with a vast red mudguard was edging its way over the stone step.

Seconds later there was a loud burst from an engine and Hugo thundered into the kitchen on a vast motorbike which he proceeded to ride around in a wide circle, practically mowing down several party guests including Sophia.

'God, he's a immature prat, isn't he?' Sally giggled with relish.

Tash, who had been rather carried away by the sexiness of the whole thing, took a hasty swig of wine and tried hard to agree. But there was no denying that Hugo looked obscenely good.

His hair, wet from the drizzle outside, gleamed like Medusa's snakes around his laughing face as he dodged in and out of the guests, long legs dangling to either side of the huge bike and scuffing the floor to keep balance as its back wheel slithered on the flagstones. Wearing a vast sheepskin flying jacket and scruffy, rain-soaked jeans, he looked more like a hell-raising gate-crasher than a party host.

'He's so bloody attractive, it's unfair,' Sally sighed. 'I'd love to think he's got a small prick, but Lisette assures me otherwise.'

Tash breathed a great mouthful of wine into her wind pipe.

Bringing the beast to a skidding halt on the flagstone floor, Hugo cut the engine and whooped delightedly. 'Thanks, Ma!' He blew his mother a kiss and removed a large red satin bow from the handlebars.

'That monster is Alicia's present to him,' Sally muttered to Tash. 'It seems the old dear's quite keen to kill him off young so that she can get her court shoes through the door here again.'

'But Hugo already has about three cars.' Tash watched as he attached the vast bow from the bike on to the collar of one of the dogs that was milling about at knee height.

'Ah, but they've all got air-bags and anti-roll bars.' Sally winked.

Looking at Hugo's big smile and glittering eyes, Tash could tell he was in a dangerous, reckless mood. She had seen him like this before and knew just how unpredictable and nasty he was capable of being. Recently she had been the victim of that relentless, mercurial need for entertainment far too often. Deciding to steer well clear, she slipped into the room which Sally had nodded to when talking about Niall.

He was sprawling loose-limbed on a sofa with Zoe and the local vet, Jack Fortescue. Lounging on the arm beside him, a long thin strip of unlit fuse, was Lisette.

Tash was about to back out again when Niall caught sight of her and bounded upright, almost tipping Lisette into a vast, dead-looking fern.

'Tash angel, I've been searching all over for you.' He laughed, clearly already very drunk. 'You having a good time?'

'Terrific.' She smiled stiffly as she caught a strong whiff of whiskey. 'Lots of familiar faces.'

'Sure, there are, there are – and one of them's right here.' He gripped her arm. 'Come and say hello to Lisette. Doesn't she look well?'

'Terrific,' Tash repeated hollowly. She looked more than well, she looked ferociously beautiful, those huge haunted eyes almost bottomless in their magnetism, the curling mouth strangely reminiscent of Hugo's with its drooping sensuality and sloping curves. With a free-falling heart she realised that no amount of primping and preening would ever make her that beautiful.

Expecting a gushing faux-welcome in return, Tash was rather surprised to be on the receiving end of a frosty glower.

'Hi.' She swallowed uneasily.

'Hi.' Lisette stretched out a slender arm.

Thinking she was expected to shake her hand, Tash made a fumbled grab for it before realising too late that Lisette was simply reaching for her drink. A split-second later three inches of red wine cascaded down her own leg and into her ultra-trendy long boot as a result.

'Christ!' Tash leaped away, shaking her leg as though performing a spontaneous hokey-cokey. 'I'm sorry – it was my fault. So clumsy.'

Lisette didn't argue. Instead she sighed patiently and signalled for one of the roving local girls to bring over the bottle of red. She held up her glass to be refreshed, brushing a few imaginary drops of wine from her own dress. As it had almost all tipped into Tash's boot, this was pure showmanship.

Suddenly she flashed the big, sexy smile that could floor an entire rugby team at twenty paces.

'I hear you're going to let me borrow Niall back for a few weeks?' she said smoothly.

'What?' Tash was preoccupied with the damp vintage whooshing around inside her boot. It felt as though her right foot was plugged into an electric foot spa.

'The film, Tash.' Niall was smiling through gritted teeth.

'Oh, yes. That.' She nodded vaguely.

'I'm glad you're so enthusiastic.' Lisette's smile flashed off as instantly as it had beamed on.

Tash was wriggling her toes uncomfortably amid much squelching of claret.

'Oh, I am.' She tried to ignore her wet foot. 'I loved the script – it's terrifically funny.'

'She was the one who bullied me to take it.' Niall touched her arm lovingly.

Lisette flashed the smile on and off again so quickly that she looked as though she had a facial tic. Then, with a malicious glint in her eye, she proceeded to go into every boring, finite detail of the casting, crew and schedule. Having an active interest, Niall was the only rapt listener. Even Zoe, who was killingly polite, stifled a yawn.

Tash caught her eye and was grateful for the sympathy, noticing that Zoe's long, subtly clinging midnight blue dress brought out her cool blonde colouring perfectly; she looked like a glamorous ice queen in a fairy tale. It was the first time Tash had seen her dressed up since New Year's Eve, and she was startled by the change it effected. She looked ravishing. Had Zoe gone the whole hog on a more regular basis, she guessed she would be hopelessly intimidated by her.

Sticking out Lisette's monologue for a couple more minutes so as not to appear rude, Tash finally limped off to locate a loo in which to rinse her foot.

All the downstairs ones were occupied and it appeared that the more riotous the party grew, the less they were being used for their natural purpose. From one, Tash could distinctly make out the sound effects of some very unpleasant projectile vomiting; from another came the zealous grunts and groans of mutual tongue-swallowing.

Now walking with a very strange gait, she headed upstairs. Again, the lavatories with which she was familiar were locked. She knew the house pretty well from previous parties and occasional teaching sessions with Hugo, who had given her some dressage coaching during their brief moment of friendship and even once, on a memorable day, asked her in for doorstep-thick sandwiches and wine afterwards. But her knowledge of Haydown stopped just several yards along the landing and she looked around rather forlornly as she tried to figure out where another bathroom might be.

It was a very long, dark, galleried landing, its wooden floors dull and pock-marked from the dashing of booted feet, its tapestried upper walls torn, dusty and faded. To her left, an ancient horse-hair chaise was oozing out stuffing like a splitting soufflé, beside which a low Pembroke table was groaning beneath the weight of a dozen dusty silver photograph frames. Tash hobbled over to take a peek. They were almost all of dogs and horses, she noticed, some clearly dating back several generations. From one, Hugo's despotic late father glared at her beadily, seeming to accuse her of snooping.

Backing off, she headed through a nearby door and found herself in a vast bedroom, dominated by an unmade four poster, the sheets pouring over the end like a bursting dam, the pillows scattered beside it like a giant's slippers and a great pile of unmated clean socks littered on top. A tatty biography of Montgomery sat on the bedside table with a pair of spectacles perched on top, and several acres of old newspapers lay on the floor, fluttering in the breeze from an open window.

To her relief Tash spotted what appeared to be an interconnecting bathroom and darted guiltily inside.

There was no lock, so she shut the door firmly and perched on the edge of the bath with her feet inside it to remove her wet boot. The dregs of Lisette's wine spattered out as she pulled it off, staining the white enamel of the bath like diluted blood. It smelled foul – a nose-punching mixture of hot foot and fruity Brouilly.

Popping the boot on the loo seat, Tash pulled a lime-encrusted brass shower attachment from its antique telephone-like rest above the taps and twiddled the knobs to rinse her foot. The water that jetted out on to her red-stained toes was at first icy cold and then almost immediately so scalding that it almost took her skin off. Letting out a yelp of pain, Tash drenched most of the bathroom as she fell backwards off the bath rim, landing on a scratchy, balding rug and knocking all the air painfully from her lungs.

From her upside-down position, she watched with motionless,

winded horror as the bathroom door was pushed open above her head and a pair of long legs walked in, trouser fly already being wrenched open in anticipation of a quick slash. Craning her neck, Tash could just make out the bottom of Hugo's chin, and was perfectly positioned to look up both of his nostrils.

'Hi,' she croaked as, not spotting her at his feet, he almost trod on her face.

Stumbling around to avoid falling over her, he backed away in astonishment as he took in her supine position and the fact that she was clutching his shower attachment to her chest.

'I might have bloody guessed,' he sighed, squatting down so that she could see up his nostrils in even closer focus. They were remarkably clean and hairless, she noted with interest, taking advantage of her rare stance to have a good peek. She was starting to get her breath back at last, although it was still shallow and gasping. She tried to get up, but something seemed to be holding her down.

'Tash, what the hell are you doing?' He glanced across at her damp boot, which had landed in a large money plant when she'd knocked it off the loo seat in falling.

'Cleaning my foot.' Tash smiled weakly up at him, realising that her only escape was to brazen the circumstances out honestly. She was having considerable difficulty getting up now. 'It got covered in wine, you see.'

'I see.' He plainly didn't, blue eyes narrowed with irritation and mistrust. 'Wouldn't you be better off doing it in the bath?'

'Well, I was, but I . . .'

'In your own bathroom,' he added, leaning across her to turn off the shower which was still dribbling on to the floor beside Tash's knee.

In doing this, he practically had to clamber over her, and Tash found to her horror that her face was pressed into his hard, muscular stomach just inches above his waistband. She lay flat against the floor like a corpse to avoid touching him. He was wearing a crisp cotton shirt that smelled deliciously of aftershave and deodorant as it brushed against the tip of her nose. She fought an urge to breathe in more deeply.

The shower curtailed, he backed off hastily and regarded her from a safe distance. Tash made another effort to get up and was again cut short.

'Are you hurt?' Hugo muttered coldly.

'Er – no.' Tash smiled apologetically, wriggling around on the floorboards. 'But my dress appears to be attached to the floor.' She rolled her eyes upwards, indicating the back of her neck where her zip had become intimately involved with a large amount of tassel, tethering her to the ancient rug like a prisoner-of-war pinned out in the midday sun.

Swearing under his breath in exasperation, Hugo moved forward to free her – cursing as the tassel refused to budge, and finally using his teeth on the knot. As his hot breath involuntarily caressed the top vertebrae of her spine, Tash tried not to enjoy the sensation at all, but her pulses had started to skip disobedient beats. Flinching away as his lips accidentally made contact with the back of her neck, she didn't like the ominous ripping sound with which she was finally freed.

'Thanks.' She clambered up, using his leg as support before realising what it was and hastily letting it go.

'Now can you push off so that I can take a piss in private?' He nodded impatiently towards the door.

As Tash dashed out, she was unpleasantly aware of a chill breeze against her back. But even more discomforting was the pronounced limp she now had as a result of wearing just one boot. The other was still in with Hugo. She couldn't realistically expect to head downstairs and mingle into the background with one leg four inches shorter than the other and her dress undone. She groaned to herself quietly. However much distance she was longing to put between herself and Hugo's wet bathroom, she would have to wait for her hostage boot to be released.

Feeling her face start to burn, she sat on the edge of his bed and waited for him to emerge. Fiddling awkwardly around behind her neck with her hands, she managed to get her zip about two-thirds of the way up but beyond that it gritted its teeth and refused to budge, like Snob on a bad day.

He took ages. Waiting nervily, Tash gnawed at her nails and gazed around the room, now realising that it must be his. He was pretty messy, although nothing on Niall's grand scale of chaos. The huge, dark wardrobes had gaping doors with ties hooked over them like thirsty tongues panting at a trough; a dressing gown was tossed over an old altar stool and a pair of trousers were trying to kick their way back out of a laundry bag. The open drawers of a tall chest were spilling out clean socks and underpants – natty black jersey ones, Tash noted. From the state of the room, she guessed his mind wasn't set on seduction that night. Even given his devastating good looks, it was pretty off-putting. None of the eventing groupies putting themselves on offer downstairs would mind, but Hugo wouldn't see them as conquests. Tash doubted he was planning to take Lisette later – not unless he tidied up first.

Lisette struck her as a woman who wouldn't just want a man to take his socks off before sex – she'd prefer that all eighteen pairs were off the bed too.

For something to do, she matched a few clean pairs together and balled them up before stopping herself, realising what Hugo would make of her if he caught her pairing up his socks like a crazed Mary Poppins when he re-emerged. He was taking positively ages in there, she realised worriedly. She hoped he wasn't ill. She had read somewhere – in a Robert Maxwell biography, she suspected – that men's blood-pressure could fall dramatically when they relieved themselves, making them drop in a dead faint. She hoped Hugo hadn't passed out. Men's lavatorial habits were largely a mystery to her – she tried to discourage Niall from wandering in to take a slash while she was in the bath because she felt some things should remain a mystery, her bath-time habits for one.

Gazing at the walls, she wondered whether his bed was a mess because Kirsty's boyfriend was shacking up at Lime Tree Farm, meaning that she would go home with him and not stay on at Haydown. He was certainly in a pretty stinky mood considering it was his own birthday party. Perhaps he minded turning thirty, Tash mused, looking at her watch. He really was taking ages in the loo. She hoped he wasn't doing anything gruesome to her boot; her one bare foot was starting to get seriously chilly.

His taste in pictures was a conservative mix of hunting oils, naive square farm animals and a couple of family portraits, although she was wildly flattered to spot one of her own oils of his old event horse, Saxophonist, in amongst the far grander marques.

There were piles of papers, schedules, notes and coins on every surface, as though he had emptied his pockets all over the room and never bothered to fill them up again. Tash could see two mobile phones, a Walkman and a digital organiser on one vast dressing table alone. It, too, had gaping drawers, from one of which poked a very tempting-looking hunk of family-sized Galaxy bar, the foil glinting seductively in the dim light.

Her stomach was growling and pleading like a small child tugging its mother's skirt outside a sweet shop. Tash gazed at the chocolate longingly. It had been a stressful night, and she was certain that Hugo wouldn't miss a couple of squares. He was still busily occupied, water swooshing now, hot pipes clanking. She briefly wondered if he was having a shower or, even more uncharacteristically, cleaning up after her boot blitz.

Dashing across the room, she broke off several squares of chocolate and was chomping frantically when something caught her eye in the drawer below. With bulging cheeks, she rooted urgently amongst the teenage fan mail, bank statements and credit card slips to extract it.

There it was in all its dreadful splendour – her mis-routed Valentine's card, complete with lipstick kisses and semi-nude photographs.

Looking at it once again, Tash gasped in horror as she took in the full implication of sending Hugo such a thing. The pictures were simply ghastly – more like mug-shots of a dead prostitute in a Lynda la Plante mini-series than titillating self-portraits. She had been far bigger then, positively bursting out of some of the underwear, and her mastery of the timer on the Polaroid had clearly not been great – most of the pictures were at very odd angles, cutting off a vital limb, her head or most of her body altogether. Sadly, they were all in clear focus. Squinting at a close-up of her cellulite-and-G-string look, Tash wanted to curl up and die with shame, particularly when she spotted the pizza delivery boxes and empty wine bottles in the background of the shot. What was even more ghastly was that Hugo had kept it to gloat over. She hoped to God he wasn't planning to blackmail her with it.

Springing upright, Tash realised that she had no time to lose; she was going to have to destroy the evidence.

It was too big to fit into her bag to steal away and dispense with in private later, and the cardboard was too thick to rip. When she tried, she merely bent it around and caused two of the photographs to fall to the floor.

Hearing the loo flush on the other side of the bathroom door, she looked around desperately for inspiration. Bingo! In front of her was the open window, and on a table in front of that were several match books.

Not thinking too far ahead, Tash fumbled with the matches until one spluttered and took. The card was largely made up of glue and photographic card so went up like a toxic bomb, blue-black smoke licking towards her fingers in seconds. Victorious, Tash threw it out of the window.

Gusted by the wind, it flew straight back in again and landed on the laundry basket.

In a panic, she ran over to it and tried to pick it up, but it was a ball of foul-smelling flame now and threatening to ignite the basket and its contents within seconds. Hugo's trousers were already developing scorch marks. Tash searched madly for something to pick it up with, but there were no tongs to hand.

In a total flap now, she grabbed the two mobile phones from the top of the dresser and, extending the aerials, carefully used those as metal chopsticks to lift the flaming card from its wicker tinder and rush it towards the window.

She almost made it, but at the last minute her flaming bundle crackled loudly, shooting sparks into her face before plunging to the floor.

'Shit!'

Wailing, Tash started to stamp on it with her one boot. It stuck fast to the plastic sole, threatening to burn off her leg. She let out an anguished shriek and started to hop around like a crazed hopscotch champion.

Wandering out of the bathroom at long last, Hugo was remarkably quick at sizing up the situation. Within seconds he had sped back into the bathroom, fetched a plastic cleaning bucket of water and tossed it over Tash's melting boot, extinguishing the flame instantly.

She was breathless with relief and mortification, but as she opened her mouth to gulp her apologies, Hugo held up his hand, face stony with fury.

'Don't even bother to explain,' he hissed. 'I can't take it right now.'

Shutting her mouth again, Tash swallowed and nodded meekly.

He started to pace around the room as though chained there, his tortoiseshell hair on end where he had rubbed his hands through it, blue eyes searing into the furniture with such angry intensity that Tash expected every piece spontaneously to combust.

She backed away slightly, aware of the water in her boot starting to warm up. A repulsive smell of burning plastic lingered in the air. Biting her lip, she wondered whether she should boldly walk into the bathroom, extract her boot and then leg it, but she supposed that wouldn't be diplomatic. After all, she had just tried to flood his bathroom and burn down his bedroom. They were tremendously competitive with one another, but these acts of sabotage were rather too much even by Hugo's Machiavellian standards.

Thankfully he had stopped pacing and was staring at her with an unreadable expression that could register anywhere between utter contempt and mild fear on the emotional scale.

'Er – sorry,' she muttered, but Hugo butted in before she even got the word fully out.

'Shut up.' He started pacing again.

Clearly not the right move, Tash realised. In fact, she had regressed the situation somewhat.

The pacing was really fraying her nerves. She thought about joining in and pacing – or limping – around with him, but decided not to risk it. He wasn't beyond hitting her when he was in this state. Besides, she was standing in a pool of water and figured that wading it around the room wouldn't go down too well.

She was dying to escape back to the party and dive into a huge drink. Niall would think she'd gone home without him at this rate. But Hugo was pacing between her and the door now, barring her way. And she really needed that other boot. Keeping an eye on his restless stalking, she started to edge towards the bathroom.

He stood stock still and swung around to her, making her jump backwards in fright and almost land on the bed.

'You've already done in there,' he drawled. 'Don't you want to throw paint over one of the drawing rooms, or torch my kitchen instead?'

'Er, good point.' She swallowed, not liking the menacing glint that had returned to his eyes. There was no mistaking this expression. It was pure evil, and she was suddenly certain that he was pacing in order to determine which form of punishment would be most satisfactory to make up for her vandalism that night.

'Just getting my boot,' she yelped, diving into the bathroom and almost crowning herself on the bath as she slithered over the wet floor.

As she picked her boot out of the money plant and hastily sat on the loo to pull it on, she noticed that half a bottle of whisky was standing on the cistern. She was certain it hadn't been there before. Nor had the newspaper which was open at the sports pages and now sucking up water from the floor.

Tugging up the zip of her sodden boot, it dawned on her that Hugo had been sitting alone in a distant bathroom at his own party, swigging whisky, compelled by some deep well of unhappiness to seek solitude and drunkenness. She suddenly felt a great wave of pity for him.

Wandering back out again, however, she found that he had gone. So had the two photographs which had fallen from the card when she had tried to rip it.

The party was raging at full throttle now. Squelching back downstairs, Tash was faced with the sight of two of the country's top event riders re-enacting the show-jumping final of last year's Badminton in the hall. Using a mixture of pot-plants, umbrellas and walking sticks as fences, one rode piggy back on the other as they stumbled and toppled their way into each 'jump', spreading plant, soil, leaves and laughter throughout the room.

Sliding around the walls behind everyone's backs, Tash crept into the room where Niall had been talking to Lisette and Zoe earlier.

They were no longer there but, disastrously, Hugo was, sitting in amongst a noisy group which included Sophia and Ben, Stefan, the Lime Tree mob and Sally, who hailed Tash like a long-lost friend stumbling off a ship in port.

'Honey!' she whooped. 'Over here! We're playing truth or dare, like a bunch of teeny boppers. I'm trying to persuade Hugo here to spin the bottle.'

'Christ!' Tash muttered under her breath before shaking her head with as big a smile as she could crack open. 'I'm just going to find Niall – see what time he wants to leave.' She peered quickly at Hugo to see what sort of mood he was in after the loo fiasco, but he was staring bleakly into his glass of scotch, a fingernail broodily tapping its rim.

'He's gone already.' Sally waggled her hand to coax Tash towards them. 'Zoe found Rufus wrapped around one of the downstairs loos and needed a hand getting him home. He said to tell you he'll try to get a cab back here as soon as they've put him to bed. Zoe's whacked, so she's not planning to come back. Here – have some champagne.' She held up the bottle as Tash shuffled within reach, her boots quacking like ducks as wet skin sucked against wet leather with each step.

Sitting as far away from Hugo as possible and determinedly not looking at him, she squashed herself between Sally and Ben, who was absolutely plastered – his usual state at parties. Sophia, as sober as a school bus driver and thoroughly disapproving, narrowed her eyes as Tash, who had lost her glass, took a quick swig straight from the bottle.

'Isn't that a little unhygienic?'

'No – it's very sexy,' Stefan butted in on Tash's behalf, taking the bottle and swigging from it himself.

'I can't believe how many people gave you booze for your birthday, Hugo,' Sally giggled, regarding a vast stack of bottles to one side of them. 'It's like a millionaire's cellar in here.'

'I always get bottles for my birthday.' Hugo shrugged, his face guarded and sulky. 'I should just lodge a list with Majestic. I'll probably chuck most of it up later – talk about many happy returns.'

'I suppose it's the obvious gift for the man who has everything but a drinking problem.' Sally swigged from her glass, her face pink from overindulgence. 'I'm sorry mine was just some old plonk. Did you and Niall get Hugo booze too, Tash?' she looked across with slightly unfocused eyes.

She was about to say yes when Hugo muttered icily, 'Tash and Niall didn't, so far as I know, bring anything but their fame and glamour – although Tash seems quite keen on toasting the birthday boy and lighting up the candles on his cake.'

Flustered, she muttered something about leaving it at home.

'I thought I told you to leave Niall there too,' Hugo said suddenly, his tone deliberately light and flip.

Looking at him, Tash found his eyes boring into hers and was totally thrown. 'Er, I'll get a drink,' she muttered.

'Take your pick,' Stefan laughed, starting to rifle through Hugo's clanking gifts, his long legs stretched to either side of the cache. 'There's Bollinger, Moët, Taittinger, Lanson – Christ there's even a couple of Krugs here. Or if you want something stronger there's—'

'Ben and I gave Hugo a Trollope first edition,' murmured Sophia, who had recently taken to giving 'cultural' presents. Tash had received a very odd compact disc of a trendy modern composer for Christmas; one minute of it was enough to evict Niall to the pub and cause Beetroot to try and hide in the coal cupboard. Twenty minutes later it had still sounded as though the orchestra was tuning up.

'I'd rather have just had a trollop.' Hugo smiled malevolently, and looked up. 'Talk of the she-devil . . .'

'Hi, guys.' Red-faced Richie grinned over them, dwarfing them in large, square shadow. 'Is this a private party or can anyone join in?'

Hugo winced at the cliché and shot Kirsty a dirty look before shrugging. 'Why not? After all they let anybody in these days, according to my mother.'

'In where?' Richie looked confused, square forehead creasing.

'In Kirst—'

'Why don't you sit down next to me!' Tash beamed brightly up at Richie, aware that Hugo was at a pitch of drunkenness that was dangerous when whetted.

Hovering behind her gargantuan fiancé, Kirsty was clearly gibbering with nerves, but far too eager to keep Hugo in view to be subtle about it. She perched on a foot stool opposite him, eyes darting towards his face as often as a darts player checking the scoreboard. Even sitting on the floor beside Tash, Richie towered above most of the assembled company, red face grinning inanely. She decided she rather liked him.

'Actually we were playing a game of truth or dare.' Penny was pulling the foil from another champagne bottle, her feet hooked up on to Gus's knees. 'You can join in. It was Tash's turn, wasn't it?'

She wanted to dare herself to tell the truth for once and announce that she refused to play, but she was feeling far too gutless, aware that Hugo was taking brief breaks from shooting Kirsty evil looks to shoot them at her.

'I'll do a dare,' she croaked.

Gus rubbed his hands together with delight. 'Now we should be able to think up something really juicy. Particularly as Niall has bunked off early.'

A quarter of the way down a fresh bottle of scotch, Hugo glanced up, eyes glinting as never before. 'I think,' he drawled, letting the words roll slowly from his pink tongue, 'that she should ride my new toy to the bottom of Twenty Acres and back.'

'Christ – you'd trust her with your bike?' Ted was wide-eyed with amazement and jealousy. 'You only dared me to pinch your mother's bum!'

'That,' Hugo smiled, 'was far more dangerous.'

Looking at Tash's white face, he watched her flinch as Penny's champagne cork flew out, jumping almost six feet into the air. Catching him watching her, Tash stared defiantly back at him.

'Haven't you got livestock in there?' Ben asked, a hiccup coursing up his throat so that he sounded as though he was speaking with a gob-stopper in each cheek.

'Nope.' Hugo continued staring straight at Tash.

She didn't dare look away. He was challenging her loud and clear. This was her punishment.

'It's too dangerous,' Penny protested, sucking froth from the top of a Bollinger bottle. 'It's pitch dark out there.'

'Don't do it, Tash.' Sophia was, for once, genuinely concerned. 'You could kill yourself.'

'I'll do it.' Tash lifted her chin and stared Hugo out.

'Good girl.' He grinned. 'Let's go.'

Eighteen

A LARGE CROWD ASSEMBLED out on the gravel driveway. Many of Hugo's guests had already left, but of those still there, none headed for their cars as they filed out into the cool, damp March night. Hot breath clouded and mingled in front of flushed faces as a nightjar chattered in the garden and Hugo's two guard dogs barked from the yard.

Twenty Acres was a large, claggy field that sloped at an acute angle down from the house towards the valley below. It was perilously steep and pitted, and useless for anything other than rough grazing as the sheer incline was too acute for most farm vehicles. One or two timber and tyre fences were dotted sporadically around it, which Hugo used to train his horses over. It was also host to several small coppices and a couple of deep ponds where the heavy clay soil held on to water in the damper months. In the past, Tash's heart had caught in her throat just cantering at half-pace down it. The prospect of racing down it on a large motorbike was making her feel physically sick.

Laughing and chatting with the milling party guests, Hugo was extremely drunk but still walking and talking fairly normally. Only his glinting eyes gave him away. When he tossed Tash the ignition keys, they landed plum in her hands.

She was trembling with cold now, her teeth chattering like a rattling window, her back tightening like a drum skin where her dress was gaping open at the top.

It took her several moments to figure out how to turn on the bike's ignition. Tash had spent a considerable amount of time the previous summer rattling around the fields of the Moncrieffs' farm on board an old scramble bike that had belonged to one of the part-time grooms. She was fairly familiar with staying on board over rough terrain – even in the dark. But Hugo's bike was far bigger and more powerful than the scrambler. She could barely touch the ground with her damp, booted feet as she pushed it off the rest and switched on the lights.

The next moment, she let out the throttle and it roared into life like a minotaur chasing a piece of string.

As a whooping Ted opened the gate which led straight on to the drive, the bright halogen headlight slashed through the dark, highlighting churned up mud in the gateway, the crystal tips of the dewy grass, and the top of a distant tree. The field wasn't even visible as it sloped out of sight within metres, disappearing into a darkened chasm.

Tash caught her breath. It would be like riding off a cliff.

'Tell her not to do it, Gus.' Penny was trying to galvanise some help to stop the dare. But Gus stood stock still, arms crossed against the cold, and simply shrugged, enjoying the show.

'I think thish could be rather rash, Tash old thing.' Ben approached her, smoothing his messy hair and lurching drunkenly where he was being prodded by Sophia from behind. 'Think how ghastly it would be if you hurt yourself all over a shilly game.'

But Tash was revving the engine and didn't hear him. All she could think was how much this would tick off Hugo. He'd clearly expected her to wimp out, and she hadn't even complained.

Those party guests lining up by the fence to watch were swigging from bottles and cans as they giggled and gossiped and chatted, seeing this as an entertaining side-show, numbed by drunkenness to the idiocy of it.

Sally had drunk far more than usual too, but suddenly felt horribly sober. As she dashed towards the puttering bike, she crashed into Lisette who had wandered outside to watch, swathed in a long velvet coat, glass in hand.

'What's going on?' Lisette took in her panic-stricken expression.

'I've got to stop this,' wailed Sally. 'Tash is planning to ride round that bloody field like some sort of teenage joy-rider. It's Hugo's fault. I'm going to kill him.'

Lisette's warm hand entrapped her wrist and held it tight. 'Don't. Let her get on with it.'

Sally tried to wrench her arm away, but Lisette clung on tightly.

'You may want Niall back,' Sally hissed, 'but letting Tash try and kill herself isn't the best method, believe me.'

Lisette's huge, painted eyes glittered in the steely light and she tightened her grip so much that Sally winced.

'I don't want Niall back,' she whispered. 'But if I did, Tash is certainly helping me all the fucking way. Why d'you think Niall was drinking for England, Ireland and the States tonight and looking as though he'd had teeth pulled with every drink, huh?'

Only half listening, Sally was craning around to see Tash talking to Gus and Stefan, trying desperately hard to laugh even though she was shivering madly and pasty white with fear. She had lost so much weight that she looked like a fragile, leggy bird perched on the great bike with her ridiculously flimsy party dress rucked up to show a lot of slim, pale thigh. Sally wanted to throttle Hugo who was standing alone a short way off, bottle to his chest as he tugged sporadically on a cigarette, its long red end sparking in the dark.

'Tash is in love with *him*.' Lisette jerked her head towards the solitary figure. 'Not Niall. That's why he's miserable, why he's fucking around with actresses, drinking himself to death and clinging to the apron strings of that ageing mummy tonight. Don't feel sorry for Tash – feel sorry for Niall.'

Not bothering to respond, Sally finally broke free just as Tash rolled the bike into the field entrance to yells and claps of excited encouragement. She raced up to Hugo, whose own teeth appeared to be chattering like mad now as he tried to swig from his whisky bottle and spilled most of it.

'Stop her, you bastard!' yelled Sally. 'You'd never ride down that fucking field yourself at this time of night. Stop her!'

Hugo seemed on the brink of telling her to get lost, but then he looked across at Tash, who was borrowing a pair of gloves from Stefan. They were far too big for her and made her look like a member of the audience at Gladiators waving great rubber fists around.

Muttering 'Fuck this' under his breath, Hugo thrust the scotch bottle at Sally and ran to the entrance, long legs eating up the ground. To even louder whoops and cheers, he clambered on to the bike behind Tash.

'Let's go cycling,' he murmured into her ear.

As he wrapped his arms tightly around her waist, she tipped the bike over the brow of the hill and twisted the throttle so that it let out another great pride-leader roar. Moments later they were speeding off down the hill in a flurry of mud and churned grass, red tail light streaking away from the gate.

'That's it – call Mummy and let her know the wedding's off but she can wear the hat to the funeral.' Sophia turned to Ben and burst into unexpected tears.

He gave her a stiff hug and bit back a comment about over-reacting. He and Hugo had tobogganed that hill hundreds of times as children and apart from a couple of twisted ankles they'd survived intact. Pressing his chin lovingly to the top of her head, he let out a slight hiccup.

'Don't do that with your chin, Ben,' Sophia snivelled. 'It flattens my hairdo.'

Out in the field, mud was coating Tash's face, her hands were freezing despite the gloves, her eyes were full of hair and scoured dry by the wind, and her heart was so far up her throat that it was doing a double-act with her tongue.

Nonetheless she was whooping with exhilaration as well as the pulse-stopping punch of fear. It was a heady, drug-fix mix – the most exciting cross-country ride ever, a mile-high roller-coaster run and great one-night-stand sex. She'd never experienced anything quite so terrifying, exhilarating, or cold.

Behind her, Hugo was laughing his head off, relishing the thrill. It was only when they sped towards the bottom of the hill perilously fast that his grip tightened on her waist.

'It's wet down here!' he warned, but Tash couldn't hear.

Still very drunk, Hugo was not the best judge of speed, but even he could tell that Tash was going to go straight through to the next field if she didn't brake soon. At the bottom of the hill the wet, claggy clay was like an oil slick.

'For fuck's sake, slow down!' he yelled into Tash's ear as she narrowly missed a water trough and slithered around to track the rails on the left, back tyre skidding perilously close to them.

The wind whipped his words away and she sped towards a blackened coppice, avoiding it by inches and ducking to let the low branches scrape overhead.

'Get your head lower!' Hugo yelled, pressing a hand to her head and pushing it forwards so that she was crouching over the handlebars. His grip loosened on her waist and she could feel him frantically shifting to keep balance, his chin digging into the soft flesh beside her spine.

A huge branch came out of the gloom, too high to be caught by the headlight until the last moment, swinging towards Tash's forehead like the boom of a yacht in a gale.

'Ohmygod!' she wailed as she pressed her face to the dials in an attempt to avoid it.

It was a few seconds before she realised she had lost Hugo – the bike was suddenly lighter, faster and more manageable. And her back was a hell of a lot colder.

Skidding to a slippery halt, she looked over her shoulder. She could see nothing but damp, squally gloom and the jagged black silhouette of the coppice.

Tash scoured the gloom for Hugo, terrified that he was out cold somewhere and in desperate need of medical attention. She could barely see a thing in the peaty dark and drizzle. Swinging the bike around so that its headlights were facing in the direction she had come, she saw nothing but thin, sinewy tree trunks and the raw gash of the tyre tracks splitting the wet grass.

She was about to cut the engine so that she could call for him when he loomed out of the darkness to her left, only a few yards away, reeling slightly, his breath pluming in front of him, shirt torn on the shoulder. For the first time Tash noticed that he wasn't wearing his flying jacket – he must be frozen through. Her own jaws were chattering like wind-up teeth from a joke shop.

'Are you hurt?' she asked anxiously as she noticed a big graze on his forehead.

'I'll live.' He put a trembling hand on the leather seat behind her to steady himself.

'Sorry.' She bit her lip, 'It was my fault for going too fast.'

He looked slightly dazed for a moment or two and then managed a sudden, unexpected smile.

'It beats an Alka-Seltzer for sobering one up. I deserved it.' He shrugged, stretching across her thigh to reach for the key and cut the engine.

'What are you doing?' She gulped nervously, intimidated by the sudden silence. Her ears were still ringing from the noise of the bike.

'We need to talk.' He touched his forehead tentatively and winced.

Unaware of the wind buffeting around her or the hollow booming of music coming from the house up above, Tash fumbled for the key fob in the ignition. She didn't trust herself to speak and her heart was doing a maddened dance in her chest, almost winding her. She knew she should feel angry and indignant, or even frightened, but she didn't; she couldn't pin down the precise emotion but knew that it was dangerously close to hope.

'I don't want to talk.' She started the engine again.

His hand closing over hers, Hugo cut it and pulled out the key. Very gently, he prised the fob from her fingers and stepped back.

'Give them back!' Tash bleated, but he ignored her, shoulders hunched against the cold, face in the shadows.

'I didn't want you to do the dare.' He played with the keys, not looking at her. 'I wanted you to tell a truth.'

'Oh, yes?' She realised her heart was doh-si-dohing with her tongue once more. Her voice sounded ridiculously high and tight, as though she'd been sucking helium balloons.

He suddenly laughed – a low, husky sound that didn't stem from amusement.

'You once told me you'd had a crush on me – as a kid. Nothing serious, I know, but . . .'

Tash nodded, desperately defensive of her pride. 'So?'

'Was I truly awful to you, Tash?'

She gaped at him through the gloom, astonished that he should think to ask. But his face was still in darkness, with only the whites of his eyes glinting.

'Pretty bad, yes,' she managed to croak, eyeing the keys that dangled less than a metre from her hand, catching the light like icy leaves on a branch. 'But that was years ago,' she added dismissively.

'Poor little Tash.' He seemed to mock her, his voice as low and soft as a sigh. 'You only needed to ask.'

Someone was yelling from the top of the field, but they were too far away to be audible, their words snatched back by the wind.

The keys continued glittering. Tash gazed at them, mesmerised. She was so bitterly cold that her arms and legs were shuddering as though jabbed with electric probes, her jaw clenched to stop her teeth chattering. Hugo was as still as an ice carving; despite the thin cotton shirt, gaping where it was ripped, he wasn't even shivering.

'Give me the keys,' Tash pleaded, stretching out for them. She shifted in the saddle as she did so and her bare upper leg touched the hot engine casing, jerking in a spasm of pain. Unbalanced, she and the bike almost went over.

'We haven't talked properly yet.' Hugo stepped back again until the keys were just out of reach once more. 'I want to know what it felt like.'

'What what felt like?' she groaned in exasperation. Boy, was he going for big time humiliation here, she realised. He really wanted to make her squirm. Not content with asking her to risk her life on a dare, he wanted to punish her with a truth too. She wished she'd gone the whole hog and burned his bed now.

'Fancying me so much when I felt nothing for you?' he snapped through the darkness. 'Did it really hurt?'

Not answering, Tash made a final lunge for the keys, but her oversized gloves made her grip clumsy and they flew from her fingers as soon as she pulled them from Hugo's hand.

'Shit!' she wailed, only just stopping the bike from capsizing, her boot heel sinking deep into the mud to the left as she fought to hold it up.

Hugo stooped down, cursing under his breath as he fished around in the damp grass to retrieve them.

'Now look what you've bloody done!' he hissed.

'You were the one giving me the third degree.'

'I was just interested,' he muttered, wiping his hands on his jeans and resting on his haunches as he peered at the muddy ground for the key fob.

'Well, I suggest you develop an interest in something different then,' Tash muttered. 'Like flower-pressing.'

Looking up at her, his face was still in complete shadow, but she could just make out his eyes in the dim, steely light from the turbulent sky. They seemed to be raking her face as though searching for a completely different key. She almost fell off the bike in shock. He's hitting on me, she realised in utter amazement. Hugo Beauchamp is hitting on me.

Tash took a deep breath, knowing that she had to act quickly to stop herself free-falling delightedly into something very dangerous and almost guaranteed to hurt everyone she loved and decimate her pride as surely as appearing naked in *Playboy* alongside Elle MacPherson. She kept thinking of the unmade bed – not made up for anyone special, but perfectly prepared for a casual screw. Old Tash had always lumped around after him like a love-sick groupie; she was keen and available and it would make Hugo feel great to lay Niall O'Shaughnessy's future wife at the same time as his ex-wife was trying to lay Hugo. It was typical of Hugo when very drunk to choose such a childish, egotistical goal. He had already tried to humiliate her that night – why not go the whole hog and give her that big come-on she'd longed for during all her confused, hellish teenage years? He was bound to think that killingly funny. Beating her at the trials the next day would make a neat hat trick.

Still crouching on his haunches beside the bike, Hugo was looking for the keys again, his hair gleaming in the pewter light, clean and shiny. It had always been her weakness, that hair which she had once dreamed of touching – a silly daydream that had been her idea of a risqué sexual fantasy in her early teens, when details of the actual lights-out act had still been woolly and based largely on a battered copy of *Fear of Flying* that she'd bought from a jumble sale in the hope that it would cure her aeroplane phobia. Yet it was a fantasy that had stuck and still caught her in the groin with leaping excitement every time she contemplated it.

She quickly looked away, crossing her arms to hug herself for warmth, her huge gloves feeling like a stranger's hands on her shoulders.

The next moment she realised that a third hand was joining the fray, sliding slowly and snugly up the outside of her boots and then under the nub of her knee as it headed upwards – gentle and unhurried.

For a moment Tash didn't move as she felt a container-load of fire-crackers go off in the pit of her belly and several pulse-points she'd never known existed suddenly leapt into life as though making up for lost time. As the hand slipped up to her thigh, she realised that she'd stopped breathing and couldn't remember how to start again.

Fighting like mad to get a grip on herself, she squeaked in a more helium-enhanced voice than ever: 'I don't think you'll find the keys there.'

The fingers continued their steady ascent without hesitation.

'Maybe not,' he laughed huskily, 'but I'm having a great time looking.'

Tash closed her eyes and allowed the fire-crackers a moment's more life before dousing them in cold water and anger.

'You're drunk, Hugo.'

'I know.'

'You've been downing scotch like a tramp all night,' she spluttered, trying to sound logical. 'It's made you bad-tempered and childish and I think you should stop this before you really regret it.'

'I thought you fancied drunks,' he murmured. 'After all Niall's usually plastered – I figured I might stand a chance if I drank for England. Might be more your type. Isn't that what you go for?'

'Niall is not a drunk!'

'No, you're right.' His hand suddenly gripped her leg tightly, almost pinching. 'Niall is an alcoholic.'

'How dare you say that!' Tash howled.

'Because it's true,' he said simply. 'And you know it. Which is why you're starting to go off him. Because, in your heart of hearts, you know that one of the reasons he drinks is you. He's hitting the wedding Bell's and toasting the bride until he passes out at night. Now are you going to help me out down here?' He calmly let her go and started looking for the keys once more.

Tash wanted to kick his face in. She wanted to leap off the bike and flatten him with her heels. She wanted to drop the bike right on top of him. Because cruelly, hatefully, there was some truth in what he said.

'I'm madly and crazily in love with Niall, Hugo,' she spluttered, hooking the bike up on to its rest as she climbed clumsily off. 'Now I'm going to walk back up to the house and try to track him down.'

As she walked away, he leaned his forehead against the spokes of the bike wheel. She had a horrible feeling that he was laughing.

Tash stumbled through the dark field, tripping over the uneven ground as she raced up the hill.

'Tash, come back!' he called behind her. Far from laughing, his voice was hoarse with guilt.

Tash blocked out the sound. All she could hear as she walked away was the squelch of her boot heels plugging her into the mud with every step. She couldn't wait to throw them out – they had brought her nothing but bad luck.

Halfway up the hill, she did just that, walking the rest of the way on bare feet so numb with cold that she kept thinking they'd dropped off.

Catching sight of her as she moved into the light, coated with mud and bare-legged, the gathered guests raced forwards demanding to know what had gone wrong, whether the bike had crashed, where Hugo was and whether he was hurt? Tash shrugged them all off and headed indoors to warm up and collect her coat.

The forge was icy cold as the Rayburn had puttered out again. Howling and whimpering sulkily, Beetroot was shut in the bedroom away from Niall's ankles.

He had all but polished off the bottle of malt they had been going to give Hugo for his birthday when Tash rolled in. 'I got a lift back with Godfrey Pelham.' She watched him closely, anxious to gauge his mood.

But, shrugging, he said nothing. He looked impossibly depraved and poetic – dark hair tickling his bloodshot eyes, stubble pricking out of his cheeks, body an indolent, slothful sag of alcoholically relaxed muscles. He didn't even comment on her bootless feet or muddy face and clothes. Nor did he complain when she clambered on to the sofa beside him and curled up into a tight foetal ball in his arms.

'D'you have a good time tonight?' She clenched her eyes shut and pressed her nose against one of his shirt buttons.

'No.' He stroked her ears softly as though distractedly caressing a cat.

'Me neither.'

'I love you so much.' He pressed his lips into her hair, breath as usual smelling of whisky. It reminded her of Hugo's. She wished hell-raising men would stick to something more appetising, like vodka. Or Listermint.

'I love you too.' She pressed her cheek to his wide, warm shoulder. 'To distraction, to bits, to death and too much.'

Drifting off to sleep, she dreamed that Hugo was licking her legs while she was trying to perform a dressage test on Snob. Snob had just very alarmingly turned into Niall giving her a piggy-back when she was woken at four in the morning by Niall – who was absolutely paralytic – dropping her as he tried to carry her upstairs.

Nineteen

THE NEXT MORNING, TASH encountered Zoe and Gus in the kitchen at Lime Tree Farm, gossiping happily about the party. Zoe, who had left early with Niall to ferry the drunken Rufus home, was dying for news. Gus and Penny had stayed to the bitter end and had therefore got a lot of bad behaviour to report – mostly details of eventers getting off with one another, which was not unusual, especially amongst the younger ones. The fact that two of them had chosen to rise to the pelvic trot in Hugo's bedroom while Alicia was using the lavatory three yards away was alarming but not as shocking as the rumour that Hugo himself had been in bed at the time and had slept on throughout.

Trying to listen in, Tash drank strong, black coffee on the run and fell over Beetroot who was following her around imploringly, her breakfast having been overlooked in the rush.

She was running late and had just under an hour to get Snob ready to travel to the Lowerton trials with Hugo and Stefan, who were due to collect them at seven.

Not really following the rather fanciful tales of party antics, she only picked up a few bald facts, snatched as she dashed around in search of drying numnahs and clean shirts. Ted had stayed the night with Hugo's buxom head girl Franny, with whom he was now seemingly reconciled, and was in Gus's bad books as he hadn't yet arrived to do the feeds and mucking out. After Tash had left the night before, Sophia had gone into hysterics on discovering her Trollope being used as a beer mat, Hugo had later been hauled up from the bottom of Twenty

Acres almost an hour after Tash had walked up, blind drunk and very bloody-minded. He had then downed yet more scotch before passing out on a sofa, at which point Lisette had coiled herself into the space beside him and asked him yet again to agree to Haydown's being used for the Four Poster Bed shoot.

'She was all over him like aftershave,' Penny giggled. 'There were all the other men in the room with their eyes on stalks, absolutely spitting with envy, and Hugo could hardly open his eyes.'

'He only woke up when she practically grabbed his groin to get his attention,' Gus said in near-disbelief as he wandered through the kitchen to fetch another sweater.

'Did he say yes?' Zoe asked. 'To the location shoot, I mean.' For some reason she looked at Tash when she said this. Flustered, Tash pretended to be engrossed in untangling a pile of exercise bandages.

'Not sure.' Penny wrinkled her nose as she downed Alka-Seltzers dissolved in orange juice. 'I think he might have been concussed from coming off that bike with you, Tash. How you could just leave him down there with a head injury, I'll never know. Everyone at the party was talking about it.'

'He was fine!' Tash bristled, a blush curling into her cheeks. 'He was walking and talking perfectly well. It was just a scratch.'

Penny gave her an old-fashioned look. 'Bloody foolhardy thing to do, if you ask me.'

'Why did you do it?' Zoe joined her sister in looking disapproving. 'I'm sure Niall would never have left the party if he'd thought you were going to start leaping on motorbikes and careering around Hugo's fields the moment he turned his back.'

'It was a dare.' Tash was aware that she was slouching around like a surly teenager. 'And, anyway, I thought Niall was coming back.'

'Sorry, my fault.' Zoe looked apologetic. 'It took ages to persuade Rufus that it wasn't a good idea to go to bed in the back of the car. Niall was wonderful with him so I offered him a coffee for his efforts. Then we started talking and we didn't notice the time.'

'You drank coffee?' she asked casually.

Zoe nodded. 'Gallons of it. Niall was just telling me about the Anne Brontë adaptation when India wandered in – she got a lift back from the party with the Cubitts. *Wildfell Hall*'s one of her set texts at the moment, so they were discussing it forever – they were like a couple of swots revising for Oxbridge entrance. He said she'd given him such good ideas that he wanted to rush back to the forge to go through the script and make notes.'

Instead, he went back to the forge and drank a bottle of scotch while waiting for me, Tash realised with a plummeting heart. She could still hear Hugo's words of the night before stinging in her ears. She longed to confess her fears to Zoe, but had to race outside to bandage up Snob so that he would be ready to load the moment Hugo's box arrived. With Ted not on hand, she had a pile of things to do.

Tripping over a hungover Gus who was listening slyly to Today on the tack-room wireless, she was still well behind schedule when Franny drove into the yard, glowering behind the wheel of Hugo's vast high-tech lorry, stereo pounding out the Chris Evans morning show.

Scruffy and unshaven, Ted leaped down from the cab, grinning the happy, Cheshire cat smile of the recently shagged. He had a woolly hat pulled over his shorn scalp to protect against the early-morning chill.

'Hugo's conked out in the back, so don't panic.' He started to gather up tack and heave it over to the huge holds at the base of the lorry. 'Christ knows how he'll get round – he's been vomiting rainbows all morning, and Surfer hasn't qualified for Badminton yet, so they have to go clear.'

With a grumbling Gus roped in to help, they were on their way within half an hour, Snob trying to kick his way out of the rear as he always did on his way to competitions, thoroughly het up with excitement, like a football hooligan on his way to a grudge match.

'Shut that fucker up or I'll shoot him!' came a deep voice from the living compartment.

'Hugo's unusually cheerful.' Ted didn't look up from the *Sun*.

In the cab, Tash and Franny tried not to giggle. Stefan, in the back with Hugo, was throwing up over and over again in the tiny loo cubicle.

'He looks hellish,' Franny whispered as they raced up the slip road and on to the M4, her rubber t-shirt straining over her vast chest as she craned to look in the wing mirror. 'And I'm sure he's still half-cut. Everyone at that party was off their heads – I reckon there'll be a lot of falls today. You were one of the only ones to stay sober and leave early, Tash. You should coast it.'

Walking the course before her dressage test, Tash had grave doubts that she would coast it at all. She had even less hope of Hugo being capable of mounting, let alone riding his nervy, clever liver-chestnut, Surfer. Thankfully it was a two-day event, which meant that both the show-jumping and the cross-country phases were to follow the next day. All they had to do that morning was perform their dressage tests.

They were walking the course early because another intermediate competition was running alongside the more senior class, and those entrants went across country that afternoon, using part of the same course. It meant it would be hard to get close enough to the fences to study them any later that day, but both Stefan and Hugo grumbled like mad at the early start.

Lowerton was an extremely tricky, undulating course on which it was almost impossible to get a good, flowing rhythm as the track twisted around like a snake with colic, forever changing direction and gradient. The fences themselves were a tricky bunch of corners and arrow-heads which needed supreme accuracy and strong control. The latter was something Tash had lacked of late with Snob. She was certain that she'd have a battle on her hands the next day trying to hold him on line. These days he took more diversions than the North Circular.

Hugo made no comment about the night before. Hardly speaking to Tash at all, except to snap at her to hurry up as they walked the course with Stefan, he was sullen and jittery, eyelids dropping over diabolical bags beneath.

He barely seemed to be taking in the fences as they tottered around, meeting a lot of other green-faced eventers en route – all of them gossiping about the party and muttering darkly about deliberate sabotage on Hugo's part. It was only when they saw his pale green face that they realised he was feeling the roughest of them all.

'Are you two planning to ride pillion across country, like you did last night?' Lucy Field giggled, digging for gossip.

'Tash never lets me ride Snob,' Hugo muttered darkly. 'She thinks I might show her up.'

'You wouldn't know which way to point him if you rode him tomorrow,' Tash said pettily, noticing that he'd given one of the hardest fences on the course – a vast bounce over a footbridge – only the most cursory of glances.

'I've ridden this course for the last four years,' he muttered as she pedantically paced out a double of bullfinches at the brow of a hill, which gave one the impression of jumping into the sky.

'There are a couple of new fences this year,' she pointed out, retracing her steps to check she had counted right.

'Well, I'll make sure I introduce myself to them then.' He staggered off, hardly glancing at the bullfinches.

Rolling her eyes, she carried on with her meticulous appraisal of every fence and alternative route into them. Tottering wanly beside her, Stefan threw up behind practically every single one, but at least he diligently worked out the distances and approach lines, unlike his crabby boss.

'I can't think what's got into him,' he complained as they trailed through ominously slippery mud. 'I've seen him hungover before, but never like this. I'd say he was under a black cloud, but then again we all are.'

The sky was so heavy with rain, it seemed to be dropping by feet every second, like a plunging grey parachute canopy, yet no drops fell as a squally breeze buffeted hoods against the backs of heads and knocked bush hats into adjoining fields where they had to be chased along like stray kites.

Back at the lorry, Ted and Franny had settled the horses in the temporary stabling nearby and were huddled in the living quarters microwaving mugs of coffee and looking glum. Franny's straining leather trousers were covered with purple antiseptic spray.

'Bodybuilder cut his fetlock slipping down the ramp.' Franny tipped the peak of her baseball cap away from her nose and gazed at Tash forlornly. 'Hugo's just fired me for the third time today.'

Tash winced. 'So he's just got Surfer to compete?'

She nodded. 'No bad thing – he has such bad shakes, he'll be using the reins as divining rods in the dressage.'

Later that afternoon, Tash managed a fairly respectable dressage score, enhanced by the fact that everyone else, hungover to the back teeth from Hugo's party, performed abysmally. She had never known so many top drawer eventers forget their tests.

'It's bloody sabotage,' cursed one of the best British riders, Brian Sedgewick, whose lop-sided rugby-player's face was almost grey with nausea. 'Hugo should be shot.'

But the grumblings stopped when Hugo's own test was the worst he had executed in over five years. Surfer was a lean, graceful liver-chestnut with long, nervy rabbit's ears that twitched like antennae with concentration as he listened to his rider's every breath. They were usually a lethal combination, with Hugo's fluid, almost imperceptible aids spurring the horse into balletic brilliance. All the other riders envied Hugo like mad for clicking with him. But today those Cadbury brown ears were flat to the horse's neatly bobbled plaits as Hugo sat hunch-backed in the saddle, his concentration in tatters. He forgot his way twice, flopped around in the saddle like an amateur, and his mouth disappeared entirely for the last few moments as he battled not to throw up. Riding out of the ring, he was off Surfer in super-quick time and, chucking the reins to Franny, hared off to the Portaloos.

A bleach-faced Stefan received the dubious honour of being the first person ever to fall off during the Lowerton dressage phase. He came out looking very hang-dog with a muddy top hat and pride as bruised as a windfall.

No one was feeling particularly social that evening; Tash had been invited to a pasta session in a nearby box, but just wanted to use the cab phone to call Niall and then go to bed in anticipation of the dawn start the next morning. At least Hugo had stomped off in high dudgeon to spend the night at his friend's farmhouse and was no longer lurking around to snarl and mob her up.

The following morning everything was freshly rinsed and still dripping. Drizzle leaked through layers of clothing, left tiny droplets on hair and made the competitors' paper numbers as soft and rippable as damp tissues. Most kept theirs inside the plastic bibs they wore on their chests, but for the few who didn't it was a case of shouting out their number each time they passed a fence judge.

Tash, who had an early cross-country draw, walked the course one last time before taking Snob out for a pipe-opener and some basic schooling to calm his nerves.

Wet, muddy and cast in early-morning shadows, the fences looked even less appetising than they had the day before. One fence particularly worried her – a sunken road that one had to jump in and out of before coming straight up against the narrowest of arrow heads. Coming near the end of the course, it required a die-straight line with no room for error. Combined with the wet, slippery ground it would be like trying to sword dance barefoot on an ice rink.

'Bloody nasty object.' Lucy Field, the diminutive blonde eventer, caught her up as she stared at it. 'I'm going the long way. My nag'll glance off that in this weather.'

Imagining the speed at which she and the headstrong Snob would be travelling by the time they reached it, Tash decided she should play it safe too. Going early, they had little chance to see how other riders tackled it. Their draw also meant that the ground would be very slippery. The more horses that went around, the more cut up and grippable would become. Tash and Snob followed fewer entries, so would be galloping on something close to an oil slick.

Back at the make-shift wooden stables that had been erected for the weekend, it was all activity. Snob didn't have to be pretty and plaited for the two phases that came that day, but he had been shampooed anyway, to remove his stable stain, and was sulkily allowing himself to be vigorously rubbed by Ted, looking like a young rugby player, furious that his mother was washing away the mud from his first ever scrum.

'Hugo's still in bed.' Ted dodged Snob's snapping teeth. 'Says he doesn't need to walk the course again. Now Bod's been scratched, he doesn't have to ride until after lunch.'

'Lucky for him.' Tash watched as Snob tore a piece out of Ted's denim jacket. 'He in a good mood?'

'You mean Snob or Hugo?'

'Both.'

'No.'

To prove his point, Snob smashed his way around the show-jumping course that morning like an over-sprung pin-ball, demolishing two flower arrangements and splitting a pole with his hind legs as he kicked back so hard at the final fence that Tash left the ring with her chin between his ears.

Later, she finished her cross-country round with aching arms, a red face and a pounding heart. They had survived by the skin of their teeth, although Tash was amazed that she had any teeth left, she had gritted them so much on the way round.

Huddling in wax coats and bush hats, Ted and Stefan were whooping their support and congratulating her as she slithered to a halt close to the weigh-in trailer, but she knew that, despite the clear, she hadn't ridden at all well. Most of the round had been spent trying to pull Snob's head up from between his legs as he fought to get away from her and go faster. He was wearing one of the strongest bits available and yet she was a hair's breadth away from losing control. She had schooled and schooled him for weeks to no avail. He was simply too strong and she was in despair. He might love and honour her, but, like an errant husband, he no longer obeyed.

At least the weather was on her side. Half an hour after she weighed in and cooled Snob off, the rain was coming down in sheets, jumping high off the horse-box roofs and driving into the entrances of the few trade stands that had turned up for the day.

Changing into dry clothes, Tash was fairly certain that her bad show-jumping would have left her unplaced, and she would have liked to box up and head home to Fosbourne Ducis and a few snatched hours with Niall, but they had to wait for Hugo and Stefan to finish.

Trying to make up for his appalling dressage of the day before,

Stefan rode as though he had the devil at his back, securing the fastest clear round of the day, although he took some near-suicidal risks to achieve it. He was the first rider of the day to tackle the direct route of the sunken road, riding it as though it wasn't there, which belied the tremendous skill involved in jumping it.

'My heart was jumping higher than the horse,' he confessed to Tash as he crashed around the box afterwards peeling off his wet clothes. 'That fence won't give you an inch, and the arrowhead is straight on top of you as you jump out of the road. Yeach!' He shuddered, wandering around in his underpants. Stripped off, he was incredibly thin and bandy, like a long strip of trailing ivy.

Despite a commendable clear round at show-jumping, his dressage had been so bad that he, too, was unlikely to be placed. Once he was dressed in an Asterix sweatshirt and old navy cords, he and Tash cracked open a couple of cans of Tango and huddled together in the tented competitors' area to listen to the commentary and smoke lots of nervous cigarettes. They knew that they had both been lucky to get around. The weather and the tricky course were causing havoc among less experienced competitors, and riders were being stopped out on the course over and over again as it had to be rebuilt, or the ambulance had to trundle over to collect a broken-boned competitor.

Having knocked out just one fence during his show-jumping round, Hugo was in with a far better chance than anyone could have anticipated the evening before. With multiple faults and high finishing times, most finishers had three-figure penalties, and the dressage score was a far less significant factor than usual. If he went clear and fast across country, Hugo had a good chance of being placed. To qualify Surfer for Badminton, he absolutely had to go clear.

But the ground had turned into a quagmire by the time he and Surfer were due to set out. Their start had been delayed over and over again by the stoppages on the course, and Surfer was as wound up as an over-twisted coil.

Tash and Stefan wandered to the start to offer support, but Hugo was in no mood to take it. The ribby liver-chestnut was dancing around excitedly, eyes bulging, rabbit ears twitching. He looked far too eager and fresh, whereas Hugo looked jaded and preoccupied.

'I feel like shit,' he muttered through clenched teeth, leaning down to steal a puff from Tash's cigarette. 'I think I'm coming down with something.'

'Alcohol poisoning,' Stefan looked up at him with a sly grin. 'Christ knows why you got so smashed at your party.'

'Lost my heart over a woman, haven't I?' Hugo hissed, looking to the starter who was counting him down. Surfer gave a flurry of half-rears like a small child trying to see over heads at a football match.

Delighted, Stefan caught Tash's eye and mouthed, 'Lisette!'

Tash glanced up at Hugo. His beautiful, angular face as grey as the sky, he looked truly ill. He could ride better than anyone she knew across country, but even a virtuoso violinist couldn't play in tune if he'd put on a pair of gloves.

'Go safely,' she urged him. 'Don't take any risks in this weather.'

For a moment he looked down at her as though noticing her for the first time, eyes raking her face, but then he resumed his visored look, and ignored her as he waited for the starter to shout: 'Go!'

Thundering out of the start box, Surfer's studded shoes kicked up such enormous divots that the starter got a mud cake right in the face.

'Typical Hugo,' Stefan laughed, watching the combination streak for the first fence as though riding the Cheltenham Gold Cup.

As soon as he was off, it was obvious that safety was well down on Hugo's list of priorities. He was clearly attacking the course with the same intention that Stefan had – trying to make up for his abysmal dressage with a fast time and the quickest routes.

Surfer was a gutsy, athletic horse with a lion's heart in his narrow, ribby chest. But he had been bred and trained in Australia where the ground was hard and dusty, the light searing, the air dry. The gloomy, slippery sludge of England confused him and snatched at his confidence. Of all the riders in competition, Hugo was the bravest and most inspired. He could see a line from half a mile away, could judge pace and attack like no other. But his eyes were pinched by a hangover, his reactions dulled, his body sweating as he detoxified from two days of very heavy drinking. He couldn't rely on his usual second-sight judgement. But still he tried, convinced that he knew the course too well to be fooled by a bit of wet weather. His arrogance was his undoing.

Listening to the tannoy, Tash, Stefan and Franny waited in the shelter of the riders' tent with bated breath as reports came back of Hugo clearing fence after fence in record time. He went over the bullfinches without breaking Surfer's stride, it was reported, and the tiny, malevolent crowd around the river fence were to be disappointed as the combination streaked through it without a slip.

Two easy galloping fences later and they were just four from home and well within the time limit – unheard of on such a wet day. Even Stefan, who had been the fastest so far, had been ten seconds over it.

'If he goes clear, how close to winning will he be?' Tash asked fretfully.

Pushing back her baseball cap, Franny looked at the board. 'Well, Graham's ahead by a mile, and Becky Holdsworth looks pretty unbeatable too. You're fifth. If he gets inside the time, he'll sneak ahead of you, I'm afraid.' She rolled her dark-rimmed eyes.

'Great,' muttered Tash. 'I hope he falls off. No one should ride that well after drinking that much.'

It was a feeble, bad-spirited joke made in a weak moment. The second she said it, she regretted it and was grateful to the others for letting it pass. It was only when the next tannoy announcement came through that she felt her heart kick out at her ribs in shame. It was the first of many, many moments in which she would re-live her bad sportsmanship and cruel wish with deep regret.

'Hugo Beauchamp and Surfer are down at the Sunken Road in what looks like a nasty fall. They tried for the direct route and failed to make it. Horse and rider have still to get up . . .' The microphone was muffled and, after a moment of crackling interference, fell silent.

While Franny raced out of the tent, Tash and Stefan waited for a few more seconds in case there was another announcement, but, after a long break, the PA crackled into life to warn of yet another course stoppage, inducing impatient, exasperated groans amongst those waiting for the final score.

Tash and Stefan legged it out of the tent to be met by Ted bolting the other way. He was carrying Surfer's headcollar and a waterproof woollen blanket in anticipation of collecting him.

'D'you know what's going on?' he panted. 'I've just come from the stables.'

'Hugo's down and they've stopped the other riders on the course,' Tash explained, her throat cramped with fear.

'I know that, idiot,' he snapped. 'They've just called for the course vet – he was looking at Bod's pastern again. Sounds like Surfer's more than just winded.'

'Shit!' Stefan rubbed his spiky wet hair nervously.

'What about Hugo?' Tash muttered, feeling bile rise in her mouth.

But Ted and Stefan were already heading out on to the course. She raced after them, heart crashing in her chest like a hammer against an anvil.

Together they ran and stumbled towards the fence, which was almost

half a mile away. There were very few spectators around as the weather
was too wet and the competition too unglamorous, but those that were
there were knowledgeable and experienced. They mostly knew Tash
and Stefan, shaking their heads when asked whether they knew what
was going on, offering concern and sympathy. An older woman with
a fat spaniel on a lead was walking from the fence as they approached
it, face ashen beneath her battered waterproof hat.

Lagging behind the others because she couldn't run as fast, Tash
watched as Stefan paused for a second to speak to her while Ted dashed
on. As she caught up, she heard the tail end of a sentence that seemed to
drain the blood from her face as surely as if her throat had been cut.

'—lost his footing and fell back in. Smashed his spine, I think.
Poor lad.'

Whimpering, Tash bolted past them, tripping on a divot and crashing
to her knees in her haste, her cold face feeling more and more numb.

She could see the cluster of people around the fence now, heads
bowed, shoulders slumped, an air of desolation permeating the wet
air. Several course Land-Rovers and an ambulance were parked nearby.
She couldn't see Hugo anywhere.

Slithering past the deserted steward's chair, she found Ted talking
to the course organiser. His usually merry, ladsy face was a mask of
tightly controlled pain as he fought tears.

'Surfer's had to be destroyed.' He turned to her, eyes dead with
sorrow. 'They came at the fence too fast and he slipped. He had
no hope.'

'And Hugo?' She could barely get the words out, her eyes darting
madly around the faces nearby for his.

'Not a scratch on him,' Ted hissed. 'Bastard!'

Tash burst into tears, as instant a response as screaming when one
felt pain. She was deeply ashamed of her reaction but couldn't help
herself, dissolving into Ted's arms.

Closer to the fence, there was an air of menace and misery. Officials,
spectators and organisers milled around despondently. A clerk of the
course was barking into a walkie-talkie and glancing at his watch.

Already on the scene, Franny was totally inconsolable. At last
catching up, Stefan found her being patted rather ineffectually by
a St John's Ambulance volunteer just beside the jump, which had
been screened off with make-shift wicker fencing while a tractor
backed its trailer close enough to collect Surfer's huge, motionless
body, now covered with a tarpaulin. Tash looked away, her chest so
heavy that it seemed to creak under the strain. Her tears now at the

gulping stage, she left Ted and Stefan comforting Franny and searched for Hugo.

Even though they were thick with mud and rain, his red eventing colours stood out like a splash of blood against the sludgy landscape. Sheltering under a tree, his shoulders hunched, head hanging, he was talking quietly with two officials and a fence steward, drawing on a borrowed cigarette. She could hear the accusing tone of the officials' voices, and the monotone bleakness of Hugo's replies, but couldn't make out the words. He seemed to be getting a very severe dressing down and precious little sympathy. Whatever had happened to make Surfer fall, it seemed that Hugo was being entirely blamed by those who had witnessed it.

Hovering a few metres away, Tash could see that his eyes were red from crying. She had never, ever known Hugo cry. It hadn't seemed possible until now, and her heart crashed in pity for him. He could be a bold, bloody-minded rider, but that was why he was at the top of the tree. However rash and dangerous he had been that day, he didn't deserve this tragedy or the blistering condemnation that followed. Eyes hollow and wild under his wet hair, he looked perilously close to cracking up.

As the officials drifted away, he suddenly gazed across to where Tash was standing, not seeming to see her at all. His helmet was in his hands, his number bib tattered, breeches black with mud and rain. A huge, angry bruise was starting to form on his right cheek and his nose had clearly been bleeding. He still had the faintest trace of a graze on his forehead from falling off the motorbike, and his cheeks were splattered with mud and blood from the nose-bleed.

Not thinking, Tash bolted forward, desperate to support him but not knowing how.

'He's dead, Tash.' Hugo blinked at her forlornly, seemingly trying to get this to sink into his own head. 'He's dead. It was all my fucking fault – oh, Christ!' And he buried his face in his hands.

'Shh, shh – don't say that.' Tash put her arm around his shaking shoulders, and reached out her other hand to stroke his wet hair. That hair – her fantasy. Such an awful time for a day-dream to come true. It had turned into a nightmare. There was no pleasure in the touch of it now, just desperate compassion.

The next moment he stumbled forward and, almost knocking her over with the violence of his movement, was gripping her for support, head buried in the crook of her neck, hot, rapid breathing hitting her throat. He clung there for a long time, his body trembling, eyes tightly clenched, shoulders taut, knuckles white. Then, pushing her away almost as aggressively as he had grabbed her, he turned and walked to the far side of the tree and slumped against the trunk where he couldn't witness Surfer's carcass being edged slowly on to the trailer.

Supervising the brave horse's ignoble removal from the fence was hellish. What had been a trembling, excitable bundle of primed muscle and eager energy just minutes earlier, was now just half a ton of impediment which had to be swiftly and quietly removed from the course to allow the competition to continue. Realising that Hugo wasn't up to it, Stefan and Ted waded in to let the officials know where to take him while Tash was allotted the task of getting Hugo and Franny back to the box.

The long, wet walk seemed endless. Franny couldn't stop crying; Hugo was walking like a zombie, saying nothing, gazing ahead fixedly. They were stopped over and over again to be asked what had happened, with Tash only able to shake her head and hustle her charges on, as the slightest mention of 'destroyed', 'put down' or 'dead' sent Franny into complete free-fall hysteria.

Back at the box, Tash poured her a huge brandy and tried to make Hugo change out of his sodden clothes, but he just sat at the table, staring into space, surrounded by the bedding of the night before. He tried to light a cigarette, but his hands were shaking so much that he couldn't spark the flint, finally letting Tash light it for him. As she did so, he reached out and grabbed her wrist, looking up at her with feverish eyes.

'You don't blame me, do you, Tash?' he barked, sounding strangely angry and savage. 'After all, you're in love with me, aren't you?'

She gaped at him in amazement, too shocked to speak. Behind her, Franny was still sobbing too loudly to hear.

'Well, aren't you? Christ, I thought I could at least rely on you to be loyal and wet and stick by me through this!' He dropped his head into his hands, gloved fingers raking through wet hair.

'I'll pretend I never heard you say that.' Scarlet with fury, Tash stomped back to the sobbing Franny and gave her a huge hug.

Over the next half-hour, several fellow eventers knocked on the door offering support but Tash fielded them, thanking them politely and asking them to leave it for a while. Even worse, a couple of local stringers from the papers tried to get in and talk to Hugo, muttering darkly about animal cruelty. Surprised by her own resilience, Tash booted them out and shut the curtains to stop them taking photographs.

The medicinal brandy had not been one of her wisest moves,

however. Before long, Franny had stopped crying and was laying into Hugo, blaming the incident entirely on him and his reckless riding.

'You're such a competitive fucking idiot!' she screamed, her eyes so puffy and bloodshot that she looked as though she'd had chlorine thrown in her face. 'You as good as killed that horse because you wanted to win so badly and save your pride. You spoilt shit!'

Hugo didn't respond, lighting one cigarette from the butt of another with shaking hands and staring at Tash in a desperate plea for help. He was still wearing his tatty gloves and the stopwatches on his arm were still clocking up the time from the moment he had raced out of the start box, full of hot-headed determination.

Dropping her gaze, Tash stood back, no longer willing to rush to his aid.

'Everyone was telling you to go the safe routes,' Franny raged on, her voice climbing. 'But you wouldn't sodding listen, would you? You blazed out there thinking you could sodding well conquer the world and instead you killed your horse. You might as well have got up this morning, taken a couple of Alka-Seltzer and shot him in his stable.'

'Shut up!' Hugo suddenly stood up and lunged across at her, sending mugs flying from the table

But Fanny just dodged sideways and screamed on, 'You were still pissed today, weren't you? You went out there so blind drunk you couldn't see straight, figuring that if Stefan could do it, so could you. You're a disgrace to me, to your poor, doomed horses and the whole sport. And don't bother firing me this time – I'm quitting. I wouldn't work for you again if you trebled my wages. You're a loser, Hugo.'

As she made to turn and leave, he bolted forward and lifted his arm to slap her.

Yelling at him to stop, Tash jumped between them and received a crowning blow to the side of her face, the sharp edge of his glove buckle catching her cheek just millimetres from her eye.

'Shit!' He backed away as Franny charged out of the box, running slap into Stefan who made a grab for her and missed as she bolted towards the stabling area, blind with tears. Seconds later, Stefan had been jumped on by the stringers outside. Beside him, the door slammed shut in the wind.

Inside the box, Tash was reeling, her eye smarting with pain as she reached up to her face and felt the damp, hot trickle of blood.

'You shouldn't have got in the way.' Hugo cleared his throat defensively, backing off even more.

'You were going to hit Franny.' Fighting not to cry, she headed

towards the lavatory and fetched some toilet paper to stem the
bleeding.

'You guys okay?' Stefan clambered into the box, having told the
reporters to get lost.

'Terrific.' Hugo started to pull off his gloves, his voice icy cool now.
'We're in roaring party spirits, in fact. Can I get you a drink or a canapé
or something?'

'Hugo, I think you need to sit down, mate.' Stefan watched him in
concern.

'I have full use of my legs, thank you,' he snapped. 'I think I need
a change of clothes.' He started to strip off.

Coming out of the loo and mopping her eye, Tash stood beside
Stefan and watched for a moment in appalled bewilderment as Hugo
frantically tugged off his clothes, ripping them as he went. Down to
his underpants, his body as lean and mean as a marathon runner's, he
turned to face them once more.

'Flattered as I am by having an audience,' he drawled, 'I'd far rather
you pissed off and left me alone. Don't you two have prizes to collect
or something? And you can stop staring!' he snarled at Tash. 'Seeing
as you no longer seem to want the goods, just fuck off.'

Twenty

ABSOLUTELY LIVID AT BEING left alone for so long, Snob napped and misbehaved in the ring when Tash rode in to collect her prize, picking up on her gloom. He bit the rather grand peer who was handing out the awards, and then reared up and refused to leave the ring while the overall winner, Brian Sedgewick, was performing his lap of honour. When Tash finally coaxed him out in a crab-like canter, he almost flattened a spectator's dog.

'You're all bloody animal killers!' the woman shrieked after her as Tash frantically fought Snob all the way back to the stabling area which was now almost deserted as most of the competitors, knowing they had no chance of being placed, had packed up and left long ago.

Ted was waiting for her, his bush hat rammed down over his nose like Clint Eastwood riding into a strange town.

'Sorry I wasn't around,' he apologised, gathering tack into the big lockers that would be carried to the box. 'I was arranging for Franny to get a lift home in Isabel Pike's lorry. She refuses to go back to Maccombe, so I said she could stay at the farm tonight.'

'Why didn't you get her a lift with the Stantons?' Tash asked tiredly. 'They're going to the farm anyway to drop Kirsty off.'

'They left hours ago.'

'So Kirsty doesn't know about the accident?' Tash started to take off Snob's tack, sighing impatiently as he danced around on the spot, eyes rolling.

'Oh, she knows about it all right,' Ted muttered through clenched teeth. 'That's why they left early, I figure. She didn't even pass on a message for Hugo.'

'Shit.'

'Bod and Happy Monday are boxed already, so we just have to get this fella padded up and we're off.' He started to lug the crate in the direction of the horse-box area. 'Stick his kit in that one, will you?' He nodded towards the one remaining tack trunk.

Looking inside as she tossed in Snob's tendon boots, she caught her breath. Surfer's bridle, with its distinctive red rubber cheek protectors, was resting on top. Seeing it made a lump the size of the wicked step-mother's poisoned apple leap up into her throat. Poor old Surfer, the nervy, eager-to-please gentleman who had the grace of a Burmese cat and the over-enthusiastic boldness of a setter puppy. It may have been Hugo's fault that he had fallen, she realised, but it was in the nature of the horse to take on the fence with all guns blazing. The reason she herself had chosen to take the longer route there was because she had been almost certain that, faced with the same decision Surfer had faced, Snob would have tried for the same huge, fatal leap. And riding early in the day, she hadn't known, as Hugo had when he set off, that it could be jumped safely. She dreaded to think what might have happened had the roles been reversed, and she'd set off across country after Stefan's successful jump.

With Snob padded out in blankets and travelling boots like a nervous roller blader about to hit Hyde Park, Ted took him off to load in the box and Tash scoured the make-shift yard for the last of her belongings. She was one of the final competitors to leave and the place seemed eerily abandoned, like a fair-ground after all the rides had been switched off, the revellers long gone.

Gathering a stray head-collar and Stefan's black jacket, which he had left thrown over Happy's door, she headed towards the horsebox, now parked alone in the churned-up, tyre-marked field. Hugo was coming the other way, face set angrily, blue eyes narrowed.

'There you bloody are.' He threw up his hands impatiently and turned on his heel to march back towards the box. 'We were giving up on you. Hurry up – we're practically the last here.'

'Who's driving?' Tash asked, trailing behind him. With Franny not with them, someone else would have to take the wheel of the huge box.

'I am,' he muttered.

Tash started to lag back, fear squirming in the pit of her stomach. 'Let me,' she urged. 'You've been through one hell of a shock.'

'I'm fucking driving – now get in and shut up. Ted and Stefan are staying in the back. You can come in the front with me.'

The journey home started badly as Hugo punched out the glass of the indicator light by brushing the post of a gate on the Lowerton rear drive. Again Tash offered to drive and again she was told to go to hell.

The last grey streaks of light faded out of the sky as they charged along the M4. Tash could hear Ted and Stefan talking in low voices in the rear. Normally they played raucous games of poker – often with Hugo – as Franny drove the long-haul home. But today was different as gloom prevailed. Tash had been careful to hide her rosette in the bottom of her trunk. With her knees tucked up to her chin, she chewed her way through nine-tenths of her nails and only had one little finger to last her the rest of the journey.

Although Hugo tried his damnedest to kill them all on the last stretch, the high-tech coach-built box lived up to its design standards superbly, power-steering and braking them to safety every time he lost concentration. Even so, Tash felt as though she had lived eight of her nine lives in several incarnations by the time they reached Fosbourne. As a result, she and Hugo were no longer speaking at all and Tom Waits had been around on auto-reverse several times.

'Be quick, I want to push off home,' Hugo muttered as he pulled up outside Lime Tree Farm, not even bothering to turn into the yard.

They had to unload hurriedly in the lane, further pressured by a weekender's very clean Rhino jeep thundering up and, finding it couldn't get around the box, hooting its horn angrily. Snob became increasingly maddened and unruly as a result. When they were finally out and the ramp was up, Ted thrust two fingers up at the angry jeep driver and stalked into the yard.

Tash made her way to the cab with Stefan to say farewell, but Hugo didn't even look at her, his white knuckles clasping the steering wheel as though it was the safety bar of a fair-ground fright-ride.

Giving her a hug, Stefan breathed in her ear, 'Thanks for your help today, darling – you were great. I'll take care of him, I promise. Is Franny staying here tonight?'

'I think so.'

'Get her to call me on my mobile at seven, will you?' He winked.

Nodding, Tash watched him climb up on his long, long legs, blond hair gleaming in the cab light before it was extinguished as he slammed the door. With Tom Waits still booming, Hugo drove off so fast that he took most of the hazel hedge with him.

Having settled Snob and checked him over thoroughly for bumps and cuts, Tash left Ted mixing up his feeds and wandered into the kitchen, longing for warmth and sympathy.

India was doing her homework at the table, chewing a pen thoughtfully, her blonde hair curled up on to her head and secured with a sock.

'Good day?' She looked up, pretty face scrunched in inquiry.

Tash shook her head. 'Kirsty hasn't said anything, then?'

'Haven't seen her.' India shrugged. 'She dumped poor Betty and charged upstairs for a bath before heading off to London with thick Richie. They're seeing some play with Maggie Smith in it. Richie was seriously pissed off because he'd got her muddled up with Maggie Thatcher and was desperate to try and meet her backstage.'

'I see.' Tash wasn't taking much of this in.

'Penny and Gus aren't back yet.' She stood up and put the kettle on. 'Mum and Niall are in the sitting room. Tea or coffee?'

Not answering, Tash wandered into the sitting room, eager for a hug.

Niall and Zoe were sitting on the sofa, feet tucked beneath them, elbows on arm rests as they watched an old film over the rims of their tea mugs. They looked like a pair of matching book-ends. Even though they were sitting a respectable two feet apart, there was an air of intimacy between them that made her stop in her tracks.

Neither looked up until Beetroot raced across the room and welcomed Tash with an excited series of yelps, her long, frayed-rope tail quivering with joy.

'Tash – we didn't hear the lorry.' Zoe put down her mug and stretched back over the sofa arm with a smile. 'Win anything?'

'Hugo dropped us in the lane.' Tash noticed that they were watching an old black and white film of the soppy, sentimental sort that Niall normally loathed. From the flickering rectangle, Bette Davis was dabbing a diamond-like tear from her cheek with a crisp white triangle of hanky, her gloved hand quivering along with her lips.

'What is it, Tash?' Zoe was watching her with concern.

'Surfer had to be destroyed.' She watched as Bette lit a cigarette, lips still quivering. 'He fell – I'm not sure quite what happened. Broke his back.'

'Christ!' Niall covered his mouth. 'I'm so sorry, Tash angel. Oh, my poor love. Which one was he?' he asked. 'That big bay fella? Were you hurt at all?'

She shook her head. 'Surfer was Hugo's horse, Niall.'

'Oh, I see.' Niall seemed to perk up at this, imagining it made things better. 'Poor old Hugo.'

'But you did okay?' Zoe asked, reaching for her zapper and muting Bette who was throwing a bit of a distracting blue funk on screen, lips still quivering.

Tash suddenly found she didn't want to talk about the day with either of them. Although they would offer all the support and sympathy she could ask for, they simply would not understand what it was like. They loved horses, but they weren't their life and that made them impossibly distanced from people like herself, Hugo and Stefan. Worse still, they were both regarding her with soft-eyed kindness, like a pair of parents preparing to listen to a teenage daughter ranting on about being dumped by a boyfriend. The stance made her feel impossibly uncomfortable.

'Forget it – I'm going to have a bath.' She stood up again, dropping Beetroot to the floor.

'There are plenty of clean towels in the laundry cupboard,' Zoe called after her. But, slamming the front door, Tash decided to head to the forge with Beetroot.

Having fed Giblets and taken a long soak in the chipped bath, she curled up on the sofa with a trashy novel and ate her way through a packet of Just Brazils that a fan had sent Niall. After he claimed on Desert Island Discs that they would be his luxury, he was currently receiving about six boxes a week. Her feet warming on Beetroot's tummy, she lobbed the odd one at the dog's eager mouth. Beetroot had put on a growth spurt recently and was starting to look alarmingly like her father – the deceased, shaggy Lothario, Rooter. Tash no longer wondered why Niall was afraid of her; she was already bigger than Wally and, although most of her was gangly legs, she had a lean, mean lurcher look that was pretty terrifying when she growled.

'You have to learn to love him,' Tash told her, adoring the way her envelope-flap ears sprang forward, head cocked, eyes adoring – although Tash suspected she was more interested in the Just Brazil than the line of conversation. 'Promise you'll try to like Niall, huh? Just for me.'

Beetroot chomped up the chocolate with great white teeth and looked at her benignly.

He came in half an hour later, just as Tash was breaking into a second packet.

'I stayed to the end of the film,' he explained rather sheepishly.

'Fine.' She stuffed another chocolate in her mouth.

'Was it pretty hellish today then?' He slumped down beside her and took a Just Brazil, ignoring Beetroot who was growling ominously from beneath a cushion.

'Very hellish,' Tash passed the box to him. 'Do you want something to eat?'

He shook his head. 'Zoe made me a big plate of some odd lentil stew stuff. Amazingly tasty. Everyone jokes about her cooking, but she's bloody good, if weird. She says she finds ordinary ingredients limiting.'

She watched as he headed into the kitchen to fetch the inevitable bottle of Bushmills, stooping to avoid the low overhead beams that he would no doubt crack his head on fairly soon after he had cracked open the bottle. She could always tell how drunk he was by how loud the smack was on impact.

'Want one?' He waggled the bottle at her, searching for a clean glass amongst their mountain of washing up.

'No, thanks.' She rubbed her chin awkwardly. 'Do you have to tonight?'

'Have to what?'

'Drink.' She smiled apologetically. 'I thought we could have a chat – we haven't talked properly in ages.'

'Sure.' He was already pouring himself out three inches. 'We can talk while I have a wee night-cap, angel. What d'you want to talk about?'

'Oh,' she kept her tone light and vague as she fiddled with a cushion tassel, 'the wedding and stuff.'

There was a bitter edge to his laugh. 'In that case, I definitely need a drink.' All three inches slid down his throat and, banging the glass down, he immediately poured himself another, dark hair flopping over his face.

'I can't talk to you if you get drunk, Niall,' Tash said softly.

He looked at her, a smile playing on his lips as he held the glass to them, eyes merry.

'That's your problem, angel, not mine,' he said softly, taking a long sip, his gaze raking over her indulgently. 'You look so sexy tonight – all clean and scrubbed and fresh. Will you tell the dog to get in its basket so I can sit down and touch your skin?'

Tash closed her eyes for a brief second. It was hopeless talking to him when he was like this – it was Niall in deNiall; he was impenetrable in his cheerful, insouciant assertion that nothing was wrong. She had tried it before, but he would be a wonderfully attentive listener who heard nothing. His eyes would blaze into hers throughout, he would touch her and kiss her and tell her he loved her, which was just what she wanted to hear. Almost inevitably they would end up in bed – Niall's answer to all rows. But they never had rows, Tash realised. That was the problem. Who could have a row with someone when they agreed with everything you said and tried to take your clothes off while you were saying it?

'Have the whole bottle.' She stomped off with Beetroot, too tired to face the battle which he always won by not fighting at all.

When Niall tried to climb in with her later, Beetroot growled so much that he elected to sleep on the sofa. Although Tash slept on throughout, Beetroot cocked her head with interest as she heard him trip clumsily down the stairs and stagger into the sitting room. A moment later there was a loud thwack as he hit his head on the low beam in the kitchen.

Sitting in the dark in his own vast kitchen, Hugo could hear the electric clock on the oven creaking through the seconds, could see the shadows of the looming, old-fashioned furniture lit by the various pilot and power lights that gleamed from every electrical appliance.

In his hand was the brown and blue rosette Tash had won on Snob earlier that day – one of the grooms had found it at the bottom of a tack trunk and handed it over to him, assuming it was his. The memory of how lousily he had treated her was twisting in his stomach like cramp. He'd been so wrapped up in his own failure, jealousy and confusion that he'd blown everything.

For a moment he considered driving down to the farm to apologise, but he knew that Niall was around at the moment. In other circumstances he might have gone ahead for the hell of it, but he had ridden his best horse to its grave today and his confidence and pride were shattered. He was deeply ashamed of himself and shaking with nerves and self-doubt. And the hundred-weight straw bale that was breaking the camel's back was the fact that he was now absolutely certain Tash no longer wanted him. She was going to marry a man who, worse than anything, Hugo genuinely liked, a man who was kinder and brighter and far more likeable than he himself was. That hurt more than hell itself.

Grabbing the phone, he searched around for his wallet and pulled out a business card, flipping it over to read out the home number written on the back.

'Lisette? Hugo – yes, fine, thanks. The place is all yours as long as you can guarantee that the running of the yard won't be interrupted. That's great. Yes – next week, then. Call me.'

Tash woke after midnight and, finding herself alone with Beetroot, had a brief moment of panic before she heard the muted sound of the television floating up through the door to the stairs. Niall was clearly still up and, from the sound of it, watching Beavis and Butthead. She could hear his low, melodious laugh breaking in every now and again over the television's gruff American chatter and strident music.

Staring at the phone by the bed, she wondered whether she should call Stefan and check that Hugo was okay. But she didn't dare call straight through to the house in case Hugo picked up the call and took it to mean she was panting away fantasising about him, and besides her diary with the number for Stefan's mobile written in it was at the farm.

Nestling deeper into her pillow, she hoped to God he was all right. When she closed her eyes, she could see him back in the cramped horsebox, his beautiful face desolate. Part of her still loathed him for the shabby way he'd treated her, his appalling contempt and the childish pleasure he seemed to derive from reminding her of that awful, fierce crush she had wasted on him for so many years. But she knew that, unlike Niall, attack was Hugo's first, second and third line of defence – he was savagely private and proud. Today he had, for the briefest of moments, broken down and shown a weak side she'd never known existed. And he'd done so to her of all people – shy, useless Tash whom he thought hopelessly wimpy. But instead of digging deeper and trying to extract the pearl, she had let him clam shut again. She was gnawed through with guilt and, though she hated admitting it to herself, raging, heart-pounding disappointment.

Twenty-One

THE NEXT MORNING, NIALL left for Yorkshire to start the location shoot for The Tenant of Wildfell Hall.

Determined not to pine, Tash threw herself into work.

At last given the all-clear to bring Hunk back to top-level competition fitness, she launched into an intensive training programme, relishing his eager obedience compared to the struggles she'd been having with Snob of late. A gentle giant bay with a Roman nose and knowing eyes that reminded Tash of Leonard Rossiter, he was the comedian of the yard, known for his face-pulling stunts and incurable greed for Polos – no other mint had the same effect on him. Biddable, armchair-easy and a great listener, he was a joy to ride.

Over the next week, as Hunk got better, Snob went rapidly downhill. Penny and Gus had decided that it would be fun to train him to pull a carriage for Tash's wedding. After one session in the menage with Ted long-reining him from behind while Snob dragged a tyre around to accustom him to tugging, he tugged so hard Ted and the tyre travelled several hundred yards at full gallop. The incident left the horse jittery and mistrustful. The next day a loose plastic bag sent him into such a panic out hacking that he chucked Franny and returned to the yard alone, leaving her to limp the three miles back with a twisted ankle. Thankfully, she hitched a lift with Stefan who was popping down to see her.

'I'm never riding him again,' she announced huffily afterwards.

No one complained. After all, having quit Hugo, she was currently working for just food and keep so she could dictate a few rules. The only person who couldn't stand the loud-mouthed, sexy new arrival was Kirsty, who conducted heated and very public rows with her almost every morning as Franny continually pointed out how slap-dash and sloppy her work was.

'I'm a senior rider here,' Kirsty yelled. 'No' a groom. I shouldna even have to muck out.'

'No, you should bloody well muck in like everyone else,' Franny hissed.

With thick Richie still in tow, Kirsty huffily decamped to visit her parents in Scotland, telling her gullible fiancé that Franny was the unrecognised love-child of Pavarotti and Janet Street Porter. She had already nick-named Franny the Stable Rubber because of her second-skin PVC and rubber wardrobe.

'And she's the sporran of Satan,' Franny hissed. 'That big Australian beefcake she's engaged to must have Scotch mist before his eyes not to see through her. She'll be back in Hugo's bed before he's through customs next week. She's known as Lassie at Haydown because she's always whimpering at Hugo's bedroom door.'

With Sally out of the Richmond house so much these days, Matty suddenly started realising that, far from being a fifty percent chore-sharer since becoming a parent, he had, for years, been a five percent stake-holder and sleeping partner. He found it impossible to work during the day when Sally was out and the two youngest children were in the house, needing to be fed, cleaned and entertained. Missing his mother, Linus cried almost incessantly. Tor was old enough to be posted in front of the Disney Channel (of which Matty had once thoroughly disapproved) which provided at least a brief period of quiet while Linus had his afternoon nap, but she was notoriously troublesome and, left alone for more than a few minutes, would grow bored and seek distraction. She had already pulled apart the television remote, torn up several of Matty's research books and pulled out the reels of half a dozen videos, two of which were Matty's only copies of Forty Minutes documentaries that he had directed in the eighties when he was just starting out. He was livid.

Things came to a head when, distracted by a duster salesman at the front door, he returned to his study to find that Tor was colouring each of the keys of his laptop with indelible marker pens, and that she had covered his screen with breakfast cereal stickers of the latest cartoon craze, Mega-Galactic Space Squirrels.

'Pressy for Mashy!' she announced happily, her face covered with coloured stripes like an African bride. 'Make Mashy happy again!'

Mashy was far from happy. He was going demented. The house was a tip, washing-up crowded every surface of the kitchen and the dirty laundry pile was now so high it doubled as a bouncy castle for the kids. They had been eating microwave food out of the freezer for weeks because no one had done a supermarket shop and, most distressingly, Tor's beloved guinea pig had died two days ago because, Matty suspected, no one had remembered to feed it. He had buried the little body in the weed-choked garden which no one had mown that year. The image of the neglected little animal starving to death tortured him.

Tor's decorative attempts to please him had wiped the letter he'd been writing to a Channel 4 producer, following up a possible commission which had been discussed before Christmas and then left unchased. He knew that he was not working as hard as he should to get a new project off the ground, but looking after the children exhausted him, and he missed having Sally around during the day to pop her head past the door and ask him how it was going, or bring him cups of tea and let him bounce ideas off her. She stabilised him and, although he was loth to admit it, she did a lot more donkey work than he had ever given her credit for. Without her the post was neglected until after lunch, bills turned red before they were paid, the phone went unanswered and his filing system went to pot.

'I can't cope with the kids and work at the same time,' he told her that night.

'You were the one who's always said you wouldn't condone a stranger looking after our children,' she reminded him as she searched through the diminished contents of the freezer for something to defrost.

'Their mother's becoming a stranger to them these days,' he snarled.

Sally let this pass, not wanting a blazing row. She was too tired to face one tonight, too satisfied with her day's work to taint it by scrapping.

'We can't afford a nanny,' she reminded him gently. 'Lisette isn't paying me enough to cover one yet, and you haven't earned anything decent for months. We're currently living off an overdraft again, as you well know.'

'How can I work on anything when it's a full-time job looking after the kids?'

Leaning away from the freezer, Sally looked at him for a long time, letting him realise the implications of what he had just said. She was looking pale and uptight, but there was no denying she had really pulled herself together lately. Trips to Lisette's apartment block gym had started to tone her body, firming the softness where motherhood had fleshed her out. Her hair, with its new feathery cut, framed her made-up face nowadays rather than blinkering it, and her slick little power suits gave her an authority and glamour that unsettled Matty. He found it both unexpectedly attractive and unnervingly emasculating.

'I'm doing this for me, Matty,' she said gently. 'It's only until summer. I have to get out and do something for myself for once.'

'Like shopping. You must have forked out a bit on clothes lately,' he pointed out peevishly.

Sally let out an exasperated breath and turned away to switch on the oven, not bothering to descend to his level of snide remarks.

'So how *was* your day at the office?' he asked with blistering sarcasm. 'Or did you go to another shoe shop today?'

Sally ignored him.

'Lisette's only using you,' he ploughed on, desperate for a reaction. 'To get closer to Niall.'

'Hardly!' Sally laughed sarcastically, banging the oven door shut. 'She's hired him for her latest film. You can't get much closer than that. They'll be working together soon. I had nothing to do with him accepting the role.'

'I can't imagine she was too happy to hear he's marrying Tash,' Matty sniped.

'You couldn't be more wrong,' Sally sighed, starting to wash up two plates. 'Lisette's even giving them the wedding photographs of a lifetime – a seven-page spread in *Cheers!* magazine. It's great publicity for the film.'

'The photo tabloid for the culturally illiterate,' Matty scoffed. 'I can't imagine anything more ghastly, although I suppose it's about Lisette's level; she's always been so brazenly commercial that one keeps expecting her conversations to end in a pack shot. I'm amazed Niall agreed to it.'

'He needs the money.' Sally shrugged.

'Because Lisette herself takes practically every penny he earns!' Matty laughed bitterly. 'Her fat cat Los Angeles lawyers saw to that.'

'Well, now she's in a position to repay him, she's doing all she can.' Sally squeezed Fairy Liquid straight on to the plate, knowing that Matty would disapprove of such wasteful abuse of detergents. 'And she is happy that he's marrying again, whatever you say. She thinks Tash is perfect for him. She's even juggled the shooting schedule to give him a fortnight off for the honeymoon.'

'I'm surprised she hasn't organised a fly-on-the-wall documentary team to follow them on that as yet more publicity,' he sneered. 'In fact, she should have asked me – I could use the work.'

'She probably doesn't realise you're still making documentaries.' Sally rinsed the plate under the cold tap. 'It's been so long since your last one.'

'My wife's taking a sabbatical from her children,' he muttered. 'I'm too busy wiping baby food, crayon and Squirrel stickers from the wall to be a fly on it.'

'Makes a change from banging your head against it, I suppose,' she muttered through tight lips, turning the taps on harder. 'At least Lisette takes my ideas seriously, which is more than you've ever done.'

Matty watched her dabbing water splashes from her chic suit. 'Don't tell me you suggested a different restaurant for lunch today? Or did you change her mind about the purchase of some new designer outfit?'

'I came up with a publicity proposal, if you must know,' Sally said through gritted teeth. 'And she's letting me run with it.'

'Oh, yes?' He looked unflatteringly pompous. He still wouldn't believe that she was doing anything more on the film than making coffee.

'Yes.' She refused to let him belittle her. 'I suggested that the film company should buy an event horse as a wedding present.'

'You did what!' Matty howled with laughter.

'You heard me,' she hissed. 'It could be renamed *Four Poster Bed*. Tash would compete on it at Badminton this year – that's just a week before they get married and bang in the middle of the film's first location shoot. All the press will catch on to the idea, Niall O'Shaughnessy's bride riding her wedding present, which is named after his latest film. Then, if we're lucky, it could go on to compete at Burghley – that's the other big televised three-day-event, I gather – in September when the film's released.' She pulled off her rubber gloves and turned towards him, face triumphant.

Matty was still laughing disbelievingly. 'And where do you find this wonder horse? They take a hell of a long time to train if Tash is to be believed. And they cost millions. You can't just buy a ready-made one on the cheap and start at the top.'

'Oh, but you can.' Sally looked rather pleased with herself. 'We've been working on that all this week – Lisette has been grilling Hugo and apparently the answer's on the Lime Tree Farm doorstep. Lisette already owns a half-share in an event horse. She almost died when she found out.'

'She what?' Matty looked astonished.

'She half owns Tash's top horse – Snob is it called? Apparently Niall bought him from Tash just a month before Lisette and he divorced – something to do with importing him to this country. The horse was even listed among his assets in court, but Lisette has never cared that she was entitled to fifty percent – she simply wasn't interested. And you know how little Niall had to do with the settlement – he just let her take what she wanted for the sake of an easy life. He probably didn't even notice the horse was part of it. She had a meeting with her solicitor today to see where she stands. All she has to do is lease the other half-share on the film company's behalf and they're away. She says she'll buy me a magnum of champagne if the deal comes off.'

'Oh, c'mon, Sally.' Matty shook his head. 'She's humouring you. You don't think she'll really invest money in the idea? The fiscal effect of sports sponsorship is notoriously difficult to assess, even on huge international football matches watched by millions. And eventing is a minority sport for thick aristos and horse-mad teenage girls. There's no publicity mileage in it at all.'

'Well, Lisette doesn't agree,' Sally said hotly. 'She thinks the film company will benefit from the investment.'

'Oh, it'll benefit all right,' he sighed. 'But not in the way you think. Lisette's absolutely brilliant at marketing films on a shoe-string – it's her trademark. That's why she wouldn't touch your idea – it has no spin. She knows that the way to make a mediocre low-budget comedy into a surprise box-office hit is to involve the press every step of the way. This *Cheers!* tie-in is typical of her, and it'll almost certainly help her first feature film to turn over a fat enough profit to guarantee her a future in the industry. And she's desperate for that. But making films eats money, like Tash's valuable event horse eats hay. She's shoe-stringing you along, Sally.'

'What do you mean?'

'What's she going to do after the film's out?' Matty pointed out nastily. 'She'll sell her share to the highest bidder and Tash will lose her horse. Great idea, Sals.'

'Rubbish! She'll sign her share over to Tash for free as soon as the lease runs its course.' Sally lifted her chin angrily. 'Like I say – it's a wedding present.'

Matty started to laugh. 'You don't really believe that?'

She nodded. 'And the idea *has* got spin, Matty. It's wonderful merchandising – what better Four Poster Bed asset than a four-legged animal?'

'The only thing with four legs that Lisette has time for is two men,' Matty hissed. 'And one of them's Niall. I'm just wondering who the other one is . . .'

When thick, amiable Richie finally flew back to Australia, Kirsty – who had hardly been seen for a fortnight – raced up to Haydown at the earliest opportunity, only to arrive back twenty minutes later and slam her way to her room in tears. The next day, she set off to Scotland for an unannounced visit to her parents, who were rather surprised as they had only seen her three days earlier with her fiancé.

'Hugo told her to Fuck Oz,' Stefan told Tash afterwards. 'He seems to have gone right off her, poor cow. She ripped up all his pictures of Surfer before she left, which was a bit bloody bitchy, but she was really upset. She even offered to dump Richie for him and he laughed in her face.'

Tash winced, easily picturing Hugo's reaction. His blistering rejection would have come as news to Kirsty who, despite behaving with galling lack of tact by parading her big, thick lover around in the past week, had clearly assumed that their relationship would take off again the moment he left.

'I reckon she only allowed Richie to come over here to make Hugo jealous,' Stefan told her the next day when he drove down to help her with Hunk's rather lacklustre dressage. 'Apparently that relationship is far from healthy and Richie is getting cold feet. He flew over here to issue ultimatums, but she kept that quiet to wind Hugo up.'

'Richie has cold feet?' Tash was surprised. 'Not Kirsty?'

'She wants to get married and have babies,' Stefan reminded her, admiring her bottom as she leaned down to tuck in a stirrup leather. 'But Richie is no longer so keen, particularly as she wants him to move over here after they're married. Hugo says she bosses him round like a kid.'

'Do you think Hunk over-bends?' Tash set Hunk off into his rather lumbering trot.

'No – he looks great.' Stefan was still staring at her bottom. 'The ironic thing is,' he started shouting out the gossip to her as she rode around the menage, 'that while Kirsty was hawking poor Richie around in the hope that it might push Hugo into some sort of proposal himself, Hugo was over the moon to have an excuse to dump her – he's been trying to get around to it for months. Told me last night.'

'Why didn't he? He's not the type to spare anyone's feelings.' Tash rode past at a walk, trying to encourage Stefan to talk a bit more quietly.

'He says she's amazing in bed.' He winked slyly as she drew level. 'His relationships are frighteningly shallow – not like you and Niall. I think he envies you.'

Riding away, Tash laughed at this, but Stefan kept going, again talking so loudly that Franny, Ted and Gus, who were all out in the yard, were bound to hear every word.

'Don't take any notice of Hugo's flippant façade, my dear.' He lolled against the rails. 'That man is going for the full hearts and flowers deal, believe me. He's looking for true love. He's always so sarcastic about you and Niall that he can only be wildly envious of what you two have together.'

'Or just bloody perceptive,' Tash muttered under her breath, urging Hunk into a trot again.

'I wonder just how amazing in bed Kirsty is?' Stefan sighed thoughtfully, not hearing her.

Even though she was wrapped up in work, Tash couldn't fail to notice that Niall had only rung once from Yorkshire, just to tell her he'd arrived safely. Since then it had been the same story as ever – she'd left endless messages at his hotel reception, with assistant directors, on his mobile answering service. But the pattern had changed slightly – this time the return messages and faxes from him were not in evidence.

'He's probably frantically busy,' Zoe reassured her.

Tash tried desperately hard to believe it.

On the weekend after Lowerton she travelled to Dorset with Gus and Penny to compete at some novice trials which included an open competition, thus allowing Hunk his first outing of the year. Revelling in the soft turf and low fences, he pounded around clear and was only beaten by a young lawyer called Roger Monk, whose brown mare had been walking away with all the smaller competitions that year.

'See you at Badminton!' he called after Tash as they pounded out of the ring after the prize-giving.

'What did he mean?' she asked Penny when they were back at the box. 'Surely that mare of his isn't experienced enough?'

Penny shrugged awkwardly, her berry eyes dull. 'Gus has sold him Sex Symbol.'

'No!' Tash wailed. 'But he won you your gold medal.'

'Gold medals don't buy hard feed, Tash.'

'Gus has had him for ten years. He's fifteen. You can't sell him now.'

'Roger paid through the nose,' she explained sadly. 'He's dying for a crack at Badminton, and he himself is qualified and entered – but his senior horse went lame. He knows Symby is on his last furlong. Says he'll give him a good retirement, which we can barely afford. His parents have a huge farm in Suffolk, so Symby will have a great old age.'

Tash travelled back to the farm in sombre mood. She wanted to commiserate with Gus who had now lost his ride at the event he had always coveted, on a horse who was amongst the favourites to win. But he seemed chipper and chatty, hiding his disappointment with pleasure at the money he had gained through the sale, money that would help them limp along for a few more months.

'I've still got Fashion Victim to take there,' he consoled himself. 'Although I suspect the lazy devil's odds would be longer than his teeth. And I'm talking to some more potential sponsors this week – one looks promising. They want to ride me off against Brian Sedgewick to see who gets the deal.'

'Isn't that a bit mercenary?' asked Tash.

'It's business, darling.' He gave a withering look. 'We're all mercenary. Why do you think I took you on in the first place?'

'What do you mean?' She was baffled.

'Shut up, Gus,' Penny hissed from behind the wheel where she was trying to get past a clutch of spring cyclists out on a wobbly jolly.

Tash was gazing at Gus enquiringly, desperate to know what he meant, but he raised a sardonic blond eyebrow and said no more. Later, she asked him where this 'ride off' for the sponsorship deal would take place if it went ahead.

'Ah, you'll like this bit,' Gus laughed dryly. 'Badminton. Ironic, huh?'

He'd just sold the one horse he possessed that stood any chance of winning. However much she wanted to rant and rage on his behalf, Tash knew that he'd had no choice. The farm's scarlet bank balance couldn't hold out for three more months to keep Sex Symbol in the yard until June. By then the debts would have become so crippling that they'd be spending Badminton weekend in the bankruptcy courts.

Twenty-Two

IN LATE APRIL, NIALL came back from Yorkshire and stayed at the forge while he commuted to London for studio work on Wildfell Hall. This involved hellishly early starts but, as Tash herself was unwillingly up at the crack of dawn each day, she felt this was one of the few things they had in common.

As usual when engrossed in a part, he took a lot of adjusting to. At first Tash was wary and more than a little frosty, brooding on his recent neglect. But he was too excitable and attentive to sulk at for long. Spending almost twenty-four hours a day in character, he was a lovable bounder. This struck Tash as odd since the character that he was playing, Arthur Huntingdon, was a singularly unpleasant individual – a hell-raising, Byronic rake who treated his wife appallingly. He'd been spoilt rotten throughout his life, but deprived of emotional support to such a degree that he had matured without humanity. His world was peopled by free-loading lechers, card sharks and other hell-raisers who indulged him in his insatiable lifestyle. Despite being graced with tremendous charm, wit and good looks, his immoral greed for kicks prevented him from denying himself a single indulgence.

Reading the novel in the lorry as the Lime Tree contingent drove to events, Tash was appalled by the character's nastiness, and even more alarmed when Niall announced that he had based the character almost entirely on Hugo.

'Rubbish!' she railed. 'Hugo can be bloody mean-spirited and self-indulgent, but he's got some compassion.'

'Admittedly he treats his dogs better than Huntingdon, but I 'clare, they have everything else in common.'

'Well, Huntingdon would have been okay if he hadn't had such depraved friends and such a pious, unloving wife,' Tash bristled. 'He adores her in the book, but she shrugs him off every time he wants to grope her.'

'Which is more than can be said for you,' growled Niall, pulling her into a clinch.

The one thing that had to be said for this Niall-as-Huntingdon character, Tash realised, was that he was irresistibly sexy, despite the rather off-putting sideburns that the director had insisted he grow. She loved the way he couldn't keep his hands off her and made it so obvious what a turn-on he found her. Their sex life owed everything to Anne Brontë right now.

'I'd have quite gone for Huntingdon,' Tash admitted. 'Gambling, womanising and all – he just needed the love of a good, racy woman up to his rakish Regency ways.'

'At least he has a sense of fun.' Niall started to undress her with his teeth amidst much shrieking. 'I think I'm beginning to rather like the old sod.'

So much so, Tash noticed, that he was living life in his guise. Gradually, Niall became more and more demanding and dictatorial, less sympathetic. Increasingly, he was making no secret of the fact that he resented her time away competing. He helped less in the forge, drank even more than ever, and his sex drive shot through the roof. Not only was he dragging her off to bed earlier each night, but he was flirting more unashamedly than ever. No one was safe as he used his towering charms on everyone from Penny, Denise in the Olive Branch, his co-star Imogen Glenn, Godfrey in the local shop, Zoe, and even Kirsty, who was back from Scotland and throwing herself into her work to compensate for not throwing herself on to Hugo. Worse still, the dreaded Minty was playing the demonstrative, adulterous friend, Annabella Wilmot, with whom Huntingdon has a wild affair. Tash became accustomed to dropped calls and enigmatic faxes which she was certain were from the infatuated actress. Only Niall's derisory indifference to them saved her from the jealous demons. He was living the part to the hilt.

'What's got into him lately?' Zoe laughed one night when they had all been drinking in the Olive Branch. 'He seems to have had a new lease of life.'

'Character acting,' sighed Tash.

'Well, I'm not sure I'd give him a character reference. He's jolly headstrong at the moment.'

'D'you think so?' Tash looked to the bar where he was flirting with one of Denise's daughters. 'I rather like it. He's more fun.'

He was difficult, argumentative and selfish, but Tash found him far less withdrawn than he had been all year. Together, they started to laugh again, play silly games, dare to be sarcastic or confrontational, and she had to admit the sex was great. Even Beetroot called an uneasy truce, cowed by his new found domination. In a moment of excitable master-and-faithful-hound role-play Niall even spent a day off from filming teaching her to sit, stay, beg and shake hands.

He was so delighted with his conquests that he insisted on showing Tash as soon as she walked through the door, returning whacked from a competition the other side of Windsor. She didn't have the heart to tell him that Beetroot knew every one of the tricks he had 'taught' her already.

'I walked up to show Zoe earlier,' he told her. 'And she kept laughing at me. Can't think why. I said I'd give Rufus a couple of driving lessons if I get the time.'

'In what?' Tash giggled. 'The design classic?'

'Of course. It's the greatest car ever created, so it is.'

'Its gear-stick is above the steering wheel,' she pointed out. 'And it has no clutch.'

'So? If he can drive that, he can drive anything.'

Tash hugged him for being so hopelessly gorgeous.

Glowing with radiance, she found herself winning everything in sight. Hunk, who was growing stronger every day, couldn't put an oiled hoof wrong and was looking increasingly likely to go to Badminton after all, for which he was still entered. Even Snob was starting to come into hand again, seemingly bowled along by her ebullient mood, although he was always ratty and difficult after a 'driving lesson' with Penny.

'Do you have to teach him?' Tash asked. 'I'm quite happy with a hired Bentley and a few ribbons.'

'Nonsense,' she pooh-poohed. 'He's doing brilliantly. He's quite used to shafts now.'

Tash, who had picked up a new line in double-entendres from Niall, stifled a giggle.

'Gus long-reined him in full harness twice this week without a single wobbly,' Penny went on regardless. 'And I have to push on somewhat as we've only a couple of months to go.'

That scared Tash. Even more so when Henrietta drove to Fosbourne

Ducis the following weekend with a stack of invitations, stamped envelopes and various proposed guest lists which she and Alexandra had concocted during their innumerable wedding-plan phone conversations. Although the original plan had been to hold the reception in the grounds of Fosbourne Holt House, where the wedding ceremony was being conducted, Gus was now rather magnanimously suggesting that it be held in the untended gardens at the farm.

'Too mean to get a taxi home,' Penny had moaned, dreading the litter on the lawn.

'Rubbish!' Gus had railed. 'I'm too mean to buy them a decent present – this is it.'

Henrietta would rather have gone for the glamour of the stately home and its grand lawns, but at least this way saved James and Pascal a few hundred pounds and she expected the numbers would have to be kept quite low too.

'Now there are bound to be bags of people you want to add from the eventing and acting worlds, plus friends and locals and what-not.' She smiled at Tash and Niall when she finally cornered them together in the forge. She noticed fondly that they had that new-love inability to keep their hands off one another.

'Sure,' Tash giggled, not really listening because, unseen by Henrietta, Niall had his fingers between her legs underneath the stone-topped table and was doing quite miraculous things with them.

'But your mother and I have tried to work out most of the family for you to save time.' Henrietta cleared her throat and went on, 'We really have left this terribly late, you know. Now, I was a bit woolly on your family, Niall, so you'll need to help me out on the cousins etcetera. Plus telling me who you want to come along to the ceremony, or just reception.'

'Fine.' Niall went on to reel off a list of names so long that it sounded as though he was role-calling the entire cast of Ben Hur. All the time his fingers played delightfully with Tash. He even had the nerve at one point to fumble for a cigarette with his left hand and then ask her to light it for him.

Given the job of looking up the addresses in Niall's falling-apart Filofax, Tash kept writing them down entirely wrong on the envelopes. At one point she realised that she'd written '*Oh Christ yes*' instead of a London post code.

'We'll have to pare these down.' Henrietta gaped at the list nervously afterwards.

'Oh, sure – most of my family won't be able to come over

anyhow.' Niall shrugged. 'Now, I'd better give you the names of my friends too.'

Henrietta almost fainted, her pen seeming to smoke as she scribbled them down. Getting bored of writing envelopes, Tash lolled against Niall, indulging him in a long, slow finger massage to the back of the neck while she grinned rather inanely at Henrietta.

Her own list, although long by her standards, was pathetically scant compared with Niall's.

'Well, I think we need to lose at least two-thirds, don't you?' gulped Henrietta, looking down at her three-page list and imagining James's reaction if she went home with the news that he was footing half the bill for a reception for four hundred actors, Irish Catholics, starving artists, rowdy eventers, and Tash's old school friends as well as his first wife's awful family.

Deciding who should attend the civil ceremony was easy, as the long hall at Fosbourne Holt House would only fit in one hundred.

The big marquee reception in the Moncrieffs' garden, however, was a nightmare to write a list for.

Tash ended up having a blazing row with Niall about it.

She was even more alarmed when he started mulling over who was to be his best man, tossing around the names of several wild men of films, including the self-proclaimed bastion of all 'lads', the comic Rory Franks, who had only recently been all over the papers for getting a fifteen-year-old girl pregnant. He was a well-publicised alcoholic and coke addict with whom Niall had once had a tumultuous friendship before backing off, announcing him too dangerous.

'But I thought Matty was going to be your best man?' Tash tackled him after Henrietta left.

They were heating up an M and S ready-meal in the little kitchen and had been arguing so animatedly that both had failed to notice that the microwave wasn't plugged in.

He looked at her thoughtfully. 'I've asked him, yes. But he wasn't very keen.'

'What do you mean, not keen?' Tash laughed, turning her back on him to get the meal out of the microwave. 'He's my brother.'

Niall cleared his throat uncomfortably, suddenly putting his arms around her and resting his chin on her shoulder so that she seemed to have four hands grappling at the rock-hard meal.

'Not keen means he refused point blank.' Niall nuzzled her neck, eager for the row to be curtailed. 'He says he won't be seen to condone a marriage which he doesn't believe will work.'

'He what?' Tash put the plastic tray of food on to a work surface and, with Niall still draped over her shoulders like a shawl, started to try to hack the still-frozen contents apart, too abstracted to notice.

'It's what he said.' Niall's lips were eating up her neck now. 'I'm going to stay up there a couple of days next week. I'll try to bring him round, huh?'

Tash chiselled a piece of frozen courgette out of the tray with a knife.

'In order to do that,' she said hollowly, 'you'll have to knock him out first.'

'I'm not hungry.' Niall slid his hands over hers and pulled them away from her frosty forage. 'Let's go to bed. I'm determined that today, at least, you are going to ride me more often than your damned horses.'

As the pressure of the early starts got to him, he spent several nights a week staying with Matty and Sally in Richmond, which meant the driver could collect him an hour later each day. Whenever he returned home to the forge afterwards, Tash found him distanced and tetchy. It took several hours before he was back to normal. She blamed it on the pressure of work, and having to adjust from the pampering on set to the do-it-yourself relaxation of the village. It never occurred to her that the reason he seemed detached was as a result of talking to her own brother.

Twenty-Three

SALLY WAS NOT GETTING on at all well with Matty. She had tried to ease his load by enrolling Tor in a local nursery for three afternoons a week and arranging for a neighbour to look after Linus most mornings, but Matty remained sullen and uncommunicative.

He thoroughly disapproved of her renewed friendship with Lisette and made no secret of the fact. As she devoted more and more time to mugging up on the film industry and helping Lisette set up the first May shoot for Four Poster Bed, he had become increasingly detached and sulky, burying himself in work. That was not in itself a bad thing as he'd done precious little of it in previous months, coasting along on the odd bit of project consultation without getting a good new film of his own underway.

But with work came the age-old, brooding resentment that he was still trapped producing low-budget commissions from satellite channels and, if he was lucky, Network television, whereas Lisette was now whooping it up within the luxurious echelons of the film industry.

'The British film industry is a charity, Matty,' Sally protested, stealing a line that Lisette was always using.

'Not if it's co-produced with Americans, it isn't,' he sneered, 'which is where Lisette's little piece of porno trash is coming from.' He liked to refer to the film as some sort of blue movie because, stealing a look at the script when he thought Sally wasn't looking, the only bit he had managed to read was a rampant sex scene between Niall and an as yet uncast actress whom Lisette wanted to be American but the casting director and director, David Wheaton, wanted to be a Brit.

'And what exactly is your job on this film?' he wanted to know.

'I'm assisting Lisette.'

'So you're the production assistant? That's quite a responsible role.'

'No, not that. I'm just sort of helping out.' She wished she knew herself, Lisette was being infuriatingly vague about it, just promising lots of fun and a fat salary. So far all Sally had done was sit around Sleeping Partners' plush Marylebone office, gossiping and getting in the way.

'You spend more time lunching with her than working with her.' Matty was deliberately scathing.

'I came up with that publicity idea,' she pointed out hotly.

'Which Lisette hasn't taken up, thank God.'

'She's working on it!' Sally protested furiously. 'We're drawing up a proposal.' She thought that sounded sufficiently grand. Emboldened, she added, 'And I'm doing a lot of PR liaising for her.'

'But why does she need you on location?' he persisted, still sceptical. 'She won't need to be there much.'

'She's the producer, of course she will – she'll need to see the, er, rushes and dailies and things,' Sally blustered, trying to remember the lingo. 'And talk to all the, um, different directors and stuff.'

'Rubbish. That's the production manager's job – Flavia Watson. Lisette's role is much more hands-off than that.' Matty's eyes sparked suspiciously. 'If she wants to be hanging around the location shoot so much, she's up to something.'

Finally Sally caved in. 'She's after Hugo Beauchamp.'

'Ah,' he laughed delightedly. 'Now that does make sense. Didn't I tell you that Lisette had a nose-job for trouble? And Hugo's definitely trouble. It couldn't happen to a nastier chap.'

Sally avoided arguing with him about Lisette wherever possible.

She made valiant attempts to keep the friendship distanced from the marriage but this just infuriated Matty even more, as he convinced himself that she was being deliberately elusive to hide her secret life from him.

He still had odd bouts of explosive fury. When he found out that she was planning to stay in the crew hotel for the duration of the Berkshire location shoot, he went so far through the roof that he could have fixed the guttering on his way up.

'We need the money, Matty – you can't deny it,' she pleaded. 'And it means I'll be near Niall and Tash. I can even keep an eye on things in case Lisette winds them up.'

'And what are you planning to do with the kids while you're earning all this cash and acting as guardian angel?' he hissed. 'Shall we have them put into care?'

'Don't be facetious,' she snapped. 'My parents have said they'll have Linus and Tor to stay with them. And you can look after Tom until half-term when he'll go down and join them. The shoot is only a couple of weeks long. We'll just have to coast the last few days. I can look for a temporary child-minder if you want.'

'Some stranger looking after our kids? I'd rather take time off and do it myself,' he said to make himself look martyred.

'Oh, would you?' she beamed. 'Well, that's settled then.'

Which it wasn't. Life became even more unsettled after these brief confrontations, especially when Niall started to use their house as a hotel. He had a flat of his own in London, but it currently had sitting tenants whom he was too kind to boot out, and he found the hotel that the BBC put him up in too professional and soulless to suit him – it was full of salesmen on conferences and American tourists who recognised him at breakfast and came rushing over to ask him to autograph napkins. As most of the other actors in the project lived in London and went straight to work from home, he lacked company. The only actors who stayed at the hotel were those in minor roles who were only called for a couple of days' work before leaving, thus giving them the transitory feel of the businessmen whose faces changed as often as the restaurant menus.

Sally was only too happy to have Niall to stay at first, hoping that he would cheer up Matty and ease some of the pressure off their marriage. But she was anxious how Lisette would react to news of their temporary lodger. When she broke it to her, Lisette was delighted, her rasping voice dropping excitedly over the phone line.

'Oh, would you have a talk with him about your fucking brilliant event horse idea, Sally hon? I've tried to set up a meeting through Bob, but Niall's been away on location most of this month. Don't push him hard – if he thinks it's a bad idea we'll forget all about it. Is Matty out at the moment?'

'Yes. He's sloped off to Manchester for an overnight recce researching some project.'

'Then I'll fax you the proposal.'

Sally was over the moon that her idea was being taken seriously. With Matty away, she couldn't wait to put it to Niall. Having plied him with wine later that evening, she discovered that he had forgotten he even owned Snob.

'He's Tash's horse, so he is,' he shrugged, not understanding what Sally was suggesting. 'She'd never sell him.'

Sally bit her lip. 'She already has. You bought him, remember? To get him imported?'

'So I did!' Niall's face lit up and he cackled, rubbing his Huntingdon sideburns theatrically. 'Christ, my money troubles are over. I'll sell him straight away and pay the tax man. He's worth at least half a million. I can buy Tash and myself a house with what's left over.'

Sally stared at him in amazed delight. 'Do you mean that?'

He cocked his head. 'What d'you think, angel? Tash would murder me. She dotes on that animal. Like I say, he's her horse – whether it's my name on his papers or not makes no difference.'

'Ah, but it does . . .' Sally looked at him excitedly.

Ten minutes later and Niall was rubbing his chin thoughtfully, his reaction to the news surprisingly muted. 'You say Lisette definitely isn't interested in selling off her half?'

'Not at all,' Sally shook her head earnestly. 'Although I'd keep quiet about his being worth half a million if I were you. She thinks all nags bar racehorses are bought and sold for cat food. She just wants the publicity for Four Poster Bed.'

'But she's already got the *Cheers!* deal,' said Niall, shifting uncomfortably at the thought.

'This was my own idea, actually.' Sally bit her lip, unable to hide her pride. 'I originally suggested that the film company buy Tash a horse to compete on this year. Lisette was as surprised as you to discover from Hugo that she owned half of Snob already, so we just worked out a way to capitalise on that instead. Lisette wants to lease your half-share from you. It's just until the film is released – we could draw up a contract if you're worried. She's offering to cover all the horse's costs for the remainder of this year in return for the publicity, and then at the end of the year's lease, she signs her share over to Tash.'

'Won't she want half his value?'

Sally shook her head happily.

Niall enveloped his neck in his long, bony hands and mulled this over. 'Tash will kill me when she finds out Lisette technically owns half of her horse.'

'She'll be a lot happier if you tell her Lisette is signing over her share for nothing in eight months' time,' Sally said logically, refilling their wine glasses. 'And it's not as though Lisette is being difficult about it.

She's more or less offering to sponsor Tash and Snob for a year then give her share back for free. And, as Tash doesn't have a sponsor right now, I think she'll jump at the offer.'

He rubbed his head anxiously. 'Are you sure she's right about this? About being entitled to half?'

'Apparently it's all there on the settlement papers. Her solicitor checked them over last week.'

'Jesus, I never even read the things – just handed them over to my accountant,' he groaned.

'Listen, Lisette says she'll forget all about it if you think the idea will upset Tash,' Sally said reluctantly, longing for him to agree. 'She's happy to leave things as they stand. There's no pressure. But she's willing to pay the Moncrieffs a hefty fee for his year's keep, and I gather they need all the help they can get at the moment.'

'True,' Niall agreed, remembering both Zoe and Tash telling him how broke the Moncrieffs were. 'How much exactly?'

When Sally told him – upping Lisette's offer by twenty percent in her desperation – he chewed his lip pensively. 'I'll think about it, angel.'

'Will you talk to Tash?'

He shrugged.

Yet when Niall returned from a weekend in Berkshire and Sally eagerly asked what Tash thought about the proposal, he claimed he hadn't had time to mention it.

'Do you two speak at all?' she laughed.

Niall looked awkward. 'She was away competing. We're both working flat out at the moment – I'm trapped here in London all this week. I'll try to talk to her next weekend, angel.'

Which was not at all satisfactory. Particularly as, when Lisette called for an up-date the following morning, Matty picked up the call and was blisteringly rude to her.

'Couldn't you bring yourself to be civil, at least?' Sally implored when he hung up on her as though she was a pest caller. 'After all, they've been divorced for nearly two years, and Niall's about to get married to a girl he truly loves. She's trying to build bridges now – Christ, she's just got him one of the best roles of his career.'

'The only bridges Lisette builds are new ones for her nose.'

'Will you shut up about her bloody nose-job!' Sally wailed. 'Christ, I wish I'd never told you about it now.' She was relieved that she'd kept quiet about the boobs; Matty would never let it drop – rather like Lisette with her bust-line.

'She was unspeakably cruel to Niall, as you well remember.' He stomped around slamming kitchen cupboard doors as he searched for a clean mug. 'He went completely derailed when she pushed off.'

'And now he's happily connected to Alexandra and your step-mother's runaway bridal train, and too madly in love with Tash to care,' Sally sighed dreamily. 'Can't you see that now is the perfect time for Lisette and he to make friends again?'

'Don't be so sure.'

'He wouldn't have taken the role if he was still cut up about Lisette, Matts,' she persisted. 'He just wants to move on and forget it all.'

'I meant,' Matty stood up and looked at her, a chipped mug in his hand, 'that he's not necessarily happy with Tash.'

'That's an awful thing to say. She's your sister!'

'Which is why I know her well enough to say it,' he sighed. 'Because from the way she looked at the christening, I'm pretty damned sure she isn't happy either.'

He played a waiting game as Niall lolled around their house, drinking too much, eating junk food and watching television late into the night even though he had early-morning starts. The strange, reckless mood that was possessing Niall at the moment rather frightened Sally, and she sloped away from the house as often as possible when he was around – more often than not to meet Lisette and moan about Matty's suspicions. But Matty gently and persuasively worked on Niall, asking and probing and pulling information from him like silk threads from a scarf until he had enough to weave an argument.

One Tuesday night, the inevitable confrontation came.

Sally was grumpily loading the dish-washer after they'd pigged out on a takeaway. She was always happy to eat out of the cartons, but Matty believed in warming china plates and sitting around a table, considering formal meal-times an essential opportunity for 'family bonding'. He did not, however, believe in clearing away these plates afterwards, preferring the far more demanding job of going upstairs and reading Tom his bedtime story. The other kids had conked out hours ago, but Tom had been allowed to stay up for the takeaway as a rare treat because he saw so little of his godfather, Niall, whom he adored.

Carrying the wine glasses through to Sally, Niall was wearing his overcoat and a thick jumper. He found their house unbearably chilly.

'How do you cope at the forge?' Sally laughed, watching him put the glasses on to the wrong rack of the dish-washer, but grateful that he was trying – Matty would have just dumped them on top.

'I spend as much time as possible at the farm, so I do,' he shuddered. 'I try only to be in the forge when Tash is around to warm me up. Most of the time I sit and chat with Zoe by the range in the farm. She's a sweet woman.'

'She is lovely,' Sally agreed. 'I was rather hoping to develop her as a friend, but Matty hates going to Berkshire.'

'You'd think it was several time zones away from his reaction every time Tash invites you two down to supper,' Niall agreed. 'Not that her cooking is much of an attraction; Tash doesn't cook, she warms up, like an athlete.'

Sally stiffened. 'I wasn't aware that she had invited us to dinner lately.'

'She's asked twice this month – we're trying to persuade Matty to change his mind about being best man.'

Sally looked even more irate. 'I wasn't aware of that either.'

When Matty wandered back downstairs, he was faced with two pairs of critical eyes watching him from either end of the checked sofa in the sitting room.

'What?' He looked from one to the other in mock enquiry.

'Why,' Sally took a deep breath, 'are you refusing to be Niall's best man?'

Looking cornered, Matty rubbed his mouth and shrugged.

'C'mon, Matty, my son,' Niall laughed. 'You've done it once before, so you should know the job by now.'

'I don't think I'm the right person.'

'You're one of my oldest, dearest friends,' protested Niall. 'I think that qualifies you perfectly.'

'Niall really wants you to do it, Matty,' Sally urged.

'And I don't think I should.'

'Whyever not?'

'Don't push me on this one.' He backed away, about to head to the dining room for the open bottle of wine.

'I'm damned well going to push you to give me a good reason for refusing.' Niall leaped up and stood in the doorway. 'After all, you'll be coming along anyway. It won't take that much more effort to bring a ring and stand next to your old friend for an hour or so, will it? And you don't have to think up a new speech – just use the old one and substitute "Tash" for "Lisette"'.

'Well, that fucking says it all, doesn't it!' Matty suddenly raged.

'I'm sorry?' Niall reeled at the venom in his voice.

'She is just that, isn't she? A substitute. I don't know how you can be so sodding glib and flip about it. This is my sister we're talking about here!'

'And I hope I'm going to make her very happy indeed,' Niall said slowly, refusing to raise his voice to Matty's feverish pitch.

'Well, you're doing a bloody lousy job of it right now,' he snarled, 'so I hope to God you buck up after this farce of a wedding.'

'Their wedding isn't a farce, Matty,' Sally interrupted.

'Oh, yes it is,' Matty stared at Niall. 'Look me in the face and tell me honestly that you haven't had second thoughts?'

Niall gave a brief laugh and shook his head. 'Jesus, it's a lucky man that doesn't! Of course I have, but no more than anyone else.'

'Well, I'd lay my life that Tash has them far more than anyone else.' Matty sat down on a creaking kitchen chair despairingly. 'Christ, is it only me that thinks you've changed beyond recognition since you agreed to get married?'

'I haven't!'

'Yes you bloody have! You make less effort to spend time with Tash, you drink more, you're more ambitious, less loving, less communicative, more forgetful.'

'I've always been like that,' Niall laughed, trying to lighten Matty up, but he would not be deflected now that his resentment had been punctured, allowing his rage a release.

'I've listened to you over these past few evenings,' he said forcefully. 'You talk about your fellow actors in Wildfell Hall – Greg, Emma, Minty – especially Minty – Jude Wells the director, Bob the kleptomaniac camera-man. Fine, that's understandable; you work with them. You talk about America and how much you hate working there; you talk about how much Beetroot the bloody dog is starting to like you; how lovely Zoe Goldsmith and her kids are . . .' Clearing his throat uncomfortably, he rushed on: 'You can bore for your native country on the various members of that bloody farmhouse, human and animal. And sometimes, just very occasionally, you mention Tash.'

Niall was watching him, very still and calm now, big dark eyes taking it all in. He had heard Matty on a rampage before and knew to sit through and listen to the end.

'Not once this week, not one single time until just now, have you mentioned the wedding to me,' Matty went on. 'Isn't that strange? You are getting married in less than two months yet without the invitation – which we only got this week incidentally – propped up on the mantelpiece to remind me, I wouldn't know. And I find that bloody unsettling. Admittedly I haven't made it easy for you, but

I know damned well you're supposed to be asking me again to be your best man. So this week I've waited and waited and you've not so much as dropped a hint. The only reason you've brought it up tonight is because Sally's found out, isn't it?'

Niall shifted uncomfortably, still standing in the middle of their rather grubby if beautifully decorated kitchen, next to a fridge-freezer that was covered with the kids' drawings. He was so tall and wide that he seemed to dwarf everything around him, the ridiculous sideburns lending him a demonic air. Wavering uncomfortably in the corner, Sally looked tiny and fragile by comparison, her new boxy trouser suit ridiculously slick and tailored next to his great, crumpled shagginess.

Matty raised his palms in a strange, Jesus-like manner and looked at him imploringly. 'I really do want you to ask me again, Niall. I want you to persuade me, to be as alive and vibrant and buzzing with enthusiasm for this marriage as you are for that Brontë film, Rufus Goldsmith's driving lessons and even training that bloody dog. There's nothing I'd like more than to be your best man, but I have to hear that old Niall enthusiasm ringing in my ears, and there's none. Even tonight, it was Sally who rounded on me for saying said no, not you. I know you love Tash, I know that. I've never doubted that for a minute.' He sighed. 'But I don't think you want to marry her and I'm certain she doesn't want to marry you.'

'Has she told you that?' Niall went pale.

Matty shook his head, rubbing his creased forehead tiredly. 'And that aside, supposing this absurd situation goes ahead, you don't seem to have asked yourself just what sort of a couple you and Tash will make once you are married.'

'Pretty much the same as we were before, I should think.' Niall shrugged.

'And what is that? I mean, how long have you really spent together since you met? In between your films and her awayday competitions, I bet it only amounts to a few weeks. How many holidays have you been on together? Who shops and looks after the house? Who pays the bills, phones a plumber in a crisis, cooks the food?'

'Well, neither of us is much use at that to be honest.' He didn't seem too bothered. 'If I was after a servant I'd be marrying a butler.'

Matty banged his palms down on the table in frustration. 'I'm not saying that you should strut around like that character you're playing – what's his name? – Huntingdon. All I'm saying is, look at how impractical you two are as a couple. You're appallingly late everywhere when you're together, you kill yourselves with fags and booze, you are both hopeless with money and so cowardly that you're never entirely honest with one another about your feelings. Christ, it's like booking two gambling addicts into the same room in a recovery clinic and handing them a pack of cards for entertainment!'

'I think you make a lovely couple,' Sally said rather hopelessly, knowing that it would be impossible to stop Matty now that he was in mid-flow. Niall, head cocked, shoulders relaxed, was taking the diatribe with remarkable calm.

'At least Lisette was a control freak who didn't allow all your bad habits to run riot.' Matty waved his hands around expansively. 'Tash has all those habits too and you act as catalysts to one another, feeding from one another's laziness and paranoia.'

'Glad you think so highly of us.' Niall reached for a cigarette.

'You're so similar it's hardly any wonder you adore one another, but I think you both know that you're basically incompatible because of those similarities.' He tried to soften his voice but the blows were still raining hard and fast. 'You'll be self-indulgent parents, terrible hosts, perennially broke and constantly jealous of one another. Even now you're convinced she's still hankering after Hugo Beauchamp and she's knocked sideways every time one of your many drunken bloody flirtations gets out of hand.'

Sally, listening in, felt her ears ringing. She had been telling Lisette for weeks that the notion of anything between Hugo and Tash was absolute rubbish. Now she wasn't so sure.

'You're both driving each other to extremes of behaviour,' Matty was saying. 'You do exactly what you want when you're apart and exactly what everyone else wants when you're together, which is why this ridiculous wedding is going ahead at all. You make a great combination, but a lousy couple. You both need far stronger partners.'

'Any suggestions?' Niall muttered caustically, taking a deep drag on his cigarette, eyes narrowed. 'Think I should ask Lisette back?'

'Of course I don't!' howled Matty. 'But I don't think you should marry Tash, and I'm pretty damned certain that you both know that already. I just want you to bloody well admit it before it's too late.'

Niall was silent for a long time. Then, gathering up his cigarettes, he headed to the hall to fetch his bag.

'So I'll take that as a "no" to being best man then, shall I?' he called over his shoulder with studied casualness.

'Oh, for Christ's sake, Niall!' Matty followed him. 'I know I'm being bloody brutal, but I'm the only friend you have who's honest enough to tell you all these things before you make the biggest cock-up of your life. Can't you see that?'

'No, Matty. The biggest cock-up I made was thinking that you were my friend.' He dropped his voice so that Sally, still hovering red-faced in the other room, couldn't hear. 'And given the appalling state of your own marriage, I hardly think you're in a position to preach.'

Just for a moment Matty looked stricken, and Niall's insouciance seemed about to crumble, but instead he looked back towards the kitchen. His voice boomed out once more: 'Bye, Sals – I'm staying in the hotel tonight after all. Thanks for the food, angel.'

Dropping a tea-towel mid-wipe, Sally rushed through to the hall to dissuade him from leaving, but Niall was already halfway out of the door and simply kissed her farewell, ignoring her entreaties.

He looked over her shoulder to Matty.

'May the best man win, my son.' He gave a bitter laugh. 'Because he sure as hell isn't you.'

Hugo was already regretting his decision to let Lisette film at Haydown. He needed all his concentration right now as the season reached its peak, and his peace was being continually interrupted by calls from Lisette demanding dimensions, or a diary-check, or the number of local council departments to clear road filming – why she needed to bother Hugo with such matters was beyond him. She had even taken to calling him on his emergency mobile number, catching him when he was hacking out nervous youngsters, schooling his internationals or shouting at the grooms. This morning she had managed to call when he was taking a pee behind a bush on his way to catch a horse in one of the bottom fields. If it was like this now, he reasoned, then what on earth would happen when thirty or forty arty-farties, techies and luvvies minced over his land and through his house in May? His concentration would be shattered.

In reality, he knew that he was searching for excuses when he only had himself to blame for a dramatic drop in form of late. Without Surfer, he was down to just two really top-grade horses, but that was two more than many other competitors had and was no reason to fail. In truth the accident had knocked a lot of the confidence and enthusiasm out of him, and he no longer entirely trusted his judgement. For the first time in his life, he was riding cautiously across country and it was taking its toll in the form book as he dropped lower and lower down the ranks.

The enquiry after Lowerton had cleared him of blame – rumour had it that this was under the duress of one particularly exigent Olympic selector – but the mud still clung to him, and he was uncomfortably aware that his reputation was tarnished. At least his sponsors were sticking by him, but two private owners had taken their horses elsewhere – one, rather gallingly, to Gus Moncrieff, who had backed off considerably since Surfer's death. Two days after the accident, he had turned up on Hugo's doorstep with a bottle of wine and a sympathetic ear, only to be told sharply to bugger off. Hugo was deeply ashamed of his acerbity, but far too proud to do anything as simple as apologising. Gone were the easy days when he could hack down to the Moncrieffs' for a long, lazy afternoon drinking coffee and talking horses. He didn't want to risk bumping into Kirsty or Franny there, knowing that they would remind him of his headstrong, thoughtless ability to screw up. He also knew that the Moncrieffs were in dire financial straits, and that Gus bore a burning resentment towards him for being comparatively buoyant. He'd deliberately not stopped Franny's wages while she was staying with them, knowing that they couldn't afford to pay her, but he longed to do more and had been searching out likely sponsors for them, although the current black cloud of bad publicity hanging over him wasn't helping.

He would willingly have bought another Lime Tree horse to tide them over, but the Moncrieffs had sold so many horses this year that the only one who was still officially on the market was the crabby, slothful, know-it-all Fashion Victim. Hugo would never dream of depriving Gus of his Badminton run, especially as Stefan had hinted there was a potential sponsorship deal hanging on it. He was also not having the best of times with his last Lime Tree purchase. The hapless Mickey Rourke, though tremendously willing, was a disaster, constantly getting thoroughly overexcited and tripping over his own feet. The last time they had competed he had failed even to exit the start box as, bouncing around in his eager, clumsy manner while they were being counted down, he'd caught his legs in the rope barrier and brought himself crashing down to terra firma, trussed like a suckling pig. Hugo only persisted because he knew that Tash had such faith in Mickey, and because he didn't want to be seen as failing where she had triumphed.

In truth, there was one overriding reason that he steered clear of the farm, and he had to endure vivid descriptions of it day after day as Stefan chattered cheerfully about what a great bunch of people they were. The Moncrieffs, it seemed, had been caught up in the Wedding of the Year, and no wonder, for Niall almost lived there at night, sitting in that messy kitchen helping India with her homework, Zoe with her cooking, Rufus with his Highway Code swotting and Tash, no doubt, with just about everything.

When Lisette took him out to dinner at the Olive Branch that evening, Hugo barely spoke, drank or ate. He felt unbearably nervy being there at all, certain that one of the Lime Tree Farm contingent – worse still, all of them – would troop in at any second. He wondered if Lisette was deliberately hoping to bump into Niall.

'C'mon,' she goaded, 'what happened to the sexy, dynamic Hugo I fancied rotten for years?'

'He went off,' he snapped. 'Tell me, d'you want Niall back?'

His directness didn't throw her for a second. She smiled, luminous grey eyes dancing at him through the candlelight. 'That depends.'

'On what?'

'Whether I get a better offer first.'

Hugo raised his chin, eyes unfriendly. 'They don't come much better than Niall.'

'Oh, I don't know,' she breathed.

A few years ago he would have sparred back, loving the direct ballsiness of her come-on. All through his adult life he had actively searched out partners who could take him on that level – Amanda, Kirsty, and countless others who had made it perfectly clear what they wanted from the start. But now Hugo felt no pleasure at all, no sexual kick. He wasn't even flattered. He rubbed his forehead tiredly, wishing he hadn't come. He was wasting her time as well as his own; he had no desire to lead her on. She was a phenomenal woman, deserving a far more worthy target to set her sights on. He was too full of bullet holes already.

Suddenly his face drained as he watched a couple come in through the door, faces turning pink in the sudden heat, laughing as Ange swooped on them with coat-taking bonhomie. It was Tash and Zoe. Hugo studied them, as still as a sniper.

'Ah.' Lisette, in turn, was watching him. 'I think I've just spotted my rival.'

'What?' he snapped.

Lisette smiled. 'You don't think I mean Tash?'

'Well, she and Niall *are* getting hitched,' he hissed.

Still smiling, she dropped her voice to a breath so light it would barely mist a glass. 'And I'm very pleased for them. I can assure you, I have absolutely no interest in winning Niall back.'

'Sure you haven't,' Hugo sneered, glancing towards Tash again.

'You don't have to believe me.' She played with the stem of her glass.

He took a slug of mineral water. 'So who is this rival, then?'

'Actually, it's you.' She winked and gazed across again as Tash and Zoe settled at the opposite end of the bar with glasses of red wine and a stack of crisps, well out of earshot. Neither of them appeared to have noticed that she and Hugo were there.

'Me?' Hugo sounded appalled. 'What on earth are you talking about?' He wondered for a horrifying moment if she thought he had some sort of homo-erotic crush on Niall.

But Lisette just smiled. Tilting her head, she smoothed back a long, glossy tress of hair. 'I never would have believed it of Tash French.'

'Believed what?' He pushed his plate away, longing to leave. He hadn't a clue what she was prattling on about.

'That she had such exquisite taste in men. It's the one thing we have in common.' Lisette laughed, and then dropped her voice to a near-whisper. 'Tell me, Hugo, how would you like to buy a half-share in an event horse from me?'

'You own a half-share in an event horse?' He looked at her disbelievingly.

'Shh.' Lisette rolled her eyes towards Marco Angelo who was hovering nearby, her voice even lower. 'I was rather surprised too. It was something you said in passing that made me realise in the first place.'

'Shit!' Hugo closed his eyes as he realised which particular horse she was talking about. He'd hankered after it for years, admiring its phenomenal talent, its monumental athletic power, and above all its unbreakable spirit. He'd wanted the horse from the first moment he had ever seen it at Alexandra D'Eblouir's house in France two years earlier, and jealously watched it take the sport by storm ever since. It was just the sort of animal he adored, knowing that he had the experience and strength to control that famous explosive ability which many condemned as dangerous. On the very few occasions he'd ridden it, he'd experienced that elusive click that sometimes took years to achieve with a horse. With this one it was instantaneous.

'I gather you rather tragically lost one of your top nags recently,' Lisette was saying without a trace of sympathy. 'So I thought you might be interested.'

'That horse belongs to Tash,' he said flatly.

'No, he doesn't,' she breathed. 'It was you yourself who told me Niall owns him. Or rather, half of him as it turns out. And I'm willing to sell you my share. Perhaps we should discuss this somewhere more – intimate.' She pressed her ankle against his beneath the table.

Unsmiling, Hugo looked at her for a long time, his cool blue eyes so intent that he could have been counting the flecks on her corneas. He was wearing that curious half-smile that Lisette could never read but found wildly sexy.

'Perhaps we should,' he drawled softly. 'Come back to the house for a drink.'

Twenty-Four

IT WAS NOT UNTIL the day after Niall flew to America to promote Celt that Tash realised he had gone at all. Humiliatingly, it was Zoe who told her.

'I thought you knew,' she gasped in surprise. 'He popped in to say goodbye last night. You hadn't come back from the Tewkesbury trials.'

'Oh, I see.' Tash bit her lip. 'We had a flat tyre. I thought he was going next week – after my birthday. I assumed he was up in London last night.'

Zoe looked away, embarrassed for both of them. 'He didn't mention your birthday. Anyway, he should be back by then.'

He wasn't.

Tash's birthday fell on a Sunday. The day before, she took her two 'seniors', Snob and Hunk, to Ratchet Trials, getting a lift with Hugo and Stefan, as Gus, Penny and Kirsty were competing elsewhere.

It was the first time that she had travelled with Hugo since the day of the accident and she had barely seen him in the few weeks since then. They had competed at the same events, but he had grown increasingly aloof and detached towards her, simply nodding 'hello' when they encountered one another. He no longer joined in so much with the tomfoolery and high jinks of the other riders, and his fuse was currently so short that they steered clear of him too.

'Honestly, he's intolerable,' Brian Sedgewick complained as he returned from walking the Ratchet course. 'I asked him what the best approach to the saw-mill drop was, and he said "on foot". Then he nicked a fag and bogged off.'

Tash found that by the time she was changing for her dressage test, they had exchanged all of three sentences. To add to her unease, Hugo was immediately after her in the running order and wanted to change in the lorry at the same time.

'Can you wait two minutes?' Tash asked at the door, suddenly suffering a fit of modesty. 'I'll give you a shout when I'm done.'

'No, I can't.' He pushed past her and started to strip off. 'Bodybuilder needs a lot of working in, and I don't trust Jenny with him. She seems to get him leaning into his forehand like a pit pony heading down to work.'

Jenny was Franny's replacement, an eager ginger-haired youngster fresh out of training college, with a huge crush on Hugo. She was really too inexperienced for his yard, but he had been in a hurry for someone and he knew her father well. What she lacked in maturity, she made up for with boundless enthusiasm, good humour and immunity to Hugo's tongue-lashings. Her slavish adoration had won her ridicule from many of the other eventers, but Tash found her charming and far easier-going than the irascible Franny, who was still shacked up with Ted. With her pretty, pixie face and outlandish taste in jumpers and hats, Jenny had also won the affection of Stefan, who doted on her like a big brother.

Tash had India grooming for her that day and was worried that she might be finding it hard to handle Snob's over-boisterous strength. India loved helping out at events, and thought of it as her Saturday job, but she was inexperienced and not as strong as Tash physically. Stuck in the horse-box with Hugo, Tash knew that she was leaving her to cope all alone, and longed to escape and see what was going on. Hugo seemed to be taking an unusually long time to change.

'I won't look if you want to get your kit off,' he said as he re-tied his stock for the third time, fiddling with the pin.

'It's all right, I'll wait for you to go.' She was sitting at the table with her back to him, watching out of the window as Stefan helped one of Hugo's younger grooms to get Happy Monday to open his mouth for the bit.

'Are you that afraid of me?' he muttered edgily, stabbing himself in the finger with the pin and wincing. 'What do you think I'm going to do – pounce on you in a fit of passion once I see your bare legs?'

'Of course not!' She squirmed, ashamed of her own silliness. It was ridiculous that she found herself so mawkish and uncomfortable with him when she thought nothing of stripping off and changing in front of Gus, Ted or even Stefan, which she had done hundreds of times in cramped lorries. There was no room for modesty in eventing, yet with Hugo her face flamed as though given an Eric Morecambe cheek-slapping.

'Well, you'll have no time to ride Snob in,' Hugo snapped, stooping down to pull off his old cord breeches ready to don his whites. He perched on a chair to do this and spent ages easing them off over his feet.

Staring fixedly out of the window to stop herself ogling his rower's legs and trendy underwear, Tash was also aware that she was wearing her grottiest sports bra, which had a ladder on one nipple, and that she had that morning resorted to the kinky knickers that Niall had given her for Christmas because she had no others clean. Perhaps worse was the fact that it was a cold day and she had hastily fished a pair of tights from the laundry basket which, although only worn once before, had that stale, unpleasant smell of dirty washing. She had no desire to flash all this in front of Hugo and receive the usual derision and ridicule.

'Get your finger out, Tash,' Stefan yelled through the door. 'You're on in three, and India's had to get off Snob because he's all over the place. He's really lathered up now.'

Hugo was still sitting on the chair, his muscular thighs shimmering in the neon lights as he tugged the jaunty red wool socks upwards.

Dog in a bloody manger, Tash fumed, realising that she had to get outside soon or forfeit her chances.

Succumbing to shame, she pulled off her jeans and, grabbing the white breeches from the back of Hugo's chair, tugged them on as fast as she could. They were incredibly long and narrow, with a vast, gaping waist as though the elastic had lost its stretch. She must have boil-washed them by mistake, she realised, as she dived out of her sweater and into a sweatshirt which would be hidden by her dressage jacket. Because she had lost so much weight of late, she could really pad up beneath her black jacket, a godsend on days like today. And not being a stock snob, she had wrapped her made-up one around her neck in seconds, adhering the Velcro and jumping into her boots practically en route for the door.

To her chagrin, Hugo watched her throughout, a big grin on his face for the first time in weeks.

'I know you like to wear the trousers around here, Tash,' he laughed, 'but isn't this going a bit far?'

'Glad you find me so amusing,' she mumbled, dashing out and ignoring his sudden shouts of protest behind her.

Snob was indeed in a sweat, but Tash was too busy trying to stop her breeches falling down to allow him to get the better of her. Somehow, with her buttocks clenched and her elbows stapled to her sides like a guardsman on parade, she steered him through the test with hardly a faulty move. Afterwards she whooped in amazement, exchanging a high five with Stefan, who was warming up his elastic little bay gelding, Happy Monday, for the show-jumping.

'It's psychology.' He rode alongside her as she patted Snob on the rock-hard neck muscle. 'For once you weren't wound up about his temper and mood, you were too busy concentrating on something else to let it bug you. He picked up on that and, given a bit of trust for once, he got on with the job like a champ.'

'Rubbish,' she laughed. 'I think India fed him some dope cake.'

'I didn't!' India protested, throwing a blanket over Snob's rump as she followed them on foot.

'Now, if it's not too much trouble, Hugo would like his trousers back.' Stefan pointed to a burger stand behind which Hugo was gesticulating madly. 'They're his lucky ones and you know how superstitious he is – we got a fifteen-minute delay by telling the judges that Bod's cast a shoe, but you'd better hurry up.'

For a moment Tash's brows shot up as she gaped at Stefan in bewilderment. Then, slowly, she lowered her eyes to her clean, white thighs encased in the impossibly tight-legged, baggy-waisted breeches.

'These are Hugo's?' she breathed disbelievingly.

Grinning broadly, Stefan nodded. 'I suggested he wore his spares, but he insisted he wants those back.'

Still high from her recent test, Tash started to giggle. Sliding from Snob and handing him over to India before she lost her composure completely, she laughed so much that her stomach was pinched with cramps and her eyes glistened with tears, star-fishing her lashes. As she ran towards the stand, her movement crab-like as a result of the tight breeches, she was almost bent double.

'Don't, whatever you do, wet yourself,' Hugo hissed, dragging her behind the stand and starting to unbuckle his jeans. 'I'm hiding from the dressage judges in case they smell a rat. Quick, we'll swap.'

'I'm not changing here!' she wailed, noticing that a man with a large, panting mongrel had paused close by and was feigning interest in the menu on the side of the stand.

But Hugo was already holding the jeans out for her to take.

Very reluctantly, Tash prised off her boots and tried to pull down the breeches. The man with the dog was gawping openly now, and had been joined by the burger bar's two spotty traders, who were peering over a stack of buns in the greasy rear window. The breeches got stuck at her knees.

'Oh, for Christ's sake, lie down and I'll pull,' Hugo snapped.

'Get lost.' Giving the breeches a tug, she got her foot caught in the waist and fell over anyway.

With her head next to a spluttering petrol generator which was gushing out foul-smelling heat, Tash watched in horror as Hugo grabbed her by the ankles and pulled the breeches hard. The peering youths were pressing down on their burger buns now, and mongrel man was starting to breathe audibly. I've still got my dressage topper on, Tash realised, feeling the brow tip towards her nose as it hit the generator. Matched with her gloves, stock and hairnet, she must look like some sort of hard-hunting over-sexed aristo desperate for a rogering. Hugo was lifting her right off the ground with every tug now.

'In other circumstances this might be rather enjoyable,' she joked in embarrassment.

He gave her a withering look and told her to hold on to the base of the burger-bar trailer while he pulled. They were gathering quite an audience. Mongrel man, in the front row, was almost on top of them, his panting dog's very pink tongue lolling inches from Tash's face.

Everyone around was getting a glorious view of her stinky tights and kinky knickers – especially Hugo. She peered up at him, still tugging between her ankles. He was starting to look rather frantic, teeth gritted with effort. Because he'd already taken his jeans off, he was wearing his underpants and red socks below his fully jacketed upper half, his boots lying alongside him ready to pull on the moment he was in his breeches. It was simply a matter of getting her out of them first.

'I can't get – blast – them – blast – off – ah!'

One ankle suddenly came free and Hugo lurched backwards, almost losing his balance. The second didn't take much more force and Tash sagged back on the ground for a second in relief before reaching for his discarded jeans, her topper right over her nose now like something from Cabaret.

Humiliatingly, his jeans were also far too tight on the thighs and clung to her in all the wrong places like a pair of seventies slacks. She couldn't wait to get back to the lorry to change, but their boots had become muddled up in the tug of war, and she waited an interminable amount of time while Hugo stepped in and out of footwear like Cinderella's ugly sister, red socks bobbing.

'Mine are the small ones,' Tash said helpfully, and almost got punched in the face.

He had less than five minutes to ride Bodybuilder in, which was a ridiculously short space of time. The huge black horse was notoriously temperamental and, like Snob, could explode in the dressage phase, but, also like Snob, he relished a challenge. And this day he rose to it.

At first Hugo was spitting, but having performed his best test in weeks followed by a clear jumping round, he was willing to be conciliatory and gradually thawed to see the funny side of the incident. In fact, slouching in the lorry drinking coffee with Tash as he waited the half-hour before he needed to warm up Bodybuilder for the next phase, he was momentarily back to his old form, laughing and teasing and generally immeasurably improved from his glum sulks of the morning.

Changing for the cross-country phase, Tash scoured the box for her kit which had as usual spread itself everywhere. Now buried behind *The Times*, Hugo swigged from his coffee mug and talked about the four Poster Bed shoot.

'They won't leave me alone,' he complained. 'This art director chap, Sean, keeps wandering around the house as though he owns it. Yesterday he walked in on Stefan having a bath, said, "Don't mind me," measured the window, and walked out again.'

'Sounds like Gus when he's decorating,' Tash muttered, pulling on her scruffier breeches, no longer caring if he saw her tights as he'd had such a long close-up of them earlier. But *The Times* didn't move.

'Gus says he hasn't spoken to you for ages,' she said tentatively, having heard Gus say quite a lot more than that recently – all of it unflattering. 'You never come down to the farm anymore.'

'I came to pick you up today. Anyway, none of you lot ever come up,' he pointed out.

'Gus did,' she reminded him, wondering if she was being suicidal breaking his good mood. But she knew that Gus was deeply hurt by the slight. Zipping up her body protector, she braced herself for an old-fashioned Hugo snarl.

He stayed behind the paper, but sounded quite regretful. If Tash hadn't known better, she'd have said he sounded guilty.

'I should have called him to apologise. Truth is, I was all over the place that night – I'd just been summonsed by the BHS and the press were all over my back about the barbarity of the sport. But that was no excuse to take it out on Gus. He was being a good mate and I was being a prat.'

Diving into her number vest, Tash couldn't wait to tell Gus off for calling Hugo a bloodless Vulcan.

Outside, she could see India calmly walking Snob around in his cross-country armour, bandages stitched in place, bridle sewn to his top plait so that it wouldn't be pulled off in a fall, grease on his legs to help him slither over fences if he hit them. She had even tied his tail up to the bone with a matching bandage to stop it getting coated with mud – Ted could never be bothered. Tash was impressed. She searched for her coloured hat silk to swap it for the black one.

'That was a bloody good dressage test you just rode, by the way.' Hugo drained his coffee mug. 'That big chestnut of yours has really improved – you could hardly hold him last month.'

Tash pulled a sceptical face. 'He comes to hand or goes to pot depending on his mood, but he's still so strong my arms ache to buggery by the end of the course.'

Hugo looked over his paper seriously. 'If you don't entirely trust him, Tash, you shouldn't be competing him. You have to know him inside out or you're truly in danger.'

'I think I know him pretty well,' she bristled, locating her silk amid a pile of spare number vests.

'I know that sounds rather damning, but I'm just thinking of your safety.' His face was open and honest. 'You can't let a horse think he can take over the reins and choose which line he wants – if he suddenly goes through the bridle halfway round Badminton, you could be leaving Gloucestershire in a blood wagon. He has to obey you even if he'd rather go faster or jump bigger or muck around.'

Tash fiddled with her crash helmet, pursing her lips as she absorbed his criticism so that she looked as though she was sucking an oversized gob-stopper. Finally irritation got the better of her.

'Surfer obeyed you,' she reminded him. 'He trusted you.'

'Perhaps too much,' Hugo answered smoothly, not losing eye-contact for a moment. 'Yes, they need to obey you, but sometimes they have to put in that extra stride, or apply the brakes if their rider gets it wrong, It's called self-preservation and the best horses – including Snob – have it in spades. Surfer had too little, took on everything I asked him to, and to my everlasting shame I abused that.'

Tash stared at him, barely able to believe her ears. Admitting he was in the wrong was as rare for Hugo as poetry recitals and Buddhist chants.

A cool blast of air preceded India's popping her head around the door and tapping her watch. Tash nodded, grinning as she spotted

Snob's pink nose resting on top of India's green lace hat. She was one of the only people he would abide wearing hats.

Not taking any notice, Hugo continued lecturing.

'What I'm talking about,' he went on, 'is bullish over-enthusiasm, and that's far more risky than Surfer's obedience. Because when it happens there's nothing you can do about it.'

'*If* it happens.' Tash reached for her stopwatch and started to strap it on her arm, along with her marker times.

'I'll give you a couple of hours' work together next week, if you like,' he offered, watching her struggling into her armour. 'Hack up to Maccombe one day and we'll see what we can do – I've got some ideas that might help.'

'Thanks.' She looked at him in amazement, astonished by the offer. It was almost a year since he'd given her any help. 'That would be great. When?' She blushed slightly, aware that she was sounding over-eager.

'Tomorrow suits me.' He shrugged indifferently, lighting a fag.

'Fine.' She looked away, trying not to smile stupidly.

Still waiting in the doorway, India caught her eye, her expression strangely devious.

'But tomorrow's your birthday, Tash!' she complained. 'Gus said you could laze around all day eating the chocolates you'll get given and watching junk TV.'

'I'm not too good at lazing,' Tash said quickly, and then blushed even more when she realised how ridiculous this sounded. She was famous for being hugely lazy. At Lime Tree Farm, she'd had one well-chronicled day off when she'd slept right through till the next morning, not getting out of bed once.

Snatching at his newly imported strong bit, Snob was eager and over-fresh as Tash circled him at the start. She had spent twenty minutes working him in circles to calm him, but her effort seemed wasted as he rotated on the spot, dragging his head between his knees and then snatching it up as he fought for control, not understanding why they couldn't launch themselves on to the course right away instead of waiting for the man in the hat to count them down. Apart from India's, Snob was not keen on hats. Each time he clapped eyes on Jenny, who was wearing a red fake fur pork pie number today, he feigned hysteria. Tash only just held him as she bounded up to wish them luck.

'Hugo says he'll catch you up on the way round,' she giggled, bouncing on the spot so that she and Snob, opposite one another, resembled energetic disco dancers at a club.

'He'll be lucky.' Tash gritted her teeth as Snob practically pulled her arms from their sockets.

'I wish he was chasing me,' Jenny sighed, looking wistfully into the far corner of the collecting box.

Following her gaze, Tash could see Hugo circling nearby on the tall, regal Bodybuilder, his face shadowed by the peak of his red silk, his attention rapt, entirely into getting in tune with his horse.

She wanted to ask Jenny exactly what she meant, but there was no time. Checking her stopwatch, Tash felt a skip of nerves in her chest as the starter gave her thirty seconds and Stefan, who had been around the course already, issued last-minute advice about the way it was jumping which she was far too nervous to take in.

India had already raced back to the horse box to collect Hunk, whom she was going to ride in as he was due in the dressage ring almost as soon as Tash completed with Snob. She wished she was nearby with the reassuring smile she had inherited from her mother, and the loud whoops of encouragement she normally let fly when Tash set off. Stefan and Jenny were far too pragmatic to bother.

'Be careful and don't take risks, remember?' Stefan was admiring Jenny's rear as she bent down to haul up a welly sock, crimson leggings straining over two round, plump buttocks. He liked red-heads with round bottoms.

'Yes – be safe.' Jenny caught Stefan looking and grinned delightedly.

By the time Tash and Snob were streaking towards the first fence, Stefan had already wandered away to help India, and Jenny was attending to Hugo's girths. Only he watched Tash's departure, his face pinched with concern.

Splattered with mud and grinning from ear to ear, Tash almost mowed India down as she galloped through the finish five minutes later and turned in a wide circle to slow Snob gradually to a walk. Pulling up too quickly could jar a horse's legs, although she didn't have to worry with Snob, who always took several hundred yards to battle down to a walk.

'Fantastic!' India whooped when they finally united. 'That was really fast.'

Tash shook her head. 'We had a stop at the ditches – he got his legs in a mess in the middle because we jumped the first part too big. But he was really obedient, so yah, boo and sucks to Hugo.'

She jumped off and started wrestling to undo the breast straps of the martingale.

'I didn't hear them mention the stop.' India took Snob's head. 'Hugo's still clear according to the tannoy. I've got Hunk ready – he's by the box. You'd better go and get changed as soon as you've weighed in. And wash your face if you want to impress those judges.'

Tash grinned, amazed by India's super-efficiency. She had only come to help at all because Franny, hearing that Hugo would be involved, refused point blank to care for Tash's two horses that day. Tash was now pleased that she had.

She was so busy with Hunk that she didn't see Hugo again until just before her second crack across country. Finished for the day, he was wearing a large grey sweater over his muddy breeches and sharing a cigarette near the start with the sport's craggy-faced old timer Brian Sedgewick, a can of lager in his hands.

'I hear we have you to beat,' Tash called as she rode past them.

'No chance,' Hugo laughed. 'You need to go inside the time to do that, and you'll never make it on that old cob.'

Her competitive streak aroused, Tash exploded on to the course in a flurry of kicked mud. Although shorter-striding and less energetic than Snob, Hunk was more economical across country as he wasted less time pulling and fighting. He simply settled into his plodding, easy stride and bounced over the fences as though skipping for joy and simply taking a pipe-opener across the fields at home. Feeling him back to his full strength and running for fun underneath her, Tash barely glanced at her stopwatch. This competition was a confidence-bolster for Hunk, a dress rehearsal for Badminton without the pressure of the full event. Her primary objective had never been winning, she mainly wanted to give Hunk a big dollop of encouragement, but he was going so well that she was confident enough to tackle most of the direct routes to keep in touch. But even she was surprised when she glanced down to her watch at the final time-check to see that she was almost ten seconds ahead of the clock.

Another rider – delayed by a stop and a fall – pulled to the side as Tash and Hunk scattered dead leaves in their wake and bounded out of the final woods over the Elephant Pit. Then they raced up the hill to whistle over a pile of logs and pound through the finish, where Hunk proved a great deal easier to rein down to a walk than Snob.

'Christ, that horse is fit.' Stefan loped up, stuffing a hotdog into his mouth as he freed his hands to help her remove the saddle. 'What's your secret?'

'Neglectful fiancé.' Tash jumped off. 'I've put a lot of work into him during the lonely evenings.' She gave him a kiss on his black muzzle. Hunk threw a delighted, lip-smacking raspberry and hunted her pockets for Polos.

'Well, unofficially you've won.' Stefan spoke with his mouth full, winking at her as she undid the surcingle and pulled Hunk's ears with delight. 'I make you inside the time, and you were the only pair who could catch Hugs – he's pretty pissed off with you for denying him his first win in weeks.'

But far from seeming pissed off, Hugo slapped her on the back and handed her a can of lager as soon as he caught sight of her.

'Well done.' He grinned. 'Bloody brilliant. Have a fag and talk me through it.'

As Tash walked around with him and related, jump for jump, the delights of taking Hunk around the course, she shivered with happiness. It was so rare to be able to yak on about a triumph to someone who seemed eager to listen. Gus and Penny generally wore the 'heard it before' faces of those who had won and lost too often to want to pick the bones of each event anymore, and Niall – when he was in evidence – tried to join in her enthusiasm but bored easily.

'Listen, there's someone I want you to meet.' Hugo led her towards the bar tent once India had emerged to take Hunk off for a cold sponge-over and a handful of Polos.

Twenty minutes later and Tash was even more ecstatic. She had an appointment for the following week with the marketing and managing directors of Mogo clothing, a very upmarket manufacturer who was breaking into the fleece and waterproof markets so favoured by events' sponsors. They had initially approached Hugo with an offer, but he was tied up in an exclusive deal with an investment bank that he was eager to keep sweet, so he'd suggested Tash and had been politely haranguing them to attend the event that day. Having seen her compete, the two men seemed enthusiastic. Riders normally had to chase sponsors and badger them for funding and endorsements. To be approached by one was almost unheard of. Tash almost exploded with gratitude.

'I can't believe it.' She wandered back to the lorry with Hugo to collect Snob for the presentation. 'Why me? Why not Stefan – he's independent right now, isn't he?'

'He's foreign, Tash, and they wanted a Brit.'

'What about Gus? He's gagging for a sponsor.'

'Tash!' He swung her round by the shoulders, laughing with frustration, his straight dark brows diving towards one another in disbelief.

'Hasn't it occurred to you that for all the respect and experience the Moncrieffs have in the field, you have better horses right now and you're winning more comps? Your profile is far higher than Gus's. How many interviews or features have you had written about you this year in the horse rags?'

She shrugged uncertainly. 'Half a dozen maybe.'

'Which is half a dozen more than Gus.' He clutched her shoulders and faced her. 'Look, Gus might be a bit jealous if you pull this off, but the yard needs the money, whether it's you or him pulling it in – you'll get entry fees and petrol-money, insurance costs covered; your top nags will get nice new rugs to show off the Mogo logo, their grub paid – maybe even new transport if you're very lucky. And their mistress will get a lot of two-tone designer fleeces, which beats those holey old jumpers she slopes around in now.'

She hung her head and realised he was speaking a lot of sense. Glancing up through her lashes, she saw him still watching her, hands gripping her shoulders bolsteringly.

'You fit their product.' His blue eyes were warm with encouragement. 'Just believe that next week. You're a winner.'

'Today, I am.' She shrugged. 'Lots of unsponsored riders are winners – look at Brian Sedgewick; he's one of the top riders in the country.'

'He doesn't look like you, though, does he?' Hugo sighed despairingly.

Tash wrinkled her nose thoughtfully. 'Brian's very – distinctive,' she said kindly.

'Brian's very ugly,' Hugo laughed. 'Whereas you are very beautiful indeed.'

Tash gaped at him. She couldn't believe he'd just said that. She was longing for him to repeat it just to make sure, but he was still giving her that kind, encouraging big-brother smile that said nothing at all.

On the return journey, she sat between Stefan, who was driving, and Hugo, who slept throughout, his long thigh resting carelessly against hers, head lolling alternately against his breast bone and her shoulder. At one point her face seemed to be full of his slithering, sweet-smelling hair. With a great squirm of fear tightening in her stomach, she realised that the old magic was working again. Her crush was coming back like some terrible childhood illness one thought one couldn't catch twice, but that hit ten times as hard when it returned.

Eating a Zoe special – cauliflower and carrot chilli – that night at Lime Tree Farm, Tash broke the news about her meeting with Mogo to Gus.

'I see,' he said after a long pause. 'Well, that would be good if it worked out, but don't build your hopes up – you know how things can go phut when it comes to sponsors.'

'Sure.' Tash forked her food around the plate unenthusiastically.

'Well, I think it's fantastic!' India told everyone eagerly. 'Tash rode brilliantly today – even Hugo called her "shit hot and bloody scary".'

'Language!' Zoe laughed in mock-horror. 'Although perhaps I should call Hugo and say that.'

'I shouldn't bother.' India wrinkled her nose. 'He's got a hot date tonight. Stefan says she's drop-dead gorgeous.' She peeked furtively at Tash.

Tash was chewing on a whole green chilli, seeming not to notice.

'Well, I'm jolly pleased you did well today, Tash.' Penny cleared her throat and reached for the wine bottle. 'We have a lame horse, twisted wrist, kicked shin and torn shoulder muscle between us to show for our day's work.'

Tash kept quiet, not certain how to respond to that one. At her feet, Beetroot was licking the flagstones thoughtfully.

'Niall phoned,' Zoe told her as she started to collect up plates.

'Did he?' Tash looked at her watch to see what time it was in the States. 'I could call him back now – where's the number?' The chilli was starting to bite and her mouth suddenly burst into flames.

'He – er – didn't leave one.' Zoe bit her lip. 'He was mid-way on his coast-to-coast promo and calling from some airport – even he didn't seem to know which. Says he's spent every day trapped in a hotel suite with a different journalist poling up every five minutes on roster to ask exactly the same questions. He sounded terribly tired.'

'Did he leave a message?' Tash's eyes were starting to stream, her mouth positively dissolving now, her throat one big fireball of pain. She was trying to keep her dignity, but it was hard when one's nose had started to dribble with chilli blast-back.

Zoe was looking at her in concern. 'He says he loves you,' she said unconvincingly, 'and that he forgot to mention that he's free for that weekend at your ma's if you make it the second in May.'

'But that's just before Badminton!' she howled, sounding like Darth Vader.

'I shouldn't worry, Tash,' Gus stood up, his voice caustic. 'You're doing so well at the moment, you won't need the practice.' He walked out, taking the wine bottle with him.

Tash sank her head into her hands, nose going like an outlet pipe now, a blow torch blasting through her mouth and aiming into her throat, bonfire coming the other way. The only reason she was doing well right now, she wanted to yell if she only could, was because she had all the time in the world to practise. She was supposed to be getting married in two months and she had seen far, far more of her horses this year than of her lover. What was worse, she was finding she missed him less and less.

Twenty-Five

THE NEXT DAY, HUGO greeted her with a cup of undrinkably bad instant coffee made in the tack room and a big, genial smile. She still kept having to double-take when he smiled at her, it was incredibly hard to adjust to. She couldn't wait to say hi to Mickey, who was looking spectacular now that his dull, clipped winter coat had been replaced by the glossy steel of his summer one. His lop ears waggled back and forth with amazed delight when he saw her and, thoroughly overexcited, he tried to thrust a mouthful of hay into her face.

Holding the jealous Snob at a safe distance, Hugo laughed in amazement. 'He looks like some sort of camp make-up artiste.'

But he was far from friendly once he had her and Snob circling around him in the indoor school. Out of necessity rather than cruelty, he revealed all of their weak spots as easily as the king revealing the four and twenty blackbirds. One by one, he picked on her legs, her hands, her back, her head and her feet.

'Okay, drop the reins but keep riding forward. Where does he go?'

'To the left.' Tash almost fell off as Snob veered dramatically to one side.

'Know why he does that?'

'Because he favours that side.'

'Nope.' Hugo walked forward and grabbed the rein to slow up Snob. '*You* favour that side. You might not realise it, but your weight is almost entirely on your left buttock – here.' He slipped a warm hand beneath her rear. 'He pitches that way to compensate for all the pressure bearing down on him.'

Tash shifted away, not wanting him to have a chance to assess the pudginess of her bottom.

'That's better.' Hugo removed the hand, unsmiling. 'When he gets overexcited across country, he veers left because it's now ingrained. The same happens show-jumping, especially when he's had a couple down and tenses up – I've seen him do it. Now go through those canter transitions down the centre line again, this time trying to place your weight evenly.'

Tash did and Snob veered left.

'And again – concentrate.'

Again he veered left.

'Once more!'

And so on for almost an hour until Snob was heading in a straight line but was looking exceptionally fed up.

'That'll need a lot of work,' Hugo commented afterwards as they took a break, sitting on jumping barrels sharing a cigarette. 'You both have a very stubborn habit to break. Right, let's work on your confidence. Get that kit off.'

'What?' she yelped.

Hugo looked withering. 'The horse's, Tash, the horse's. I want to lunge you both.'

'Without the saddle?' Her eyes narrowed. She knew this trick.

'Yup.'

Ten minutes later and she was swearing every blue word she knew under her breath as Hugo lunged Snob around a jumping grid, letting him shoot out all manner of bucks and leaps and swerves which sent her sailing through the air time and time again. This was one of Hugo's favourite old training methods and he had used it before on her – it was a guaranteed bum-crushing, bone-aching short-cut to shame. Black and blue after half an hour, she called it a day.

'What possible good can this do?' She limped furiously up to him. 'Me getting flung off just encourages him to misbehave.'

'No, it doesn't.' Hugo patted Snob and checked his legs for heat. 'From where I'm standing he's getting more careful and you're less terrified every time he dips his head to take a pull or lets out a happy buck. You know the reins will drag you off if you check too hard, so you let him get on with it.'

'Bollocks! Without a saddle on, I fall off every time he lets out—'

'Not *every* time,' he corrected. 'And when you do stay on – which you certainly would if you had a saddle between you and his back – you are so pleased to have sat through it that you trust him to get over the fence without jabbing his mouth.'

'God, you're the sort of man who throws babies into swimming pools to teach them to swim, aren't you?' she muttered.

'Only some babies.' He smiled right into her eyes and she suddenly remembered with a great body-blush that one of the first conversations she had ever had with him – bang in the middle of the worst excesses of the Crush – had ended up with her falling into her mother's swimming pool.

'Are you saying I jab Snob in the mouth?' she spluttered, trying to remain furiously indignant about her bruised behind.

'Yup, but you can't really help it – it's a natural reaction to his pulling, but it's habitual and the one leads to the other. You think he's going to pull so you take a tug, and check and panic and check until he's off balance and dragging you into a fence like a bolting bison – it's no wonder he can't settle between fences, because he's so worried about what will happen when he gets there. It's why you keep having to put him in stronger and stronger bits, because he keeps fighting through them.'

'Oh.' Tash blinked. She suddenly realised that she'd only caught about two-thirds of what he'd been saying. She'd been watching his mouth, those curling lips, cool white teeth and healthy pink tongue. She wondered what it tasted like.

'Er . . .' She tried to remember what he'd been driving at. 'Well, it never happens with Hunk,' she said lamely, noticing that Hugo's eyes were the same searing blue as a Savlon tube. She would never look at a Savlon tube the same way again, she decided.

'That's because you don't do it with Hunk,' he was saying calmly. 'It's largely about the mental attitude of your partnership, and you and this guy need some serious marriage therapy. Now get his saddle on again and we'll go once around the course here to cheer you both up before calling it a day.'

Hugo rode around with her on one of his novice hopes, The Broker. They stopped after every fence to discuss how she'd taken it and, if Snob had charged into it, what she had done wrong. Tash found his advice immensely useful, although she continued to grumble and gripe and eye him up like mad when he wasn't looking. By the time they walked away from the last fence on a long rein, the sky was darkening ominously overhead and there were already lights on in Hugo's house.

'Is that Stefan?' Tash looked up at the beautiful building, its

climbing ivy fat and vivid from late-spring growth, like a revitalised perm.

'Probably.' Hugo rubbed his nose with the nub of his crop. 'He's been
with the blacksmith all afternoon. You off out with Niall to celebrate
your birthday tonight?'

Amazed he'd remembered that it was her birthday, she shook her
head. 'He's still in the States.'

'Oh.' He looked across the valley, where the last reds of the sun were
fading into the mackerel sky above the ridgeway crest.

Tash watched him in profile for a second, drinking in the straight
nose, well-defined chin and long-lashed eyes before turning to stare
fixedly between the two red points of Snob's ears.

'You looking forward to seeing him again?'

'No, I'm dreading it,' she snapped sarcastically, and then instantly
regretted it as he shot her a scornful look.

They rode on in silence for a few minutes, listening to the mournful
two-tone call of a distant cuckoo and the jangling of Broker's snaffle as
his head bobbed while he walked.

As they squelched up Twenty Acres in sombre silence, Tash felt a
long nail of skin-splitting dissatisfaction claw at her spine. I don't want
to marry Niall, she thought wretchedly.

Then she almost fell off as she realised the implications of her
thought, her hand flying to her mouth.

She wasn't sure if Hugo noticed, but thankfully he said nothing,
instead whistling for his terrier, Plod, who was snorkelling a hole
behind them.

In the floodlit yard, Jenny and another groom were giving the horses
their penultimate hard feed and supervising two youngsters from the
village who came in to clean tack for pocket money.

'Good session?' Jenny looked up at Tash from beneath the brim of
a baseball cap shaped like a banana.

Trying to stop Snob from taking flight as he clocked the cap,
Tash shot a sideways look at Hugo and nodded. 'Very construc-
tive.'

'Meaning he yelled at you a lot?' Jenny winked.

'I was a perfect gentleman.' Hugo jumped off Broker and led him
alongside Snob who was preoccupied with gaping at the banana. 'D'you
want to come in for a drink?'

Tash felt a little skip of longing in her belly as she watched him pull
off his crash cap.

She looked at the ever-blackening sky and shook her head, relieved.

'I'm risking it hacking back in this light as it is. Can I borrow some reflective stuff?'

'Nope.' Hugo scratched Snob's nose and looked up at her.

'You haven't had your present yet,' he said, watching her with amusement.

'My present?' Tash asked in confusion.

'It is your birthday today, isn't it?' he laughed.

'Yes, it's my birthday.' She grinned rather goofily because she was so pleased with this new, nice Hugo with whom she wanted to loll around all evening.

'In that case you must have a present,' he said. 'Everyone should have a present that really means something on their birthday.'

Tash quailed, aware that her – rather dull – gift for his thirtieth had disappeared into Niall's stomach.

'You don't have to give me anything,' she said, to let him off the hook. 'I mean it's not as if . . .' She trailed into an awkward silence, her pride getting in the way.

'As if what?' he asked gently.

'As if you knew today was my birthday until India mentioned it yesterday.'

'Of course I knew,' he said matter-of-factly, leading Broker off to the boxes in the far yard which were out of sight.

After he'd gone, Jenny took off her banana cap and sighed, fanning her face with it.

'You're so lucky, Tash.' She leaned across to give Snob a pat, face dreamy. 'I do envy you.'

'Why?' Tash was preoccupied watching Plod the terrier trotting towards the far yard to follow his master. She longed to do the same thing. She really had to get a grip on this resurgent crush, she told herself. She was a mature, enlightened woman and should act like one.

'I wish Hugo was as nice to me as he is to you,' sighed Jenny again, suddenly looking terribly young and insecure. 'He's hell to work for really. I wouldn't be here if I didn't fancy him so much.'

At that moment, Stefan loped out of the tack-room on his long spidery legs. Pretending to be devastated, he groaned, covering his face. 'What do I do wrong?'

'You're just too nice, Stef,' Jenny shrugged. 'And too promiscuous – everyone here knows you're called "Groom Service" because you sleep with all the prettiest stable girls, whereas the only passes Hugo makes are in the dressage ring – more's the pity.'

Empathy drenching her every pore, Tash smiled at Jenny and shook her head.

'You don't want Hugo really,' she told her rather unconvincingly. 'I used to have a honking great crush on him myself,' she confessed. 'Years ago now – before Niall,' she added quickly. 'I used to moon around at my elder sister's house staring longingly at him from behind bits of furniture. He still laughs about it.'

'You fancied Hugo?' Stefan gaped at her. 'He's never even mentioned it.'

'Hasn't he?' Tash was surprised. 'I was Jenny's age – younger even.' She glanced at Jenny in embarrassment, desperate not to sound condescending considering her own recent hormonal crisis. 'It's a bug most young women who meet him get, and it's a sign of great taste.' She smiled and then, deciding that was perhaps not strictly true, rushed on, 'I suppose fancying Hugo is like spots – you have to suffer them at one time, and they seem like they'll never go, but they do.'

'You still have them,' Stefan said with a wicked grin.

'I what?'

'You still have spots,' he pointed out. 'Well, one big one on your chin at least.'

'Thanks, Stef – no one can say you knock spots off other men.' Tash jumped off Snob and loosened his girths, suddenly longing to slope off to a loo mirror and examine her chin.

Then she spotted a streak of grey passing through the courtyard beyond and caught her breath.

The next moment the dividing gate had swung open and, with a loud clatter of hooves on flagstones and a nervous whinny, Mickey Rourke appeared through it with boggling eyes and clumsy feet that flattened Hugo's in his wake.

'Ow – get off, you bugger!' he wailed, eyes watering.

Looking confused, Mickey stood stock still and gazed worriedly around him, his dinner-plate hoof still pressing down on Hugo's foot. He was wearing an over-sized glittery 'Happy Birthday' gift tag like a rosette on one side of his big white face, obscuring most of one wall eye.

Tash let out a brief whimper of joy. Spotting her, Mickey's vacuous eyes lit up and, chortling a volley of whickers from deep within his throat, he broke free of Hugo and clattered across the yard to see her, sending two feed buckets and a wheelbarrow flying before he could dive for her pockets and head-butt her shoulders, almost pitching her into the tack room in his relief at seeing her.

Realising that Snob was looking furiously put out and gearing up for a fight with the hapless Mickey, Stefan hastily took hold of the jealous chestnut and led him away. Tash barely seemed to notice as she read the gift tag on Mickey's headcollar in near-disbelief.

'Happy Birthday,' Hugo drawled from the yard gate. 'Now don't you dare look in his mouth.'

Pressing her face into Mickey's huge grey cheek, Tash tried not to cry, knowing that her déjà vu crush was making her a risky emotional cocktail right now.

'You can't just give him to me, Hugo.' She pulled back as Mickey spotted a discarded feed bucket and clattered off to investigate, the rope from his headcollar tripping him up as he went. 'You paid tens and tens of thousands for him.'

'He's the clumsiest, stupidest horse I have ever encountered,' Hugo confessed as Mickey picked up the entire bucket between his teeth and turned to face Tash proudly. 'I don't know how the hell you got a tune out of him, but I'm going nowhere very slowly every time I get on him. He's all yours to ride on my behalf.'

'Ohmygod – thank you!' Tash raced over to him.

But Hugo hurriedly held out his arm to stop her hugging him. 'I'm not saying I'm handing over a twenty-grand horse just like that,' he went on. 'I'm technically still his owner, but you can train and compete him for me. I'm hoping the Mogo team will take on the cost if they sign you up, but that's still up in the air. I mentioned him to them, though – playing down his stupidity, of course – and they certainly sounded interested.'

'Oh, thank you so much!' Tash bounded forward and succeeded in giving him a clumsy hug.

Clearing his throat and backing away, he wandered towards the tack-room door. 'Jenny can take him back to his box while I phone the trials secretary for tomorrow's start times.'

'Shit, I forgot!' Stefan looked at his watch in horror.

'I know.' Hugo gave him a withering look. 'I just hope to God she's still around. Then we'd better all push off to the pub for a drink – it's far too dark for Tash to hack home now. Snob can stay here tonight – I'll let Gus know. Could you do him after Mickey, Jen?'

Nodding and donning her banana cap once more, Jenny shot Tash another dreamy, disbelieving look of envy and persuaded Mickey to part with his bucket.

Once they had clattered out, Hugo headed into the tack room to make the calls, Plod still at his heels.

Lounging against an open box door-frame, having taken in all the proceedings with a passive thoughtful smile, Stefan handed Snob's reins back to her. 'Happy birthday, darling.'

'Thanks.' She tickled the chestnut's twitching ears to cheer him up, goofy grin now impossible to lose.

'Why d'you think he did that?' He slouched back against the frame again and watched her closely.

Tash totally failed to notice how loaded the question was.

'He said why.' She was still reeling happily from the idea of having darling, ebullient Mickey back to ride. 'He says he can't get a tune out of him.'

'Sure.' Stefan let out a dismissive breath, the smile fading from his face. 'And you know Hugo – he's always handing over rides from the goodness of his heart.'

Not quite certain what he was driving at, Tash squinted across the yard and watched as Jenny led Mickey back to his stable, a plastic bucket handle still poking from his mouth like a belligerent teenager being hauled out of a raucous party by a concerned parent.

'Jenny's great with the horses, isn't she?' she mused. 'She has a lot more heart that Franny. I know that's mean to Franny, but she was sometimes—'

'I asked you why he's letting you have Mickey back, Tash?' Stefan straightened up. 'He's only had the horse a month. It's madness quitting so soon. Please think about it. For me.' He walked towards the house.

Tash buried her face in her hands for a moment, trying very hard to do just that. She felt as though she had been held upside down today and shaken until all her silly, preconceived ideas about Hugo had dropped out of the top of her head. Yet with the tragedy of only the best of badly timed ironies, this had coincided with her exploding hormones and dreadful, aching yearning of old. How could she hope finally to befriend the man she had coveted all those wasted years, she reasoned, when the coveting itself was making her blind again?

Hugo seemed not to notice her agitated state as he wandered back into the yard.

'We'll set off in a minute,' he told her, taking Snob and leading him into the empty box to await Jenny's attentions. 'You going to Lockington Down this year?'

Unable to look at him at all, Tash shook her head. 'I was balloted out. Niall and I are going to France that weekend instead.'

He paused for a beat, and when he spoke his voice was as smooth as black ice and tinged with the old arrogance. 'Visiting the lovely Alexandra?'

'That's it.' She watched as he tied Snob's reins out of harm's way and undid his nose band.

'Sophia and Ben are going too, aren't they?' He closed the box's half door behind him.

'First I've heard of it.' She was hardly concentrating on what he was saying at all. She felt hopelessly wound up and fretful, her attitude to him in complete tatters. She wanted to race up and down some stairs like a bush-tailed cat, clawing at the carpet to defuse her fraught nerves.

'Ben mentioned it on the phone, along with the astronomical cost of the dress Sophia has bought for the wedding.' He moved away to search for his car keys in the tack room. 'He reckons it's costing more than the bride's.'

'Knowing Mummy, I doubt that.' She closed her eyes at the thought of all those faxes of designs she had received last month, finally picking one at random just to shut her mother up and clear the fax in case Niall got in contact.

'Going for broke, huh?' Hugo had re-emerged and was watching her intently from the doorway. 'Christ, Tash, you're monumentally spoiled, aren't you?'

She glared back at him until they resembled top-seeded tennis enemies limbering up on the Queen's centre court.

'I mean, you can't even really be bothered with your own wedding, can you?' he breathed icily. 'Just let Mummy get things perfect for her little sweetheart. Talk about being joined in holy mater money!' He headed back into the tack room to fetch his coat.

'Shut up!' Tash marched after him.

'You should float your fucking wedding on the Dowry Jones index. You really do get life on a plate, don't you?' He glared at her over his shoulder.

'An L-plate maybe,' she croaked, close to tears.

'Don't be fucking flippant. You were born with a *s'il vous plaît* spoon in your mouth, Tash. All you ever say is please, please, *please*. And you've even been given a horse for your birthday to win you lots more pots. Talk about trophy wife.'

She took a deep, galvanising breath that seemed to pull air from the entire room. Jenny was clattering around in the box next-door with Snob now, cursing as he tried to nip her. But Tash didn't take her eyes from Hugo.

'If you think I'm so spoiled,' she whispered, 'then why do you spoil me too? Last year you sold me Hunk – he was one of your best horses – for peanuts. You've ferried me to events, found me a sponsor, lent me equipment, schooled me for free. Now you've lent me Mickey Rourke back again. And I've even heard that you—' She shut abruptly up as his face contracted with wariness.

'Heard what?' he breathed.

Tash gnawed her lip uncertainly.

'I've been hearing this rumour around the farm,' she started falteringly, in case she was wrong. 'About my being "subsidised". By you of all people, Hugo. I simply don't understand what's going on. I can't figure it out.'

'Well, if you can't,' he murmured, 'then I'm sure as hell not giving you the satisfaction of telling you.' But there was a nervous tic in his cheek and, despite his flippant tone, his eyes were almost eating her up.

She felt weak with fragile, terrified expectation now, blinking towards that cool, chiselled face.

'I want to think you're doing it because you might – just perhaps – quite like me?' She cringed at her inability to risk honesty.

'Gus is an old friend in a continual financial crisis,' he said levelly. 'This is one way of helping without his pride getting in the way.'

Horrified by her complete misjudgement, Tash turned to run, but Hugo was as agile as a cat. Grabbing her arm at the elbow, he stopped her in her tracks and pulled her back towards him, pinning her still in mid-swing like a stuck revolving door.

'Get one thing straight, Tash,' he said, his voice a hoarse, cracking breath. 'I'm not here for you to rebound off when Niall neglects you for a couple of weeks. I swear to you on Bod's life that I will never try to kiss you, never ask you how you feel about me, never make a move on you again.'

Wrenching her arm from his grip, Tash bolted from the tack room, crashing straight into Stefan who was coming the other way. Diving to one side like Rory Underwood on a long try, she fled past him.

'Where's the fire?' he asked with a nervous laugh.

'Burning boats,' Hugo said bitterly. 'Best tinder in the world.'

Tash escaped home as soon as she could to find that Giblets, accidentally locked inside all day, had crapped extensively over the latest dialogue script of Four Poster Bed. There were several long messages on the phone from her family wishing her a happy birthday and telling her how excited they were about the wedding.

As a special birthday treat, Polly had faxed her a charming drawing of Tash and Niall getting married – both looking scruffy, stick-legged and, Tash personally thought, spaced out on heroin.

The only person from whom there was no fax or message or card was Niall. Tash tried to kid herself that, as there was no post that day, she would get a card the next, but she didn't really believe it. She had no contact number for him in the States besides the Los Angeles film publicist's office number which, she had learned to her peril, was attached to an endless computerised phone system. Whenever she called, she was told by a simulated voice to dial '0' for the switchboard or to key in the extension number of her choice. Each time, she had tried both to no effect; the system required a touch-tone phone and the one in the forge was an antiquated Bakelite one which Niall himself had bought, thinking it another unrivalled design classic.

Hoping in vain that he would call her, she waited up by the phone and munched Just Brazils – the influx was down to one box a week now. Eventually she fell asleep on top of it, knocking the receiver off.

She woke at three in the morning to hear a strange woman's voice telling her to replace the hand-set. It was only then that she remembered Beetroot was still at the farm. A headache was already crunching at her temples.

The next day brought numerous cards, but none from Niall.

Jogging to the farm in the early-morning light, Tash arrived to find that Hugo had already dropped off both Snob and Mickey on his way to a Bank Holiday Monday event, and that she was as popular as a molehill on a bowling green.

'How are we going to afford to feed that bugger?' Gus whinged, already sour-faced from his turn at early-morning mucking out.

'Hugo said he'd cover it.' She winced at the thought.

'Sure,' he snarled. 'That man covers just about everything here – including his tracks.'

Tash froze. 'He what?'

But Gus was already heading into the next stable with his wheel-barrow.

In the kitchen, Zoe was still in her dressing gown and spitting with anger.

'Where the hell were you last night? We had a big birthday meal waiting for you for hours and you didn't even call to say you weren't coming. India is devastated – she cooked most of it.'

Tash covered her mouth in horror. 'But Hugo called to explain where I was – it got too late to hack back.'

'Don't lie, Tash.' Zoe pushed past her towards the stairs which were stacked with piles of washing to take up. 'And Niall called twice to wish you a happy birthday too. You'll be pleased to know that I lied and said you were out with some girlfriends rather than telling him the truth.'

'Why?' Tash wailed, but Zoe had already reached the landing.

Later that day India returned from school and, spotting Tash's wiped-out face, forgave her, sharing a Mars bar whilst perched on a railed fence waiting for her friend, Sadie, to come around for a pooled make-up session.

'You can join in too if you want,' India offered. 'I'll show you how to cover that spot on your chin.'

'That's really kind, but I'm a bit busy, thanks.' Tash smiled, her spot suddenly throbbing self-consciously.

India passed across her can of Coke.

'Niall didn't really phone,' she confessed, thinking she was cheering Tash up. 'Mummy made that up.'

'Why?' Tash was amazed.

'She feels protective towards him, I think.' India looked guarded. 'She thinks you might neglect him a little bit.'

'We neglect each other,' Tash sighed sadly.

Later, she cornered Gus in the tack room, spot glowing angrily.

'Why didn't you say Hugo had called last night?'

'Because he asked me what I'd say if he gave you Mickey to ride again.'

'And what did you say?'

His blond brows creased angrily. 'That you didn't deserve it.'

The atmosphere towards her at the farm remained frosty up until her meeting with the Mogo men on Wednesday. No one wished her luck or even noticed her and the design classic leaving the yard and heading towards Marlbury just before midday.

The lunch, in an exclusive ivy-clad restaurant that Tash had been to several times with Niall in happier days, went well. Whether they agreed to take her on for the rest of the season because they genuinely thought she'd be good for business or just because her dress split at the front halfway through dessert, Tash couldn't be sure, but she raced back to the farm afterwards dizzy with delight, not even caring that the design classic was hopping along as though driving over corrugated steel the entire way. She thought about popping in at the forge to change en route, but was too eager to tell her news to bother.

Her reception was far from enthusiastic. Only Ted seemed pleased for her, cracking open a bottle of Newcastle Brown Ale in her honour and admiring her bra.

'I can see what I've been doing wrong all these years,' Gus said nastily. 'I've been wooing potential sponsors with all my clothes on. Now I know what getting abreast of the competition means.'

Tash's face flamed with humiliation.

'Does this mean I might get paid now?' Franny asked hopefully. 'Only Hugo asked for his money back when he dropped Tash's horse off this morning.'

A week later and Niall still hadn't called. Realising that she had shared her bed more often with Beetroot than with Niall of late, Tash knew something had to be done. She was now absolutely certain that she no longer wanted to marry him. She couldn't last a weekend in his company without longing for someone stronger, less paranoid, less emotional. Not that she got the chance to spend a weekend in his company very often, she realised. She loved him with a furious, proud devotion and she missed him desperately, but she no longer spent sleepless nights squirming with desire for him, conducting imaginary conversations and staring tearfully at the phone as though it personally was to blame for his not calling. She yearned for someone with whom she could share common interests, common friends, time. More than anything she longed for Hugo, but he had made it patently obvious that he was out of bounds, that he despised her shallow, drooling crush and had only ever helped her as an indirect way of bailing out his old friend Gus from the debt-swamp. He'd made it as patently obvious as a pimp's loafers that he still saw her as a childish, lusting push-over and played on that for his own entertainment. The memory of her awful, clumsy attempts to draw him out haunted her night after night.

Ten days after her birthday, a huge, tacky, fake-fur Vegas card arrived by Data-post along with half a dozen bottles of Chanel nail varnish in colours unavailable in the UK. The card read:

Darling Tash.
Happy Birthday.
Back in UK next week, so muzzle Turnip. (This had been scribbled out and 'Beetroot' written over it.) *The nail varnishes are an absolute die-for-it necessity amongst women according to my publicity girl. These things are a mystery to me but I'm sure you'll know all about them.*

Hopelessly in love with you, as always.
Give my love to Zoe.
Niall.

His handwriting was all over the place, showing how much he'd had to drink when scribbling it.

As she had practically no nails at all, Tash used the most garish pink among the bottles to stem the ladders in all her tights and then painted Beetroot's claws, which looked wonderfully jaunty. Even that failed to cheer Tash up.

She was as wrung out with guilt as a chamois leather in a desert. Niall had written that he was hopelessly in love with her. That sentence bored holes the size of meteor craters into her soul, and Tash picked up the card again and again to scour the words and torture herself.

Zoe was right. She did neglect him. She was totally incapable of looking after him, simply didn't possess the confidence to chase him through international time zones and telephone systems, gutlessly wimping out at the first dropped call. Yet he still invested so much of his huge, boundless faith in her. It terrified her that he loved her so much when her own enthusiasm for the relationship – and for the wedding – had drained away like sand through splayed fingers. If he'd held her hand over the past few months, the grains might have stayed put, but he continually shifted like the sand itself. He was the chameleon and she the faithful old stick of a reliable hue he habitually returned to in order to ground himself. Tash felt utterly wretched that her feelings towards him had changed so irrevocably. He was the one who reinvented himself with every role, turned from all-conquering hero to faithless bounder at the drop of a script. And yet he still loved her 'hopelessly'. She wanted to die of shame and self-hatred. The one comfort, she thought forlornly, was that she was in an ideal position to wear a horse-hair shirt.

Zoe seemed incredibly touched that Niall had remembered her in his card, asking if he was truly okay.

'I think he was pissed when he wrote it,' Tash confessed. She kept remembering Hugo saying at his party that Niall was an alcoholic. He had said it with the same total conviction as if asserting Niall was Irish.

'Oh, Tash,' Zoe sighed in despair. 'Only you could possibly say that at this stage.' She sounded genuinely furious, curtailing the confession Tash had been working up to about her current emotional turmoil. She found Zoe increasingly difficult to approach these days.

Her mother called the weekend before they were due to fly to France.

'Are you both terribly excited?'

'Well, I haven't spoken to Niall recently, but I think he's looking forward to having a rest and seeing you and Pascal, yes,' Tash hedged. She had been dreading the trip all week.

'I meant, are you excited about the wedding?' Alexandra laughed. 'Not long now, huh?'

'No, you're right,' Tash sighed. 'I haven't got long at all.'

Twenty-Six

LE MANOIR CHAMPEGNY GLOWED like hot, buttered toast in the evening sun, its medieval turrets pointing manicured fingers to the sky.

Bumping the hire car over the cattle grid at the entrance of the long front drive – once neglected but now restored to its endless, straight-spined splendour – Tash glanced across at Niall and noticed that he had finally woken up and was staring at the house in rapt awe, his mouth open.

'I always forget how stunning it is,' he murmured. It was the longest sentence he had spoken to her since they had got off the train, so she supposed she should be grateful.

The sun was now so low that it just peeked over the horizon, blushing furiously and squinting through the pollarded poplars that lined the drive, striping the pale Tarmac with shadows like a humbug.

Alexandra was in her usual state of crisis, surrounded by panting spaniels, fabric swatches, wedding magazines and faxed florists' quotes, but still looking radiant in a bubblegum pink tunic dress. She'd recently had her sleek bob cut into a neat pageboy's mop, revealing her face and adding yet more to her awesome, age-defying glamour.

'You look wonderful, Mummy.' Tash raced forward to give her a hug.

Finally pulling out of the clinch so that she could look at her daughter properly, Alexandra longed to be able to say the same thing in return but found she couldn't. Tash looked tired, drawn and spotty; her hair hung lankly and her eyes were dull and spiritless.

'You look rapturous, Alexandra,' Niall said flamboyantly, giving her a stubbly kiss which Alexandra noticed had a strong taste of Irish distilleries about it.

'I've embarked on a long term tart-up programme for the wedding,' she explained. 'I've been slapping on tightening, softening, smoothing and invigorating balms every morning after my shower. Pascal is convinced I'm going embalmy.'

Both Tash and Niall took a couple of beats before they laughed along with her. They were impossibly tense-necked and nervy.

'You must be quite exhausted, you poor things,' she soothed. 'You've both been working so hard lately. You simply have to loll around and relax this weekend – I insist.'

She led them through the ornate, echoing house to her favourite retreat, the China Room, which was packed to the skirting boards with all manner of pots and vases like a hollow Giant's Causeway across the floor with paths between to allow access to the furniture.

'Now sit down while I fetch you a drink.' She pushed yet more wedding magazines from a threadbare red silk sofa. 'Pascal is in Paris today – he can travel back with us all tomorrow night.'

'He can what?' Tash watched her mother in confusion as she dashed out of the room.

She looked at Niall quizzically, but he was too busy saying hello to the spaniels to have heard. He still had his sideburns from playing Huntingdon, although the shoot had been wrapped several weeks earlier. He had grown rather attached to them now and had an irritating habit of stroking them absent-mindedly with the back of his finger so that they stood out like fans. Tash loathed them.

'What did you mean about Pascal travelling back with *us* tomorrow, Mummy?' she asked as Alexandra wafted back into the room with a bottle of local Blanc de Saumur and three rather smudgy glasses. 'We're already here.'

'Oh, didn't I say?' Alexandra laughed gaily, placing the glasses on a low table and gazing around for the corkscrew – Pascal was famous for keeping one in every room, like Liberace's pianos. 'I'm going to drive you to Paris tomorrow morning. You have an appointment with the dressmaker at three,' she explained breezily. 'So I've arranged to meet Sophia, Ben and Pascal at Le Grand Véfour for a boozy lunch, then we girls can leave the chaps to their brandies while we get you kitted out before driving back here in the Espace. It'll be fun.'

'Kitted out?' Tash repeated weakly.

'A dress-fitting, darling!' Alexandra exclaimed disbelievingly. 'You can't expect to get away without one, surely? Sophia simply can't *believe* we've left it so late as it is. She and Ben have come over here specifically because she wants to be on hand to advise you, which I think is jolly kind, darling, don't you?'

Tash noticed Niall was tweaking his sideburns rather maniacally now.

'Christ!' She gaped at Niall, who was still offering no reaction. 'I didn't know about any of this.' But Alexandra's mind had moved on to menus as she started to lay out prospective ideas in front of Tash, catering for vegetarians, diabetics and Hay Diet followers.

Half an hour later and Tash and Niall were briefly relieved from discussing the various merits of turbot over salmon by the distant ringing of a phone.

'Drat – I'll be right back. Think about wild strawberry mousse with three-chocolate sauce while I'm gone, will you?'

'Shit – she's turned into Sophia,' Niall groaned after Alexandra had left the room. 'I always wondered where your sister got it from. I've never seen so many lists – it's like being trapped with a manic production secretary.' He picked up several menu mock-ups and waggled them around in despair before throwing them over his shoulder.

'It's all got a bit out of hand, hasn't it?' Tash winced. 'I had no idea they'd done this much – and on this scale.'

'Well, it makes it bloody tough to back out now.' He stood up and grabbed the wine bottle. 'I'm going for a walk.'

Tash watched him stepping out of the high french windows and on to the terrace, now swamped in darkness. Soon his footsteps retreated and she could only hear the creaking of the crickets outside, sounding as though they were all tipping back and forth on individual rocking chairs as they enjoyed the evening air.

It was the first time Niall had broached the subject of calling the wedding off – however glibly. Tash felt as though she had been punched in the chest. Relief was drenching her with heat, but it still hurt so much that tears kissed her eyelids.

She closed her eyes. She had known for ages that she and Niall were no longer communicating properly, talking honestly or making one another happy. They hadn't had a decent conversation or laughed together in weeks. If they had argued endlessly, Tash would be able to understand things better, but it seemed they had simply stopped caring for one another in that delightful, mutually reliant way they once had. Outsiders might blame it on wedding nerves and stress from so much planning, but it was evident that neither of them had done any planning at all; they had simply allowed others to assume the task, hoping that somehow, if they ignored it, it would go away. And now that they were less than a month away from the day itself, they were both completely appalled that it was really happening after all. It was like getting into a drunken conversation at a right-on party and casually agreeing to do some voluntary work for a charity, only to find weeks later that one's flight was booked to a war-torn African state, the bullet-proof vest ordered and a date fixed for swamp-fever immunisation.

Weeks ago, during Niall's giddy Huntingdon phase, they had travelled to Marlbury for a boozy lunch with his agent, Bob Hudson. Two bottles of wine up and giggling like kids, they had filled in a marriage notice at the register office. Their names had been pinned up outside ever since, along with those of countless other young local couples. On the odd occasions Tash had passed by, she had longed to take a great, black marker pen and cross them out. Calling everything off had seemed that simple but in reality it was infinitely more complicated, and she had absolutely no idea where to start. She felt desperately alone.

The prospect was made even harder after a day in Paris.

Niall elected to stay behind at the *manoir* and lounge by the pool, claiming exhaustion. Tash envied him, settled in a sun lounger with a long, cool drink and a hot, hot sun overhead.

Insects danced in Pascal's rampant, overgrown garden and the only noises that split the warm, dusty air were the distant grumble of a tractor criss-crossing a field and the rhythmic lapping of the pool against its tiled edges, tempo as leisurely as a tired, drunken blues band.

In contrast, the tooting, hooting traffic en route to Paris was a fanfare of mosquitoes hungry for blood. Endless rows of cars stretched out along the heat-hazed roads, as shiny and colourful as the long strips of plastic-encased bon-bons that hung outside the streetside shops.

Feeling sick the entire way, Tash alternately breathed in the lung-freezing, plastic smell of the Espace's air conditioning and then buzzed down the window for a hot chestful of fresh exhaust fumes.

Alexandra didn't once stop talking about weddings.

In central Paris, the tourists were out in force, clogging up the roads in hire-cars, taxis and coaches, and grid-locking the pavements in a shuffling, sight-seeing crocodile of bad-taste shirts. Alexandra drove around in endless circles searching for somewhere to park close to Palais Royale. As a result they arrived at the restaurant almost an hour late, to find Sophia holding court as she was fawned over by Ben and Pascal, and even her young half-sister, Polly, who was eight and had recently developed a keen, if eccentric, fashion sense. Allowed to run amok by her indulgent father, Polly was wearing a bizarre orange rubber t-shirt, lime green velvet hot pants and a pink beret. Finished off with Lolita sunglasses and badly applied red lipstick, she looked like a paedophile's hot date. In contrast, Sophia was even more understated than ever in knee-length, bias-cut Galliano.

'I keep telling her to wipe that stuff off, Mummy,' Sophia greeted her mother with a kiss and a hiss. 'But she just slaps more on – and it's Lancaster. I assume it's yours?'

'It must be,' Alexandra greeted Pascal and Ben with a kiss before enveloping her daughter in a big hug. '*Chérie!* Did you have a good week at school?'

'*Oui, Maman.*' Polly kissed her mother's nose, leaving it port-drinker's crimson with lipstick. 'I kissed two boys and I get ze top mark for my *histoire.*'

'Well, I'm delighted for you on both counts.' Alexandra let her daughter struggle free as she raced to Tash for a hug. 'Have you ordered for us, darling?' She looked to Pascal. 'So sorry we're late.'

'Ees okay,' Pascal patted the seat beside him. 'But I order for Niall too – he coming, *non?*'

'No,' Alexandra dropped her voice furtively, checking that Sophia and Ben were still busy talking to Tash about the awful traffic. 'All is definitely not right there – both the pour souls look washed up, over and out. We must talk later.'

Pascal nodded tactfully.

'Still dieting?' Sophia asked pointedly as Tash fiddled later with her cherry *clafoutis.* 'You'll have to stabilise your weight once the dress is fitted, you know – for God's sake don't do a Princess Di and walk up the aisle with enough room for Will Carling in your bodice.'

The wedding-dress fitting was something Tash could never have dreamed up during all her youthful illusions of fairytale weddings and floating silk organza – most of these involving Hugo waiting for her at the altar, eyes ablaze with love.

The design house was halfway along avenue Montaigne, and one had to ring a bell and wait to be shown in by a very sleek woman with a huge bun as shiny as patent leather and green suit cut so sharply, Tash was afraid she would gash herself on it as she brushed past. Upstairs, they were ushered into a large, overtly Baroque cream room littered with plump footstools, curvaceous sofas and hour-glass mirrors. The whole effect was as succulently feminine as a Rubens nude. Tash was terrified to tread on the plush cream carpet for fear of staining it. The place horrified her – it was like a sterile, man-made cream womb.

She was ordered into a cubicle with vast mirrors set in each of its cream marble walls and told to strip. Waiting in her bra and knickers – thankfully a matching pair, although she was ashamed of their three-year-old M & S status – she almost fainted as the door was whipped open and she was tutted at by Patent Bun before it was slammed closed again. Moments later, items of cream silk underwear were being thrust at her, price tags swinging. One garter belt cost more than a winter coat.

Outside, Tash could hear Alexandra and Sophia chattering, but above them was the unmistakable squeak of rubber as Polly approached the door.

'The lady, she ask you to leave your pants on when you put on the lingerie,' she translated. 'But she wants the full effort – I mean, effect, *oui*?'

'*Oui*.' Tash struggled into the underwear, which was far more complicated than her usual type – all cross-lacing, multiple hooks and delicate ribbon ties. Once she was ensconced, and feeling like a trussed turkey, she was fitted into a part-silk, part-calico mock-up dress which was full of pins, loose stitches and strange holes. It was like clambering into a kinky S & M kit, although she doubted they usually came with a watered cream silk fish-tail skirt.

Tripping out of her changing room – pleased to move away from so many reflections of her sun-reddened face and dreadful hair – she was greeted by muted reactions from Alexandra and Sophia, although Polly wolf-whistled and expressed admiration for the pins.

'It's a bit of a tent on her, isn't it?' Sophia tilted her head. She and their mother were sitting on a cream chaise-longue, drinking espresso from tiny ivory cups. Tash was certain that, had she been holding one, she would have thrown it over the hated dress – and legged it towards the gare du Nord and the Eurostar express.

But, aware that her mother was spending a fortune on it, she said nothing.

'You've lost so much weight since I took your measurements last Christmas,' Alexandra sighed, watching as Patent Bun twitched around Tash, pulling pins from between her teeth and tightening the fit.

Tash felt as though she was being fitted into a strait-jacket. With every tuck and fold, she lost a little more freedom.

Patent Bun was waffling on about the need for further fittings, but Alexandra shook her head. '*C'est impossible – ma fille demeure en Angleterre.*' She raised her hands in apology.

Eyes narrowing, Patent Bun thrust a pin deep into Tash's bottom.

There then followed a trail of head-dresses, veils, shoes, stockings and jewellery which Tash couldn't hope to take in. She listlessly picked several at random and then acquiesced as Sophia and her mother argued her towards others. She didn't care. She wasn't going to marry Niall. This was all an awful, expensive mistake and she wanted to scream it in Patent Bun's face as she frisked around as attentively as Cariola attending the Duchess of Malfi during her last desperate hours of life.

As soon as they were out of the cosseted cream womb, Tash grabbed her mother's arm. 'I need to talk to you, Mummy – can we go for a coffee?'

Looking at her watch, Alexandra grimaced. 'You were due at the salon quarter of an hour ago, sweetheart. And I said I'd go and fetch Pascal and Ben while you're there.'

'Salon?'

'The top hair-stylists in Paris,' Sophia corrected. 'And I'm being done too, so we can sit and gossip beneath the drier – I'm dying to know which of Niall's famous friends are coming to the wedding. Has Brad Pitt said yes? He's frightfully dishy.'

Twenty-Seven

WHEN THEY RETURNED TO the *manoir*, Niall was already two-thirds of the way down a bottle of wine, and fell about laughing when he caught sight of Tash.

'Christ, angel, you look like Crystal Tips!' He bounded over to kiss her and say 'hi' to the others, spinning a delighted Polly around and around in an exuberant hug until she was screaming with laughter, her rubber-top squeaking.

Despite the disastrously unflattering new cut, Tash cheered up considerably; his mood was much, much cheerier than the night before. Relaxed by a long sleep in the sun and a ramble down to the village bar for a baguette and beer at lunchtime, he was bright-eyed and animated.

Outside on the terrace, Tash sat in one of the last patches of evening sun, finding herself between Sophia and her mild-mannered brother-in-law, who was having considerable difficulty erecting a wooden Raj chair which collapsed every time he sat in it. Once he was finally on board, its long leg rests swung round and trapped him inside like a child in a high chair. Not seeming to care, he placed his drink on the wooden bar in front of him and donned a pair of scratched dark glasses that made him look like a blond Hank Marvin.

'You seen much of old Hugo lately?' Ben asked her, scratching his chin with the rim of his glass.

She shook her head, watching Niall wander towards a balustraded wall to stare out across the darkening valley, his dark eyes crinkled against the sun so that he almost looked to be wincing in pain.

'He's been keeping a pretty low profile lately,' said Tash, unwilling to say too much. 'I saw him at the Blewford trials last week, but he left early.' He had fallen off a novice that day, cracking a rib and consequently scratching all his other entries and leaving in a high old rage. Stefan, who had also been competing, had been forced to beg a lift back to Maccombe with the Moncrieffs after Hugo had sulkily abandoned him.

'You won a couple of classes there, didn't you?' Ben tried to cross his legs and found that the bar in front of him prevented it. Instead he sat knock-kneed like a bashful debutante.

'Just one.' She took a slurp of her drink and winced as she realised how strong it was. Alexandra always poured pastis as though it would evaporate on contact with the glass. 'I won an intermediate class with Mickey Rourke.'

'Is that the chestnut beast?' asked Sophia, who never kept up with Tash's horses.

'Dappled grey,' she corrected. 'Hugo bought him from Gus a while back, but they didn't get on, so he's given me the ride. My new sponsors are covering the cost.'

'I must say, Tash, you're doing exceptionally well – bloody well.' Ben raised his glass approving. 'I keep hearing your name being bandied around as a new hot shot – should be capped soon, huh?'

Hating to tempt fate, Tash shrugged.

'Surely you wear a cap, darling?' Alexandra asked in concern. 'I thought they made you these days – for safety reasons?'

'Are you going to take more of a back seat in the sport once you're married?' Sophia asked rather crushingly. She hated to hear about her sister doing well, especially from Ben.

'Of course not,' she muttered, not wanting to talk about it.

'But you'll want to start a family soon, surely?'

'Nope.' She noticed that Niall had already drained his drink and was still staring out at the valley, eyes performing their Clint Eastwood enigmatic trick.

'Oh.' Sophia looked across at Niall as well. 'I must say you've both lost bags of weight recently – have you been dieting together?'

'No, we're just starved of conversation,' said Tash sadly.

That night, Tash was hugely grateful to Niall for holding their shabby act together at dinner. He regaled them all with scandalous anecdotes about his recent films, didn't drink so much that he lost his edge and only flirted a moderate amount with Sophia, who looked delighted by his sparkly-eyed flattery and obvious admiration for her beauty. Even Ben seemed delighted that his wife merited such attention. Tash privately thought him a terrible wimp, and found to her horror that she was comparing Ben's reaction to that she imagined from his closest crony, Hugo. He would have made no secret of the fact that he was irritated by Niall's behaviour and either bawled him out for it or employed the subtler tactic of flirting twice as brazenly with Tash in return. The thought made her feel rather heady.

'What are you sinking about, Tash?' Pascal asked, pouring her another glass of wine, his wise eyes watching her affectionately.

'Oh – only Hugo,' she said mindlessly. Unfortunately this came at a lull in the conversation at the table and the others turned to her in astonishment.

'I was – er – just thinking how awful it would be to lose Snob as he did his horse Surfer,' she went on, flustered into an obvious, ham-fisted lie.

'Oh, I see.' Pascal turned back to fill his wife's glass, dropping his voice and whispering in her ear, 'I was just going to say 'ow 'appy she was looking. I assumed she was sinking about the wedding.'

'Right now,' Alexandra regarded her daughter over her husband's head, 'I think that's the last thing on Tash's mind.'

In bed that night, Sophia removed the witch-hazel aromatherapy pads from her eyes, rubbed in the last of her lipo-reactive, sebocel-firming face cream and turned to her husband.

'Am I right in thinking that you once – mistakenly – believed Hugo to be rather fond of Tash?'

Ben guffawed affectionately and put down the copy of the *Telegraph*, which he had bought at the Waterloo Eurostar terminal three days earlier and had been reading ever since; he had yet to reach the Court and Social pages.

'Yes – barking up the wrong tree there, huh?'

'I'm not so sure.' Sophia slipped off her wrist watch and stretched across to the bedside table to put it down. 'I rather think I underestimated your judgement, darling.'

'Oh, do you?' Ben – who was very seldom complimented on his acumen and perception – looked delighted. 'What makes you say that?'

'Whenever one talks to Tash about Niall, she adopts the look of a long-suffering sister excusing the antics of a ruffian brother. But when one mentions Hugo, she looks just as she did as a teenager – all flustered and guilty and rather on her nerves. She had a huge crush on him for years, you know.'

'So she did – rather a hoot that.' Ben folded the *Telegraph* into a very neat triangle and cast it to one side. 'But what makes you think I was right about old Hugs's feelings?'

'Because, my darling,' Sophia kissed him on the nose before turning to the bedside light, 'he looks exactly the same way when one mentions her.' She flicked the switch. 'But without the flustered bit, natch.'

'Natch.' Ben head-butted his way into the bolster beside her before stretching a tentative hand across to her thigh.

'Not now, darling.' Sophia firmly steered it away. 'I've got fat-reducing cream on my stomach. Tomorrow perhaps.'

'Oh – right-oh.' He gave her hand a squeeze. 'Night then.'

'Night.' Sophia strained her ears for sounds of activity in the next room, but there were none.

Tash lay awake for hours, trying to muster the nerve to elbow Niall awake and have everything out, but she couldn't pluck up the courage and besides, she told herself, he badly needed his sleep at the moment. She waited and waited for her own dreams to arrive and deaden the panic in her head, but they would not come. Instead she once again watched the dawn lighten the room and listened to the morning chorus rise and work through its vocal exercises.

Sophia and Ben were already taking morning showers and chatting loudly over the gushing water in the next room when she fell into the bottomless pit of a dreamless sleep.

She woke at midday to find the shutters and windows open, and sun drenching her body. Beside her, Niall's side of the bed was creased and vacant. Blinking and peering out of the window whilst wrapped in a sheet, Tash could just see the corner of the balcony which overlooked the pool. A cloud of cigarette smoke was drifting from it, signifying that Niall was there. He was the only guest other than herself who smoked.

Dressed in a borrowed bikini of her mother's and Sophia's apple green sarong, Tash took her very pale and rather stubbly body outside to be put on show beside the pool.

Sophia was already reclining on a sun lounger looking as though every ounce of her had recently been tightened and glossed at great expense. Beside her Ben was turning the subtle pink of uncooked turkey flesh, only his nose having burnt to a rare beefsteak red.

Reading a book on wedding etiquette, Alexandra was sensibly confined beneath a sun-shade, wearing a bright yellow bathing suit that showed off the mahogany glow of her skin.

'Tash darling!' she greeted her delightedly. 'I so envy you your ability to sleep – do have a swim.'

Beside her, Pascal sipped pastis and read the papers, his own deep, burnt oak tan confined beneath cream chinos and a pale blue shirt.

'Tash, *chérie*,' he looked up from *Le Monde*, 'you look sensational – the pale English skin is so *délicat*, like a rose petal, *non*?'

'Er – *non*.' Desperate to hide her midge-bitten paleness, she greeted Polly, who was splashing around in the pool wearing a super-trendy crocheted bikini. Badgered endlessly, Tash joined her in a raucous game of 'dive for the brick' followed by 'singing underwater' and then 'race widths with arm-bands on ankles and floats stuffed down tops'. Tash longed for the confidence boost of winning something right now but she lost everything, her concentration in smithereens. All the time she was aware of an audience from high up on the balcony as Niall sat chain-smoking, drinking black coffee out of a bowl and watching them all like a psychologist regarding specimens of human behaviour through a two-way mirror.

This is where we fell in love! Tash wanted to scream up at him. What went wrong?

But she simply swam widths and lengths and dived and forward-rolled until her eyes were red and stinging from chlorine, and her fingers were as wrinkled as tinned chestnuts.

'I love you, Tash!' Polly screamed happily as she pinned her half-sister to a flapping pool filter with her water-gun. '*Je t'aime!*'

'Will you marry me then?' Tash asked bleakly.

After lunch, she and Niall found themselves side by side at the pool's edge sunbathing. Unknown to Tash, Alexandra had spread the word amongst the rest of the family to leave them alone together for a couple of hours. She had spotted the heavy silence between them and wanted to give them a chance to kiss and make up. Tash felt more like socking Niall's kisser in a punch up, but knew that she was just channelling her frustration at her own dithering inertia into illogical hatred, like Hamlet screaming at Ophelia to get to a nunnery. She wondered vaguely whether she herself might take advantage of a few years in a novice's wimple? Swapping wedding vows for those of chastity and silence seemed quite tempting right now.

Niall seemed oblivious of her mental churning as he dozed and reposed, buried behind a very intellectual biography of Goethe.

Tash, who was being bitten to itchy distraction by hungry May midges, scratched her stubbly legs and reached alternately for the sun-oil and the insect repellent. Niall only spoke to her when requesting one to be passed in his direction, as formal as a fellow client in a sun-bed salon.

He was buried deep within his book, reading as quickly and avidly as ever; Tash had always envied him his ability to get thoroughly absorbed. She found herself struggling with a magazine these days, which she believed to be a give-away sign of deadened braincells and lack of depth. She had once guzzled literary worthies, biographies, escapist trash and art books with a devotee's relish – just as she had been able to reel off the Radio 4 schedule, the latest music sensations, best exhibitions and thought-provoking films. Nowadays she was stretched to remember the news headlines. However busy he was, Niall would never fail to keep up with the news, views and previews of the world's opinion-pollsters. Tash, raced off her feet and confined within the insular world of eventing, knew more about the latest craze in tendon-protection than the latest Terry Johnston play. She sometimes wished she was like Zoe who, although living within that world too, kept her intellectual life intact; Tash had often found her at the kitchen table poring over the review section of the Sunday papers, or covertly watching an arty video which she had recorded whilst the others were glued to *Soldier Soldier*. Tash was acutely aware of her intellectual inadequacies, and of the way she had changed since meeting Niall. Their mutual interests were crumbling away, and it was almost entirely her fault. He remained within his ivory tower while she'd clambered down a rope-ladder and run away to the stable-yard.

He finally looked up from his biography after almost an hour to tell her off for leaving the sun-oil out of the shade so that it sizzled against his skin like hot cooking fat when he rubbed some on his belly – nowadays quite ample from so much drinking.

'You had it last,' she reminded him, flicking a fly from her face.

'Well, in that case you should use it more often,' he snapped. 'Or you'll burn.'

'I tan more easily than you.'

'But you have moles which are a danger sign,' he said priggishly, picking up his book with a haughty sigh.

'They're not moles, they're isolated freckles,' she grumbled, but he was feigning fascination with a foot-note now. She stared at the pool, ultra-violet bright in the sun. 'You once said you loved every one of my moles, Niall.'

'All the more reason for not wanting them to develop into skin cancer now.' He didn't look up. 'And I thought they were isolated freckles?'

She propped herself up on one elbow and shaded her eyes with one hand to look at him.

'You still love them?'

'Course I do.' He turned a page with a carefully licked finger.

'Is the biggest one to the left or the right of my belly button?'

But he considered this question too petty to answer.

Twenty minutes later she could bear it no longer.

'Please stop stroking your sideburns like that,' she pleaded. 'It's driving me to distraction.'

'They itch in this heat.'

'Well, shave them off.'

'I like them.'

'Fine – just don't stroke them.'

He stopped, burying himself so moodily between the pages of his book that he was practically wearing it as a nose-shield.

Minutes later he had thrown it down.

'Will you stop doing that!' he snarled.

Just drifting off to sleep, Tash jumped so much that she pitched off her lilo, landing on the insect repellent which oozed out on to the paving stones.

'Doing what?' She blinked at him in bleary-eyed confusion. There was a foul smell of citrus and eucalyptus everywhere.

'Those sort of shuddery sighs.' He propped himself into a half sit-up and peered at her over his dark glasses, belly creasing like a German sausage.

'Sorry.' She clambered back on to the lilo. 'I wasn't aware that I had been. I was falling asleep.'

'That stands to reason – you do it in bed too.'

'Well, you should have mentioned it before.'

'You were always asleep.'

Tash irritably wiped insect repellent from her knees.

'Do you have to smear so much of that on?' He rolled on to his side so that she was faced with his red, towel-pocked back, sweating at the neck where it had been in contact with the hot plastic of the lilo.

Ten minutes later they were both at boiling point, swatting flies and picking dust from their swimwear as they desperately sought excuses to pick on one another.

Ironically the final straw came from an entirely innocent source as one of Alexandra's spaniels came trotting up, stumpy tail gyrating as it offered them a well-gnawed tennis ball to be thrown.

'The dog wants a game.' Niall didn't look up from his book.

'It's asking you, not me,' Tash pointed out as the dog dropped the ball eagerly on Niall's sunburned bare foot.

'I'm reading.' He flipped a page with a morose snatch.

'Well, I'm going to have a swim.' Tash started to get up.

'Oh, for Christ's sake, play with the wee dog for a few minutes first, huh?' He glared at her angrily.

'I'll play with it afterwards.' She pulled down her swimsuit where it was rucked up her bottom and searched for her scrunchy.

Niall was determined to win this bout. 'Meanwhile it's going to bug me, so I can't concentrate on my book,' he complained.

'Well, you play with it then.' Tash found her scrunchy half-hidden beneath Niall's lilo and scrabbled to extract it.

'What the fuck are you doing?' He shifted away.

'Getting my hair-band.' Tash noticed that the spaniel, thinking this was all part of the game, had started to join in, barking excitedly, snatching for the scrunchy and finally sinking its teeth into the lilo, which gave an ominous hiss so that the dog leaped away in alarm and almost fell in the pool.

'Now look what you've done!' Niall grumbled, shifting around as the lilo started to lose air like a hovercraft clocking off its shift.

'I didn't bite the bloody thing.' She began to tie back her hair so furiously that her wrists became entrapped in the velvet band along with great hunks of hair until she had effectively tethered her hands to the back of her head.

'Bugger – my – ouch – hands are – shit!' Struggling to free herself, she tripped over Niall's legs, now flailing around beneath her as he fought to stay comfortable on the sagging lilo. As she pitched forward, hopelessly off-balance, she was faced with the split-second choice of falling on to hard tiles or soft Niall. The latter seemed the more attractive option in the moment that she had to contemplate it and she landed quite hard on top of him.

'Fucking ouch!' he howled, trapped underneath her. 'I think you've just smashed my ribs – get off.'

'I'm trying!'

Still unwillingly adopting the armpit-flashing position of the hands-on-head scrunchy prisoner, Tash tried and failed to roll away. Their skin, oiled and re-oiled in the past hour, formed a messy suction which let out scatological noises every time she moved, but stubbornly glued them together.

'Just came out to see if you wanted a drink!' cried a cheerful voice from the balcony. 'Oh – on second thoughts.' Alexandra slipped tactfully away, calling back the excited spaniel which was now trying to devour the belt string on Niall's trunks, pulling them almost over his hips as part of the fun.

Finally freeing her wrists, Tash heaved herself off him and straightened up sheepishly, surveying the damage. He was looking exceedingly pissed off and his book was very flat and oily, but his body seemed relatively uncrushed.

'What the hell did you do that for?' he complained, dusting himself down and peeling the book from his chest, eyes blazing furiously over his sun-specs.

'You tripped me up,' she muttered, backing away and turning to dive into the pool before he could push her in.

Unfortunately she belly-flopped in her haste, stinging her chest and legs as though diving on to burning sand, and sending up a great splash of water which doused Niall and his precious book.

When she resurfaced, he was waiting on her lilo for the attack, his own having deflated fully now.

'Okay, what is it?' he growled as she clambered out of the pool via the slippery ladder and headed for her towel, inadvertently dripping all over his melting packet of M and Ms.

'What is what?' She wrapped herself in the fluffy rectangle and searched for somewhere to settle. Niall's slippery, deflated lilo didn't tempt her, so she perched on a grubby sun-lounger instead.

'You obviously want to have a go at me.' He brushed his hair out of his eyes and glared at her. 'So now's your chance.'

Tash felt her heart lurch, aware that he had stopped peering at her frustrated moodiness through the letter-box and had now opened the door to beckon her in. This was her chance. She just wished she didn't feel quite so sun-boiled, tetchy and baited. She longed to be serene, sympathetic and sophisticated, and approach him as Zoe would – all gentle probing and quiet persistence. Instead she felt like listing every single complaint she had about him, down to leaving the loo seat up.

'I don't want to have a go at you, Niall,' she started cautiously, anxious not get this wrong. 'It's just that you've been so uncommunicative and grumpy lately, I feel very uncomfortable with it, that's all.'

'I've been fine,' he protested sourly. 'It's you who's been snappy and sulky.'

'I'm under a lot of pressure right now!' She rubbed her forehead.

'Me too.' He rubbed his too until they resembled a pair of chess masters stuck in stalemate.

For a moment they stared at one another in silence. Tash wished he'd take his dark glasses off; it was like trying to talk nicely to a beefcake bouncer at a night-club – the dark wraparound goggles were terribly confrontational.

'You have no time for me or my interests anymore,' she tried again, horribly aware that she was starting to recite a list. 'You keep cutting me out of your life.'

'So do you!'

'I don't think our lives encompass one another's any more – they're in different universes.' She reached for a cigarette. 'I'm frightened by the people you work with, Niall – they're arrogant and self-seeking and capricious. I have nothing in common with them, and sometimes, when you seem to be so in love with them, I wonder if I have anything in common with you.'

'How dare you say that of my friends!' He snatched the fag packet from her and lit one up himself. 'Especially when the eventers you hang out with are snobbish, shallow, and boorish to buggery.'

Tash took a deep breath. 'Perhaps that's how you see me too?'

He didn't answer, confirming her worse doubts and pinning down her determination to have this out.

'We shouldn't be getting married, should we?' she whispered.

'Maybe not.' He shrugged, tugging at his cigarette and looking up to the house, from which they could just make out Polly shrieking as her father played chase with her through the rooms.

For a second they lapsed into silence, both realising that this was the moment they'd been waiting for with squirming, agonising self-doubt, terrified that the other would not feel the same way. Yet now that the fuse had at last been lit, there was the inevitable explosion of disappointment and failure to be faced. So they hovered on the brink, almost too afraid of facing such catastrophic emotions.

It was a case of the bravest risking the first step forward. After an aching pause, Tash knew it had to be her. Niall had always been a terrible coward.

'I think we should come clean before you pickle yourself in Bushmills and I expire in a puff of Camel Lights.' She sighed sadly. 'We're both monumentally unhappy with the way things are right now. We have to sort this out.'

He let out a breath that went on for so long Tash wondered if he'd somehow punctured the second lilo. Then, his lungs empty, he croaked out a low half-laugh, half-sob which twisted her chest with emotion. Pulling off his dark glasses he rubbed his face furiously with his palms, breath sharp and laboured as the feelings he had kept bottled up for so long tried to rush out all at once.

'Do you love me, Tash?' He suddenly gazed up at her, his eyes huge and troubled.

She didn't hesitate. 'To distraction – you're the kindest, brightest, funniest and most talented men I've ever met.'

His face was alight with relief. 'I love you too, Tash – you're gentle and loving and totally bloody potty to boot.' He had tears in his eyes.

'So why do we drive one another to distraction?'

'Because,' he laughed sadly, tears seeping out on to his craggy, tanned cheeks now, 'love is bloody blind, and we're a classic case of the blind leading the blind.' He leaned forward and brushed away a petal which had stuck to her calf.

They looked at one another, eyes searching for reassurance. Tash wanted to melt into his arms and make up now that they were talking honestly at last, but she found that she couldn't. There was still a barrier between them, as thick and impenetrable as bullet-proof glass, and there was no way that Cupid's arrow was going to get through it this time. She loved Niall, she always would, but she no longer wanted him for good, bad and ever. And, looking at his tears, she knew that he was crying because he had finally accepted that something had died, not because it had suddenly been given a chance to live again.

'Like a house on fire, sweethearts!' Alexandra whispered happily. 'I think we must have read it all wrong – they were all over one another. I felt a bit of an old voyeur out there.'

Sophia wrinkled her nose. 'I don't really believe it, Mummy, I'm sorry. Every time one mentions weddings, Tash looks as though she's having her teeth pulled, and Niall just shuts up completely, as though his have already come out. I think they're in a real pickle about this. Let's face it, they haven't lifted a finger to help organise it.'

'They are terribly busy, darling.' Alexandra scratched a spaniel's head. 'And all this friction between them could just be wedding-day jitters.'

'Jitter-bugs, judging by Tash's legs. Bitten to shreds, they are,' Ben snorted, finding his own brand of humour acutely amusing.

The others stared at him blankly.

'So do you want me to cancel zis reservation or no?' Pascal was pacing around in the door, anxious for a decision.

They were all supposed to be setting out that night for a very expensive meal at Alexandra's favourite local restaurant, La Filature, yet again paid for by the reluctantly benevolent Pascal. It was intended as a celebration both of Tash's recent birthday and the forthcoming nuptials. He was eager to scrap the plan as the nuptials looked increasingly unlikely.

'Oh, let's go, darling.' Alexandra turned to him dreamily. 'I do really have a feeling that everything is going to be just glorious between Niall and Tash.'

'She said that about Fergie and Andrew,' Sophia told Ben in an undertone.

At the restaurant – a spectacular converted industrial mill – Tash and Niall could barely bring themselves to talk to one another, despite the recent truce. There was so much that had been left unspoken, so little of their real feelings that had been confessed and such confusion as to their future, that they were desperately coasting through the night, like actors improvising a show in a nightmare with no script, plot or set and with endless corridors between them and the stage.

Her doubts confirmed by their odd behaviour, Sophia spent a large portion of the night winking at both her mother and Ben, to such a degree that Niall politely enquired whether she had something trapped beneath her contact lens.

Pascal was privately furious that, of his guests at dinner, only his wife and Ben ate a respectable amount of the ambrosial food on offer. Sophia, competitively watching her weight because Tash had grown so slim recently, picked at her poached chicken mousseline and undressed green salad as though her jaws were wired. And Tash and Niall – who had both ordered the most delicious *Rognons d'agneau grillés chivry* – watched it congeal on their plates with barely a prod of their forks. They had been equally disrespectful to their stuffed artichoke hearts in sorrel sauce, and had skipped the fish course entirely, smoking cigarettes throughout. To a gourmand like Pascal this was the equivalent of someone taking one-hundred-pound seats at the opera and sleeping throughout the performance, or driving a Ferrari at a constant thirty miles an hour on an unrestricted autoroute. Such abuse of good food appalled him. He returned to the *manoir* spitting for a fight, but they both sloped off to bed early.

Still fretful, he produced his favourite cognac and pronounced it a night to get drunk.

Looking eager, Ben settled down on the tattered red silk sofa and loosened his tie in anticipation.

'Bed, I think.' Sophia hauled him back up.

'But it's still early, darling,' Alexandra protested. 'Stay for one drink at least.'

'No – Ben and I promised ourselves an early night, Ma.' Sophia tugged his arm, eager to get up the stairs. 'Sorry.'

Suddenly realising what his wife's fervour might indicate, Ben's face lit up and he himself took up the dragging as they dashed out.

'Lord.' Alexandra sagged on to the sofa as Pascal poured their drinks. 'One knows one's getting dreadfully old when one's children start to go to bed before one –'

'Get off me, Ben, I'm trying to listen.'

'But I thought . . .'

'Oh, that – maybe later. This is far more important.' Sophia craned her neck to pick up on the argument that was raging next door.

When Ben persisted in his nuzzling, he was ordered to have a bath.

'We're making one another unhappy, Niall!' Tash was crying. 'However hard we try to make it work, our lives are incompatible.'

'Which means your career is more important than I am to you, doesn't it?'

'No!' she wailed. 'But if I gave up my job, it would make me explosively unhappy – and I know the same would be true for you, so I would never ask you to do it.'

'I should bloody well hope not, so I should,' he raged. 'I was acting a long time before you started riding horses around rich bastard's estates. All this only started when your mother gave you that horse. You weren't like this when I met you. You were sweeter, less hard. You've changed.'

They were facing one another across the bed like adversaries in a billiards match, stalking around it as they assessed the best angle of approach.

'I started working for Penny and Gus just weeks after we met!' she argued. 'You can hardly say I changed as a result – you barely knew me before.'

'When I met you,' he said quietly, 'you lived in London, scratched out a living as an illustrator and took each day at face value, so you did. Now you socialise with landed gentry, get fat sponsorship deals and plan our dates three months in advance. I call that change.'

'I call that our relationship, Niall. If I didn't plan ahead, we would never see one another. And I got that deal less than a fortnight ago, as you well know. I could barely afford to stand a round before that, let alone race round the world trying to meet up with you.' She stalked around to the foot of the bed.

Niall relocated to the bedside table. 'I'll pay for you to do that! Christ, I've always offered to pay for you to do that.'

'That's not the point. I can't afford to be away right now, paid for or not. If I miss an event, my edge goes and my horses suffer. I don't qualify, I don't get asked to endorse products, owners don't see me as a potential jockey.'

He looked down at the table which was covered with the Four Poster Bed script.

'You love those horses far more than you love me.'

'I love you more than anything, Niall,' she breathed. 'I probably always will. But I don't want to marry you.'

'I don't want to marry you either,' he echoed, staring at her. He seemed almost surprised.

The pause was like a power-cut, suspending everything except their angry, shallow breathing.

Colour was licking its way into Tash's cheeks and she could see Niall blinking nervously over and over again as though suddenly blinded.

'There – we've said it,' he breathed hoarsely.

'Thank God.' Tash bit her lip, eyes still glued to his.

Suddenly letting out a furious, big-cat bellow, he spun around in a discus-thrower coil, arm outstretched so that he swiped every book, lamp, photograph frame and the entire Four Poster Bed script from the bedside table. Then he slumped on the page-strewn bed, head in hands, utterly defeated.

Climbing on to the bed behind him, pages of script crunching beneath her knees, Tash edged forwards until she could reach out a hand to his shoulder. A second later his arm had shot behind his head and he was gripping it tightly, fingers lacing through hers. She pressed her forehead to his warm back and clenched her eyes shut. The release of tension was so great that she felt weak, her limbs chewed to string, her lungs shallow and perforated, hardly able to hold air.

Niall shifted as he glanced around at the pages of script littering the room. It looked as though it had just snowed inside, everything was so white.

'I always said that script was all over the place,' he sighed.

Despite the awfulness of their predicament, Tash felt a giggle rip through her chest. Then, goaded by the highly charged emotions that had been battling away inside her, it started to catch. Soon she was shaking with laughter and crying at the same time. Twisting around, Niall enveloped her in a vast, warm hug.

'Just how on earth,' he wiped her eyes gently, 'are we going to tell your mother?'

Sophia was absolutely furious. Just as she had been listening to the vital moments of the argument next door, Ben had emerged from the bathroom and pounced on her, his libido at a rare high.

Rather swept away by his enthusiasm, she had humoured him for a while before wriggling away to remove her make-up, hoping to catch some more of the fascinating denouement next door. But all had fallen silent, and she retired to bed unsatisfied. She rather wished that Ben would remain the same way, but somehow she didn't have the heart.

'Will you put on your stockings?' he pleaded, tickling her neck with his fingertips.

'No, Ben – not after last time.'

'I didn't mean to rip them, Sophs. Bloody wrist watch got in the way.'

'They were La Perla.'

Taking in his desperately disappointed, hang-dog face, she was shot through with guilt, realising what a negligent snoop she had just been, caring more about family gossip than her sensitive giant of a husband. Freshly scrubbed and baby pink from his bath, he actually looked quite presentable for once, his wet, blond hair combed slickly back from his noble, aristocratic face, teeth squeaky clean, skin smelling of soap and talc. Feeling beastly and suddenly rather horny, she decided really to cheer him up by doing something frightfully risqué and talking dirty.

'Come here, you beast, and roger me senseless,' she growled, turning red.

'Who's Roger?' Ben looked horrified.

Twenty-Eight

NEITHER TASH NOR NIALL was able to confess their monumental decision to Alexandra the next morning. Humming old Supremes hits, she was in such an ebullient mood as she fried eggs English-style and supervised Polly squeezing oranges, that they simply didn't have the heart.

'You do it – she's your mother,' Niall hissed after breakfast as Alexandra headed off to make more coffee, still humming.

'No, that would make it far harder – you're more impartial if she gets hysterical,' Tash whispered back. 'And she's less likely to try and argue with you.'

Despite their nervous asides and rising panic, they said nothing over coffee and avoided Alexandra throughout the morning, behaving ludicrously like children unwilling to confess to breaking a favourite mirror or chair.

Tash suddenly found that she and Niall were talking as though given an intravenous truth serum. Bathed in relief and mutual gratitude, they could afford to be absolutely frank. They were friendlier to one another, more honest and less touchy. Escaping from the *manoir* for a long mid-morning ramble, they chatted easily about the pressure they had both been under, the ghastliness of the last few weeks, and the problems they were going to have to face in the future. Talking with him, Tash experienced the strangest sensation of meeting up with an old ex-boyfriend that one hasn't seen for years, yet finds oneself opening up to with amazed, heart-skipping delight and nostalgia. There was the awful, aching 'what could have been' mixed with astonishingly easy 'what did I ever see in him to make me so unhappy?' She felt almost revitalised.

Their new-found affection was quickly picked up on by Alexandra, who was now under the impression that her weekend break had truly smoothed out the pre-wedding nerves and provided a much needed tonic for them both. Throughout a glorious al fresco lunch of pea salad gleaming with vinaigrette, wine-rich pâtés and dry toast, she watched them both indulgently, clapped her hands together with delight whenever Niall cracked a joke, and even managed to lay off the subject of weddings for their benefit. She just poured the Kir and smiled indulgently.

Keeping a close eye on the couple, Sophia was far more sceptical than her mother, but Alexandra wouldn't be dissuaded as to the efficacy of her little plan.

'They look so wonderful together!' she sighed as Sophia helped her make coffee in the cool of the kitchen whilst the others basked outside. 'I think they're madly in love. You know, I've had my doubts about them in the past, but I truly think they're kindred spirits.'

'They had a blazing row last night.' Sophia wrinkled her nose. 'I couldn't help overhearing it. They said some dreadful things to one another.'

'Well, they're both very emotional, highly strung people.' She waved the information away with her hand as though it was a bothersome wasp. 'And rowing can lead to glorious frissons in bed, darling – Pascal and I often have a bicker when we're cleaning our teeth to spice things up.'

Packing to go back to England that afternoon, Tash knew that she had to say something within the next hour, or it would be too late.

After lunch, Pascal had taken Ben and Niall to the village bar for a final drink, leaving the women to 'talk weddings'. As they were setting off, Tash had darted up to Niall.

'You tell Pascal and Ben that the wedding's off while you're there, and I'll break it to my mother and Sophia.'

'Are you sure, angel?'

'We have to, Niall.'

This way, she figured that the onus was on both of them to do it, and they would be spurred on by the knowledge that when both parties came together again, life would be very complicated if only half of them knew the news.

Yet she had been working herself up to it for almost an hour now, and still she couldn't bring herself to join her mother on the covered terrace and broach the subject.

She sat on the floral bedspread in the turret room she had been sharing with Niall and gazed mindlessly at the wall, wondering what to do. If she told them now it would put an end to their immediate panic, cauterise that leaping nerve of fear that they were running out of time. Yet to do so would trigger off the far greater trauma of cancelling every part of her mother's and Henrietta's meticulously organised event. Her head was pounding again. She blinked several times to try and clear it.

Suddenly she noticed that she was staring at one of her own paintings – not a very good one at that. It was of Rooter, the shaggy old canine lothario that Alexandra and Pascal had adopted for a couple of years, and who had gone on to father most of the local dogs, including little Beetroot. Tash's picture made him look like a large, shaggy hearth-rug with mad eyes and paws like joke slippers, rather detracting from his noble looks. Her eyes misted over as she looked at it, remembering his big personality, over-exuberant affection and total lack of morals.

'If Niall was a dog, he'd be a bit like Rooter,' she muttered aloud.

She was just wondering what sort of a dog Hugo would be – something sleek and proud and disobedient, she mused – when Sophia wandered in under the pretext of getting back her sarong.

'I put it on your bed.' Tash dragged her eyes away from the painting.

'Oh – right.' Sophia hovered in the doorway for a couple of seconds before walking purposefully over to the bed and perching beside Tash.

'Are you okay, Fanny?' she asked gently. 'With Niall? You both seem a bit tense.'

Tash started slightly, caught off-guard by the use of her childhood nick-name and the gentleness in Sophia's usually brisk voice.

'Why do you ask?' She looked at her, noticing the kind expression on her sister's beautiful face. As children they had often been known as 'china doll' and 'rag doll', for Sophia's face had been cool, set and exquisitely pretty, whilst Tash's had been soft, padded and smiling. Yet on the few occasions that Sophia dropped her guard, her face was transformed and one wanted to pour out every woe to those huge, sympathetic eyes.

But Tash had poured out enough woes in the past to know that Sophia was also appallingly indiscreet – often barely listening to the end of a tearful confession before she sprinted off to spread the word. Tash was acutely aware that in this case, that was precisely what she needed, but she was still wary, still balancing on the precipice of the awfulness that lay ahead.

'I ask because I care about you,' Sophia was saying. 'And I think you're very unhappy with the way things are going. And I also know that there is one person in particular who is simply longing for you to have a change of heart.'

'Who?' Tash gaped at her in amazement.

Sophia's perfectly arched eyebrows shot up at the look of excitement in Tash's eyes. She hadn't expected her to react quite so enthusiastically.

'Granny,' she said smoothly. 'She's absolutely livid that your wedding clashes with the final round of her bridge tournament. She's threatening not to come.'

When Niall returned from the bar, very tight, with Ben and Pascal using his broad shoulders as arm rests, Tash and the others were drinking tea on the terrace, shaded by green parasols. The garden, soaked in that afternoon's brief storm, left knee-high wet stains like wellington boots on the men's trousers as they took a short cut through it and stumbled merrily up the steps.

From the raucous bonhomie of the new arrivals, Tash guessed that Niall hadn't been able to tell them either. She caught his eye in despair.

Sitting beside her, he shook his head. 'Sorry, angel, I just couldn't do it.'

Touching his arm, Tash looked across to her mother who was sitting with Polly on her knee, telling her what a gorgeous bridesmaid she'd make with or without a navel ring. Polly was nodding thoughtfully.

'I couldn't either,' she whispered.

Watching Tash's tender touches, Sophia narrowed her eyes. Her sister was more of a fickle minx than she had ever given her credit for, she realised.

Once Tash and Niall were on the train home, their mood grew heavier as they realised the enormity of their cowardice. They would now be forced to perform the ultimate gutless act and let everyone know that the wedding was off by writing to them.

'We'll compose a letter tonight,' Niall promised. 'After we've seen Zoe and the others.'

Tash wasn't aware that they were seeing Zoe and the others – she had simply planned to slip up the road from the forge alone later to collect Beetroot and check on the horses.

Instead, Niall instructed the cab driver to take them straight to the farm from Marlbury station. It was past nine and the yard was in darkness. Tash could just make out Snob's white blaze bobbing sulkily out of his top door in the gloom as Niall whisked her past.

They arrived just as everyone was sitting down to eat. Zoe's usual reaction would have been to laugh and fetch two more place settings. Instead, rather alarmingly, she burst into tears.

'Angel!' Niall rushed over to comfort her. 'What is it? Shh, shh . . .'

Standing behind him, Tash hovered uselessly and glanced at the others. Gus and Penny looked embarrassed. Catching her eye, Rufus pretended to slit his throat and rolled his eyes upwards to indicate bad news. Only India got up and touched Tash's arm, her big, blue eyes soft with pity.

'Mummy ran Giblets over this morning,' she said. 'He just came strutting out into the road – there was nothing she could do without killing herself. She's been crying on and off ever since.'

'We've been spending all afternoon clearing up feathers so that they wouldn't be the first thing you saw when you got back,' Rufus sighed. 'It took bloody ages.'

'I didn't see any feathers,' Tash said distractedly, looking across to where Zoe was weeping in Niall's arms while he told her that it was much more important that she was okay than that poor old Giblets was.

'I'm so sorry!' she was saying. 'He just suddenly waddled out – I wasn't even going that fast. He simply didn't give me a chance to stop.'

'It's okay, angel,' soothed Niall. 'He was only a foul fowl so he was. We love you much more.'

'He probably wanted to end it all anyway,' Tash said awkwardly, feeling surplus. 'He wouldn't want to be the victim of a broken home.'

Gus gave her an odd look at this, but Tash was too busy watching Zoe and Niall to notice.

There was nothing romantic in their posture – just a friend comforting a friend – but it betokened a closeness and an ease with one another that she hadn't really taken in before. She felt no jealousy or even surprise – she simply felt rather stupid for having overlooked it for so long.

Stiffening her resolve, Tash opened her mouth to deliver the unthinkable news about their decision, and then shut it again as Rufus started to gossip loudly and excitedly.

'Hugo's got all the film crew milling around his place now – and word on the village grapevine is that he's got a new lover too. You'll never guess who it is?'

'Who?' she asked croakily, feeling as though both her lungs were collapsing inside her chest.

'Well, you'll love this,' Rufus grinned wickedly. 'It's your ex-wife, Niall.'

'Lisette?' Niall started to laugh, not noticing that Tash had turned so white she was blending into the wall tiles.

'And this came this morning.' Rufus waggled a Sleeping Partners postcard around. 'It's an invitation to a party.'

'A party?' Niall was still laughing. 'Don't tell me they're getting engaged already?'

'No, it's a Slumber Party – at the Olive Branch.' Rufus started to read the card aloud. '"A double celebration of the wrap of the first Four Poster Bed location shoot, and the forthcoming wedding of its star, Niall O'Shaughnessy, to Natasha French. Strictly by invitation only". And this is the best bit – "To be covered exclusively by *Cheers!* magazine".'

'Shit!' Niall suddenly covered his face. He looked as though he'd just been kick-boxed on the forehead.

Tash stared at him. 'What is this?'

He groaned, still keeping his eyes covered. 'It's written into my contract. Oh, Christ, I'd forgotten.'

'What, Niall?' Tash froze, her eyes darting around the room.

'I didn't really think about it at the time,' he muttered, removing his hands and staring at her, his face tortured. 'Lisette inserted a publicity clause into my contract, so she did. It was a last-minute thing. She and Bob Hudson set up a deal that bumped up my fee by fifty percent. It's a huge tie-in deal with *Cheers!* magazine.'

'This *Cheers!* magazine?' Penny asked excitedly, holding up a weekly glossy packed with photographs of the stars at home and at play. She was mortally ashamed of buying it but, like watching Through The Keyhole, too salaciously delighted by the contents to stop herself.

'That's the one.' Niall was looking into Tash's face in abject apology. 'They're paying multiple thousands for exclusive rights to cover the wedding – pics of the ceremony and everything.'

'That's fantastic!' Rufus cat-called. 'You're going to be in *Cheers!* Christ, I can't wait to tell the guys at school.'

Tash caught Zoe's eye behind his head. That soft blue gaze – still tinged with red from crying – emanated such pity that Tash wanted to crash across the kitchen and weep into her arms. It was such an awful, sordid mess, she realised, and she had no idea how they were going to get themselves out of it.

Twenty-Nine

'SO YOU'RE REALLY GOING to stay in Berkshire for the whole fortnight?' Matty watched as Sally packed enough clothes to be leaving him for good. He was sitting tight-limbed on the button-backed chair in the corner of the bedroom, as forlorn as a dog knowing he's about to be left in kennels.

'Yup,' she muttered, not looking at him. 'I think I can trust you on your own for that long.'

'I might throw wild parties every night and enrage the good citizens of Richmond,' he joked feebly.

'Feel free,' Sally muttered, marching past him to the wardrobe. 'Just try not to leave ring marks on the furniture.'

'I could even conduct a torrid affair in your absence.' He watched her stalk back past with a pile of sweaters, resentment clawing at his chest. 'A steamy fortnight stand.'

'I very much doubt that.' Sally threw her pile on to the bed and started to sort through it.

'What's that supposed to mean?'

'Well, if you're as horrible to other women as you are to me, you don't stand much chance of getting into their knickers in just two weeks.' She grabbed a jumper and balled it up.

He blinked in astonishment. 'I'm not that horrible to you, Sals.'

Throwing the jumper into her case, she glared at him. 'You've been diabolical to me lately, Matty. You've put me down more often than a vet going through a crate of rabid cats. Sometimes I don't think you have one ounce of respect for me.'

'Of course I respect you.' He stared at her, his eyes huge.

'So much so that you laugh at the one creative thing I've tried to do in years,' she hissed. 'All you've done since I've taken this job is snipe and sneer and try to ridicule me.'

'That's because it's not creative. Lisette is using you as a dogsbody. I just wish you could see that.' He buried his face in his hands despairingly.

'And that's your prerogative, I suppose?' she muttered. 'Treating me as a dogsbody? At least Lisette pays me.'

'What?'

'If you think what I'm trying to do is so petty then you should try looking at your behaviour recently. For the past year I've watched you get up every day and stare at that computer screen for hours on end doing practically nothing – you play games of Patience more often than you write. When was the last time you really chased any work instead of wandering after it half-heartedly, only to find you've arrived there months after someone else?'

He found he couldn't answer.

'I expect you've forgotten, it's so long ago,' she sighed. 'I want you to enjoy yourself again, Matty, to love what you do for a living instead of living through hell trying to do it at all. What do you think it's felt like watching you hating your days, watching you trying to force yourself to work for months on end, when I've just longed and longed to get out of the house and work myself?'

'You felt that trapped?' He covered his mouth.

'Not always.' She rubbed her forehead. 'I adore looking after the kids, after you even, although I'd be grateful for a scrap of thanks occasionally. But it riles me when you talk down to me all the time. You seem to forget that I had a career once, that I was once something other than a mother, cook and laundry woman. It's as though you think I've lost a few million braincells with every labour I've been through, as though my intellect has shrunk every time my belly has swelled.'

'So why didn't you tell me? You didn't even say that you were planning to take this job – you just sprang it on me.'

'I wasn't aware I had to ask permission.'

'These things need to be discussed.' He watched her trying to click shut the suitcase latches. 'There's such a thing as compromise.'

'Oh, yes, I know. You decide and I compromise. Well, I thought that it was about time you experienced what it's like to be taken for granted.'

Matty gazed at her in appalled horror. 'Christ, Lisette's really turning you into a selfish bitch.'

'And you've been turning into a fucking misogynist for years, Matty.'

'I have not!'

'You act all high and mighty and as politically correct as an American job application form, but underneath it all you're as prejudiced and reactionary as your father, aren't you? I just can't believe it took me so long to see through you.'

'Don't you dare suggest I'm like my father!' he wailed. 'I do not take you for granted, Sally. And I would never look elsewhere for comfort like my father did when his marriage was on the rocks. If you were a bit less insular and self-obsessed you might have noticed that I've been a bloody good, faithful, self-denying husband recently. Christ, I wish to hell I hadn't bothered now.'

'What do you mean?' Sally froze.

'I was bloody tempted to have an affair not too long ago,' he muttered accusingly. 'She was bright and witty and educated, and by God we were close to getting it together. I was certainly lonely enough. But I love you, Sally, and I was simply torn apart by guilt and self-loathing. I couldn't go through with it. Now I know what you think of me, I almost wish I had.'

'Well, now's your chance.' She dragged her case from the bed, stifling a sob. 'Why don't you give her a call this week?'

Niall and Tash had chosen the worst possible time to try to call off a wedding. It was the week before the Badminton three-day event, the trials on which the entire Lime Tree Farm yard had been focused for months, and Tash had two horses to prepare during the final, vital run-up. Four Poster Bed was due to begin shooting at Haydown on Wednesday, and Niall was committed to a non-stop round of read-throughs, costume-fittings and rehearsals before that. They were both so tied up that finding time to sort out the mess they were in was next to impossible, and out of cowardice they wasted hours discussing the best way to approach their dilemma instead of tackling it head on.

Tash now knew that Lisette's company, Sleeping Partners Productions, was relying upon the publicity that the *Cheers!* wedding coverage would provide to promote their first feature film. It would be hard enough to cancel the wedding as it was, without the further trauma of extricating Niall from his disastrously misjudged obligation to the glossy coffee-table weekly. But until they tackled that problem, they couldn't whisper a word to anyone about their decision. The moment it was common knowledge, the promotional deal would collapse like a house of cards and Niall's career could fall apart with it.

For two days, they stalled for time they didn't have. Almost out of habit, they still shared the forge, still slept in the same bed – although he crashed into it hours after she did. They slept together like old friends doubling up in a two-man tent on a camping trip. Working flat-out with the horses, Tash was too shattered to care that his warm, heavy arm still crushed her face when she woke each morning, but the situation was ludicrous. Just as they had been terrified of committing to marriage, so it seemed they were equally unwilling to commit themselves to parting.

On Tuesday night, she knew they couldn't put it off any longer. Dodging wedding talk at the farm was like trying to avoid talking politics in the House of Commons, and Niall was getting increasingly jittery that the Four Poster Bed production secretary had approached him twice that week, eager to get him to agree to *Cheers!* photographing an 'at home' spread at the forge.

Having sloped away from the farm early that evening with a feeble excuse about checking on Beetroot, who was in season and confined to the chastity of the forge, Tash poured out two vast glasses of red wine and persuaded Niall to call his agent, the mercenary Bob Hudson.

'I'm not going to say anything to my mother until we know where we stand on this publicity deal,' she explained. 'As soon as we break it to her that we've decided to call things off, she'll broadcast the fact faster than CNN reporting a first Sino-nuclear strike on Taiwan.'

'You're right.' Niall looked about as eager to face the music as Jarvis Cocker at a Michael Jackson concert. 'I'll get Bob to look at my contract.'

Watching him as he called, Tash noticed that he'd had his hair cut for the film – a close-sided, loose-topped flop of thick curls that wiped years off him, giving him a sleek, roguish attraction that once again jabbed the blunt, bruising sadness of what they had lost into her chest. It hurt her more than anything that they had failed, that they hadn't been able to hold on to something which, for a short time, had seemed to drench their lives with colour.

Tash buried her chin in her palms as she realised that they'd both wanted the happy ending without recognising that their stories followed different plots. And by letting someone else write their fairytale wedding for them, they'd got themselves into terrible trouble. Without an editor to help them out, they were going to end up with Grimm reality rather than the happy ever after of waking up and realising it was all a bad dream.

Watching Niall's shoulders slump lower and lower as he talked to Bob, she had a terrible foreboding that she might even be being a bit optimistic.

'I'm finished,' he said bleakly when he put down the receiver almost an hour later. 'Bob reckons *Cheers!* will sue Sleeping Partners if they don't get their photographs – they've already invested heavily in the film on the promise of them. If that happens, the film company will almost certainly sue me blind. He's just looked at my contract and it's as watertight as a depth probe. Even waiving my fee for the film wouldn't release me from it.'

'You mean you can't buy yourself out of the contract?' Tash asked in horror.

He shook his head. 'Not at this late stage. Bob says I'll have to buy myself out of the whole promotional deal, which is worth far, far more money to Sleeping Partners in potential box office returns than the amount they're paying me to act in the film.'

'How much?' Tash asked nervously.

'That's a piece of string question, so it is.' He flopped down beside her, utterly defeated. 'I'd call up Lisette right now and try to thrash something out but, when I suggested that, Bob blew his lid faster than a faulty pressure cooker. He pointed out that she has me over a barrel financially – a double-barrelled shotgun wedding, in fact. I've got about as much room for negotiation as an estate agent in a prison cell.'

'But she chased you!' Tash pointed out. 'You only agreed to take the part in the first place because I said I liked the script so much, and David Wheaton had agreed to direct it. She needs you.'

'That's exactly my point,' he sighed. 'My role has a lot to do with the film's commerciality.' He leaned back as Beetroot snarled her way past his legs to settle at Tash's feet. 'I didn't just get the part because I was the best actor for the job, Tash. I got it to sell the film to America.'

'What do you mean?'

'Lisette cast me because my media following out there means I'll get bums on seats,' he explained. 'And she got *Cheers!* in when she found out you and I were getting hitched because she knew those seats would develop superglue as a result. It could make all the difference once the magazine's photographs are syndicated to magazines and tabloids in the States. I'm the best known of her cast out there by far, and the American movie-theatre audience latch on to publicity like this in a big way. It's not just the *Cheers!* deal that counts. It's the knock-on effect – three *Cheers!* for the Bride and Groom, and so on ad infinitum. This is Lisette's company's first feature film. She's sweated blood for three years to get this far, and if I blow it for her by deciding to pull out of a key promotional arrangement a day before shooting starts, she'll have no choice but to sue.'

'Can you really not afford to buy your way out?' Tash asked without much hope.

He shook his head. 'I'm sorry, angel. You know how terrible I am with money – I've just given the Inland Revenue my last thirty grand, and I owe them thirty more in July. I can't afford to pay off my credit card bills at the moment, let alone this. If Sleeping Partners sue me and win, I'll probably have to declare myself bankrupt. That means my passport stays in this country and so do I. Bye-bye America. My career will be washed up for a few years at least.'

'Oh, Niall.' Tash put her arms around him. 'I'm so sorry.'

'Jesus, I wish I'd never signed the damned thing!' He clenched his eyes shut. 'But it seemed so unimportant – a last-minute deal to bump up my price, and a free wedding photographer to boot. I even laughed when Bob insisted on including an opt-out clause in case the wedding was cancelled. It simply didn't occur to me at the time that we'd change our minds about getting married.'

Tash bit her lip guiltily, and then, realising what he was saying, her heart skipped a beat of hope. 'But surely if there's an opt-out clause, that means we're okay?'

'There was a deadline attached,' he sighed, taking her hand in his. 'It expired a fortnight ago. If we call off the wedding now, Bob says I'm contractually obliged to cover any losses Sleeping Partners incur as a result of lost publicity. That could be hundreds and hundreds of thousands if they take me to court over this – perhaps more. Like I say, one daft little publicity clause could bankrupt me.'

'Talk about making a contract killing.' Tash closed her eyes. 'It's almost as though Lisette planned it.'

'I honestly don't think she did, angel.' He cupped her face in his hands, dark eyes tortured. 'That's the terrible thing. I think she meant this to be an added extra which helped us both on our way. There's a saying in the film industry – "making a marriage". It means a producer getting guaranteed backing for a script. If we don't get married, she stands to lose a lot of her publicity as well as backing, and there's no way she'd have deliberately planned that. When she finds out the wedding's off, she'll be as devastated as anybody. This film is her baby

– she'll panic if she thinks I'm pulling out of the *Cheers!* deal. Which is why we must keep it from her until we can sort this thing out.'

'Or you'll be in court publicising the film a different way,' Tash groaned, realising just how compromised his position was. 'So what does Bob think we should do?'

'He had two suggestions.' He released her face and started to chew his thumb-nail uncomfortably. 'The first was that we keep quiet about this until I somehow raise the money to pay off Sleeping Partners.'

Tash rolled her eyes. 'And the second?'

Niall's tragi-comic face twisted into a sad clown's smile. 'That the wedding should go ahead as planned.'

'It can't!' she gasped.

'He came up with some demented idea about going through with it until the last possible moment,' Niall laughed, shaking his head. 'He thinks we should stage some crazy theatricals at the altar with you refusing to say "I do" and running out halfway through the ceremony while *Cheers!* photographs the lot. He figures that way, Sleeping Partners would get better publicity than they could have dreamed of and the contract would be honoured and obeyed even if I'm not. I've always said he had a criminal mind. He says it could be our pretend-nuptial agreement.'

Tash gazed at him in absolute horror. 'We can't do that, Niall. I simply couldn't do it to my family for one thing.'

'I know, angel, I know. And I'd never ask you to.' He pressed his hand to her cheek. 'I told Bob they could sue me to hell and back before I'd do that to you.'

'What did he say?'

Niall grinned. 'That in that case, he'll sue me too.'

Tash buried her face in her hands. 'There must be another way out of this,' she groaned. 'I can't stand by and watch you being dragged through the courts because my potty grandmother mistook a cracker ring for an engagement one. It was my bloody family that got us into this mess in the first place. We should never have gone along with it.'

'We'll think of something.' He hugged her tightly. 'We just have to brazen this out until we do.' He got up to open another bottle of wine.

'But for how long?' Tash went pale. 'The wedding's in less than three weeks.'

'I'll just have to figure out a way of coming up with the money,' he sighed, searching for the corkscrew. 'Bob's working on it – I read for a couple of screen tests when I was publicising Celt in Los Angeles last week which he's going to chase, but it means keeping things monastically quiet at this end for at least a few days. You know how litigation-phobic the Americans are. One sniff of a law suit against me at the moment and the Hollywood casting couch will turn into a bed of nails. If nothing comes up soon, I'll just have to come clean to Lisette and take the consequences. Like I say, I won't let you go through with this thing just to save the shirt off my back. You're worth more than that.' He settled beside her again, ignoring Beetroot's snarling protests.

'Oh, Niall, I'm so desperately sorry.' Tash pressed her forehead to his. 'I just wish I could help, but the only way I could lay my hands on any cash at the moment is to win Badminton next week. And even if by some fluke I did, that wouldn't be nearly enough.'

'Brilliant!' Niall whooped, his face suddenly alive with smiles, as though she'd solved it.

'Oh, Niall, I haven't a hope.' Tash laughed, despite herself. 'I think Bob's idea is more likely to work than that, to be honest.'

'We'll see.' He kissed her on the nose and splashed out the wine into their glasses. He'd already drunk most of the first bottle himself, she noticed worriedly. 'I think you might just have given me an idea.'

'Yes?' Tash brightened. 'What?'

'Give me until tomorrow.' He took a great gulp, giving himself a dark red moustache. 'I've got to test the ground first and I'm not sure you'll want to agree to it.'

'Agree to what?' she asked uneasily.

But he just kissed her on the nose again and reached for his script. 'Don't tell a soul what's happening until then – least of all your mother.'

Alexandra called from France just as Tash was clambering into the bath to soak away her saddle sores. Dripping water everywhere, she stood in the bedroom with Beetroot frantically trying to lick her legs dry, listening as her mother launched excitedly into a description of the bridesmaids' dresses which were now complete. 'And, I've been in touch with Niall's mother, darling – extraordinary woman, kept calling me "child" as though I was ten,' she breathed. 'She says that she's coming over to England to stay with some relative in Liverpool this week, and then Niall's father is joining her just before the big day. She seems to think that Hugo is putting them up, which is odd as I'm sure he said nothing of the kind when we chatted last week. He refused point blank to put anyone up, in fact; said he was too ashamed of his interior decor right now. Honestly, he's such a dry chap – I was falling around laughing for hours afterwards, which rather pissed darling Pascal off as his brother had just had a minor heart attack that night.

'And have you made a definite decision about whether we go for rose buttonholes, or naff-but-trad carnations? Henrietta *has* to know by next Monday. And she says she's persuaded James and the girls to go to Badminton and support you this year. Won't that be super?'

Thirty

FROM WEDNESDAY, THE EFFECT of the filming on Hugo's house and the surrounding villages was enormous. A cool, slow-release summer was rudely interrupted by the sounds of cars and lorries roaring past first thing in the morning, the cordoning off of roads as shooting took place, and the boisterous presence of the cast and crew in the Olive Branch, which had been designated the 'shoot pub' to Ange's delight.

Hugo, who had been assured that the filming would take place with the minimum of interruption to the running of his yard, was furious as he was prevented from entering certain rooms of his house, made to walk the long way around the garden to get to the yard, and told to keep his dogs under lock and key after they had bounded in front of the camera during an intimate scene between two of the leads. Hugo had even been booted out of his own bedroom to the attic rooms to accommodate Niall's multiple love-scenes.

The film company had wanted to move him out of the house completely at first, offering to pay for his stay in the Marlbury hotel where the cast and crew were staying, but he had refused point blank.

'I'd rather move in with one of the grooms – I can't come into work like other people each morning. Horses aren't like an office desk.'

To add to his annoyance, Niall was playing the charming, good-for-nothing owner of the house and spent all day being filmed pacing around Hugo's rooms in baggy guernseys and old jeans, seducing ravishing women. The previous day he'd had his hair cut suspiciously like Hugo's too – militarily short around the ears and nape and longer and floppier on top. Not liking the way Niall had taken to talking in a throaty, upper-class drawl, Hugo thought murderously about investing in a crew cut and putting on a Berkshire accent.

'He's bloody aping me,' he fumed.

'Well, he is supposed to own the place in the film,' Lisette explained.

'I've just heard they're going to be filming him shagging in my bloody bed all next week.'

'You should be flattered.' She smiled nastily. 'It's more than you've been doing in it lately.'

To compound Hugo's fury, he found that he couldn't drive the horse-box out of his own yard that afternoon because the entrance was blocked by a huge pantechnicon from which various film heavies were unloading vast, spider-like lighting rigs. He was due to take Bodybuilder to use the all-weather gallops of a racing trainer mate in Lambourne and was already running late.

'Can you shift that?' he yelled at one of the heavies.

'Half an hour.' The man shrugged, not looking up from his copy of the *Sun*.

'Now!' Hugo barked.

But the heavy ignored him.

Pacing around by the box as he waited for the men to finish, Hugo noticed Sally French wandering past towards one of his paddocks which was being used as a caravan park for all the cast, costume and make-up trailers. He hardly recognised her at first, she had glammed up so much. Dressed in an overtly fashionable pair of velvet hipster trousers and nipple-hugging t-shirt, her hair scraped back with wraparound sunglasses, she looked like any number of the trendy young babes who had been floating around his house all week clutching a clip-board and trying to look important. But her face was tired and drawn beneath its thick layer of make-up, and she looked as though she was more used to clutching at straws lately than clip-boards. Wondering if she was all right, Hugo was about to call hello when he saw her stop to talk to his copycat, Niall.

Not wanting to get embroiled with the naked ape-artiste, Hugo leaned back against the box and lit a cigarette, glancing irritably at his watch. If the heavies didn't get a push on, he was going to miss his trainer mate entirely, and he badly needed to ask his advice.

Suddenly, he heard Niall's melting Irish voice mention a familiar name. And it was the last one Hugo would have expected. As far as he recalled, it was a name Niall seldom even remembered.

'But I thought she was keen to lease him for a year?' Niall was saying. 'You said she wanted the publicity?'

'I'm sorry, Niall.' Sally sounded incredibly tired. 'It was some silly idea of mine. I don't think Lisette ever took it seriously, to be honest. She certainly wouldn't be interested in substituting it for the *Cheers!* coverage.'

'It's just that Tash's family aren't too keen on being photographed for the magazine,' said Niall. 'You know how snobbish her old pa can be now.'

'Tell me about it.'

'And he *is* footing half the bill for the wedding,' Niall went on, sounding strangely desperate.

'But you agreed to this months ago, Niall. It's all arranged.'

'I know, I know. It's just that you'd mentioned this idea about running Snob at Badminton under the film's title and we thought Lisette—'

'I doubt she'd even consider it.' Sally's voice was flat and listless. 'She's terribly keen on this wedding feature. She even told me to pass on some message about a photographer coming to see you today, actually. God, what was it again? I don't think it was very important. Do you want me to ask her to meet up with you later to discuss it, then you can tell her about this idea yourself? I've left her diary in the house somewhere.'

'No, no, I'm sure I can persuade Tash's family to agree,' Niall said hastily. 'I just thought this sponsorship idea might be an alternative, that's all.'

'I'm sorry,' Sally sighed. 'Like I say, I think Lisette only let me moot the idea to keep me occupied. But there was one good thing to come out of it, you'll be pleased to know.'

'Oh, yes?' Niall sounded extremely distracted.

'She told me she was going to sign her share of Snob over to Tash when you two get married,' Sally said more cheerfully. 'As her wedding present.'

'You what?' Niall seemed appalled at the prospect.

'She's arranged it with her solicitor,' Sally told him. 'Her share in Snob becomes Tash's property when you two get married. It's all legal and above board. The moment you two are hitched, she'll have no claim on him. I thought you'd be pleased.'

'Sure, sure,' Niall was croaking now. 'I'm delighted, angel, honest to God I am. In that case, I'll definitely persuade Tash's pa to go through with the *Cheers!* thing. Do me a favour, Sals, and forget I ever told you he wasn't keen, huh? I don't want to upset Lisette. Especially not as she's doing this for Tash.'

'Sure,' Sally said vaguely. 'Listen, I must go, only I said I'd take these sandwiches to the costume lorry hours ago and you know how bitchy they are. I'll be fired if I don't get a move on.'

Hugo ground his cigarette out on the gravel and watched as Niall wandered past in the direction of the house, far too absorbed in thought to spot him standing just yards away. He looked absolutely haggard, as though he'd just been told of a fatality, not received the news of a wedding present to die for.

Hugo walked around the lorry to bawl out the heavies once and for all. He was amazed by what he'd just heard: he didn't know what to make of it at all.

The *Next Directory* lay open on the Lime Tree Farm kitchen table, surrounded by the debris of lunch, so that it crunched breadcrumbs every time a hand reached out to smooth a page. Several of the lingerie pages had already been ripped out to adorn Rufus's bedroom walls, and a corrugated coffee ring indented a pale green silk suit which would be perfect for a bright June wedding spent swigging champagne and nibbling on salmon parcels in a cool marquee.

'Do you think green's very ageing?'

With less than three weeks to go, even Penny Moncrieff had started debating whether to buy a new outfit for the day.

In response, Zoe said nothing. In fact, Penny noted, she had gone particularly quiet lately, especially when the conversation turned to Tash's and Niall's wedding. There was something strange in her behaviour that Penny couldn't quite figure out. If she wasn't absolutely certain that all was quiet on the man front, she would have sworn that Zoe was infatuated with a new lover. She was wildly distracted at the moment, always sloping off to be alone, getting unexpectedly agitated when there was a crisis and forgetting to cook meals or post letters. All this was totally out of character.

'Are you engrossed in a new book?' she asked casually, flipping past pages of spill-thin models wading over sandy beaches.

'What?' Zoe had been gazing through the window. 'Oh – no, nothing like that. I'm going to take Enid out – I might march her up to Hugo's place to see a bit of the first day's filming. I thought I'd ask him and Lisette Norton down to dinner this Friday if they're free. Get Tash and Niall along too.'

'Is that such a good idea?' Penny was slightly aghast. 'They're hardly a chummy bridge four, are they?'

'I think it could be rather fun.' Zoe watched for a moment longer as, through the window, Tash clattered into the yard on Hunk, along with Gus on his old campaigner, Fashion Victim. They appeared to be arguing heatedly. 'I might ask Sally French too – Tash's sister-in-law. She's working on the film apparently. I've always liked her.'

'That doesn't mean you're going to invite Tash's awful brother along, does it?' Penny looked aghast. 'He's dreadfully anti-social – just lurked around in here shooting disapproving looks at the hunting prints last time he came. He didn't even leave the kitchen.' She thought the idea of a dinner party the weekend before Badminton generally ridiculous – the whole house would be in chaos.

Zoe cleared her throat uncomfortably. 'I might. I'll let Sally decide – she might not even be free. I gather Lisette's got her running around like a messenger all day, poor thing.'

Penny eyed her thoughtfully, wondering how she knew all this. She supposed Tash must have been gossiping. 'Don't you think it could be a bit of a strain on poor Tash? I get the impression she's terrified of Lisette.'

'So is Niall – they're both terrible cowards, and they have absolutely no reason to be.' Zoe coughed and smiled rather guardedly. 'Lisette is terribly pleased that Tash and Niall are getting married. In fact, I gather she's almost as enthusiastic about it as Tash's mother.'

'Gosh – how very liberal. So are she and Hugo really an item now?'

'The local gossip-mongers seem to think so.' Zoe started searching for Enid's lead, her pale-blonde bob tipping back as she stretched up to the coat hooks. 'But, if you remember, they linked me to Godfrey Pelham for months just because we were doing the same evening course in advanced oriental cookery at Marlbury College.'

'Kirsty will be devastated.'

'Well, I'll leave it up to her whether she wants to join in or make herself scarce.' Zoe clipped an old lead-rope on Enid, having failed to unearth her lead. 'But I'll ask Stefan too, so that might ease things.'

'Stefan?' Penny was mentally counting numbers and starting to panic. They couldn't afford to cater for that many – especially not big drinkers like Stefan and Niall. The trip to Badminton – with four horses running – was already costing them a fortune. She shut the *Next Directory* rather pointedly.

Zoe was at the door now, stepping into her wellingtons. 'I think

Stefan's rather sweet on Kirsty.' She made it sound gloriously old fashioned. 'He's been down here every two minutes since her affair with Hugo ended. Haven't you noticed?'

'But he's years younger than she is!'

Zoe looked slightly uneasy. 'Does that make such a difference? You're a few years older than Gus.'

'And she's supposedly engaged to be married.' Penny looked thoroughly disapproving.

'So she is.' Zoe smiled stiffly, leaning back as Gus stomped through the lobby door looking ratty and almost falling over Enid who cowered into her mistress's legs.

'If Tash behaved to Niall the way Kirsty does to poor Richie,' Penny tutted, 'there wouldn't be a wedding in a fortnight.'

'Don't talk to me about that bloody wedding.' Gus fumed, heading straight for the biscuit tin. 'Tash is totally riddled with nerves and it's still over a fortnight away. Christ knows what she'll be like next week. At this rate, she'll never get through Badminton alive – her riding's atrocious at the moment. I've just had to bawl her out. She's got her head so far in the clouds, she should be forecasting the weather.'

'What d'you mean?' Zoe watched him intently.

'I just asked who was giving her away at the ceremony, and you know what she said?' He turned back, Bourbon cream in mouth. 'She said, "I keep thinking I'll give myself away first." She's coming unhinged. I've sent her home early.'

To Tash's absolute horror, a simpering *Cheers!* photographer and a puff-wielding stylist were waiting on the forge doorstep when she returned from the farm, tut-tutting about how late she was. Barging inside with a barrage of vacuous hello kisses and hardly a word of explanation, they spent an hour going through her wardrobe and pronouncing everything highly unphotogenic with shrieks of laughter.

'I remember when these were in fashion!' The stylist fell about when she spotted Tash's favourite pair of baggy palazzo pants.

'Do you have anything that isn't black?' The photographer peered into her wardrobe forlornly.

'Only my reputation,' she muttered.

Exhausted from her day in the saddle, Tash hadn't the energy to complain as coathangers clattered and the duo chattered. She simply sat with Beetroot on the bed while they threw her clothes around and wondered whether they'd mind if she crept beneath the duvet and clamped her eyes tightly shut. Perhaps, she hoped vaguely, they would have disappeared by the time she opened them again?

'Can we do anything with this, Marcelle?' the photographer sighed, holding up Tash's hair, which was flat and dull from being confined under a crash helmet for ten hours.

'I'll back-comb it.' Marcelle whipped a menacing-looking steel comb from her vast make-up case. 'Get some body into it.'

'Get anybody into it, love. Just change it.'

Niall arrived just as Tash – made up with so much red lip gloss that she looked as though she had just sucked a virgin's neck – was leaning against the range posing for a ridiculous shot which involved her holding a glass of champagne in one hand, her Burghley trophy in the other, a riding crop under her armpit and blowing a kiss at Beetroot at the same time. Eventing rosettes and publicity shots of Niall littered the Rayburn lids, and the row of Niall's drying jockey shorts on the rail had been replaced by a crisp, unused 'Rules of Hurling' tea towel which had been a Christmas gift from his sister Nuala, alongside a pair of oven mitts that had never been out of their plastic shrink wrapping.

Tash's hair was so big, it was threatening to glue itself to the overhead beam, and she was dressed in her full dressage regalia – tail coat, waistcoat, boots, breeches and stock. She looked both ravishing and utterly miserable, her huge, painted eyes pleading for help the moment Niall wandered into the room. Beetroot, who had also been back-combed, snarled menacingly.

'Niall, love. At last!' the photographer greeted him as though they were old mates, although it was the first time they'd met. 'Marcelle will just dust you down and we'll have a couple of shots outside before the light goes.'

'What the fuck's going on?' Niall stormed.

'They're from *Cheers!*' Tash said weakly. 'They say they arranged this session with the film company. We were supposed to be here at three.'

'We won't occupy too much of you two lovebirds' time.' The photographer schmoozed towards Niall with a light meter.

'We've laid a few casual clothes out for you on the bed, Niall – take your pick.' Marcelle was powdering Tash's forehead again. 'Gosh, you're shiny, darling. You must have overactive sebaceous glands.'

'Can we see Natalie in the red satin party dress now, Marcelle?' the photographer called over his shoulder as he wandered outside to peer at the light.

'Jesus!' Niall stayed glued in the doorway.

For a moment Tash thought he was going to throw them out, but instead he meekly complied, his face suddenly adopting the easy, charming smile of his daytime film role. Within minutes, he was totally in character, laughing and joking with the photographer as he took shots of them perched on the sofa, the bed and the tatty garden furniture. Tash was so pole-axed, she did everything asked of her, even leafing through the back copies of *Cheers!* that the duo had brought along and grinning inanely over them.

'It's a bit messy in here, innit?' The photographer sniffed disapprovingly. 'People usually tidy up for us. Can you hold down that dog, love? Only it looks like it's going to bite Niall.'

Suddenly Tash had to fight hard to control a fit of giggles. The situation was too absurd to take seriously. But catching Niall watching her, she saw that, despite the relaxed smile and comic charm, his eyes were almost black with misery. It was as though someone had dropped an ice cube down her back. Saying 'cheese' this late in the day was going to give her nightmares.

Niall practically had to throw them out in the end. The moment they had gone, his cheery façade dropped with an almost audible clang. He was as jumpy as a cat in a thunderstorm, Tash noticed. No wonder Beetroot had looked eager to savage him during the farce of a photo-shoot.

'I can't believe we just went through with that,' she whispered, watching him worriedly as he poured himself a scotch. His hands were shaking so much that most of it slopped over the stone-topped table.

'I honestly didn't know they were coming.' He turned to her, his face white. 'Lisette must have organised it and forgotten to tell me. Jesus!'

'Has something happened?' Tash sat down heavily on the sofa, not liking the way his eyes were staring at her with that baleful, apologetic sadness that always preceded bad news. 'You told me you were going to try and sort something out today?'

'Christ, I thought it might work.' He rubbed his forehead in agitation. 'I'm sorry, Tash. So fuckingly, hellishly sorry. I've just made things worse.'

'What do you mean, made things worse?' Tash gazed at him. 'I thought they were about as bad as they could get?'

'Oh, no.' He shook his head. 'Last night all we had to worry about was the fact that I stand to get sued once we break the news that the wedding's off.'

'I think breaking it to my family might cause us a few headaches,' she reminded him. 'I'm pretty certain that my father, for one, will never forgive me for doing this to him.'

Another gill of scotch slid down his throat in one. 'I'm sorry, angel, I know they're going to freak – my mother will be out for my blood too. But, believe me, I wouldn't ask this of you if it were just a matter of saving my skin.'

'Ask what of me?'

He was already hitting his third glass. 'You have to promise me something.'

'What?' Tash wanted to dive-bomb the bottle and throw it from the window. He was escaping into it faster than a fox into a familiar den, and within minutes he'd be back in character again, fobbing her off with that trust-me charm that belonged to the irresistible liar from Four Poster Bed.

'You must promise me,' he said shakily, eyes locked on hers in desperation, 'that you'll pretend the wedding is going ahead for a while. You have to believe me, Tash. If we don't act like we're getting hitched a fortnight this Saturday, you stand to lose almost as much as I do.'

'What?' Tash froze. 'What do I stand to lose?'

But he closed his eyes tightly to evade the question. 'Promise me, Tash!'

Something in his tone made Tash's skin feel as though she had just been plunged into a liquid nitrogen bath. She gazed at his creased, unshaven face with its familiar grooves gouged out into far deeper troughs by tension and tiredness. He looked absolutely desperate.

'What do I stand to lose, Niall?' She suddenly felt terrified.

Starting to cry, he pressed his forehead to his clenched fist and shook his head. 'I'll find a way out of this, I swear to God I will. But you have to promise me you'll keep quiet.'

Unable to bear seeing him so unhappy, Tash stumbled across the room to hug him in her arms, resting her chin on his head like a mother with a distraught child.

'I promise,' she said hollowly.

That seemed to satisfy him. He bounced back to his energetic Tigger charm, drinking his way through the rest of the bottle and telling her about his day as though his recent weeping had never happened. Trying to get him to talk about it again was impossible – his light, witty, dilettante character role was impenetrable. Battling to get through, Tash was almost demented with frustration and worry. Half an hour later, and he had sloped off to the Olive

Branch to meet 'the guys'. He even had the nerve to ask her along too.

'Hugo and Lisette might be there,' he told her, as though that was a selling point.

Tash shook her head, horrified how easily the mention of that particular couple could thump the air from her chest.

She was left to stew in solitude, appalled by what she had just agreed to. Starting to feel paranoid, she almost wondered if he'd tricked her into it, if he was somehow trying to get her to agree to Bob's ridiculous altar-cation idea after all. He'd said she had as much to lose as he did, but she was wary of him at the moment, uncertain how much of what he told her was the truth, and how much was some fabrication he was dreaming up in his new character. If only he hadn't looked so completely wretched, she might have challenged him. But, however good an actor he was, he couldn't cry like that on cue. Nor could he feign the inebriated ramblings he came out with when he staggered back in at midnight. He could hardly walk, let alone put in a Bafta-worthy performance.

'Stefan was there – with Kirsty.' He fell over Beetroot, not noticing when she sank her teeth into his ankle. 'We had a chat about Snob, so we did.'

'Oh, yes?' Tash watched with alarm as he tripped into the kitchen with Beetroot still attached.

'They say you stand a good chance of winning Shuttlecock.'

'Badminton.' Tash whistled Beetroot away.

'That too.' He head-butted a cupboard as he searched for a fresh bottle of whiskey. 'Kirsty claims the horse is one of the top five in the country. Worth almost a million, so she says.'

'That's right.' She tried not to notice that he was now trying to pour Bushmills into a small glass measuring jug by mistake.

'But Stefan said you'd rather sell your soul than sell Snob,' he slurred, and then giggled as he realised that he was tipping up the bottle without unscrewing the top.

Tash froze. He couldn't be suggesting what she thought he was, could he? That she should sell Snob to pay his way out of the publicity deal? Then she almost blacked out as she remembered that Snob officially belonged to Niall anyway. There was nothing stopping him from selling her beloved, rebellious chestnut friend if he wanted to. The money he would get from it would almost certainly solve his problem. He'd probably even have enough left over to purchase a yacht and take out a lifetime's off-shore subscription to *Cheers!*

'What are you saying, Niall?' she croaked, her voice almost packing up on her as she fought not to cry.

He settled back against a kitchen cupboard and gazed vaguely in her direction, eyes crossing and uncrossing as though he was trying to count the freckles on his nose.

'Will you marry me, Tash?' he hiccuped.

She shook her head in bewilderment.

'Will you?' he repeated.

'No, Niall.' She carried on shaking her head.

'In that case,' he closed his eyes, 'we've both sold our souls. I always said we were soul mates.'

He was so drunk that he passed out on the floor of the kitchen, sleeping soundly with his mouth open, the empty measuring jug gripped tightly in his hand.

He was far too heavy to lift, so Tash could only settle for making him more comfortable with a pillow and a blanket, positioning the washing-up bowl beside him in case he felt sick in the night. He was so desperately pitiable that she felt no anger, just a hollow drum-roll of panic booming through her chest.

Thirty-One

BY THE FRIDAY OF Zoe's dinner party, Tash was aware that she was falling apart big time. Her riding was going to pot and neither of her Badminton horses was giving an inch. Unable to concentrate, she was only making things worse by letting them get away with murder.

Her more experienced ride, Hunk, was suffering a fit of dressage boredom and shuffling around the schooling ring like a toe-scuffing teenager forced to endure a seaside trip with his grandparents, and Snob was behaving even more badly – treating each training session as a rein-wrestling match where he took her on and won almost every time. He had never behaved as atrociously as he was now, and Tash knew that it was largely her fault. He was a horse who required endless riding in and calming down, but she simply hadn't had the time lately. Over the past month, wrapped up in her worries about Niall and increasingly involved in promotional work with her new sponsors, she had started to neglect the enormous input Snob had grown accustomed to. With a bigger, stronger rider on board he wouldn't need the same hours, but because Tash simply wasn't physically strong enough to hold him when he became overexcited, she had to rely upon having his total concentration and confidence at all times, particularly now that she had got him so fit for Badminton.

With her nerves as ragged as they were right now, she found it almost impossible to rally her usual gritty determination and patiently bring him around to her way of thinking.

Trying to persuade him to take a row of fences in the menage on

Friday morning, she suffered the shame of being spotted by Gus just as Snob ducked out of the middle element and sent the wing crashing to the sand.

'Christ!' He covered his eyes and headed back towards the house. 'I can't bear to watch.'

Tash felt her face flame. She knew that her riding was abysmally shabby at the moment, but it didn't make the humiliation any the less. She was also aware that, despite his cynicism, Gus was extremely concerned about her. He'd already bawled her out earlier that week, telling her that for someone who had more talent than any pupil he'd ever worked with, she was currently displaying the riding skills of a dead antelope strapped across a pack pony's shoulders. It was the first time he'd ever admitted she had talent at all.

She watched as Ted bounded into the ring to haul up the wing for her, cackling loudly.

'Don't worry, Tash, it's not the winging that counts, it's the taking part!' he hooted.

'Thanks,' she muttered glumly.

Later on Snob was in no mood to mooch around the lanes idling a few hours away. He was fit and primed and overexcited because one of Gus's mares was in season. As a result, he left Tash up on the ridgeway five miles from home, and she was forced to call in on the Haydown yard en route back to the farm to beg a lift to search for him.

She hoped to God that she encountered Stefan or one of the grooms. The thought of bumping into Hugo with her red, unrested eyes, greasy hair and nervous spots appalled her. She had battled and battled to keep him to the back of her mind this week, not altogether successfully. Images of Hugo and Lisette entwined like two sleek, spoiled cats, writhing playfully in his huge, archaic bed, haunted her. Yet lately, her thoughts about him had turned unhealthily quixotic too. She'd needed a fix to stop her cracking up, and she had been hitting the imagination juices almost as often as Niall had been hitting the bottle.

One of the things that was keeping her sane throughout this nightmare was a silly, crazed fantasy which she clung to in the worst moments of free-fall panic, like a refugee child clutching a bright bobbing balloon while the city around her was being razed to the ground. In her most escapist moments, she let herself dream that Hugo would save her from her predicament. She'd started imagining a scenario in which he leaped up during the wedding ceremony, just as the registrar was asking the guests whether they knew of any reason for the marriage not to take place.

'Yes!' he'd drawl. (He always drawled in her fantasies, she noticed. And his hair was always wind-swept – even indoors, as though there was an electric fan on the go.) 'I do!'

At this point all the guests would turn, gasping, to face him, and he'd stride up the aisle (wearing his dressage breeches usually) to take her hand.

'Tash is one half of my beating heart,' he'd drawl more softly, his voice hoarse with love, blue eyes devouring her face. 'And without her by my side for the rest of my life, I'll have no heart to live. Sorry, Niall mate.' At which point he'd whisk her into his arms and carry her from the room to Niall's intense relief and her father's apoplectic fury.

Her mind fully occupied by this fairytale, Tash walked into the location shoot in full swing.

The place was crawling with film types, indulging in the usual tea-swigging from plastic cups, huddled chatter and clip-board waggling. There were several equipment lorries, plus over a dozen vans and cars parked randomly on the drive, and Hugo's front lawns were scattered with huge tripods holding powerful film lights like great mutant lollipops.

She could not even get through the front gates as the team was frantically filming establishing shots before they lost the light. A minion with a walkie-talkie hustled her away as officiously as a royal body-guard, and she had to run on through the narrow Maccombe lanes and then half a mile into the countryside to Hugo's back driveway. Trudging along the pitted mud track, her ribs pinched with a stitch now, she suddenly spotted him in a nearby field, pounding Bodybuilder around in circles over the dusty tracks of an old sand school. Flame-faced from running and drenched in sweat, she ducked behind a spindly hawthorn bush and caught her breath so that she could leg it past without being seen. But it was as though a great elastic band was pulling her eyes towards him again and again.

Creeping closer to the railed fence that divided them, Tash paused to watch through the hawthorn leaves, revelling in the skills of horse and rider. Bod was as supple as a snake, twisting and flexing under Hugo's effortless control, his sleek, black body glistening in the sun like crude oil being poured around the ring, red nostrils arched in two angry blazes of colour like second eyes, muscles taut as they flexed in tight constraint beneath the drum-tight black skin. In many ways, the horse reminded her of Snob – he had the same explosive temperament, endless stamina and determined, hell-bent will. Like Snob, he was as heavily built as a Mercedes, exquisitely proportioned and as brave as a lion. Unlike Snob, he was utterly obedient to Hugo's every whim.

Feeling deflated, Tash slipped away before Hugo could notice her and, keeping her head ducked below the hedgerow, wandered up the long track to the yard.

Stefan was one of the first people she saw, lounging on an upturned feed bucket and smoking an illicit cigarette, which had Hugo been around, he would have been hosed down for. Hugo smoked like a chimney, but would not condone a fag within fifty yards of his stables.

'Tash darling – he's here!' Stefan bounded towards her on long thin legs.

'What?' She looked around in confusion, taking in several comely girl grooms eyeing her thoughtfully, and Hugo's head girl, Jenny, grinning broadly as she led a tall, ugly bay from the stalls building, her curly hair confined beneath a knitted rasta cap.

'Snob.' Stephan took her arm and led her to a distant stable. 'He trotted straight through one of the film crew's establishing shots of the house and started to eat geraniums out of one of the poncey hanging baskets they've put up.' He laughed. 'We stuck him in here – guessed you'd turn up if you had any sense. Which reminds me . . .' Leaving her at the door, he headed into the tack room to use the phone, looking up a number on the wall-board above it.

When he returned, Tash had already reacquainted herself with a still very surly Snob, and having checked his miraculously unscathed legs for heat and cuts, was assessing the damage to his tack – which only amounted to some broken reins and a lost knee boot.

'He get a bit stroppy on you?' Stefan asked, sliding his dark glasses up on to his blond head.

Tash nodded, listening as a distant tannoy announced silence on set.

'Is it hell with them around?' she asked, noticing that a large screen of fake hedgerow had been erected where the yard normally faced on to the house and garden beyond. It meant they were entirely concealed from filming and also acted as a sound-barrier to cut out any chance of a whinny disrupting an exterior scene. To the right, Hugo's old pony paddock, known unromantically as Flat Pad, was littered with yet more vans and trailers, their windows glittering in the sun. It looked like a very smart New Age camp.

'Murder,' Stefan agreed. 'Now come with me to giggle at them over a coffee while we wait for Hugs – he says he'll be here in a minute. He asked me to call when you poled up.'

'But I—' Tash looked flummoxed.

'He has his mobile with him,' Stefan explained. 'He was the only one who could catch that chestnut bugger of yours. He caused chaos out there – there were camera-men running for their lives. David Wheaton's livid. He says your horse has wasted acres of film.'

'Oh, God.' Tash covered her eyes. Niall would be even more eager to sell him off now.

'When Hugo took Snob away from the carnage,' Stefan was saying merrily as he led her the back way to the house, through the unused and overgrown metropolis of potting sheds and hot-houses, 'Niall was out there denying all knowledge of him. Said he'd never clapped eyes on the horse before, which confused everyone as Snob kept chasing him for Polos.'

Inside Hugo's kitchen a lot of strange film types were milling around, along with Alicia, who had her pug, Gordons, in her arms and was grumbling that 'that cad Wheaton' had told her to 'eff orff'. She was wearing full make-up and a brand new wax jacket complete with matching hat, despite the heat.

'I have to walk purposefully, Tash,' she explained. 'I thought this garb would add to my character.'

Alicia had been allotted an 'extra' role as a rather grand local who could be seen walking her dogs around the estate at various points in the film. As such even Gordons – who was so evil-tempered that he was known to all but his mistress as Thug – was given a small role.

Together they had become a regular fixture in the tatty library which had been transformed into an actors' green room with a coffee percolator, tea urn and trays of nibbles. Taking full advantage of the excellent caterers, Alicia had behaved like a true film star all week, swanning in and out of the house in Gloria Swanson fashion, demanding constant attention, and endearing herself to no one. Niall had told Tash that they'd been sacked after Thug had bitten the sound engineer, third assistant director and two camera-men.

'I thought she'd been fired?' she whispered to Stefan as Alicia marched around the kitchen practising her 'walk'.

'She was, but she kicked up such a stink that David re-hired her,' Stefan giggled. 'Said she was deliberately trying to sabotage his film. She kept looming up behind hedges with a pair of secateurs and a big smile whenever they were shooting an exterior scene. He obviously decided she was safer in than out.'

Tash found herself smiling for the first time in ages. It was such a relief that Stefan was being nice to her again – he had been terribly frosty since the night of her birthday, but today he was bouncing around in the old, familiar, leggy puppy way, eyes rolling as he described the worse aspects of the house's being used as a film location.

'Hugo and I are living out of the attics and this kitchen – he says it reminds him of being back at school, but I swear there are mice up there.'

'I thought Lisette was staying here?' Feeling a great, red blush stain her cheeks, Tash looked around the kitchen nervously, but the chattering film-types were all jeans-wearing techies.

Stefan shook his head and stifled a laugh. 'Christ, no! She's booked into the best hotel in Marlbury.'

'But aren't she and Hugo an item now?' Tash went an even deeper scarlet. The Lime Tree mob were convinced that Lisette had at last hooked Hugo, but a tiny little prayer kept Tash's day-dream alive – albeit on a respirator and fading fast.

'Shhh!' Stefan rolled his eyes towards the nearest gaggle of filmies, who thankfully hadn't heard. 'Why do you ask? Has Niall let something slip?'

'Niall's let everything slip this week,' she said sadly.

'He's really excited about the wedding, isn't he?' Stefan opened a fresh bag of coffee with an indulgent sniff.

'He what?' she bleated.

'Everyone here's talking about it.' He grinned, starting to spoon out grains. 'Niall keeps the crew entertained during the breaks with descriptions of all your mother's extravagant arrangements. I had no idea it was going to be such a grand affair. He seems to have invited practically everyone from the cast to the reception already.'

'He has?' She almost fainted, her stomach churning with fear.

'*Cheers!* are going to have a field day with all those celebrities milling about getting smashed on champagne,' Stefan went on cheerfully. 'Talk about shooting reels.'

She smiled weakly. Right now the only thing she wanted to shoot was Niall.

Just as she was settling down to an eye-wateringly strong black coffee as only Stefan could make it, Hugo strolled in, his t-shirt drenched with sweat, breeches grass-stained and hair wild from removing his crash hat and running his gloved hands through it. That hair! Tash gripped her coffee cup tightly. She was fighting an urge to race across the room and leap on him like a waggy-tailed dog. Down, girl, she told herself furiously. He's sleeping with the enemy.

'Hi, there.' He grinned easily. 'You finally caught up with him then?'

'Yup,' Tash croaked, looking him in the eyes and finding to her terror that she was sinking. 'He's a bit tetchy today – the heat, I should imagine. How's Bod anyway?' She looked away, breathless from gabbling her words.

'He's bloody marvellous.' Hugo eked half a mug of coffee from the pot and settled beside his mother who was re-doing her make-up at the table. He leaned well away from Thug who was grinning menacingly. 'He's going so well at the moment he scares me,' he went on happily. 'Christ, I wish I could find another like him. The old bugger's knocking on – he should be rolling around in clover by now if only I could get a deputy.'

'I thought he was only eleven?' said Tash in surprise.

For a moment Hugo's eyes seemed to harden, the blue developing its frost-bitten chill.

'He is,' he said levelly. 'But I need to bring on another top horse pretty soon or I'm in deep shit.'

Tash thought briefly about Surfer, but said nothing. Hugo's enthusiasm was too rare and too ebullient to be dampened. She already had a feeling she'd just said something wrong, although she had no idea what.

'So you're confident for Badminton?' she asked, shifting her coffee mug around like mad on the table to earth her nerves. Being so close to him was giving her the shakes now. She felt like a dieting chocolate addict, deprived of her fix for weeks, suddenly finding a family-sized Galaxy bar dangling around in front of her.

He shrugged. 'One never wants to tempt fate, but I guess it's our last crack at it together, and I've never denied I've wanted to win it more than any other. You?'

Tash shook her head. 'I'm not sure it's going to be my year – both my entries are a bit stale right now. Snob's all over the place.'

'How's Mickey?' he asked calmly, apparently unaware of her turmoil.

'Great.' Tash tried to get a grip on herself. 'He's still a big baby, but he's trying to listen at long last. I think his time with you really helped him mature,' she added guiltily.

'Glad I was of use.' Hugo sounded narked.

'Oh, you were!' Tash realised how insensitive she was being with a great, guilty gulp. Hugo had given her the ride back, after all, even if he had told her afterwards that it was just to help Gus out. 'He's much more – um – together now. And far fitter. You should see him. He's looking terrific.'

'Perhaps I'll pop in on him and say hi tonight.'

Tash closed her eyes. She had forgotten about Zoe's dinner party. When Niall had told her about it, she'd been horrified that he'd accepted on her behalf, but it had paled into insignificance compared to the rest of her worries. She now wondered if it was too late to develop twenty-four-hour 'flu.

'I always look forward to Zoe's meals,' Hugo was saying lightly. 'She seems to go completely deranged when it comes to buying the ingredients; it's the one thing in her life she doesn't quite have under control. Gus says it's her way of cooking the books – apparently she thinks up the steamiest scenes for her erotic novels while she's slaving over a hot stove.'

'That's so cute!' Stefan hooted in delight. 'No wonder her recipes are always so hot.'

'She calls them her aphrodizzy spells,' Tash said weakly, her face starting to colour. Feeling horribly shy at the conversational line, she couldn't bring herself to look at Hugo at all and found, rather alarmingly, that she kept catching Alicia's eye.

'I gather there's something of a party going on at the farm tonight,' she said jealously.

'You would be invited, Mother,' Hugo muttered, 'but the Moncrieffs are frightened that Thug will eat one of their Badminton hopes as a horse d'oeuvre. He tried to savage one of Gus's brood mares the last time you visited, if you recall.'

'I could leave him behind,' Alicia grumbled. 'And don't call him that, Hugo. His name is Gordons. That charming Lisette gel said he had star qualities today.' She pressed her lips to the little dog's head and he almost took her hand off.

'Dog Star qualities.' Hugo smiled at Tash. 'I should be flattered, Mother. It means she's taking you Siriusly at last.'

Tash, who was desperate to know more about what was going on between Lisette and Hugo, realised that her opportunity was almost knocking her heart out of her chest. She took a deep breath.

'It'll be the first time I've seen Lisette since your birthday party,' she said leadingly and scoured his face for give-away signs of passion, but he looked the same as ever – beautiful, laser-eyed and utterly dead-pan. He possessed the most guarded face she had ever encountered.

'Oh, I think you'll still recognise her,' he said dryly. 'Sally's coming tonight too, apparently – the last I heard, she was monopolising Lisette's mobile phone trying to persuade Matty to get a biodegradable babysitter for those brats of theirs and drive down here this evening.'

'Sally's here?' Tash was surprised. In all her recent panic, she had forgotten that her sister-in-law was working on the film.

'Has been for almost a week,' Hugo murmured, the uncut sapphire eyes becoming icy once again, voice laced with its old mockery. 'Christ, you really aren't interested in your fiancé's day job, are you?'

Tash squirmed, her gaze glued to the table which, she now noticed, was covered with dark, wet splashes from her recent coffee-cup shuffle. She wanted to scream out the truth at the top of her voice – tear outside and dance around, rampaging through Hugo's beautiful gardens yelling that she wasn't going to marry Niall at all, they weren't going to honeymoon in the Cayman Islands or dance to 'Unchained Melody' at the reception or any of the other ludicrous stories he'd been drunkenly spouting this week to get himself into character. She wanted the crew to film every second of her doing so. In close up, spots, greasy hair and all. But if she did that, she would wreck Niall's career, blow Bob's horrific plan sky-high and lose any hope of keeping hold of dear, difficult Snob who – for all his ridgeway gallivanting – was more precious to her than a whole Moonie sect's worth of multiple weddings. Instead she watched her coffee spills sinking slowly into the scrubbed wood of the table, disappearing into it along with her nerve.

'Well, Niall's around here somewhere, so you must say hello,' Hugo muttered. 'If he's in his trailer, it's the first one you come to in Flat Pad – the one with cigarette smoke pouring out of the windows.' He waved her away as though dismissing a loitering secretary.

'I'm sure he won't want to be interrupted while he's working,' gulped Tash.

'For Christ's sake, you're marrying him in a fortnight!' Hugo snapped. 'Don't be so wet.'

Terrified that she would blow her cover if she said another word, Tash sloped out of the house and in the direction of Flat Pad, trailing past half-empty costume-rails covered in plastic sheeting, to locate the rather rickety, if modern, trailer housing Niall, along with a make-up girl, leather-faced director and a mobile phone into which he was purring in his melting Irish brogue.

He flipped up the base the moment Tash poked her head around the door and, looking embarrassed, gave her his big, charmer's smile. 'Hi, angel – come in.'

The lofty, leather-faced David Wheaton, who was in the middle of telling the girl to buzz off, sharply added that Tash could fuck off too.

'Listen, we are seriously behind time on this one,' he blazed at Niall, not noticing that Tash was taking her time to go. 'And you keep fucking back here to call your girlfriend, when she only lives two miles down the fucking road! Much as I admire your loyalty, and sympathise with the fact that you are about to get married, I have to INSIST on some fucking input from you here. I was told you were a bloody professional, not some sort of love-sick drama queen!'

'Er, David,' Niall looked at Tash, 'this is—'

'And you fucking drink too much!' David broke in, glaring at the glass of scotch on the table. 'I gather you're going to AA with your beloved future wife right now, but I need you to cut down when you're on set – it puts the others off.'

Picking up the glass, Niall poured its contents slowly and deliberately out of the window until he had gained David's attention and shut him up.

'Forgive me, David.' He smiled apologetically. 'This is Tash.'

David was all oozing charm the moment he realised that Tash was the mysterious fiancée. He kissed her on both cheeks with very chapped lips.

'Delighted to meet you at long last, poppet.' He beamed out a high-wattage smile, although his eyes were looking her up and down in amazement, taking in the dusty breeches, flat, dirty hair and spotty face. She knew she looked a complete, haggard wreck, a fact which hadn't helped her hopeless gaucheness with Hugo in the kitchen.

Her face was aflame and she found that she couldn't look at Niall at all.

'I'm sorry to barge in, I can see you're busy,' she spluttered, turning to Niall and staring at his legs, aware that his smile had not faltered. 'I just came to remind you about your AA meeting tonight.'

'It's Zoe's dinner party tonight, angel.' Niall smiled easily, but his eyes were hollow.

'So it is,' Tash said helplessly. 'Silly me – I must have muddled the days up. What a prat I am.' Trying to give a gay little laugh, which came out as a sort of guinea-pig's death-cry, she escaped to collect Snob.

In the yard, Hugo was wearing a fresh t-shirt and conducting a fierce argument with Stefan and a groom about the fact that someone had cancelled an order of horse supplements. He barely noticed Tash creep past and collect Snob, fumbling hastily to tie his broken reins together to get them home, then tightening his girths with her hot face pressed to his smooth, twitching belly.

It was only when she led him out into the yard that Hugo shut up and watched her mount, blue eyes taking in the svelte bottom twisting up into the saddle.

'You and Niall have a nice chat then?' he asked disparagingly.

It was too much for Tash. She trotted off without another word, Snob's hooves hammering out great echoing sounds on the Tarmac that caused a furious voice to shout 'Cut!' over a tannoy on the far side of the false hedge.

'Apparently not.' Hugo turned back to the others. 'Now where were we?' He glared at them for a brief moment before starting to walk towards the house. 'Oh, fuck this,' he sighed, 'just order some more.'

Stefan and the groom exchanged astonished glances.

Half an hour later, Stefan tracked Hugo down in the attics, where he was buried in *Horse and Hound*, looking murderous.

'The answer's no,' he said without glancing up.

Stefan hovered in the door. 'I'm really worried about Tash,' he started cautiously.

'Oh, yes?' Hugo flicked a page in boredom.

'Well, aren't you?' Stefan looked at him in amazement.

'Not particularly,' he muttered. 'Should I be? Don't you think she'll be happy with a bed canopy as a wedding present then? I thought it was rather apt given that Niall wakes up with a hangover every morning.'

'Oh, c'mon, Hugo my friend,' laughed Stefan. 'You can see how unhappy she is too, don't pretend otherwise. For someone who's more or less sponsored her career, you sure as hell cop out when it comes to any emotional support.'

'I pay her way to help Gus,' Hugo snapped. 'And because she's a bloody good rider who deserves a break – you know how impossible it is to get started in this game without money. Her private life has nothing to do with me.'

'So you wanted me to call you when she arrived today so that you could rush up to the house to check your investment, did you?'

'Something like that.'

'I don't believe you.'

'You,' Hugo looked up at him, his face ashen, 'are not paid to believe me. And you'd do well to remember that the same bank account that covers Tash French's expenses also mops up your exorbitant cost of living. You're a superb jockey, Stef, but if you don't shut up right now, you may well find yourself riding off into the sunset tomorrow.'

'You can't buy her, Hugo.' Stefan shook his head. 'Haven't you realised that by now?'

'Stef . . .' he warned icily.

'Your father left you with one hell of a financial legacy, but without a legacy to stand on emotionally, didn't he?' Stefan blinked his huge, pale eyes in astonished disbelief so that the blond lashes tangled like threshing chaff. 'Kirsty thinks you're a barbarian with women because you were so starved of love as a child, you are terrified of falling in love. You think it's a sign of weakness, don't you?'

'Get out!' Hugo snarled. 'Don't you fucking dare to condescend to me and make dim suggestions about my father based on the Scotch Brothel's amateur psychology.'

'But she's right, isn't she? I bet the old bugger's way of stopping you crying was to buy you another pony, or send you packing on a skiing trip, or just thrust a tenner at you, wasn't it?'

'Not exactly.' Hugo's jaw was quilted with fury, his eyes so angry that Stefan blanched in terror. 'He used to beat the shit out of me, if you must know. And unless you want me to do the same to you, I suggest you get out of here and leave me alone.'

'Okay.' He started to back hastily out of the room. 'You win.'

'That,' Hugo said bitterly, 'is one thing I haven't done in a long time.'

Thirty-Two

THAT NIGHT, AS TASH and Niall walked to the farm from the forge, she finally tackled him about his drinking.

'You have to come clean with me,' she pleaded. 'David Wheaton said how grateful he was that I was going with you to AA, and I simply didn't know where to look. Plus he kept going on about the phone calls and the long lunches, and that's just rubbish. You can't use me as a cover up.'

'My drinking's not out of control, angel.'

'It is, Niall,' she protested. 'I know I agreed to keep quiet about what's happening between us for a while, but it's killing me. I just can't stand by and watch you drink your way into even more of a mess than you're already in. I had no idea what ludicrous things you'd been telling people until today. I thought you were trying to sort things out, not make them worse.'

'I am, angel, I am.' He took hold of her hand and squeezed it. 'But Lisette was getting suspicious that you never came to see me on set, so I started talking about the wedding to convince her that all was well. It just got a bit out of hand, that's all.'

'Out of hand?' Tash laughed hollowly. 'Christ, Niall!' she snatched her hand away from his grip. 'Can't you see how much worse you're making things? How long is this ridiculous charade going to go on?'

She wanted to scream, How long until you admit that the only way out of this mess is for you to sell Snob? But to say that was to accept it as a fact, and she simply wasn't brave enough. However hard she told herself that there was no other solution, she was still clinging on to the tiny belief that a miracle would happen – she'd even blued a fiver on Lottery tickets in the desperate hope that she might scoop the Jackpot on Saturday night.

'We wrap this location shoot in a week.' He rubbed his forehead agitatedly, starting to walk faster, as though trying to run away from her. 'If we can keep it up until then, things might work out, I promise you.'

'But that's not until after Badminton!' she breathed, suddenly terrified.

She knew why he wanted to spare her until then. Waiting until afterwards to tell her would allow her one last ride with the horse that had taken her to such a giddy height professionally – at the biggest competition of their career. Yet if Snob performed at the trials as he had today, she realised, no one would want to buy him anyway. She felt utterly torn.

'I spoke to Bob Hudson today.' Niall was marching faster and faster along the lane now. 'He's working on one of the Hollywood deals, but it might take until the end of next week to come through – particularly as he's demanding money up front and adding half a million on my asking price. If it pays off then I'll be able to negotiate my way out of this thing.'

'And if it doesn't?' Tash was almost running to keep up.

Niall put on another spurt of acceleration. 'I think we should agree to keep quiet until Lisette's wrap party – that's the night you get back from Gloucestershire. If I still can't get hold of the money by then, I'll come clean there and take the consequences, I swear I will.'

'But we'll only have a week to cancel.' She shuddered. 'We can't do it.'

'We have to, Tash.'

'I can't let you carry on putting on an act and drinking yourself silly for another week just to let me ride at Badminton.' She shook her head, knowing that to accept his offer would be hopelessly selfish. 'You'll be dead of alcohol poisoning by then. How on earth you had the gall to tell them you were going to AA is beyond me.'

'Because I am,' he said quietly.

'You what?' Tash stood stock still in the road.

He waited patiently beside her, hands thrust deep in his pockets, heels rocking. It was an intensely close night, forewarning a racketing storm later, and the hedgerows seemed to be drooping in the heat, the cow-parsley looking bitty and brown, like dispersing froth on a pint of beer. When Tash made no apparent move, he heaved a deep sigh.

'I know I'm still drinking like a fish with a sore throat, angel, but I'm trying to get help. I truly want to stop.'

'But when? I mean, how?' She stared at him, still not quite able to believe it.

'Zoe is going with me,' he said after a pause. 'To Marlbury – on Thursdays. We went last night. It's in the United Reform Church Hall after the—'

'Flab-busters session,' Tash finished, not certain whether to laugh or cry. 'I know when it is. Why didn't you tell me?'

'I thought you might be angry,' Niall said, not quite meeting her gaze.

'Angry?' She felt her eyes filling with unexpected tears. 'Christ, I'm so proud of you – I've wanted you to do something like this for weeks.'

'You never said,' he sighed, starting to walk towards the farm again. 'You never even acknowledged that there was a problem. I thought you didn't care.'

Tash bit her lip, knowing that however much she had cared, she had failed him again by not confronting him. 'And Zoe saw it?'

He nodded. 'And was brave enough to tackle me on the subject, put up with my denying it for weeks on end, and then bully me into going. She reminds me of Matty sometimes – ironic really.'

Even more ironic that Matty and Zoe were the first two people that Tash and Niall saw as they headed into the kitchen, fighting off the dogs' exuberant welcome and handing over their gifts of wine and early-summer strawberries.

'How lovely.' Zoe took them, her arms now full of bottles, strawberry punnet under her chin. 'Matty was just saying that he's working on a new project about corruption in the racing industry. You should be able to help him out there, Tash.'

'Yes, that's a thought,' Matty said, smiling stiffly.

Gaping at them both, Tash couldn't possibly think how. She knew as much about racing as she did about industrial engineering. Then, looking from one to the other, it suddenly hit her that Matty was the man that Zoe had kissed at the party two years earlier. She found she couldn't stop smiling as the penny finally dropped. She had always assumed it was Hugo, but one look at her brother's guilty face told her otherwise.

Hugely embarrassed at meeting up again, Zoe and Matty were both behaving so politely to one another that they could have been two hosts of a regional TV news round-up, trading inane comments on a pastel settee. Zoe, floating around in an exquisite steel-grey dress which Tash was certain had once been a costume she had made for Rufus's school play, was as cool and classic as an Art Deco statuette. She looked ravishing, if nervous.

'I dressed to kill time,' Zoe smiled when Tash complimented her. 'You look gorgeous, too.' Her eyes widened slightly as she took in what Tash was wearing. 'In fact, you look amazing.'

Desperate to salvage some pride after such a hellish day, Tash had made a valiant effort to pull herself together and stop slobbing around like a heroin addict in the last stages of cold turkey. She knew she hadn't a hope of competing with Lisette's taste in couture, but she couldn't bear the thought of Hugo seeing her looking as gross as she had earlier at Haydown. If he went for such overtly seductive women, she decided that she had to try and play the game. It was hopelessly shallow of her but she couldn't stop herself. She'd even spent hours scratching around the forge for a pair of earrings shaped like stirrups which he'd once admired in passing.

She almost fainted when her brother nodded at her in polite approval and agreed that she looked very slick. He *was* on his best behaviour, she realised in amazement. It was the first compliment she had ever heard him pay her.

'Thanks,' she gulped gratefully, starting to feel slightly more positive about her choice. She was dressed in a pair of exquisitely soft DKNY leather jeans which Niall had bought her back from the States and she'd never mustered the nerve to wear. They were wildly sexy and made her legs look endless, but they were really far too hot for the sultry evening. Her plunging blue silk shirt was already sticking to her moist chest, and it was too humid to get away with much make-up – she'd just settled for covering her spots and pulling her hair back into a ponytail. At least working outside so much had given her a tan which her recent weekend in France had deepened, leaving a pink tinge in her cheeks that made her look healthier than she felt.

'Don't you think she looks great, Niall?' Matty asked his friend.

'Terrific,' he said, but he was looking at Zoe, not Tash.

'Help yourself to drinks,' Zoe told them, a nervy edge to her voice. 'Good of you to dress up too, Niall.'

His jumper was an ancient spinach-green turtle-neck that was covered in dog-hairs and reeked of local pub. Unshaven and detoxifying like mad from his recent drink binges, he looked dreadful. He poured

Tash a glass of wine and himself a Coke, but his hand shook so badly that most of it went over Wally, who was frantically sniffing Niall's legs because Beetroot, still back at the forge, was just coming out of season and reeking wantonly.

'I can guess why you're done up like a New York raver tonight, Tash.' Matty inserted himself beside his sister, grateful for the company which would disperse the tension between himself and Zoe.

'Oh, yes?' she bleated.

'You always did hide a fearsomely competitive streak under that shy exterior,' Matty laughed. 'Trying to show queen bitch that you're younger and slinkier, huh? Do you still think she's going to try and seduce Niall away from you?'

'What d'you mean?' Niall looked unexpectedly furious.

'Zoe has just broken your dreadful secret to me,' Matty told him.

'Our what?' Niall gulped nervously, eyes darting towards Tash.

'I assume the reason Tash is looking so sensational tonight,' Matty rolled his eyes, 'is because the Wicked Witch is dabbing sulphur behind her ears and heading this way. A case of out-tarting the enemy, huh?' He gave his sister a malicious wink.

'You've lost me there, old friend.' Niall shook his head, still looking edgy.

'He means Lisette, Niall,' Zoe sighed.

'I had no idea that bloody woman had been invited,' Matty sniffed. 'Had I known, I would never have come.'

'She and Hugo are going to be late,' Zoe explained hastily, uncorking another bottle of wine. 'Hugo called two minutes ago to say that Lisette was still going through the rushes or something biblical like that. They're bringing Sally and David Wheaton. The numbers keep going up and up. I almost phoned you to beg more crockery and chairs.'

'Niall and Tash don't have any dining chairs,' Matty pointed out, flushing slightly because he himself was a last-minute addition. 'They've only got cast-iron garden furniture.'

'We're going for a co-ordinated look,' Niall said lightly. 'They match our cast-iron constitutions.' He seemed tremendously relieved suddenly, his whole mood lightening.

'I doubt you'll need that tonight,' Matty said cheerfully, watching Zoe as she moved a vast foil package from top to bottom oven. 'Something smells delicious.'

Tash noticed that her brother was looking fatter than usual, which seemed remarkable given the fact that Sally continually referred to him as being miserable these days. In her experience, Matty had only ever run to fat when he was happy and contented, which was so seldom that he was usually as gaunt as a male ballet dancer – all angry, tensed sinew and tendon. He looked tougher and more robust, had colour in his cheeks for the first time in years, and reminded Tash strikingly of their father. The illusion made his crocheted cap and ethnic waistcoat look even more ridiculous than usual, like dressing up a Power Ranger in the seventies tuxedo belonging to Barbie's boyfriend, the thatch-haired Ken.

'How are you?' she asked cautiously. 'You look incredibly well.'

'I am.' He smiled his nervy smile – another rarity. 'I've finally got a couple of good commissions this week and, better still, I've secured a co-producer on both deals who lets me do what the hell I want so long as it's brilliant, which it will be.'

'Christ, that's excellent – Jesus!' Niall bounded up to him and shook his hand vigorously, slopping yet more drink on Wally. 'Who is it?'

'A guy called John Merchant.' Matty smiled cautiously, backing off slightly under his friend's high-spirited congratulations. 'He's a great bloke – been in the business for years. I've been chasing him for almost as long, and he finally caved in last week.'

'You've waited ages for a break like this!' Tash smiled at him in delight. 'I'm so pleased for you. Sally must be over the moon – I mean, it really takes the pressure off you both.'

But Matty looked uncomfortable. 'She doesn't know yet.' He grimaced. 'I haven't had a chance to tell her – it's partly why I came down here tonight, to tell her face to face.'

'She'll be chuffed to bits,' Tash assured him, certain that Sally would cartwheel with relief at the end of the prolonged stale patch in Matty's career.

'Well, we'll see.' He glanced briefly at Zoe again, clearly doubting the wisdom of coming to the farm at all. 'I gather you're doing pretty well too,' he told Tash, not sounding particularly interested.

'Not bad.' She shrugged, helping herself to a handful of crisps from a bowl on the table. She was amazed that she felt so calm and relaxed when Zoe, Niall and Matty were all as jumpy as coins on a spin dryer. She'd decided that she was going to do it once and for all tonight. However much Niall wanted to keep it covered up, she was going to come clean about the wedding. She'd go crackers if she didn't. If it meant selling Snob, then she'd just have to accept it, however agonising the loss. Instead of feeling panic-stricken, she was washed with relief. She just wanted to get it over with. But she knew she had to wait until everyone was gathered first – especially Lisette. Until she and Hugo had arrived, Tash had to keep coasting. She knew that tonight was a perfect time to do it; Lisette would have no choice but to come to some sort of compromise with so many people around. If that compromise was for Niall to sell Snob and pay her off then the obvious buyer was at hand – Hugo had been wanting to get his hands on Tash's talented red rebel for years. He'd have his chequebook out within minutes, thus saving the day as she'd predicted, only not with the impassioned declaration of love she'd allowed herself to fantasise in her more deluded moments of day-dreaming.

The thought made her throat cramp with a sudden, unexpected burst of emotion, and she had to turn away from Niall and Matty so that they couldn't see her fighting to get a grip on herself. But Zoe saw her face and her own blue eyes seemed to fill with tears too. Blinking, Tash looked at her in confusion, not understanding why she seemed to be so overwrought.

'Film going well, is it?' Matty was asking Niall.

He nodded. 'Bloody rushed. We've only got two weeks on this location, then we're breaking for a fortnight and shooting in London after that.'

'And you're both still set for the seven-year hitch?' Matty gave him a pointed look. 'Or are you planning to make this particular marriage last longer?'

Thankfully Rufus loped in at that moment to ask if he would be allowed a rare can of lager as it was a special occasion. He was wearing a pair of high-fashion checked yellow trousers that made him look like Rupert Bear, particularly as he'd had his sleek blond hair shaved into a fuzzy crew cut that week to look like Ted's.

'What's so special about it?' Zoe watched him plunder the fridge for a can before he joined Tash in the crisp corner, begging a fag on the way. He ogled her jeans excitedly.

'Well, it's a dinner party, isn't it?' He made an expansive gesture, slopping lager over Wally, who was now looking like a shaggy sponge. 'We don't have too many of them. A motorbike and a car have just arrived, by the way, and Penny's still in the bath. She keeps complaining that you nicked all the hot water.' He lit the cigarette inexpertly, yelping as he burned his nose with the lighter flame.

Zoe was gazing out of the window. 'Oh – it's only Stefan on that ridiculous bike of Hugo's. And that looks like Sally getting out of the car. Gosh, she looks lovely. Who's that with her?'

Niall, who was standing at her shoulder, squinted out too.

'Shit and Christ alive!' His eyes went wide with fear. 'It's my mammy.'

Tash felt her face drain to an unattractive washed-out grey, and listened as Ma O'Shaughnessy's booming, merry voice floated in from the yard, punctuated by her industrial-waste hacking cough.

'No, Sally child, I will not be helped from a car like an old crock – I have the strongest legs south of Dublin, and a bloody great arse to land on if I fall, so I do. Now where's that son of mine?'

Moments later she was almost filling the room, not simply with her enormous bulk but also the ringing, musical tones of her loud voice, her frizz of unsculpted black hair and the overpowering waft of lavender oil, which she always wore as a perfume.

'There you are, boy!' she cried, pressing down on Niall with a hug of such power that his spinach jumper almost fell apart. 'Christ, but you smell of the drink, just like your Godforsaken father. So, are you pleased to see your old ma?' She let out a volley of high-tar coughs.

'Ecstatic.' Niall finally extricated himself and straightened up to look at her, groping for a platitude. 'Whatever brings you here?'

'You're too thin.' She regarded him slyly for a moment before scanning the room for Tash, saying, 'I'm staying with your Aunt Maria in Liverpool this week – she's having her gall bladder out on Monday, so she is – and I decided to visit my son for an evening to check out what was going on about this wedding thing. Ah, there's the child!' She lumbered forward to crush Tash in her embrace. 'I don't trust those two silly girls you have organising this thing – a right pair of eejits, if you ask me. One of them's your mother, is it not, Tash? Bejasus, you're too thin too. It's like hugging a bar stool, so it is.'

'You should know, Mother,' Niall said unkindly, still white beneath his stubble.

Free at last, Tash brushed down her rucked-up shirt and regarded Ma O'Shaughnessy with a mixture of fear and astonishment.

'What a wonderful surprise,' she gulped. 'When did you get here?'

'Sure, I rolled up at that posh eejit's hotel just an hour ago. Jesus, what a fool the man is!' She sat heavily at the table, causing one of the Moncrieffs' old wicker chairs to groan like a ship in a storm. 'Now, who's going to get me a drink, or must I get it myself?'

While Niall dashed off to fetch his mother a family-sized scotch, Tash sat dutifully beside Ma and listened as she rambled on in her husky baritone, floridly describing the snooty local hotelier who had refused to carry her bags when she'd arrived.

'He sounds like Basil Fawlty,' sympathised Tash.

'I've never met such a rude young tearaway in all my days,' Ma sniffed. 'I didn't tip him, you know.'

Known simply as The Ma to everyone of her acquaintance, she was well over fifteen stone, although most of this was pure muscle, not fat. Despite her vast frame, wild hair and drinker's nose, she was a powerfully attractive woman, with the same huge, dark liquid eyes as her son, cranberry red cheeks and gloriously pale, freckled skin, as smooth as bone china. Her laugh was famously raucous, and she claimed to be the best cook in all Ireland, a fact which Niall was fairly hasty to dispute when he and Tash had visited the family the previous year. Tash had left the house almost half a stone heavier with an intimate knowledge of the multifarious uses of the common potato.

'Where is this hotel you're staying at?' she asked when Ma finally paused for breath and a tot of scotch.

She pulled a face which clearly said the whisky was appalling, and nodded towards Sally and Stefan, who were creased up with laughter by the door.

'Same place as these two youngsters are staying, am I right?'

Sally, speechless with giggles, could only nod. She had yet to say 'hello' to Matty, Tash noticed. Instead she was leaning against Stefan and chewing her knuckles with glee.

'Beauchamp Towers.' Stefan had pulled himself together and was nodding sincerely. 'It's not in the tour guides, but its reputation is well known around here.'

'Well, I 'clare, I won't be suggesting it to me friends now,' sniffed Ma, her voice pure gravel. 'I can't understand why your dear mother recommended it to me, Tash. To be sure, it's a terrible place. And he's a horrible fellow who runs it. I mean, I've only come from Ireland, but this young man is on holiday from Sweden, are you not?' She nodded at Stefan, who collapsed into laughter again.

'Are you telling me that you're staying at Hugo's place, Mammy?' Niall was aghast.

'If that's the fellow, then yes – until I can make other arrangements, for I won't be staying long.' Ma took another slug of scotch and again pulled a face. 'Jesus, that's a rough mouth o' malt. Not only are the rooms appalling,' she went on, 'but they seem to be filming some sort of advert for the place – there are lights and cables all over the floor, so there are. It's a Godforsaken health hazard.'

Niall shot Sally an exasperated look. 'Haven't you explained to her then?'

She wiped her eyes and fought for breath through her laughter.

'Believe me we've tried. Boy, have we tried. She thinks Lisette's the receptionist.'

'Oh, Christ, Mother!' Niall sighed.

'Don't blaspheme, lad. I'm allowed to do it as I have a spotless soul and go to mass. You may just be struck down as you stand there like a great lump of sin, so you may,' she snapped, patting Tash's hand. 'Now, I want my future daughter-in-law to tell me all about the wedding. I don't trust her idle lump of a betrothed to know a thing about it.'

Tash winced and caught Niall's eye, but he was looking towards Zoe and trying not to laugh himself.

'I'm having a bloody great drink,' he sighed, heading for the scotch bottle. 'I need one.'

Zoe's face tightened, but she said nothing.

Taking a deep breath, Tash decided that it was now or never. They'd just have to break it to Lisette when she arrived. If Niall got pissed, she'd have no hope at all. They had to face this thing together.

'The thing is . . .' she tried to make herself heard above the babble as Gus wandered into the kitchen, announcing loudly that he'd asked Ted in for a drink. They were followed by India, packing the kitchen into a tight party of people like a London Underground lift.

'Are there any more crisps, Mum?' Rufus was shouting.

'The thing is . . .' Tash tried again.

'Can I have a spritzer as Rufe's on lager, Mum?' asked India. 'You look fantastic, Tash. I love those jeans.'

Ted and Gus were arguing loudly about whose turn it was to check the horses, and Stefan was trying to talk over them as he told Niall that one of the camera cranes had collapsed on Hugo's conservatory that night.

'Niall and I have decided that perhaps . . .'

'Can everyone get out of here while I cook!' yelled Zoe. 'It's a mad-house. I can't even reach the Aga.'

Moments later, Niall was ushering everyone, including Tash, out of the room.

'I was trying to tell them,' she hissed as he pushed her out.

'Jesus, not now – not tonight!' He looked horrified. 'We'll have enough of a job on our hands trying to explain that Hugo's place isn't a hotel. For Christ's sake don't complicate things more. For my mother's sake, Tash, I'm begging you!' He sounded absolutely desperate.

Tash had little chance anyway, as Ma marched into the Moncrieffs' messy sitting room and immediately settled herself between India and Rufus on the best sofa, delighting them with outlandish and much-embellished tales of Niall at their age. Tash was glad that he wasn't around to listen in. She had heard most of the stories before on their visit last year, and they were grossly unflattering and largely untrue. Mercifully, Niall appeared to have stayed in the kitchen with Zoe, and wasn't around to hear.

Matty had cornered Sally by the long dresser at the gloomy far end of the room and was conducting a low, animated conversation with her as he told her his news. From her roaming eyes and bored expression, Tash had a feeling that Sally wasn't as delighted by the break as her brother had anticipated. She looked mildly put out, if anything.

Tash busied herself helping Gus to get everyone drinks, and finally settled beside Stefan who was lounging like a long piece of string on the broken-legged sofa, with an adoring Wally washing his hands. Enid was no doubt hiding in the bathroom, her favoured retreat during social gatherings.

'I thought Kirsty would be here,' he said sadly. 'But Ted says she's gone out for a pizza with Franny tonight.'

'I don't think she fancied seeing Hugo and Lisette, to be honest,' Tash whispered, knowing exactly how the buxom Scot felt.

'Whyever not?' Stefan looked confused, pale lashes batting.

Tash bit her lip, remembering that Penny had been gossiping only that morning about the fact he had a huge crush on Kirsty at the moment. 'Oh, no reason.' She watched as Sally started to snarl something to Matty in an undertone.

'You got back okay today, huh?' He smiled at her.

'Oh, yes, fine.' Tash dragged her eyes away from her brother and sister-in-law's argument and felt her face colouring. 'So – er—' She searched around for a change of subject, watching as Matty stormed out of the room to fetch another drink, his face set with irritation. 'What do you think of Niall's mother?'

'She's totally mental,' said Stefan simply, adding in an undertone, 'Hugo thought she was a stray loon, or some sort of practical joke set up by the film crew, but she's completely convinced the place is a hotel. Is the rest of the family like that?'

'Mostly.' Tash nodded.

He started to giggle delightedly. 'Your wedding is going to be hysterical.'

'Hugely funny, yes.' Not noticing how closely he was observing her face, Tash watched as Sally wandered over, looking surprisingly perky despite her husband's recent huffy exit. Her usually scruffy hair had been slicked back into a satin clip, emphasising her merry eyes and shapely neck, already glowing pinkly from several gin and tonics at Haydown. Her soft, angora dress – absurdly fashionable – was far too hot for the close summer evening, making her cheeks flame with colour like a naughty schoolgirl who's just hidden a toad in her room-mate's sock drawer.

'Darling Tash, you look as overdressed as me – and almost as trendy. We must both be sweat-shopaholics.' She perched on the arm next to Stefan and scratched Wally's nose. 'We never see you at the shoot – I thought you'd be up every day checking that Niall's behaving himself, which he isn't, as always.' She winked cheerfully. 'Always sloping off to see you instead. Lisette's furious.' She brushed a few imaginary dog hairs from Stefan's shoulder. It was a curious gesture, which Tash couldn't quite figure out – part habit, part mother, and yet indicating a flirty intimacy that surprised her.

But she was too distracted by what Sally had just said to dwell on it long.

Half tempted to say that Niall had not been sloping off to see her – to the pub was far more likely – she buttoned her tongue and offered Sally another drink.

'Wine, please – and could you check that Matty's okay? He was in his usual stinky mood just now.'

'He seemed quite cheerful earlier,' Tash said in surprise.

But Sally was already distracted chatting with Stefan and sliding in beside him on the sofa now that Tash had stood up and released a space. 'Did he?' she muttered vaguely, long after Tash had left.

In the kitchen, Niall was sitting at the table with a now furiously moody Matty and the scotch bottle whilst Zoe chopped up salad beside the sink, cursing Hugo for being so late.

'What are he and Lisette up to, for Christ's sake?' she moaned. 'I said eight at the latest – does your mother have a large appetite, Niall? Only I'm going to have to stretch the salmon.'

'Huge, she'll think it's a whitebait.' Niall smiled up at Tash. 'Okay, angel?'

'Fine.' She headed for the fridge to fetch more wine, longing to corner him and demand that they make an announcement together.

'Knowing Hugo and Lisette, they'll be in bed,' Matty said acidly, his earlier good mood absolutely shot to pieces now.

Her head in the fridge, Tash found her nose pressed to a very musty cauliflower, heart racing.

'Rubbish!' Niall scoffed. 'He and Lisette aren't involved – I should know.'

'Really? So you keep tabs on them throughout the working day, do you?' Matty muttered, anger coming to the boil. 'Come off it, Niall, it's not as though you have a claim on her anymore. Like you keep saying, you're marrying Tash in a fortnight. And I get the impression from Sals that Lisette's finally got her claws into Hugo's back each night and is drawing blue blood.'

'Well, she's lying then,' Niall said cheerfully, not rising to the jibe. 'The reason I should know is because Lisette is currently shacked up with David Wheaton – they're even sharing a room in the hotel, for Christ's sake, although they've got two booked for form. I hardly see her sloping back to Haydown for a nightcap with Hugo when she and David have only been together a month, do you?'

'It wouldn't be out of character,' Matty said nastily, turning to watch his sister with irritated, scornful eyes. 'Tell me, Tash, are you cooling your face in there, or have you inadvertently become welded to the ice box?'

Re-emerging with a bottle of wine, she found that her face, despite the icy chill of the fridge, was burning.

'Are you feeling okay, angel?' Niall watched her with concern.

Gripping the work surface for support, Tash stood up and nodded. She was so relieved to find out that Hugo wasn't sleeping with Lisette after all that she wanted to run around the room kissing everyone. Whilst Niall and Zoe probably wouldn't mind, she had a feeling that it would finish her brother off. She felt almost giddy, and hopelessly confused. She simply had to force Niall to come clean tonight. He was already half-cut, and leaving it any longer would just compound the awfulness of their ridiculous pretence.

'I think Niall and I should get a couple of things straight.' She cleared her throat loudly. 'And you two should perhaps be the first to know.'

Niall shot her a warning look. Opposite him Matty was knocking back scotch – he normally never touched it – and glaring at her witheringly, as though she was about to announce a change in bridesmaids or something equally petty.

'What's that, Tash?' Zoe was transferring pans across the Aga lids, her hands buried in oven mitts. Tash couldn't tell whether her face was flaming from the rising heat or because she had guessed what Tash was about to announce and was quietly, sympathetically embarrassed for her, but she looked likely to combust.

Clutching the cool bottle tightly to her blue shirt, Tash looked at her brother's clever, nervy face and gave him an apologetic smile that wobbled so much she had to bite her lip. He glared back unsympathetically, but she launched on anyway, determined to get it over with.

'You were right all along, Matty,' she started, her voice croaking with the effort of at last coming clean. 'You always were the cleverest of the bunch. When we were in France, Niall and I decided that we—'

'I am not going to be your fucking best man!' Matty exploded furiously.

'I'm not talking about that,' Tash bleated. 'Well, I am, but not like you think . . .'

'Just shut up about you and Niall, okay? I've told you my feelings on this bloody marriage,' he raged on, undeterred, his anger now too explosive to be defused. 'And right now, tonight, it's the last thing I want to fucking discuss. I don't care if you get married anymore – go ahead, get hitched, kill yourselves with unhappiness for all I care. I certainly am.' He buried his head in his hands, anger evaporating as he descended into his black gloom once more.

The wine bottle was being pressed so hard to Tash's chest that she was almost cracking her ribs. She glanced desperately at Niall, but he was reaching across to take Matty's hand, his craggy face wreathed in sympathy.

Tash backed away in confusion. Matty had seemed so cheerful earlier and now he was positively spitting with brooding, wrathful unhappiness. Yet Sally was, apparently, chirpily unaware. Then she remembered her sister-in-law asking her to keep an eye on him and flushed even more guiltily.

'Sally seems worried about you,' she told her brother as she frantically fished through the drawers for a corkscrew. 'She asked me to check you were okay.'

'How very civil of her,' he hissed, only just controlling another explosion. 'I'm surprised she could bear to drag herself away from her Swedish toy boy.'

'Stefan?'

'Is that what he's called?' Matty shuddered. 'Sally's behaving like a bloody sixteen-year-old tease with him tonight, I can't bear it. She's only doing it to wind me up, but it still bloody hurts.'

'Stefan's probably to blame,' Zoe told him gently. 'He's a terrible flirt, and he's in a bit of a strop that Kirsty isn't here.'

'No, it's entirely Sally,' Matty sighed, looking up and rubbing his mouth sadly. 'Listen, I'm sorry for being such a self-pitying jerk, but

I'm at my wits' end. I can't do anything right at the moment. I keep expecting a divorce petition to land on the doormat.'

'Are things really that bad?' Niall asked in horror, pouring Matty another vast scotch and an even larger one for himself.

'Worse if anything. Why d'you think I came here tonight? I'm clutching at straws like a faulty combine harvester. She hasn't called all week – now she summons me down to rub my face in it and make me look a fool. And it's all my fault for mentioning . . .' He cleared his throat uncomfortably and glanced at Zoe. 'For mentioning what – er – happened.'

'You did what?' Niall was appalled.

'She was laying into me, saying how useless and apathetic I was, and I just snapped – I blurted something stupid about almost embarking on an affair. I suppose I wanted her to realise how much she was taking for granted.' Matty clammed up embarrassedly.

'But it wasn't as bad as that!' Zoe gasped, abandoning the dill she was chopping.

'I know. I'm sorry.' He looked up at her pleadingly. 'I didn't mention any names.'

Listening in, Tash had pulled the cork so badly that most of it was now floating around in the bottle. It was incredible enough that her brother had been the mystery man who had engaged Zoe in a long, flirtatious kiss at the Moncrieffs' barbecue two summers ago. But what was harder to get to grips with was the extraordinary way she and Niall were now talking Matty through it. They sounded like Richard and Judy gently working out a distraught caller's marital crisis during a This Morning phone-in.

'Perhaps you should have done,' Niall was telling Matty. 'Sometimes you have to stick your neck out to find out that your head's not going to get cut off after all.'

'If she knew the whole picture, she might stop trying to pay you back,' Zoe added gently. 'After all, it was terribly innocent. At the moment her imagination must be running riot.'

'You're right,' Matty groaned. 'She's playing games, and that's one thing she's never done before – we've always tried to be die-straight with one another when we've hit a rocky patch. I'm certain Lisette is to blame – the marriage guidance counsellor from hell. She's just counselling us down the river.'

'Talking of which . . .' Zoe craned towards the window. 'Here they are – Christ, Hugo drives fast.'

'Shit.' Matty rubbed his face with the palms of his hands as though trying to get some colour back into it. 'I bet she'll just love seeing me like this.'

'Don't let her then,' Niall said quickly. 'Put on a front.'

'You'd know all about that, wouldn't you?' Matty looked at him with a sad smile.

'I'll give you tips.' He stood up. 'I think I'd better go and stand by my mother in case she accuses Hugo of leaving the hotel unstaffed or something. I wouldn't put it past her to provoke a punch up.'

He wandered out, followed by a despondent-looking Matty.

Still fishing cork out of her wine bottle, Tash looked up at Zoe and paused, desperate to talk, however bad her legendary lousy timing was. Standing directly beneath an angled kitchen spot light, Zoe was whisking dill mayonnaise now, blonde hair gleaming almost white. In the silver dress, she looked ethereal and angelic.

'He told me about the AA meeting,' Tash said cautiously.

'I'm glad.' Zoe didn't look at her. 'I told him to, but he was too ashamed.'

Tash listened as the dogs, hearing a car engine, scuttled through the house from the sitting room to perform their door duty.

'You're so good to him.' Tash swallowed, her throat suddenly bone dry as though she'd had an emergency tracheotomy.

'Not especially.' Zoe was looking more and more uneasy, her whisk rotating madly. 'I've just been around when he needs a chat – I'd do the same for you, darling.'

Tash shook her head. 'I don't think so.'

'Of course I would!' She looked up from the bowl, blue eyes worried. 'I love you, Tash, – you're one of the family to me.'

The dogs were barking like mad in the hall now as Hugo reversed his car loudly out of the courtyard, which was already too full of cars to park in.

Tash took a deep breath, knowing she had just a little borrowed time while Hugo parked in the lane. She had to speak to Zoe before he came in, was determined to get at least a part of her messy life sorted out before she saw him.

'This might sound strange, but you two look like a couple.'

'What?' Zoe jumped nervously, glancing towards the window where the Range Rover was reversing at a frantic pelt down the muddy drive.

'You do,' Tash insisted. 'I keep noticing it recently. You and Niall, you look – act – like a couple who've been together for years.'

Blonde hair tickling her eyes, Zoe barely dared move, her whisk slowed to a stop, the bowl held at an angle under the crook of her arm.

'Really?'

Tash nodded, listening to the car engine cut out in the lane, and Ma, having just been warned of Hugo's imminent arrival, booming, 'Not that Godforsaken man!' from the sitting room.

'You know we're washed up, don't you?' said Tash in a low, urgent rush.

Zoe nodded, her clever blue eyes softening.

'H-how long have you known?' Tash asked.

She shrugged. 'Officially, a few days, I suppose. Since you got back from France. Niall was in an awful state before you went away. But I've guessed for weeks – maybe longer.'

'He didn't used to phone the farm to speak to me, did he?' Tash watched her face, hearing car doors banging in the lane now, followed by the electronic chirrup of an alarm being activated. 'I mean, maybe at first, but he calls here all the time now, and you can't pretend it's to get hold of me any more.'

'No, I can't.'

'Are you – I mean, have you—'

Zoe shook her head violently. 'No! Not at all. We're friends, Tash, no more. I swear the most secretive thing we've done all week is have a couple of lunches to talk about how hellish he feels about what's happened with you – and a furtive trip to an AA meeting. It's hardly a whirlwind affair.'

Figures were moving along the drive now. Tash could hear Lisette's rasping, sexy voice raised in anger as she complained about Hugo's driving. She wanted to lean out of the window and scream at them to wait a few minutes, longing desperately to resolve a situation in which she felt she was slowly suffocating to death.

'He won't let me tell anyone,' she muttered hoarsely, hearing Hugo's voice floating in from the courtyard now, soft and drawling as ever. 'I want to say something tonight, but he won't let me. He's convinced we should keep it quiet for another week.'

Zoe turned away, her voice cracking with emotion. 'I've talked to him until I'm blue in the face, Tash. It's like his drinking – telling him to stop won't help. You have to take hold of his hand and keep holding it until he knows for certain you're not going to let it go, not going to let him down.'

'I've already let him down,' Tash whispered bleakly.

'And he's covering up,' Zoe went on urgently. 'He's tucking away the truth in the same way he hides countless bottles around the forge, thinking you won't notice. He's terrified that you'll never forgive him once he tells you what this mess he's got himself into might cost you. I'm sorry, darling, but it's going to tear you apart when you find out.'

'I know,' Tash muttered, finding that tears were starting to leak from her eyes and slip warmly down her cheeks. 'I know I'll lose Snob. And if that's what it takes to straighten him out, I'll do it. Niall will just have to sell him.'

'Is that what you think?' Zoe gasped. 'That Niall is planning to sell him?'

'Isn't he going to have to?' Tash asked in confusion. 'To get the money to buy himself out of the *Cheers!* deal?'

'Darling, he'd never do that to you, even if he could. He knows how hard you've worked on that horse. That's why he's desperate for you two to go to Badminton without the tabloids on your back, sniffing around for a cheap quote, hounding you endlessly, putting you off while you're working the horses, shattering your concentration – because that's what will happen when this news breaks, believe me. It will be simply awful for you. Can't you see that's why he's keeping up this act for you both?'

'And afterwards?'

'Oh, Tash! I simply don't know.'

Slamming the bowl down on a surface, Zoe turned and raced across the kitchen to give her a hug. Letting out a stifled sob, Tash breathed in her lovely, cool scent and felt Zoe's strength and warmth seeping into her, giving her a tremendous, almost drug-like boost.

The dogs were barking like mad once more. Hugo and his coterie were moving through the parked cars outside, taking their time as they paused to look at Zoe's ancient Mercedes, but almost at the door.

'You have to help me, Zoe,' said Tash desperately. 'You have to be completely honest with me. Do you love Niall?'

Zoe pulled back to look at her, blue eyes suddenly guarded. 'Of course I do – I love both of you.'

'Not like that,' Tash gabbled her words to get them out. 'Do you love him? I mean love, love. Because I'm almost certain he loves you. Is in love with you – over, under and upside down with love for you.'

Zoe froze, stiffening in her arms. 'Don't talk rubbish,' she scoffed dismissively.

'Oh, I know Niall.' Tash laughed through her tears. 'And I know what a cretin he is about telling someone how he feels for them at first, how terrified he is of rejection – we're both exactly the same, it's why we're so hopeless together. You have to do it for him, Zoe. If you feel the same way, you have to hold his hand like you said. Because he won't let go of mine until you do.'

Zoe stared at her in silence and Tash was suddenly terrified that she'd got it wrong.

'You d-do love him, don't you?' she stammered.

Zoe smiled – that warm, luscious smile that melted the beautiful, glacier-smooth face into warmth and sympathy, her blue eyes glistening with tears.

'I think I'm starting to.' She nodded, giving Tash a tight squeeze. 'I think one day very soon I could find myself loving him almost as much as you love Hugo.'

Tash bleated in shock.

'Oh, darling, it's patently obvious you adore him,' Zoe laughed through her tears. 'It always has been.'

A sharp rapping on the yard door separated them, and Zoe reached for a tea towel to swab her eyes. Tash searched desperately for something absorbent too, but she was too late. Hugo and Lisette were already entering the room with bottles of champagne and yet another extra guest as David Wheaton – tall, leather-faced and frighteningly cerebral – followed behind them wearing a comfortingly old-looking pair of cords and exactly the same checked Marks & Spencer shirt that Gus had on that night.

'Sorry we're late, darling.' Hugo moved across to give Zoe a kiss. 'Hope you don't mind David coming too – I said you're always blissfully informal about these things. You haven't done individual *boeuf en croûte* or anything?'

'No, no – it's a whole salmon, we're fine,' Zoe said rather weakly.

'Hi, Tash – still dewy-eyed, I see.' Hugo turned to her with a caustic smile.

Saying nothing, her chest absolutely exploding with emotion, Tash headed for the cutlery drawer to grab another place setting, turning her back to him. Why was he always so killingly cruel? She was acutely aware of what Zoe had just said, and consequently paranoid that she'd been wandering around for ages making it patently obvious that she adored Hugo. Quite what exactly had made it so patently obvious was a mystery. She was pretty certain that she'd never mooned around gawping at him with her tongue hanging out, but she was almost doubting her memory on that one. She realised that she'd have to keep a closer guard on her emotions in future.

Ever the smooth social engineer, Lisette was introducing David to

Zoe, telling him loudly about Zoe's former fame as a top-ranking features journalist. She seemed to know a remarkable amount about it.

'I really wasn't around for very long,' Zoe said modestly, picking up her congealing dill mayonnaise. 'And I wrote an absolutely appalling column for the *Sunday Telegraph* which pretty much killed my career off.'

'Oh, I wouldn't say that,' Lisette said easily.

Tash stiffened as she felt Hugo move in behind her. Suddenly a hand reached around and stopped hers from scrabbling loudly in the cutlery drawer. Very slowly and carefully, he removed her fingers from their kamikaze blade-rummage and pulled her round to face him.

'What's wrong?' he muttered, not altogether gently, his cool blue eyes raking her face. 'Because that's a bloody silly way to cut your wrists.'

Wearing an old rugby shirt and black jeans, he seemed to have made even less of an effort than Niall had. Tash noticed that he had hay all over one sleeve and he'd slipped his watch on the wrong way round – probably after a hasty shower. She longed to reach out and put it right for him.

'What's wrong Tash?' he repeated, backing off a couple of feet as though worried she might do just that.

Not really thinking, she mouthed, 'You are!' and headed through to the dining room to lay yet another place and search for a spare chair strong enough to hold Ma.

She felt tearful and childish. The titanic conversation with Zoe had absolutely drained her and yet, she realised, she was not really much further on than she had been at the start of the evening, except that she was no longer so sure that Niall was planning to sell Snob. She just wished she knew quite what he was planning to do, other than wait for Lisette's party to stage something dramatic. This evening, he seemed hell-bent on convincing everyone that the marriage was very much on – especially if he carried on drinking and adopted his garrulous, compulsive-lying character from the film, which he was certain to do with such a large audience to play to.

Tash wasn't sure she could get through the night ahead, let alone another week of pretending like this. Hugo was obviously setting out to stalk around her, hissing and snarling, when all she longed for him to do was throw her over his shoulders in a completely brutish, Neanderthal way and whisk her back to Maccombe to ravish her and tell her that he loved her and would sort her life out for her. She knew it wasn't a very politically correct, feminist fantasy, but she was feeling far too exhausted and stressed to throw him over her shoulder and sort her life out for herself.

It was hot, sticky evening, and Tash's jeans became more and more clammy as she circulated the sitting room before dinner distributing wine. The room was full of strange cross-currents of which no one was oblivious. The talk before they ate was, predictably, all about films and weddings. Far too much about weddings for Tash, who hardly spoke for fear of screaming.

Desperately avoiding looking anywhere near Hugo, she found that she was catching Niall's eye over and over again as he drank too much on an empty stomach and played the dutiful fiancé. Yet throughout his utterly convincing act, he continually kept tags on Zoe, eyes glancing towards her when she moved or laughed, always offering to help when she was buckling under a tray of drinks or trying to open a door with a platter of hors d'oeuvres in her hand. It was so obvious that they were attached by invisible strings to one another now that Tash wondered why no one else commented on it. Yet to the rest of the party, who spoke of little else than the doomed wedding, it seemed that the forthcoming nuptials was a dream match.

As they chatted in the sitting room before going through to eat, Niall became more and more convincing in his role, seeming to revel in his skill.

'Tash and I aren't doing a stag night, hen night thing,' he told his avid audience. 'Instead we're both having a huge final fling with one another at the location wrap party next weekend.'

'A chicken night,' Tash muttered, but no one was listening.

'How romantic,' Sally giggled, still trying to wind up Matty. 'I had my final fling with a red-haired bar-man called Jerry. I only got off with him because I was absolutely plastered from running up to the bar every ten minutes, saying, "I want a gin, Jerry, and make it a stiff one," to amuse my girlfriends.'

'Which says a lot for her girlfriends,' Matty said witheringly, shooting Lisette an evil look which she ignored.

'What hymns are you having, son?' Ma boomed. Having worked her way almost single-handed through all the crisps, she was now halfway through Zoe's tray of rather odd hors d'oeuvres which consisted of a piece of raw vegetable draped with a whole anchovy.

'We're not having hymns, Mother.' Niall's dark eyes glittered. 'We're having a specially commissioned concerto from a mate of mine who writes film scores.'

'I 'clare, that sounds a bloody awful idea, so it does.' Ma chomped her way through an anchovy-draped carrot stick. 'You had some lovely hymns at your wedding to that skinny woman. What was her name?'

'Lisette,' said Lisette huffily.

'That's the one!' Ma took a slurp of scotch – she'd had at least three now – and eyed Lisette thoughtfully. 'Actually, d'you know, she looked a little like you, child. She had a bigger nose, though, and a chest like a slip of a boy.'

'This is Lisette, Mother.' Niall was almost crying with laughter. 'My first wife. The one you keep telling me I'm still married to in God's eyes.'

'And may the Lord forgive us for it!' Ma's mouth vanished with disapproval and she went almost purple. Then she gave Lisette a beady look. 'God can sometimes turn a blind eye, you know. What's she doing here anyway?'

'I was invited,' Lisette said simply. Ma had never been her biggest fan, particularly as Lisette equated pregnancy with fatal illness.

Completely ignoring her, Ma turned to talk to Tash, her voice so loud that it was almost impossible for anyone else to conduct a conversation in the room.

'I'm going back to stay with my sister in Liverpool tomorrow – she's having her gall bladder out on Monday, so she thinks she'll not be well enough to come to the wedding. She's a terribly hypochondriac, always has been.' She let out a flurry of coughs. 'But she's got you and Niall a wedding present. It's the most beautiful little cot you'll ever see.'

Tash gaped at her.

'Kids!' Niall raised his glass cheerfully. 'We can't wait to have them.'

Begging his help in the kitchen at every opportunity, Zoe was obviously doing all she could to temper his enthusiasm for lying about the wedding, but he was thoroughly in character now and impossible to stop.

For something to do, Tash started wandering around the room filling glasses again, a task she had been performing with increasing randomness all evening – she was so distracted that she kept pouring people the opposite type of wine to the one they'd been drinking. Luckily most of them were now too tight to notice. Rufus was already on his third can of lager and starting to talk too loudly and ogle Lisette, whom he clearly thought awesome.

Lisette, Tash noted, looked predictably ravishing – all cream skin, glossy hair and honed physique, the neat little Hollywood nose tipped towards leathery David in constant, rapt attention, huge eyes drinking him in. She really was a devastating seductress. Tash felt like a St Bernard plodding up to a whippet every time she approached her to re-fill the glasses. She supposed her technique with Hugo had similar parallels; while Lisette slithered and wriggled, coquettish and slinky at the same time, Tash lumped herself down beside Hugo occasionally and panted passively – tongue lolling lovingly, eager to slurp him up. Tonight he was sensibly steering clear, huddled in a corner with Gus and Penny talking about Badminton. She was surprised Stefan hadn't joined them, but he seemed to be giving Hugo a wide berth, and was consequently falling prey to Sally's charms as she tried to get Matty's back up.

'Your legs are so long, I'm surprised they don't trail the ground when you're on horseback,' she murmured, making a show of measuring Stefan's legs alongside her own, which involved a great deal of angora fluff being transferred on to his jeans.

'I usually ride with my leathers very short,' he explained.

'Sounds wonderfully kinky,' Sally giggled. 'Is that like *Lederhosen*?'

'No, they're leather shorts.' Stefan smiled kindly.

'I thought that's what you said.'

Tash noticed when she refilled her brother's glass that he was looking totally fed up.

She plodded up to the whippet again.

To her amazement, Lisette was being nicer than she ever had been, asking after her horses – and seeming to know the names of an alarming number – apologising for keeping Niall working such long hours, and telling Tash how pleased she was to be arranging a party which was as much to celebrate their wedding as for the wrap of the location shoot.

'I'm sure Niall must have told you about my little wedding gift?' She smiled her sexy, wicked smile. 'It was supposed to be a surprise, but I gather Sally let it slip out this week.'

Tash shrugged rather hopelessly, wondering what on earth she was talking about. She started pouring white wine into leathery Davids' still half-full red wine glass. The resultant mix looked revoltingly like fruit cordial.

'Well, it's not as though I'm really interested in eventing – although Hugo assures me it's almost as good as sex and just as messy,' Lisette was saying airily, glancing around the Moncrieffs' tatty sitting room which was littered with horse-trials memorabilia. 'And I thought it would be a rather nice gesture – signing my share of the horse over to you on your wedding.'

'Y-your share?' Tash croaked, starting to pour wine all over a chair arm without noticing. Thankfully Ma thrust her glass underneath the deluge.

'It was all a bit silly, my ending up with it in the first place,' Lisette laughed, genuinely amused. 'I don't think any of us even realised until this year. But it hardly matters now, does it? I'm going to get my solicitor to draw up the papers, so it's all legal.'

'That's very kind of you,' breathed Tash weakly.

'Too bloody kind!' David laughed heartily. 'I don't think you have any idea what that animal's worth, Lisette.'

'Oh, I think I can make a shrewd guess.' She shot Tash a wink. 'And, as I'm still officially his half-owner for another fortnight, I'm going to get all the cast and crew of Four Poster Bed rooting for you at Badminton, Tash – we'll be glued to the box to cheer you on between takes. If you win, I might even demand my first and last owner's pat. *Cheers!* are very keen to get some pics of him, by the way, did Sally mention? Especially now we know he's going to be pulling a carriage at the wedding.'

'It's a trap,' Tash muttered.

'What?' Lisette gave her a sharp look.

'He's going to pull a trap, not a carriage,' she said.

Christ, Tash thought as she moved away, so that's it. She owns half of Snob already. And, unless Niall and I get married, she stands to gain the other two legs along with anything else she could sue him for.

She glanced over to where Niall sat slumped in the corner seat beside his mother, who was still booming loudly about what ravishing children he and Tash would have. The smile that was glued on to his face suddenly reminded her of a strip of gaffer tape gagging a hostage.

No wonder he was so desperate to keep things quiet. Tash could suddenly understand why he'd been drinking himself into oblivion and living in character all week. He hadn't been building himself up to tell her that he was going to have to sell Snob at all. He'd been trying to hide the fact that he'd signed her talented, hot-headed chestnut friend away long before he'd agreed to take on the part in Four Poster Bed. As Snob's half-owner, Lisette had the legal right to stop Tash ever riding him again. Even if, by some miracle, Niall could get the funds to negotiate his way out of this *Cheers!* deal, she'd retain that right. Whether Niall was sued or not, Tash stood to lose the wilful, spirited horse to whom she owed her career. In all probability, her last ride with him would be at Badminton.

She sat down heavily on the sofa, gripping the wine bottles in each of her hands like a terrified skier clinging on to her sticks as she tackles her first black run.

After a few moments a firm hand prised first one and then the other out of her grasp, which was no mean feat as she was clinging on for dear life. Tash carried on staring fixedly ahead, not caring how freakily she was behaving. Someone sat down beside her on the sofa and asked a question. Tash took no notice.

Then a familiar smell drifted towards her. Breathing a lungful of the lime-sharp aftershave, she only just stopped herself from sighing like a Bisto kid.

She gazed fixedly at a pale patch on the threadbare carpet where one of the dogs had once been sick and India, thinking she was being helpful, had poured bleach on to it. I must not cry, she told herself firmly. I must be cool and collected and noble. I still have nine days left to get through before my world falls apart, after all.

'Everyone gets scared their first time at Badminton,' Hugo murmured smoothly.

'What makes you think I'm nervous?' she said in what she hoped was a cool, noble, martyred sort of a way.

'I thought that was why you're so uptight.' He looked at her curiously.

'Oh – yes. It is,' she murmured, rather appalled that a crisp fragment chose this moment to fly out from between her teeth and land on his wine glass where it stuck fast. It somewhat spoiled the mood of ethereal fragility.

Pretending not to notice, he dropped his voice so that no one could overhear.

'Tash, are you in some sort of trouble?'

Looking up in alarm, she gazed into his eyes and, finding herself getting hopelessly lost in them, looked hastily away. She supposed there had to be something positive to be gained from knowing one had very little left to lose in life.

'If I win Badminton this year, will you do something for me?' she asked.

'Sure,' he said warily.

Making sure no one was listening in, Tash felt herself start to colour. 'Will you kiss me?'

Not waiting for him to answer, she stood up and walked away as quickly and nobly as she could.

Thirty-Three

IT WAS FAR LATER than planned when they sat down to eat, and, because of the two extra guests at the table – one of whom took up at least two people's width – they were crammed in like a hen party at a busy restaurant.

The candles, which Rufus had eagerly lit at the beginning of the evening in an excuse to sneak a quick undetected fag, were already guttering, and one of the farm cats had walked across the pale tablecloth leaving a trail of prints which everyone except Ma politely ignored.

'I 'clare, it's like being in my own home!' she boomed delightedly when she saw them. 'I hope you're a good cook, Zoe – of course, no one can match me, but I like a good meal.'

Zoe's cooking was, as ever, something to behold. They fought their way though an anchovy and garlic salad of such strength that Sally's eyes watered throughout, and David – who had the misfortune to find himself crunching three whole garlic cloves simultaneously – had to be excused from the table to choke them up in the kitchen.

'Jesus, this is a fine dish!' Ma helped herself to Tash's leftovers. 'Are these crunchy white bits some sort of nut? Break your bread as God intended, Niall, and stop fiddling around with that knife like a murderer.'

Just as Zoe was bringing a whole salmon poached in Pernod and balsamic vinegar to the table, the phone trilled in the next room, its klaxon loudspeaker wailing in unison out in the yard.

Most of the family, eyeing the salmon suspiciously, made to get up and answer it with relief.

'I'll get it!' Gus pulled rank and edged his way hastily out of the room.

'It'll be one of India's boyfriends,' Zoe groaned. 'They always call at antisocial hours.'

'I want a mobile for my eighteenth,' Rufus grumbled. 'That way Gus won't hold the phone away from his mouth and shout: "It's Jane – is that the one you said was a lousy kisser?" He wrecks my sex life.'

'What sex life?' Penny laughed, frantically chewing on the parsley garnish to kill the smell of garlic.

Tash was standing in the kitchen and wondering vaguely whether to carry through the puréed dandelion and swede dauphinoise or the stir-fried asparagus tips with grapes and mung beans. She could hear Gus cursing as he tried to locate the phone under a pile of papers in the next room. Balancing a serving plate along her arm, she listened as he hailed the caller jovially (obviously a friend) before hushing his voice to a serious whisper and starting to talk more urgently.

Just as she was making her way from the kitchen to the dining room with the asparagus tips, he slammed his way out of the study and, almost sending her flying, called for Hugo before bolting back to the phone again.

Not picking up on the urgency of Gus's voice, Hugo sauntered out of the room just as Tash was picking asparagus tips from her cleavage. He was clearly half-cut.

'You look like a comely wench at a feast.' He regarded her with sparkling eyes that danced like fire-flies. 'Holding your salvers aloft.'

'Very *Tom Jones*,' she joked nervously, in imminent danger of dropping her salvers altogether.

'The Welsh singer?' He looked confused.

'I was talking about the book.' She cleared her throat. 'All bawdy meals and rolling in haystacks.'

Not saying anything, Hugo gazed at her for a moment, and then smiled.

'This must be the first year I've ever actually hoped I don't win Badminton,' he murmured, moving away as Gus demanded that he hurry up.

She stood in the hall for a few seconds, fighting to recover from the all-out nuclear explosion of lust that had just taken place inside her. That was a come-on, she realised. It had to be a come-on – even she knew a come-on when it came at her with the smile Hugo had just given her. It was a smile that was tattooed on her eyeballs. A smile that had made electric currents etch her body and her hair spring up from her scalp. A smile that bore no resemblance to the huge goofy, panting St Bernard one that was plastered to her face when she finally wandered into the dining room, asparagus tips sliding off the platter she was wafting around in comely wench fashion.

'Ah, you can always spot a girl who's to be wed soon by the smile on her face, so you can!' Ma boomed, already making inroads into the salmon with her dessert fork.

Tash was trying to edge a space on the table to put down the serving platter when Gus hurried back in, rubbing his hair and looking agitated.

'What is it?' Penny asked in concern.

'Hugo's horse Bodybuilder – he's cast himself in the box and Jenny thinks he's broken a leg.'

Tash froze, the smile vanishing as though shot from her face.

'No way!' Stefan stood up so fast that his plate flew out from the table and knocked over a candlestick. He hastily pushed his way from the room.

'Listen, Hugo's talking to Jack Fortescue now, but he's going to want to get up there pretty quickly and he's far too pissed to drive,' Gus said urgently. 'Who can take him?'

'I can,' Rufus offered hopefully. 'I always fancied a crack at Hugo's car.'

'You haven't passed your test yet,' Gus snapped. 'I'd go, but I'm way over the limit. Which of you two is driving?' he asked Lisette and David.

'Hugo was,' Lisette admitted. 'I thought he was staying sober.'

'Typical,' Gus hissed. 'Matty?'

He shook his head. 'I've had at least half a bottle.'

'I'll do it, so I will,' Ma offered with a mild burp. 'If I get stopped, I'll just say I'm a foreigner.'

'I'll call a cab.' Gus looked anxiously at his watch.

'There's no way he'll wait,' Zoe pointed out. 'How much have you had, Tash?'

She bit her lip, trying to think. It suddenly occurred to her that she had been far too busy filling other people's glasses to tend to her own.

'A glass, maybe,' she realised. 'No more.'

'Okay, use the Land-Rover,' Gus ordered. 'Stefan will probably want to come too.'

'You're not going, are you?' Penny looked anxious.

'Of course I fucking am!' He glared at her. 'Don't you understand? The horse is seriously injured. He might never compete again. Hugo will be all over the place.'

Numb with shock, Tash passed the study in which Hugo was still talking to the vet in desperate, urgent tones, telling him to hold on until he got there. Grabbing the keys to Gus's Land-Rover, she shot outside and started it up, thankful that no other cars were blocking it in.

There she sat in the cab for what seemed an endless amount of time, her heart churning with fear for Hugo. Bodybuilder was a big, strong horse – the sort of animal that could recover from a break if carefully tended. And in her experience, horses that cast themselves in the box seldom suffered the sort of severe break that necessitated destruction. But whatever the outcome, Hugo's Badminton chances were in ruins.

Finally, she saw him running out to join her, his face white with worry.

'Let's go!' he hissed as he jumped in beside her.

'What about Stefan and Gus?' Tash stared back to the house. 'I thought—'

'I told them not to come. Now let's fucking go or I'll drive myself.'

The journey was short, fast and silent with Hugo drumming a jittery tattoo on the dashboard and chain-smoking beside her, legs jumping with impatience and fear. With the tragedy of nature mistimed, it was a breath-taking night still caught in twilight, the downs rolling away in dark-velvet, erotic mounds, the shot-silk sky hanging warm and heavy overhead, hinting of a storm. Dead flies clustered on the windscreen as Tash twisted and heaved the cumbersome Land-Rover around the narrow lanes, groaning up the steep hills to Maccombe and finally bouncing up the back drive to the yard. Hugo was out of the cab before she had even braked and rushing to Bod's box, which had both doors closed but from which a thin line of light around the frames showed it up against the rest.

Switching off the engine, Tash hurriedly clambered out to be greeted by astonishing silence. There were none of the usual dogs barking and horses whickering, or even a radio blaring from one of the groom's rooms in the cottages to the left. Just an eerie void. Even the flood-lights were off – the night only illuminated by two exterior bulbs.

She went cold. If Bodybuilder was being urgently treated, she reasoned, surely there would be more light? More noise? More bustle and panic?

As she waited by the Land-Rover, uncertain what to do, she saw Jack Fortescue emerging from the large stable office at the opposite end of the yard, scratching his bald head and squinting at the familiar Land-Rover.

'Oh, it's you, Tash.' He walked towards her. 'What are you doing here?'

'I brought Hugo.' She noticed that he was wearing a dinner suit beneath his moleskin waistcoat and wellies.

He suddenly looked alarmed, his plump, weathered face seeming to sink back towards its bones with worry.

'Where is he?' he asked quickly.

'In the box.' Tash nodded towards it. The top half was now ajar, letting out a bright slash of light that cut left through the yard.

'Shit.' Jack rubbed his head. 'We had to destroy the horse ten minutes ago.'

'You what?' Tash bleated. 'But he only cast himself.'

Jack was already hurrying towards the box. Throwing herself after him, Tash tripped as she caught up.

'The horse was in agony,' he muttered through his teeth as they reached the door. 'It was my decision. Hugo wasn't around to take it.'

'Then you should have given Bod more painkillers until he arrived!'

He paused for a moment. 'That would have killed him too. I must speak to Hugo first, you understand? Bloody awful blow. Excuse me.' He slipped into the box, closing the door behind him.

In the briefest second that Tash saw inside, Hugo was crouched by the big, black horse's head, cradling it in his arms.

She waited outside for a few moments, but heard nothing. She wandered towards the office, but Jenny and two of the other grooms were inside crying, so she moved silently away, anxious not to intrude. Their loss was a communal one and right now she felt far more angry than weepy, rage and indignation flaming inside her on Hugo's behalf. She simply couldn't believe that Jack had made such a catastrophic decision without waiting to consult him. It was unthinkable. He was one of the best eventing vets in the county, knew full well the value of a top competition horse to its owner's happiness, living and livelihood. He had just wiped out Hugo's best horse. She wanted to throw bricks through the windows of his flashy Discovery and slash its tyres in fury.

Eventually she settled on the bonnet of the Land-Rover with her feet resting on the bumper and looked out to the shadowed storm-gathering valley, across the field that she had foolishly agreed to ride down with

Hugo all those weeks ago, when she had thought she was going to marry Niall and live happily ever after.

Then, listening to Hugo's horses shift around in their boxes, she gazed into the dark, hazily obscured distance and recalled that when Hugo had run a warm, lazy hand up her leg, she had almost disintegrated with excitement even though she had been convinced he was just trying to tease her. She had longed for him for so many years, sometimes with such titanic force that it had physically hurt, but each time he'd reached out to touch her she had recoiled, terrified by her feelings, paralysed with fear that he still held her in the same disdain he once had, frightened that he was trying to exact some sort of revenge. For the one time he had really shown his feelings, several summers ago in her mother's overgrown garden in France, she had been far too loopily infatuated with Niall to notice. The memory made her sink her face into her hands in despair.

'Do you want some tea or anything?'

Looking up, Tash noticed that Jenny, looking strangely naked without her usual hat, had tearfully wandered across the yard to the Land-Rover. She shook her head, feeling too sick to drink anything.

'I'm sorry about Bod,' she croaked, about to add how appalled she was by Jack's decision, but Jenny blew her nose loudly and squinted towards the box with puffy eyes.

'Hugo in there with Jack?'

Tash nodded. She was amazed that she couldn't hear Hugo's voice raised in anger, screaming and yelling at the vet.

Blinking, Jenny rubbed her nose and sniffed tearfully. 'He was a mean bugger, old Bod, but we all loved him – mostly 'cos we knew Hugo loved him so much. He almost fell apart when he found out he had Navicular, and now this.'

'What do you mean?' Tash was gaping at her in horror.

'He had Navicular disease, Tash,' Jenny told her in a low voice. 'Very early stages – Jack only diagnosed it a couple of months ago. Just after Hugo lost Surfer.'

'Oh, Christ!' Tash covered her mouth.

'Jack had to do it – no choice. The horse was in agony – stupid, pigheaded sod kept trying to get up even though he was almost unconscious with painkillers. He would never have recovered, not with a future like his.'

Navicular disease was one of the cruellest ailments to affect horses because it was so random, the infection of a tiny, tiny bone in the hoof that developed slowly and relentlessly and was totally incurable.

It caused excruciating pain which could be treated to a degree with drugs, shoeing and diet, but ultimately it always killed. For a horse like Bodybuilder, who lived to work and compete, it spelled the end of their lust for life long before it wiped away life itself. Tash had seen it affecting one of Gus's horses when she'd first joined the yard – an old eventer who had hobbled around on weak legs, desperate to go to every event and hollow with misery when he was left behind. Eventually he lost so much condition and became so depressed that Gus had decided it was kinder to help him on his way.

'He wouldn't have been able to event after this year,' Jenny sniffed, mopping her eyes. 'The pain would have started to slow him down within eighteen months or so, even with those funny corrective shoes he wore.'

Tash closed her eyes as she remembered joking about his roll-toed, wedge-heeled shoes at an event the previous month – telling Hugo that they made Bod look like a seventies swinger.

'Given three years or so it would have crippled him,' Jenny shrugged. 'Hugo could have had him denerved, but it's a dreadful risk. He said he was going to talk to a racing trainer friend about it just this week, but I don't think he held out much hope. Come in for tea later if you feel like it.' Giving Tash's hand a squeeze, she trailed back to the office, glancing up at the threatening storm clouds which had started to gang together overhead.

When Hugo and Jack finally re-emerged, they talked in hushed voices by the door for a few moments, their heads low as the vet passed over a couple of sheets of paper and patted Hugo on the back. Then he headed towards his Discovery, nodding briefly at Tash as he passed. Left behind, Hugo bolted both the doors on the box shut and twisted the large metal knob on the wall that clicked off the interior light, pressing his forehead to it for a moment.

Watching him, Tash wondered whether she should leave: she'd made such a bodge of comforting him after he'd lost Surfer, and now this – he would probably want her to beat it, accusing her of being cursed. But she stayed put, deciding that he could, if he wanted, just walk straight past her to be with his grooms, or head for the house alone or even come over and tell her to piss off. She didn't care, she just couldn't leave him in this state.

He walked towards the Land-Rover, eyes gazing into the black valley. Silently, he heaved himself up beside Tash on the bonnet and lit a cigarette. His hands were shaking so much that he dropped the lighter afterwards. It clanged off the radiator grille and fell to the Tarmac.

'Storm should break soon.' He squinted at the sky. 'It's bloody close.'

Tash nodded, still saying nothing. She kept trying to commiserate, but the words were sticking to the top of her mouth like peanut butter as she fought not to cry. She couldn't believe he was being so dead-pan about it. She guessed he was in shock.

'Will you stay a while?' he asked.

'Of course, as long as you like.'

'Oh, I won't keep you long.' His voice was icy. 'I know you're dying to get back to the dinner party and darling Niall.'

'I won't go back there – not after this.' She shook her head. 'I'll go home.'

He was silent for a few moments, tugging on his cigarette and staring into the distance, his profile lost in shadow. Then he dropped his head to his hands and groaned – a long, low, echoing sound that was one of the saddest Tash had ever heard.

'I can't believe this is happening to me,' he whispered hoarsely. 'Such a bloody diabolical year.'

Saying nothing, she watched as his fingers raked the back of his neck, digging into the knots of tension there.

'I worshipped that horse, Tash.' His voice was muffled, although whether it was from his sleeves or tears, she couldn't tell. 'He was so bloody-minded and so fucking brilliant. I adored that fucking horse. Why'd he have to do something as bloody idiotic as lying down and getting his legs trapped in the corner of his stable? It's so – so fucking pointless.'

'I know.' She touched his shoulder.

For a long time they remained sitting there, Hugo slumped forward in despair and Tash, feeling stiff and awkward and unable to move, touching his shoulder like an old seer bequeathing information to a disciple. The wind had started to pick up now, flattening her thin silk shirt against her arms and making goose bumps spring up all over her, and the clouds were pressing down overhead like a water-logged black tent.

At last he looked up, his hair all over the place, eyes wild.

'Twice in two months. People will think I'm jinxed. Owners will start to take horses away.'

'Of course they won't,' she assured him. 'They'll all feel desperately sorry for you, and angry at how unjust life is.'

'Is that how you feel, Tash?' he asked, turning to her, his eyes suddenly focused and glittering through the gloom. 'That life is unjust?'

'Sometimes,' she hedged uneasily. 'It certainly has been to you this year.'

A loud drum roll of thunder rattled in the distance, making the horses start in their boxes. Tash jumped nervously.

Hugo didn't even seem to notice. He was still staring at her, eyes haunted.

'So far it's been the worse year of my bloody life – which is pretty good going as it's still only May.' He rubbed his hair. 'Let's see. What more have I to lose between now and December? So far I've lost my best horses, my heart and my house to a bunch of idiots with clapper-boards. Will you come to bed with me? I hate storms.'

For a moment Tash wondered whether she'd heard him right.

'Will you come to bed with me?' he repeated in a low, level voice.

If the circumstances hadn't been quite so awful, she would have laughed. She had wanted him to ask her that for almost half of her life – and here it was, the offer, on possibly the worst night they had ever shared.

'No,' she said firmly, not moving and not dropping her gaze.

'No?'

'No.' She shook her head, jumping as another clap of thunder boomed across the valley, much closer this time.

'Okay then.' He shrugged. 'Just thought I'd ask, seeing as you're hanging around. I thought that was what you were after.'

Tash sighed. 'Please, Hugo, don't start all this again. Not here – not tonight.'

'All what?' he demanded, his face momentarily illuminated by a flash of sheet lightning, pale and wild-eyed.

'This "You're gagging for me, Tash" line you keep feeding me. It's hurtful and humiliating and I wish you'd get off my back about it.'

'You were the one who asked me to kiss you if you won Badminton,' he snapped.

Looking insolent, he watched her through narrowed eyes.

'I know I did.' She stared to the turbulent sky in shame. 'I'm sorry. It was a stupid thing to ask.' She pulled her hair back from her face.

'Well, why did you then?'

She blinked as a huge splash of rain ricocheted off her nose. She badly wanted to gibber a great, long explanation, but he was staring at her with such wild-eyed, distraught intensity, she bottled out. It was probably the last thing in the world he wanted to hear right now. If she told him what was going on, she knew she'd crack up completely, and she owed it to Hugo to be strong.

She had no right to suck him into her own swamp of problems.

'My heart goes out to you tonight, Hugo,' she said. 'I'd give anything to take time back, to restore Bod to you. But I can't. All I can be is your friend, and be here for you, but you make it so bloody difficult sometimes.' She stretched out her hands to clutch his, but his fingertips slithered away as silently as a spider.

A steady patter of rain had started tapping on their skulls as the heavens started to open – tentatively at first as though checking that the mechanics were working before opening the sprinklers to full power until it was rattling on the roof of the Land-Rover cab like shingle thrown against a window.

'I've tried to make it difficult.' He suddenly grabbed her wrist tightly. 'Christ, I've been trying to make it impossible. I don't want to be your fucking friend, Tash! Can't you see that? Haven't I been trying to tell you that all year?'

She tried to pull her hands away, but he had a tight hold. The patter was intensifying on their heads now, like the drumming of impatient fingers. Tash's hair was being plastered to her face and her silk shirt was starting to wrinkle and cling like old skin.

'I don't want you as a friend,' he repeated, fingers digging into her tendons like piano wire. 'I can't bear that – it hurts too much. I thought I could hack it, but I can't.'

Wrestling free, Tash rubbed her wrists and watched him hunch away from her, head hanging in utter despair, hair dripping water on to his nose. Her heart had started to do its mad leap-frogging act again and she was fighting for breath. This was absolutely the wrong time to discuss her feelings for him, she realised, but her timing always had been lousy.

'What do you want then?' she managed to croak.

He looked up, his eyes red and hooded with tiredness. 'What's the point? What's the point in fucking telling you?'

Tash realised she had started to shake as the biting wind and driving rain seeped into her skin. The rain was being thrown down in such stair-rods now that it seemed they were almost underwater. It was running into her eyes, trickling into her shoes and pouring in rivulets along the creases of her leather jeans.

Still neither of them moved.

There was a distant rattle above the heaving rain as a motorbike started to approach the yard from the long back driveway. Tash glanced at the headlight bobbing in the distance, refracting in the pressure-hose angled rain, and then back to Hugo.

'I think that's Stefan.' Her voice was drowned by a heavy crash of thunder. A moment later and an arrow of forked lightning unzipped the valley.

As it abated, Tash could hear the bike roaring into the yard entrance behind them, its engine cutting almost immediately.

'I've loved the same man for years and years,' she told Hugo hurriedly, her voice wavering all over the place in her haste to get out the confession before Stefan got close enough to hear. 'And it's not Niall.'

Hugo turned to stare at her, his gaze devouring her face, sad eyes as dark and misty as bilberries. Behind them, Stefan was already wading through the puddles in the yard.

'I've only ever been in love once,' Hugo suddenly muttered, his voice almost inaudible under the din of the storm. 'Bloody awful emotion – I couldn't cope with it at all. I suppose it's okay if you both do it – like eating garlic. I just couldn't get rid of the taste.'

'And now?'

He shrugged bleakly. 'Whoever said it was better to have loved and lost than never to have loved at all was just a loser.'

'Tennyson.' Her voice wobbled.

'You always were better read than me.'

'There are lots of poems about unrequited love,' she croaked. 'And I've had a lot of years to read them.'

He said nothing, bilberry eyes blinking away the rain which was beading his lashes.

The next moment Stefan was towering over them, absolutely sodden, looking the picture of sympathy, his schoolboy face pinched with worry.

'Shit, I'm cracking up for you, my friend.' He loped over to Hugo on his long, thin legs, dripping water everywhere from his cycle leathers. 'Jack phoned the farm to say what had happened.' He wiped water from his face with the back of his glove. 'God, you're both drenched. Come inside.'

'Ah – the next nursing shift, how timely.' Hugo smiled at him before turning back to Tash. 'You can piss off now, Sister French.'

'Hugo—'

'PISS OFF!' His face was venomous.

'Steady on, Hugs.' Stefan held him back as he made a lunge for Tash who scuttled off the car bonnet, tripping in her haste.

'You've had your fun and heard all you wanted to hear to make you feel good.' Hugo spat out his words. 'Go back to Niall and tell him what a sad bastard I am.'

'Hugo, please listen to me—'

'Fuck off, fuck off, FUCK OFF!' he yelled, burying his face in his hands and starting to sob. 'For Christ's sake, get rid of her, Stef. Get her out of here.'

As Hugo wandered unsteadily towards the house, Stefan hastily kissed Tash's cheek and pushed her into the Land-Rover, ducking as the rain flattened his spiky hair and ran into his eyes.

'I'd better follow him,' he yelled over the machine-gun rattle of the downpour on the cab roof. 'I'm sorry, darling. Take no notice of what he said – he's feeling so hellish about Bod that he needs to savage something. I'll look after him. For Christ's sake, drive carefully.'

Tash cried all the way back to Fosbourne, which barely mattered as she couldn't have seen a thing through the windscreen even had she been dry-eyed. The wipers were next to useless in the downpour, and she relied upon knowing the lanes to get her back. Even though she took large chunks of several verges with her, she made it safely. There were floods in several spots, some already almost a foot deep. Had she been in the design classic, she would have been stranded miles from a phone.

She knew she should deliver the car back to Gus and tell them what was going on, but she couldn't bring herself to.

The forge was in power-cut darkness and poor Beetroot, who was terrified by the storm, crawled out from her hiding place beneath the coffee table, positively trembling with fear.

Tash collapsed on the sofa and cuddled her.

'He thinks I'm so blissfully happy with Niall,' she told Beetroot in disbelief. 'How can I adore someone who can be that thick? And so downright, pigheadedly, bloody-mindedly proud?'

Beetroot licked her tears, desperate to reassure her.

Thirty-Four

THE FOLLOWING MORNING, THE Lime Tree Farm mob were eating their usual noisy breakfast, agog to know what had happened at Haydown the night before. Only Zoe was away – out stocking up at Tesco's according to the others.

'Is it open at this time in the morning?' Tash looked at her watch tiredly. It was still before seven.

'Must be,' Penny said brightly.

Settling at the kitchen table, Tash wished that Zoe was around; she was desperate to talk to her about Hugo. His car was still parked in the lane outside the farm from the night before. She'd wanted to drive straight up there that morning to see how he was, but hadn't had the nerve. She had a pretty shrewd idea that she was the last person he'd want to see.

'Sally's just called,' Penny told her, towelling her wet blonde hair dry and eating toast at the same time. 'Apparently she turned up on location first thing this morning to find Hugo shivering in the kitchen with his dogs, and Stefan fast asleep at the table. She thinks they'd stayed up talking all night, but Hugo is still pacing around like a mad thing. I could hear him yelling in the background while she was on the phone.'

'His best horse was destroyed last night,' Tash sighed, helping herself to a coffee. 'I don't think I'd sleep if it happened to me.'

'So what exactly happened?' Gus noticed her red eyes. 'We thought you'd come back here afterwards.'

'We waited up for hours.' Penny was towelling her ears vigorously now.

The mood was all light-hearted cheer and busy activity. Tash could hear India thudding around in her room overhead, and Rufus's stereo already booming out its early-morning bass tattoo. Someone was whistling up on the landing, and out in the yard Ted and Franny were chattering loudly about some pub gossip from the night before.

Settling beside Gus at the table, Tash gave them a brief, painful précis up until her exit from Haydown House the night before. She carefully omitted to mention their lop-sided conversation about love or the fact that Hugo had practically thrown her out of his yard afterwards. The whole thing seemed like a bad dream, she kept having to pinch herself to believe it had actually happened.

'I had no idea Bod had Navicular,' said Gus, absolutely appalled. 'Shit, what a bloody awful thing to know! And Hugo didn't breathe a word to anyone. It must have been eating him up, poor bastard.'

'He was devastated.' Tash took a slug of coffee and winced as it scalded a filling. 'But there was nothing he could do. He knew Bod wouldn't have been able to compete after this year. Badminton was going to be their last big event together. Now he won't even be going.'

At that moment, Kirsty wandered in, looking ratty. 'That friend of you guys is still in the bath,' she moaned, flopping down at the table and starting to leaf through the post. 'Hi, Tash hen. Sorry to hear about last night. Is Hugo okay?'

'Not particularly.' Tash watched her, but she was calmly ripping open a letter from Australia and far more interested in moaning about the bathroom-hogger than asking after Hugo.

'Half an hour he's been in there. What's he doing? Re-tiling the walls?'

'It's Matty,' Penny explained to Tash in an undertone. 'He got totally plastered last night and had to stay here. There was a bit of a confrontation after you'd gone, actually. Poor Sally went back to the hotel – I think she called just now to check he was okay as much as anything.'

'Yes?' Tash wasn't particularly interested. Her brother's problems seemed to pale into insignificance right now.

'You'll never believe this,' Penny went pink, 'but they started having this full dress row at the dining table while we were all tucking in – just after you and Hugo left – it was wildly embarrassing. Niall's mother almost had a coronary.'

'Your brother refused to eat the fish because he's a veggie.' Gus spooned sugar into his tea. 'And Sally cracked some joke about him finding salmonogamy hard to swallow. Didn't quite get it, to be frank. Odd woman, your sister-in-law.'

'The next moment, they were accusing one another of adultery.' Penny shook her head. 'Or rather Matty was confessing to it. With my sister of all people.'

Gus cleared his throat. 'He told Sally in front of everyone that he'd had a fling with Zoe at one of our parties a couple of summers ago. India and Rufus were sitting at the table listening to it all. Poor Zoe didn't know where to look. He even asked her to back him up when he went into details.'

'I thought that was just a bit of a drunken kiss.' Tash rubbed her eyes tiredly. 'Nothing very serious.'

'You knew about it?' Penny gaped at her.

'Niall told me. Did he stay here last night, by the way? Talking to Matty or something?' She hoped he hadn't passed out blind drunk anywhere.

Gus and Penny exchanged glances. 'Yes, something like that. He persuaded his mother to stay at the cast's hotel in Marlbury – she was all set to return to Haydown, which you can imagine would have been a bit sticky. Lisette and David took her in their cab, along with Sally, who was in a state.'

'Poor Zoe.' Tash smiled sadly. 'Her dinner party was a wash-out, wasn't it?'

'Oh, I think it had its compensations.' Gus cleared his throat uncomfortably.

Tash knew she should dedicate a morning to pepping up Hunk's lack-lustre dressage, but she had to get away from the chat and babble of the yard where talk was of nothing but the disastrous dinner party and Hugo's awful loss.

She took Mickey Rourke through the Fosbourne villages and out on to the matrix of old, formal rides that criss-crossed the grounds of a local estate, which the landowner allowed them to use. As the lush green canopy enveloped her like a verdant tunnel, she tried to clear her head as she listened to Mickey's huge, soup-plate feet thud out a muffled, squeaky rhythm in the thick, emerald green grass below. The trees, still wet from the storm, dropped great splashing beads of water on to her shoulders and legs, and Mickey continually tripped over newly exposed tree roots and slithered around on the glassy grass like an oversized grey duckling on a frozen pond. What had

Hugo called him: 'the clumsiest horse I've ever encountered'? Tash bit her lip.

He had lost his two best horses in less than a year, and it was probable that he would also lose his sponsorship and backing as a result. He no longer had a ride at Badminton, a chance for international teams, a career he could reliably live off. He had several brilliant youngsters, but they were still years away from earning their keep in top-grade competitions unless he sold them all to buy a good international horse, and Hugo was unlikely to do that – he liked to make his horses from nothing, not buy them ready-prepared like cakes. His best mid-grade horse that year had been Mickey Rourke, and he had given him back to Tash. Before that it had been Drunken Hunk, and again Tash had benefited from Hugo's belief that a horse should be with a jockey he clicks with.

Tash knew exactly what horse Hugo had always clicked with and longed to have the chance to ride again. He was a horse so similar to Bodybuilder that it was uncanny. She had battled and battled to find the same chemistry with him that Hugo had discovered on the very few occasions he had ridden him, the same chemistry that she had seen him demonstrate with Bod only the previous day.

Tash gazed at Mickey's lop ears and watched them multiply like grey rabbits as tears started to sprout from her eyes. When she'd realised last night that she would lose Snob after Badminton, she'd been almost ripped apart with unhappiness. Now it seemed insignificant. At least Snob would carry on rampaging and causing merry havoc in someone else's yard. Bodybuilder, the greatest Badminton hopeful of all, would never trot out of the Maccombe yard again, never shiver with excitement when he was led into the horse-box at the crack of dawn, realising that he was off to vie for glory. There had been one final victory which Hugo had longed to give him, a ghost of a dream that he had been denied the chance to fulfil.

Tash had the same dream, the same foolish, romantic notion. But her circumstances were far less noble and her nerve far less steady. By giving up her last chance to prove herself, she knew that she could give Hugo a second one. She just wasn't certain she was brave enough to do it.

That evening, Niall returned to the forge after a very boring day's shooting, most of which had been spent waiting for the ground to dry out enough to enact a picnic scene on the downs. He was in a strange, excitable mood that Tash couldn't read, talking incredibly fast and moving around the room like a zephyr as he hastily went through his post, collected his messages and started to change his trousers for a clean pair that were hanging on the rail of the range. He didn't bother to explain why he hadn't returned the night before, nor did he ask her what had happened with Hugo at Haydown, although he had plenty to say on the subject of Bod's inconvenient death.

'Hugo was like a bloody lunatic today,' he told her, wandering around in his underpants. 'He hired this bloody great JCB which rolled up at lunchtime and started heaving chunks of earth out of the bottom of that steep field of his, what's he call it?'

'Twenty Acres?'

''S the one. Lisette is going nuts – I mean, we're shooting the quad bike scene down there on Monday, and here he is digging it up. The next thing a fucking crane turns up and before you know it there's a bloody dead horse swinging around on the end of it, headed for the hole like an oversized fair-ground game!'

It was a typical Niall story told in his hyperbolic style. Tash wanted to deck him for insensitivity. He must be wildly distracted, or drunk, or both.

'He was burying Bod.'

'So he was,' Niall nodded in agreement, pulling on the clean trousers, which were still damp. 'And Lisette is screaming at him the whole time that the horse would have to be moved before the quad bike scene, or she'd have to re-insure the actors for injury by equine grave. I 'clare, it was madness. Finally Hugo stormed off to the house and left them all to it. Jesus, but that man frightens me sometimes. I'm going out tonight, all right?' He started to look shifty, as though he was about to confess to something, but Tash was already halfway to the door.

'Fine,' she said, reaching for her coat. 'So am I.'

She drove the design classic to Maccombe in a daze, half an eye noticing the thick, heavily muddied tracks running all over the flat verges where the Land-Rover had wandered on to them during her return journey the previous night.

It was a mild, bosky evening, so different from the cloying closeness of the night before. The sun, almost resting on the distant ridgeway like a ball on a seal's nose, was drenching the valley in a last pink blush, an hour away from dropping out of view.

Haydown was still buzzing with film types wrapping up for the night as they coiled cables, moved furniture and double-checked everything against the inevitable clip-boarded list.

Hopping with nerves and trepidation, Tash encountered Stefan in the yard watching a young mare being lunged over a grid in the menage.

'I thought they weren't shooting here tonight?' She nodded towards the house.

'They weren't.' He turned to her, squinting through the lowering sunlight. 'But there's been a lot of fuss about the smashed conservatory and Hugo's big dig. They're going to have to go into extra time or something. I heard one of the crew saying they're so behind schedule that they're re-negotiating dates already. Looks like this wrap party will be an unwrapped party.'

Tash closed her eyes. It would make things ten times worse, she realised, if they announced their split at the party. No wonder Niall had looked so evasive earlier.

'I heard about the JCB drama,' she sighed, looking down the sweeping drop of Twenty Acres. Apart from some heavy tyre marks leading to and from the bottom gate and a flat, muddy rectangle beside the large chestnut tree, there was little sign of disturbance, and all the heavy mechanical equipment had long since departed. She felt a great, leaden drag of sadness weighing down her shoulders as she thought of poor, talented Bod lying there.

'It was a bloody fiasco,' Stefan sighed. 'That Lisette is such a bitch – no wonder Niall chose you.'

Tash grimaced, turning her face to the sun to avoid looking at him. 'It wasn't quite like that. Is Hugo around?' She quickly changed the subject.

'Dunno – hang on.' He leaned over the fence and yelled at the girl in the menage: 'Hugo back with The Broker yet?'

'Hours ago.' She jerked her head towards the house. 'He went in there. Follow the sound of pouring scotch.'

When Tash finally tracked him down he wasn't drunk at all. He was swigging tea in the old nursery upstairs wearing a personal stereo and reading *Eventing*. It was obviously one of the few spots in the house he could get some peace – the whole place was crawling with filmies checking off clip-boards and dismantling equipment. He looked dusty and dishevelled, still dressed in his riding gear, straw clinging to his t-shirt. To Tash he'd never looked more forlorn or more desirable, his beautiful face pinched with unhappiness. Once again she fought down the run-to-him-and-leap urge, hovering nearby until he noticed her and pulled off his headphones.

'What d'you want?' he asked guardedly. His blue eyes were squinting from lack of sleep and rimmed with red.

She stood with half the room still dividing them, desperate to remain calm and practical, not smother him with soppy tears and pity.

'I want you to help me out,' she said firmly, launching straight in. 'I need you to ride Snob for me at Badminton.'

'What?' He stared at her levelly, his face guarded.

'I need you – want you – to ride Snob. I can't do it,' she explained hurriedly, moving towards him. 'We've started to fight one another and it's not safe – everyone's been telling me that for weeks, but I couldn't pull him out because he stands such a good chance of winning. Just not with me. You could ride him; you've always handled him better than me.'

Hugo continued staring at her in silence. Close to, Tash could see how exhausted he looked with black smudges beneath his eyes and a little tic rattling in one cheek.

'I phoned the head of the entry committee today, and she told me it would still be allowed if we declare a change of rider on Monday morning. Please, Hugo.'

The muscle in his cheek was twitching more noticeably now, and he was clenching his fists so tightly that the knuckles gleamed through like pearls.

'Will you do it?' Tash asked cautiously, not liking the blue flame glitter of his eyes.

He took a deep, shaky breath and then exploded so angrily that she screamed.

'How DARE you?'

'What?' She reeled backwards.

'How dare you be so fucking insensitive and childish and downright IDIOTIC as to think this can be some sort of bloody consolation prize for my misery?'

She cowered away from him as he stood up, shaking with fury, his face a twisted mask.

'You silly little bitch!' he howled, starting to pace around frenziedly. 'I can't believe you're capable of this – it's bloody beyond me how you even got the notion into your head. Christ!'

'I wanted to help you, Hugo. Can't you see that?'

'Oh, I can see that,' he snarled. 'I can see that all right. I bet you and Niall had a good old chat about it this evening, huh? "What can I do to make poor old Hugs feel better now that his favourite horse has just croaked, Niall baby?" – "I know, Tash angel!"' he aped Niall's accent perfectly. '"Why not offer him a turn on yours?" – "Oh, Niall, you're so clever, darling. I'll do just that." Like a rich kid offering a pauper a ride on his fucking bicycle!'

'It wasn't like that! I didn't mean it like that!'

'You might not think so, but I'm afraid you did, darling,' he drawled, voice ringing with acid mockery. 'Bod wasn't a shitty toy I need a replacement to play with, or a dead hamster that the parents can whip out of a cage and replace with a new, live one undetected. I shed blood and tears on that horse – he was a fucking star and a damned good friend. And now he's dead, so don't you bloody DARE offer me an animal you've spent the best part of two years fucking up so that I can prove I'm a better rider than you. I don't need five days in Gloucestershire with your shoddy seconds to do that, darling.'

Tash couldn't speak for tears. How badly she'd misjudged the situation. She flinched as he started backing her towards a wall, his pale, furious face just inches from hers.

'I never imagined you capable of shallowness to this degree, Tash,' he whispered, voice seething with blame. 'Christ! I can't believe I thought so much of you. I was talking crap when I said I loved you last night. I was just pissed and fucked up about losing Bod.'

For a moment Tash thought she'd misheard him. She'd played that conversation over and over in her head all day. She knew exactly what he'd said. She stared into his blisteringly angry face, taking in the ice-chip eyes, snarling mouth, beautiful, straight nose with its nostrils flared in contempt.

'You didn't say you loved me, Hugo,' she said.

'Didn't I?' For a moment his gaze flickered. 'Are you sure?' He sounded as though he was confirming a feed order, voice snappy and abrupt.

She nodded frantically. 'You told me you didn't want to be my friend, and that falling in love was like eating garlic, and that Tennyson was a sad loser. And then you told me to get lost.'

'Oh.' He rubbed his chin awkwardly, moving away. 'I was obviously in a more philosophical mood than I thought.' He was looking hugely uncomfortable now, shoulders hunched, hands banging together, legs moving stiffly. Tash had never seen him so self-conscious.

'What –' she started cautiously, voice wobbling with nerves and hope '– made you think you said you loved me last night?'

He turned back to her, chewing his lip for a moment, still looking jumpy. Then the easy, mocking smile slid back into place.

'I think I probably wanted a shag.' He shrugged. 'I do seem to recall asking, now I think about it. And I certainly needed cheering up – the

"I love you" line usually works. Thank God I didn't try it after all – I was probably far too plastered to get it up.'

She yelped, backing away as though struck. 'You don't mean that!'

'Don't I?' he laughed. 'You were certainly giving me the come-on at the farm earlier. Or did you just want to make that childish kiss-the-bride Badminton deal because you know you haven't a hope? I expect that's why you're offering me Snob now. At least that way he stands a chance of winning.'

With a sob, Tash threw back her arm and, not stopping to think, swung her hand with all her weight behind it. Her palm and his cheek made contact with such an almighty smack that she winced, her hand buzzing with pain.

For a moment he gazed at her, eyes watering, one pale cheek starting to colour. Then he strode out, heels clicking on the polished floors until they faded away.

Tash raced from the house, crashing past Lisette and the ubiquitous clip-boarded minion as she ran.

'Tash – hello there!' Lisette called after her, but Tash had already pelted towards the design classic, which unusually started first time.

By the time Lisette had raced after her to the yard, Tash was shooting up pebbles and toxic fumes in her wake. Once again the lanes from Maccombe to the Fosbournes got a heavy hammering under her erratic driving.

Once again Niall didn't return to the forge that night.

The phone rang again and again but, certain that it was either her mother or Henrietta eager to discuss what shade of dog collar the vicar should wear, Tash had disconnected the fax and answerphone and simply let it drone on unanswered. Hugging Beetroot for comfort, she listened to Abba's greatest hits at full blast to punish herself some more for her idiotic attempt to cheer up Hugo and appease his pain. He was right, she was as shallow as a puddle in a drought. She'd wanted so much to believe that he'd almost confessed to loving her last night, but when she thought back with the agonising logic of hindsight, she'd dressed like a siren at Zoe's dinner party and he'd hardly noticed it when he arrived, simply making the usual derisive remarks. In fact, he'd only started flirting with her after she'd asked him to kiss her if she won Badminton. And he'd been pissed then. Later, when they'd raced up to Haydown, she'd hung around to comfort him, and instead of letting him ramble on about the horse he'd just lost, she had engineered the conversation towards their feelings for one another instead. No wonder he'd told her to piss off the moment Stefan arrived. She wanted to die with humiliation.

Her mother had always taught her the old truism that if one wanted something enough, it happened. Tash decided that she was living proof that there wasn't always truth behind clichés. If one wanted something hard enough, for long enough, the disappointment of not getting it just grew greater and greater.

'You still here?' Hugo snapped as he encountered Lisette prowling around his kitchen with a large gin and tonic – almost certainly his own. She was doubtless going to bawl him out about the Twenty Acres fiasco again.

But she greeted him with a big, slinky smile instead.

'I've been waiting for you,' she purred cheerfully. 'Stefan said you were skulking around the attics, but I couldn't get very far beyond the door. It's a pig-sty up there.'

'Do feel free to whisk around it with a duster if you want,' he snarled, stalking across to the fridge and extracting a pint of milk.

'Don't be facetious, Hugo.' She smiled, leaning back against a huge old laundry cupboard and watching him. 'I want to have a little chat.'

'Oh, yes?' He swigged back milk straight from the carton.

'About Niall.'

'In that case I certainly don't want to know,' He headed towards the hall door again, whistling for his gang of dogs.

Lisette clinked the ice in her glass and waited until he was almost out of the room.

'. . . and Zoe Goldsmith.'

He paused, framed in the doorway, and turned very slowly around to look at her, face still indifferent. 'What about them?'

'You saw them the other night, the way they kept moving together like doubles partners between tennis rallies – and you saw Tash too, watching them and looking as though her world had been wiped out. Don't pretend you didn't, darling. I could see your eyes following her everywhere. Talk about eyeball and chain.'

'A lot has happened since then,' he muttered, leaving against the door frame.

'Indeed.' She took a long sip of her drink, watching him over the rim. 'For one, I know you've been talking to Tash today. I saw her running through this house earlier looking as though there'd been a death in the family.'

'Oh, yes?' He fiddled with the milk carton.

'What have you been saying to her, Hugo?' Lisette demanded.

'That's none of your fucking business.'

She rattled the ice in her glass, voice steely. 'Did you tell her that Niall and Zoe spent last night together?'

'Did I what?' Hugo gaped at her, genuinely astounded. 'Whyever should I say that? It's not true, is it?'

Lisette opened her mouth and shut it again, her huge, feline eyes regarding his face mistrustfully. 'No, of course it's not true. Just location gossip – you know how ridiculously exaggerated these things get. I just didn't want Tash finding out and getting upset about some bitchy extra's lies, that's all.'

'Of course you didn't.' Hugo ripped a shred from the carton and smiled at her levelly.

'Well, that's okay then.' Lisette started to polish off her drink, eager to curtail the conversation.

'You're signing over your share in Snob to Tash when they marry, aren't you?' Hugo said idly.

'Yes, it's okay, I haven't abused my promise,' she muttered, picking up her handbag. 'I told you I wouldn't sell the bloody thing to anyone else, although God knows I think you were mad not to have taken me up on my offer. Stefan let slip last night that you've been after the horse for years.'

'Well, I've changed my mind.' Hugo wandered forward, not taking his eyes off hers. 'I want to buy your share now.'

'It's too late.' She waved a dismissive hand. 'I spoke to my solicitor this week. He's drawing up an official transferral document or something – I had no idea how complicated these things are. Did you know that horse is worth more than a small house in Chelsea?'

'Of course I know.' Hugo was just a foot away from her now. 'And I'll pay you what your share's worth – the full amount. No bargain offers.'

She shook her head, matching his gaze. 'I've promised Tash now. And we wouldn't want to break her little heart by going back on a deal, would we? Not your darling protégée?'

Eyes still boring into hers, Hugo smiled easily. 'I'm not interested in her. I'm purely interested in acquiring the horse.'

'Sure!' she scoffed. 'And the fact that Tash only gets my share when she marries Niall has nothing to do with your sudden change of heart? I thought of that little clause myself. Rather neat, huh? I guessed it might piss you off.'

'It might have escaped your notice,' Hugo said, his face absolutely expressionless, 'but I lost my best horse last night. I don't have another in my yard to replace him. My career is on the rocks as a result, and if I don't find another top-grade animal bloody soon, I'll probably lose my sponsors. Snob is perfect.'

'And what makes you think Niall would ever sell you the remaining share even if I do agree?' sneered Lisette, totally unsympathetic.

'Because I'll offer him so much money he can't refuse,' Hugo said simply.

Lisette laughed. 'Christ, you're a selfish bastard, aren't you, Hugo?'

They were less than a foot apart now. Lisette could feel the heat from his body and could just catch the lightest, earthy tang of sweat and straw rising from it. His eyes met hers with such teasing seductiveness that she couldn't help but smile. Boy, was he pretty. Looking at him, she knew without doubt that he was one of the most desirable men she had ever encountered, worth a dozen shallow, self-seeking Davids with their this-is-my-first-affair sham liberalism, their ageing vanity and pseudo-intellectualism. Hugo was hot-headed and physical and gloriously deceitful. Not only was he so exquisitely put together that the eye was dragged to him over and over again in disbelief at such perfection, but he had a desperate, passionate will which she also recognised in herself. They were both people who wanted things very, very badly indeed, and loathed giving up on them, however desperate the odds. And Lisette had wanted Hugo for a very long time. But she had wanted a successful career more, and for longer, and she knew she had a far better chance of keeping it. Hugo would slip through her fingers before she'd even familiarised herself with the feel of his skin. Trapping him was like trying to catch a leaf in a gale.

'Okay,' she said, voice melting with intimacy. 'I'll do you a deal. You can buy my share of the horse on two conditions. The first is that he wins Badminton next week.'

'Christ, you don't ask much, do you?' he laughed bitterly. 'What's the second? That he sprouts wings and helps slay Chimera?'

'The other,' Lisette smiled delightedly, 'is that you leave Tash French alone. If I hear that you've so much as winked at her over the next week, the deal's off. And believe me, I'll be listening hard. Steer clear, Hugo. Hands off. She chose Niall over you two years ago, and she's not about to change her mind two weeks before the wedding.'

One of Hugo's straight, dark eyebrows shot up. 'Even though Niall is having a last fling with Zoe Goldsmith?'

'I told you, that was gossip,' Lisette said lightly. 'You heard him at Zoe's dinner party. He talked about the wedding non-stop. You have to accept that Tash is going to marry him, Hugo. She loves him. Face it, the only thing you have a hope of wrapping those long legs of yours around is her horse. It's the closest you'll get.'

'Boy, you do like to protect Niall's interests, don't you? Anyone would think you were his mother, not his ex-wife.'

'I don't want you fucking this up for either of them, Hugo.' Lisette gathered her car keys. 'I'm only offering to do this because you're so bloody irresistible, I can't quite bring myself to give you a flat no. Now do we have a deal?'

Hugo shrugged. 'Sure. Snob has to win Badminton and I have to keep my hands off Tash, then I'll get to buy your share. Frankly, I think I have a better chance of marrying Niall.'

Thirty-Five

SCHOOLING SNOB THE FINAL Sunday before Badminton, Tash started to hope that she might enjoy their hardest – and probably last – test together after all. He dropped his head and listened for once and by the end of an hour-long jumping session, Gus was actually applauding them both as she rode out of the ring.

'Great! Go like that for the rest of the week and I might even put a fiver on you.'

But that afternoon, Snob disgraced himself once more as she rode him out on the heat-hazed ridgeway with Ted on Mickey and Kirsty on her great old mare, Betty Blue. Spooking at a kite being flown by a young boy, he went bananas and decided that it was in his and Tash's best interests to bolt as fast and as far from this potentially life-threatening airborne murder-weapon as possible. His flight was far more life-threatening – as Tash ducked the low branches that threatened to decapitate her, his hooves scattered large flints and divots, missing the huge track-grooves left by farm vehicles in the winter by inches, only just dodging rabbit holes and loose wire coils from the sheep fencing that was flashing past Tash's left leg at an alarming rate.

It took her almost a mile to pull him up, fighting and tugging all the way and thanking her lucky stars that he hadn't come to harm. He'd been like a bulldozer with its accelerator jammed on full and was so supremely fit that he could have carried on like that for miles if he so chose. That was a taste of what she would get if he finally fought the battle and won across country and the prospect terrified her.

When she rejoined Ted and Kirsty, they hacked back in silence while Tash descended into lower and lower spirits.

'Hunk's going brilliantly, isn't he?' Ted asked to cheer her up as they neared the farm, the horses' hooves ringing out.

Tash nodded, but it simply pointed up how badly Snob was going. And he was the one she desperately wanted to succeed, however unfair she knew it was on her dear, gentlemanly Hunk. Because Snob was the horse she was going to lose. Her short-fused, hot-headed chestnut who was as ingenious one day as he was unco-operative the next, was picking up on her nerves and unhappiness, however hard she tried to keep them covered.

To her surprise Hugo was sitting at the Lime Tree kitchen table when she walked in, chatting amicably to Gus and sipping coffee from one of the farm's assortment of mismatched, chipped mugs. When Tash slid past to fetch herself a Coke from the fridge, she noticed that it said 'Natasha' – a birthday gift from Rufus.

It was the first time she had seen him since his outburst in the nursery at Maccombe, and she felt understandably twitchy as she dug around in the fridge and then pulled the ring on the can, which predictably caused a minor explosion of froth on the front of her shirt. She couldn't even bring herself to say hello to him, simply wanted to beat a retreat as hastily as possible. But Gus curtailed her escape with a wave of his hand, indicating she should join them.

'Hugo's come over with a suggestion,' he greeted her with a sly smile. 'An idea with which I gather you are not altogether unfamiliar.'

'Oh, yes?' Tash slid into a chair at the opposite end of the table to Hugo, but on the same side so that she didn't have to look him in the face.

'I'm not sure it's really for the best, though, as I've just been telling him,' Gus went on. 'Not after this morning's performance at any rate.'

'Oh, yes?' Tash repeated, her voice growing more and more squeaky.

In her peripheral vision, she saw that Hugo had turned his chair towards her, but she remained staring fixedly at Gus. Her expression must have been fairly rabid because he shot her a concerned look.

'I'm offering to take on the ride with Snob next weekend,' Hugo said gruffly, not looking at her either. 'If you want me to. You said you'd been having one or two problems with him which you feel a change of jockey might remedy.'

Tash swallowed and said nothing for a moment. The temptation to tell him that she was having no such thing was enormous, but she knew that she would be fooling herself and that the slightest word from Ted and Kirsty – who could wander in at any moment – would blow her cover so high it would be in orbit. Yet she was loth to agree so readily after he had thrown her suggestion back in her face the night before. She couldn't believe he had the nerve to perform such a volte-face without apologising first.

'I told you she wouldn't be so keen now,' laughed Gus. 'The horse was going spectacularly this morning, and she's put a heck of a lot of groundwork into him this year, haven't you, Tash?'

'Yes,' she managed to gulp.

'Far more than the other horses, which I would tell her off about if she weren't earning more sponsorship than the rest of us put together.'

'Not for long,' Tash muttered, managing to smile at him. 'You might win the deal at Badminton.'

'Against Brian Sedgewick? I'm certainly not counting on it,' Gus said curtly. 'So I take it you're turning down Hugo's offer?'

Tash found that she couldn't answer. Much as she longed to say yes, logically it would give Snob a real chance. She may not be made for Hugo, but she knew Snob was. But by giving Hugo the ride on him, she would be giving away what was probably her last ever chance to compete the horse she loved more than any other, the horse who – for all his bad-tempered, misanthropic disobedience – she knew adored her too. In many ways she idolised Snob because he was the equine version of Hugo himself – utterly uncompromising, hopelessly proud, fearsomely loyal. And just as she had failed ever to win Hugo's respect, so she felt she was admitting defeat with the horse she had battled to prove herself with.

'Tash?' Hugo was trying to catch her eye now.

'You can ride him.' She stood up, directing her next words towards the top of his head. 'I'll let the officials know. There shouldn't be a problem – particularly once everyone finds out what happened to Bod.' She finally stole a look at him, adding smoothly: 'I'm sure you'll get the sympathy vote. Should be good for a few dressage points, if nothing else. That's his weakest phase.'

With that she stomped gracelessly out.

Her exit was ruined by both Gus and Hugo pursuing her into the yard.

Gus had not registered the acidity of her little speech.

'Great, Tash – very brave decision. I'm proud of you!' he puffed after her as she strode quickly towards the menage where Franny was giving

Hunk a quick work-out. 'If you're about to have a session, we could get Hugo up with you and you can give him some tips.'

Ahead of them by a few paces, Tash closed her eyes and let out a low groan of horror.

'Snob's been out twice already today,' she said. 'He'll be really ratty if he's hauled out to do flat-work at this stage, you know what he's like. I'd leave it until the morning.'

Gus was about to protest, but Hugo stopped him.

'She's right. I'm whacked too. I'm going to dash home for a shower and then I'm coming back to take Tash out to dinner at the Olive Branch to say thanks – you and Pen too, Gus,' he added quickly when Tash turned to gape at him in horror. 'And Franny,' he muttered rashly as his irascible, black-eyed former groom rode up on Hunk whom she'd been working in ready to let Tash take over.

'No, thanks – it'd choke me,' she hissed, sliding off the big bay and into her jazzy snakeskin cowboy boots.

'Still not my biggest fan then?' Hugo watched her impassively as she handed Hunk's reins over to Tash.

Not deigning to reply, Franny stomped off, rubber top squeaking.

'I wasn't aware that you had any fans, Hugo,' Tash muttered, leading Hunk away towards the mounting block.

'Oh, I have Stefan,' he said, starting back towards the house as she mounted Hunk.

Gus sighed, glancing thoughtfully over his shoulder at her. 'I'm rather surprised by her decision, to be honest, though not displeased – she deserves a medal with that horse, the amount of extra hours and patience she's put into him. He must drive her mad sometimes, and he's nearly killed her more than once. If he were mine, I'd have shot him by now.' He slapped his hand to his mouth. 'Shit! Bloody glib of me. I'm so—'

'Forget it.' Hugo shook his head. 'One loses horses, it's a fact. It's hell, but it happens. The thing to do is appreciate them while they're around, which isn't something I've always been good at.' At the farm door he turned back and watched Tash trotting out of the yard.

'Tash adores that chestnut bugger.' Gus greeted Wally who was waiting for them by the door, tail gyrating as he crawled along on his belly, grinning happily. Moments later Beetroot, at last season-free, had shot out too and was hurling herself delightedly at Hugo.

'I know she does,' he said, stooping to say hello and laughing as her eagerly lapping tongue smothered his chin with kisses. 'And I plan to repay her for this.'

'With dinner?' Gus looked sceptical. 'I'm not entirely sure she'll want to come.'

'No, not with dinner.' Hugo shook his head.

'What then? Don't tell me you're going to bung me another grand? I told you months ago that she was good enough to earn her own keep.'

'I'm not sure yet.' Hugo chewed his lip, straightening up from his nose-to-snout chat with Beetroot.

'What's your game?' sighed Gus irritably. 'I mean, we've played along with it here because we bloody well need the cash, but it's not like you're doing it to give her a start in the sport anymore. She's arrived. She's off to Badminton next week.'

'You said it. You need the cash,' Hugo said simply.

But Gus laughed and shook his head. 'Why don't I believe that? Why have I never quite been able to bring myself to believe that?'

'Because you're the most mistrustful, pessimistic sod I know.' Hugo grinned and headed towards the kitchen where Penny was ferreting around amongst a pile of entry forms.

'Bloody Zoe has completely gone to pot lately,' she was grumbling. 'I've just had Miranda Bingham on the phone asking why we're not doing Hyam Park this year, and when I told her we had five horses entered she told me it was the first she'd heard of it. Zoe can't have posted the sodding form and the entries are closed now.'

'Shit!' Gus looked livid.

'Tell me if I'm off beam here.' Hugo settled back at the table, letting Beetroot scramble heavily and precariously on to his lap. 'But are Zoe and Niall having a walk out?' He sounded so completely casual that he could have been asking whether the Royal family had been having marital problems.

For a moment Penny and Gus masked up with blank expressions and awkward side-glances at one another, and then Penny let out a heavy sigh and shook her head.

'Ludicrous, isn't it? I mean, I know he has a reputation, but two weeks before his wedding is ridiculous, and she is going to be so hurt. He still seems hell-bent on getting married.'

'Does Tash know?' Hugo eyed them.

'Shouldn't think so.' Gus raised his eyes to the ceiling. 'She's been so busy trying to sort out Snob, and Niall has the perfect excuse with this film thing. It's been like a French farce here – Tash heads out of one door and bloody Niall slopes in the other, all smiles, as blatant as you like. He's too likeable to be a real bastard, but I could have wrung his neck this week.'

'Be fair,' Penny pointed out. 'We think they only really got it together on Friday night, after Tash had . . .' She shut up and covered her mouth, remembering why Tash had left.

'Go on,' Hugo muttered.

'Well,' Penny was clearly being cautious, 'they seemed to change that night – become far more open about it. I can't be sure what happened, but the weird thing was that no one commented. I mean, they seem so comfortable together – so right, somehow. Even the kids adore him. India seems actively to encourage them to get together.'

'Poor bloody Tash,' sighed Gus. 'It's diabolical for her. When she finds out – and let's face it, she must – she'll fall apart. She thinks she's going to be Mrs O'Shaughnessy in a fortnight.'

Hugo's jaw tightened.

'Well, that's bloody farcical for a start!' Penny sniffed. 'I mean, does he need a British passport or something? Is that it?'

'Nope.' Hugo rubbed his chin nervously. 'But I'm pinning all my hopes on the fact that Tash needs an exit visa.'

'You've lost me.' Gus shook his head. 'Am I still a bloody usher or what?'

'Christ knows. I'm supposed to be one too. I'm just hoping I get to kiss the bride first.'

That night in the Olive Branch, Tash was uncertain how to take Hugo. She'd only come at all because Penny had pleaded with her, sounding unusually desperate. But the last person she wanted to share a table with that night was Hugo. She felt more like breaking arms than bread.

He rolled up wearing clean chinos and a baggy green Italian jacket that had Marco Angelo in raptures. He certainly looked glorious and smelled so good that Tash had to lean away. His ruffled, tortoiseshell hair gleamed like a polished desk top and his eyes were back to their clear, bright sparkle without a trace of bloodshot derision. Tash couldn't think what had got into him. He even took her coat and hung it up for her before steering her towards a bar-stool, like Fabio on a hot date.

'I thought Penny and Gus would be here?' she muttered as they waited at the bar, reading menus while Marco Angelo freed a table for them in the restaurant.

'They're coming on later – they phoned to say they'd be late. You look lovely.' This was added so quickly and quietly that Tash took a while for it to register.

She had dressed in such a tearing hurry that her clothes were still sticking to her from a rushed shower. Having worked on Hunk and settled him into a much more fluid dressage routine, she'd only had time to plunge into a polkadot red sundress that was ancient but sexy, according to Niall. She'd been halfway to the pub before she realised that the top three buttons had popped off when she was much fatter and, on close inspection, it was practically see-through, so that her black undies were perfectly visible if she stood in front of so much as a candle.

'I thought we were eating in the bar,' Tash glanced across to the formal restaurant where the women were far more opulently dressed.

'We can if you prefer it.' He gazed around for a free table.

'I don't care.' She jutted out her chin and took a slug of her gin and tonic. The chin trick had been a bad idea, she realised, as drips of frothing tonic splashed on to her chest and rolled between her breasts. She was so on edge. She longed to be cool and hostile, but it was impossible. The old magic worked every time; she only had to be in the same room as him to feel like an Alka-Seltzer dropped into a can of Fanta.

Hugo smiled, tilting his head towards her so that she had to look into those icy blue eyes. She was rather taken aback to find them melting with warmth. It was such an odd expression on his usually hostile face that she stared and stared.

'I apologise for yesterday,' he said quietly. 'I was unforgivably rude. I know you were doing it for the best of reasons.'

'Well, it certainly didn't take you long to change your mind,' she said grumpily. 'And I'm fed up with your apologies. They're as shallow as your forehead.'

For a moment he looked as though he was going to bite her head off, but held himself in check and simply said, 'I'm sorry. I was in a hell of a state.'

'I didn't mean to make it worse for you. I just wanted—' She ground to a halt, finding it impossible to explain.

'Wanted what?' he persisted.

'Nothing.' Tash shook her head, looking away. 'Forget it. You're right, my timing has always been lousy.'

'You can say that again.' He shrugged. 'This wedding for one.'

'What do you mean?' She looked up at him sharply, but his face was impassive.

'A week after Badminton – the middle of the season, Tash.' He smiled. 'What were you thinking of?'

She squirmed uncomfortably. 'It was my mother's suggestion,' she muttered hastily, desperate to shuffle away from the subject. Her stomach was heaving at the thought. She hadn't seen Niall for more than five minutes in two days, but he was still insisting that they breathe a word to no one until the following Sunday at the wrap party, still believing that some last-minute miracle solution might present itself over the next week. Tash wondered vaguely if the Lottery had been drawn yet, and then realised that her tickets had been in the pocket of a pair of jeans she'd boil-washed that morning.

'I hope the wedding justifies it,' Hugo said lazily, eyes never leaving her face.

'Oh, I'm sure it will,' she said hollowly, her head spinning. He was sounding almost as eager as her mother now. She felt slightly sick as a result. 'So do you want me to fill you in on how to get the best out of Snob?' She tried to change the subject.

'No – we'll talk about that tomorrow,' he said gently, looking up as the door to the pub opened. 'Tell me,' he dropped his voice, 'does it bother you that Niall is absolutely mad for Zoe?'

'What?' She almost fell off her chair.

'Because,' he studied his glass carefully before taking a sip, 'I'm bothered. I'm bloody bothered because I'm so mad for you I can't sleep at night. And I resent your fucking up my eight hours' kip – they'd be far more pleasant if you were with me.'

She gaped at him, jaw swinging. But the next moment Penny and Gus were settling in beside them with kisses and apologies for being so late. Hugo had timed it perfectly. There was no way Tash could tackle him about what he'd just said in front of them.

For the rest of the evening he behaved like a perfect gentleman, checking that her glass was full and her plate heaving with all manner of goodies. He talked calmly and cheerfully to them all, not favouring her and certainly not hinting at the slightest trace of flirtation. If his hand accidentally touched hers, he removed it; if his eyes met hers, he smiled and then looked calmly away. At one point a warm ankle touched hers with just the lightest pressure.

Tash felt a pulse suddenly leap to her throat as she fought to keep up the rather dull conversation she was having with Gus about Hunk's tendon whilst daring herself to return the pressure. The pulse was going so wildly inside her that she found herself waving her leg rather feverishly around under the table in her excitement.

'Are you all right, Tash?' Gus gave her an odd look. 'Only you appear to be kicking me.'

'Fine!' she gulped, pulling her leg hastily back towards her chair and blushing furiously.

I must have heard him right, she told herself. I'm sure he said it. I'm sure he said he was crazy for me. Oh, God, I want to talk to him alone, NOW. I want him to say it again.

She tried frantically to catch Hugo's eye, but he was gossiping to Penny about who was going to Lisette's party, and resolutely refused to glance in her direction.

Penny was the first to look up. 'You must be excited, Tash. First a star-studded shindig here, then only a week until you say "I do" – or are you planning to say something different?'

'What?' Tash squeaked, staring from her to Hugo like an umpire at a tennis match.

'Have you and Niall made up trendy new vows like "I promise to interact with my equal spouse for richer or more fiscally challenged"?'

'Oh, no – I mean, I don't know. Not sure.' She scrunched up her forehead in confusion. Whipping up her knife and fork with what she hoped was ravenous speed, she started on her untouched lamb. It was as tepid as ditch water in a drought.

'Glad you've noticed that at last,' Hugo laughed, lighting a cigarette.

Looking up, she realised that they had all finished theirs ages ago.

For the next ten minutes, she prayed that Gus and Penny would decide that they needed to go to the lavatory at the same time so that she could corner Hugo alone. She determinedly kept topping up their glasses with water and wine, much to the head waiter's disgust at being done out of his job. She even went herself as she hoped this would encourage them, but they made no sign of paying a visit. They must have bladders like camels' humps, she thought sourly. Finally she resorted to suggesting politely that they might be in need of a natural break, and why not do it before the desserts arrived?

'Why?' Gus gave her a puzzled look.

'Oh – no reason,' she said brightly. 'I just thought you might be holding out – to be, er, polite.'

After Gus and Hugo had ploughed through dessert and were debating what sort of coffee to go for, another ploy struck Tash and she yawned widely.

'I'm bushed,' she apologised rather hammily. 'I might just wander back to the forge and crash out – it was a lovely meal. Thanks, Hugo.'

She paused for a beat, waiting for him to offer to walk her home. But Penny got in there first with a far less welcome suggestion.

'Good idea – I'm shattered too. Come back with me to the farm for a tea, Tash, and collect Beetroot. We'll leave the men to talk horse.'

Tash inwardly cursed. She'd forgotten that she'd left Beetroot with India and Ted. She should have asked for a double espresso.

Penny said little on the walk back, although Tash had a strange suspicion that she was waiting for some sort of confession from her. She was feeling far too irritated and frustrated to talk much anyway. Dictating the pace, she marched to the farm so quickly that Penny was panting to keep up. Skirt flapping, Tash slammed her way through the front door, eager to grab Beetroot and scram.

Zoe and Niall were embracing by the fridge. Despite the awful setting – the mess, food debris, scattered tea-towels, hovering dogs – it was as tender and earth-shattering a kiss as he could ever dream of acting out on film. Tash stopped and stared in wonder.

Only Beetroot, growling furiously by the Aga, hackles up as she eyed Niall, was not a rapt member of the audience.

'I wish you'd go slower, Tash! I've been—' Penny puffed in behind her and then stopped in shock.

Instantly, Niall and Zoe swung around in horror, their faces utterly appalled as they realised that Tash was there.

'This is a Tash French farce,' she joked, echoing Gus's words earlier that day. 'Talk about fridge magnetism.'

'Christ, angel, I'm sorry!' Niall rushed towards her. 'We didn't want you to find out this way. Truly we didn't. I'm so—'

'I already knew, Niall.' She stopped him, stretching up to cover his mouth, watching the tragedian's face registering surprise, the melting brown eyes blink, the flop of black curls shadow his creased brow. She almost laughed. She had known he would react exactly like this. To the word, expression and gesture.

'I knew,' she repeated. 'And I don't mind. Honestly. I think you're both lovely.' Backing slowly away and whistling for Beetroot, she walked out on them.

Unexpected tears washed her face as she stumbled down the lane, trying to absorb what she had just seen. She might not be surprised, might not be particularly jealous or angry – she had no right anymore. Yet she still felt a great dam-burst of emotion that the affair was finally showing in Technicolor on a screen near her. Niall loved Zoe – it was written all over his face like a punk's tattoo. It was why he had been avoiding Tash so much lately; he was ashamed by the haste with which he had raced from being her fiancé to Zoe's lover. Niall had always been like that: he so loathed being alone that he sought a lover wherever he went, even if they only ever made love in his imagination. But Zoe was more than that. She suited him so well it must have been like an itch he'd wanted to scratch for months, and now it had been allowed to develop into a great blushing rash. Despite his guilt, Tash could forgive him the speed. After all, he had forgiven her the ultimate infidelity, hadn't he? He had forgiven the fact that in all the time they were in love, she had loved another more, however she'd tried to deny it.

'I love Hugo,' she said aloud, to test herself. Beetroot, trotting beside her, looked up eagerly. She seemed to approve, so Tash said it again. Several times. She even shouted it once, but they were passing the swanky mill house at the time and the heat-sensitive security light came on so she shut up.

She knew that in many ways Niall was the better man, the kinder man, the brighter man, yet her head could not reason with her unruly heart. She even loved Hugo for being scornful and headstrong and utterly spoilt, because beneath his glib, unyielding exterior there was such generosity. It surfaced at the oddest moments so that sometimes she barely noticed it, yet it was steadfast and unswerving and surprisingly selfless. Because once someone, or something, won his respect, Hugo never, ever let them down, through earning that respect seemed harder to achieve than a brass-rubbing of the Holy Grail.

Earning his respect was perhaps harder for Tash than anyone else. For two summers ago in her mother's garden in France, he had made a pass at her and she'd committed the ultimate faux pass. She'd kicked Hugo right where it hurt most – in his pride. Coming anywhere near his closely guarded emotions again was definitely trespass.

Yet even his increased nastiness had been a terrible, heart-pinching clue. She'd uncharitably assumed that his backing off and sniping simply coincided with her success in the sport they shared; but, looking back, their friendship had only really cooled off when Niall had rented the forge and they had moved in together. And Hugo had become even more explosive since the announcement of the engagement. Those terrible, spiteful passes he had made, demanding to know exactly how she felt about him and whether she still hawked her crush around in her heart like a battered keep-sake. She'd thought he was playing a game with her, when all along it seemed he'd been desperately trying to understand the rules. Being Hugo, he had wanted to lose no face by admitting his feelings and had consequently played his cards so close to his chest that even he had difficulty seeing them.

Yet tonight Hugo had said he was so mad for her he couldn't sleep: the words still rang in her ears like campanologists on an all-night ringathon. She wouldn't stop hearing them for hours, remembering that soft, deep, drawling voice, shivering as she recalled the electric reaction she'd experienced when she'd realised what he'd just said. Despite everything that was going on, he had said it.

She stood stock still as she realised that she was still officially marrying Niall in thirteen unlucky days. In all her excitement, her pre-Badminton nerves and fridge snog-watching, she'd practically blanked out the reality of the situation.

Thirty-Six

THE FOLLOWING MORNING TASH watched Hugo ride the eager Snob around the small course of solid fences that the Moncrieffs had erected years ago, and held her breath with admiration and envy. Snob respected this rider, with his longer legs, heavier body-weight and firmer aids, and he was clearly revelling in the change. At first he put up a spirited battle when he realised that he wasn't going to get his way, snatching the bit and dipping his head as of old, but it didn't take him long to settle and Tash found herself wishing he'd put up a bit more of a fight just to show Hugo what a bugger he could be.

But it seemed that he and Hugo were on their best behaviour.

'You've really taught this nag some manners,' he complimented her. 'And you must work him out more than Mr Motivator – I've never known a horse so fit and supple.'

'Lots of sex,' Tash said levelly.

'What?' Hugo gaped at her and then started to laugh. 'Oh, yes – ha! Definitely.' He rode off, sitting easily on the unfamiliar horse, his long legs with their battered black suede chaps barely moving as he set Snob into a long, liquid canter. Tash wished he hadn't worn those chaps; they made her go weak at the knees. She preferred him in a manky old pair of cord breeches and a bad temper. Later, when they all piled into the kitchen for a bread and cheese lunch, she deliberately spilled salad dressing on them, desperate to provoke some sort of reaction. Normally Hugo would have hit the roof. Instead he just brushed it off with a long thumb and laughed.

'Now I'm even better dressed,' he said, smiling at her and moving away to chat to Penny about transport the following day.

If anything, he was behaving more courteously to her than ever before. She was utterly confused and her confidence started to ebb again.

She knew that he had a ridiculously short space of time to acquaint himself with Snob, and was stupefied that he barely sought her advice at all, always deferring to Gus when he had a query.

'He's my horse,' Tash pointed out rather huffily.

'And I'm grateful to you for warming the seat for me,' Hugo told her as nicely as he could. 'But I'm on board now, and I really can't abide back seat drivers.' It was the nastiest he had been all day, but even that was said with a gentleness and warmth that totally threw her. She wanted him to yell and spit – at least that showed he cared. She longed to corner him on his own and demand to know what he had meant by his confession in The Olive Branch, but the yard was buzzing with activity and it was impossible to get a moment alone with him.

The year before, Tash had been caught up in all the pre-Badminton excitement at the yard even though she hadn't taken part as a competitor – grooming for Gus instead as Snob was not sufficiently experienced to qualify that year. This time, she was involved as a rider and the excitement was even greater. It was the biggest event in the professional calendar and as such there was a special kind of atmosphere that surrounded it. The day before they travelled to Gloucestershire, Lime Tree Farm was in a roaring party mood mixed with jangling nerves, so that everyone fell over everyone else, argued about where to find a certain piece of equipment, checked and re-checked the wall-plan that Gus had made out and talked about nothing but the big B.

The plan was for India – who was on half-term – to groom for Tash and Hunk, whilst Ted looked after both Gus's ride, Fashion Victim, and Kirsty's old mare, Betty Blue. Penny was coming along too, but as ever was far too nervous to trust herself to look after the horses and had decided instead to be general liaison and score-watcher. Franny, who should have been helping as she was now practically one of the staff, refused to come at all since Hugo was riding one of the yard's horses. She could barely bring herself to speak to Tash once the news had been broken, only muttering darkly that if she wanted Snob destroyed it might have been simpler to let him loose on the M4.

'That might well happen at the wedding,' Rufus joked. 'Penny thinks he'll head there once he's pulling that carriage.'

No one commented on this. The subject was strictly off limits.

Only Zoe missed out on the excited anticipation as she and Enid were barely seen for the entire build-up phase. Normally she was at the hub of the action, co-ordinating and keeping everyone calm, but this year, she was steering clear. She had taken to sleeping in until after all the breakfast gatherings had cleared, and then marching Enid out on a long, long walk which Tash suspected took in the film shoot at Maccombe. Returning fleetingly in the afternoon, she would borrow whichever car was available and disappear once again, leaving Enid to sulk on her bed.

Nor had Niall been seen since the night before. Tash had to face the brunt of the questions about whether the wedding was on or off, and what would happen to Lisette's party if it was indeed, as the farm mob assumed, off.

She deflected them all with shrugs and finally yelled at everyone who asked that she didn't want to talk about it, but she knew that things were getting desperate.

She returned to the forge on Monday evening to find that Niall had made a lightning visit and taken enough clothes to last him a few days, leaving a note to wish her luck at Badminton and say that he would be in touch before the party, which Tash found difficult to believe as one followed straight after the other. He had written in his loopy, scrawling hand:

> I can't apologise enough for all this. I am, as ever, behaving like a
> cowardly shit, but I need time to straighten my head out. I think
> it would be best all round if I beat it for a while, so I'm putting
> up in the cast hotel for a few nights. Please try to keep going until
> Sunday. I'll love you for ever for it.

Again the phone rang almost incessantly. This time, Tash resorted to pulling it out of the socket and spending the night watching all Gus's old videos of Badminton and blanking her mind to all but the competition ahead. Hugo was out to dinner with his sponsors so she knew it couldn't be him calling. Yet again he had spent all day being killingly polite and dodging all her attempts to corner him on his own. She was starting to doubt his motives, and to suspect he was proving as devious as ever. If Hugo felt that he had achieved victory already by duping her into thinking he loved her in order to borrow her horse, the least she could do, she realised, was beat him on the day and win on Hunk. That night, it became her sole obsession and ambition, eclipsing all her churning panic about the wedding.

*   *   *

Henrietta settled herself in the breakfast room and, checking that James was suitably preoccupied with his recently purchased sit-on mower, she dragged out the aerial on the walkabout phone and called France. James normally confined these calls to after six as he had almost fainted on espying the last quarter's phone bill with the Saumur and Paris exchanges listed over forty times, but Henrietta could not and would not wait this time.

'Sophia's just called me,' she breathed as soon as Alexandra picked up.

'Me too,' Alexandra whimpered. 'I guessed she was calling you, darling, because you've been engaged for the past twenty minutes. Do you think she can be telling the truth? I mean it's simply appalling.'

'Lord only knows, but she seems utterly convinced. Have you tried getting hold of Tash?'

'For days, darling. There's never any answer.'

'When are you coming over to England?'

'Well, we were planning to arrive a week on Wednesday, but I think I should come over straight away, and then Pascal and Polly can follow on.'

'You can stay here.'

'Won't James mind?'

'Of course not. This is an emergency.' Henrietta looked out of the window again and grimaced as she realised what she had just said.

Thirty-Seven

WHEN THE LIME TREE Farm lorry – newly refitted and emblazoned with Tash's sponsor's name on the side – rolled into Badminton park on Tuesday afternoon, there ensued a long security checking process which was only common at the largest of international events. At most competitions, practically everyone knew everyone else and the riders were used to spectators roaming around the horse-box area or stopping to chat as they sat eating their lunch in the grub tent. At Badminton, it was a very different matter and each area was strictly guarded, regulated and restricted for the five days of the competition.

They were all issued with coloured wrist bands, which would be checked by the security guards before they were allowed near the horse yard or caravan park. They were then ordered to unload the horses who were briefly inspected for identification against their passports, and then they unpacked the tack crates from the box and settled in the vast, grand stable yard that was normally used to house the horses for the Duke of Beaufort's Hunt.

Even set against a black, rain-heavy sky, its beauty stopped Tash in her tracks – low-built, graceful, a biscuit-umber in colour and curling around her like warm arms. The creamy old stalls seemed to buzz with excitement and anticipation. Grooms raced around settling in their charges, riders hailed one another eagerly, grumbling about the weather and their draw in the running order.

The Lime Tree Farm horses were all stabled according to that running order. Snob, who arrived later that morning with Hugo, was low in the draw and consequently quite close to Stefan's horse, Happy Monday, also a late starter. But poor Ted had to look after both Vic and Betty who were far apart in numbers and designated stables at the opposite side of the yard, meaning that he had to dash across it in laps to care for his charges.

'Bloody good for him too,' Gus pointed out. 'He's been getting obscenely fat lately – Franny's cooking is delicious.'

'Which is more than can be said for Zoe's,' laughed Hugo. 'I always wondered why you lot were so thin.'

'Zoe's a great cook – if wacky,' Gus said grumpily. 'The reason we're all thin is because we can't afford to buy food.'

Soaking in the atmosphere of the place, Tash wandered around in a state of fizzing excitement and nerves, saying hello to old friends and other fellow competitors.

Later, when she took Hunk out for a short hack in the park to acclimatise him – carefully sticking to the areas designated for exercising horses – she stared at the broad, grand old house and shuddered.

'I'm here,' she muttered in amazement, the realisation of just how far she'd come suddenly dawning on her. 'We're here. Bloody hell!'

With all the awfulness of the past few weeks she'd almost forgotten what an achievement it was. This was the biggest spectacle of the eventing calendar – the toughest, most gruelling event of the year. This ebullient, heart-kicking feeling of excitement was the reason that she had sweated and toiled and dragged herself up at dawn for months. She'd made it through the park gates and into the competition programmes. Whether she won or lost was immaterial, and trying to beat Hugo was a ridiculous whim. She didn't care who won, she simply wanted to have a crack and revel in the experience of making it here at all.

Letting out a great whoop of delirious glee, she set Hunk into his easy, lolloping canter – almost ploughing down Brian Sedgewick, the championship favourite, who was out walking his Doberman.

The next morning they attended the competitors' briefing in the striped marquee riders' tent, where they were allocated their large-scale maps of the courses for Saturday's endurance day, taken through the administrative procedures of the event, introduced to the main officials presiding, and told where to eat, drink and socialise for the four days of the competition.

Too excited to concentrate, Tash passed it in a daze as she gazed at the great and the good in the sport sitting alongside first-timers like herself. Gus, who had been there many times before and was shattered from the five a.m. start, fell asleep with his mouth open. Hugo, alongside him, stared fixedly ahead however hard Tash tried to catch his eye. He was blowing hugely hot and cold at the moment – like a faulty hand-dryer in a ladies' loo, Tash decided with some satisfaction at her simile. She was too swept away by the whole thing to allow him to tie cat's cradles with her heart strings. But still she found her eyes sliding towards his throughout the briefing, pulled there again and again like a ventriloquist's dummy telling witty jokes to its straight man.

The gossip was all of Bodybuilder's sad demise and Tash's amazing decision to give a ride to Hugo.

'Bloody generous of you, handing him the reins like this,' said Brian Sedgewick as they headed from the tent to the endurance box for the first official inspection of the course. From there they were to be taken around the beginning on the roads and tracks sections – known as Phase A – in four-wheel drives. Some of those who had raced ahead were already setting out in army Land-Rovers, whooping madly. It was like the first day at camp.

'I think you're mad, Tash,' Lucy Field told her, pushing her blonde ponytail into the back of her turquoise fleece jacket and ramming a baseball cap on her head to shield her eyes. 'Hugo's bound to beat you.'

'Don't be so sure,' Brian told her, hooking an arm around Tash. 'I think it's bloody wise to stick to one horse on your first try here – madness to go round twice. It's so bloody exhausting. And you've chosen the safer mount.'

'Thank you.' Tash smiled gratefully into his battered, comedian's face.

She was rather sickened halfway around the course to hear him having a ten-pound bet with the scottish eventer, Glen Bain, that Hugo would win the championships.

'He's been dying to get his hands on that horse for years . . .'

The course inspection did nothing to cheer her up.

First they were driven around both roads and tracks sections, breaking in between to spill out of their vehicles and inspect the steeplechase course – much like any used for a National Hunt race and there to test the horse's stamina. Then it was back to the endurance box to walk around the ultimate test – Snob's old favourite – the cross-country course.

This first inspection – the only officiated one – was perhaps the most communal and least serious of the competitors' several course-walks. It was the first time that the riders had a chance to see any new fences close up, although most of the course was familiar as it stayed largely the same year in and out, to be run in alternate directions year by year. As they walked the course on this occasion, the riders and owners joked and gossiped between fences, exchanging tips and advice, horror stories and anecdotes, only pausing to discuss each fence fairly seriously when they came to it. All the riders would walk the course again – some several times – to measure out paces, time checks and alternative routes in and out of each fence. The later course-walkings would be far more studied, serious affairs, conducted with measuring wheels, chewed nails and pencils and pads. This time it was more about communal spirit and gasping at new fences than technicalities.

Tash was horrified by pretty much every single obstacle and felt nothing but relief that she was not facing the prospect of riding Snob around them. Whereas other events presented challenging fences at intervals, stopping the gaps between them by 'stocking fillers' – easier, galloping fences that allowed one to gain confidence and maintain rhythm – this course was challenge after challenge without let up. Every single obstacle presented its own series of problems, requiring thought, accuracy and skill. With Snob towing her around here, it would be like driving the wrong way up the M4. At least with the safer, more reliable Hunk she could plan her lines without worrying what would happen if he trundled up to the fence with his head between his knees, looking at the ground instead of the huge jumping effort ahead. Hunk hadn't the same ability, but he was as accurate as laser surgery and tirelessly responsive.

The course was scattered with fences that had been around for years and still instilled fear into the greatest of riders – the vast, gaping angle of the Vicarage Vee, the yawning ditch beneath the Cross Questions, the twisting undulations of the Quarry, and, of course, the steep drop into the huge Lake which, if one rode it too boldly, could set a horse swimming in seconds.

Of the new fences one or two stood out as titanically difficult and had fellow competitors scratching their heads as they pondered sharp turns, tight arrowheads and, the latest craze amongst course designers, angled triple bounces which required horse and rider to head for a fence in a perfectly judged stride and line in order to make it over three jumps in immediate succession. These three fences, which

looked like Chinese hieroglyphics in high relief when you first saw
them, would be angled so acutely that the line had to be precise or
the horse would either grind to a halt or drop a shoulder and run
out at one of the elements.

The fence that worried Tash most was a new one called the Three
Scythes and involved a lethal and complex combination of fat, solid
log 'arms' and curved silver-painted arcs scattered with bundles of
cut grass. It was a rider brain-teaser that in essence could prove
easy provided the jockey had worked out exactly how to aim his
horse towards it beforehand. There was only one logical direct route,
which would save seconds but had absolutely no room for inaccuracy.
The alternatives took one all around the houses and could effectively
scupper one's chances of winning the event. Tash had a feeling that
cross-country day would be won or lost on that fence, and it was just
the sort of obstacle that Snob loathed.

'I should watch him at this one,' she told Hugo as they stood by
it, watching the beetle-browed Scottish eventer Glen Bain clambering
all over the fence and declaring it a monster. 'He might be athletic,
but three bounces on a pin-point line is stretching him and he could
go horribly wrong.'

'With you, maybe,' Hugo was staring at the line intently, 'but I'm
on board on Saturday.'

Tash refused to rise. 'I'd check out all the alternatives really
thoroughly,' she warned. 'If there's a route where you don't have to
pull him up too much or turn him tightly, I'd go for that. Anything
that allows him to keep his impetus and rhythm, even if it's longer,
will be safer. This is absolutely his worst type of fence.'

She trudged around the remainder of the course with Lucy Field
and Penny, both of whom were frantically gossiping about the fact
that Kirsty's fiancé, thick Richie, had faxed her that weekend to say
he'd been having an affair with a fellow Australian lawyer for six
months and their engagement was off.

'You'd have thought he could have waited until after Badminton!'
Lucy was appalled. 'I call that so insensitive.'

Tash hid a smile. She guessed if there was one thing that Niall had
always been, it was sensitive.

That afternoon was the first of the event's vets' inspections. It was a
rather grand affair in front of the main house with a large number of
officials in situ to preside over proceedings with the panel of vets. India
had spent a large whack of the afternoon beautifying Hunk who now

gleamed like a melting chocolate bar, his bay coat so shiny that Tash could almost see her pale, anxious face reflected in it as she waited to trot him up on the straight run of flat Tarmac which had been scraped out of the gravel carriage sweep. Although fit for over two months now, his tendon did give him sporadic stiffness, especially when it was cold and wet. So far that week the weather had held out, giving them a cool, blustery backdrop with just the odd glimmer of chilly sun, as though God was running a lighting check for the big summer stage show in a couple of months' time. But the forecast for the weekend was bad and a lot of the competitors had spent the day gazing sporadically at the western horizon from which a huge blanket of storm cloud was predicted to emerge.

Because she had originally been entered on two horses, Tash was drawn as a very early number on Hunk. Snob, who was to have been her second ride, was one of the last in the draw and so Hugo wasn't even out in front of the house as Tash trotted Hunk up before the panel. She jogged alongside him like Madonna shadowed by a huge bodyguard, trying to remember to keep his head straight as Gus had told her, which was hard as his nose kept dive-bombing her pockets for Polos.

He gambolled along happily, black ears pricked tightly forward, eyes gleaming, huge soup-plate hooves ringing out a clear, even percussion on the Tarmac. On the return leg, Tash had to sprint to keep up with him. There was no question but that he would pass. She felt immensely relieved and watched as, half an hour later, Fashion Victim passed too, although the vets were far slower in letting him through, deliberating for some seconds and calling Gus over for a quick word.

'What did they say?' Tash asked as they walked together back to the stable yard.

'Oh, the usual stuff about his wind – you know how he pants like an obscene caller. He's got a reputation for it now, so we always go through a bit of a question and answer routine about it. And they asked after his corns, like old ladies at a clinic.'

At the yard, a glamorous former Olympic eventer, Julia Ditton, whom Tash had once desperately wanted to be, was roving around preparing the pre-recorded information package that would precede the live television coverage of the endurance day on Saturday. She was interviewing grooms and riders for gossip, scratching the better-known horses' noses in front of the camera and picking through tack boxes to explain to the folks at home what a brushing boot was.

She cornered Tash by a feed bin.

'D'you mind awfully doing a little interview about giving Hugo the ride on Snob? I've already hoodwinked him into taking part. I know it's a pain, but I'd be tremendously grateful.'

Tash reluctantly agreed. She tended to get very tongue-tied and idiotic at these things, dropping malapropisms left, right and centre as she groped for words. She'd once told a Sky reporter that she was 'billed to thrits' at winning Bramham. Hugo, by contrast, was supremely fluent and sexy on screen, which in part accounted for his huge female following. Commiseration letters and fan-mail had been flooding in since the weekend. Already, Snob had hundreds more good luck cards pinned up around his stable door than any other horse. Poor old Hunk only had a card from Beetroot (in India's handwriting) and a telegram from Alexandra wishing him and Tash luck and begging the latter to call.

The television crew consisted of a bored-looking camera-man with scurf-scattered shoulders, and a balding sound recordist wearing headphones over his pate and waggling a furry microphone around. Lurking behind them was a despotic BBC sports producer called Paul who was wearing a baseball cap and a Pringle sweater and yakked into his mobile phone almost incessantly. He kept grumbling that horses were absolutely not his thing, and he gave anything with four legs – including the dogs – a wide berth, his sunburned nose wrinkling.

'Is this going to take long? Only I'm due at the vets' inspection soon,' Hugo snapped. He was looking extremely dashing, if crabby, in a cream waistcoat and navy cords, Tash noticed. She wished she'd made more effort for the earlier inspection instead of borrowing Penny's rather worn navy blazer and dragging her hair into a messy ponytail. She looked like a student with a vast overdraft at her first job interview. No wonder he was practically ignoring her at the moment. She determined to make a real effort to smarten up for the rest of the week.

At first, Paul wanted Tash and Hugo to be standing on either side of Snob during the interview, but the chestnut took an instant dislike both to Paul's hat and to the sound recordist's furry microphone, looking in imminent danger of demolishing both with his paddling hooves as he reared up, with Tash struggling to keep a grip on him. He was quickly reinstalled in his box and it was decided to interview them with Tash sitting on a bale of straw whilst Hugo stood behind her with his foot resting on the bale in romantic hero pose. The stance was extremely artificial and Julia raised her eyes to heaven in sympathy.

'Raymond Brooks Ward would never have stood for this,' she

groaned, adjusting the alice band in her short blonde hair and wiping the moisture from her forehead. 'Still, I need the cash. Right, let's get cracking.' She waited for a nod from the camera-man, did a short spiel to camera, and then turned to them with a big smile. 'Hugo, I was so sorry, as I'm sure all our viewers were, to hear of the tragic death of your great horse Bodybuilder last weekend. How are you feeling about that now?'

Behind her, Tash could feel Hugo's foot digging into the straw as he tensed.

'Not great,' he admitted. 'He was a terrific horse – perhaps the best I've ever had. He was so clever, he could tackle a fence from any direction off any leg at practically any speed. I adored him, and I'm cut to ribbons that he's gone – I'd be a liar to pretend otherwise.'

That'll get them right where it hurts, Tash realised. The gruff, drawling voice just tinged with sadness would have teenage girls and old age pensioners weeping countrywide when this was aired.

'And with the loss of Bod, you weren't expecting to come here at all, I gather?'

'Nope, I was planning my first weekend at home this season.' His foot was starting to dig into the small of Tash's back now. 'Which is rather bad timing as my house is being invaded by film crews at the moment.'

Choosing not to pick up on this, Julia pressed on. Behind her Brian Sedgewick's groom, Ursula, had wandered into shot without realising and was now trying to edge her way out again, looking wildly self-conscious. Watching her shuffling sideways like a prime prat, Tash started giggle.

'But you had other ideas, didn't you, Tash?'

Suddenly realising that the furry microphone was being waggled at her, Tash found her tongue was intent on counting her teeth one by one.

'Yes,' she managed to splutter.

Julia smiled kindly, waiting for more. Behind her, Ursula, blushing furiously, fell over a bucket with a loud clatter. Tash felt her face straining and twitching under the pressure not to laugh. Hugo gave her back a sharp prod with his foot but her chest was starting to heave now and hiccups of laughter were bubbling up in her throat so she kept her mouth glued closed as though sucking a fizzy sweet.

'Can you tell us what happened?' Julia prompted hopefully.

'I – er – I—' Tash had to shut her mouth again as her voice warbled towards the giggles.

'Tash very generously offered me the ride on one of her top horses, Foxy Snob,' Hugo cut in smoothly. 'He's a brilliant but very difficult horse who tends to drag a rider around a course, as many followers of the sport will know. Tash felt a change of rider at this stage might get Snob on his toes again and, as I was suddenly without a horse, she offered him to me. I'm just hoping I can give her and Niall the best wedding present ever and win Badminton for them this year.' His foot ground its way towards one of Tash's kidneys and she winced.

Giving Tash a very sly wink, Julia turned back to the camera again.

'Of course as most of you out there who read the gossip columns will know, Tash is marrying the actor Niall O'Shaughnessy a week on Saturday. Despite this, she's bravely riding around the toughest course in the country on her second horse Hunky Drunk on Saturday. Tell me, Tash, are you more nervous about that, or about marrying every woman's dream man?'

Tash's giggles instantly evaporated as the scurfy camera-man panned into her face in sharp close-up.

'Mmmm . . .' She started to cough. 'Both really.'

'And can we expect the gorgeous Niall to come and support you this weekend?' Julia looked girlish.

'He's – er – busy filming.'

'What a shame! I bet he's at the end of a phone all the time, hoping that you don't do yourself an injury this weekend and ruin the big day?'

Tash coughed. 'Well, it wouldn't be the first time in this sport that a bride went up the aisle with the aid of crotches – I mean, crutches,' she fumbled nervously. 'In fact, I might need a stretcher to get me up there, as the saying goes.' She wasn't sure that the saying did go like that, but anyway.

Julia's pale blue eyes were widening with surprise and she gave a nervous laugh. 'Quite. So you'll be in the unique position this weekend of competing against one of your own horses?'

'Yes.' Tash decided to settle for her old favourite answer again. Her more inventive one clearly hadn't gone down too well.

'Won't that be odd?'

'No.'

'So you've done it before?'

'Yes.' She shook her head. 'I mean, no. I mean, in the yard where I'm based we swap around horses quite a lot, so you find that the one you were working with the week earlier is with another member of the team the next week. Quite often it means I compete against a horse I've schooled myself. We often change our mind about which horse suits which rider best at a late stage. Like men, really!' she gulped.

'I see.' Julia turned to the producer. 'We'll do that bit again, shall we?'

He shrugged. 'Scrap the lot for all I care – it was dismal. I wanted to be at Silverstone this weekend. Let's get a shot of the nag now. Which one is it?' They wandered towards Snob who was being pacified by India with a carrot while Jenny plaited him for the inspection panel. The producer's eyes lit up.

'Let's have a few shots of the horse and his young groom, shall we?' he suggested excitedly, taking in the length of India's legs.

'India's not actually looking after him this weekend,' Tash explained, following them. 'Jenny's his groom.'

'It's all right, darling, we won't need you for this bit.' Paul waved a dismissive hand over his shoulder.

Tash melted away.

For the ensuing half-hour Paul presided with meticulous care over the shooting of India from every conceivable angle – leading Snob across the yard, feeding Snob a Polo mint, putting his bridle on, taking his saddle off, lifting his leg and dropping his girth. It was a dangerous escapade – Snob was notoriously evil in the stable – and she was rather embarrassed throughout, but Paul was enchanted.

Finally, Hugo insisted on dragging the horse away for the vets' inspection. After that, Paul even had the gall to suggest that India carry on the shoot with another similar-looking horse, but thankfully Julia put a stop to it.

'You might not be able to tell them apart, chum,' she smiled her delightfully disarming smile, 'but most of the viewers will – it's like sports presenters: Des Lynam and Jimmy Hill look one and the same to a BBC2 arts viewer, and horses look the same to a suburban golf-fanatic, but not to the eventing fans. Now we *must* interview Lucy Field – you'll love her. She's pretty.'

Tash sloped off to watch Snob fly through the vets' inspection, so obviously fit to run that he almost dragged Hugo into the crowd. He came away grinning broadly.

'I am going to have to pin you down soon and grill you for fitness training techniques,' he told Tash as he waited for the inevitable 'passed' to bark out over the senior steward's megaphone. 'This horse is like Linford Christie on the blocks.'

Despite herself, Tash felt her shoulders straighten with pride.

But after that he vanished like the shop-keeper in Mr Ben, leaving Jenny clinging on to Snob's bobbing pink nose. It was becoming something of a habit of Hugo's. Apart from their dreadful interview together, Tash had hardly seen him.

'Sloping off to make telephone calls to a bloody girlfriend, I'll bet,' Kirsty sniped, blowing her red hair out of her eyes. 'Stefan says he's madly into someone at the moment. He's been yakking away into that mobile all day. You think you can go the straight route on the Three Scythes?'

Shrugging, Tash chewed her lip and wondered to whom exactly Hugo had been yakking. She'd noticed him sloping off to make phone calls too – he was like a businessman constantly checking on his shares as though he knew Black Wednesday was approaching.

'Hunk won't make that last bounce,' Kirsty told her calmly. 'He's no' got enough impetus to go through with it.'

'Neither have I.' Tash went off, not thinking about the Scythes at all.

But later, in the Lime Tree lorry with Penny, she knocked back a scotch-laced coffee and tried not to shake.

'It's too big and scary,' she gulped. 'I can't do it, I simply can't.'

'Everyone says that their first time,' Penny dismissed her. 'Like weddings – you'll be saying that to Niall this time next week.' She lifted her chin, raised her eyebrows and all but held up a large question mark on a flash card.

Tash made a sort of nervy, non-committal squashed hamster noise. Right now she was battling to get to grips with the notion of tomorrow. Next week was far too much for her head to take in.

The next morning, Tash guzzled a vast fried breakfast in the Badminton kitchens – a temporary cafeteria set up in the house's old servants' hall. Twenty minutes later she was throwing it all up again. An hour later and what was left was frantic to come out of the other end.

'Is that what they call the Badminton trots?' she asked Gus weakly as she staggered out of the loo cubicle, bleach-faced.

'You've only got collected trots right now.' He looked up from the *Mail* and peered at her over his half-moons. 'Tomorrow night is extended trots. Penny's got a Valium somewhere if you want one.'

'No, thanks.' Tash shuddered. 'I don't want to perform my test high on drugs. I'll end up doing more than a half-pass at the judges.'

Despite demons of terror on her back, she managed a fairly respectable dressage test on Hunk, finishing the day in fifth place.

But with many of the top competitors – including Gus, Stefan and Hugo – performing their dressage tests the next day, she knew she wouldn't stay there for long. The wait would play havoc with her already turbulent gastric system and she deeply regretted her early draw. Yet it did have its benefits . . .

Thursday night was the official cocktail party at Badminton House – a very august couple of hours swigging champagne cocktails with all the senior stewards and event organisers in the grandest of settings before traditionally heading off to a local pub to unwind. For those competitors still to attempt the dressage it was a tense, abstemious affair, but for those – like Tash – who had already circumnavigated the dreaded rectangle, it was a time to unwind briefly, get slightly tight and let rip.

She made a concerted effort to dress up for Hugo, spending hours over her outfit and make-up until she was convinced she looked pretty knock-out, but he barely looked in her direction all night. Every time she worked her way across the room to get closer to him, he seemed to work his way in the opposite direction. She even started to test her theory by trying out the sly tactic of darting behind people and slowly creeping up on him until, at the last moment, she could pop up within a couple of feet and feign surprise at bumping into him again.

The main topic of conversation with everyone she spoke to was inevitably her wedding.

Despite his dodging technique, Hugo was a fateful few yards away when Tash finally put the spot-changing leopard among the pigeons by stopping the dashing Duke himself in his tracks with a fateful one-liner. When he politely asked her whether she was looking forward to her well-publicised wedding, she scrunched up her face thoughtfully and – several champagne cocktails up – gave him a rather loon-on-acid smile.

'It's very good of you to ask, Your Grace, but I'm still not certain whether to run at that particular event as the going's a bit too rough. Excuse me.'

She fled to the stables after that, frightening several of the security staff who demanded to see her wrist band and know what she was doing.

'I've come to see my horse,' she announced rather hysterically. 'I always talk to him the night before a major competition. I have to give him some vital last-minute advice.'

Shrugging, they took in the short, bias-cut silk dress and the dishevelled hair and let her through, keeping a close eye on her – or rather her bottom – as she headed straight for Snob's box to cry into his red, unsympathetic neck for a few minutes; he was more interested in searching for her pockets and, finding that there were none, was eager to boot her out of his sleeping space and settle down for the night.

'Do me a favour and buck Hugo off tomorrow?' Tash breathed into his twitching ear before leaving him in peace, giving Hunk a kiss as she passed.

Thirty-Eight

ON FRIDAY MORNING, THE heavens were as wide open as shop doors on the first day of the sales, and throwing down water as though baling out a sinking ark.

Top hat tilted against the driving rain, wet shoulders shining like jet and breeches sodden, Hugo and Snob displayed a mastery of horsemanship over weather conditions during the dressage test, but they inevitably suffered from the pelting rain in their faces whenever they turned towards the judges' caravan. Snob's red ears were flat back to his head most of the way round, like a hosed-down lion. Although they did have some brilliant moments, their lines were practically never straight as Snob shuffled sideways trying to turn his back on the weather, spooking at the television cameras and throwing a wobbly whenever they neared the bank of flower arrangements that were flapping around in the wind like formation swimmers wearing textured petal swimming caps. They finished the day well down the placings.

Tash spotted him afterwards, listening to one of Glen Bain's many personal theories – all of which related eventing to sex.

'Dressage is like foreplay. The more you can hold back, keep control and set yourself up, the better the big event – the cross-country,' Glen was saying earnestly.

'More like four-ply out there.' Hugo towelled his hair and, seeing Tash approaching, headed off towards the riders' tent to wait for his disappointing score.

Tash was too disheartened to follow. She'd wanted to commiserate with him, but he'd run away from her yet again. Now she felt rather proud of her red rebel for giving Hugo such a hard time and headed to the stables, where Jenny was rubbing him down, to give him a big kiss on the neck. But, breathing in his damp, familiar smell, Tash was yet again shot through with the pain of facing up to parting with him once the Sunday of reckoning was over and Lisette knew she wasn't marrying Niall.

'Nice weather for ducks,' Jenny said cheerfully as she wiped water from the sweat scraper with an old stable rubber.

'Especially sitting ones,' Tash said bleakly, moving off to watch Stefan's dressage.

By the completion of all the dressage tests on Friday afternoon, Tash and Hunk had slipped down to thirteenth place, which made her want to run around spotting black cats, four-leafed clovers and new moons to dispel the bad luck.

Having driven around the roads and tracks once again with Gus on a borrowed scramble bike, she took her final walk around the next day's cross-country alone, trying to absorb every last undulation and divot on the route, but in reality more preoccupied with Zoe and Niall. She wished at least one of them would get in touch; every night she meticulously checked Gus's mobile phone for messages, but there had been none. At the farm, Rufus reported that he had seen neither of them all week and that, as they were all away, he was having a party for 'just a few friends' on Saturday night. Penny, guessing that this meant the entire sixth form of Rufus's school had been invited, refused to let Tash tell Gus in case it ruined his concentration for the competition.

Double-checking her time check-points against the sheet of paper that she would attach to her arm the next day, Tash tried to keep her turbulent thoughts away from Hugo, but his face flashed in front of her eyes every minute, as though caught on a continual spool.

She could see him in the far distance with a group of cronies, including Stefan, Brian Sedgewick and the cheerful, libidinous Glen Bain, measuring the course with a wheel and talking strategies as they headed for the Lake which was pitted with ripples as rain lashed down on it.

Tash hung back, taking a long time to walk the long, level gallop through the park that preceded the fence. Beside her, workmen were unwinding the last of the rope barriers which would stop the crowd wandering into the tracks of the horses. Beyond these the park was now dotted with royal blue Portaloo cubicles, some singular for officials, some in multiple lines like garish phone-boxes on a railway concourse. To the left a large stand had been erected for spectators to get a good view of the Lake in case anyone had the misfortune to fall in. Tash shuddered, whistling for Beetroot who had been investigating beneath it. But when she looked for her, the dog had disappeared.

Squinting ahead, Tash saw that she had raced on ahead to join Hugo and his gang, cavorting merrily with Glen's cairn terrier, Burns. Laughing, Hugo threw a stick for her and headed towards the Mitsubishi Pick-ups fence, two huge cars parked back to back.

'At least Beetroot still gets on with him,' Tash muttered under her breath, walking the rest of the course in solitude.

When she got back to the yard, Beetroot was waiting with Ted who was giving Vic a Cromovet inhalation for his wind. She looked both very muddy and very pleased with herself, a manky-looking stick protruding from her mouth like an Argentinian siren's rose after a particularly rampant tango.

'Hugo delivered her back,' Ted explained. 'Said you looked like Ophelia out on the course, and you need a waterproof hat.'

Amazed that Hugo had even noticed her, Tash pulled her wet rats tails behind her ears and took Beetroot back to the box for a good towelling.

That night she couldn't sleep for erotic thoughts of him. Over and over again, she played back that kiss two years earlier beside her mother's pool at Champegny. Immediately afterwards, she had told herself that it had been a way of exorcising her crush, of laying a ghostly half-love that had haunted her teens. But, looking back now, she knew she had never been kissed like it before or since.

If I win on Hunk this weekend, she told herself, then Hugo has promised to kiss me. Please, please God, let me win. And if I do, let it be a kiss like that one.

Endurance day started with one of the worst storms of the week. It brought down several trees in the park – two of them across the steeplechase course – so the start of the day's competition had to be delayed and the spectators, who had braved the elements to turn up early, were asked to avoid walking directly on the cross-country course at all costs as their trampling feet could turn the going into an ice-rink.

Due to be one of the first to start, Tash – who had taken Hunk out for a quick breather already – hovered around the yard waiting for the go ahead, her heart pounding. It had only just really dawned on her what she had undertaken. Hunk was a big, easy-going horse who seldom got ruffled, ate up ground with his long, bounding stride and jumped accurately, if occasionally lazily. But he lacked Snob's athleticism and, although not one to allow himself to be fazed, had never faced a course this big in such awful conditions. Over the past year, Tash had devoted much more time to working on Snob with his doubtful temperament and hatred of flat-work. Hunk had been sidelined with lameness for a long time, and was not as familiar a ride. Tash knew he had the scope and talent, but she doubted both his stamina and her own confidence.

As she walked to the entrance of the yard to find out what was going on, she could see that out in the park the rain was still lashing down in whips and the wind bent the trees on their sides as though they were doing a communal aerobics class.

'I am about to ride Badminton in a storm,' she told herself, trying to stop her teeth chattering as she watched India stacking together all the essential equipment and spares that they would need for the ten-minute break between the roads and tracks phases, and the cross-country.

An official was waving Tash and a couple of the other early starters towards him in the yard entrance. 'We're ready to go,' he told them. 'Now the going isn't as bad as we feared but as you'll be riding on the top of the ground it'll be pretty damned slippery out there. So for God's sake, use fat studs and be careful. Best of luck.' He glanced at his watch.

Tash felt such a heaving cluster of butterflies take off in her stomach that she rushed off to be sick, finding herself chucking up in the next cubicle along to Kirsty who was due to start three horses after her.

'No need for Flab-busters now,' she joked feebly. 'This is the best diet in the world. I'll have to slip more lead into the cloth before weighing out.'

Riding Hunk on a long rein to the start box to weigh out, Tash said her second prayer in twenty-four hours. Only this time she wasn't praying for a kiss. She was hoping she'd live through the day.

The first of the roads and tracks sections, Phase A, was a fairly leisurely three-and-a-half-mile hack around the park. It was timed, but the limit was lenient and competitors could walk and trot throughout and still make it easily within the limit. It was little more than a gentle warm-up for what was to come. Tash wanted to gaze around the tracks she had walked so intently earlier that week and enjoy the breather, but she hunched up her shoulders against the wind and glanced sporadically at her watch instead, moving it around on her wrist to ensure the best position and continually cross-referring to the times on the check-list she had strapped to her left arm. The ink had started to run despite its plastic cover. She knew she was being over pedantic, but it was the only way to keep her nerves at bay.

She had longed for Hugo to appear in the yard that morning as a sort of lucky emblem but, due to his late start time, he had clearly decided to occupy himself elsewhere.

Hunk – who was a complete mudlark – was blissfully unaware of the wet, but Tash was worried for him nonetheless. His old tendon strain could flare up in this sort of weather, and the slippery conditions didn't help his balance. His ears darted around eagerly as he listened to the public address system gurgling into life in the distance, welcoming spectators to the event and explaining that the first competitor would be out on the course in just under an hour.

They reached the steeplechase course with just over a minute to spare and circled at the start in anticipation of the four-minute gallop ahead, which took place in a figure of eight over standard National Hunt fences. Penny was waiting nearby with some emergency spares, the hood of her coat pulled so low over her face that she looked as though she was about to hold up a building society.

'Looking good!' she shouted cheerfully after she had given Hunk a quick check-over. Tash smiled. It was what Penny said at every single event to cheer her gang on. She shortened her stirrups and fiddled with her watch again, ready to spring Hunk through the start.

Out on the course, he settled easily into his mile-eating stride and took the fences as though they weren't there, never having to adjust his face-chillingly fast stride to clear them. Hearing the wind rush in her ears and his hooves pound smoothly beneath her, Tash started to feel her confidence flood back. She was so used to riding Snob, who had to be treated with kid gloves all the way, she had forgotten that Hunk was the sort of horse who could run on auto-pilot. She had to make herself relax and trust him instead of continually waiting for the explosion.

Checking her stopwatch at the halfway mark, she realised to her horror that she'd somehow switched it off whilst fiddling around with it at the start. She'd have to guess the last half-mile or so. Panic pulled her tongue back in her throat again as she trusted her timing to fate and Hunk's sublime rhythm. Mud and water were flying up into her face as she crossed the finish line

His sublime rhythm was not on her side. As they slowed gradually to a canter, they passed Penny who was holding up her gloved hands in horror.

'You were almost a minute over!' she wailed. 'What happened?'

'Watch stopped!' Tash panted over her shoulder, heading straight out on to the start of phase C which was another set of roads and tracks, far longer than the first and requiring greater timing control. Her watch was flashing the date now. When she pressed the tit again it blanked out totally. She'd have to rely on her plain old wristwatch which was an ancient Swatch with a scratched face and a bent second hand.

Somehow she made it to the endurance box just within the allotted forty-five minutes, but her preoccupation with calculating the time hadn't stooped her noticing that Hunk was stiffening up badly behind. By the time they trotted towards the vets waiting in the ten-minute break box at the start of the big cross-country phase D, he was clearly not as fluid behind as he had been when starting the day. An enthusiastic India greeted them with words of encouragement as they pulled up, but one look at Tash's face shut her up.

'Okay, you can dismount now.' One of the vets approached them, clip-board in hand. For a moment he reminded Tash of one of the filmies who had been monopolising Hugo's house recently.

'Bad luck about the steeplechase,' India commiserated as Tash jumped off and started to loosen the girths straight away. Behind her, the vet was already taking Hunk's heart-beat.

'Is Gus around?' she asked, gazing round for one of the Lime Tree Farm seniors. She badly needed advice.

India was trawling around Hunk with a bucket and sponge, cooling his throat and belly and waiting for the vet to finish taking his temperature with a thermometer on a piece of string – it always reminded Tash of a Tampax – so that she could sponge between his hind legs.

'He's with Kirsty,' India explained. 'Betty cast a plate on the steeplechase and Ted couldn't find the spares – you know, those flat-fronted things she has. Gus had to race over to help out. Penny's back at the yard preparing Vic for him.'

'Shit!' Tash rubbed her head as India started to busy herself greasing Hunk's front legs with goose fat for the next section. The vet was filling in his clip-board now.

Tash reached into the tack bin to look for the spare stopwatch, and strapped it on in place of the dud, her eyes scouring the box for help. Her first priority was to decide whether or not to run Hunk, and she needed someone to make up her mind for her. Plenty of competitors were milling around, mostly preoccupied with their own impending starts, but it was too early in the day for most of the riders to be at the box – they were all concentrated at the yard.

The vet was already looking worried.

'Near hind tendon a bit of a problem area, is it?' he muttered, deferring to his partner for another opinion as he asked India to lead Hunk around for a moment so that they could check if he was level.

Suddenly Tash spotted Hugo standing close to the weighing tent, chatting to the great Australian eventer Mick James, who had been the first competitor around the course and was filling him in. Mick's craggy, bushman's face was splattered with dirt and his side darkened with mud where he had clearly taken a fall. Hugo wasn't due to start for over an hour, so he was dressed in his work-gear chaps and t-shirt with a wax coat over the top. Several young girls were lurking near the fence behind them clutching autograph books. Tash dashed over to attract his attention.

'I need your advice!' she bleated. 'I think Hunk's too stiff behind to go, but I'm not certain.'

Saying nothing, Hugo followed her and within seconds was examining the sweating horse, a hand running expertly along the back of his near hind.

The vets were still in a huddle, deliberating. Tash knew they could only disqualify her if Hunk's paces were uneven, which they weren't, but she didn't want to take any risks. Asking him every hard question across country – as Badminton inevitably did – in this sort of weather could strain his tendon again and put him out of work for months, potentially for ever. Equally she didn't want to be branded a coward for making a decision too hastily, which would incur the wrath not only of Gus but also of her sponsors, who were already grumbling disconcertingly about her decision to let Hugo run Snob. The Mogo team had a trade stand at the event and were keen for her to boost their corporate image – the managing director had already called the lorry mobile twice that morning to wish her luck. If she pulled out before even riding across country, he would be furious. She was supposed to be signing photographs at the stand later – mud-splattered and brave. A wimpy withdrawal wouldn't draw in the same crowds.

'Walk him out.' Hugo nodded at India who did as she was told, her face pinched with worry. Hunk appeared totally sound, his mouth snapping comically from the squirts of water and ion salts India had been administering, but as he turned at the end of his line, his near hind leg bowed and dipped very slightly. Hugo ran his hand down it once more, trying to feel for heat through the protective bandages that were stitched in place to stop them unravelling on the course.

He turned to Tash and touched her arm gently, shaking his head. 'Not safe to run him in this weather.' He glanced at the vets. 'What d'you think?'

'Technically he's passed all the checks.' The senior one shrugged. 'There's no swelling or lameness, and he's certainly fit enough to run as he is. But he is very slightly stiff, which could be a warning sign. It's up to you. You know the horse.'

Tash looked at Hunk, who was still all pricked ears and silly facial expressions. There had always been a residual weakness since his injury, and he tended to feel it more as a competition progressed without its affecting his performance. Yet this was no run-of-the-mill event and he wasn't as fit as Snob. He was already sweating up badly from his exertions, and the hardest work was still to come. He was a gritty, trustworthy horse who would give her his all – but that needed to be more than he had right now and she knew it. In her heart of hearts she had known it before they had even started. She'd only kept going so far in the silly, deluded hope that she would win the competition and thus her kiss. Tash gave him a big, grateful pat and searched out an official.

'We're pulling out,' she told him. 'Sorry.' She could feel the tears creeping out behind her eyes and bit her lip hard to stop them.

He nodded understandingly and patted her arm. 'Very wise decision – save his big guns for next year,' he told her, moving away to pass on the message through his walkie-talkie.

Tash walked back to give India a big hug.

'I'm sorry.' She tried to keep her voice from wobbling tearfully. 'You did a great job. He's just too precious to waste.'

'That's okay,' India said philosophically, hugging her back. 'My fingers are shredded from plaiting yesterday – I was going to resign tomorrow anyway.' She was trying frantically to be brave.

Tash smiled gratefully. Sometimes India reminded her so vividly of Zoe – gentle, strong, easy-going – it was uncanny.

It seemed like seconds later that the news was coming out over the general address and there was a disappointed groan from the spectators around the box who had rolled up to wish Tash and Hunk well. Amongst them, Tash noticed in alarm, was the *Cheers!* photographer who had snapped her and Niall 'at home' the previous week. Nikon lens flashing, his spools were clattering faster than chattering teeth in a blizzard as he caught her brave disappointment for the wedding spread.

'Hello there, love. Bad luck!' he called, shutter still clicking like fingers in a busy restaurant.

She gave them all as big a smile as she could muster and apologised, but it was all she could do to stop herself breaking down with disappointment. Walking up to her, big Mick James shot her a wink and slapped her shoulder. 'I'd've done the same,' he sympathised. 'Bad luck.' It was the first time he had ever spoken to her.

Hugo was still standing quietly beside her and Tash jumped in surprise as his arm was slotted gently around her shoulders and he hugged her to him, calling to India over her head.

'Walk him around for ten minutes more and then take him back to the yard and give him a good, long hosing on that hind leg before putting an Animalintex on it, will you? And, for Christ's sake, cheer up – you can help Jenny with Snob this afternoon. She's terrified of him. I'll look after Tash.'

Saying little, he steered her out of the box and walked her to the lorry park so that she could recover her composure before going back to support the others. Tash listened to the television helicopter fluttering around overhead like a great, flapping moth and wished more than anything that it was capturing shots of her and Hunk kicking up the Badminton turf right now. Big, childish tears started to plop from her eyes.

'I don't want t-to s-see G-gus or P-penny like this,' she wailed.

Heading right, Hugo took her to his horse-box instead of her own, where she would risk bumping into someone else from the Lime Tree Farm team. There, he made her a very strong, milky cup of tea and poured some brandy into it for good measure.

'Your sponsors here?'

Tash nodded, trying to stem the inevitable tears with the cuffs of her cross-country shirt. 'I was supposed to join their guests at the Mogo trade stand after my round.'

'Mike Seith and Peter Lisson are understanding blokes – they know the sport. They'll forgive you, and it's not as though they paid the entry fees on this one.'

Tash sniffed. 'I can't face seeing them.'

'Wait till after I've been round on Snob and we'll go together,' he suggested. 'After all, I'm riding under their corporate flag today too. I'll hold your hand – in fact, I might need you to hold mine if Snob dumps me in the Lake.'

The thought of Snob and his secret fate almost finished her off. Tash blew her nose noisily and tried to get a grip on herself. Hugo was about to ride one of the toughest rounds of his life, on her mentally deranged horse in appalling weather. She couldn't throw a wobbly now.

'Shouldn't you be getting ready?' She glanced at her watch. Realising that her spare stopwatch was still strapped to her wrist, she tugged it off and threw it on to the table.

'I've got ages yet.' Hugo settled in the seat facing her. 'Feeling a bit better?'

She nodded, not trusting herself to speak. She couldn't believe that he was being so kind.

'It's a hell of a wrench doing that.' He started fiddling with her discarded watch. 'Almost worse than failing the vets' inspection tomorrow morning. Happened to me a few years ago – awful.'

Tash shrugged. 'I didn't have much chance anyway as I buggered up the steeplechase. My penalties must have been in triple figures.'

Hugo grinned. 'After the appalling dressage test I managed, mine practically are already.'

'The penalty is mightier than the sword. Snob's phenomenal across country,' she said. 'If you go clear you could make up the deficit.'

'No one's going clear today, Tash – at least not within the time. It's Torville and Dean stuff out there. Mick says he feared for his life a couple of times.'

Tash bit her lip. It was practically a replay of Lowerton – the weather was almost as bad, their draws as far apart. Only the course was far, far harder. If he rode Snob the way he had ridden Surfer then, the consequences could be catastrophic. Running the back of her hand across her nose, she battled hard not to think about it.

'The going will get better once the ground's been cut up a bit.' She took the handkerchief Hugo was offering her and gratefully blew her nose. 'Once it churns up there'll be some grip to it.'

'That's what I'm hoping.'

'Where did Mick fall?' she asked, blowing her nose again.

'The Three Scythes.'

Tash blinked. 'Did he try the straight route?'

He nodded. 'And don't tell me how to ride it,' he said quickly, voice regaining some of its old arrogance. 'I'm making up my own mind.'

'If you head for the outer log on a left line, you can still bounce out through the last part of the direct route,' Tash told him anyway. 'I walked it last night – it's not obvious, but the striding is perfect for Snob and it wouldn't break his rhythm. You hardly lose any time by—'

'Tash.' Hugo reached across and covered her mouth with his hand. 'Shut up.'

Aware that she had a damp, recently blown nose, she flinched.

He looked mildly irritated, but said nothing, standing up and fetching his body protector from a pile of clean clothing on his bed. Before Tash could take in what he was doing, he had stripped to his underpants and was shaking out a clean pair of jodhpurs.

Tash quickly peered out of the rain-flecked window to avoid staring at that beautiful body – the long, tanned legs like slim iron girders, the stomach dappled with muscles, and the even ribs which she longed to strum with her fingers like a harp. Despite the last traces of tears and self-pity, she was fighting down the familiar lust-in-the-bus feelings of old. He had just been so nice. She mustn't ruin it now.

Hugo carried on chatting regardless, hoping that the rain would ease off, wondering whether Kirsty had completed yet, then telling her about Stefan's parents, who were over from Sweden and spoke absolutely no English. Assuming that Badminton House was open to the public, they had wandered around it for hours that morning before being discovered in the Duke of Beaufort's private chambers. He even started chatting about Zoe's erotic novels, asking all sorts of odd questions that Tash supposed were intended to take her mind off things. The trouble was, he wasn't putting her mind on to things that were any better for her erratic blood pressure.

'They any good?' he asked.

'Um – yes, well. Mmm. Very well written.'

'Not quite up to Tennyson?' He shot her a look.

Tash squinted out of the window again, turning pink.

'Will you wait at the box for my ten-minute break on Snob?'

'Of course.' She turned. 'If you like.'

He was dressed in his breeches now, but still topless. Gazing at him, Tash was mesmerised by that smooth brown chest and the strong shoulders, toughened and widened from so many hours in the saddle. She blinked in awe, instantly blaming the brandy for giving her such a hot, zippy kick in the groin. Any minute now and she'd start panting St Bernard-style again, she realised; she simply had to get a grip. Talk about Alpining passes . . . she was pining, full stop. She polished off the tea greedily, deciding that she was developing rather a taste for brandy.

'You okay?' He gave her a curious look before disappearing inside a black polo neck.

'Fine!' She had one last gawp at his stomach before his head reappeared through the neck-hole and he started to tuck the sweater in.

'Here – wear this, you'll get soaked otherwise.' He threw her a waterproof coat. It was made by Mogo's arch rivals, she noticed worriedly, pulling it on anyway. She had no idea where she'd left hers – in the yard, probably.

When Hugo was ready, she had a final blow of her nose and stood up, feeling the warmth from the brandy lingering in her stomach like a hot meal, giving her strength. Unfortunately it was also adding like mad to her lustiness too; she wished she hadn't been thinking quite so much about Zoe's erotic novels. She shuffled hastily past Hugo, anxious to get out of the box and away from such claustrophobic proximity. But at the door, she stopped and turned back, realising how rude she must appear.

'Thank you,' she said quickly. 'For looking after me just now – it was very kind.'

Picking up his crash hat from the sink drainer, he grinned. 'I assure you, it was purely selfish.'

Tash smiled awkwardly, not understanding. 'Good luck,' she added as he moved beside her. 'Give him a great ride for me.'

In the cramped space by the door they were inches apart. Tash's hand was on the handle, but her fingers were refusing to obey her head as they just gripped and clung instead of pushed and swung.

'I'll do my best,' Hugo promised, patiently waiting for her to open the door.

Still she lingered, daring herself to stretch up and kiss him on the cheek for luck. It was such a tiny gesture, one she performed practically every day of her life with the Lime Tree Farm mob, yet with him it took on enormous proportions. She took so long to galvanise her lips into action that Hugo, who had watched her mental struggle with amusement, was waiting with his cheek conveniently poised when she finally went for it. Then, at the last moment, he swung his face around so that she was planting the lightest of pecks on his lips, not his cheek.

'Good luck.' She was out of the door in a flash.

They walked to the yard in silence.

India was still hosing Hunk's leg when Tash got there. The place was buzzing with activity as horses were prepared for the gruelling challenge ahead with boots and bandages and all manner of tack being strapped to their excited frames. Tash felt another twinge of regret that she had been denied the full excitement of the day.

Ted was walking Betty Blue around with a waterproof sheet over her sweat-rug to cool her off without letting the driving rain chill her too quickly.

'How did Kirsty do?' Tash asked him, trying to be as cheerful as she could.

'Two refusals and a stack of time faults,' he groaned. 'And hers is one of the best rounds so far – she's in the TV tent with Penny. Gus is out on phase A. Sorry to hear you had to pull out. Gus was trying to track you down earlier to commiserate. And the MD of Mogo has been prowling around.'

'God!' Tash groaned, wandering into the stalls to say hi to Jenny and Snob. He was looking spectacular, his red coat gleaming like old gold, muscles shifting and glimmering beneath his skin.

'He looks wonderful,' Tash congratulated Jenny.

She pulled a face. 'He's almost had my arm off twice – look.' She showed a couple of blackening bruises. 'And it'll all go to rot the moment he's out in the rain. Brian's first ride, Babe Magnet, slid right into the Huntsman's Hangover like a duck on a frozen pond. They think he'll lose his eye – the vet's with him now.'

'No!' Tash shuddered, suddenly feeling uneasy. She watched as Snob smacked his lips and lunged at Jenny's bottom while she struggled to screw in a stud. He was looking as bullish and cocksure as ever. She hoped to God Hugo could hold him.

He was still in the yard, talking seriously with Brian Sedgewick who was as white as a sheet beneath his thick splattering of mud. From their grim expressions, Tash guessed that the horse's eye hadn't been saved. She felt sick with nerves.

'Bloody mess,' Ted tutted, walking Betty past her. 'It's the worst wash-out on record. Julia Ditton says it's even wetter and more perilous than ninety-two. The riders keep being stopped out on the course because of accidents. It's a wonder there haven't been any deaths.'

'Don't say that!' Tash crossed her fingers tightly. 'I'm going to find Penny.'

She couldn't bear to be near brave, excited Snob any longer. It would be unthinkable to pull him out just because she was a coward, she realised, but she still felt like a mother leaving her Christian son at the gates of the Colosseum on lion-feeding day. Not saying a word to Hugo, she raced towards the TV tent. As she trotted past the packed trade stands – which were doing a roaring trade in wellies and waterproof wear – she was almost brought down as a small child grabbed her coat hem, shrieking excitedly.

Looking down, Tash saw an exquisitely pretty black-haired girl dressed from head to foot in the latest Barbour childwear.

'Lotty!' she cried delightedly, stooping down to pull her delighted, giggling niece into a hug.

'Where is that revolting child?' quacked an angry voice as Sophia emerged from a stand selling novelty umbrellas. 'One looks away for a split – Tash!'

'Hi.' Tash let Lotty to the ground and noted that her sister was wearing an identical outfit to her daughter's. Waddling on child-reins beside her was Josh, also decked in Identikit attire. Only Ben, who staggered out of the stand a moment later carrying a wailing Henry, was dressed in his usual tatty old drover's coat and an unspeakably ancient Australian bush-hat that made him look like a village idiot.

'Think the young chap's just done one,' he was saying as he held his son at arm's length.

Sophia ignored him, and gathered her children close as she kissed Tash on the cheek.

'Have you seen Daddy and Henrietta?'

'No.' Tash's heart sank. She had forgotten that they'd said they would pole up and offer support. She wasn't sure she could face either of them in her current state of flux. 'Are they here?'

'Supposed to be, but we were an hour late to meet them. This weather's such a bore – multiple pile-up on the M5 slowed us down, which was highly annoying. They originally said they'd meet us by your sponsor's stand, but we keep going there and they're nowhere to be seen. We haven't been anywhere near the course yet. Are you going there now?'

'The course?' Tash looked at her rather blankly. 'Actually, I've already—'

'No, silly, your sponsors – Mogo, isn't it?' She examined Tash's coat for a label. Tash backed away.

'No, I'm not going there.' She glanced guiltily around in case there were any Mogo employees on the prowl. She'd lose the contract if she was spotted like this, or snapped by a journalist, she realised. She ducked her head beneath the lapels like a spy and buried her hands in the pockets, which were full of horse treats and other rubbish.

'Daddy and Henrietta are very keen to talk to you about the wedding, Tash – and so am I come to that.' Sophia was looking around the stands again. 'Drat, where's bloody Bernadette got to now? I bet she's having a sly fag.'

'I'm going to the tent to watch the cross-country on CCTV.' Tash started to back away. She certainly couldn't face talking about the wedding today. She hadn't even let herself *think* about the wedding today.

'Is it dry?' Sophia sniffed, looking up at the dark, squally sky.

'It's competitors and owners only,' Tash apologised. This wasn't strictly true but she had a dread of Sophia's long-suffering au pair nappy-changing in the middle of it.

'Oh.' She looked rather miffed.

'Think this chap needs changing, Sophs.' Ben was getting increasingly desperate as he waved Henry around like a loaded gun about to go off. 'You been round yet, Tash old thing?'

With enormous relief, Tash spotted Henrietta in the distance, tripping over a dog in her haste to catch up with James, who was marching ahead with his usual military gait.

'Look, there's Daddy,' she pointed out to Sophia and, the moment the Merediths started waving and shouting to attract his attention, dashed towards the TV tent. In her haste, she failed to see the elegant, slim woman stalking alongside Henrietta, her wide-brimmed leather hat tilted to shield her face from the rain.

Penny had left the tent to cheer Gus through the steeplechase, but Kirsty was still inside and looking after Beetroot, who was stuffing her face with Lucy Field's unwanted hot dog.

'Well done for getting round,' Tash greeted her.

'Bad luck for no' getting the chance,' Kirsty said. She had put on a coat over her cross-country shirt, but her sharp-featured face had the tell-tale splattering of mud that separated those who had been round from the hopefuls still awaiting their start time. Many of the competitors in the tent were fresh-faced and scrubbed-cheeked. Tash found herself in the unique position of being halfway between the two.

She took hold of Beetroot's lead and sat between Kirsty and Glen Bain as she watched a few rounds, including Stefan's, on the television monitors. Julia Ditton and her camera crew were roaming around outside to wait for competitors who had just finished, sucking up to the very few who had done well in order to chat to them, and pouncing on the majority who had been the victims of crashing falls to ask what had gone wrong. Every so often the camera loomed into the tent to focus on the white, nail-chewing faces of the current leaders as they watched their positions slide ever-downwards in the wake of better rounds. Kirsty, who was still sitting in fourth place despite her cricket score, received the odd close up while Tash tried to cower out of shot to hide her jacket. In the end she discarded it altogether, pushing it beneath her to act as a cushion, The tent – damp, moist and muggy from so many sweating bodies – was too warm to need it.

Finding that she was sitting on a lump, Tash pulled the coat out from under her and fished in its pockets. Inside one were a packet of sweets and an old leather credit card case filled with Hugo's plastic – gold Amex, banker's card, Visa, memberships to various clubs. Tash flipped idly through them, surprised that someone as punctilious as Hugo had left them lying around in a spare coat.

'He rode out in it this morning.' Kirsty was watching her. 'That is Hugo's, isn't it?'

Tash nodded.

'He rode out in it – I saw him,' Kirsty said. 'And that must be his wallet thing.' She took it from Tash and flipped through. 'Look, photos – ah! He's got one of Bod. And this must be his father, I take it . . . Christ, I recognise this!' she shrieked with amazement.

'What?' Tash dragged her eyes away from the screens, which were showing Stefan and Happy Monday squelching through the mashed-up Quarry. Looking at what Kirsty had in her hands, she almost passed out.

It was one of the kinky Polaroids of her that had been stuck to the Valentine's card she had intended for Niall. Hugo had cut it down to fit into the wallet so that thankfully only her face and shoulders showed, but the picture still made it pretty clear how little she was wearing and how pleased she was with herself.

'How can that have got there!' Tash whipped it back and threw it into the pocket it had come from, determining to extract it later and burn the photograph. Her face was on fire. 'Look, poor Stefan's had a stop at the Cross Questions.'

But Kirsty was still staring at her, her damp red hair falling across her eyes as she cocked her head with a funny half-smile.

'It all makes sense now,' she murmured softly. 'I canna believe I was so thick.'

'What do you mean?' Tash pressed her cold hands to her hot face in an attempt to ease the burning. She was uncomfortably aware that Glen Bain was pretending to watch the monitors, but listening in avidly.

'He never wanted me to go to the house where we could be private,' Kirsty breathed as though thinking it through for the first time. 'He used to want to come down to the farm. And he always asked after you – used to like me to tell him wee stories about how funny you were when you fell off or gave all the horses the wrong feeds or whatever. And he loved hearing about the times Niall couldn't get away from work to see you. In fact, he talked about you a lot – I always wondered why he bitched so much. Now I know.'

'Know what?'

Kirsty gave her a sarcastic look. 'Don't be thick, Tash. He even dragged me with him to try and persuade you to come to the New Year's Eve party.'

'Penny asked him to,' Tash remembered.

But Kirsty shook her head. 'It was Hugo's idea. As soon as you and Niall announced you were getting engaged, he went right off me. Couldn't wait to get rid of me. Christ! This woman Stefan was going on about Hugo adoring is *you*, Tash. It's you!'

There was a huge groan in the tent and Kirsty turned to look at the monitors. 'Has Stefan fallen?' Her face started to drain of colour.

'No.' Lucy Field was swigging ready-made gin and tonic from a can even though she had yet to ride. 'Happy put in another stop and he's retired.'

'But he was almost at the end!' Kirsty wailed, standing up and heading for the tent exit to go in search of him hacking back off-course.

'Kirsty!' Tash tried to call her back, but she was already through the door and hunching against the rain.

Tash watched a few more rounds without really taking them in, mindlessly chatting to the other competitors as she alternately congratulated and sympathised, although she got even that wrong, finding that she was giving a comforting hug to a New Zealand friend who had just clocked the fastest clear of the day.

People keep telling me how Hugo feels, she thought giddily, and I keep ignoring them and carrying on as though this is some dumb crush.

Grinning from ear to ear, she decided that she had better go and locate her family supporters to steer them to the start of the course where they could watch Gus and then Hugo set off.

Wandering out of the tent and shrugging Hugo's coat back on – snuggling happily into it like a dog in a basket – she bumped into Kirsty and Stefan coming back the other way. From the way he had his arm around her, she realised why Kirsty hadn't seemed too upset by her discovery in the wallet earlier.

'Congratulations, Stef,' Tash said rather vaguely and headed out into the rain.

'She okay?' Stefan watched her go with concern. 'She looked a bit spaced.'

'She's just found out Hugo fancies her rotten.'

'Oh, she must know that by now,' Stefan sighed despairingly. 'He's been after her for years.'

* * *

Taking in the crowds properly for the first time that day, Tash was amazed by the moving, sludgy sea of waxed coats, hats and green wellies. Golfing umbrellas danced through the neap-tide like floating debris, along with weaving dogs, brightly dressed toddlers and the air-borne litter of fast-food containers, paper napkins and dropped programmes, buffeted around by the wind.

Because of the awful weather, the sheltered trade stands were packed while out on the course the crowds were far thinner than usual on endurance day, spectators walking at hunched angles as they battled against the wind and rain. Umbrellas, hoods and dogs' ears were inside out and coats full of air as the onlookers squelched gallantly through the mud, eager to see their favourite combinations ride round.

Tash tracked Sophia's mob down at a trade stand decked with novelty sweatshirts featuring three-dimensional sheep and fat Friesian cows with udders that dangled like silk fingers from the embroidered design.

She was almost mown down by an elegant figure in a leather hat racing up to hug her.

'Tash darling! Henrietta and I are so, so cross with you that I should be in an awful sulk but I'm far too pleased to see you. Have you been round yet? Are you leading? Gosh, that's a nice coat – is it new? You could have done with a smaller size.'

Tash backed away to see her mother's exquisite, wide-eyed face looking at her anxiously.

'I'm no longer in the competition, Mummy,' she sighed, trying to answer the most important question first. 'And what on earth are you doing here? I thought you and Pascal were coming over next week.'

'We are – I mean, he is. But we have to talk about this wedding very urgently, darling, so I had to track you down for a chat.' Alexandra backed off and gave her a beady look from under her hat brim. 'Now say hello to your pa and Henrietta and let's all get huge drinks somewhere.'

After the hellos were done with – Tash noticed that she received her frostiest reception yet from Henrietta, but a far warmer one than expected from her father – they moved towards the start box in a straggling group. Henry was still wailing loudly, although he was now being held by the Merediths' vast French au pair who kept asking where the lavatories were.

'Is this the way to the bar?' Alexandra asked hopefully. 'I have to talk to you straight away, darling.'

Not liking the excitable tone of her mother's voice, Tash ignored her and trudged towards the ten-minute box where Gus was remounting ready to start. Not able to take her family into the horse area, she parked them at the fence.

'Tash!' he called from up high, just stopping Vic from ploughing down the ring fence as he recognised her and nosed for a mint.

Tash fed him one of the treats from Hugo's coat pocket and wished them both luck.

'Rotten shame having to pull out like that.' Gus smiled sadly, nodding to Tash's family who were all trying to say hello at once. He hadn't the time or inclination to get involved in the greetings. He reached a hand beneath his leg to check the girth a final time, face scrunching up with effort.

'I won't mind nearly so much if you go clear,' Tash told him. 'Best of luck.'

Gus pulled a face and stretched down to kiss Penny before moving towards the start box.

Once he was counted down and on his way, Penny dragged Tash to the riders' tent to watch the television coverage.

'Will your family be all right?' she asked anxiously as they found a couple of seats.

'Shit! I forgot about them.' Tash made to stand up again, but Penny gripped tightly on to her hand. 'Stay here – I need you more. Where's Ted?'

'Still in the endurance box, I should think.' Tash looked around. She wanted to slope back there too and collect her family. She was feeling hugely guilty now. But she was also uncomfortably aware that all of them – with the possible exception of Ben – today possessed the avid, earnest look of a minority pressure group marching to lobby Parliament. It frightened her. She wasn't sure she could hold out.

'Damn! I wanted him to hold my other hand.' Penny was fretting.

'I'll do that,' Glen Bain offered slimily.

Penny gripped on gratefully and watched the ensuing twelve minutes in terrified, shaking silence, punctuated only by the odd gasp of relief when Gus made it through a sticky moment or Vic slithered in the soup-thick mud.

'He'll be fine,' Tash assured her as her hand was mashed to a pulp. 'Vic has studs in the size of conkers.'

'Matches his brain then,' Penny said in a tight voice. 'How are they doing for time? If he gets a good place here, he'll have clinched the Bettapet sponsorship deal. If Brian goes faster on Foreign Agent, he gets it. It's hateful, but it's our only chance to keep going.'

They raced back to the box to watch him take the last fence, face plastered with mud and smiles.

Gus pounded through the finish just thirteen seconds over the maximum time and grinning from ear to ear. He'd had the second fastest clear of the day and he couldn't talk for excitement. When he slid off Vic, Julia Ditton thrust a microphone in his face and asked him how it had gone, but he just smiled goofily and silently into it until she gave up.

He hugged Penny until she practically snapped and loped into the weighing tent to sign in before bounding back to hug Tash, Penny and Ted, who was holding a panting Vic. Then he hugged them again. About to embark on a third round of hugs, he let out a cry of joy.

'He did it!' he wailed, giving Vic such a patting that the old horse looked likely to develop a dent in his neck.

'Tash!' yelled a voice from behind, and she swung around to see Ben waving his arms at her and pointing to the far side of the box where a familiar chestnut was looking eager to slay a few random grooms.

'Shit!' She remembered that she had promised to meet Hugo and raced off.

He was sitting on an upturned bucket as Jenny greased Snob's stamping legs, aided by India, who was holding his head to stop him from taking lumps out of her. The vets had already given the big chestnut the all clear and had backed hastily away. In contrast to Hunk earlier, he was barely sweating, although his coat was damp with rain. He gave a huge, rumbling whicker as Tash approached and delved into her borrowed coat pockets for treats.

Thankfully the downpour was at last easing off and the storm clouds seemed to be rumbling east to pester Oxford and then London.

On the other side of the fence from the box, Tash's family were rowing and fretting, still clustered together like a small group of political activists. At least the au pair seemed to have whisked Henry off to a convenient lavatory. Leaning over the fence, Alexandra was trying hard to have an animated conversation with Hugo who was sensibly ignoring her. Henrietta was entertaining Lotty and Josh by pulling funny faces, at which James was looking both peeved and jealous.

Tash squelched through the mud to Hugo's side.

'How's he going?'

'Like a bloody rhino on steroids,' he groaned, looking up through a damp forelock. 'My arms ache. I think I'll lose the use of both if I get on there again.' He rolled his eyes towards Snob.

Tash smiled. 'He's much more fun across country than roads and tracks,' she assured him. 'And his steeplechase is always done full pelt, however hard you try and pace him.'

'Tell me about it.' He flexed his fingers to get some feeling back into them. 'Jenny's just given me a ticking off for going too fast but believe me, if I could have got him to go slower, I would have.'

Tash giggled. 'He's so fit, it won't have taken anything out of him – in fact, it will have done him good. Composed him a little.'

'Practically decomposed me.' Hugo stood up, glancing at Jenny who mouthed, '*Three minutes.*'

'D'you need any help?' Tash looked around awkwardly, trying to ignore her mother's frantic hand signals.

'You can wish me luck again,' he said lightly, pulling on his gloves.

'Good luck.' She watched his clever, focused eyes.

'I didn't mean like that.'

Heart leaping, she gazed around at several adoring young female fans who had come to see him off, and her bickering family who were hissing over the fence that they simply had to talk to her right this minute. Suddenly none of them seemed to matter.

'Good luck.' She stretched up and kissed him very slowly and lightly on the mouth. Just for a second his lips yielded.

His eyes seared into hers with such intensity, she thought he was going to kiss her back properly and almost fainted with excitement. But he simply smiled broadly, leaping back on board and circling Snob at the start to try and calm him. Already snatching at the bit in anticipation, his mouth foaming, Snob looked thoroughly overexcited, his dark eyes bulging eagerly.

'Just like me,' Tash murmured to herself faintly, ducking out of the box to join her family, not hearing a word they said until Hugo and Snob bounded out of the start, mud flying.

'Can we all talk now?' Alexandra pleaded as soon as they had streaked out of view.

But Tash was already trotting through the park, her ears on elastic for the commentary.

She longed to watch the round from the comfort of the TV tent surrounded by friends who would hold her hand and understand her current free-fall adrenaline rush, but as her family contingent was far too big to be smuggled in, she rushed them and Beetroot to watch from the large stand by the Lake which, for the first time in years, had spaces in it because of the awful weather.

'You and Hugo seem to be getting on jolly well,' panted Alexandra excitedly as they climbed up to a suitable vantage point.

'We are,' said Tash, listening as the commentator announced that Snob was clear over the enormous Zig Zag. She sat down between her mother and Ben, who were the only two to have kept up with her.

'And Niall?'

'What about Niall?' Tash pulled Beetroot on to her knee and watched the rest of her family clamber up to join them, faces red with effort.

'Is he having an affair with Zoe Goldsmith?' Alexandra didn't waste time with platitudes. Settling in beside Ben, Henrietta was agog that she was being so direct. 'Sophia says he is.'

Sophia, furious at finding herself trapped at the far end of the family line, was leaning across her father, step-mother and husband in an attempt to listen in.

'Yes, he is. They're in love,' Tash said simply. 'Shut up a sec, Hugo's getting a mention.'

The public address declared Hugo and Snob were clear through the first Luckington Lane crossing and going great guns. Tash was about the only person taking in every word – everyone else around her was listening in on her family's extraordinary conversation.

'Are you seriously saying Niall is in love with someone else?' Henrietta stammered, pale eyes huge and disbelieving.

'But you're engaged to him, dammit!' James was joining in now.

Tash ignored them. The commentary switched back to Hugo again: '. . . flying over centre walk and . . . clear over the second crossing, taking the direct route. Hugo Beauchamp really attacking this course on Foxy Snob now . . .'

She heaved a sigh of relief. They were almost a third of the way around already, with some of the nastiest fences already tackled. She was drenched in nervous sweat. The Three Scythes was in just a couple of fences' time.

Alexandra and Sophia were both squawking excitedly about Niall, but their voices were drowned by an enormous cheer, and prop-forward-faced Brian Sedgewick, the country's favourite, thundered into view on his second ride, Foreign Agent. Within seconds they had splashed through the Lake in copy-book fashion, leaping out over the upturned boat and pounding towards the Pick-ups, drips flying. There was tremendous support for him at the event now that people had found out his younger horse had lost an eye. Such was the fickle nature of public sentiment, Tash realised, it had more or less eclipsed the greater loss Hugo had suffered earlier that week.

'You don't seem that bothered, Tash,' Alexandra wailed as the cheering died down.

'I'm not,' she said simply. 'Now keep quiet, I want to hear this bit.'

'. . . Hugo Beauchamp and Foxy Snob clear over the Vicarage Vee now, with a tremendous bold jump over the direct route – this combination really flying. Coming up to the Three Scythes – no one's successfully tackled the direct route on this fence so far, but Hugo seems to be going for it . . .'

Tash held her breath in horror, digging her elbow hard into her mother's side as she opened her mouth to speak again. Furious, Alexandra shut up.

'. . . but no, Hugo's tackling the fence to the left . . . first time we've seen this today . . . and he's through and clear – very clever bit of riding there. These two very much in contention despite their overnight dressage score . . . Lucinda Chucklesworth and Ravish A Radish, a refusal at the Sunken Road . . .'

Tash was grinning from ear to ear. He'd taken her advice and ridden the route she suggested. She wanted to hug him to bits, she was so proud.

'I must say, Tash,' Henrietta was talking again, her voice high and emotional, 'you're not reacting at all as we imagined.'

'Am I not?' She beamed at her step-mother.

'No – we thought you'd be terribly upset!'

'I couldn't be happier.' Tash listened as the Tannoy declared Hugo and Snob over the Leap of Luxury and heading down the long gallop to the Lake.

As whistles blew to warn of his impending arrival, Tash clutched on to Beetroot and blocked out the jabbering of her family all around her, instead craning around to catch her first sight of him. As soon as the galloping red streak was in sight, her only thoughts were for the horse she loved and the man she adored.

The Lake this year consisted of a huge leap into deep water over a fence that had been built to resemble a storm-wrecked jetty. Then one had to turn sharply right in the water to jump out over a 'ship-wrecked' rowing boat which had been hollowed out so that one jumped on to a platform then into the arrow-head of its bow, finally bounding out over the rear of its hull.

Tash could see that Hugo was having to use every last ounce of his considerable strength and skill to keep control – his face was gritted with determination and coated with mud, his steel-strong legs barely moving as he channelled all Snob's furious energy into his great, spring-like hind quarters. She suddenly knew for certain that had she been on board, she would have never been able to hold him like that. Snob was absolutely fearsome in his desperation to get going and get at it, as though terrified that the fences would walk away without him to tackle them. But, thundering towards the complex, he seemed to take in the crowd for the first time, and panic, utterly fazed by the great, gawping mass of faces, bustling bodies, bright hats and waggy-tailed dogs. Suddenly all over the place, he careered sideways and lunged into a series of terrifying, panic-stricken, nose-diving bucks that threw Hugo entirely off balance and dragged the reins from his rain-wetted gloves. The next moment, Snob was accelerating towards the Lake at full throttle, head between his knees. As they got within strides of the fence, he threw up his neck and surged forwards.

Oblivious of all around her, Tash screamed.

Battling to get Snob's head down, Hugo barely had time to check him or see a stride before the fence was upon them. They plunged into the water at a racketing pace and seemed to be leaping deeper and deeper into the Lake in great dolphin-arcs of splashing water. Tash was amazed that Hugo stayed on board amidst so much see-saw lunging and kicked-up spray. She'd almost certainly have been doggy-paddling to shore by now.

'Oh God, he's going for a swim!' Ben groaned, covering his eyes.

The crowd was starting to cheer rather uncharitably as they saw another fall coming, but at the last minute, Hugo managed to gather up the unravelling knitting of reins in front of him and pull Snob around to the right on an accurate enough line to get him clambering out over the boat in an inelegant but effective fashion before pelting towards the Pick-ups.

On the stands Tash and Ben clutched each other for support and screamed with delight.

Ben was the first to recover.

'Er – yup, jolly good that, huh? Sorry to grab you like that, Tash.' He backed off and turned pink.

Puffing loudly, the Merediths' au pair had clambered up on to the stands with a freshly changed Henry. Both Lotty and Josh, on Sophia's far side, were wailing loudly now.

'They both need the lavatory, Bernadette,' Sophia announced before the poor girl had a chance to sit down. 'Can you take them?'

'But, Madame, there is ver' long queues.'

'Now!' Sophia snapped.

'*Oui, Madame.*' Handing Henry over, she grabbed the kids and panted off again.

'Good way for her to lose weight,' Sophia said smugly, turning to Tash. 'So are you marrying Niall or not?'

'The truth is,' Tash stood up, pausing to listen as the commentary announced that Hugo was safely up the Beaufort Staircase, 'I haven't seen him lately to ask – excuse me, I'm going to run across and see Snob finish.'

Leaving them all gaping, Tash raced across the car parks and just caught Snob pounding the fastest route through the Quarry as though the mud wasn't there. As he streaked off into the distance with Hugo huddled over his neck, Tash did a little rain-dance of happiness and pelted off to wait at the finish, where Jenny, Penny and India were already installed beneath the tall copper beech, listening eagerly to the public address as it estimated that Hugo was the closest to the time yet.

'If he goes inside he could take the lead.' India jumped up and down excitedly.

Consulting her scribbled-over programme, Penny scrunched up her face as she did some hasty mental arithmetic. 'I think he would, you know. But only if he makes the time.'

'I shouldn't think there's much chance of that,' Tash laughed. 'But he should be in with the chance of an overnight place.'

Behind them, Julia Ditton had at last got Gus in a talkative mood and was asking him about his round.

'Fucking awful going, to say the least – we were bloody swimming out there. Thank God he had great big buggery studs in or we'd've been shafted by this eff-awful weather.'

Julia waved at the camera-man to stop.

'Could you not swear, Gus?' she asked politely. 'Thankfully this isn't going out live as they're broadcasting the three-forty-five from Doncaster at the moment.'

'Oh – right.' Gus grinned. 'Well, Julia,' he nodded feverishly as they shot again, 'it was a great round – just great. The horse was simply great.'

'And how did it feel to triumph over the weather?'

'Great, basically.'

'Any sticky moments?'

'Gratefully no – he did a great job.'

'Thank you, Gus Moncrieff. Now back to Mike and Lorna in the commentary box.' She turned to give Gus a kiss. 'That was crap, but thanks.' Winking at Penny, she wandered off to interview Brian Sedgewick, who had just weighed in, his prop-forward's face red with an endorphin high, and currently lying in third place on Foreign Agent – one behind Gus. The fast New Zealander was still in the lead.

Tash bounced around in an agitated state as she listened to the public address describing Hugo and Snob's rather reckless jumps over the Huntsman's Hangover complex and the windfalls in the coppice that preceded their appearing in view.

'There they are!' Penny shrieked as they came pelting out of the wood and galloped towards the Lamb's Creek, demolishing most of the top of it.

'Jesus, they're going fast.' Gus held his breath.

'That horse is so bloody fit.' Jenny stood beside Tash. 'What d'you feed him on – kerosene?'

'And sex.' Tash watched them pelting towards the last, with Snob at last seeming to ease off a little as he allowed Hugo to change his legs and balance him.

Tash felt her heart puff with pride as she watched them work together like a couple of slick old pros, pounding up to the finish – Snob with his ears pricked and eyes shining, Hugo with his stopwatch held in front of his nose and his legs urging to the line.

As ever, Snob took ages to pull up, almost flattening the finishing steward who welcomed them home with his bowler hat aloft.

'Was I inside?' Hugo panted as he finally walked Snob back to his support team.

'Think so,' Penny told him, peering at the timing clock. 'Maybe a couple of seconds over.'

Hardly seeming to take this in, Hugo was staring down at Tash as she took Snob's head and loosened his crossed noseband, her hands shaking.

'That,' he told her, laughing delightedly, 'was one of the most exciting quarter of an hour's of my life – and I'm including the three minutes before the start.'

Heart hammering, Tash buried an unstoppable smile in Snob's cheek.

As he jumped off and started to ungirth, the course vets rushed in once again to take Snob's heartbeat and temperature, and Hugo was instantly cornered by the finishing steward who went through the usual routine of asking him whether he'd incurred any penalties out on the course, waiting for him to gather up the saddle so that he could lead him off to the weighing-in tent.

Moving to Snob's off-side to help, Tash unbuckled the second breast-plate strap, catching her fingers against Hugo's gloved ones across Snob's withers as she helped heave off the saddle. For a moment he gripped them tight, but he was almost instantly swept away to the weighing-in tent, his progress being filmed eagerly by the scurfy roaming camera-man.

In the finishing area, congratulations rained down on Hugo and he was pounced upon by Julia and her TV team as soon as he emerged from the weighing-in tent, still completely breathless from his round and clutching Snob's saddle to his number-bibbed chest.

'We make you in the lead right now by one tenth of a penalty, Hugo.' Julia blocked his path before he could head back to his team. 'How d'you feel about that?'

'Well, pretty pleased, obviously, although my arms ache like an Oxford rower's after the boat race.' His eyes searched the crowd of faces around him.

He suddenly reached out and pulled a horrified Tash into shot, rival jacket label flashing madly.

'Here's the girl you should be congratulating,' he said with startling generosity. 'She put in all the hard work on him.'

'Are you pleased, Tash?' Julia asked as the furry microphone loomed large.

'We're both puffed to chieces -- I mean, chuffed to pieces,' she managed to gulp.

'And is this the wedding present you wanted?' Julia winked.

Tash looked momentarily lost, glancing from Hugo to Snob, already being sponged down by India and Penny.

'We'll have to wait for tomorrow to see about that,' Hugo said firmly.

Thirty-Nine

WATCHING THE LIVE BADMINTON transmission on the huge, high-tech television which the film crew had rigged up in the temporary Haydown green room, Lisette chewed her lip anxiously.

'Did I miss much?' Sally asked as she wandered back in with a fresh jug of water to refill the coffee filter.

'Nothing important.' Lisette watched her as she poured, slopping most of it over one of Hugo's very grand, very ring-marked side dressers. She'd really let herself go that week, and was suddenly reverting back to the scruffy hair and old leggings look Lisette despised. She also kept talking boringly about her children and sloping off to telephone them at her parents' house just as Lisette wanted her to do something.

'Who's in the lead at the moment?'

Lisette gritted her teeth. 'Hugo.'

'But that's wonderful!' Sally spilled the rest of the water as she spun round.

'Isn't it?' Lisette stared fixedly at the screen where Julia Ditton had cornered a mud-splattered Lucy Field.

'It's a shame my idea didn't work out, really,' Sally sighed. 'Just think of the publicity you'd be getting now if Tash's horse was called Four Poster Bed.'

'Your sister-in-law isn't even riding the horse, Sally,' Lisette snapped. 'It was a hopeless idea in the first place. There was never any publicity mileage in it.'

Sally looked at her in alarm, her usually merry eyes wide with hurt. 'That's what Matty said,' she whispered.

'Well, I'm afraid he was right.' Lisette's voice softened as she realised how harsh she had sounded. 'I'm sorry.'

'I was so angry with him when he told me that, I sprinkled a beef stock cube on his pizza when he wasn't looking,' Sally remembered in horror.

'Well, I'd think long and hard before you force-feed him the fatted calf after last Friday's fiasco,' Lisette muttered.

Sally closed her eyes and turned back to the filter machine.

'So have you decided whether you're going to divorce him yet?' Lisette asked bluntly.

'I haven't made up my mind.'

'But he humiliated you in front of everyone last Friday night,' Lisette pointed out. 'I couldn't believe my ears when he asked Zoe Goldsmith whether she remembered the night they got off together in the larder. I thought he was talking about some teenage necking session in a cheap Russian motorcar for a moment, and then I realised that he meant right there at the fucking farm, while you were in London, barefoot and pregnant with Linus.'

'That's hardly grounds for divorce,' Sally muttered, her face colouring with humiliation. She was terrified someone would overhear. They were working with a skeleton crew that day to save on money, but Flavia Watson – Lisette's super-efficient production manager – was only in the next room chatting on the phone, and several of the cast were milling around the house, awaiting the start of the last scene of the day which was delayed because Niall had not yet returned from lunch.

'Maybe not.' Lisette muted the television as the coverage moved on to golf and turned to face her. 'If you think you can forgive him the infidelity, that is.'

'He only kissed her!' Sally banged down the jug. 'I seem to recall you did a hell of a lot more than just kiss someone at a party before Niall divorced you. You went to parties back then where you'd slept with practically every man in the room more recently than you'd slept with Niall.'

'I'm a good mixer,' said Lisette smoothly. 'And we're not talking about Niall here, besides which I was the one who divorced him. We're talking about Matty. He deliberately made a fool of you at that dinner party.'

'Perhaps I deserved it.' Sally searched through cardboard boxes for a fresh packet of filter papers. 'I was behaving really childishly – I only invited him to come so that I could show him how well I was getting on without him, how easy it would be for me to start a new life. He genuinely wanted to tell me the truth. And I know it was an awful way to do it, but I think he was at his wits' end. It was Zoe Goldsmith I really felt sorry for. Her children were there.'

'They seemed to find it highly amusing.' Lisette's eyes flickered at the mention of Zoe Goldsmith.

'They're great kids,' Sally sighed. 'I hope my lot grow up to be as level-headed and open about everything.'

Lisette clenched her teeth, praying that Sally wasn't going to start talking about her children again. But thankfully Niall walked in before she could. He'd come straight from make-up and still had tissues sticking out of his shirt collar like a tatty Elizabethan ruffle.

'Has Tash been round yet?' he asked, peering at the muted television. 'Jesus, there are people walking all over the cross-country course with steel bars, so there are. Do you think they're animal rights protesters?'

'It's golf, Niall,' Lisette said witheringly. 'And Tash pulled out of the competition hours ago. Where have you been? Flavia's been going ape trying to track you down for the past hour. We've had to hold filming again, and we're already two days behind schedule which is largely your fault. If we go any more overbudget on this thing, I'll sue you.'

'You what?' he gulped.

'It was a joke.'

'I can't believe you didn't know Tash has pulled out of the competition, Niall.' Sally shook her head and laughed. 'You're getting married in a week.'

'I know.' He caught Lisette staring at him and suddenly flashed his big, disarming smile. 'And there's still a hell of a lot to organise, so there is. It's why I'm late. I was just dropping off my grandmammy's wedding ring at the jeweller's to be altered.'

'This wedding had better go smoothly,' Lisette told him, eyes narrowing. 'I'm banking on it being fucking spectacular – Sally tells me her mother-in-law has spared no expense. And *Cheers!* want their money's worth.'

'And they'll get it, angel.' His eyes crinkled. 'Every last penny. I think we can safely say the wedding will go ahead without a hitch.'

After Hugo's spectacular round, Tash found the afternoon passed in a blur. Sophia and Ben nipped back to their car and brought a couple of bottles of champagne over to the Lime Tree Farm lorry where Hugo and Gus were talking about their rounds non-stop. Soon the place was heaving as Tash's family crammed inside, along with Stefan's lofty Swedish parents who spoke no English and looked confused throughout. Kirsty and Penny were quaffing away too, joining in the spirit of it all. It was like playing a very damp, boozy game of sardines. Only Jenny, Ted and India stayed at the yard where they were keeping a close eye on the horses, walking them out regularly to check for any signs of stiffness or injury.

There were so many people and such a lot of noise that Alexandra and her pressure group had considerable difficulty in cornering Tash, who was herself finding it almost impossible to get close enough to Hugo to see his face. She had hardly had a chance even to congratulate him yet as they'd been swept along by the eager Lime Tree team, continually parted like two swans on a squally river. After two glasses of champagne, she was almost beside herself with the bubble-popping, nose-fizzing urge to fling her arms around him and tell him she loved him. But she had a plan.

That night was the Badminton Ball, a huge post-endurance-day party held in the rider's marquees that was an exercise in endurance itself as it usually consisted of a large number of over-fit, over-sexed eventers on the razzle – either high from their day's successes and celebrating, or low from their failures and trying to drown their sorrows. Even with another day of competition ahead, it had a reputation as a party to behold. It was the perfect setting, she decided, to corner Hugo and tell him how she felt about him. There was nothing, according to her mother, as intimate as a large party. And Tash was bursting with the need to get extremely intimate indeed.

The champagne was very quickly replaced by cheap Bulgarian Chardonnay but no one seemed to mind as they downed several glasses each and took turns to race back and forth to the course to check the last few finishers' scores. At the close of the endurance day, Hugo was still in the lead with Gus third, Brian Sedgewick fourth and Kirsty now back in twenty-eighth.

Stefan and Tash, who had both failed to finish, consoled themselves with a huge box of chocolates that a female fan had given Hugo that morning to wish him luck.

'Save me a soft centre.' Kirsty swam through the tight gaggle of revellers and joined them where they stood crushed up against the little kitchen oven. Hugo, still sitting at the packed table at the opposite end of the box with Gus, was out of view.

'Stefan and I think,' she gave Tash a beady look as she selected a strawberry cream, 'that you should make up your mind who you want – Niall or Hugo.'

Tash gulped. Sophia, who was just behind her and chattering away to Stefan's uncomprehending six-foot mother about Holdham, suddenly went quiet.

'You have to choose, Tash,' Stefan whispered, eyes raking her face. 'You can't keep stringing him along like this. You're a week away from being Mrs Niall O'Shaughnessy, and you keep looking at Hugo as though he's the one who's going to be waiting at the top of the aisle.'

The back of Sophia's head was almost on Tash's shoulder.

'Hugo must be in one hell of a mess right now, Tash.' Kirsty chomped on her strawberry cream.

'We think all those phone-calls he's been making over the past couple of days are to the Samaritans.' Stefan selected a nougat and looked at Tash earnestly.

She gulped in horror, a lump of hazelnut whirl sliding down her wind pipe and almost choking her. 'Really? He seems so together today.'

'All front.' Kirsty shook her head. 'You know how proud he is.'

'Poor Hugo,' Tash whispered.

She was horrified when, minutes later, Alexandra offered to take them all out to dinner that night.

'But it's the ball!' she wailed.

'Oh, we never go to that,' Penny said dismissively. 'And this would be far more fun. Anyway you said yesterday you didn't want to go to it.'

'Yes, come on, darling.' Alexandra gave her an unusually stern look. Squashed together nearby, Henrietta and James joined in. They should be holding up placards, Tash thought weakly.

She escaped from the heaving, airless box to see the horses for a few minutes, checking Hunk first, who was wearing a cold poultice on his weak tendon and pulling faces, greedy for Polos. She then headed across the yard to check Snob over. His legs, now scraped free of their cross-country grease, were miraculously cool and unmarred and, even though he was tired from the day's exertions, he was still boisterous enough to head-butt her a couple of times in the ribs before settling down to snatch at his net. Tash pressed her forehead to his shoulder, breathing in the warmth of his neck and the sweet scent of his highly banked alfalfa bedding.

'Give me an excuse not to go,' she moaned, turning back to lean against him. 'Give me an excuse to stay here and keep Hugo here too. Can't you put on a fake limp for a bit?'

But he merely offered silent support, pressing a warm muzzle to her shoulder and blowing out in a long, languid sigh. He was feeling extremely smug.

As was Hugo. When they walked to the cars they were all sharing that night, he fell into pace beside Tash and caught her arm in his. 'You haven't congratulated me yet.'

Tash looked up into those eager, laughing blue eyes and rippled all over with excitement. Then a booming chortle behind them made her jump out of her skin.

'You haven't won yet, Hugs.' Ben lolloped up beside them companionably. 'Listen, Sophia and I are going to push off home and skip this dinner thing. Kids are getting a bit fractious and the nanny appears to be throwing some sort of wobbly and crying non-stop. Damned inconvenient. Good luck tomorrow, Hugs.'

'Thanks.' Hugo was still looking at Tash.

Ben slapped them both cheerfully on the back. 'I suppose the next time we'll see you two is at the wedding?' He carried on walking beside them towards the car park, humming flatly.

Seeing Hugo's eyes harden, Tash wanted to scream.

After that, Hugo stomped broodily off to travel to the restaurant with Penny and Gus in the only taxi. Desperate to avoid a grilling by the pressure group, Tash leaped into the back of Stefan's parents' hire car, cramming herself alongside Kirsty and the tall Swede.

'Wouldn't you be more comfortable in there?' Kirsty nodded towards James's Jaguar.

'No, no – this is very cosy,' Tash squeaked, slamming the door shut and watching Hugo's set profile slide away as the taxi beside them drove off.

Niall, as ever, chose the most theatrical moment to get in touch. They were just settling down in a very grand restaurant near Bath, toasting the day, when Gus's mobile telephone shrilled into life, causing a lot of the other diners to tut disapprovingly. Tash cowered when he said who it was. She couldn't bring herself to look at Hugo, who yet again had been swept away from her and was sitting at the far end of the long, narrow table.

She took the phone with a shaking hand and glanced around for somewhere to escape with it in private, but she was hemmed in against a wall with two people to either side of her. Short of diving under the table, she had no choice but to stay put.

'Angel, can we talk?' breathed Niall down a crackly line. 'Are you alone?'

Tash gazed around her at almost a dozen fascinated faces and swallowed. 'Not exactly, no.'

Opposite her, Alexandra was mouthing 'Is that Niall?' like mad and Penny was nearly burning her hair off in the candle flame as she leaned forward to hear better over the restaurant chatter.

'Oh – I see.' His voice kept cutting out on the line. 'I hea . . . you had to pull out of the . . . mpetition, angel. I'm so sorry.'

'Thanks.' Tash shifted in her seat. The connection was appalling. She could only catch snatches of what he was saying. 'I'm . . . orry I haven't been in touch . . . rlier, but this we . . . been . . . urder.'

'What? Murder?' Tash craned back in her chair to get a better reception. In front of her, the pressure group craned forward to listen in, eyes widening.

The line was breaking up even more badly now. 'Angel, the film's . . . hind sched . . . and over budget. I honestly think that if I break our news at the party to . . . row night it will fin . . . . . . ette off.'

'Did you say finish Lisette off?' Tash found that the aerial was now caught up with an elaborate metal sconce behind her head, making reception even worse.

Niall sounded as though he was talking through a kazoo.

'Yes – we're carry . . . on filming at . . . down for an ex . . . two days. I've only just this minute got back from . . . sh . . . myself.'

'Sorry, I didn't catch that.' Tash was battling to get the aerial out of the sconce. 'What yourself?'

'I've just this minute got back from the shoot, angel.' His voice returned to normal as she freed herself from the sconce although the line was still crackling like a crisp packet in a jogger's bum-bag.

'Oh, *shoot*,' Tash nodded.

'Lisette seems to have guessed that something's up,' he went on. 'In her current state she might do something silly.'

'What do you mean, do something silly?' Tash asked, ignoring her mother's frantic hand signals.

The line was now coming and going as though he was swinging the phone receiver around his head by the cord. 'Listen, we have to meet up tomorrow evening,' he said urgently. 'Before Lisette's party. At the forge. I need to ask a monumental favour of you. I 'clare, it's pretty bloody gargantuan, and you might well refuse. But my future happiness is riding on it.' He sounded wildly excited and almost, Tash realised in amazement, joyful.

'Oh, yes?' Tash noticed that everyone at the table was gaping at her in appalled silence. She tried to flash them a 'just having a chat' smile.

There was a long pause and for a moment Tash worried that the line had cut out completely, but at last Niall spoke, his voice meltingly soft and persuasive. 'Angel, I want the wedding to go ahead.'

'You what?' Tash yelped.

'It was Zoe's idea,' he confessed.

'Did you say Zoe?'

Opposite her, Henrietta elbowed Tash's mother so hard in the ribs that she almost landed on James's lap.

There was another long pause, punctuated by Gus's phone letting out a sharp beep to warn that the battery was running low. When Niall finally started talking again, his voice was deep and laced with apologies.

'I love Zoe, Tash. I'm sorry, angel, but I have to be honest. She's the one person who's held me together through this. I adore her – she's so strong and good and clever. If she believes in me enough to let me risk it rather than go bankrupt, I think I have to be the luckiest, most undeserving sod on this earth.' Suddenly she could hear him laughing his lovely, abandoned, raucous laugh.

'Risk what?'

The line started breaking up badly again. 'Zoe thinks the idea of giving *Cheers!* a huge surprise next Saturday is wonderful, so she does. She says she's always believed rearranged marriages last the longest.'

Tash wondered if Zoe had been joining him on his drinking binges.

'What are you suggesting here?' She was having to tip right back in her chair to keep the connection.

'I suppose Bob Hudson should take all the credit.' Niall's laugh was fragmented by crackling interference, making it sound alarmingly manic. 'After all, staging an altar-native wedding was his idea in . . . first pl . . . I just wish I could tell him, but he . . . ight blow the whole th . . .' The line disappeared for a moment.

'Niall?' Tash waggled the phone. 'Niall?'

'. . . if Lisette found out at this stage, it would be suicide,' his voice came back.

'Suicide! Niall, if you're suggesting—' Tash was about to say that if he believed she would really agree to go ahead with Bob's ridiculous tears-at-the altar stage-show, then that would be suicide too, but the pressure group was practically lying over the table now.

'Believe me, Tash, we've talked and talked about it,' Niall urged. 'And I swear to you that, if you help me pull this thing off, I'll make it up to your family one day, I promise I will.'

The phone let out another urgent beep.

'Niall, the battery's about to cut out,' Tash said hopelessly.

'I have to talk to you tomorrow night, angel,' he begged. 'I have to convince you this thing might work. Promise me you won't breathe a word of this to anyone until then?' he pleaded.

'Okay.' Tash glanced at Hugo and then looked quickly away again, unable to bear seeing that beautiful, guarded face which almost certainly hid a seething well of anger and hurt.

'Thank you, angel!' Niall sounded like an overexcited small boy. 'If you agree to do this, we might even be able to stop Hugo getting his hands on Snob.'

'What?' She froze, looking at him once more. He was glaring at her murderously. Perhaps he wasn't so hurt after all . . .

'I overheard Lisette talking to him on the phone today, angel. I'm not sure, but I think she's agreed to sell the horse to Hugo if we call the wedding off. She was talking about their "deal".'

The phone was letting out a beep every few seconds now, obliterating a lot of what he was saying. Tash was terrified the line would go before she had a chance to find out anymore.

'What exactly did she say?'

She was astonished to hear Niall laughing once more.

'Tash, it doesn't matter. Wait till tomorrow night. Zoe's convinced that all you have to do is tell Hugo—' The line finally died with one last trill.

There was an ominous, expectant hush at the table. Tash took a deep breath and, tipping forward on her chair again, flipped the cover of the phone shut.

'That was Niall,' she said shakily.

'So we gathered,' her father snapped.

'What's happening, darling?' Alexandra's eyes were huge with concern. 'He's not threatening to do something awful to himself, is he?'

'No, Mummy,' she muttered. Not to himself, she wanted to scream. Just to me. 'He was extremely cheerful, in fact.'

'So is the wedding still going ahead?' Henrietta asked nervously.

Not trusting herself to speak, Tash nodded.

Then, as though worked by a ventriloquist's hand at her back, her eyes slithered involuntarily towards Hugo. He was lighting a cigarette with shaking hands but his face registered nothing but utter contempt, blue eyes searing into hers with such scorn that she almost flew back against the wall. She looked away in despair.

Forty

UP AT DAWN THE following morning because the others were thumping around the lorry so loudly that Tash at first thought they were hitting her over the head, she stumbled around with a crashing hangover, hardly focusing as she crawled to the yard to watch Snob being trotted out along with the other Lime Tree Farm horses to check they hadn't stiffened up in the night. Having just held her heaving stomach in check long enough to see that Snob was looking far better than she was, she bolted off to be sick.

'I think her nerves are getting to her,' India said with concern. 'She's really worried for Hugo and Snob, really wants them to win. That's so selfless.'

Having stayed in with the other grooms the night before, she had no idea of how absolutely plastered Tash had got and she had been in bed long before Stefan's huge, silent Swedish father had kindly carried a practically comatose Tash into the Lime Tree Farm box.

Stefan and Kirsty, who were watching Betty Blue trotting out, said nothing. As far as they were concerned, Tash deserved to expire from alcohol poisoning.

'I called the farm last night,' India said, cheerfully unaware of their glum expressions. 'Rufus was having one hell of a party. Gus is going to be furious. He's already grumbling about the prospect of tidying up after the wedding reception next weekend – he thinks the place is going to be wrecked.'

'The fall of the house of the usher?' Kirsty muttered, walking towards Betty to feel a hind leg with concern.

India giggled. 'Mum says that if everything works out next Saturday, it'll be a wedding deception, not reception, anyway.'

'If what works out?' Stefan looked at her in confusion.

Suddenly covering her mouth in horror, India went bright pink and shrugged, hastily rushing off to collect Vic.

But Stefan was too preoccupied with looking at Betty to notice her embarrassment.

Eyes rolling evilly, Snob passed the second official vets' inspection later that morning – again on the Tarmac strip in the gravel sweep in front of the house – striding out as though doing a strut down a catwalk and battling hard to take a piece out of Hugo the entire way. There was more deliberation over the lolloping, angular Fashion Victim, who had his legs thoroughly peered at and his wind listened to but, to huge sighs of relief from the Lime Tree Farm contingent, he also passed. Only poor Kirsty missed out on the luck as, tired and lack-lustre from her exertions the day before, Betty shambled up and down the Tarmac line with a very limp gait, like a good-time girl who'd lost the heel from one stiletto. When the senior steward announced over his megaphone that she had failed there was the inevitable groan from the knowledgeable spectators who had turned up early to watch the final inspection, but Kirsty gave a rueful shrug and, letting Ted lead her big mare away, melted into Stefan's long arms and demanded a thorough kissing to make up for her disappointment. They headed back to the yard with Stefan's stern parents following on disapprovingly, not knowing the English to ask her to lay off their young son.

'Those two must have got it together last night,' Gus told Hugo. 'Kirsty didn't come back to the box until three. I'd got up for an insomniac snack – bloody nerves playing up. Tash was still cornered in the lavatory throwing up, poor darling. I've never known her get as hammered as she did last night.'

'She's obviously in training so that she can keep up with Niall once they're married,' said Hugo.

'I can hardly believe that wedding is still going ahead.' Gus shook his head. 'It's ridiculous – even her family seem to want her to call the bloody thing off. She and Niall have hardly been speaking since they got back from France.'

'Perhaps they've called a temporary trousseau,' Hugo muttered, and stalked off to give an interview to a roaming *Daily Telegraph* sports reporter.

*   *   *

There was a long, long wait between the vets' examination and the final nail-biting show-jumping rounds that afternoon. At lunchtime, all the competitors still left in the championship were due to parade formally in the main arena, but before that it was the lower-placed riders – those who were lying below twentieth place – who coaxed their tired horses over the coloured, rain-flecked poles in the main ring. It meant that all the overnight leaders had a restless, nerve-racking wait.

Although the storms of the past few days had rumbled off to Sussex and Kent, it was still spitting down outside, and Tash ended up in the lorry playing poker with India and Ted. She was so hungover that she could barely focus. She looked like death boiled dry and her eyes – when she recovered sufficiently to examine them in a mirror – were like a major industrial town on a scale road map, interlaced with red A roads.

Demons of embarrassment were clawing at her shoulders as she tried to remember the previous night, but apart from the vague recollection of a bowl of crème brûlée coming up to meet her, the evening remained an obstinate blank.

'You should have played that, Tash!' Ted groaned, looking at her hand. 'Why did you cop out? You've got three sevens.'

'Have I?' Tash had forgotten she was even holding a hand of cards in the first place.

'Oh, it's pointless playing with you!' India laughed. 'Go and watch TV or something, then at least Ted and I can strip if we lose. I thought you'd be happier after last night.' She gave her a huge wink.

'What?' Tash looked at her exquisite, leggy groom and wished she was fourteen again. She'd never looked that good, but loving Hugo had been a hell of a lot more simple then.

'Mum said Niall was going to ring you.' India gave another wink, almost popping one huge, pale blue eye out of its socket. 'About the *wedding.*' She glanced sideways at Ted who was too engrossed in shuffling the cards to bother listening to trivial girlie-talk.

Tash was gaping at her in horror. 'You mean, you know?'

'Mum and I had a long chat about it last weekend – when she first thought the idea up. She wasn't even going to suggest it to Niall then, but Rufus and I persuaded her that you seriously wouldn't mind.'

'You did?'

'She's been leaving messages all week, so I guessed Niall had agreed. I called her at the hotel.'

'What hotel?' Tash was getting more and more confused.

'Oh, Tash, you really are preoccupied, aren't you?' India laughed. 'That's so typical. I suppose you have me to thank for everything working out really, don't you?'

'Do I?'

'Well, it was me who made you send him a Valentine's card, remember?' India looked rather put out.

Tash gazed at her in bewildered frustration. She wanted Ted to push off so that she could demand to know what India was talking about.

Ted was looking at his hand with almost equal frustration as it was obviously good enough to make India flush if she showed her pair, now that they were playing for strips rather than chips.

'I thought you were going to watch the box, Tash.' He gave her a beady look, eager for her to push off too.

Doing as she was told, Tash slumped back on a bunk and watched an episode of Little House On the Prairie on the portable, which bucked her up slightly, as it was all about Laura having the hots for a young farm-hand who also had the hots for her. They were both too shy to let their secrets out until they made friends over a pet rabbit. Reclining weakly in her bunk, Tash hoped it was an omen. She wondered vaguely if she should make Beetroot a pair of long floppy ears to entice Hugo into a tête-à-tête, but decided against it.

What Niall had said last night had shattered her confidence completely, riddling her with doubts. Yesterday, she had been so convinced that Hugo was as mad for her as she was for him, yet it appeared that he was only after her horse all along. And, when she thought about it, he had practically ignored her all week. It was only yesterday that he'd suddenly seemed keen again. If he'd made some sort of deal with Lisette on Friday night as Niall said, then it was no wonder. It was in his interest to try and seduce her into calling off the wedding at the last minute. That way, he'd get the horse for good, not just for Badminton.

Deciding that she needed some air, she took Beetroot for a walk, but it was still spitting with rain and she felt so fragile that every drop on her head was like a thump from a mallet.

She felt ridiculously tearful as she remembered that Hugo had told her she needed a waterproof hat this week. Heading groggily through the trade stands, she bought herself a jaunty yellow sou-wester before wandering back to the yard to check how things were progressing.

There was no one around from the Lime Tree Farm mob. Snob, already groomed and plaited from his morning inspection, was swathed in a quilted blanket and head-bobbing sulkily like a shadow boxer. He flatly refused to acknowledge her. Equally uninterested, Fashion Victim was snoozing with his eyes half open. Tash trailed along to Hunk's stall and fed him an entire packet of Polos, eager to secure an ally.

Back out in the yard several eventers were clustered together exchanging gossip from the previous night's raucous ball. They all shut up when Tash shuffled past. Then there was a muted titter, followed by a few stifled guffaws, followed by a gale of giggles spreading as quickly through the group as yawns through a bored class of schoolchildren.

It was Brian Sedgewick who started the chant, his battered face split with laughter.

'Where did you get that hat, where did you get that hat!'

Pulling the despised hat over her ears, Tash shot them all as brave and indignant a smile as she could muster before trudging out with Beetroot across the park, mulling over her fate. The prospect of standing at the altar with Niall in seven days' time awaiting her cue to stage a dramatic exit appalled her, but she could now see no other way out. He clearly wasn't prepared to square up to Lisette and she had flunked what would probably be her last chance to confess what a mess they were in to her family. With just a week to cancel, she almost thought Niall's idea would be easier for them to take. At least it would go down in the annals of family history as the annulled wedding to remember. A tearful last-minute change of heart would be far easier for them to forgive than the reality of a web of lies to prevent Niall from becoming an alcoholic bankrupt.

Several competitors were out for a short, leg-loosening hack before their show-jumping rounds, well wrapped up against the viperish wind and spitting rain, their horses swathed in waterproof exercise sheets and leg-protectors so it was hard to identify exactly who was who.

Rendered anonymous by the new head-gear, Tash trudged around yesterday's cross-country course uninterrupted, letting Beetroot sniff, dig and chase vermin to her heart's content. She was in no hurry; she'd got a lot of thinking to do. She kept thinking about her fantasy – the ridiculous dream she had clung to where Hugo would leap up at the wedding and announce just about every impediment he could think of. Suddenly it didn't seem quite so ridiculous after all.

Tash walked for such a long time that she missed the lunchtime parade of the top twenty competitors and only just settled in beside Penny in the stands as Lucy Field, who was lying twelfth, rode into the ring on her nervy youngster, Treasury Spokesman.

'How are they all doing?' she asked.

'Well, the course isn't exactly taxing, but yesterday's weather's really taken it out of a lot of them and poles are flying like a windy day in Warsaw. That hat is truly awful, Tash.'

Still stewing over her decision, she watched Lucy more or less demolish the course for twenty-five penalties and a fast descent to eighteenth place.

Subsequent competitors did not fare much better. The purpose of the final show-jumping day in a three-day event was not to tax the horse by demanding that he tackle a grand-prix height course of the sort undertaken by professional show-jumpers – the fences were deliberately inviting and placed on clear, basic lines. The twisting, well-spaced course was to see whether a horse was still supple on both reins, fit and obedient enough to jump the day after such a draining test on his stamina. It was also to judge whether the horse would respect flimsy fences that could be knocked down with a tap of the hoof as much as it did the large, solid obstacles across country. Snob was notorious for not respecting them at all.

'Hugo took him out to the practice ring an hour ago and he ploughed through everything like a ram-raider in a hurry – the parade thoroughly overexcited him,' Penny told her. 'Hugo was searching for you everywhere for advice. Where have you been?'

'I took Beetroot for a walk.' Her stomach lurched as though the stands were experiencing airborne turbulence. 'Was he really looking for me?'

'For a bit.' Penny shrugged vaguely as she watched Glen Bain come out of the ring with five penalties, to tremendous applause. 'He's taken Snob out into the park to try and calm him down now. Hugs says he's going to aim to get to the collecting ring just before they're due in.'

Disappointed, Tash snuggled deeper into her seat as she spotted the MD of Mogo waving at her from one of the VIP seats. He was being very civil to her while Hugo was still in the lead on a Mogo-sponsored horse, but Tash had a feeling that he would change his tune faster than a pianist playing a medley if Hugo ballsed up the jumping. At least she was wearing the right jacket today. She pulled up her lapels so that the distinctive Mogo labels were shown off fully and tried to grin at him encouragingly.

'Are you feeling all right?' Penny watched her in horror.

'Fine. Much better in fact. Why?'

'You looked as though you were about to be sick.'

'I was smiling.'

'Oh. Will you hold my hand when Gus comes in?'

Tash winced at the prospect. She still had no feeling in her little finger from Gus's cross-country round.

'You feeling better, Tash?' Stefan asked nastily as he and Kirsty moved in on either side of her and Penny twenty minutes later. They both looked rumpled and Kirsty had appalling stubble rash. Matched with her red hair, she looked like a very minxy Yosemite Sam.

'Enjoy last night, did you, hen?' she asked with equal venom.

Tash wanted to hide under her seat with shame.

'It just about compares to the night I tried to slit my wrists with a Bic disposable razor at the age of ten because I finally realised David Cassidy would never fancy me,' she muttered, not taking her eyes off Roger Monk clearing every jump on the lovely, rock-solid Sex Symbol for seventh place.

'That's only because you should have told David Cassidy exactly how you felt about him,' Kirsty said darkly, settling in beside Penny who was getting more and more nervous as Gus's round approached, her berry eyes staring madly, her face lab-coat white and pinched with mounting tension. She immediately gripped Kirsty's hand.

Tash was fixedly watching a German ride into the ring. 'Actually I wrote three letters and sent him a Terry's Chocolate Orange that cost me a week's pocket money.'

'He can't have been much of a romantic if that didn't get you a date.' Stefan shrugged. 'Still, he probably realised you'd run off and marry someone else in the end.'

'No, I wouldn't!' She shifted in her seat.

'Are you wearing that hat for a bet?' Kirsty asked.

Tash couldn't bear it any longer.

Transferring Penny's vice-like grip to Stefan's far bigger and more robust hand, she slipped out of the stands and went to the collecting ring in time to see the last four horses out, so that she could wait with Gus and Fashion Victim, offering them support. She looked around for Hugo, but he and Snob were steering clear until the last moment. Julia Ditton and her roving TV team were again hovering like market researchers in a busy high street, eager to snaffle victims. Tash pulled down her hat brim and darted past.

Vic was looking very undignified in his plaits, like a lurcher given a Yorkshire terrier cut in a pooch salon. Because he was a big, gangly and rather battered old horse, he always looked ridiculous when turned out properly. He rolled his eyes as Tash approached, searching for a solacing carrot.

'You nervous?' She smiled at Gus, glad that her eyes were at last opening enough to look up. It had taken most of the day.

'Bricking it,' he muttered through clenched teeth. 'Hugo's done a bunk and the officials are doing their nut – they think the competition leader won't be here to bloody compete. That hat is diabolical by the way.'

'I thought he was taking Snob around the park until the last minute?' Tash asked worriedly. Again her stomach lurched. She felt like one of Pavlov's dogs – except she needed the word 'Hugo' rather than a bell.

Standing by Vic's head with a bucket of equipment, Ted laughed. 'Look to your left, darling.'

Doing as she was told, Tash saw Snob – also plaited up and looking far more glamorous than poor old Vic – being walked around on a long rein, his rugs still slung over his rump for warmth. On board, chewing at a Mars bar and chatting to one of the dishier young male eventers, was India. Hugo was nowhere to be seen.

'So where is he?' she asked, but Ted and Gus were both intently watching Brian Sedgewick, who was halfway around the course and still clear, if painstakingly slow.

'If he goes clear but gets more than two time faults, then I have a fence in hand.' Gus turned Vic away and walked him around, unable to watch.

Brian had almost four time faults, but he had one of the first clear jumping rounds of the day and kept hold of his fourth place to cheers of delight from his supporters in the collecting ring. As he rode out, his wife practically pulled him off his horse as she leaped up to hug him.

Tash dragged the rug from Vic's behind and handed it to Ted as Gus rode into the ring, his red coat three shades paler than Brian's because it was so old and faded.

'Good luck!' she called anxiously.

'Where's Penny?' Ted asked as they moved to the arena entrance to watch.

'Staying in the stands because she can't let go of Kirsty and Stefan's hands,' Tash said nervously as Gus dipped his head to salute the judges, his ancient black hat silk flapping in the wind where it was ripped at the peak. 'They were talking about getting a doctor to surgically remove her.'

'Must have done already,' Ted pointed out. 'Here they are.'

Arms hooked around one another despite an eighteen-inch height difference, Stefan and Kirsty joined the nervous huddle to watch from the entrance as the buzzer rang out in the ring.

'She's hiding behind the stand smoking a cigarette,' Kirsty muttered, her arm reaching so high in the air to encompass Stefan's shoulder that she looked like she was answering a question in class.

'She doesn't smoke.' Ted chewed a thumb-nail as he continued watching Gus.

'She's on Rothmans.' Stefan whistled in admiration. 'The farm's future's riding on that ugly bastard out there.'

'Vic isn't ugly!' Tash wailed. 'He's heroic-looking.'

'I wasn't talking about the horse.'

Vic lumbered through the start in his usual cart-horse way, hind hooves seeming to drag along the ground like a surly teenager scuffing his feet. He was a terrifically ungainly horse and several spectators started to laugh, but once he began jumping, they applauded instead. It seemed unfeasible that something as unaerodynamic and bored-looking as Vic could be such an accurate show-jumper, but it had always been one of his best phases and he didn't let them down, galumphing easily around the ring and heaving himself over the fences with the minimum of effort, like a skipping boxer who barely seems to leave the ground yet clears the rope every time. There was an almighty groan from the crowd as he kicked out one of the planks, and Tash was certain he'd done it out of spite, just to show that he could. One of his half-closed eyes almost seemed to wink towards the Lime Tree Farm mob as he lolloped towards the final line.

'Penny should come out now.' She closed her eyes as he lumbered up to the final combination.

'I'll get her.' Kirsty raced off, still staring over her shoulder to watch Vic clear the last three fences with ease, receiving a great roar of applause and slowing to a walk the moment he was through the timer beam. He had been at the game long enough to know what was needed and to offer absolutely no more.

As Gus rode out and the second-placed New Zealander rode in, the Lime Tree mob went mad. Julia's camera team, lurking nearby, got a long, lingering shot of Gus jumping off Vic and hugging everyone in sight, including two strangers and Captain Mark Phillips, who took it in very good part. Then like an athlete spotting the tape, Penny raced forward shrieking like a banshee and jumped right into Gus's arms, her legs straddling him as she covered his face with kisses.

Soon afterwards tens of hands were patting Gus on the back. He was such a popular figure in the sport that his success touched everyone who knew of Lime Tree Farm's terrible recent financial struggles. He was congratulated so much, it was almost as though he had won the championships overall.

'Well done! I'm so chuffed for you.' Tash gave them both a massive hug, backing off as Julia Ditton hoved in with her mike.

Her eyes immediately started scouring the collecting ring for Hugo, but India was still walking the bit-snatching, spooking Snob around and looking increasingly anxious herself. With only one round before his, Hugo was leaving it ludicrously late – especially on a hot-head like Snob who needed to be settled. She wondered if he was somehow doing it to punish her for the way she had behaved the night before. Yet she knew how badly he wanted the Badminton title, how frustratingly it had eluded him all these years. He was within a hair's breadth of snatching it at last and he had done a bunk. She chewed her knuckles in agitation.

Having said 'great' a lot to Julia Ditton, Gus joined Tash and turned back to gaze into the ring as the buzzer went for the New Zealander to start.

'No sign of Hugo?'

Shaking her head, she watched India riding Snob towards them, her pretty face pale with worry. 'I've asked around – no one's seen him for ages.'

'Did he say where he was going?' asked Tash as India jumped off.

She shrugged. 'Something about ringing a friend. God knows who. They've put out a call for him around the grounds, but it's getting desperate. If he doesn't turn up soon, he'll forfeit the championships.'

Again, Tash gazed around the collecting ring where the horses that had already jumped were being led around to await the prize-giving ceremony, rugs slung over their saddles and coats slung over their riders' shoulders. Hugo was nowhere to be seen.

The New Zealander was halfway around the course now, and had already kicked a pole from an upright for five penalties. If she had another fence down, she would drop behind Gus and Brian to fourth.

With the sportsmanship of true professionals, Gus and Brian were standing side-by-side, watching anxiously and sharing a cigarette. They were far too good friends and far too nervous about the final result to let sponsorship rivalry get in the way.

'Someone had to win the deal.' Brian shrugged rather bleakly, his battered face still watching the New Zealander. 'It was a bastard thing of them to do – setting us up against one another like that.'

'How's Babe Magnet?' Gus, tugging on his cigarette, asked after Brian's young horse that had been injured the day before.

He laughed. 'Vet reckons he'll still be able to event – he only ever had one eye on the fences anyway.'

Gus grinned and gave him a huge pat on the back which was caught on camera as they flashed between the action in the ring and that just outside. The television crew was now aware that the overnight leader had gone AWOL, and great excitement was going on around Julia Ditton in the collecting ring as she prepared to go on air live the moment the New Zealander's round was over.

To a hearty round of applause, she came out on five penalties with her second place still intact and was swallowed into the whooping bosom of her back-up team and fellow competitors.

Standing nearby, Julia gazed into the camera and started to talk in a breathy, excited voice.

'Well, the latest news is that Hugo Beauchamp has still not reappeared and the officials are giving him ten more minutes to materialise or he forfeits his chance to compete for the trophy, and Kerry Maguire will automatically be elevated to first place. As you can imagine there is terrific excitement and speculation around here as the other competitors – and his own increasingly desperate team – wonder what could have happened to one of Britain's top riders to make him go missing like this.' As she spoke, she was edging closer to Tash who was edging rapidly away.

From behind the stands, Hugo's head groom, Jenny, came racing up wearing an identical hat to Tash's, her face bright red from the exertion of running to the yard, the lorry park and then back again.

'No sign!' she panted, sliding to a halt in front of Gus and Stefan. 'No one's seen him.'

India was leading around Snob who was looking increasingly put out as he realised he had somehow missed out on a vital piece of the action. As they walked past the camera crew, the scurfy camera-man panned a shot of him with his ears flat and head bobbing. The next moment he had turned to lunge at the sound recordist's furry mike, taking a large chunk out of it.

'Tempers are clearly starting to flare here.' Julia talked to camera.

Dashing into the collecting ring behind her was Paul the Pringle-wearing producer who had just come from the commentary box and was looking highly put out. He marched straight up to Tash.

'Is your fucking boyfriend turning up or not, because we're supposed to be going to the rugby now.'

'In that case I'd better press on,' said a smooth voice. 'I've set my video to record the match at Twickenham, so I'd be bloody furious if it started late.'

'Hugo!' Tash spun around to see him walking leisurely up to them, buttoning his red jacket as he came, cheeks high with colour from a recent sprint. 'Where on earth have you been? They're waiting for you.'

'Just phoning an old groom for advice.' He checked Snob's girths and nodded to India to hold his head while he hopped on. 'A leg up would be appreciated.'

Tash grabbed his waggling boot in shocked silence, watching as he swung into the saddle and found his other stirrup, his thigh now level with her eyes. It took all her strength not to reach out and touch it.

'Wish me luck,' he murmured as two course hands pulled back the rope at the entrance to the arena.

'Good luck,' she said bleakly.

'I didn't mean like that. Nice hat, by the way.'

For a moment their eyes met and he smiled such an open, genuine, carefree smile that Tash almost fell over backwards. Then, as he rode towards the arena, Snob's head swung around and, teeth bared, he lunged at her hat, neatly removing it and carrying it in with him to the crowd's shrieking delight.

He deserves to knock down every jump for this, Tash thought darkly, grinding her teeth. How dare he be so nonchalant and glib! Snob would be all over the place after such lousy preparation, his concentration in ruins.

As she suspected, Snob was shaking his head like crazy and dancing around in a maddened tango through nerves and impatience to be at the fences, hat flapping from his teeth so that he resembled a rabid big cat with a recent cull. In this state he would plough every one, Tash realised in despair. To the crowd's even greater amusement, Hugo waited until he had stopped to salute the judges before leaning forward on his stirrups and gently tugging Tash's mangled hat out of his mount's mouth then hooking it on a wing upright.

'Bloody exhibitionist!' she groaned, waiting for Snob to explode out on to the course like a dust-devil in a hurry the moment the bell rang.

But instead of heading straight through the start, Hugo took his time, cantering the big chestnut around in wide circles to calm him, his hands so still he could be carrying an egg and spoon, his legs barely shifting as he waited for the edgy, darting stride to move down a gear and engage all four legs before getting underway. His mouth was moving all the time as he rode.

'Bloody hell!' Gus exclaimed in astonishment. 'That's the first time I've ever known him talk to a horse. I think he's been around the back of his lorry shooting up drugs.'

'He hasn't – I'd've seen him,' Jenny panted earnestly.

'He'll be disqualified for leaving it too long to go through the start,' Penny fretted, grabbing Tash's hand first, then India's. 'The bell went ages ago.'

'It's okay.' India winced as her hand was suddenly gripped in her aunt's. 'He's on his way.'

Tash wasn't sure if she breathed at all as Hugo and Snob went around the course, but she certainly left the ground every time they did, jumping on the spot at each fence as though skipping, her face frozen in total fear. She didn't even notice the roving collecting ring camera focusing on her, its red light flashing on and off as the round progressed. Nor did she hear Penny squeal when she tightened her grip to a clamp on her hand as the combination approached the last line, Snob's powerful hind legs collected underneath him like spring boards. Hugo had him superbly collected, but he was fighting all the way there, face clenched with effort. Unable to watch, Tash closed her eyes and braced herself for a communal groan from the crowd. Instead there was a slight rattle, then another, but no hollow bouncing of poles. Seconds later, a tumultuous amount of yelling and cheering all around was splitting her eardrums and she opened her eyes to see Penny smiling at her through streams of tears.

'He's won, Tash,' she said through gritted teeth. 'He's got the Championship. Now will you let go of my hand, only I think you've broken my thumb.'

As Hugo rode out of the ring, Tash was being squashed from all sides as she was hugged and kissed as though she had ridden to victory herself. But she knew that she could never have ridden that round. She wouldn't have had the nerve to take time out to settle him like that – her head, legs and hands would have gone to pieces.

'You made him, Tash.' Gus gave her a hug. 'You worked and worked to get that chestnut thug here, and that bloody counts. Believe me, that counts.' For the first time since she'd known him, he gave her a huge kiss on the mouth. 'I'm bloody proud of you.' That was a first, too. She almost broke down.

Backing away in a daze, she tried to fight her way towards Snob and

Hugo, but now that they had won it was like trying to get to the front of a rock concert.

When Hugo jumped off, there were at least ten people between them including Julia Ditton, desperate for a few seconds of interview before they were cut from live transmission in favour of the rugby. He ignored them all and, giving Snob a brief pat, handed him over to Jenny and shouldered his way towards Tash, face triumphant. Pulling the chin protector from his crash hat with a gloved hand, he dragged it from his head and shook his hair, face dancing with laughter.

'That horse is something else,' he whistled as he stopped in front of her. 'And it's all your doing, darling.'

Tash gazed at him, her mouth unable to do anything but smile. She kept trying to look serious and sincere as she had intended, but the smile twanged back as though on elastic.

'Congratulations,' she laughed. 'You were utterly, utterly brilliant.' She longed to add, And I love you, but bit it back with all her might, knowing that to say it would be to open more cans of worms than an angler trying for a world record. Doing that in public – on national television – would be kicking poor, cornered Niall so hard in the teeth that his fillings would end up stapling his stomach. She had to wait until she could tackle Hugo in private, but was so overexcited that she wanted to rugby tackle him into a private room right this second.

Hugo was watching her with a look of such ebullient glee that she found her eyes getting hopelessly lost in his and not wanting to find their way out.

'You seem to have a new car,' he said smoothly. 'So I was rather wondering if you could give me a lift back to Berkshire this evening?'

'It's your car,' she gulped. 'You won.'

'I know, but I can't bear to see you polluting the countryside in that French banger any longer.' He was already being dragged away by Julia.

Now that, Tash realised, was just the sort of private vroom she needed to rugby tackle him in.

Watching the royal prize-giving twenty minutes later, Tash clapped until her hands were buzzing. Beside her, Penny was weeping buckets. It was the first time Tash had ever known her to cry. She kept claiming it was the pain in her thumb, but Tash thought it had more to do with Gus's longed-for victory and the financial boost it was going to give the farm's ailing bank account.

'I'm so proud of him!' Penny sobbed, staring through her tears as Gus shook the hand of the Princess Royal. 'I hardly ever tell the disagreeable bugger how much I love him but I think I will tonight.'

'Me too,' Tash laughed, thinking of how many Polos she would stuff Snob with later.

''Bout time too.' Penny turned to her. 'You're the only person who hasn't told Hugo how much in love with him you are this week. The rest of us have been like cracked records.'

Forty-One

THEY WERE ALMOST AT Marlbury by the time Tash plucked up courage.
Hugo, who had been swigging from a bottle of champagne throughout,
was playing with some of the high-tech dials on the dashboard of the
new Mitsubishi that was part of the first prize and alternately blasting
Tash's face with hot and cool air. He was in a hyper-excited mood but
had said little except politely to suggest that she change gears when
she had done a continuous thirty in second for several miles. Tash was
finding the huge new car very hard to adjust to after the wrecks she was
used to driving, especially in her current state of nerves.

She pulled up in a lay-by and groped around to turn off the CD
player, blasting the volume up to full and shifting the balance around
the speakers before she finally silenced it.

'Hugo, I love you,' she said, so quickly that she wondered at first if
he had heard her.

There was a long pause as he stared at his champagne bottle and then
tossed it out of the window before tilting his head to look at her.

His eyes glinted as they studied her face, the black pupils almost
drowning out the cobalt blue. As ever, his expression was unreadable.

'Nicely put,' he finally said.

A car swept past the lay-by, shaking the new Mitsubishi in its
slip-stream and sending up a great splash of water from the road
which whipped the windscreen before starting to slide away, leaving
a snail's trail of dripping dirt. Tash watched its progress and licked her
lips nervously.

'Just thought I'd say it.'

'Thanks.'

There was another long pause. She fiddled with the ignition keys. She had never felt so disappointed in her life.

'Right then.' She slotted them in and started the engine. 'We'd better get you to this party Lisette's hosting. I'm sure you two have a lot to chat about.'

Hugo leaned slowly across her and cut the engine, pocketing the keys before leaning back in his seat again.

'Is that all I'm getting?' he muttered.

Tash's libido was all over the place as a result of his leaning across her. She had been certain that he was about to ravish her and had been all geared up to ravish him in return. Now they were back to square one and her heart thudded into its resting place in her chest like a cricket ball landing in the wicket keeper's glove.

'What more did you expect?'

Another car splashed past as he lit a cigarette.

'Well, if you're asking for a date, I'd expect a bit more than a window in your dowry,' he sighed, clicking his lighter shut, his hands shaking. 'Unless you've forgotten, you're rather booked up this week. For a start you've got a twelve o'clock appointment pencilled in to marry Niall O'Shaughnessy next Saturday.'

'Yes. Well, it's all a bit of a mess.'

'So I gather.' He took a deep drag and turned to look at her.

'But I'm not really marrying him,' Tash said encouragingly. 'Just pretending to.'

'How original. The bride wore white lies.' He seemed remarkably unsurprised by the news and extremely on edge, eyes still searching hers as though there was an iridologist's treasure map written on them. 'I suppose you're waiting until there's a total eclipse of the honeymoon to tell your family?'

'Oh, God, I've made such a terrible hash of things,' she groaned, sagging back in the seat.

'I know that.' He looked away, the end of his cigarette glowing like a warning light as he took another sharp drag.

'You do?' She was finding his reaction to her dramatic pronouncement of love not at all encouraging.

'Tell me,' he gazed out of the windscreen, eyes narrowing as though squinting into sunlight, 'have you decided to come out with this now because you really do love me, or just because Niall's rejected you and gone off with Zoe Goldsmith?'

'Niall didn't reject me!' she wailed, pride flaring. 'We rejected each other. This wedding was a ludicrous idea in the first place. It's been like some sort of bad dream for months, with neither of us wanting to go through with it. Our relationship was never strong enough for marriage. It wasn't even strong enough for us to live together. How could it be when I was hopelessly hooked on you throughout?'

Hugo chewed his thumb, still staring through the windscreen as though fascinated by the graffiti-emblazoned road sign ahead, its wording obscured by thick black spray-paint contesting a proposed by-pass.

Catching up on their head start now, the Lime Tree Farm lorry suddenly drove past in a cloud of spray, making the new car rock from side to side in its slip-stream. Not recognising the new Mitsubishi, Ted – who was driving – didn't even hoot. Tash watched its tailgate disappearing, the new Mogo motif on the ramp already coated with mud.

Turning to look at him again, she felt an involuntary corkscrew of lust. As ever, he turned each of her limbs into tendrils that wanted to wind their way around him and cling there for ever.

'I've been in love with you for years, Hugo,' she croaked. 'I've grown up with it – like a birthmark. However hard I've tried to scrub it away, it's still there.'

'Glad you've enjoyed the experience so much,' he muttered.

'You haven't exactly made it easy,' she sighed. 'Especially recently.'

'Well, you have rather given the impression that you're determined to marry that bloody feckless Irish drunk.'

'I know.' Tash bit her tongue.

'Even though he's patently madly in love with Zoe Goldsmith.'

'I know.' Tash bit her tongue harder.

'Christ, Tash, I even resorted to calling your sister and telling her that the reason Niall had only bought you a rolled gold wedding ring was because he was rolling Goldsmith.'

Tash almost bit the tip of her tongue clean off. 'You told Sophia that?'

'I'm not particularly proud of it.'

Looking at Hugo's profile – the outline of which she could draw in her sleep and suspected she did on regular occasions – Tash felt as though her heart strings were frantically trying to knit one, purl one as they began to pull the wool from her eyes. His face was totally unmasked and riddled with doubt.

'When you announced that the wedding was still going ahead last night,' he said edgily, 'I couldn't fucking believe it. Everyone's been telling me this week that you and Niall are kaput. Even Lisette is certain you two are all set to call it off at the party tonight. From the way you were talking to him on the phone, I thought that bastard was threatening to kill himself if you didn't agree to go through with it.'

'You thought what?'

'Last night I was convinced Niall was threatening to kill himself if you didn't marry him,' he repeated, still sounding irritable. 'So was your mother come to that – probably still is for all I know.'

'Mummy thinks Niall's going to kill himself?' Tash was aghast.

'I was rather hoping he bloody would, to be frank,' Hugo muttered. 'This mess is all his fault. I can't believe what a total fucking cock-up he's made of it. Talk about putting you through the Bushmills and then taking you up the Jacob's Creek. All he needed was a couple of Alka-Seltzers and a bloody good lawyer. Instead he's made things ten times worse by stalling. Thank heaven for Zoe – without her Lisette would be financing twelve more movies out of this fiasco.'

'So you know? About Lisette suing him if we don't get married? About the stage-show Niall's planning next Saturday?'

'I do now, although I bloody nearly missed jumping off this afternoon trying to find out. Why in God's name didn't you tell me what was going on, Tash? I could have helped.'

'I wasn't sure you wanted to,' she said hollowly, thinking of Snob. 'After all, you've practically bitten my head off every time I've come close to telling you how much I adore you.'

'I haven't!' he snapped.

'There you go again,' she sighed. 'If I wasn't absolutely out of my mind bonkers about you, I'd have gone off you long ago for being so horrible to me. I should be hitting you right now, not hitting on you.'

He looked at her, eyes burning with shame. 'I wanted to punish you for putting me through so much fucking agony,' he said. 'For not loving me as much as I love you.'

'You do love me then?' she gasped, almost expiring with relief.

'Don't state the bloody obvious,' he muttered.

'But you've never told me.'

'Wasn't sure you wanted to hear it.'

'How can you say that?' she wailed indignantly. 'I think I've loved you since the first time I ever saw you – handing Bea Meredith a spiked drink at my sister's engagement party. You were giving her this smile that was so downright wicked that I think she would have drunk it even if it was the chalice of poison at Hamlet's sword fight.'

He took another sharp puff of his cigarette and then tossed it out of the window, turning to her at last, eyes almost liquid with relief.

'I love you to bloody distraction,' he breathed, 'even if you are always rabbiting on about English literature. Christ, Tash, if you only knew the self-control I've had to exhibit over the past few months! I thought you really were going to marry him. Everyone kept banging on about this bloody wedding, and all the time I was so eaten up with jealousy and anger I just lashed out at you. I even convinced myself that you were using me to get back at him for playing around. After all, you knew how much I felt for you.'

Looking into his beautiful, sincere face, Tash found a great smile wrapping its way around her cheeks.

'You really think I knew how you felt?' she watched his eyes.

They didn't flicker. 'Of course you did. It was obvious,' he said rather indignantly, groping for another cigarette. Then he turned to her again, all wide-eyed concern, cigarette dangling from his mouth. 'Wasn't it?'

'Oh, Hugo, I do love you,' she laughed, removing the unlit cigarette from his lips and throwing it to one side.

Kissing him was like bungee jumping – such a terrifying prospect that one hovered on the precipice for far too long, feeling sick with fear. But on jumping, it was one of the most exquisite sensations she had ever experienced.

As his mouth yielded to hers and his tongue slipped between her lips, Tash wound her hands around his warm, strong neck and allowed herself an all-time indulgence, slithering her fingers into his hair and letting its silken weight caress the soft flesh between each one. She had never felt this high, horny or happy.

As the kiss became more unruly and ungainly, Hugo pulled her on to the passenger seat with him and they started to laugh as clothes became caught on gear and brake levers and wrists trapped in head rests. Yet still they kissed, totally unable to stop even though their feet kicked plastic stereo speakers and their shoulders crashed against seat-belt fittings. Tash's bottom knocked the glove compartment open, Hugo's elbow pressed down on the centre control panel and whizzed windows and sunroof open and shut. Even when the seat flew back six inches, almost giving them both whip-lash, they couldn't stop laughing and kissing and making up for more lost time than Buck Rogers at a reunion party.

'I've wanted to do this for so bloody long.' Hugo kissed his way down her throat with delicious short, deft bursts, like a flautist performing scales.

'And I've wanted you to do that for so long.' Tash squirmed delightedly. She was bobbing around on a great lagoon of lust now. Every new touch sparked off another fast-burning fuse of excitement that fizzed down through her and let off great depth charges in her pelvis.

They were beginning to break up the car like teenage hooligans. As they started to slide limbs against limbs and delve hands into clothes, they twisted around in the confined space, crashing against the dashboard, the side window and the hand brake. The rubber casing spun around on the gearstick, the rear-view mirror smashed against the windscreen, the stereo speaker flew off. Coming up for air and pressing her palms on to the head-rest so that she could stretch back her neck, Tash pushed the padded rest right out of its metal sockets and landed back at Hugo's mouth again. Laughing, she pressed her lips to his once more. Who needed air? She'd never been able to breathe properly when she was near him anyway, so she'd had a lot of practice holding her breath.

Another lorry rattled by, shaking the car on its wheels. Falling back across both front seats now, Hugo and Tash didn't even notice. Nor did they notice as they pulled shirts from trousers and coats from shoulders, that the car had started to creep forward very slowly. Starting to touch more skin than cloth for the first time, they had no idea the car was gaining momentum. It was only when, as Hugo's hands slid into Tash's waistband and her fingers traced every rib of his chest, there was a loud, shuddering crunch that they looked up. At precisely the same moment two airbags flew out from the dashboard and the steering wheel, like parachutes snapping open at five thousand feet, thwacking Tash in the face and Hugo in the knee.

They had rolled forward and crashed into the road sign. It wasn't a great impact – the bull bars at the front of the car were barely dented – but this was a super safety-conscious, ergonomically designed luxury penthouse of a car and it pampered its occupants accordingly. Or, in Tash's and Hugo's case, squashed them against the plush leather seats with two plump, fabric marshmallows, like contestants in some bizarre X-rated game of It's A Knock Out.

'What happened?' Hugo looked up at her.

'Well, either the earth moved or the car did.' Tash removed her face from a taut white airbag and squinted out through the driver's door window. The hedge opposite had a distinctly different profile from earlier, with a gate in the middle. 'Yup – the car moved.'

Laughing, Hugo groped around in his discarded coat pocket for his folding binder-twine knife and, having turfed out several packets of Polos, his mobile phone and a great scattering of old receipts, finally located it.

'Isn't that a bit rash?' Tash pulled back her chin. 'I'm sure there's an instruction manual around here somewhere which says how to let them down.'

'I'm sure there is.' He smiled up at her. 'But the only thing I never want to let down again is you.' And, calmly popping both bags, he pulled her back into a long, luscious kiss that left Tash so breathless she wished he'd left one airbag to puncture later – she could use the oxygen.

'Let's go back to the forge,' he breathed as his fingers inched inside her shirt again.

'We can't,' she gasped, shivering with excitement as his thumb brushed over her nipple. 'Niall said he'd meet me there.'

The thumb was abruptly withdrawn.

'Why?'

'To talk about these awful wedding theatrics.' Tash felt reality crash its way into the car as fast as a juggernaut through the windscreen.

'What's so awful about them?' Hugo was playing with a button on her jeans, his face incredulous.

'You're not serious?'

His eyes were drinking her in now.

'Why not? It seems a perfect solution to me. Admittedly, Niall's buggered things up totally by leaving it so long – I'm pretty certain Lisette wouldn't have sued him at all if he'd let you call off the wedding a fortnight ago. But that's academic.'

'What do you mean?' Tash was amazed he was so relaxed about the idea of staging a fake wedding. The prospect appalled her.

'There's no way she'd sue Niall,' Hugo laughed. 'Think about it – he already gives her practically half his earnings which is bloody criminal in this day and age, especially given how well she's doing now. There's not a court in the country that would let through a case brought by an alimony-grabbing divorcee, suing her ex for calling off his second wedding. The tabloids would have a field day.'

Put that way it did seem rather ridiculous. Tash wondered why Niall had made it sound so convincing at the time. His melodramatic, overactive imagination had, as ever, improvised a five-act tragedy from the flimsiest of synopses.

'But then surely we can just come clean?' she said excitedly. 'Why have a wedding at all?'

'Well, firstly because Lisette's film is depending upon it, and secondly because it could be bloody good fun.'

'Fun?' Tash gulped.

'I'm sorry, darling. I'm not thinking – you must feel awful about deceiving your family this way.'

Tash was so horrified, she couldn't speak. This is the man I've just declared a lifetime's love to, she thought weakly, and he's suggesting I go through with the pretence of marrying Niall for 'fun'.

'The trouble is,' he went on, not seeming to register her momentary loss of faith in him, 'that Lisette must have realised last week that you and Niall were hitting stony ground faster than a hydraulic drill, and she started to panic. Ironic really that she invested so much in you two getting married – I mean, she can hardly have been pleased about it, but she saw too much profit in the whole thing to be emotional.'

'Go on.'

'Well, she'd already tried to sway it by telling you that she would only sign her share of Snob over if you and Niall got married,' he started.

Tash closed her eyes.

'Don't worry – I think I can help you on that one,' he said smoothly. 'But what I can't do a hell of a lot about is the fact that she's now quite prepared to swap one kind of publicity for another. She thinks Niall is going to announce that the wedding's off tonight, remember? And she's got half the tabloids queuing up at the Olive Branch as I speak to report on it, although she's lured them there without breathing a word of her suspicions in case she's wrong and you really are potty enough to marry Niall. I must say, you're a bloody good liar, Tash. Even she's not certain.'

'Thanks,' she said weakly.

'And as her scoop de grâce,' Hugo went on, running an idle finger up and down the inside of Tash's thigh, 'she's lined up a particularly sordid exclusive to feed to one grubby Sunday rag outlining the full details of Niall's drinking problem and his affair with Zoe. It's pretty career-wrecking and there's a lot of stuff about Zoe's first marriage which would absolutely crucify her and the kids if it was made public. You know Si Goldsmith's schizophrenic? And Lisette has written in a lot of balls about Zoe being involved in the porn industry, which is absolute rot. Even your brother gets a mention.'

'Matty?'

'Yup – Lisette was party to some sort of confession of childultery between Zoe and him. That's like adultery but without the sex, I gather. Of course she's added it in spades. She has them bonking against a shelf of pickles in the larder of all places. If Niall stands up in front of her high-powered guests tonight and tells them that you're calling off the wedding, Lisette's little ex-file lands on a hack's desk before you can say knife in the back. That hack will think all his Sunday exclusives have come at once. Compared to that, posing for *Cheers!* next Saturday seems a pretty small price to pay, doesn't it?'

'Christ!' Tash was reeling. 'How do you know all this?'

'It might have escaped your notice, but I've been wearing my mobile phone like a piece of costume jewellery this weekend.' Hugo grinned.

'Stefan thought you were calling the Samaritans because you were pining for me,' Tash remembered.

Hugo looked absolutely revolted by the idea.

'But why go to such lengths to find out?' she went on hastily. 'Are you mentioned in Lisette's story? Is that it?'

'I made it my business to find out.' Hugo looked at her, a smile spreading across his face. 'Because I've made it my business to look after you over the past two years, Tash. And, lord, do you take a lot of looking after.'

She bit her lip, suddenly remembering what else he seemed to have done for her. It was the very thing that had made her doubt him and she burned with shame. 'And does that include buying Lisette's share of Snob?'

'Ah.' Hugo looked awkward. 'I've taken a bit of a gamble there, I'm afraid. You see, I couldn't handle her terms, so yesterday I told her to stuff the deal. I was all set to reap the benefits when you blew it by telling everyone that you were still marrying Niall.'

'What were Lisette's terms then?' Tash asked.

He took hold of her shirt collar and pulled her towards him. 'That I wasn't allowed to do this.'

Lord, but kissing him was fun, she thought headily.

'Stefan once accused me of trying to buy you,' he said when he finally broke away. 'And he was right – what's that poem Niall's always quoting when he's pissed? The one by Sir Walter Raleigh? About throwing things over puddles.'

Tash hid a smile. 'I think you mean Yeats: *"Had I the world's embroidered . . ."*'

'That's it,' he nodded. 'Well, I was so busy throwing the world's embroidered cloths under your feet that I didn't realise you had your head too far up in the clouds to notice. Then you gave me your dream – your ride on Snob at Badminton. I was so fucking diabolical to you that day because I suddenly realised how shallow all my efforts had been. There was nothing I could give you that meant that much – I thought maybe buying Snob back for you, but that was just money again. I wanted to give you a dream. I still do.'

'You just have.' She looked into his lovely, curling-lipped, blue-eyed face and was almost wiped out by happiness. 'You've told me you love me. I've dreamed of that for years.'

Laughing, he reached out a hand to stroke her cheek. 'You are so incredible. Christ, you are just so beautifully bloody, unbelievably incredible.'

His hand slipped from her cheek to the back of her neck, thumb caressing the hollow of her ear. Then he slowly sat up and pressed his nose against hers, eyes fixed on her imploring.

'Do you really have to meet Niall at the forge? I want you all to myself for tonight. Can't we just go straight back to Haydown?' He kissed her so long and hard on the mouth that Tash practically melted into the dashboard.

'I owe it to Niall,' she panted, fighting an urge to pull Hugo on to the back seat and forget all about Niall and the wedding charade.

'You don't owe that bastard anything.' He pressed his lips to her ear.

'I haven't told him that I'm willing to go ahead with next Saturday yet,' she realised with a start.

Hugo gave her a curious look, then shrugged. 'I suppose it is your family's big occasion, although I'm certain they'll enter into the spirit of things once they realise what's going on.'

Tash thought that was perhaps a bit optimistic.

'God knows how I'll be able to pay back all the money Daddy and Pascal have forked out.' She closed her eyes at the thought.

'Sell the car.' Hugo started to kiss her mouth again.

'It's your car,' she murmured. Not that there would be much of it left to sell even if it were hers, she decided, as they started sending the windows up and down again.

'I was talking about the French banger.' Hugo kissed his way down her throat once more. 'That thing's a death trap. I thought I was going to lose you that day you set out to Scotland in it. I had half a mind to drive after you in the horse-box and bar your way like a French farmer staging a port protest.'

'I wish you had,' she sighed.

'I thought,' he pulled back and looked her in the eyes, hands holding her face like a trophy, 'that you would never tell me how you felt – I kept trying to make you, but you ran away.'

'You never told me how you felt!' she protested.

'Christ! We were like two kids saying "you go first", weren't we?' he laughed, eyes lingering on her. She'd never have believed they could look so loving, so completely without scorn. 'Everyone told me to fight for you – Penny, Stefan, your mother, Zoe – even that hippy brother of yours. The only person who seemed to think I was wasting my time was you.'

'I'm pretty gutless when it comes to men,' she confessed. 'You have to declare undying love to get me to believe you.'

'Which was why O'Shaughnessy did so well – he declares undying love to every woman he meets. Lisette says it used to drive her wild.'

'Thanks a bunch!' she sighed.

'I'm wildly jealous so I'm allowed to snipe.' He pulled an apologetic face and kissed her again. 'I know he adored you – and I wanted to kill him for it. But I also know he changes his mind as often as the shape of his facial hair, whereas I stick to a decision like gum on a shoe. So you have to bloody believe me when I say I love you, Tash, because I fucking well mean it.'

She kissed him and laughed. 'Nicely put.'

'I've wanted you for myself for two years.' He smiled. 'I've never wanted anything that long.'

'I've wanted you since I was a teenager.'

'Don't try and beat me here,' he growled. 'I'm sure I wanted you more intensely.'

'No way!'

'Did.'

'Didn't.'

'Did.'

'Come here.'

It took a long time to drive back to the forge because they had to stop at every gate-way, lay-by and wide verge to kiss one another breathless.

'There is one other dream you could give me,' Tash sighed delightedly as they indulged in one last delicious kiss before going inside. 'I've just remembered it. I was going to suggest it earlier actually.'

'Oh, yes?' Hugo cocked his head towards her.

The boom of music was already throbbing out from the Olive Branch a hundred yards away. Tash listened to it for a second or two, wondering if she dared ask him.

'It's a bit of a fantasy really,' she confessed. 'And please say no if you think it's too soon. But next Saturday – at the wedding – when the registrar asks if there are any just impediments or whatever, would you mind awfully standing up and saying yes?'

'Why on earth should I do that?' He looked bewildered.

'Well, I assumed you might want to.' She scuffed her feet against the pedals. 'Seeing as you love me. I thought it might be in your interests to stop the wedding – you could be doing your bit to help out with the authenticity of the whole thing.'

Suddenly he started to laugh. 'Oh, Tash, you still haven't realised, have you? No wonder you were so reluctant. I think there's something I should explain before we go inside . . .'

Forty-Two

AT THE OLIVE BRANCH, the Four Poster Bed location wrap party was in full swing.

Stefan and Kirsty, who had driven back earlier in the day from Gloucestershire with Jenny and the two Maccombe horses, arrived tarted up in their party best to find themselves thoroughly out-tarted by the film world. Stefan had brought his towering, austere parents with him because they were staying at Haydown, and the Swedish duo retired hastily to a quiet corner and drank orange juice, clearly overawed by the drunken, debauched joviality of the rest of the guests.

By far the largest contingent, and the most raucous, was the technical crew from the location shoot who stood in a loud, cheerful mob at the bar chatting up Marco Angelo's staff and stuffing back as much food as they could manage. In the main, the actors clustered together in a separate and slightly disdainful group.

'It's ridiculous having a wrap party three days before we finish shooting,' moaned one of the supporting leads. 'I've never heard of anything so nonsensical.'

'We went over-schedule. This was the only day Lisette could organise,' explained the production assistant patiently. 'It was going to be next weekend, but that's Niall's wedding.'

'Hmmph.'

Wearing a pair of satin trousers that she couldn't sit down in, Sally was helping Lisette to host the evening. Or at least she had imagined that would be her role until she was posted at the door with a clip-board to check the guests off as they arrived, and gently turn away people who had rolled up not realising there was a party on.

'I'm afraid it's strictly by invitation,' she told a couple of local lads at the door. 'You'll have to go to The Terrier in Fosbourne Dean if you want a pint.'

They headed back to the car park at the rear, grumbling loudly. The next moment their Escort XR3i was revving at the gates, halogen fog-lights flashing and two-tone horn singing out into the night before they raced off, almost wrenching out the gear-box in the process.

'No sign of Niall or Tash?' Lisette breezed up to her, hair slicked back into such a tight ballerina's bun that she looked as though she'd had a face lift, emphasising her gamine face and huge eyes.

'Nope.' Sally pulled a face. 'Tash probably won't be back from Badminton yet. But Niall should be here. He said he was only popping back to the hotel for a quick shower.'

'A wedding shower,' Lisette pursed her lips worriedly. 'I bloody well hope they turn up soon. I might have a surprise waiting for them.'

'What is it?' Sally demanded. So far Lisette had flatly refused to tell her.

But she simply winked and drifted off to David's side.

Sally sighed and welcomed a new batch of incomers that included Penny and Gus, both looking hopelessly scruffy as they hadn't bothered changing from the clothes they had worn to pack up and leave the trials earlier.

'Where's Tash?' she asked anxiously.

'Driving her prize back, I should imagine.' Penny grinned, winking at Gus.

'I thought Hugo won?' Sally looked confused. 'We all watched it at Maccombe. Niall kept running in between shots to cheer. Even Lisette whooped at the end.'

'Hugo did win.' Penny seemed highly amused, wet berry eyes gleaming.

'And I must say he's bloody smug about it,' Gus sighed, removing a piece of straw from his jumper. 'He's positively crowing. And he was fairly pleased about winning Badminton too.'

Sally was even more bewildered. They both still had their security wristlets on, she noticed, like his and hers friendship bracelets

'Gus came third,' Penny announced, proudly slotting her arm through her husband's. 'Are Niall and Zoe here yet?'

Sally glanced at her clip-board tiredly, not noticing the leading way Penny had linked the two names together. 'Not yet,' she said, running her eyes over the long list of names beside most of which was a neat tick. 'Wasn't Zoe at the farm?'

'No – just Rufus, a gaggle of friends, a blocked loo and a lot of empty cans of lager,' Gus groaned. 'He's not allowed to come here tonight, by the way, unless he's cleaned up the place as requested. Tell me if he tries to sneak in, will you?'

'Sure.' Sally was easing her feet in and out of the court shoes she was wearing. She longed to bunk off and have a drink; she'd been standing at the door for over two hours now and Lisette hadn't once offered to help or find someone else to take over.

'There are a hell of a lot of press here, aren't there?' Gus was asking as Penny elbowed her way to a tray of drinks. 'I had no idea it was going to be this high-powered.'

'I know,' Sally groaned. 'And Lisette's starting to get edgy. Niall's committed to be here for *Cheers!* tonight. Plus the local television news crew rolled up over an hour ago to get an interview with him and some footage of the party and they're all too pissed to do it now. They're supposed to be going to your place afterwards and filming the horses coming home from Badminton or something.'

'Well, they're too late.' Penny came back clutching three glasses and dripping champagne everywhere. 'Ted's tucking them up in bed right now for a well-earned rest. They can come over and film tomorrow if they want.'

'Tell them that.' Sally nodded to the bar where a young female reporter with a spray-welded blonde bob was giggling hysterically with a bunch of the lighting engineers from Four Poster Bed. Behind her a man wearing a *Southern News Round-up* bomber jacket with a television camera at his feet was tucking into a huge plate of bruschetta.

'I had no idea that this many reporters were coming tonight.' Sally rubbed her forehead tiredly. 'They were all added at the last minute.'

'Does that mean,' Gus said as Penny handed Sally a drink, 'that Lisette knows what's going to happen next weekend? I thought it was meant to be a secret.' He spilled the lot down his shirt as Penny elbowed him hard in the ribs.

'Sorry?' Sally looked bewildered.

'Oh, look! There's Godfrey Pelham. We must go and thank him for the good-luck carrots.' Penny dragged Gus off in the direction of Godfrey, who was chatting up a young male extra.

At that moment another gaggle of guests arrived and Sally was once again distracted as she juggled her champagne, clip-board and pen.

'Thanks.' An arrogant young actor who was the son of an RSC star took the glass of champagne from her hand and downed it in one. He had caused merry hell at the shoot all fortnight because he generally turned up on location either stoned, or drunk, or late, or – most often – all three. Eventually David had told him he'd be fired if he didn't stay sober for the remainder of his scenes. Sally knew for a fact that he had a five a.m. call tomorrow because they were now shooting in extra time.

'Anyone worth talking to here or shall I get hammered straight away?' He handed the glass back to her.

'I'd stay sober if I were you.' Sally ticked him off her list and squinted across the room. 'That chap over there is co-producing the next James Bond film – it's being shot in Stockholm. Butter him up and you might find yourself trying to drive a tank over Pierce Brosnan. But be warned, he's a staunch tee-totaller.' She pointed out Stefan's father.

Lisette breezed past again, shooting her a grateful wink.

'Lisette, I'm getting terribly—'

But she'd already inserted herself into a group of VIPs and wasn't listening.

'—tired,' Sally finished with a sigh.

Finally kicking off her shoes, she gritted her teeth and decided that she badly needed Matty around to make sarcastic comments and be rude to people on her behalf. She wanted him to be especially rude to Lisette, who was treating her like a lackey on work-experience.

She gazed around the party longingly, wishing that she could chat and laugh and booze the night away too.

Calling in every favour she had ever been owed, Lisette had provided a truly splendid array of headlining guests and society journalists. There were so many celebrities on show that a couple of freelance paparazzi had even got wind of the event and were lurking outside to take snaps for the tabloids, much to the annoyance of the official *Cheers!* photographer who was prowling around inside, darting into groups, rearranging them, snapping them and then leaving them to try and remember what they had been talking about. The tables in the restaurant heaved with the most succulent of food in such abundance that a prominent bearded stage star was already going up for fifths. Moving slickly around the chattering guests, Ange's team of waiters and bar staff – largely consisting of members of his extended Italian family – made sure that every glass was kept brimming with chilled champagne. Ange himself beamed benevolently from the bar, confident that he had put on a magnificent spread worthy of his beloved Michelin star. Nothing in his slick, professional demeanour gave away the fact that Lisette had demanded a twenty percent reduction of costs at the last minute. Had he not been so madly in love with her, he would have refused to heat up a single roasted pepper canapé.

Sally knew that Lisette could ill afford to put on this sort of corporate show, especially this early on in filming. The cast and crew had now nick-named the film Four-tune Poster Bed because it was costing so much to make. Lisette had been forced to turn a small, private party into a much larger networking affair in order to try and secure more funds. Several key backers had been invited along at the last minute in the hope that she could persuade them to stump up a little more cash. As a result, the occasion was a lot more formal than at first planned. She needed to put on a great performance, and Sally suspected that the sudden inclusion of so many press boys was part of her strategy.

It was unfortunate, therefore, that by nine-thirty the two guests of honour had yet to make an appearance.

Wearing his favourite blue shirt, Ted – who had not strictly been invited – poled up towing Franny who caused quite a stir in a crotch-length PVC mini-skirt and cross-laced velvet bustier. Before they had even made it fully through the door, Lisette screeched up to him, demanding to know where Tash and Niall were.

'Haven't seen them.' Ted shrugged. 'But a bright yellow helicopter's just landed in Gus's sheep field – we thought Fergie had turned up, but it's just Tash's ma. She's completely fucking demented, that woman.'

'What?' Lisette wasn't in the slightest bit interested in Tash's lunatic family, however unconventional their means of transport.

'We're here on Rufus's and India's invites if that's okay.' Ted grabbed two glasses of champagne from a passing waiter. 'They're not coming. Is the food here free?'

'No, it was bloody expensive,' Lisette snapped.

She searched around for Sally, who was supposed to be at the door keeping unwelcomes like the Lime Tree Farm grooms away, but she had deserted her post and was nowhere to be seen. Only her two Patrick Cox shoes – borrowed from Lisette – remained posted on sentry duty, as though their occupier had recently exploded.

'Where's that Irish bugger?' asked David, sliding up behind Lisette and cupping her bottom in a warm hand. 'I thought you were going to give him and his fiancée a present?'

She brushed his hand away in case one of the journalists saw it; the last publicity she wanted for the film was to find herself exposed in a national paper's diary.

'If Niall takes any longer then I'm giving them more than a present

– it's more of a past really. Certainly not a future,' she muttered sourly. 'I can't think where he's got to.'

By ten o'clock things were getting desperate. Some excitement was caused as a tall, slim woman bearing a startling resemblance to Charlotte Rampling dashed through the door, her face desperately scanning the room. But Lisette recognised her straight away as Alexandra D'Eblouir, Tash's mother. She seemed to be in a raging hurry.

'Have you seen Tash French anywhere?' she asked several people by the door.

'Niall's Tash?' someone laughed. 'I don't think she really exists, does she?'

'No one's even met her, darling.' A chippy leered down Alexandra's silk blouse. 'Are you a journalist? I'll give you a quote.'

'He'll just measure you up first!' cackled another chippy, who was familiar with his friend's one and only joke.

Lisette ground her teeth as Sally, recognising her mother-in-law, dashed over to see what was going on. For the past ten minutes, she had been hiding in the kitchens with Ange's chatty wife Denise and a large glass of brandy. Her eyes, Lisette noticed irritably, were red from crying. She simply couldn't take the pressure.

'Where have you been?' she hissed as Sally panted past her. 'All sorts of gate crashers are rolling up.'

'Phoning Matty to ask for a lift home.' Sally shot her a dirty look and rushed over to rescue Alexandra from the leering chippies. 'What's the matter, Xandra?

Alexandra's eyes were alight with agitation and secrecy. 'I have to find Tash. I simply can't believe what they're planning. It's *so* romantic.'

'What who are planning?' Sally asked.

Alexandra opened her mouth and then suddenly shut it again as the *Cheers!* photographer lunged forward excitedly, demanding that she and Lisette stand side by side.

'I didn't think you were coming over from France until Wednesday?' Sally watched Alexandra produce her ravishing smile for the camera, which remained on her lips for just as long as the automatic flash brightened her beautiful, worried face.

'I came to England because of – er – Badminton.' She was as bad a liar as Tash. 'To cheer her on. I've been staying with James and Henrietta.'

'Oh, yes?' Sally didn't register this at all, even though it was just the sort of family gossip she normally devoured with relish; Alexandra being invited to spend Badminton weekend with her irascible, disapproving ex-husband was almost unthinkable. It also augured some serious family calamity.

Alexandra was still frantically scanning the room. 'Is Tash here? Only I'm in a bit of a hurry – I've got a helicopter waiting.'

'I haven't seen her.' Sally shuddered, biting her lip worriedly, eyes darting towards Lisette who was schmoozing one of her little power-groups and trying to listen in at the same time. 'Did you say a helicopter?'

'I'm on my way back to France,' explained Alexandra, absent-mindedly accepting a glass of champagne from a roving waiter. 'I couldn't get a flight, so darling Pascal arranged for his company chopper to fly over and collect me – it's waiting in one of the Moncrieffs' fields now. I'm looking for Tash. I said I'd get the pilot to do a detour and give them a lift.'

'To France?' Sally froze, mindlessly fishing in her pockets for a tissue.

'Yes, darling.' She was bubbling over with excitement. 'Tash phoned her father's house earlier to say that Niall wasn't going to kill himself after all, and that the wedding was still on, so I offered them the Loire house for a couple of days' well-deserved rest before the fun started.'

'Tash and Niall?'

'No, of course not!' Alexandra laughed and then gulped guiltily. 'I mean, yes. Well, Tash certainly. Hmm.' She scanned the room, frantic to cover up her blooper.

Then, glancing at Sally again, she took in her swollen-eyed face with sudden concern. 'Are you all right, darling? You look as though you've been crying.'

'Conjunctivitis,' Sally lied. 'So how long are they staying in France with you? I thought they'd only just come back?' She rubbed her forehead fretfully, looking tense and preoccupied. Lisette was edging her group closer now, still unable to hear properly over the party babble.

Bubbling over with nervous excitement, Alexandra completely forgot to lie.

'Oh, just a couple of nights. They're using the Loire house while we're in Paris – it's only lying empty and the weather's so lovely there at the moment. They both need a break. I think it's so devilish.' She smiled dreamily. 'Tash says they're saying goodbye to England and helloping to France.'

'They're eloping?' gasped Sally, who'd been too distracted to concentrate fully. 'Niall and Tash are eloping?'

There was a shocked lull immediately around them.

'What!' Lisette howled, abandoning her power-group altogether and rushing up to them. 'But the wedding's next weekend. They can't go off on the sly and get hitched beforehand.'

'But they're not, darling,' Alexandra said hastily, frantically trying to remember where she'd seen her before. 'The wedding's still going ahead – I can't wait to be there. I do so adore them, don't you?'

'I'm sorry. My fault. I think there's been some sort of misunderstanding.' Lisette's slinky smile sprang back into place as her eyes darted nervously towards the power-group she had deserted, a lot of whom were influential film industry high-flyers she had begged, bribed and bullied to come that night.

'Oh, there has been, darling!' Alexandra laughed delightedly. 'There was a misunderstanding right at the very beginning of this fiasco and it was all my batty mother's fault.'

'What's Etty got to do with this?' Sally asked in confusion.

But Lisette was already cutting across her with another furious realisation, this time far more quietly spoken for fear of being overheard.

'Hang on – are you telling us they're going to fucking France tonight?' she hissed in a voice so low that it seemed to come from the spikes of her three-inch heels.

Not hearing her properly, Alexandra looked rather shocked. 'Well, darling, it's not something I'd actually planned to ask them. These things are rather private and Tash has never been a great one for telling her mother all the gory details.'

'I should hope not,' said a dry voice as Hugo wandered in. He was still wearing his breeches and a dog-eared jumper, his blue eyes gleaming. 'Hello, Alexandra darling. Did you know there's a helicopter pilot helping India with her French homework in the Lime Tree Farm kitchen? He says he's something to do with you.'

'Hugo – there you are!' Alexandra looked delighted. 'I've been searching everywhere for you. Where on earth—'

'—are my manners? I know.' Stooping down to kiss her on the cheek, he muttered 'Belt up' very kindly in her ear before straightening up again. 'Listen, Zoe's pretty keen to boot this pilot out so that she can have a word with her kids. Shall we walk up to the farm to stop him drowning in young India's eyes?'

Giving him a beseeching look of apology, Alexandra laughed. 'Of course, though lord knows why he's helping her with her homework. He's Yugoslavian. His French is absolutely dreadful.' She headed outside.

Hugo glanced back at Lisette for a moment. 'Give me five minutes.'

'Where are Tash and Niall?' she demanded furiously, but he'd already gone.

'Perhaps they're not coming.' Sally chewed her lip, her eyes almost hopeful.

'I'm employing Niall – he still has two scenes to shoot! He can't swan off to France,' Lisette spat at her. 'And whilst I'm on the subject, I thought I was employing you too. You're supposed to be on the door.'

'Not any longer,' Sally told her. 'I'm quitting – had I known six months ago that you wanted to be my friend again just so that you could act out some silly revenge mission on darling Tash, I'd have taken Matty's advice and told you to swivel on your barbed tongue once and for all!'

'You what?' Lisette licked her lips nervously and glanced at her power-group who were still hovering nearby quaffing Krug. A few of her invited journalists were milling around within earshot too.

'You've used me, Lisette.' Sally's eyes were stinging with tears but her voice stayed calm and level. 'You only employed me to get closer to Tash's mob. It's why I've done nothing for you but run errands that have been run already. You weren't trying to help me build my confidence and get away from the kids a few days a week. You just realised what an indiscreet blabbermouth I am and hoped it would be useful. And it bloody well has been, hasn't it?'

'You've got me all wrong, Sally.' Lisette tried to pull her away from the gathering crowd of fascinated onlookers. 'Let's talk this through in private.'

'No!' She pulled away. 'I will never forgive myself for being duped like this. I've probably wrecked poor Tash's career and I hate myself to hell for it!'

'Sally!' Lisette hissed desperately, directing her eyes towards the journalists.

'It's okay, for once my trap is shut,' she sighed. 'I'm too mortally ashamed of my involvement in all this to tell tales. After all, there's nothing I can do to stop you selling the horse to Hugo, is there?'

'Don't talk rubbish.' Lisette was trying to tow her away by the arm now.

'If I hadn't suggested that childish sponsorship idea, you would never have known you were entitled to half that horse, would you?' wailed Sally. 'And now, instead of giving it back to Tash as you promised, you're going to sell it to that bastard Beauchamp, aren't you? Knowing full well that he and Tash loathe one another.'

'I'm not.' Lisette's eyes flashed.

Shaking her head, Sally sobbed on, 'You are, Lisette. I've seen tonight's surprise wedding present. While I was in the kitchen, I spotted the golden envelope you've got hidden back there and I'm afraid I peeked at the winner. Imagine my surprise when I found out the show was rigged. Well, I'm nominating you for the worst friend of the millennium awards. You're so full of acid, I'm surprised you don't dissolve yourself.' She walked off, leaving all the onlookers wildly frustrated that such a show-grabbing scrap had yielded practically no gossip at all.

Lisette straightened her skirt, took a deep, shaky breath and flashed a smile at them all. 'Silly bitch!' she chirped brightly, heading off to fetch herself another drink. She looked at her watch. It was almost half-past ten; some people were already leaving.

David slid over to her, hand discreetly tracing her bottom, leathery face dipping towards hers. 'Looks like the star attraction and his future wife are having an early night.'

'They'll be here,' she muttered through gritted teeth, as much to convince herself as him. 'Niall never can resist the chance to make a speech.'

In the corner, the arrogant young actor was not progressing very far with Stefan's austere father. With the aid of a lot of miming and wide hand gestures, he had managed to get across the fact that he was an actor, but Stefan's father merely nodded politely that he understood, repeating the word: 'Actooor.'

'James Bond?' the young rake said slowly and clearly, his eyebrows nudging towards his hairline eagerly. 'Double O Seven. Yes?'

'Yes! Yes!' Stefan's father had heard of that too. 'Bond!' he said in a strange, loopy voice, putting his hands together in a gun gesture and blowing the tips of his fingers with a cackling laugh. Beside him, Stefan's mother fell about too. It was the first time they had so much as cracked a smile all night.

Draining his third unadulterated orange juice, the actor closed his eyes and groaned.

Hugo reappeared five minutes later, pushing his way through the gaggles of now very drunken party-goers until he located Lisette in one of her power-groups. She was all oozing, delighted charm in front of the money-men, but the moment she had apologetically excused herself and gone into the kitchen, she dropped the smile as fast as an armed robber pulling off a plastic cartoon mask and rounded on him, huge eyes flashing. 'What's going on, Hugo? Where are they?'

'Well, Tash is in the bath,' Hugo lit a cigarette, oblivious of the hustle of waiting staff and pot-washers around them. His eyes didn't leave her face.

'So they are definitely coming here tonight?'

'Well, Niall is.' Hugo clicked his lighter shut and watched her like a hawk sizing up a snack. 'He has a little announcement to make.'

Lisette went pale. 'Shit! But I thought Tash's mother said—'

'Alexandra was overexcited,' Hugo cut in evenly. 'Although I think you'll be rather pleased with what he has to say. You certainly won't need to blow the view halloo to that little pack of news hounds you've got gathered out there.'

Glancing sideways at the busy kitchen staff, Lisette blanched. 'You know?'

'Of course I know.' Hugo shot her a withering look. Then he leaned back against a stainless steel surface, eyes narrowing. 'I couldn't believe you took it so calmly yesterday when I told you I refused to abide by your conditions in our Badminton arrangement. It didn't take much effort to discover that you had more cards up your sleeve than a pick-pocket in a department store. Reporters' personal business cards mostly. It's like a seventies Fleet Street pub in here tonight.'

'If Niall makes an announcement, then they're all going to hear it. I can hardly throw them out.'

'And your grubby little exclusive?'

She backed towards a juddering industrial dishwasher. 'If the wedding's called off, then I can't stop that happening either.'

'Sure.' Hugo snatched another puff of his cigarette. 'Just as you couldn't have stopped Bob Hudson telling Niall that he was going to be sued by Sleeping Partners if he approached you about pulling out of the *Cheers!* deal?'

'Don't talk shit!'

'We both know that greedy little Bob has never said no to a fast buck, fuck or tummy tuck.' Hugo watched her as she tripped over a trolley stacked with plates. 'How much did you offer him to pretend that contract of yours was as binding as a kidnapper's gaffer tape? Don't tell me you traded in below the belt liposuction?'

'You bastard!'

'It's true, though, isn't it?' Hugo laughed. 'You cooked up a fat little deal with that criminal agent of Niall's to convince the great, gullible Irish idiot that he'd be put through the mill faster than a green peppercorn if he tried to pull out of your sham contract. You've been spreading Chinese laundry whispers lately, haven't you, Lisette? No wonder Niall's been shitting himself. First you made him think you were going to take him to the cleaners, now he believes you're planning to air his dirty linen in public.'

'I don't want to hurt him!' she bleated. 'I just want him to marry Tash.'

'Exactly.' He cocked his head, watching her face with growing amazement. 'Boy, have you given out the wedding marching orders recently, Lisette. For a long time I was convinced that you were intent on roasting the bride and groom, but I've changed my mind about you. I think you've been trying to keep as quiet as a church spouse all along, but your faith in Niall back-fired on you.'

'I need this wedding to go ahead!' For a moment she looked distraught with fear, the huge eyes luminous with tears, red mouth gashed apart with a wail of absolute desperation.

'And you'll get it.' Hugo walked across to the kitchen until they were almost nose-to-nose. 'On two conditions.' He suddenly smiled.

Too frantic to see the irony of the situation, Lisette gnawed at a glossy red lip. 'What conditions?'

'Firstly, you guarantee me that your grim ex-file never sees the light of a Sunday exclusive.' His blue eyes danced as coolly as light refracting through ice. 'Not that you'd ever show it to anyone unless you were certain your film was going to crash and die anyway. After all, publishing it would leave you without a leading actor. You could hardly expect Niall to roll up to work after the printing presses roll with that.'

'He's under contract!' she ground her teeth.

'Con being the operative word.' Hugo backed away and started to scan the steel shelving to their left. 'You're bloody lucky he hasn't drunk himself to death over this. If it weren't for Zoe Goldsmith he probably would have done.'

Lisette looked at him for a long time, ignoring the kitchen help who was trying to edge his way behind her to open the dishwasher.

'Niall wasn't really threatening to kill himself, was he?' she asked worriedly, her voice dropping to a hushed croak.

Searching through a shelf of catering-sized sauce bottles now, Hugo grinned over his shoulder. 'And deprive you of an income? He's far too kind. Anyway, he's got Tash and her mother on his side now. And he's getting married next Saturday – provided you agree to condition number two.'

'Which is?' She watched as he peered between two jars of mustard.

'Come Saturday, you give your share of that horse back to its rightful owner.'

'And who's that?' Lisette lifted her chin, eyes glancing towards a shelf on the right.

'That's for you to decide.' Hugo backed away, following her gaze and finally locating an envelope hidden there, tucked beneath a vast tin of tomato purée. 'I want you to be a maiden name of honour at the wedding, Ms Norton. And you know, I rather think you have it in you. That's the ridiculous thing. You really do want Niall to be happy, don't you? You want him to be as content in his second marriage as you are in yours – to your bloody career.'

'And you?' She watched him in disbelief. 'What's in this for you? You love that bloody scatty, mixed-up creature.'

'Oh, I'll cope with the loss.' He turned the envelope over in his hands. 'After all, love and marriage need their horse and carriage, don't they?'

He calmly ripped up the rectangle without gazing at its contents.

'You knew I was going to sign the bloody horse over to you all along, didn't you?' Lisette laughed in amazement.

'I'm a professional eventer.' He shrugged. 'I always examine the mouth of any nag I'm offered. You didn't really believe that I couldn't see the wooden gift horse for the trees, did you?'

'And you're still willing to let Niall marry her on Saturday?'

'I'm all for it.' Hugo smiled. 'She's one of the loveliest women I've ever encountered. He's one hell of a lucky bastard, if you ask me.' He glanced at his watch. 'I must go. Do I take it I have your agreement? Only I said I'd get back to Niall ten minutes ago.'

Lisette nodded mutely.

'Good.' Hugo ran his hand through his hair. 'Don't look so glum, darling – you're going to one hell of a wedding next weekend. Now I must push off, there's a rather affectionate pack of spaniels I'm eager to reacquaint myself with.'

As soon as he'd gone, Lisette escaped to the loo and pressed her burning face to the cool window at the rear of the cubicle.

To her amazement, Niall was in the bar when she came out, knocking back mineral water and charming everyone in sight. Standing at the huge, unlit fireplace, he made a brief announcement.

'Tash apologises that she can't make it,' he said loudly, with a strange glint in his eyes. 'But the wedding is still very much on, and we all look forward to seeing you next weekend, if not at the ceremony then at the reception afterwards. It should be a bloody brilliant affair.'

He walked up to Lisette and gave her a soft kiss on the cheek. 'Sorry I'm late, angel. I'll pose all you like for the *Cheers!* guy now I'm here.'

Lisette's eyes were brimming with tears as she took in his kind, craggy face which bore not one streak of malice.

'You don't have to,' she found herself saying.

He shrugged. 'I don't mind. I know how much this means to you.'

She shook her head very slowly and determinedly. 'Nothing means that much, Niall. Please don't get married next weekend.'

'But I want to.' He smiled easily. 'You see, you've done me a favour, angel. You've given Tash and me the chance to show just how much we care about one another.'

Lisette stared at him in horror.

'Does she know you've been seeing Zoe Goldsmith?' she managed to splutter.

'Of course,' Niall told her calmly. 'She knows everything. We have no secrets – I can safely say she's the best mate I have, which is why she's going to be standing at my side on Saturday morning.'

'Rather forgiving, isn't she?' Lisette frowned, trying to keep calm.

'She's an extraordinary girl, so she is.' He grinned. 'And so's the chap she wants to spend the rest of her life with.'

'He's an unfaithful bastard!'

'Shh.' Niall winked. 'Don't tell her that. Jesus, I've tried enough times, but she's ludicrously attached to him.'

Forty-Three

TO ALLAY HER NERVES, Tash walked to Fosbourne Holt House very early on Saturday morning while the grass on the verges was still misted by a patina of dew, like the skin of a ripe Muscat grape dusted with the first mildew of noble rot. Behind her, Beetroot dived in and out of the hedgerows, snorting madly at molehills so that her pale muzzle was covered with earth like a finger dipped in cocoa powder.

Fosbourne Holt House was the sort of country pile that Tash had day-dreamed of living in as a child, long before she developed an adult understanding of the cost of central heating. Although large, it wasn't as sprawling or decrepitly stately as Ben Meredith's family seat, Holdham Hall, which had been gaining a wing per century since Jacobean birth. But Fosbourne's solid, muscular bulk, strawberry pink brick walls, glittering windows and tall, fat chimneys had appealed to Tash ever since she'd been to a hunt ball there the year before and glimpsed it properly for the first time. Before that, she had hacked past it almost daily for a year, standing up on her stirrups time and time again like a jockey riding into the winners' enclosure as she'd sought to see more of the seventeenth-century house than its lichen-speckled roof and multiple chimneys. Set in acres of hilly, flint-strewn parkland, it hid its beautiful face like a bashful, fan-wielding courtesan, peeking up behind a high brick and flint wall.

Walking the final few hundred yards across the fields, Tash caught her breath as the house finally crept into view beyond a mist-drenched pheasant copse. Last winter, it had been a floodlit, unset jewel nestling amidst a black, moonless velvet night – cool, steely and romantically remote. Now it was enveloped in the ornate, sculpted setting of daylight, and glittered all the more brightly for it.

It was surrounded by soft, sumptuous grounds. Tall, isolated oaks dotted the parkland at intervals like proud bodyguards on the look out for danger, and there was such a profusion of green everywhere that Tash felt as though she should burst into strains of 'Jerusalem' and encourage Beetroot to stop rubbing her neck in goose crap and start showing a bit of respect by kneeling down or something.

'Verde que te quiero verde,' she sighed, transfixed. Beetroot panted alongside her, entering into the spirit of things with a fresh green stain on her neck.

Yet it was the house itself that provided the richest colour in the park, like a jaunty brooch pinned to Robin Hood's doublet. Decked out in its midsummer finery, it was coated in variegated ivy, honeysuckle, mauve wistaria and a climbing quince that was dropping the last of its tomato red blooms like feathers from a scarlet boa. Zandra Rhodes couldn't have designed a brighter outfit for a wedding.

The bulk of the building now housed the British headquarters of a high-flying electronics company, with partitioned offices which fragmented most of the grand old halls and rooms. But the commercial owners had sympathetically left the entire first floor untouched and hired it out for conferences, parties and – now that wedding ceremonies were allowed to be conducted in specially licensed venues – marriages. Today's was only the third to be held in the house, and to Tash's alarm the owners had taken out an advert in that week's *Marlbury Weekly Gazette* proudly declaring that Niall O' Shaughnessy was using it for his celebrity marriage 'to be covered by *Cheers!* magazine'.

Tash closed her eyes and hoped to God that everything went to plan.

Not wanting to disturb the security staff, she settled on the roots of one of the guardsmen oaks and looked at the house for a self-indulgent few minutes. At her feet, amid the dried humus and warty toadstools, a small clump of clover was battling for life in the shade. Bang in the middle of it was a four-leafed one, so small that Tash wondered if her ropey botanical skills had identified it correctly at first. But, as she turned it around in her fingers, she knew she was right. It was the first one she'd ever found, and there seemed to be something prophetic in it, however tiny. Standing up, she whistled for Beetroot and started trailing back to the house.

'C'mon, Bee,' she sighed, carefully pocketing her find. 'You need a bath, and I have a speech to rehearse.'

From eight o'clock that Saturday morning, florist's vans started rolling through the high security gates at the entrance of the park and unloading their contents from the gravel car park at the side of the house and into a side entrance which led directly to the back stairs. When the flower arrangers ran out of foliage, a Sloaney girl was despatched into the park with a pair of secateurs to pillage from the hedgerows. Soon, several rhododendron bushes and a climbing ivy to one side of the house were starting to look suspiciously bald.

Later that morning, a piano tuner poled up to perfect the tone on the Steinway grand which was due to be played during the ceremony by Niall's great friend, the film-score composer Roger Allice, who had written a wedding anthem especially for the ceremony.

'It sounds like he's head-banging the piano, so it does,' Niall had moaned when it was played down the phone to him earlier that week. 'I think perhaps we should have stuck to Handel.'

By lunchtime the imposing double front doors of the house had been opened by security staff and the first of the groom's party started to arrive in anticipation of welcoming guests. With them was Beetroot, her biscuit-coloured coat gleaming like a wire brush from an early-morning bath, a huge ivy-coloured ribbon tied to her collar which caused her to sit down and scratch frantically every few paces.

The three ushers – Gus, Hugo and Rufus – were relieved to see that no guests had turned up yet. Niall's family had a reputation for arriving so early at weddings that they regularly attended other people's ceremonies before waiting through to see their own family member getting hitched. Ma claimed it got her in the mood – like watching a short at the cinema before catching the main programme.

'No sign of *Cheers!* yet then?' Rufus looked around eagerly, clutching on to Beetroot's lead as she tried to drag him towards a potted bay tree. His new crew cut was hidden beneath an old dressage topper, and he had borrowed Gus's yellow dressage waistcoat. A can of Becks was poking from each pocket.

'Obviously not.' Hugo glanced up the steps, which were covered with quince petals like a very ragged red carpet. He was pale-faced with sternly controlled nerves, blue eyes watchful, mouth curled into that half-smile he always wore when he was uncertain. Yet such was his remarkable sang-froid that the only real outward sign of anxiety was a tendency to tug at his shirt-cuffs beneath his well-cut, well-brushed and well-used morning suit.

Gus was holding together less well. Despite his own smart, hired morning suit, his shirt was already stained with horse slobber and his straw-coloured hair was clumped into tangled tassels because he hadn't combed it after his shower that morning. His thin, angular face was as bleached as a piece of Bondi Beach driftwood.

'I feel like I'm about to ride for England on a strange horse.' He wrinkled his nose as he paced around outside with a last, nervous cigarette. 'And that dog still smells.'

'She's probably decomposing a wedding anthem,' Hugo muttered.

'Two to one she'll bite the groom.' Gus winced against his cigarette smoke. 'That animal seems to have it in for Niall.'

'On the contrary, I'm sure she's Beetrooting for him,' a voice pointed out calmly and, giving Beetroot a big pat, the best man dashed up the grand staircase to check that all was well above.

'I don't have a great deal of confidence in Niall's choice.' Gus watched the long legs bound up the stone steps. 'Doesn't strike me as very organised – no use at all at the stag night. Didn't even hire a stripper.'

'Oh, I don't know,' Hugo said lightly. 'You didn't stay as long as I did. Shit, here come the superficial wedding photographers.' He nodded towards a silver hatch-back that was turning into the gates, the rear of its driver-side sun-visor plastered with *Cheers!* stickers.

Inside Fosbourne Holt House, the long hall ran for the entire length of the first floor, with huge floor-to-ceiling windows to one side which let in thick, slanted stripes of sunlight, dancing with shadows from the rampant wall-climbers. Today, the hall had been set out to resemble a church with a wide central aisle, a vast bank of flowers and candles where there would normally be an altar, and row upon row of 'pews', which in this case were the far more comfortable and ornate gold banqueting chairs that belonged to the house. One of the staff was busily ripping seat numbers from the back of them, left over from a recent music recital staged in the same room.

'It looks jolly lovely,' she called out cheerfully as she spotted the morning suit wandering in. 'The floral arrangements are simply super, aren't they?'

The hall was decked entirely in white summer flowers which had given the florists no end of nightmares as James French was very snobbish about carnations or chrysanthemums and had banned them entirely. As a result a wildly expensive range of roses, lilies, irises, phlox, jasmine and orchids dripped and drooped from the foliage-strewn walls with the languid decadence of porcelain-pale nymph's fingers beckoning from a mystical forest. There were so many flowers banked on the grand piano that it looked as though it had been planted out like a novelty wheelbarrow in a suburban garden, and the florists had even trailed jasmine and ivy around its legs and those of the stool.

'Where shall I set up, mate?' The *Cheers!* photographer wandered into the hall behind the best man, loaded down with padded bags, his creased suit scattered with red petals. 'Christ, it's like walking into a garden centre, innit?'

Behind him, a scrawny, long-haired assistant was buckling under a tripod, his pockets bulging with film reels. 'Over here okay?' He dropped the tripod to one side of the flower 'altar'.

'Have we met?' The photographer scratched his head. 'Don't tell me – you were in a film with this Niall geezer? The one about the Scottish rebel, wonnit?'

'No – but you're right. We have done some pictures together – quite a few, in fact.' The familiar face flashed him a wicked smile. 'And we're about to star in the best one yet.'

Driving around the narrow, interlacing Fosbourne lanes with an out-of-date ordnance survey map, and a very simplified set of directions drawn by Henrietta which made the tiny, winding Berkshire C roads look like the gridded streets of New York, Matty French found himself ploughing the Audi through the same ford in alternate directions several times. Because his window was open from asking directions, his right arm was now soaked with muddy water. At least it cooled him down slightly; the car was unbearably stuffy.

'You should know the area better than me,' he told Sally. 'Surely you remember where this house is?'

'I never saw the place.' She was hurriedly coating her legs in fake tan make-up, most of which was splattering over the car's upholstery. 'Why don't we drive back to the farm and ask?'

'Shouldn't think they'd be too keen.' He turned Henrietta's instructions upside down and peered at them again. 'Gus Moncrieff was hardly friendly earlier. If we'd stayed any longer, I think he'd have seen us off the premises with a shotgun.'

'He was behaving a bit oddly, wasn't he?' Sally wiped her hands on the chamois leather from the glove compartment. 'So was Penny come to that – she grabbed the kids as though it was a ransom swapover. I thought they'd at least invite us in for a cup of coffee until Tom and

Tor were settled and dressed. Penny even tried to whip Linus away until I pointed out he wasn't one of Tash's pages. I mean, he can barely walk – he'd never make it up the aisle.'

'Nor will Niall if he's as pissed as he was the last time I saw him,' Matty said darkly, trying out a lane he hadn't attempted before, only to realise that it was the driveway to a remote farm with nowhere to turn the car around until they were practically in the milking yard.

By lunchtime, it was absolutely classic wedding weather. Now flying high in an unblemished forget-me-not sky, the sun hadn't been crossed by a cloud since dawn, and had strengthened enough to drench the house and grounds in sumptuous, saturated warmth. Arms were bared, sunglasses donned, faces tilted upwards and tights discreetly removed in the privacy of cars before the wedding guests drove into the Fosbourne Valley and tried to decipher Henrietta's map.

Growing tired of holding on to Beetroot while he waited outside to welcome guests, Rufus tied her to the bay tub – in which he had stashed his cans of lager – and told her to guard them. Donning a pair of dark glasses, he lolled on the steps and lifted his topper as the first cars started rolling up the carriage sweep.

'Here come the innocents.' Gus narrowed his eyes against the sun as he and Hugo bounded down the steps from the house, both loaded up with service sheets. 'I thought you were going to show people where to park, Rufe?'

'I am.' Rufus grinned idly and waved his hat in the direction of the car park as a flashy Discovery trundled past. 'I'm sure that's Alan Rickman.'

'It's Jack Fortescue,' Hugo said witheringly.

The mildest of veil-lifting breezes cooled the faces of the early arrivals as they clambered from their cars in the vast gravel stretch of car park beside the house and stared up at the multi-coloured foliage bobbing jauntily and shaking pollen on them all. Close to, the house smelled as glorious as it looked – a heady mix of honeysuckle, jasmine and trailing roses.

The wind was just light enough to keep hats on heads without the need of a protecting hand, yet cool enough to stop those hats feeling as though they were made of thermal wool with bobbles on top.

'Couldn't want for a better wink from God, could you now?' pointed out one of Niall's relations who had arrived predictably early and whose rose button-hole was failing to counter-balance the hip-flask weighing down the opposite inside pocket.

Hugo, who was ushering him inside, nodded vaguely and handed him a service sheet. He hoped the day went according to plan, whether or not God was winking at them; he felt unusually nervous. He'd only just realised quite how newsworthy Niall's wedding was.

The *Cheers!* photographer, who had set up his tripod inside the hall, had left his lanky assistant to guard it and was now roaming around outside taking shots of the arriving guests in the hope of catching one or two celebrities flashing serene smiles. He was furious to find his pitch being queered yet again by a small gaggle of freelance tabloid paparazzi who had been tipped off and were hoping to catch celebrities flashing their knickers as they clambered from the rear of Mercs.

'Clear off!' he told them huffily. 'I'm on an exclusive job here. What are you lot after?'

'Same as you, mate.' One of the paps shot him a wink. 'Piccies.'

They all surged forward as a car drew into the carriage sweep with someone who looked startlingly like one of the Baldwin brothers in the passenger seat, but it turned out to be Tash's cousin Olly and his boyfriend Ginger, who was most alarmed to find a man leaning on his bonnet and pressing a camera lens into the windscreen of his Porsche.

'I had no idea wedding photographers were so adventurous these days,' he said in surprise. 'I thought it was all about getting into a line and trying not to stand with a tree behind your head.'

The *Cheers!* photographer, who had wasted almost half a reel of film on Olly before he realised his mistake, was furious.

He then enlisted the help of a burly security guard to throw the tabloid stringers out into the lane. But confined there, they simply rushed to their cars, drew step-ladders out of the boots, and set them up at the far side of the brick and flint walls, over which they pointed their zoom lenses.

'You'd think Princess Diana was coming,' the *Cheers!* photographer hissed through his teeth, and then almost fainted as a convertible Audi crunched on to the gravel.

'I say,' called a soft, plummy voice tinged with shyness, 'is this the O'Shaughnessy-French wedding?'

'Y-yes, ma'am,' the photographer gulped, trying to peer beneath the broad-brimmed hat and dark designer glasses. She was certainly radiant, and blonde, and very, very classy. His eyes automatically darted to the boot, wondering if she had a date stashed in there.

She giggled. 'Please don't call me that, however flattering. I'm here incognito – I do so hate being recognised these days.'

'Of course, I quite understand,' he oozed, slyly checking the amount of film he had left in his camera.

'Are you from *Horse and Hound*, then?' she asked as she put the car into reverse and looked around for a parking space.

'Er – I don't quite understand?'

She started to laugh. 'I thought you knew who I was?'

'Um—'

'Julia . . . ?' she coaxed teasingly.

He started to colour, realising the enormity of his mistake.

'Sorry, love, I thought you were the other one,' he gulped.

'What? Lucinda Green?'

'Who?'

She laughed even more. 'Darling, my name's Julia Ditton. I wouldn't bother photographing me – I'm not nearly famous enough for you. But I overtook Minty Blythe rattling along the A34 in a Beetle convertible about ten minutes ago, so she'll be here any sec.'

'It must have been left back there!' Matty sighed, close to despair. 'That bloody ford is straight ahead.' He started a three-point turn.

'No, we've already tried that left turn.' Sally was spinning the map around and around almost as frantically as her husband was spinning the wheel. 'It just goes to Fosbourne Dean, which is useless. What about the lane on the right?'

'That takes us back towards the farm.'

'We'll just have to go back there and ask.' Sally looked at her watch. 'We could be driving round in circles for hours. I told you we should have followed that Volvo with all the hats in it – they had to be wedding guests.'

'I hope not – they looked like retired barmaids on an outing to the races.' Matty was appalled. 'Although, in retrospect, it could have been a contingent of Niall's aunts.'

'For a card-carrying socialist, you can be such a snob!' she laughed.

Suddenly he started to laugh too. 'But I always carry my card in the correct pocket of my ratcatcher, darling.'

Casting the map aside, Sally smiled. If she had levelled the same accusation at him a fortnight ago, he would have bitten her head off and retreated into an indignant sulk.

She tilted her head towards him as they sped along the lane that led back to Fosbourne Ducis. 'You know Lisette's been invited to this wedding, don't you?'

He shrugged, slowing down at a turning point to let a Land-Rover get past.

'Do you mind?'

'Do *you*?' He glanced across at her with his wary yellow eyes.

'A bit.' She wrinkled her nose. 'But I guess we have a lot to thank her for.'

'I hope that's supposed to be a joke?' Matty still had his foot on the brake as he gazed at her.

But she nodded, eyes bright with belief. 'If she hadn't tried so hard to persuade me that our marriage was over, I might still believe it. Instead, I realised how far down my roots have grown since we married and how irretrievably entwined in yours they've become.'

'You didn't take much persuasion to uproot and rush down here as I recall,' Matty pointed out, but his tone was gentle and teasing rather than accusatory. They had talked this through many, many times over the past week.

'And I missed you like mad,' Sally sighed. 'Lisette's commitment to any one thing lasts about as long as it takes to shoot a film – she finds it as easy to leave a man as a hotel room, and usually in the same total mess. Even if it weren't for the children, I simply can't do that to you, and the easier she told me it was, the more I missed you and wanted to make our marriage work, rather than make myself work.'

Matty started to smile. 'I suppose the fact that she thinks I'm an all-out failure isn't such a bad thing either. Before she came along, I was the only one allowed to think that. Wallowing in self-pity isn't nearly so much fun when someone starts calling you a self-pitying jerk.'

'Did Lisette really call you that?' Sally looked indignant. 'The cow!'

'You called me that, actually.' He grinned. 'But it was only when she started luring you away to The Ivy every day to help her lunch a thousand shits that you called me anything at all. Before that you only ever called me into the kitchen for supper. The moment Lisette-your-teeth-on-edge came on to the scene, you developed terminal termagancy.'

Sally stretched back to tickle Linus who was just waking up on the back seat with a groggy, grumpy wail.

'Lisette didn't really take me to The Ivy on her important business lunches.' She bit her lip guiltily. 'I only said that to get at you. Mostly I just hung around her office feeling surplus and gossiping. That's why it's my fault that Tash has probably lost the ride on her best horse.'

Matty's face tightened at the mention of his sister's name. 'The blushing bride – and no wonder! Niall has a lot of groom for improvement too. How they can go through with this bloody ridiculous wedding at all is beyond me. It might be the biggest organisational triumph of my mother's life, plus a huge media exercise for Lisette, but they'll make one another miserable. Both Niall and Tash have always been pathetically eager to please. Anyone else would have called things off weeks ago. Knowing them, they'll probably wait until they're at the altar to have second thoughts.'

'You don't really think that, do you?' Sally gasped.

'I'd like to.' Matty started driving towards the farm again. 'And I don't think I'll be the only one who'll be crossing their fingers and hoping Niall forgets his lines for once in his life when it comes to "I do".' He chewed his lip and thought briefly about Zoe Goldsmith.

'So by that I take it you haven't had a last-minute change of heart about handing the ring to Niall?' Sally smiled sadly.

'No. I might be a new man, but I'll never be a best one under these circumstances.'

She sighed. 'I wonder who Niall's got after all?'

'Rory Franks, I think.'

'That hell-raising louse?' Sally looked horrified. 'Talk about "with this vice ring I thee wed". He'll have pawned it to buy a gram of coke by now.'

'He's been in re-hab, apparently.' Matty slowed down as a deer dashed across the road. 'So he says, anyway.'

'Then he's a re-habitual liar.' She muttered. 'When Rory Franks sneezes, half of Colombia comes out of his nose.'

'In that case, I think we should drop in at the forge, don't you?' Matty sighed.

At Fosbourne Holt House, the rows were starting to fill up, especially on Niall's side of the hall where a large contingent of his raucous family was already ensconced, chattering, laughing and scrapping as they passed around sweets, hip-flasks and a creased copy of the *Sporting Life*. One uncle had already borrowed Hugo's mobile phone to put a bet on the one-forty at Newbury.

It was still over half an hour before the ceremony was due to begin, and as yet Tash's side of the hall resembled the auditorium of a regional theatre box office flop with just one or two seats taken up by old friends and eager locals.

'You don't think her family's found out what's going to happen, do you?' Gus muttered to Hugo in an undertone. 'Alexandra swore she wasn't going to tell a soul.'

'She's certainly told an arsehole.' Hugo glanced around anxiously. 'I wouldn't put it past James French to have fucked this thing up deliberately out of spite. He hasn't stopped grumbling all week about recouping the cost. It's not as though he's paying a penny towards the wedding now – he just can't resist getting at Tash. Apart from the divine Alexandra, her family are almost as hellish as mine.'

'Who is paying for all this?' Gus whispered.

Hugo grinned. 'Niall.'

'But he's totally strapped for cash, isn't he?'

'Not since the horse he owns a half-share in won twenty grand at Badminton.' Hugo winked and then groaned as he looked towards the door. 'Shit! I think Tash's family is finally arriving. Here's Cass-tration. You deal with her, Gus.'

He hastily tried to hide behind a vast arrangement of lilies as he recognised a familiar figure in a hat like a blue chiffon bee-hive, which exactly matched her floating sky blue chiffon empire-line dress. But fluttering a couple of blue-pearlised eye-lids, she had already spotted him and was trotting up on two sky blue satin pumps. She looked like a huge Wedgwood tea-pot on the move.

When Gus gallantly sprang forward to intercept her, she simply brushed him to one side with a blue patent leather kelly bag and kept going.

'Hugo, isn't it? Cassandra – you must remember? Tash's aunt.' She puckered her lips and aimed for his cheek with the same expression as someone frantically sucking the last fizzy pop out of a can with a straw. 'We holidayed together with Alexandra at Champegny a couple of years ago. And, of course, I've seen you at darling Sophia's social functions several times.'

Hugo flashed a non-committal smile. 'You look wonderful, Cassandra. And this is Marcus, isn't it?' He peered at a pasty-looking youth wearing a garishly striped velvet trouser suit, with a face full of double-topping pizza acne and straggly hair hidden under a shapeless black cottage loaf hat.

Cassandra let out a ringing laugh that set his teeth on edge.

'Always the joker, Hugo.' She gave him a wise look. 'This is Sooxiee.' She pronounced the misspelling with distaste. 'Marcus's girlfriend. And this is Marcus – my youngest son. You remember Hugo, don't you, darling?'

An identical acned youth wearing pretty much the same get-up as his girlfriend – with the addition of a drooping rose in his buttonhole

– shuffled up behind them, giving Hugo a cursory nod. Hugo gave a cursory nod in return.

'Marcus is at Manchester now. He's reading European fiscal law and monetary incrementals,' Cass announced proudly.

'Sounds riveting,' Hugo muttered. 'I must ask my local library to reserve a copy.'

'I want to sit in a row with enough space for Sophia and Ben,' Cassandra insisted as he moved them up the aisle.

'What about your husband?' Hugo asked carefully, worried that Pa Hennessy had croaked recently. He remembered that Marcus's father was knocking on in years and had a gouty leg.

'Michael? Oh, he's parking the car. He can go anywhere – better near the back as he insists on singing incredibly badly at these things. I can't believe Tash has hooked someone quite so – successful as Niall.' She hated to admit to people being famous, considering celebrity distasteful. 'Can you, Hugo?'

'Niall's a very lucky man.' Hugo flashed a wary smile and thrust a service sheet under her nose.

'But, my dear,' Cass's voice dropped to a hush-hush breath, 'he's *bound* to be unfaithful. All these film types are. They're forever being exposed for it in the gutter press – or so my char tells me. We only read the *Daily Telegraph*, of course.'

'Of course.' He backed off hastily. He was in a cold sweat now, certain that the whole idea was doomed to failure.

In a bedroom at Lime Tree Farm, two women were ignoring the shrieks of impatient, dolled-up children coming from the next room and concentrating on a far more pressing dilemma as they prised and squeezed and forced flesh beneath fabric.

'I'm sorry, Penny, I simply can't wear this corset thing. It's far too tight. I'd pass out from oxygen deprivation before I got through Niall's five christian names.'

'What are we going to do then?' Penny's eyes widened. 'The dress simply won't do up without it.'

'I don't suppose you've got one I could borrow?'

The first thing Niall did when Sally and Matty walked through the door to the forge was offer them a drink.

'A drink?' Matty's eyebrows headed rapidly towards his hairline and he slid Sally a knowing look. But the next moment Niall was lunging into the kitchen to fetch a half-full cafetière.

'Do either of you take sugar? Only I don't think we have any.' He started slopping it into two mugs, trying not to get splatters on his trailing shirt-cuffs. 'I just went over to the farm to borrow some cuff-links, but Tash's mother was so frantic to throw me out before I bumped into the bride that she handed me a pair of gold earrings by mistake.'

He was dressed in just his shirt, trousers and braces, with no waistcoat or cravat. The jacket from his morning suit was slung over the back of one of the cast-iron chairs, and a pair of glossy shoes was sitting on a polish-smudged rectangle of newspaper nearby. Glancing down, Sally realised Niall wasn't even wearing socks.

'I can't find any that match.' He followed her gaze with an apologetic grin. 'I don't suppose you're any good at tying cravats, are you?'

Laughing, Sally set about smartening him up. 'You are hopeless. I thought this was the best man's job?'

For a moment Niall caught Matty's disapproving eye, but he said nothing.

'I think the best man's a little the worse for wear,' Matty muttered sourly, looking down to where Rory Franks lay stretched out on the sofa like a teenager after his first drink binge – all floppy-haired, bruised-eyed good looks and charm mixed with an almost pathetic depravity. At least forty, he had been to more parties than a hired tuxedo, worked his way through more drugs than a small NHS hospital, and broken practically every law at least twice, yet was far too charming to dislike. He possessed the sleepy decadence of someone who should know better if only they could remember. His thickly lashed gaze crept over to the new arrivals and he shot them both a big, sleepy wink before closing his eyes.

'My best man's already at the hall,' laughed Niall. 'Rory's only here to give me immoral support. He says he's my bestial man.'

Matty let out an anxious sigh. 'Niall, it's not too late to—'

'Don't even try to persuade me to change my mind,' he butted in, lifting his chin as Sally tied his cravat for him.

'But you're only going through with this because you've been pressurised into it!' he exploded.

Niall's huge, dark eyes regarded him thoughtfully. 'And you want to pressurise me out of it, I suppose?'

Glaring at him, Matty said nothing.

'There's only one person who's put me under absolutely no pressure at all recently.' Niall's voice shook as he spoke. 'She's stood by me quietly and supportively throughout the past few hellish weeks, and

– instead of bullying or manipulating or panicking – she's stayed calm. She didn't tell me what to do. She's never once told me what to do. Yet having her around, seeing how strong and firm and kind she is, has caused me to do things for myself instead of other people. She's made me realise that, just sometimes, the only way to help other people is to be selfish yourself. And today I'm – we're – planning to do something that's entirely selfish, that's entirely for us. The fact that it will also make a lot of other people very happy doesn't really matter. It doesn't matter about the pressure we're under any more, d'you see? We're doing this for us. We want to do it.'

'You do?' Matty still looked highly sceptical.

'Yes!' Niall laughed. 'It's been practically impossible to let people know what's been happening, and this seemed the perfect way to come clean. I can't wait to be asked if I'll take her hand in marriage. It'll be the most moving moment of my life.'

'You sound very sure.' Sally was leaning back and staring at him in amazement.

'I am. I'm also so bloody scared, it's just taken me ten minutes to do up each button on my shirt.'

'I guess there's not a lot I can do to dissuade you then, is there?' Matty sighed. 'Since you're so determined to take a stable hand in marriage.'

'Oh, I don't know.' Niall winked. 'I don't suppose you guys could give us a lift to the wedding? Only I don't think Rory's up to driving and I'm far too nervous. If you really don't think I should be doing this, Matty, you can always groomnap me.'

Sally didn't like the way his eyes flickered.

'I'm driving,' she said hastily. 'And if we don't get going soon, we'll be following the bridal train there. Do you know where this house is, Niall?'

He nodded. 'Sure, angel. There's a little ford about a mile away from here – it's right next to that, behind a bloody great wall. You can't miss it.'

Forty-Four

IN THE LONG HALL at Fosbourne Holt House, Niall's mother and father were arriving very noisily, having brought their presents along with them. Thankfully Ma didn't seem to recognise Hugo as the slack hotelier when she bore down on him.

'Ah – here's a person, so he is!' called Ma O'Shaughnessy, a terrifying fifteen stone of muscle in a tent dress with red wine stains on the collar. 'Can you hold on to this for us, child?' With unstrained ease, she handed over to Hugo a huge parcel which almost broke his back. 'Are we right or left now?'

'Right.' Hugo looked around for somewhere to put the parcel. It weighed a ton.

'Case of Bushmills.' Ma winked at him.

'That'll go down well.' Hugo smiled, knowing that Niall had been on the wagon for the past fortnight without lapsing. He had even stuck to orange juice at his stag night.

Pa O'Shaughnessy, who was twice as tall as Ma but a third the width, tugged the collar of his shirt with a nicotine-stained finger and grimaced. 'Jesus, I can't wait to take this ting off. Sure, Niall'd not mind if I wasn't wearing this neck-tie ting during the ceremony, would he? I wore the dratted article last time he got married, so I did.'

'You'll wear it, Daniel O'Shaughnessy, or you'll not touch a drop of liquor this afternoon, do you hear me?'

He hastily left his collar alone and groped for his tobacco tin.

Leaving them in Gus's capable – if shaking – hands, Hugo heaved the Bushmills to the back of the room and hid it behind the grand piano, where Roger Allice was trying to play some lightweight Bach between blowing his nose.

'Bloody hay-fever,' he cursed. 'When I played at the Royal Festival Hall last month, I was crying throughout. The audience thought I was moved to tears by the music, but they'd stuck me next to a huge pot of lilac.'

Hugo wandered off to ask around for some anti-histamine tablets, carefully avoiding Ted and Franny who had both just rolled up reeking of Calvin Klein One. Franny was wearing a red second-skin rubber dress that emitted puffs of talc from the neckline when she sat down and strained over her ample bosom like cling film stretched over two apples. Pa O'Shaughnessy, who was smoking a hand-rolled cigarette in the front row, almost swallowed the plastic roses on his wife's hat as he craned around to gawp at her.

Outside, Beetroot was now guarding Rufus's lager cans so officiously that she wouldn't let him anywhere near for a cooling swig.

He fanned himself with his top hat and watched as the *Cheers!* photographer danced around the arriving hordes, snapping madly. Beyond the wall, the tabloid paparazzi had attracted a group of minor stars who were trying to make sure they were snapped before they went into the house.

'I was in that episode of *Casualty* where Baz and Charlie had a clinch over an artificial lung, remember? My ribs had been crushed when a parachutist landed on me?'

Having shown two more O'Shaughnessy arrivals to their seats, Hugo retired to an ante-room at the rear of the hall to swig from his mug of lukewarm coffee and sneak a cigarette, leaving Gus to cope alone for a moment.

'This could be an all time bloody cock-up,' he told the best man. 'That prat from *Cheers!* has just spent five minutes photographing Niall's brother, thinking he's Johnny Depp. I hope to Christ Niall turns up – he's cutting it finer than Rory Franks's cocaine.'

'They're on their way. Niall called on the mobile twenty minutes ago to say he was out of bed, he's lost his cuff-links and the washing-machine door at the forge has stuck so he can't get his socks out. I still think I should have stayed with him.'

'No way,' Hugo growled. 'Even if Niall behaved himself, Rory Franks would try to get inside your Y-fronts within five minutes.'

'I'm not wearing Y-fronts.'

'Make that two minutes then.' He handed over his half-smoked cigarette and dived back out of the door again, slap into Sally and Matty.

'You look gorgeous.' Sally wandered in wearing a creased pink suit from the early-summer sales and kissed Hugo straight on the mouth.

Behind her, Matty had Linus strapped to his chest in a nylon padded Mothercare papoose, and was glowering perceptibly. He wasn't wearing a suit, and his dung-coloured desert boots were filthy and tied with red laces, but at least there was no sign of the crocheted peace-cap.

He shot Hugo a dirty look. 'I still can't believe they're going through with this,' he hissed. 'It's a bloody farce. I've just seen Niall and he actually seems happy about it. I think he's been drawing on the short straw again – no wonder Rory Franks is suddenly on the scene and looking as though snow wouldn't melt.'

Sally gave Hugo a big wink and pushed her tousled hair back from her face. 'Ignore him, he hates civil ceremonies because they're so civilised. We brought Niall with us, by the way – he's still outside getting snapped up.'

'Thank God,' Hugo sighed with relief. He caught Matty's eye and looked hastily away.

'So who is this best man Niall's roped in?' Matty asked, trying to sound casual.

'Funny-looking bloke.' Hugo shrugged, trying to sound the same. 'Met Niall on holiday once apparently.'

'Isn't it beautiful here?' Sally was gazing around dreamily. 'Can we go near the front?'

'I wouldn't advise it – think of Flanders,' Hugo muttered.

Several eventing friends of Tash's had appeared with yet more presents.

'I got them an alarm clock because I know Tash always oversleeps,' giggled Lucy Field. 'Terribly unromantic, but I couldn't see her ever using a fondue set. Do you know what her dress is like?'

'I think it's well suited.' Hugo took the presents to add to the expanding pile.

Twenty minutes later the rows had almost filled up.

Having been monopolised by the *Cheers!* photographer for a flattering five minutes, Sophia arrived with a very dour-looking Ben, who hadn't been monopolised at all and was longing to be at an agricultural show in Malvern. Sophia was looking ravishing in a very short, very glossy red Gucci suit that would have made anyone else look like a roasted red pepper balanced on two wooden skewers. Her hat had such a wide brim and was so tightly pinned to her head that she was knocking off top hats all around her.

'Isn't this dreary compared to a church?' she sniffed disapprovingly, then hissed, 'I don't want to sit near Matty. His kids are loathsomely boisterous and they look frightfully scruffy in their attendants' outfits.'

'You've been at the farm?' Hugo gaped at her.

'Of course.' Sophia gave him an odd look. 'Bloody Mummy seems to have been at the vodka all morning and wouldn't let us upstairs at all, but I sneaked up to look at the children in their outfits just before we came here. Of course, my two look divine but Sally's are a disgrace. Tor has already eaten the bow off the front of her dress. I can't think why Tash asked them to follow her; they'll be up her skirt in a trice.'

'Can't say I blame them,' Hugo said smoothly, showing them into the seats beside Cass.

Ben gave him a sad look and patted his back before sitting down.

'Bloody brave of you to do this.' He coughed awkwardly. 'Know how you feel about her.'

Hugo gave him the ghost of a wink and whisked off to welcome Tash's rakish, heavy-lidded Uncle Eddy, who had brought along his wild-child wife Lauren, decked out in see-though purple plastic. She and Franny were already exchanging competitive glances.

Ben settled in beside his wife and scratched the back of his ear mindlessly with a service sheet. 'Hugs is taking this awfully well,' he said.

Sophia, who was gossiping madly with Cass, ignored him.

'Awfully well,' Ben repeated, moving up to make room for Eddy and Lauren. He thought it very odd that they hadn't seen Tash that morning at the farm when they had arrived to deliver the kids. Alexandra had told them that she was in the shower, but they'd stayed for two coffees and a long bridesmaids and page-boys outfitting session and she'd apparently remained there throughout. He supposed women did strange things on their wedding day. Sophia had sucked breath-fresheners throughout the ceremony at theirs, one of which had flown out during the vows.

On the opposite side of the aisle, Gus was having trouble knowing where to seat Niall's family as they all seemed to have long-running feuds with one another.

'I'm not sitting next to me brother!' snarled Niall's sister Nuala. 'He owes Sean three thousand, so he does.'

'Perhaps here then?'

'No way! My Auntie Kathleen hasn't talked to us in years.'

'Would you like to sit here?' asked Gus in desperation, noticing the queue starting to buckle at the door as they waited to be seated.

'Are you losing you mind, man?' Nuala gaped at him. 'I'm not spending an hour sitting beside my good-for-nothing lazy lump of a husband!'

'Hello, Huggy Bear,' purred a soft Scottish voice as Kirsty sidled alongside Hugo, looking ravishing in a long, clinging slither of oyster silk. She was clutching tightly on to Stefan's vast hand in a proprietorial show as there were a lot of very pretty actresses eyeing him up from Niall's side of the hall, the formidably beddable Minty Blythe included.

'Bride or groom?' Hugo said vaguely as he spotted the *Cheers!* photographer run inside to collect more films.

'Well, I know you've been treating me like a stable hand all year,' Stefan looked at him worriedly, 'but I was originally taken on as a working pupil. Are you all right, Hugo my friend?'

'Hmm?' Hugo watched as the *Cheers!* photographer paused to talk to his assistant.

'You seem just a wee bit fraught.' Kirsty gave him a kiss on the cheek.

'That's because my main fraughts are with the bride and groom.' He showed them both to a row near the back.

'Are you sure you're all right?' Stefan's huge eyes regarded him anxiously. 'Only you seem to be coming out in a rash.'

Hugo had been pecked on the cheek by so many female guests that his face was streaked with lip-stick stripes like some tribal warrior. He had another brief fag-break in the ante-room, where Niall was now sitting with a huge black coffee looking terrified as he shared a cigarette with the best man. He'd slipped into the little room by the lobby door to avoid being mobbed by his family in the long hall.

'They'd frighten me out of my wits, so they would. That tabloid gang outside and the *Cheers!* guy almost finished me off. Talk about being shot to fame, I can't face my Uncle Seamus's box brownie right now.'

His morning suit had toast crumbs attached to the front and he had lost the top stud to his shirt so that it gaped open showing a few coils of chest hair. Instead of cuff-links, he had a couple of bendy bag seals wound through his button-holes. With his chaotic mane, wild black eyes and emerging stubble, he was the worst-groomed groom Hugo had ever encountered. Even his button hole appeared to have some sort of weed poking out of it. Peering closer, Hugo realised it was a tiny four-leafed clover.

'I'm turning over a new leaf,' Niall followed his gaze and laughed.

Outside on the gravel carriage sweep, Gus had just encountered Niall's short, rapacious agent, Bob Hudson, and was trying to persuade him to relinquish his mobile phone, on which he was still talking.

'I need it, mate.' He gave Gus a wink. 'I'm trying to get Dec Wiseman to confirm Niall as the lead for his next movie, The Quack Down – it's all about an LAPD cop who gets a talking duck as a partner.'

'Sounds very lame to me.' Gus took the phone, switched it off and pocketed it. 'Bride or Groom?'

'Which is tastier? I go either way.'

'Right, I should think.' Gus marched him upstairs and placed him beside Rory Franks on Niall's side of the hall, which at the moment had far fewer incumbents than Tash's mainly because all of his acting friends were turning up appallingly late.

Reeking of stale whisky and still wearing his dinner suit from the night before, Niall's old drinking partner, the morals-free Rory Franks, was flying on his first half-gram of coke of the day. His sexy, red-veined eyes scanned the room for talent. They briefly alighted on Minty Blythe before he remembered that he'd had her before. Then, having dismissed Franny as cheap and Lauren as jail-bait, he flashed Sophia a huge, let's-fuck smile.

Turning as red as her suit, Sophia hastily looked away, almost blinding her aunt as the wide brim of her hat wiped away a lot of pearlised blue eye-shadow and a top set of false eye-lashes. A moment later and Sophia was screaming her head off as she mistook the eyelashes – which had landed on her sleeve – for a spider.

'They're mine!' Cass whipped them back and, furtively pretending to look in her handbag, stuck them back on inside out.

Quickly giving up on Sophia, Rory decided that Franny wasn't too cheap after all and flashed her the same smile he had afforded Sophia. She returned it with bells, balls and brio. Grinning to himself, Rory girded his loins in anticipation and hoped it was a short ceremony.

Sitting beside Franny, the lapels of his borrowed suit dusted with talc, Ted glared out front and decided to have another crack at India at the party that night. He was sick of using up his entire supply of KY Jelly every night just to get Franny out of her clothes. But, gazing around the hall, he realised that there was no sign of India at all – nor had Zoe or Penny appeared yet.

Five minutes before the ceremony was due to start, Pascal D'Eblouir strode through the high double doors wearing a very jazzy morning suit made from the lightest of pale grey wool, his topper almost twice the height of any of the others to make up for his short stature. He was sporting a bright green waist-coat and already wafting wine fumes.

'*Allo, mes braves!*' His grey eyes twinkled merrily as he opened his arms, ready to fall on the ushers' cheeks. 'It go well, *non*?'

Hugo shot him a warning look. 'All according to plan so far.'

'*Bon!*' Pascal nodded. 'I am late because I bring my mozer-in-law 'ere. Etty need the lavatory every half-hour – not to pee, but to check 'er *maquillage*. She 'as not shut up for two hours talking about weddings.'

'Does she know then?' Gus whispered.

'*Dieù, non!*' Pascal looked horrified. 'Wiz any luck, she weel not even notice. She 'as just met anozer *madame* – er, mad woman – outside. They are posing for a magazine photographer. I sink they tell 'im they are two of ze Beverley Sisters.'

Hugo showed him to the front of the bride's side, where Cass was currently squawking back across five rows to some distant great-aunt with a hearing aid that Tash couldn't have hoped to do better than Niall.

He felt sick with trepidation. Particularly as his own mother had just swanned through the doors sweating in her show-off mink and dripping with the family's paste jewels, accompanying a very grandlooking old woman who was so thin that her skin hung gracefully from her bones like a silk drape over a parrot's cage. They were both wearing ostrich feather hats, although Hugo's mother's had considerably fewer feathers in it and the odd cigarette burn dotted randomly on the front.

'Hugo darling, I want to sit with my new best friend!' demanded Alicia with her usual plethora of decibels. For a moment the room – which was now almost full – fell silent.

'You have no friends, Mother,' he said dryly. 'And what is he doing here?'

He backed away as Thug the pug emerged from his mother's fur coat to snarl at him. As a concession to the wedding theme, Alicia had tied a white bow to his thickly studded collar. He had worn a similar – black – one to Hugo's father's funeral. Alicia was so mean, Hugo suspected that she had simply bleached it.

'He didn't want to stay at home. Anyway, Tash's dog is outside with young Rufus.' She thrust her chin out rebelliously, paste earrings swinging in time to her booming epiglottis. 'I hear she's to be married in cream – Etty told me. Terribly unflattering colour, especially on a rather ungainly girl like her.'

Hugo turned to the woman he took to be 'Etty'. She looked unspeakably noble, and knew it, her wrinkled neck choked with genuine pearls and diamonds, her bony frame swathed in a beautifully tailored fifties suit that Hugo guessed was original and barely worn. She was the sort of woman who hadn't increased a dress size since puberty.

A perfectly clear rouge thumb-print was dotted on to each of her jutting cheekbones and her eyes were gloriously knowing and dissipated.

'I need to sit down, young man,' she demanded grandly. 'My knickers are slipping.'

Hugo hastily showed them both to a row at the rear of Tash's side within convenient distance of the loos. He doubted either of them would be frail enough to need them, but he knew Thug had a tendency to throw up choc drops on the hour. The moment they sat down, Etty started announcing to all within earshot that it was she who was behind the wedding in the first place.

Vying to be the last to swan into the hall, Niall's film friends were finally starting to arrive en masse now, pausing theatrically at the door to check that their outfits and celebrity status were clocked before entering. They were all madly discussing the press contingent which was gathered outside the gates.

'Well, I was done by the *Mirror* and the *Mail*, darling, but bloody Terry Gale just ignored me.'

'Only goes for girls with big tits, sweetie. Did that freelancer with the divine bum get you?'

'In both directions. I'm sure the light was behind me – I'll have ears like barn doors in the shot.'

'Shouldn't worry, love, – I just saw Lisette Norton getting out of a limo with a tit flashing. She'll be everywhere – can't you see it? "Niall's ex makes boob at wedding."'

'No – "Niall's first wife throws confet-tit." She only just made it before the bridal cars too – now that's what I call upstaging.'

Hands damp with trepidation, Hugo backed off to the ante-room as Gus dealt with them.

'Think you're needed out front,' he told Niall, offering him a slug from his hip-flask.

Straightening his crumpled morning suit, Niall shook his head.

'Sorry – thoughtless of me,' Hugo apologised, putting it away. 'You feeling okay?'

'Fucking terrified.'

'Lisette's turned up after all,' Hugo told him, expecting a tirade.

But Niall merely shrugged. 'Bloody brave of her,' he said simply. 'Sit her next to someone sympathetic, huh?' He kissed his best man on both cheeks. 'See you in a minute. Thank you so much for doing this.'

Hugo's eyes narrowed jealously, but he followed him out without complaint.

Standing nervously in the hall, Lisette was wearing a very demure grape-green trouser suit with her slinky mane neatly pinned beneath an oversized citrus orange top hat. Apart from a plunging neckline, which clearly revealed that she had nothing but hot skin underneath, she looked remarkably lacking in the usual carnality. Even her huge, hungry grey eyes were naked of their usual smudgy kohl.

'Don't look so miserable, darling.' Hugo took her arm. 'I think you might rather enjoy this.'

'I nearly didn't come,' she muttered, sounding almost wretched. 'I can't believe they're actually going through with it. It's all my fault.'

'Now that's a confession I never thought I'd hear.' Hugo found himself smiling delightedly. 'You almost sound like a guilt-complex-wife.'

He sat her next to Cassandra's rheumy husband Michael, who gave her an approving look.

'Haven't we met?'

Lisette flashed a wary smile. 'As long as you're not my maker, then I hope so. Weren't you in the Loire with the D'Eblouirs a couple of years back?'

'Thought I recognised you. Never forget a face.' His little rat's eyes weren't looking anywhere near her face as he said this.

Leaving them to it, Hugo checked on Niall, who was in an arm-lock and being thoroughly wept over by his mother.

'I'm fine!' he spluttered breathlessly when Hugo asked. 'There's Henrietta at the door – check everyone's on their way, will you? I'm sure they're late. Ouch – that hurts, Mother!'

'She's a lovely girl, son. But I'll always be your mother!'

Beside her, Pa O'Shaughnessy lit another rolly. 'Jesus, I tink the boy knows that.'

'Don't blaspheme in church, Daniel!'

'This isn't a church, woman.'

'And may the merciful Lord forgive us for that!' Ma burst into more racking sobs, almost breaking Niall's neck. 'Sure little Lisette's at the back there, son, looking terrible sorry, so she is. Perhaps she's not such a sinner after all. It's not too late to change your mind. If you tell Tash you're a good Catholic boy, she'll understand.'

'She'd kill him, so she would,' Pa muttered, pulling a stray strand of tobacco from between his teeth. 'And so would I.'

Hugo found Henrietta chatting to the butch female registrar by the door. An absolute bag of nerves, she was dressed in a very smart Windsmoor suit and cream trilby that matched her pale face. She was shaking so much that her pearl earrings rattled like chattering teeth.

'How's it going?' she asked nervously as he showed her to the front pew.

'Okay so far.' Hugo glanced around. 'I think we can safely say merry hell will break loose in about ten minutes, though. Bride on her way?'

'Yup, they're just doing another circuit of the village because that *Cheers!* chap was being horribly pushy – James is outside talking to him now. It's his fault we're late, I'm afraid. He held things up because a bird dropped a what-not on his suit while he was waiting by the car at Lime Tree Farm.'

'Lucky then.' Hugo settled her in and dashed back to check on the best man, passing the *Cheers!* photographer who was running into the hall from the opposite direction looking terrified.

Joining his lanky assistant, he hastily clipped his camera on to the tripod with shaking hands.

A moment later James French strode into the hall, looking thoroughly disapproving and extremely haughty, his fleshy face absolutely immobile as he stalked to the front row and sat down beside his wife. There was a slight hush amongst the guests.

Two rows from the front, Cass was clutching Sophia's red satin arm in alarm. 'I thought your father was giving Tash away?' she hissed, pointing to the front where James's head was dipped towards his wife's now.

'She wouldn't let him,' Sophia sniffed. 'Poor Daddy was terribly upset. They had a frightful row at Henry's christening, don't you remember?'

'So who is giving her away?'

'Mummy.'

'How ghastly.'

'I know.' Sophia wrinkled her nose. 'Very Islington.'

Gus was at the long gallery door now, welcoming Penny with desperate relief. She had brought along Wally the farm collie and Zoe's paranoid Dalmatian Enid, both of whom were wearing the same fat, ivy-coloured bows. Despite looking enchanting, Enid was scrabbling to escape, her clipped nails sliding around on the polished wood floor, her pale brown eyes rolling in terror.

'Hope the bride doesn't behave like that,' Gus watched her warily. 'All set?'

'On their way.' Penny winked. 'She didn't fit into the dress Alexandra brought. We had to dig mine out of the loft in the end, but it's covered with fake blood from the time Rufe wore it to a fancy dress as the Bride of Dracula. We've been at it with the Vanish all morning.'

'Hope the bride doesn't do that either,' Gus gulped anxiously.

Rufus wandered in behind Penny. At his feet, Beetroot was still scratching madly at her bow.

'The car's had to go around again – a whole load more guests have turned up.'

The very last arrivals were several eventers who had come straight from a competition the other side of Reading and were hugely embarrassed to be still wearing their grass-stained cross-country gear.

'It started late,' Brian Sedgewick muttered apologetically. 'Someone let cows on to the course last night and they ate the entire centre of the Hay Wain water complex. I bought Tash and Niall an alarm clock as a wedding present.'

Gus had to put them on Niall's side as there was no room left on Tash's. Several actors in front craned around enviously.

'Starring in the latest Jilly Cooper adaptation?' one asked enviously, eyeing a jodhpured thigh. 'I went up for that. Bastards threw me out because I couldn't ride. I ask you! I said, "Darling, I'm an actor – I can *act* riding." Oh – here they come!'

Suddenly Roger Allice clicked his knuckles theatrically at the rear of the hall and launched into a very depressing Grieg concerto as the female registrar walked slowly to the top of the aisle, smiling benevolently at everyone. She looked like a wannabe vicar in a black suit with a very narrow white collar as she flicked open her service book and waited for the bridal party.

'One of us,' said an actor delightedly. 'Check the Doc Martens.'

'Where's the bloody best man?' Matty asked fretfully, gazing around the hall. 'He isn't here yet. I absolutely refuse to get up there if they're short-staffed.'

'I'll do it then,' Sally told him, consulting the service sheet. 'Bloody hell – Rory Franks is reading a Yeats poem – "All Things Can Tempt Me". One would imagine so. Or perhaps "An Acre of Grass". Oh, look, your mother's here.'

Dashing through the doors, Alexandra raced to the front pew wearing an amazing lilac trouser-suit ensemble that fluttered around like a dropping sail. Her floppy seventies hat looked likely to render her airborne at any second, flapping madly in her haste. Only Alexandra could look so ludicrously chic and fragile in such an outfit.

'Bloody hell, my mother's dressed as one of Pan's People,' Matty groaned, closing his eyes.

Sophia was clutching Cass's arm this time. 'That's Mummy!'

'So who is giving Tash away?'

'The mysterious best man?' Sophia suggested vaguely.

'I could do with a Best man,' Marcus piped up, suddenly taking an interest. 'Or a Guinness. Or even a lager, man.'

'Trust Niall to have a hippy wedding,' Cass sniffed disapprovingly. 'I've always said Tash was too good for that druggy Irish layabout.'

Alexandra was settling between Henrietta and Pascal in the front row. 'All going well,' she informed them excitedly.

Henrietta bit her lip edgily. 'Are Emily and Beccy behaving themselves?'

'Having great fun, darling.' Alexandra was craning around to wave cheerfully at members of her family. 'Isn't this a hoot?'

Henrietta swung around too as a noisy chattering from the stairwell beyond the doors heralded the imminent arrival of the bride and her raucous attendants.

'Where's the bloody best man?' demanded James French, noticing that there was still a gap at the front like the missing black piano key where Niall and the registrar were standing with a one-man space between Hugo, Gus and Rufus lined up to their right.

The next moment, the ante-room door swung open at the rear of the hall and a tall, slim figure in a very baggy morning suit raced up the aisle on endless legs to take up the empty space beside Niall, topper still in place. Only a few wedding guests got to view the best man's face as the figure flashed past. Of those that did, Bob Hudson let out a low whistle.

'Bloody attractive man. Should be in films.'

Rory Franks watched the passing bottom impassively. 'Sometimes I wish I was gay,' he sighed, rubbing his itching nostrils.

'Sometimes I wish you were too.' Bob gave him a game wink.

As soon as the best man was in place beside Niall, the topper came off and revealed hair scraped back into a chaotic pony tail.

'A bit eighties,' Sophia sniffed disapprovingly. 'Who d'you suppose it is?'

'One of his dreadful acting cronies, I suppose.' Cass craned to see. 'Looks a bit of a – you know – a woofter.'

Rufus was fighting to keep hold of Beetroot, who was straining her head towards Niall's right-hand man, her rope-thin tail spiralling joyously.

'For Christ's sake, don't let her go,' Niall muttered as he stared out front. 'She'll have my leg off. And she smells something awful.'

Beetroot let out a couple of high-pitched barks of frustration.

'I'm sure I know the best man from somewhere,' mused Julia Ditton.

But the wedding guests were suddenly distracted by the emergence of the bride, absolutely swathed in silk and lace. For a moment she stood alone in the doorway – pale, fragile and solitary.

There was a general hush of anticipation as the guests craned around to get the first view of her. On Niall's side a couple of flash cameras went off and an actor could be heard muttering in a loud stage whisper: 'Dreadful dress.' The *Cheers!* photographer was clicking away like mad from his standpoint at the front of the aisle.

There was certainly nothing spectacular about her dress – it emphasised her narrow waist and slender shoulders, but was essentially a large frou-frou meringue – and her veil was far too thick and heavy. Yet she radiated such total calm and confidence that eyes remained glued to her as though hypnotised. She looked absolutely beautiful.

Jiggling Linus distractedly, Matty drew in a sharp breath of admiration. 'Tash looks staggering,' he whistled.

'Who on earth's that walking in behind her?' Sally muttered. 'Bloody rude turning up so late.'

There was some puzzled murmuring amongst the guests as an exquisite, tall, blonde figure in a simple dark green dress came through the door and walked to the bride's side. To the guests' utter astonishment, she then took her left arm and started to lead her towards the aisle.

'Who is that giving Tash away?' Etty was peering with interest. 'Is that one of my grandchildren?'

'Search me.' Alicia offered Thug another choc drop. 'I hope this is a short ceremony – Gordons is looking a bit fragile. What is that dreadful racket?'

At the rear of the hall, Roger Alice had paused momentarily to sneeze and then struck up his own specially commissioned composition which Niall had asked for as an alternative to the wedding march. It was a very Phillip Glass number full of rhythmic repetitions and twirling top notes. The beat was so fast that for a couple of seconds the bride and her entourage were thrown into a confused quick-march, but they slowed as a bridesmaid tripped over the train and almost brought them all down.

Smiling behind a misty lace veil, the bride turned to face the long expanse of aisle and finally spotted the wide shoulders of her extremely scruffy groom.

Behind her, the bridal party was a glorious hotchpotch. Henrietta's elder daughter Emily smouldered sexily in a very short dark green dress. Beside her, her sister Beccy looked like a close relative of Mary Poppins in a broad-skirted number of a similar design, but possessing about six times the fabric. Tottering after them came Sophia's sickly children, Lotty and Josh, who were both starting to snivel loudly as they spotted their sympathetic au pair clutching Henry in a back row.

They were followed by Sally and Matty's two elder children, Tom and Tor. Crew-cut Tom, who was decked out in a bottle green Victorian suit, was discreetly playing on a computer game and Tor was grinning broadly at everyone in sight, most of her front teeth missing and her white rose head-dress falling over her eyes. She was the only bridesmaid not carrying a flower basket because she'd thrown it from the car window on the journey there. Bringing up the rear was Polly, wearing a version of the green silk number that was wildly fashionable and bore no resemblance to the rest – it had a button-though A-line hipster skirt, Vivienne Westwood-style corset bustier and a flowered head-dress in the shape of a baseball cap. She was also carrying a video camera, its red light flashing as she frantically caught all the action on VHS.

'Oh, doesn't Tor look sweet?' Sally gazed at them indulgently.

'Who's that giving Tash away?' Matty was peering at the figure in green. 'She looks terribly familiar.'

'It's Zoe Goldsmith's daughter!' Sally let out a surprised laugh. 'It's India. India Goldsmith.'

The motorised drive of the *Cheers!* camera had started to clash with Roger's Phillip Glass composition, which was getting thoroughly carried away now and had reached an extraordinary movement that sounded as though he was hitting the piano keys with a mallet. Cowering beside Penny, Enid the Dalmatian started to howl with distress.

At the top of the aisle, Niall was shaking so much that the best man had to take his hand and root it to a chair for support.

'She's here. She looks terrific. You're about to be married. Good luck.'

Niall finally managed to look around, dark eyes swimming with pride. 'Jesus, she's beautiful, isn't she? Utterly beautiful. I can't believe she's going to be my wife.'

At the rear of the hall, Lisette was watching the bridal train with increasing suspicion and listening avidly to the conversation in front of her.

'I must say Tash has put on a lot of weight again,' Cass was saying. 'She looks terribly squat – shorter, if that's possible.'

'That's not the dress I saw in Paris,' Sophia gasped. 'She must have positively porked out recently – she can't fit into it anymore, I bet. That must be hired.'

'Jolly thick veil, too. D'you think she's developed spots?'

'Bound to, she was always prone to them. She must be stooping or something – she almost looks shorter than Em.'

'Was she looking fat at Badminton then?'

Sophia turned around so sharply that the brim of her hat poked her aunt in the eye once more. Behind her, Ben was almost floored as it smacked him simultaneously on the forehead 'That's the odd thing – she looked rather slim then. It's hardly possible to pile it on in a week, is it?'

'My dear, we are talking about Tash here.'

'True.'

Lisette watched the bride pass and grew even more suspicious. Standing to the right of Niall and his strangely familiar best man, Hugo suddenly craned around and caught her eye in the briefest of winks.

Lisette looked from him, to Niall, to the *Cheers!* photographer and then the bride. Something about the stance was uncanny; the way she walked reminded her of someone. Then she caught sight of the neurotic, bow-decked dalmatian at Penny Moncrieff's feet, positively gyrating with recognition as the bride passed, and found herself starting to smile. Dear, theatrical Niall had finally found a woman who could match him in the imagination stakes. Moments later, to the astonishment of all around her, she started to laugh out loud too.

Niall wasn't marrying Tash French at all, she realised. He was marrying the woman that her last-ditch tabloid story had accused him of sleeping with for the past month. The woman with whom he was hopelessly in love. Niall was marrying Zoe Goldsmith.

She was way ahead of the rest of the guests in her mental gymnastics. When the veil went back, there were a few exclamations that Tash had gone blonde. When the best man twisted a long neck around to check for the ring in a waistcoat pocket, there were a few more intakes of breath, and confused murmurings.

But it was not until the registrar cheerfully announced that they were gathered together to watch Niall being united in marriage with Zoe that the communal gasps seemed to suck all the air from the room, and the *Cheers!* photographer got so thoroughly carried away that his camera fell off its tripod.

'I don't know the bride from a bar of soap,' Alicia told Etty loudly as she fed Thug yet more choc drops. 'But I know the best man – friend of Hugo's. Nice chap, can't remember his name . . .'

When the new bride and groom retired to the ante-room to sign the register, Rory Franks was prodded hard in the ribs and realised that this was his cue. Fumbling and swearing for a few seconds as he searched for his photocopied words under his chair, he finally clambered over Niall's agent and staggered to the front, tripping over several bridesmaids.

Tall, hugely attractive but utterly wasted by booze and drugs, he scanned the page with his reddened eyes and, finding that he couldn't focus, threw it over his shoulder and trusted to memory. He was supposed to be reading 'He Wishes For the Cloths of Heaven', but didn't know that by heart, and resorted to Shakespeare instead. Shooting Franny a top-shelf wink, he started to recite in his gruff, feral voice:

> 'Oh never say that I was false of heart,
> Though absence seemed my flame to qualify!
> As easy might I from myself depart,
> As from my soul, which in thy breast doth lie:
> That is my home of love; if I have ranged,
> Like him that travels I return again
> Blah blah blah blah . . .'

He paused as he forgot a few lines, but such was his magnificent presence that only a few guests noticed. Striking up again with a wide smile, he went on:

> 'Never believe, though in my nature reign'd
> All frailties that besiege all kinds of blood,
> That it could so prepost'rously be stain'd,
> To leave for nothing all thy sum of good:
> For nothing this wide Universe I call,
> Save thou, my Rose: in it thou art my all.'

Forty-Five

'I THINK NIALL WAS weeping with joy when he said "I do",' Penny sighed dreamily. 'That is *so* romantic.'

'I was crying too,' Gus grumbled. 'That dog of Tash's smells so high, all our eyes were watering.'

Posing for *Cheers!* photographs on the rear lawns of Fosbourne Holt House, Tash stood beside Niall's mother for a brief moment. At first hysterical, then struck dumb and finally apoplectic at the bridal switch, Ma had now been pacified by several large tots of Bushmills from her own case and was crying openly once more, delighted that her son appeared to be so deliriously happy with his new bride.

'She seems a sweet thing, so she does,' she wept, giving Tash a huge kiss on the cheek, leaving a great smear of lipstick that would be immortalised in photographs for generations to come like a strawberry birthmark. 'But you could have warned me, child. I've given yourself and Niall a decanter with your initials engraved on it. D'you think you can change a T to a Z?'

'Easily,' Tash assured her.

'Perhaps I will, perhaps I won't,' Ma eyed her sagely. 'You may yourself marry a man whose name begins with N.'

'I doubt that.' Tash spotted Hugo watching to see that she was okay.

'Ah, well.' Ma pulled the cigarette from her husband's mouth and re-did his tie as the photographer started barking orders. 'I might be able to give it to another couple if not. I 'clare, I go to enough weddings, but none quite like this.'

Sally and Sophia were gathering the bridesmaids and page-boys together, most of whom were either in tears, riot or revolt.

'You *will* smile for the camera, Lotty, or all your teeth will fall out,' Sophia told her wailing daughter.

Sally removed Tom's Nintendo and tried to stop Tor from stuffing her rose head-dress up her skirt.

'I always think we girls should wear hats and no knickers,' she told her, plonking it back on her head and turning to Sophia. She was thoroughly overexcited by the day's events.

'Did you have any idea?' she asked breathlessly.

'Well, I was rather amazed that they were going through with it all, and I had guessed something was awry,' Sophia told her, pulling up Josh's trousers by picking the little boy up by the waistband and waiting for him to drop further into them. 'But I never would have believed this, no. I mean, is it legal?'

'Apparently Niall sorted it all out last week – although I think several cases of champagne changed hands to speed things through. It's not like church where one has to call the banns and all that religious stuff – one just reapplies for a licence, warns the registrar to say a different name in the ceremony, and you're hitched.'

'Gosh.' Sophia kissed Josh on his curly blond head and let him go. She squinted across to Zoe who was being blissfully calm and serene as she was introduced to most of Niall's confusing, bickering, hard-drinking extended family. 'What's she like? I've hardly met her.'

'Lovely,' Sally sighed, glancing briefly towards Matty. 'Perfect for Niall. I think she'll calm him down without knocking the spirit out of him. Very strange cook.'

'Jolly attractive, though,' Sophia sniffed rather resentfully. 'Cass was so shocked that she walked straight into the gent's loos after the ceremony by mistake.'

'I know.' Sally giggled. 'Apparently Rory Franks was in there sniffing coke. She thought he was stooping over a mirror because he'd lost a contact lens and offered to help him find it, telling him he hadn't a hope of spotting it with "that dusty-looking glass". The next moment she's whipped it off him and wiped it clean with a hanky. He's distraught.'

To the front of Fosbourne Holt House, glowering beneath a flower-strewn harness, Snob was waiting on the impressive gravel carriage sweep, pawing angrily at the pebbles with a front leg and glaring belligerently at all around him. His pink nose bobbed as he flicked flies from his twitching ears, and he snapped at the harsh driving bit, loathing its presence in his mouth.

The whites of his eyes rolled menacingly as the bride and groom approached.

'Jesus, I'm not getting in that thing with him in front.' Niall regarded him in terror. The borrowed trap, despite its lick of polish, was desperately woodwormed and rickety, and Snob looked far too eager to rev off the grid and race everyone to the reception party.

'You'll be fine,' Zoe told him, letting Enid jump into the trap first, her green bow tattered from being chewed by Wally during the ceremony. 'Gus slipped him a huge tranquilliser in his morning feed – I saw him. He's tottering around like a seaside donkey.'

Niall looked disbelieving but, as promised, when Gus climbed up in front to drive them back to Fosbourne Ducis, Snob set off at a steady if grumpy amble, shooting Tash a resentful look as she stood alongside with the cheering wedding crowd, throwing confetti and swallowing most of it as it flew back in her face.

Watching them go, Tash realised that her cheeks were streaming with tears. She looked around for Hugo, but before her eyes could search him out, found herself catching sight of Lisette hastily dabbing a tear from her own cheek, her back turned so that only Tash saw. It was so utterly unexpected that she stared in amazement. Looking up, Lisette suddenly smiled and moved forward until they were standing just a foot apart. Her huge, luminous eyes were glittering with emotion.

'You must loathe me, Tash, and I can't say I blame you.'

Tash shook her head. 'Why should I loathe you? If it wasn't for you, none of this would have happened.'

'That's what I mean,' Lisette groaned, closing her eyes. 'I'm sorry. I've made you terribly unhappy, haven't I?'

Tash blew her nose. 'I don't think I've ever been happier in my life,' she said truthfully.

'I'll get my solicitors to sign my share of the horse over to you first thing next week,' Lisette was muttering. Suddenly the huge eyes opened wider. 'Did you say you were happy?'

Tash was gaping at her too. 'Did you say you were going to sign Snob over to me?'

'My half of him.' Lisette nodded. 'And the money he won at Badminton – I certainly didn't earn it, and after today I don't think I'll need it. But I have a condition to attach.'

'Oh, yes?' Tash asked shakily. She knew only too well how unpleasant Lisette's conditions could be.

'You know how Hugo feels about you, don't you?' Lisette suddenly smiled. It was such a sweet smile and so totally without malice that it transformed her face entirely.

'Yes.' Tash sucked her bottom lip.

'And you feel the same way about him?'

'Yes.' Tash sucked her top lip too, heart hammering.

'In that case, I want you to add a line to your best man's speech.' Lisette suddenly took hold of her hand and squeezed it. 'I think I owe Hugo a favour, and this might just be it . . .'

Guests were milling about on the gravel now, offering or begging lifts, gossiping like mad about what had happened and telling each other the quickest route to the farm.

There was a small press pack prowling around too, originally there just to get a few celeb shots of Niall for the Sunday supplements and gossip columns, but now snapping everything in sight – especially Tash – and barking into mobile phones as they realised they were on to a wonderful front-page splash.

Trying to hide behind a bay tree, she found herself standing next to Matty who was both hugely put out that he wasn't in on the secret and hugely relieved that his friend had married a woman of whom he thought the world, not his feckless sister.

'I owe you an apology for not coming clean.' Tash scuffed her black brogues on the gravel as she mindlessly covered up the hoof slides. 'But we thought the fewer people who knew the better.'

Matty nodded, stroking Linus's fine, silken hair and squinting across the park to the largest of the sun-drenched lakes.

'Mother knew, I take it?'

She grinned. 'We tried to keep it a secret from her, but you know what she's like. If she'd still thought I was marrying Niall this morning, she'd have drugged me to keep me away. She guessed that I'd changed my mind, but Niall got into such a panic that everything snowballed and we left it far too late to explain to everyone. The only thing we could do was ask for her help. And Daddy's.'

'But not mine?'

'The more people who knew, the messier it was going to become. It seemed much easier to do it this way. We didn't tell Sophia either.'

'Oh, c'mon!' He laughed bitterly. 'Credit me with a bit more sense than her. I'm one of Niall's oldest friends.'

'Who hasn't called in weeks,' Tash reminded him. 'Listen, you're one of the reasons that Niall noticed Zoe in the first place.'

'I what?'

Tash smiled, reaching out to tickle Linus's hand which was grabbing for her rose buttonhole. 'It was only when Zoe told Niall about you two having a bit of a flirt that he saw her for what she really is – a sexy, desirable, clever woman, not a general skivvy and mother-figure for the rest of the Lime Tree Farm mob. You opened his eyes, Matty. And yet you've avoided coming near any of us all year for fear of seeing her and feeling guilty. What you did was shitty, but no one blames you anymore. Niall is positively grateful – he told me so. Even Sally is, I think.'

'Sally?' He looked bewildered.

'If you think how it made Niall see Zoe, imagine how the news made Sally re-evaluate her reliable, pompous, eco-friendly husband. Especially when she hopped over the fence for a while herself and found that the grass on the other side was covered in weedkiller.'

Matty looked furious. 'I am not pompous!'

'Of course not.' Tash kissed him on the cheek and wandered off to find Hugo and walk back through the fields to the farm with him.

At the Lime Tree Farm reception, the notion of a formal line-up to shake hands was abandoned altogether and Zoe and Niall wandered around hand-in-hand instead, laughing delightedly at people's reactions as the same story spilled out again and again yet never lost its shine.

Zoe was glowing and utterly content. With India roaming around making sure that all Niall's relatives were eating and drinking enough, and Rufus frantically chatting up Henrietta's daughter Emily in a corner of the marquee, she dragged Niall into the house for a few moments alone. It was full of eventers who had sequestered themselves to talk shop. Finally, they resorted to shutting themselves in the laundry room to be alone.

'I have a confession to make.' Niall was looking very hang-dog. 'In all the last-minute changes, I forgot to phone the airline and change the name on the ticket for tomorrow's flight.'

'It doesn't matter,' Zoe laughed, kissing him. 'The name won't be any different. I'm Mrs O'Shaughnessy now, remember? No one's going to quibble over an initial when we're waving a marriage certificate in their faces.'

His face lit up and he started to kiss her back delightedly. 'Christ, I love Zoe O'Shaughnessy.'

'Now this,' Zoe sighed as he lifted her on to the tumble dryer and dropped down to disappear beneath her skirts, 'is what I call married bliss.'

'Wow!' he let out a muffled laugh, 'I can see my wife flashing before my eyes – I must have died and gone to heaven.'

Having thundered around the marquee with Tom and Tor for twenty minutes playing 'Chase the Big Bottom', Tash collapsed exhausted at the top table beside Hugo and plunged into the glass of champagne he had collected for her.

'You're simply marvellous with kids,' he laughed.

'I love them,' she said simply, feeling champagne bubbles pop in her nose. She ducked as Polly threw a handful of confetti at her before running away giggling.

'Then we'll have lots.' Hugo's eyes were watching her closely for a reaction, but Tash hadn't heard him.

'I can't believe it's gone so well today,' she sighed, leaning against him and pressing her chin to his shoulder. 'You were so terrific. I'm hugely proud of you.'

'You do realise that once we've all stuffed our faces you're going to have to make a speech, don't you?' he asked as she grinned happily at him, blown away by the fact it had all worked out so well.

'I love you,' she breathed, her face flushed from her recent exertions, dark hair escaping from its ponytail and clouding around her face. Her eye make-up was smudged, her tie lop-sided and she still had a huge red lip-stick stain on her cheek.

'You are so beautiful, Tash, I can't wait to move you into Haydown properly and start to look after you.'

'Do you really mean that?' she gulped, almost beside herself with excitement.

'Of course I do.' He started to kiss her mouth with a cool, skilful tongue until she felt like jelly on a spin dryer. Pulling away, he cupped her face in his hands and looked at her seriously, his face suddenly anxious. 'You do want to move in with me, don't you?'

She nodded, still staring at him with eyes as misty as Lalique glass. 'More than anything.'

Hugo's curly mouth suddenly couldn't stop smiling.

'Now I've finally got you,' he pressed his lips to her ear, his voice no more than a breath, 'there's absolutely no way I'm going to let another bounder like Niall O'Shaughnessy swagger in and steal you away from me again.'

'That'll never happen.' She kissed him back, sliding a hand beneath the table and feeling him quiver as her fingers started to perform some dressage of their own on his thigh.

'Too right it won't,' Hugo laughed, pushing her hair back from her face and looking at it. Tash was almost blown away by the intensity of those laser-blue eyes. 'Tash, there's something I've got to ask you –'

She pressed her lips to his mouth and kissed the question clean away, knowing what he had been about to ask. When they finally surfaced, Hugo was feeling far too randy to remember what he'd been saying.

'Christ, I love you.' He gently levered open a stud and slipped his hand into her shirt. 'I want to take you away and ravish you right now, Tash French. Let's go home.'

'We can't.' She pressed her nose to his, shivering deliciously under his touch. 'I've got a speech to do, people to thank and stacks of telegrams to read out – there's even one from Steven Spielberg. I'm taking my job very seriously, you know.'

'You know,' Hugo started to kiss the hollow of her throat, lips pressing so gently that she arched against them, eager for more, 'I've kissed a lot of bridesmaids in my life, but this has to be the first time I've necked the best man.'

'Good grief, there's two men over there kissing one another!' gasped Alicia Beauchamp. She frantically scrabbled for the glasses on a loop around her neck. 'And I think one of them's my son.'

'I believe you're right.' Lisette drained her champagne flute and immediately whisked another from a passing tray. 'You know, I never thought he was that way inclined. I could have saved myself a great deal of time.'

'Oh, it's all right, it's just Tash.' Alicia whipped off her spectacles, hugely relieved. She turned back to Lisette and gave her an appraising look which stretched down the entire length of her beaky nose. 'Don't worry, you'll definitely find the right chap soon. You're a good-looking gel.'

Lisette smiled gratefully. 'Thanks – but I'm rather bored of men reaching for their wallet at the end of a meal and blushing when their wedding ring falls out. I think I might buy a dog.'

'Jolly good idea.' Alicia looked at her approvingly. 'Get a pug.'

'That woman just has to Veuve Clicquot her fingers and men come running,' Sally muttered, watching as both Rory Franks and James French hovered close to Lisette with bottles of champagne, waiting for her to drain her glass.

Sitting beside her with Linus on his lap, Matty watched as Niall's ex-wife gazed round the marquee with her haunted eyes, seemingly oblivious of the drooling attentions of the men. She had a strange, excited look on her face that took Matty back years. He hadn't seen her look like that since their early BBC days when she was less confident and less obsessed by her career. It was the same look of anticipation she'd once worn before her very first dates with Niall. She seemed to be waiting for something to happen.

'I think I could finally get around to forgiving her,' he said levelly.

'You what? Blast!' Sally knocked her glass over. Matty rarely forgave anyone – it was an honour he bestowed as rarely as beatification.

'I think you were right when you pointed out that we have a lot to thank her for.' He smiled. 'It's like Niall said, sometimes truly selfish acts can help other people far more than so-called charitable ones.'

Sally started to laugh. 'Well, she's certainly going to get enough publicity out of this wedding to guarantee that Four Poster Bed will be a huge hit.'

'Yup.' He traced a finger across her cheek, his eyes softening. 'Plus she gave Niall a great part, you a chance to see how dull and fickle her so-called glamorous life is, and me a huge great slap in the face that made me get off my arse and get a decent contract.'

'And Tash's horse?' She bit her lip.

'I have a strange feeling he might just trot off into the sunset too.' Matty was still stroking her cheek, amber eyes full of bolstering confidence. 'That's the funny thing about Lisette's films. Not only are they marketed brilliantly, but they all have happy endings.'

Rolling her eyes, Sally dropped her voice to a whisper. 'I hate to say this, but your mother's bearing down on us.'

'Darlings, hasn't this all worked out gloriously?' Alexandra inserted her floppy purple hat between them in a waft of Arpège. 'Pascal is unspeakably excited – he's just sold Polly's home video to that Satellite Showbiz gossip channel. I can't get him off his cell-phone. And just think – we may all be doing it again in a few months' time!'

'What?' Matty said darkly.

Alexandra nodded excitedly across the tent where the chief usher was kissing the best man in a most ungentlemanly fashion.

'Oh, Christ, no.' Sally closed her eyes. 'Not her again. She'll go off with one of her horses this time.'

'Don't be ridiculous, sweetheart,' Alexandra said sharply. 'Pascal has already agreed to foot the bill. And there's no reason why we can't go for a church this time – in France maybe? The local one at Champegny is divine around Christmas, and I've always adored winter weddings – all those romantic long coats, squashy hats and flickering candles. What do you think?'

But Sally and Matty were already backing quietly away to escape into the garden together, grabbing full champagne flutes on their way out.

Standing up after the long, boozy and gloriously informal wedding lunch, Tash kept her speech short and to the point, partly because she wasn't particularly adept at speaking publicly, and partly because Hugo – who had moved into the seat beside her during coffee – had started playing on the back of her thighs with his fingers which made her forget most of what she was going to say, a lot of it mid-sentence. As his fingers moved idly upwards, so did her voice until she was squeaking away like a fledgling.

In his own very funny, articulate speech, Niall had already thanked so many people so profusely, and with so much easy, off-the-cuff wit, that she could do little more than endorse his sentiments and add her own grateful thanks to her family. Telling everyone how perfect the bride and groom were for one another was easy too – it was so screamingly obvious that it hardly needed to be said at all. Even in the few short hours since the wedding, Niall's entire family seemed to have fallen as head-over-heels in love with Zoe as he had, and Ma was already calling her 'daughter'.

But there was one thing that Tash was determined to say, and as soon as she had read out the last of the telegrams, she looked out across the vast marquee and swallowed nervously, suddenly not knowing how to start. Feeling herself colour, she searched around the faces in a panic until she finally spotted Lisette, sitting at the very back of the tent, her beautiful face smiling encouragingly. The next moment she was holding up both hands, long, slim fingers crossed in a message of good luck.

Laughing, Tash felt a great wash of confidence.

'This has almost certainly been the oddest wedding most of you will ever have attended,' she started boldly, then swallowed down her squeaky voice as Hugo's fingertips slipped around her leg to touch her hand. 'And I'm afraid that, just before I propose a toast to the bride and groom, I'm going to make it even odder.' She smiled broadly as she felt Hugo's fingers slide between hers.

There was a disconcerted stir throughout the tables and any chattering voices were rapidly hushed.

'You see,' she cleared her throat and looked down at him, finding herself trapped in the familiar, hypnotic tangle with his eyes, 'I'm pretty certain that none of you has ever been to a wedding at which the best man has proposed marriage to one of the ushers . . .'